EVERYMAN,
I WILL GO WITH THEE,
AND BE THY GUIDE,
IN THY MOST NEED
TO GO BY THY SIDE

DAPHNE
DU MAURIER

REBECCA

WITH AN INTRODUCTION
BY LUCY HUGHES-HALLETT

EVERYMAN'S LIBRARY
Alfred A. Knopf   New York   Toronto

THIS IS A BORZOI BOOK
PUBLISHED BY ALFRED A. KNOPF

First published 1938
First included in Everyman's Library, 2017

Published by arrangement with the Chichester partnership.
REBECCA. Copyright © 1938 by Daphne du Maurier Browning

Introduction Copyright © 2017 by Lucy Hughes-Hallett
Bibliography and Chronology Copyright © 2017
by Everyman's Library
Typography by Peter B. Willberg

All rights reserved. Published in the United States by Alfred A.
Knopf, a division of Penguin Random House LLC, New York, and in
Canada by Penguin Random House Canada Ltd., Toronto.
Distributed by Penguin Random House LLC, New York.

www.randomhouse.com/everymans

ISBN: 978-1-101-90787-0 (US)

A CIP catalogue reference for this book is available from the
British Library

Book design by Barbara de Wilde and Carol Devine Carson
Typeset in the UK by Input Data Services Ltd, Bridgwater, Somerset
Printed and bound in Germany by GGP Media GmbH, Pössneck

R E B E C C A

———

June 30 2019 Baker Taylor $15.42

INTRODUCTION

Daphne du Maurier's publisher, Victor Gollancz, announcing *Rebecca* in 1938, called it an 'exquisite love-story', which says more for his salesmanship than it does for his truthfulness. Du Maurier herself was closer to the mark when she described the novel as 'a sinister tale about a woman who marries a widower ... Psychological and rather macabre.'

There are few kisses in *Rebecca*, most of them swift pecks, and the only person who is frequently caressed is Jasper the dog. It's a novel full of powerful emotions – jealousy being the dominant one. In it love is a disappointing thing. 'We are happy, aren't we?' asks the narrator, 'Terribly happy?' 'If you say we are happy,' says her husband, 'let's leave it at that.' There is romance in this book, but it's not about courtship and marriage. Rather it is the romance of place.

Daphne du Maurier started writing *Rebecca* in Egypt, where her soldier husband, Major 'Boy' Browning, was stationed. She seems to have taken little interest in the Egyptians or in the country's tremendous monuments, and she couldn't abide the social life of the regimental club and the regimental wives. 'The effort of talking! I don't know how people stand it.' It was so hot that her sweaty fingers stuck to the typewriter keys. The novel she began in Egypt is shot through with nostalgia for Cornwall, and a house she loved there.

To begin then, as the novel does, with Manderley. It is one of the most haunting of fictional houses – more imposing and mysterious than Howards End, more solidly concrete than the 'lost domain' to which *Le Grand Meaulnes* so persistently seeks readmittance, more powerfully infused with a half-sinister vitality even than Wuthering Heights. It sits amidst lawns and rose gardens overlooking the sea. It is grand and ancient and serenely beautiful. But it is also a dark and hidden place. Mrs Van Hopper, a comically insensitive character who several times voices a truth from which the politer characters shy away, says 'I'm told it's like fairyland.' Its bewilderingly long drive winds through woods that threaten to close over it. Great banks of rhododendrons covered with 'slaughterous' blood-red flowers bar the way to it. It is a labyrinth within which something uncanny lurks: it is very, very difficult to work out its floor plan. It is the immaculately maintained and smartly furnished residence of a gentleman of the 1930s who drives too fast, eats scones for tea and keeps up with the cricket. But it also resembles the castles and palaces in which the Beast awaited Beauty, in which Psyche foolishly insisted on discovering the truth about her lover Cupid, or in which Bluebeard murdered his wives.

I'm getting close to giving something away here. Those coming to *Rebecca* for the first time should stop reading at once, and return to this introduction only when they have finished the book. *Rebecca* is satisfying on many levels, but its framing narrative is a mystery. The suspense in which the reader is kept is brilliantly achieved. This is a book that can be read over and over again, but I don't want to be responsible for spoiling the delicious repeated shocks to which the first-time reader is subjected.

*

So – to speak now to those already in the know – let us go on from a place to a person, to the second Mrs de Winter. She has a 'lovely and unusual' first name, but we are never told it. In order to write about her, though, I must give her one. Let us call her 'N', for narrator, a more appropriate epithet for this lank-haired, diffident person than 'H' for heroine would be.

She addresses us from a point in time after the story is over. *Rebecca* has often been described as a reworking of *Jane Eyre*. There are obvious similarities between the two novels' plots (impoverished young woman marries rich older man, encounters problems connected with his first wife, and finally achieves a satisfactory relationship with him after the burning down of his house has left him a sadly reduced and pathetic figure). More subtly, du Maurier also follows Charlotte Brontë in giving her heroine a double nature. Just as Jane Eyre is both the young woman of the story and the much older narrator, so du Maurier's heroine is at once the socially clumsy, yearning girl that she is when the action begins, and the poised, carefully self-censoring wife that she is as she launches – we don't know how much later – into her retrospective narrative. That dual consciousness gives her psychological verisimilitude and complexity, as the twin lenses of a pair of binoculars give a greater depth of focus than a single glass can do.

Reader, she marries him – not in the final chapter, as Jane Eyre does, but early on in the narrative. That getting her man is a far, far different thing from achieving happiness is evident from the very moment of the proposal. 'I'm asking you to marry me, you little fool,' says Maxim de Winter. In a less subtle work his rudeness might seem thrillingly masculine – kind of Rhett Butlerish (*Gone with the Wind* was published in 1936, two years before *Rebecca*), kind of hard-boiled Humphrey-Bogartian cool – but our narrator knows that it is a sign of something wrong, of an emotional flaw in her suitor. As so often in this book, a psychological clue is conveyed by a sensual detail. The tangerine he has offered her is sour. 'I had a sharp, bitter taste in my mouth.'

Du Maurier's biographer Margaret Forster has written that in Maxim de Winter du Maurier 'created a man the reader is bound to dislike ... harsh, dominant, bad-tempered'. She overstates the case. Maxim is alluringly sophisticated, and his evasiveness and moodiness can be read as Byronic mystery, Byronic melancholy. He is just the sort of man a naïve girl might fall in love with. But Forster is right that it's immediately obvious this is not going to be an easy marriage. At the time of their courtship N thinks 'It was foolish to go on having that pain in the pit of my stomach when I was so happy. Nerves of course.' But we sense that her instinct is sound when she wishes, for a moment, that 'none of this had happened', that she was still unattached, 'going for a walk, and whistling'.

*

N longs to be a woman of thirty-six in black satin rather than a gauche young person in home-made jumpers and a sensible brown frock. She repeatedly makes a fool of herself. The passages in which she does so are wonderfully observed pieces of comic writing: we groan as we read of her mortification. Too shy to ask the way around her own new home, she crosses the hall, watched by the imperturbable butler, opens a door with an air of assumed confidence and finds herself in a back room full of stacked-up chairs and mackintoshes. She sees a maid examine her vests, and, ashamed of them, orders some fine lace-trimmed underwear, only to cancel the order when the sneering maid is replaced by a less intimidating girl. Yet this abject, rather ridiculous young person has one great power – her imagination.

Rebecca's narrative is ostensibly realistic. It is full of material details, of buttered crumpets and dog-hairs on the sofa, and handkerchiefs forgotten in mackintosh pockets. Yet a surprisingly large proportion of its narrative consists of scenes N is imagining. In any life, actual events are only a part of experience – fantasies fuelled by hope and apprehension making up the rest. This novel is one of the very few that give those might-have-been experiences their proper place.

When Mrs Van Hopper announces they are leaving Monte Carlo N imagines boarding the train with her, 'holding her jewel case and her rug, like a maid'. She imagines appealing to Maxim, blurting out 'I love you so much. I'm terribly unhappy.' She imagines not doing so, and wasting her last few minutes with him exchanging small talk, 'my dreadful smile stretching across my face'. Fantasies like these give *Rebecca* its remarkable emotional density.

They allow comparisons between what is and what might have been. As N and Maxim rise from the table after his brusque proposal she thinks he might take her arm, and 'smilingly' tell the waiters, 'You must congratulate us.' The juxtaposition of that fleeting fantasy with his actual behaviour – abruptly walking out of the room ahead of her, before telling her (telling, not suggesting) that there'll be no church wedding – is sufficient condemnation of that behaviour.

Above all, the contrasts between young N's hopes, and the older N's knowledge of what awaits her, provide a rich seam of dramatic ironies. The first time N and Maxim have tea in the library she imagines their future there. She pictures a period of 'glorious shabbiness' when their as-yet-unborn sons sprawl on the sofa in muddy boots. And then she imagines a tranquil old age – she and Maxim, with other dogs, but in the same room, following the same routine of four o'clock tea. (Daphne du Maurier treasured routine – what she called 'routes'.) This vision of peaceful security is exquisitely poignant because we know – we have known since the very first sentence – that it will not be realized. There are reminders, scattered throughout the narrative, of how this story will end – glimpses of hotel rooms devoid of atmosphere, of 'harsh' blue Mediterranean skies so different from Cornwall's lush dampness, of a childless couple isolated abroad.

*

Rebecca is an intensely erotic novel, but its eroticism is of a queasy kind. Daphne du Maurier herself said it was 'about my feelings of jealousy *re* my husband and Jan Ricardo', Ricardo being an ex-girlfriend of Browning's. N is jealous from the moment she sees Rebecca's handwriting. Jealousy is morbid and obsessive. Jealousy drives a person to indulge in shaming, self-tormenting fantasies about the loved one and the other. Jealousy conjures up imaginary rivals. Jealousy infuses even innocent situations with sexual meaning.

During their courtship Maxim hugs N to him in the car but he kisses her only, as one might kiss a child, on the top of her head. She says that their honeymoon was full of gaiety and laughter, but once back in Manderley the newly-weds sleep in separate beds. When, after confessing to murder, Maxim kisses his wife passionately, we are told he is doing so for the first time. There is a suggestion that – however often others give N a quick up-and-down to check for signs of preg-nancy – their marriage may not yet have been consummated. For all that, there is a lush sensuality to the life they lead at Manderley.

The charge vibrating through the narrative is almost all displaced from people to inanimate objects: the house, its fur-nishings, the meals consumed there. The prodigal breakfasts – the silver chafing-dishes full of sausages and scrambled eggs – and the equally lavish teas are voluptuously suggestive of sen-sual gratification. Food is sexy. So are flowers. The crimson rhododendrons are terrifyingly carnal: the scent of a crushed azalea petal is a heady intoxicant. And so are clothes, as N's first visit to Rebecca's room, with Mrs Danvers as her guide, makes clear.

*

The only unreserved passion described in *Rebecca* is that felt by the sinister Mrs Danvers for the beautiful dead young woman who was her charge and her employer.

As a child Daphne du Maurier fantasized about being a boy. She called herself a 'half-breed'. She had an imaginary alter ego called Eric, who went to Rugby School where he (unlike stay-at-home, governess-taught girls like her) would have got a proper education. In her late teens she put the boy that was in her, she said, in a box. But her sexual identity remained more complicated than she ever liked to acknowledge.

Her first love was a female teacher at the Parisian finishing school to which she was sent at the age of eighteen. She loved Fernande Yvon, whom she called Ferdy, 'in every conceivable way'. In a car driving back from the Opera Ferdy put her arm around Daphne's shoulder and 'sort of pressed me'. 'You'll think, "Ugh, sordid and low,"' she wrote to a friend, but 'it gives one a sort of extraordinary thrill.' She spent the summer vacation with Ferdy. 'I only hope I haven't got Venetian tendencies,' she wrote ('Venetian' was her code-word for female homosexual). She evidently had. Her later loves included Ellen Doubleday – her American publisher's wife – who didn't respond to her amorous advances, and the actress Gertrude Lawrence, who did. When Gertie died du Maurier took to her bed for ten days, prostrated by a grief that must have been all the more painful for the difficulty she had in accepting its nature. She was not, she said, a lesbian. 'By God and by Christ,' she wrote, 'if anyone should call that sort of love by that unattractive word that begins with 'L' I'd tear their guts out ... I refuse to be classed with that gang.'

It's perhaps no wonder – given this background of repressed feeling in the author's own experience – that Mrs Danvers' love should be seen as malign. Alfred Hitchcock rose with gusto to the task of bringing her character to life. In his hugely popular film of *Rebecca* (made in 1940, only two years after the novel's publication) in which Judith Anderson played her, she is far and away the most powerful presence – despite the bravura performances of Laurence Olivier and Joan Fontaine as the de Winters. Hitchcock scarcely needed to ramp up the gothic horror that pervades du Maurier's descriptions of the housekeeper. Mrs Danvers dresses all in black. She has a 'skull's face' and a 'skeleton's frame'. 'Cold … lifeless … deathly'; these words – insistently repeated – toll through the passages in which she appears. But du Maurier redeems her from horror-movie cliché by making her emotionally vulnerable. After the turning point of the narrative – the discovery of Rebecca's body – she becomes pathetic. N finds her grief repulsive. It is the manifestation of the inadmissible love whose suppressed energy pulses through *Rebecca*, charging the novel with an explosive strangeness.

The book 'is not a ghost story,' said du Maurier. But Mrs Danvers does her best to turn it into one. 'I feel her everywhere,' she says to N. 'You do too, don't you?' Young N, prompted by Mrs Danvers's suggestions, goes into the west wing. 'My heart was beating in a queer excited way.' She enters Rebecca's room. She sees Rebecca's clothes hanging in the wardrobe. She sees Rebecca's immense bed with its satin coverlet. She is prying. She can't stop herself. (Elsewhere, when she is questioning Frank about Rebecca, the narrator likens her younger self to 'a poor person in a tenement building, when someone had died, asking if I might see the body'. She apologizes to Frank for seeming to be 'curious, in a rather beastly way', but curious she is, in a way that seems 'unpleasant' even to herself.)

She fiddles with Rebecca's most intimate possessions. She sees 'with a sick dull aching in my heart that there were creases in the nightdress'. Filmy, apricot-coloured, still carrying a musky, intimate scent, it hasn't been laundered since it last lay next to the dead woman's bare skin. And there, suddenly, is Mrs Danvers, also 'excited in a strange unhealthy way', making N feel the softness of Rebecca's wine-coloured velvet gown against her cheek, making her put her hands in Rebecca's narrow slippers, showing her the hairbrushes, unwashed, on Rebecca's dressing table, showing her Rebecca's beautiful silk underwear. Mrs Danvers is familiar, fawning, ingratiating, her manner 'sweet as honey'. This is a seduction, and it is as terrifying as the later scene when Mrs Danvers is coaxing N towards suicide.

'Do you think the dead come back and watch the living?' Mrs Danvers asks slyly. Is Rebecca watching N and Maxim together? That idea is distressing enough. But even worse is what Mrs Danvers is making N do: she is coercing her into watching Rebecca and 'Max' here together (as they probably never were) in this big luxurious bed.

*

Mrs Danvers is a figure from a nightmare, but she is the exception. Most of *Rebecca*'s characters are vividly realistic, their foibles observed by the beady-eyed narrator. *The Times*' reviewer, struggling to understand *Rebecca*'s power, described du Maurier as 'an odd writer ... hard to pigeon-hole ... mixing the grossest fantasy with the most admirable transcription of little scenes'. Those 'little scenes' are superb. Who, after having read this book, can forget Mrs Van Hopper's habit of stubbing out her cigarettes in jars of cleansing cream?

N has a sardonic wit. When Maxim tells her that there's 'no humbug' about his sister Beatrice – 'If she doesn't like you she'll tell you so, to your face' – N remarks 'I ... wondered if there was not some virtue in the quality of insincerity.' But Beatrice is a wonderful creation. When Beatrice describes the fun to be had at her house at Christmas-time – the charades ('We all roared'), the pranks with the soda syphon ('We were all in fits') – N makes a mental note not to accept any such invitation, but she is as fond of her as we are. This novel is full of finely-shaded dialogue, replete with ambiguities and misunderstandings: one of the most exquisitely painful exchanges is Beatrice's telephone call after the coroner has declared Rebecca's death a suicide. Beatrice is so indignant, so morally straight, so far from being capable of imagining her brother a murderer that she can hardly be restrained from doing the very thing that will bring about his downfall.

Frank, correct and dull, and yet heroic in his non-judgemental loyalty; Jack Favell, a copy-book bounder who suddenly springs – in a shockingly hilarious moment – to vivid life when he asks whether cancer is contagious; Ben, another stock figure (the sinister imbecile) whose fear of the asylum animates and particularizes him; all of these people form a part of the audience before which the de Winters' marital drama is being played out. That audience is essential to the story. An insistent theme of this novel is the vital importance of keeping up appearances. It is because a divorce would be so shaming ('the publicity I dreaded') that Maxim agrees to tolerate Rebecca's misbehaviour.

N always feels on show, always subjected to judgement. No wonder she fumbles, disabled by self-consciousness. When Maxim is bad-tempered, her main concern is that Frith, the butler, mustn't see her cry. (In a house full of servants, surveillance is constant.) Her most private griefs are amplified by anxiety about what others will think of them. On the morning after the dance she wakes alone, thinking that Maxim will never forgive her, and telling herself that she could bear it 'so long as the outside world should never know', because there was 'nothing quite so shaming, so degrading as a marriage that had failed'.

Du Maurier was critical of this insistence on superficial propriety. She herself was boldly unconventional. Her background was a world away from the horsey country gentry upon whom young N has to call. Her grandfather was George du Maurier, Punch cartoonist and author of the hugely popular novel, *Trilby*, set in the Parisian milieu of *La Vie de Bohème*. Her father was the actor-manager and matinée idol Gerald du Maurier. He and Daphne had a complicated relationship. Gerald was a philanderer himself, but he couldn't bear to think about his daughters' love lives, prowling the hall to yell at them when they came home after evenings out with young men. Daphne defied him, and managed – by slipping out in the afternoons – to have a happy affair with film director Carol Reed. By the time she met her husband she was living much of the time alone in her family's Cornish holiday house. On being told of her engagement her father said 'I thought she'd have had a baby by a Cornish fisherman by now.'

It was she who proposed to Browning, not because she yearned to be a wife but because he was divinely handsome.

She knew he thought extra-marital sex 'sleazy', and 'I'm scared of giving him a shock.' Tommy, who was 35 to her 24, was taken aback by her boldness, but accepted. While he was away fighting she wrote a play about the difficulty faced by married couples reunited at the war's end (she certainly didn't share Maxim de Winter's horror of exposing private matters to the public eye.)

Her novels tell of women carelessly jeopardizing their reputations for the sake of adventure or an irresistible man. The plot of *My Cousin Rachel* is piquantly complicated by the fact that a young man imagines that when a woman – older, more sophisticated – welcomes him to her bed she is tacitly agreeing to marry him. The woman is amused: she had meant no such thing. When Maxim describes Rebecca as 'vicious, damnable, rotten through and through', he is not speaking with his author's voice. Daphne du Maurier was far more like the first Mrs de Winter than she was like the second.

*

Rebecca's other great theme is that of time and mutability. Repeatedly N reminds us that she is telling a story that is long over. 'I can see her as though it were but yesterday,' she writes. 'I can close my eyes now, and look back on it.' That retrospective view brings with it a sense of loss. N has lost her youth, her hopefulness. But beyond that is the more general sense that every moment that passes, passes for ever, irrecoverable.

Before they leave Manderley for the last time N indulges in the most poignant of her fantasies, the dream of continuance. Waking early, she looks out over the garden and imagines how soon the house will begin to stir. Smoke will rise from chimneys. Rabbits will peep from the shrubberies. 'No matter what tears were shed, what sorrows borne, the peace of Manderley could not be broken or the loveliness destroyed. The flowers that died would bloom again another year.' We know she is wrong, that soon Manderley will lie 'like an empty shell amidst the tangle of the deep woods'. Nostalgia is the keynote of this book.

Blissfully happy as she sits by Maxim's side in his big car, young N says, 'If only there could be an invention ... that bottled up a memory, like scent ... And then, when one wanted it the bottle could be uncorked, and it would be like living the moment all over again.' Maxim, in flight from the past, scoffs at her, but her desire to bottle the past is no more foolish than his attempt to drown it. And he too has moments when he wants to stop the clocks. 'It's a pity you have to grow up,' he says.

It can't be done. Time's onward progress is inexorable. By the book's end the Hôtel Côte d'Azur is under new management. Manderley is a ruin. Maxim's old life, which seemed so stably established, is closed to him.

But though the past is ever receding, its influence on the present and future is ineradicable. Rebecca's boat is called *Je Reviens* – I will return. Mrs Danvers tricks young N into dressing up as Rebecca for the dance, and even stolid Beatrice admits 'For one ghastly moment I thought ...' She thought that Rebecca was back. Even when N has changed into her ordinary blue party-frock (not forgetting to iron it first, because at the most eerie moments du Maurier keeps us rooted in practical realities) she looks, says a tipsy guest, like a 'forget-me-not'. There is no forgetting Rebecca, or what Maxim has done to her.

In N's frantic mind the dance becomes a ghastly sequence of recurrences. Du Maurier's narrative shifts into a state of haunted irrationality, like a filmed dream sequence. The band plays a waltz that seems to go on and on. The same woman, her smile fixed into a grimace, passes repeatedly. Round and round the dancers go, getting nowhere, like promenaders circling on a liner's deck. Du Maurier's description is a virtuoso piece of writing. Beautifully modulated sentences trail through sequences of subordinate clauses to their exhausted close. 'I can see her now ...' says N. 'I remember Robert dropping a tray.' For the majority of the narrative older N effaces herself, allowing young N to engage all our attention, but at moments of heightened emotion she steps forward again, reminding us that this story will have repercussions reaching far forward into the future. The past cannot be held and treasured, but neither can it be erased. Like Rebecca's boat, it will return.

REBECCA

*

Rebecca's success was immediate and immense. The reviewers were sniffy, as they would remain all du Maurier's life. Critics, she believed, would 'never forgive' her 'for being a best-seller'.

'Unashamed melodrama', wrote one about *Rebecca*. 'Nothing in this is beyond the novelette', wrote *The Times*' reviewer, but he had to concede *Rebecca* had 'an atmosphere of terror which ... makes it easy to overlook ... the weaknesses'. Those weaknesses should more properly be called novelties. Du Maurier's editors complained that her spelling was shockingly bad, and her grammar unreliable. Those editors were simply more conventional that she was, thrown by the confidence with which she omitted main verbs, or segued without warning from interior monologue to lucid factual description. To modern readers it seems that she commands her medium. She can be repetitive, especially when she is cranking up the atmosphere of horror around Mrs Danvers, but she is more often acute. Her prose is by turns fluent and piquant, swooningly mellifluous and tartly sardonic.

She has a great gift for conveying emotion by indirect means. N doesn't have to tell us how upset her younger self is when Mrs Van Hopper says how much Maxim adored Rebecca. Instead she says 'Her visitors came in. I handed them their drinks dully, saying little; I changed the records on the gramophone, I threw away the stubs of cigarettes.' And she has a sure sense of drama. The scene when N and others visit Dr Baker in his comfortable suburban home, and he hands them a key to the mystery (the wrong one, as we know) is brilliantly played out against a soundscape of an offstage tennis game, boys shouting, an old Scotch terrier scratching himself, an aeroplane passing overhead. The whole sequence is low-key and banal in its content, while being audaciously strange in its technique, a long stream of consciousness from a distraught mind which fixes, absurdly, on a picture-postcard of the Tyrol as a steadying point. Those critics who undervalued *Rebecca*, and failed even to review her subsequent books, demonstrate how badly the British book world needed the feminist publishing houses that came into being a generation too late to benefit du Maurier.

INTRODUCTION

She was a writer whose prose could swerve from laconic simplicity to flaring lyricism. She was also a boldly unconventional observer of people. She could write romantic fiction – her *Frenchman's Creek*, with its artistic gentleman pirate, is an enjoyable example of the genre. But *Rebecca* is something much subtler. Gollancz's 'exquisite love-story' is actually the story of two people who barely know each other. To N, Maxim is 'inscrutable', 'hemmed in by shadows', 'secret'. He is like a Renaissance portrait, aptly named – given how little she understands him – 'Gentleman Unknown'. To him she is a child, on whom he polishes his wit. He bullies and taunts and snubs her. There is a neat little exchange between them in the style of Noel Coward:

'I wish you would not treat me as if I was six,' I said.
'How do you want to be treated?'
'Like other men treat their wives.'
'Knock you about, you mean?'

Maxim's comic timing is good, but his humour is repellent. His is a profoundly damaged psyche, and his wife's isn't much better. The narrator's response to the news that her husband is a murderer is extraordinary – 'My heart was light like a feather floating in the air. He had never loved Rebecca.' This is a mind so corroded by jealousy as to have lost all moral sense. It is all the more interesting for it.

There will be no happy ending for these two. In an early draft du Maurier left Maxim crippled after driving his car into a tree. In the final version he is not disabled physically, but emotionally, by the loss of the house that had defined him. His wife is better off. She has gained confidence and achieved self-possession. She once asked herself despairingly if they would ever be together as man and woman, equals, walking side by side. The answer is no, they won't, but there comes a time when it is she who dominates. Her husband is finally her own, but he is no longer the dashing fellow she fell for. She says 'I suppose it is his dependence upon me that has made me bold at last.'

Daphne du Maurier, finishing the book, thought it was 'a bit on the gloomy side ... a bit grim.' She thought, therefore, despite its 'atmosphere of suspense' that it was unlikely to be 'a winner'. How wrong she was. *Rebecca* was, deservedly, an instant best-seller, and has never since ceased to be popular. The reading public, it turns out, likes grim tales.

Lucy Hughes-Hallett

S E L E C T   B I B L I O G R A P H Y

AUTOBIOGRAPHY
Growing Pains: The Shaping of a Writer, Gollancz, London, 1977; published in the USA as *Myself When Young: The Shaping of a Writer*, Doubleday, New York, 1977.
The Rebecca Notebook and Other Memories, Doubleday, New York, 1980; Gollancz, London, 1981.

BIOGRAPHIES
MARGARET FORSTER, *Daphne du Maurier*, Chatto & Windus, London, 1993.
JANE DUNN, *Daphne du Maurier and Her Sisters*, HarperCollins, London and New York, 2013.

NOVELS INSPIRED BY *REBECCA*
SALLY BEAUMAN, *Rebecca's Tale*, Little, Brown, London, 2001; HarperCollins, New York, 2001.
SUSAN HILL, *Mrs de Winter*, Sinclair-Stevenson, London, 1993; W. Morrow, New York, 1993, HarperCollins, New York, 1994.

CHRONOLOGY

DATE	AUTHOR'S LIFE	LITERARY CONTEXT
1907	Birth of Daphne du Maurier in Regent's Park, London (13 May). The second of three daughters, du Maurier is born into a prominent literary and artistic household. Her grandfather was the famous *Punch* caricaturist and author George du Maurier (d. 1896), her father is the highly successful actor-manager Gerald du Maurier, and her mother the stage actress Muriel Beaumont. J. M. Barrie, author of *Peter Pan*, and writer Edgar Wallace are both frequent visitors to the family home.	Granville-Barker: *Waste*. Shaw: *Don Juan in Hell*. Von Arnim: *Fräulein Schmidt and Mr. Anstruther*. Rudyard Kipling wins Nobel Prize for Literature.
1908		Forster: *A Room with a View*.
1909		Wells: *Ann Veronica*; *Tono Bungay*.
1910		Forster: *Howards End*.
1911	Birth of du Maurier's younger sister, Jeanne (Angela, the eldest, was born in 1907).	Barrie: *Peter Pan and Wendy*. Conrad: *Under Western Eyes*.
1912		
1913		Alain-Fournier: *Le Grand Meaulnes*. Proust: *Swann's Way*. Conrad: *Chance*.
1914		Shaw: *Pygmalion* (London première).
1915		Woolf: *The Voyage Out*. Ford: *The Good Soldier*. Richardson: *Pointed Roofs*. Maugham: *Of Human Bondage*. Buchan: *The Thirty-Nine Steps*.
1916	The family moves to Cannon Hall, a large house in Hampstead, London.	Joyce: *A Portrait of the Artist as a Young Man*. Wells: *Mr. Britling Sees It Through*.

Triple Entente between Britain, France and Russia. Suffragettes storm Parliament (13 Feb); some 60 arrested. Baden-Powell founds Boy Scouts movement; first camp on Brownsea Island, Dorset.

Asquith forms Liberal government with Lloyd George as Chancellor of the Exchequer. Austria annexes Bosnia and Herzegovina.
House of Lords rejects Lloyd George's Budget: constitutional crisis. Ford's Model T car. Blériot crosses the Channel by monoplane.
Death of Edward VII. First Post-Impressionist exhibition held in London. Suffragette 'Black Friday' demonstration (18 Nov).
Coronation of George V. Agadir crisis. Industrial unrest in Britain.

The *Titanic* sinks. Captain Scott's Antarctic expedition ends in tragedy. Crisis in Ireland: Ulster opposes Home Rule.

Outbreak of World War I.

Asquith forms wartime coalition with Conservatives. Zeppelin raids. Gallipoli landings. *Lusitania* sunk by German submarine. Einstein's general theory of relativity.

First battle of the Somme. Battles of Verdun and Jutland. Lloyd George becomes Prime Minister (to 1922). Easter Rising in Dublin.

DATE	AUTHOR'S LIFE	LITERARY CONTEXT
1917		Barrie: *Dear Brutus.* Eliot: *Prufrock and Other Observations.*
1918	Arrival of Maud Waddell, 'Tod', one of several governesses to educate the du Maurier children, and Daphne's favourite amongst them.	West: *The Return of the Soldier.* Strachey: *Eminent Victorians.*
1920		Christie: *The Mysterious Affair at Styles.* Lawrence: *Women in Love.* Wharton: *The Age of Innocence.* Mansfield: *Bliss.*
1921		Maugham: *The Trembling of a Leaf.*
1922	Writes first short story, 'The Seekers'. Gerald du Maurier is knighted.	Woolf: *Jacob's Room.* Mansfield: *The Garden Party.* Sinclair: *The Life and Death of Harriett Frean.* Colette: *La Maison de Claudine.*
1923		Macaulay: *Told by an Idiot.* Wodehouse: *Leave It to Psmith.* Huxley: *Antic Hay.*
1924		Forster: *A Passage to India.* Webb: *Precious Bane.* Irwin: *Still She Wished For Company.* Kennedy: *The Constant Nymph.*
1925	Attends finishing school in Camposena, a village near Paris. Close relationship with French teacher, Fernando ('Ferdy') Yvon.	Wharton: *The Mother's Recompense.* Fitzgerald: *The Great Gatsby.* Coward: *Hay Fever.*
1926	First stay at the family's new holiday home in Bodinnick by Fowey, which kindles du Maurier's life-long passion for Cornwall, an area that provides the back-drop for many of her works. Meets Sir Arthur Quiller-Couch, a prominent writer and Cambridge academic who lives half the year at Fowey. Writing for just one hour a day.	Maugham: *The Casuarina Tree.* Wallace: *The Ringer.* Warner: *Lolly Willowes.* Parker: *Enough Rope.*

CHRONOLOGY

February and October Revolutions in Russia; civil war begins. US joins World War I. Battle of Passchendaele. Balfour Declaration on Palestine.

Execution of Nicholas II and his family. Second battle of the Marne. Armistice (11 Nov). Women over 30 gain vote in Britain. Sinn Féin win Irish elections (Dec) and declare independence the next month, initiating Ango-Irish War (to 1921).

League of Nations formed. Prohibition in the US.

British Broadcasting Company founded.

Irish Free State established. Civil war in Ireland. Fall of Lloyd George. Soviet Union established. Mussolini marches on Rome. Tutankhamun's tomb discovered.

Hitler's coup in Munich fails. Women gain legal equality in divorce suits.

First Labour government formed by Ramsay MacDonald (Jan–Nov). Conservative election victory; Baldwin Prime Minister (to 1929). British Empire Exhibition in London (to 1925). Death of Lenin.

Locarno Conference. Hitler: *Mein Kampf.*

British general strike. First television demonstrated by J. L. Baird.

DATE	AUTHOR'S LIFE	LITERARY CONTEXT
1927	Continues writing. Her short stories attract the attention of literary agent A. P. Watt.	Cather: *Death Comes for the Archbishop.* Woolf: *To the Lighthouse.* Holtby: *The Land of Green Ginger.* Lehmann: *Dusty Answer.*
1928		Radclyffe Hall: *The Well of Loneliness.* Woolf: *Orlando.* Lawrence: *Lady Chatterley's Lover.*
1929	Meets and has a brief affair with film director Carol Reed. Publishes her first story, 'And Now to God the Father', in the *Bystander*, a magazine edited by her uncle. Signed up by the literary agency Curtis Brown. Begins writing in earnest.	West: *Harriet Hume.* Priestley: *The Good Companions.* Compton-Burnett: *Brothers and Sisters.* Hemingway: *A Farewell to Arms.*
1930		Lawrence: *The Virgin and the Gypsy.* Christie: *Murder at the Vicarage.* Walpole: *Rogue Herries.* Delafield: *The Diary of a Provincial Lady.*
1931	First novel, *The Loving Spirit*, is published by Heinemann and is an immediate success.	Sackville-West: *All Passion Spent.* Rhys: *After Leaving Mr. Mackenzie.* Ferguson: *The Brontës Went to Walworth's.*
1932	Publishes second novel, *I'll Never be Young Again*. Marries Frederick (known as 'Tommy' or 'Boy') Browning, a major in the Grenadier Guards, whom she had met the year before in Cornwall.	Gibbons: *Cold Comfort Farm.* Huxley: *Brave New World.* Waugh: *Black Mischief.* Macaulay: *They Were Defeated.*
1933	Birth of first child, Tessa. *The Progress of Julius* (novel) published.	Brittain: *Testament of Youth.* White: *Frost in May.* Sayers: *Murder Must Advertise.* Maugham: *Ah King.*
1934	Death of father; du Maurier publishes *Gerald: A Portrait*, a biography of her father, within months.	Waugh: *A Handful of Dust.* Christie: *Murder on the Orient Express.* Irwin: *The Proud Servant.* Graves: *I, Claudius.*

CHRONOLOGY

Stalin expels Trotsky from Communist Party. German economy collapses. Lindbergh's Atlantic flight. 'Talkies' popularized by *The Jazz Singer*.

Women over 21 enfranchised in Britain. Stalin launches Soviet collectivization. Fleming discovers penicillin.

Wall Street crash. Beginning of worldwide economic depression. Second Labour government under MacDonald.

Gandhi begins civil disobedience campaign in India. Nazis win seats from the moderates in German election. Amy Johnson flies from London to Australia.

Britain abandons the Gold Standard. MacDonald forms National Government (to 1935).

Unemployment in Britain reaches 3.4 million. Hunger marches. Mosley's British Union of Fascists formed. F. D. Roosevelt's landslide victory in the US. Geneva Disarmament Conference. Cockcroft and Walton split the atom.

Roosevelt announces 'New Deal'. Prohibition repealed. Hitler becomes Chancellor of Germany. Nazi persecution of Jews begins.

Stavisky scandal in France. Riots in Paris: Doumerge forms National Union ministry. Hitler becomes Führer.

DATE	AUTHOR'S LIFE	LITERARY CONTEXT
1935	Presented at Court.	Isherwood: *Mr. Norris Changes Trains.* Bowen: *The House in Paris.* Compton-Burnett: *A House and its Head.*
1936	*Jamaica Inn* (novel) published; within three months it sells (in England) more than her first three novels put together. Sails to Egypt, where her husband's battalion has been posted.	Mitchell: *Gone with the Wind.* West: *The Thinking Reed.* Holtby: *South Riding.* Lehmann: *The Weather in the Streets.* Stevie Smith: *Novel on Yellow Paper.* Warner: *Summer Will Show.*
1937	*The Du Mauriers*, a history of her family, published. Returns to England. Birth of second child, Flavia. Moves to Fleet, Hampshire, where her husband is now stationed.	M. J. Farrell: *The Rising Tide.* Priestley: *Time and the Conways.* Forester: *The Happy Return.*
1938	*Rebecca* (novel) is an instant hit upon publication.	Bowen: *The Death of the Heart.* White: *The Sword in the Stone.* Pritchett: *You Make Your Own Life.* Waugh: *The Code of the Woosters.*
1939	Moves to Hythe, in Kent.	Greene: *The Confidential Agent.*
1940	*Come Wind, Come Weather* (short stories) published. Laurence Olivier and Joan Fontaine star in Alfred Hitchcock's film version of *Rebecca*, which wins Academy Award for best picture. Moves to Langley End, Hertfordshire. Birth of third child, Christian.	Hemingway: *For Whom the Bell Tolls.* Stead: *The Man Who Loved Children.*
1941	*Frenchman's Creek* (novel) published.	Coward: *Blithe Spirit.* Angela du Maurier: *The Little Less.*
1943	*Hungry Hill* (novel) published. Obtains a twenty-year lease on Menabilly, a run-down mansion in Cornwall which had caught her attention as a child and was the inspiration for Manderley in *Rebecca*.	Colette: *Gigi.*
1944		

CHRONOLOGY

Italy invades Abyssinia. Baldwin Prime Minister (to 1937). Penguin publishes first paperback books.

Death of George V; abdication of Edward VIII and accession of George VI. Spanish Civil War (to 1939). Hitler and Mussolini form Rome–Berlin Axis. German troops enter Rhineland. Churchill calls for rearmament. Blum forms Popular Front government in France. Jarrow Crusade. BBC begins television broadcasts. Alan Turing invents the principle of the modern computer.

Guernica, Spain, bombed by German planes. Chamberlain's policy of appeasement. 'Hindenburg' disaster. First jet engine and nylon stockings.

Fall of Blum and collapse of the Popular Front in France. Germany annexes Austria. Munich crisis. Germany occupies disputed areas of Czechoslovakia.

Molotov–Ribbentrop pact between Germany and the USSR. Germany invades Poland; Britain and France declare war (3 Sept).
Resignation of Chamberlain; Churchill leads wartime coalition government (May). Fall of France. Evacuation of Dunkirk. Battle of Britain. The Blitz. Home Guard formed. Rationing introduced. Italy joins the war in alliance with Germany.

German army invades USSR. Japanese attack Pearl Harbor. US joins war.

Russian victory at Stalingrad. Germans surrender in North Africa. Allies invade Italy.

Normandy landings. Red Army reaches Belgrade and Budapest. Butler's Education Act.

DATE	AUTHOR'S LIFE	LITERARY CONTEXT
1945	*The Years Between* (play) opens in London.	Waugh: *Brideshead Revisited.* Orwell: *Animal Farm.* Graham: *Ross Poldark.* Mitford: *The Pursuit of Love.*
1946	*The King's General* (novel) published.	Taylor: *Palladian.* Rattigan: *The Winslow Boy.*
1947	Visits the US to defend herself (successfully) in court against a charge of plagiarism for *Rebecca*. Meets Noël Coward and develops a passionate friendship with Ellen Doubleday, the wife of her American publisher.	Priestley: *An Inspector Calls.* Williams: *A Steetcar Named Desire.* Bradbury: *Dark Carnival.*
1948	Visits America again.	Bowen: *The Heat of the Day.* Greene: *The Heart of the Matter.*
1949	*September Tide* (play) opens in London, starring the actress Gertrude Lawrence, with whom du Maurier develops a close friendship. *The Parasites* (novel) published. Visits Italy with Ellen Doubleday.	Dodie Smith: *I Capture the Castle.* Mitford: *Love in a Cold Climate.* Orwell: *Nineteen Eighty-Four.*
1951	*The Young George du Maurier: A Selection of His Letters, 1860–1867* and *My Cousin Rachel* (novel) published. Angela's memoir, *It's Only the Sister*, published.	Taylor: *A Game of Hide and Seek.* Powell: *A Question of Upbringing.* Greene: *The End of the Affair.*
1952	*The Apple Tree* (short stories) published, which includes 'The Birds'. Film version of *My Cousin Rachel*, starring Richard Burton and Olivia de Havilland.	Pym: *Excellent Women.* Waugh: *Men at Arms.* Allingham: *The Tiger in the Smoke.* Rattigan: *The Deep Blue Sea.*
1953	*Happy Christmas* (novella) published.	Pym: *Jane and Prudence.* Lehmann: *The Echoing Grove.* Hartley: *The Go-Between.* Fleming: *Casino Royale.*
1954	*Mary Anne* (novel) published. Visits Greece.	Murdoch: *Under the Net.* Taylor: *Hester Lilly.*
1955	*Early Stories* (1927–1930) published.	Highsmith: *The Talented Mr. Ripley.*
1956		West: *The Fountain Overflows.* Macaulay: *The Towers of Trebizond.* Bedford: *A Legacy.*

CHRONOLOGY

Roosevelt dies; Truman becomes US President. Death of Mussolini and Hitler. Germany surrenders. World War II ends after nuclear bombs are dropped on Hiroshima and Nagasaki. United Nations founded. Attlee forms Labour government.
Nuremberg trials. Churchill's 'Iron Curtain' speech. Beginning of Cold War.

Independence of India and Pakistan. Marshall Plan: US gives aid for European post-war recovery.

National Health Service founded. Postwar immigration from the Commonwealth begins. State of Israel established. Soviet blockade of Berlin and Allied airlift. Communist coup in Czechoslovakia. *Apartheid* becomes official policy in South Africa. Assassination of Gandhi.
NATO founded. Germany is divided into East and West. Communist revolution in China. Ireland becomes a republic and withdraws from the Commonwealth.

Defection of Burgess and Maclean to USSR. Churchill returned to power.

Accession of Elizabeth II. Eisenhower is elected US President. Britain produces its first atomic bomb. The 'Great Smog' in London kills 12,000.

Stalin dies. Tito becomes President of Yugoslavia. Korean War ends. European Court of Human Rights set up. Hillary and Tenzing reach summit of Everest. Watson and Crick describe the structure of DNA.

Vietnam War begins. Nasser gains power in Egypt. First commercial TV station in Britain.
Warsaw Pact formed. Churchill retires and is succeeded by Eden.

Khrushchev denounces Stalin. Invasion of Hungary by USSR. Suez crisis. Britain's first nuclear power station opens.

DATE	AUTHOR'S LIFE	LITERARY CONTEXT
1957	Death of her mother. *The Scapegoat* (novel) published.	Pasternak: *Doctor Zhivago*. Highsmith: *Deep Water*.
1958		Murdoch: *The Bell*. Renault: *The King Must Die*.
1959	*The Breaking Point* (short stories) published.	Spark: *Memento Mori*. Jackson: *The Haunting of Hill House*.
1960	*The Infernal World of Branwell Brontë* (biography) published.	Manning: *The Balkan Trilogy* (to 1965). O'Brien: *The Country Girls*. Dahl: *Kiss, Kiss*. Lee: *To Kill a Mockingbird*.
1961		Spark: *The Prime of Miss Jean Brodie*.
1962	Completes *Castle Dor*, an unfinished historical novel begun by Sir Arthur Quiller-Couch.	Lessing: *The Golden Notebook*.
1963	*The Glass Blowers* (novel) published. Release of Hitchcock's film *The Birds*, inspired by du Maurier's short story of the same name.	Le Carré: *The Spy Who Came in from the Cold*. Plath: *The Bell Jar*. Spark: *The Girls of Slender Means*. McCarthy: *The Group*.
1965	*The Flight of the Falcon* (novel) published. Death of husband.	Drabble: *The Millstone*. Spark: *The Mandelbaum Gate*.
1966		West: *The Birds Fall Down*. Rhys: *Wide Sargasso Sea*. Scott: *The Jewel in the Crown*.
1967	*Vanishing Cornwall* published, which includes reminiscences of du Maurier's childhood.	
1968		Yourcenar: *The Abyss*.
1969	*The House on the Strand* (novel) published. Created Dame of the British Empire. Moves to Kilmarth at Par, on the Cornish coast, where she spends the last twenty years of her life.	O'Brian: *Master and Commander*. Fowles: *The French Lieutenant's Woman*. Drabble: *The Waterfall*.

CHRONOLOGY

Macmillan becomes Prime Minister (to 1963). Treaty of Rome: EEC founded. Soviet Sputnik flight. Ghana becomes the first African country to gain independence from Britain.
Campaign for Nuclear Disarmament (CND) founded.

'Most of our people have never had it so good' – Macmillan celebrates British postwar economic recovery. De Gaulle becomes French President (to 1969). Castro seizes power in Cuba.
Macmillan's 'Wind of Change' speech, accepting the inevitable wind-down of the British empire. Sharpeville massacre in South Africa; African National Congress (ANC) outlawed. J. F. Kennedy elected US President.

Berlin wall erected. Yuri Gagarin becomes first man in space. Bay of Pigs invasion. Britain applies to join the EEC; membership blocked by De Gaulle throughout the 1960s. Contraceptive pill becomes generally available in Britain.
Cuban missile crisis. Anglo-French agreement on the construction of Concorde.

Assassination of President Kennedy. Civil Rights March on Washington. Profumo affair. Douglas-Home becomes Prime Minister. Beatles' first LP released.

Comprehensive education introduced by Harold Wilson's Labour government. Death of Churchill.

Mao launches Cultural Revolution in China.

Arab–Israeli Six-Day War. First heart-transplant operation. Homosexuality and abortion legalized in Britain.

Soviet invasion of Czechoslovakia. Widespread student unrest in Europe; massive anti-Vietnam War protests in US. Assassination of Martin Luther King. Enoch Powell's 'rivers of blood' speech against Commonwealth immigration to Britain.
Americans land first man on the moon. Violence in Northern Ireland; British troops made responsible for security. North Sea oil first discovered. Capital punishment abolished in Britain. Voting age lowered from 21 to 18. First Booker Prize for fiction awarded.

DATE	AUTHOR'S LIFE	LITERARY CONTEXT
1970		Spark: *The Driver's Seat.*
1971	*Not After Midnight* (short stories) published, which includes 'Don't Look Now', later turned into a film starring Julie Christie and Donald Sutherland (1973).	Forster: *Maurice.* Munro: *Lives of Girls and Women.*
1972	*Rule Britannia* (novel) published.	
1973		J. G. Farrell: *The Siege of Krishnapur.*
1974		Bainbridge: *The Bottle Factory Outing.*
1975	*Golden Lads: Anthony Bacon, Francis and their Friends* (history) published.	
1976	*The Winding Stair: Francis Bacon, his Rise and Fall* (biography) and *Echoes from the Macabre* (short stories) published.	Bawden: *Afternoon of a Good Woman.* Rice: *Interview with the Vampire.*
1977	*Growing Pains: The Shaping of a Writer* (autobiography) published. Defends her late husband against his unsympathetic portrayal as commander of the British Airborne Corps at the battle of Arnhem in the film *A Bridge Too Far*. Beginning of sustained periods of depression.	Bainbridge: *Injury Time.* Pym: *Quartet in Autumn.* Rendell: *A Judgement in Stone.* Atwood: *Dancing Girls.*
1978	Receives the Mystery Writers of America's Grand Master Award.	Byatt: *The Virgin in the Garden.* Murdoch: *The Sea, The Sea.*
1979		P. Fitzgerald: *Offshore.*
1980	*Rendezvous and Other Stories* published.	P. Fitzgerald: *Human Voices.*
1981	*The Rebecca Notebook and Other Memories* (an account of writing *Rebecca*) and *Classics from the Macabre* (short stories) published.	Keane: *Good Behaviour.* Yourcenar: *Anna, Soror.*

CHRONOLOGY

HISTORICAL EVENTS

Edward Heath becomes Prime Minister (Conservative). The Beatles
break up.
Industrial Relations Act curbs power of trade unions. Decimal currency
introduced as part of programme of metrication.

Miners' strike over pay (Jan–Feb); power cuts introduced and state of
emergency declared. Bloody Sunday in Northern Ireland. Direct rule
imposed by Britain. USSR and US sign SALT I.
Britain and Ireland join EEC. Arab–Israeli war. Middle East oil embargo
causes energy crisis in West. Miners' overtime ban; three-day week comes
into operation to save energy (Dec). IRA bombing campaign hits London.
Virago Press founded.
Harold Wilson Prime Minister; draws up Social Contract with trade unions.
President Nixon resigns after Watergate scandal.
Vietnam War ends. EEC referendum – Britain votes to stay in. First North
Sea oil pumped ashore.

James Callaghan Prime Minister (Labour). Carter elected President in US.
Soweto massacre in South Africa. National Theatre opens in London.

Queen Elizabeth's Silver Jubilee. First Apple computers go on sale.

Camp David agreement between US, Egypt and Israel. P. W. Botha comes
to power in South Africa. Birth of first 'test-tube baby', Louise Brown, in
England.
'Winter of Discontent' – strike of public sector workers. Margaret Thatcher
becomes the UK's first woman Prime Minister. Ayatollah Khomeini heads
new Islamic republic in Iran. Carter and Brezhnev sign SALT II. Soviet
forces invade Afghanistan.
Housing Act introduces 'Right to Buy' scheme for council tenants.
Republican hunger strikes in the Maze prison, Belfast. Lech Walesa leads
strikes in Gdansk, Poland.
Race riots in Liverpool and London. Social Democratic Party (SDP)
founded. First cases of AIDS detected in US and UK. Wedding of Prince
Charles and Lady Diana Spencer. Ronald Reagan becomes US President.

DATE	AUTHOR'S LIFE	LITERARY CONTEXT
1981 *cont.*	Suffers a heart attack while in hospital. Increasing ill health leads du Maurier to stop writing and gradually withdraw into herself.	
1982		P. D. James: *The Skull Beneath the Skin.*
1983		Le Carré: *The Little Drummer Girl.* Hill: *The Woman in Black.* Weldon: *The Lives and Loves of a She-Devil.*
1984		Wesley: *The Camomile Lawn.* Brookner: *Hotel du Lac.* Carter: *Nights at the Circus.*
1989	Dies at her home in Cornwall.	

HISTORICAL EVENTS

Falklands War.

Reagan announces Strategic Defence Initiative ('Star Wars'). Britain, formerly the 'workshop of the world', becomes a net importer of machinery. Microsoft Word launched.

British miners begin year-long strike. British Telecom is the first public utility to be privatized, initiating the era of 'popular capitalism'.

Collapse of Communism in Eastern Europe. Fall of the Berlin Wall. Tiananmen Square massacre in China. Tim Berners-Lee invents the Worldwide Web.

REBECCA

1

LAST NIGHT I dreamt I went to Manderley again. It seemed to me I stood by the iron gate leading to the drive, and for a while I could not enter, for the way was barred to me. There was a padlock and a chain upon the gate. I called in my dream to the lodgekeeper, and had no answer, and peering closer through the rusted spokes of the gate I saw that the lodge was uninhabited.

No smoke came from the chimney, and the little lattice windows gaped forlorn. Then, like all dreamers, I was possessed of a sudden with supernatural powers and passed like a spirit through the barrier before me. The drive wound away in front of me, twisting and turning as it had always done, but as I advanced I was aware that a change had come upon it; it was narrow and unkept, not the drive that we had known. At first I was puzzled and did not understand, and it was only when I bent my head to avoid the low swinging branch of a tree that I realized what had happened. Nature had come into her own again and, little by little, in her stealthy, insidious way had encroached upon the drive with long, tenacious fingers. The woods, always a menace even in the past, had triumphed in the end. They crowded, dark and uncontrolled, to the borders of the drive. The beeches with white, naked limbs leant close to one another, their branches intermingled in a strange embrace, making a vault above my head like the archway of a church. And there were other trees as well, trees that I did not recognize, squat oaks and tortured elms that straggled cheek by jowl with the beeches, and had thrust themselves out of the quiet earth, along with monster shrubs and plants, none of which I remembered.

The drive was a ribbon now, a thread of its former self, with gravel surface gone, and choked with grass and moss. The trees had thrown out low branches, making an impediment to progress; the gnarled roots looked like skeleton claws. Scattered here and again amongst this jungle growth I would recognize shrubs that had been landmarks in our time, things of culture and grace, hydrangeas whose blue heads had been famous. No hand had checked their progress, and they had gone native now, rearing to monster height without a bloom, black and ugly as the nameless parasites that grew beside them.

On and on, now east now west, wound the poor thread that once had been our drive. Sometimes I thought it lost, but it appeared again, beneath a fallen tree perhaps, or struggling on the other side of a muddied ditch created by the winter rains. I had not thought the way so long. Surely the miles had multiplied, even as the trees had done, and this path led but to a labyrinth, some choked wilderness, and not to the house at all. I came upon it suddenly; the approach masked by the unnatural growth of a vast shrub that spread in all directions, and I stood, my heart thumping in my breast, the strange prick of tears behind my eyes.

There was Manderley, our Manderley, secretive and silent as it had always been, the grey stone shining in the moonlight of my dream, the mullioned windows reflecting the green lawns and the terrace. Time could not wreck the perfect symmetry of those walls, nor the site itself, a jewel in the hollow of a hand.

The terrace sloped to the lawns, and the lawns stretched to the sea, and turning I could see the sheet of silver placid under the moon, like a lake undisturbed by wind or storm. No waves would come to ruffle this dream water, and no bulk of cloud, wind-driven from the west, obscure the clarity of this pale sky. I turned again to the house, and though it stood inviolate, untouched, as though we ourselves had left but yesterday, I saw that the garden had obeyed the jungle law, even as the woods had done. The rhododendrons stood fifty feet high, twisted and entwined with bracken, and they had entered into alien marriage with a host of nameless shrubs, poor, bastard things that clung about their roots as though conscious of their spurious origin. A lilac had mated with a copper beech, and to bind them yet more closely to one another the malevolent ivy, always an enemy to grace, had thrown her tendrils about the pair and made them prisoners. Ivy held prior place in this lost garden, the long strands crept across the lawns, and soon would encroach upon the house itself. There was another plant too, some half-breed from the woods, whose seed had been scattered long ago beneath the trees and then forgotten, and now, marching in unison with the ivy, thrust its ugly form like a giant rhubarb towards the soft grass where the daffodils had blown.

Nettles were everywhere, the vanguard of the army. They choked the terrace, they sprawled about the paths, they leant, vulgar and lanky, against the very windows of the house. They made indifferent sentinels, for in many places their ranks had been broken by the rhubarb plant, and they lay with crumpled heads and listless stems, making a pathway for the rabbits. I left the drive and went on to the terrace, for the nettles were no barrier to me, a dreamer. I walked enchanted, and nothing held me back.

Moonlight can play odd tricks upon the fancy, even upon a dreamer's fancy. As I stood there, hushed and still, I could swear that the house was not an empty shell but lived and breathed as it had lived before.

Light came from the windows, the curtains blew softly in the night air, and there, in the library, the door would stand half open as we had left it, with my handkerchief on the table beside the bowl of autumn roses.

The room would bear witness to our presence. The little heap of library books marked ready to return, and the discarded copy of *The Times*. Ash-trays, with the stub of a cigarette; cushions, with the imprint of our heads upon them, lolling in the chairs; the charred embers of our log fire still smouldering against the morning. And Jasper, dear Jasper, with his soulful eyes and great, sagging jowl, would be stretched upon the floor, his tail a-thump when he heard his master's footsteps.

A cloud, hitherto unseen, came upon the moon, and hovered an instant like a dark hand before a face. The illusion went with it, and the lights in the windows were extinguished. I looked upon a desolate shell, soulless at last, unhaunted, with no whisper of the past about its staring walls.

The house was a sepulchre, our fear and suffering lay buried in the ruins. There would be no resurrection. When I thought of Manderley in my waking hours I would not be bitter. I should think of it as it might have been, could I have lived there without fear. I should remember the rose-garden in summer, and the birds that sang at dawn. Tea under the chestnut tree, and the murmur of the sea coming up to us from the lawns below.

I would think of the blown lilac, and the Happy Valley. These things were permanent, they could not be dissolved. They were memories that cannot hurt. All this I resolved in my dream, while the clouds lay across the face of the moon, for like most sleepers I knew that I dreamed. In reality I lay many hundred miles away in an alien land, and would wake, before many seconds had passed, in the bare little hotel bedroom, comforting in its very lack of atmosphere. I would sigh a moment, stretch myself and turn, and opening my eyes, be bewildered at that glittering sun, that hard, clean sky, so different from the soft moonlight of my dream. The day would lie before us both, long no doubt, and uneventful, but fraught with a certain stillness, a dear tranquillity we had not known before. We would not talk of Manderley, I would not tell my dream. For Manderley was ours no longer. Manderley was no more.

2

WE CAN NEVER go back again, that much is certain. The past is
still too close to us. The things we have tried to forget and put
behind us would stir again, and that sense of fear, of furtive unrest,
struggling at length to blind unreasoning panic – now mercifully
stilled, thank God – might in some manner unforeseen become
a living companion, as it had been before.

He is wonderfully patient and never complains, not even
when he remembers ... which happens, I think, rather more
often than he would have me know.

I can tell by the way he will look lost and puzzled suddenly,
all expression dying away from his dear face as though swept clean
by an unseen hand, and in its place a mask will form, a sculptured
thing, formal and cold, beautiful still but lifeless. He will fall to
smoking cigarette after cigarette, not bothering to extinguish
them, and the glowing stubs will lie around on the ground like
petals. He will talk quickly and eagerly about nothing at all,
snatching at any subject as a panacea to pain. I believe there is
a theory that men and women emerge finer and stronger after
suffering, and that to advance in this or any world we must endure
ordeal by fire. This we have done in full measure, ironic though
it seems. We have both known fear, and loneliness, and very great
distress. I suppose sooner or later in the life of everyone comes a
moment of trial. We all of us have our particular devil who rides
us and torments us, and we must give battle in the end. We have
conquered ours, or so we believe.

The devil does not ride us any more. We have come through
our crisis, not unscathed of course. His premonition of disaster
was correct from the beginning; and like a ranting actress in an
indifferent play, I might say that we have paid for freedom. But
I have had enough melodrama in this life, and would willingly

give my five senses if they could ensure us our present peace and security. Happiness is not a possession to be prized, it is a quality of thought, a state of mind. Of course we have our moments of depression; but there are other moments too, when time, unmeasured by the clock, runs on into eternity and, catching his smile, I know we are together, we march in unison, no clash of thought or of opinion makes a barrier between us.

We have no secrets now from one another. All things are shared. Granted that our little hotel is dull, and the food indifferent, and that day after day dawns very much the same, yet we would not have it otherwise. We should meet too many of the people he knows in any of the big hotels. We both appreciate simplicity, and we are sometimes bored – well, boredom is a pleasing antidote to fear. We live very much by routine, and I – I have developed a genius for reading aloud. The only time I have known him show impatience is when the postman lags, for it means we must wait another day before the arrival of our English mail. We have tried wireless, but the noise is such an irritant, and we prefer to store up our excitement; the result of a cricket match played many days ago means much to us.

Oh, the Test matches that have saved us from ennui, the boxing bouts, even the billiard scores. Finals of schoolboy sports, dog racing, strange little competitions in the remoter counties, all these are grist to our hungry mill. Sometimes old copies of the *Field* come my way, and I am transported from this indifferent island to the realities of an English spring. I read of chalk streams, of the mayfly, of sorrel growing in green meadows, of rooks circling above the woods as they used to do at Manderley. The smell of wet earth comes to me from those thumbed and tattered pages, the sour tang of moorland peat, the feel of soggy moss spattered white in places by a heron's droppings.

Once there was an article on wood pigeons, and as I read it aloud it seemed to me that once again I was in the deep woods at Manderley, with pigeons fluttering above my head. I heard their soft, complacent call, so comfortable and cool on a hot summer's afternoon, and there would be no disturbing of their peace until Jasper came loping through the undergrowth to find me, his damp muzzle questing the ground. Like old ladies caught at their ablutions, the pigeons would flutter from their hiding-place, shocked into silly agitation, and, making a monstrous to-do with their wings, streak away from us above the tree-tops, and so out of sight and sound. When they were gone a new silence would come upon the place, and I – uneasy for no known reason – would realize that the sun no longer wove a pattern on the rustling leaves, that the branches had grown darker, the shadows longer; and back at the house there would be fresh raspberries for tea. I would rise from my bed of bracken then, shaking the feathery dust of last year's leaves from my skirt and whistling to Jasper, set off towards the house, despising myself even as I walked for my hurrying feet, my one swift glance behind.

How strange that an article on wood pigeons could so recall the past and make me falter as I read aloud. It was the grey look on his face that made me stop abruptly, and turn the pages until I found a paragraph on cricket, very practical and dull – Middlesex batting on a dry wicket at the Oval and piling up interminable dreary runs. How I blessed those solid, flannelled figures, for in a few minutes his face had settled back into repose, the colour had returned, and he was deriding the Surrey bowling in healthy irritation.

We were saved a retreat into the past, and I had learnt my lesson. Read English news, yes, and English sport, politics, and pomposity, but in future keep the things that hurt to myself alone. They can be my secret indulgence. Colour and scent and sound, rain and the lapping of water, even the mists of autumn and the smell of the flood tide, these are memories of Manderley that will not be denied. Some people have a vice of reading Bradshaws. They plan innumerable journeys across country for the fun of linking up impossible connexions. My hobby is less tedious, if as strange. I am a mine of information on the English countryside. I know the name of every owner of every British moor, yes – and their tenants too. I know how many grouse are killed, how many partridge, how many head of deer. I know where trout are rising, and where the salmon leap. I attend all meets, I follow every run. Even the names of those who walk hound puppies are familiar to me. The state of the crops, the price of fat cattle, the mysterious ailments of swine, I relish them all. A poor pastime, perhaps, and not a very intellectual one, but I breathe the air of England as I read, and can face this glittering sky with greater courage.

The scrubby vineyards and the crumbling stones become things of no account, for if I wish I can give rein to my imagination, and pick foxgloves and pale campions from a wet, streaking hedge.

Poor whims of fancy, tender and un-harsh. They are the enemy to bitterness and regret, and sweeten this exile we have brought upon ourselves.

Because of them I can enjoy my afternoon, and return, smiling and refreshed, to face the little ritual of our tea. The order never varies. Two slices of bread and butter each, and China tea. What a hide-bound couple we must seem, clinging to custom because we did so in England. Here, on this clean balcony, white and impersonal with centuries of sun, I think of half past four at Manderley, and the table drawn before the library fire. The door flung open, punctual to the minute, and the performance, never-varying, of the laying of the tea, the silver tray, the kettle, the snowy cloth. While Jasper, his spaniel ears a-droop, feigns indifference to the arrival of the cakes. That feast was laid before us always, and yet we ate so little.

Those dripping crumpets, I can see them now. Tiny crisp wedges of toast, and piping-hot, floury scones. Sandwiches of unknown nature, mysteriously flavoured and quite delectable, and that very special gingerbread. Angel cake, that melted in the mouth, and his rather stodgier companion, bursting with peel and raisins. There was enough food there to keep a starving family for a week. I never knew what happened to it all, and the waste used to worry me sometimes.

But I never dared ask Mrs Danvers what she did about it. She would have looked at me in scorn, smiling that freezing, superior smile of hers, and I can imagine her saying: 'There were never any complaints when Mrs de Winter was alive.' Mrs Danvers. I wonder what she is doing now. She and Favell. I think it was the expression on her face that gave me my first feeling of unrest. Instinctively I thought, 'She is comparing me to Rebecca'; and sharp as a sword the shadow came between us . . .

Well, it is over now, finished and done with. I ride no more tormented, and both of us are free. Even my faithful Jasper has gone to the happy hunting grounds, and Manderley is no more. It lies like an empty shell amidst the tangle of the deep woods, even as I saw it in my dream. A multitude of weeds, a colony of birds. Sometimes perhaps a tramp will wander there, seeking shelter from a sudden shower of rain and, if he is stout-hearted, he may walk there with impunity. But your timid fellow, your nervous poacher – the woods of Manderley are not for him. He might stumble upon the little cottage in the cove and he would not be happy beneath its tumbled roof, the thin rain beating a tattoo. There might linger there still a certain atmosphere of stress . . . That corner in the drive, too, where the trees encroach upon the gravel, is not a place in which to pause, not after the sun has set. When the leaves rustle, they sound very much like the stealthy movement of a woman in evening dress, and when they shiver suddenly, and fall, and scatter away along the ground, they might be the patter, patter, of a woman's hurrying footstep, and the mark in the gravel the imprint of a high-heeled satin shoe.

It is when I remember these things that I return with relief to the prospect from our balcony. No shadows steal upon this hard glare, the stony vineyards shimmer in the sun and the bougainvillaea is white with dust. I may one day look upon it with affection. At the moment it inspires me, if not with love, at least with confidence. And confidence is a quality I prize, although it has come to me a little late in the day. I suppose it is his dependence upon me that has made me bold at last. At any rate I have lost my diffidence, my timidity, my shyness with strangers. I am very different from that self who drove to Manderley for the first time, hopeful and eager, handicapped by a rather desperate gaucherie and filled with an intense desire to please. It was my lack of poise of course that made such a bad impression on people like Mrs Danvers. What must I have seemed like after Rebecca? I can see myself now, memory spanning the years like a bridge, with straight, bobbed hair and youthful, unpowdered face, dressed in an ill-fitting coat and skirt and a jumper of my own creation, trailing in the wake of Mrs Van Hopper like a shy, uneasy colt. She would precede me in to lunch, her short body ill-balanced upon tottering, high heels, her fussy, frilly blouse a compliment to her large bosom and swinging hips, her new hat pierced with a monster quill aslant upon her head, exposing a wide expanse of forehead bare as a schoolboy's knee. One hand carried a gigantic bag, the kind that holds passports, engagement diaries, and bridge scores, while the other hand toyed with that inevitable lorgnette, the enemy to other people's privacy.

She would make for her usual table in the corner of the restaurant, close to the window, and lifting her lorgnette to her small pig's eyes survey the scene to right and left of her, then she would let the lorgnette fall at length upon its black ribbon and utter a little exclamation of disgust: 'Not a single well-known personality, I shall tell the management they must make a reduction on my bill. What do they think I come here for? To look at the page boys?' And she would summon the waiter to her side, her voice sharp and staccato, cutting the air like a saw.

How different the little restaurant where we are today to that vast dining-room, ornate and ostentatious, the Hôtel Côte d'Azur at Monte Carlo; and how different my present companion, his steady, well-shaped hands peeling a mandarin in quiet, methodical fashion, looking up now and again from his task to smile at me, compared to Mrs Van Hopper, her fat, bejewelled fingers questing a plate heaped high with ravioli, her eyes darting suspiciously from her plate to mine for fear I should have made the better choice. She need not have disturbed herself, for the waiter, with the uncanny swiftness of his kind, had long sensed my position as inferior and subservient to hers, and had placed before me a plate of ham and tongue that somebody had sent back to the cold buffet half an hour before as badly carved. Odd, that resentment of servants, and their obvious impatience. I remember staying once with Mrs Van Hopper in a country house, and the maid never answered my timid bell, or brought up my shoes, and early morning tea, stone cold, was dumped outside my bedroom door. It was the same at the Côte d'Azur, though to a lesser degree, and sometimes the studied indifference turned to familiarity, smirking and offensive, which made buying stamps from the reception clerk an ordeal I would avoid. How young and inexperienced I must have seemed, and how I felt it, too. One was too sensitive, too raw, there were thorns and pin-pricks in so many words that in reality fell lightly on the air.

I remember well that plate of ham and tongue. It was dry, unappetizing, cut in a wedge from the outside, but I had not the courage to refuse it. We ate in silence, for Mrs Van Hopper liked to concentrate on food, and I could tell by the way the sauce ran down her chin that her dish of ravioli pleased her.

It was not a sight that engendered into me great appetite for my own cold choice, and looking away from her I saw that the table next to ours, left vacant for three days, was to be occupied once more. The *maître d'hôtel*, with the particular bow reserved for his more special patrons, was ushering the new arrival to his place.

Mrs Van Hopper put down her fork, and reached for her lorgnette. I blushed for her while she stared, and the newcomer, unconscious of her interest, cast a wandering eye over the menu. Then Mrs Van Hopper folded her lorgnette with a snap, and leant across the table to me, her small eyes bright with excitement, her voice a shade too loud.

'It's Max de Winter,' she said, 'the man who owns Manderley. You've heard of it, of course. He looks ill, doesn't he? They say he can't get over his wife's death . . .'

3

I WONDER WHAT my life would be today, if Mrs Van Hopper had not been a snob.

Funny to think that the course of my existence hung like a thread upon that quality of hers. Her curiosity was a disease, almost a mania. At first I had been shocked, wretchedly embarrassed; I would feel like a whipping boy who must bear his master's pains when I watched people laugh behind her back, leave a room hurriedly upon her entrance, or even vanish behind a Service door on the corridor upstairs. For many years now she had come to the Hôtel Côte d'Azur, and, apart from bridge, her one pastime which was notorious by now in Monte Carlo, was to claim visitors of distinction as her friends had she but seen them once at the other end of the post-office. Somehow she would manage to introduce herself, and before her victim had scented danger she had proffered an invitation to her suite. Her method of attack was so downright and sudden that there was seldom opportunity to escape. At the Côte d'Azur she staked a claim upon a certain sofa in the lounge, midway between the reception hall and the passage to the restaurant, and she would have her coffee there after luncheon and dinner, and all who came and went must pass her by. Sometimes she would employ me as a bait to draw her prey, and, hating my errand, I would be sent across the lounge with a verbal message, the loan of a book or paper, the address of some shop or other, the sudden discovery of a mutual friend. It seemed as though notables must be fed to her, much as invalids are spooned their jelly; and though titles were preferred by her, any face once seen in a social paper served as well. Names scattered in a gossip column, authors, artists, actors, and their kind, even the mediocre ones, as long as she had learnt of them in print.

I can see her as though it were but yesterday, on that unforgettable afternoon – never mind how many years ago – when she sat at her favourite sofa in the lounge, debating her method of attack. I could tell by her abrupt manner, and the way she tapped her lorgnette against her teeth, that she was questing possibilities. I knew, too, when she had missed the sweet and rushed through dessert, that she had wished to finish luncheon before the new arrival and so install herself where he must pass. Suddenly she turned to me, her small eyes alight.

'Go upstairs quickly and find that letter from my nephew. You remember, the one written on his honeymoon, with the snapshot. Bring it down to me right away.'

I saw then that her plans were formed, and the nephew was to be the means of introduction. Not for the first time I resented the part that I must play in her schemes. Like a juggler's assistant I produced the props, then silent and attentive I waited on my cue. This newcomer would not welcome intrusion, I felt certain of that. In the little I had learnt of him at luncheon, a smattering of hearsay garnered by her ten months ago from the daily papers and stored in her memory for future use, I could imagine, in spite of my youth and inexperience of the world, that he would resent this sudden bursting in upon his solitude. Why he should have chosen to come to the Côte d'Azur at Monte Carlo was not our concern, his problems were his own, and anyone but Mrs Van Hopper would have understood. Tact was a quality unknown to her, discretion too, and because gossip was the breath of life to her this stranger must be served for her dissection. I found the letter in a pigeon-hole in her desk, and hesitated a moment before going down again to the lounge. It seemed to me, rather senselessly, that I was allowing him a few more moments of seclusion.

I wished I had the courage to go by the Service staircase and so by roundabout way to the restaurant, and there warn him of the ambush. Convention was too strong for me though, nor did I know how I should frame my sentence. There was nothing for it but to sit in my usual place beside Mrs Van Hopper while she, like a large, complacent spider, spun her wide net of tedium about the stranger's person.

I had been longer than I thought, for when I returned to the lounge I saw he had already left the dining-room, and she, fearful of losing him, had not waited for the letter, but had risked a bare-faced introduction on her own. He was even now sitting beside her on the sofa. I walked across to them, and gave her the letter without a word. He rose to his feet at once, while Mrs Van Hopper, flushed with her success, waved a vague hand in my direction and mumbled my name.

'Mr de Winter is having coffee with us, go and ask the waiter for another cup,' she said, her tone just casual enough to warn him of my footing. It meant I was a youthful thing and unimportant, and that there was no need to include me in the conversation. She always spoke in that tone when she wished to be impressive, and her method of introduction was a form of self-protection, for once I had been taken for her daughter, an acute embarrassment for us both. This abruptness showed that I could safely be ignored, and women would give me a brief nod which served as a greeting and a dismissal in one, while men, with large relief, would realize they could sink back into a comfortable chair without offending courtesy.

It was a surprise, therefore, to find that this newcomer remained standing on his feet, and it was he who made a signal to the waiter.

'I'm afraid I must contradict you,' he said to her, 'you are both having coffee with me'; and before I knew what had happened he was sitting in my usual hard chair, and I was on the sofa beside Mrs Van Hopper.

For a moment she looked annoyed – this was not what she had intended – but she soon composed her face, and thrusting her large self between me and the table she leant forward to his chair, talking eagerly and loudly, fluttering the letter in her hand.

'You know I recognized you just as soon as you walked into the restaurant,' she said, 'and I thought, "Why, there's Mr de Winter, Billy's friend, I simply must show him those snaps of Billy and his bride taken on their honeymoon", and here they are. There's Dora. Isn't she just adorable? That little, slim waist, those great big eyes. Here they are sun-bathing at Palm Beach. Billy is crazy about her, you can imagine. He had not met her of course when he gave that party at Claridge's, and where I saw you first. But I dare say you don't remember an old woman like me?'

This with a provocative glance and a gleam of teeth.

'On the contrary I remember you very well,' he said, and before she could trap him into a resurrection of their first meeting he had handed her his cigarette case, and the business of lighting-up stalled her for the moment. 'I don't think I should care for Palm Beach,' he said, blowing the match, and glancing at him I thought how unreal he would look against a Florida background. He belonged to a walled city of the fifteenth century, a city of narrow, cobbled streets, and thin spires, where the inhabitants wore pointed shoes and worsted hose. His face was arresting, sensitive, medieval in some strange inexplicable way, and I was reminded of a portrait seen in a gallery, I had forgotten where, of a certain Gentleman Unknown. Could one but rob him of his English tweeds, and put him in black, with lace at his throat and wrists, he would stare down at us in our new world from a long-distant past – a past where men walked cloaked at night, and stood in the shadow of old doorways, a past of narrow stairways and dim dungeons, a past of whispers in the dark, of shimmering rapier blades, of silent, exquisite courtesy.

I wished I could remember the Old Master who had painted that portrait. It stood in a corner of the gallery, and the eyes followed one from the dusky frame . . .

They were talking though, and I had lost the thread of conversation. 'No, not even twenty years ago,' he was saying. 'That sort of thing has never amused me.'

I heard Mrs Van Hopper give her fat, complacent laugh. 'If Billy had a home like Manderley he would not want to play around in Palm Beach,' she said. 'I'm told it's like fairyland, there's no other word for it.'

She paused, expecting him to smile, but he went on smoking his cigarette, and I noticed, faint as gossamer, the line between his brows.

'I've seen pictures of it, of course,' she persisted, 'and it looks perfectly enchanting. I remember Billy telling me it had all those big places beat for beauty. I wonder you can ever bear to leave it.'

His silence now was painful, and would have been patent to

anyone else, but she ran on like a clumsy goat, trampling and trespassing on land that was preserved, and I felt the colour flood my face, dragged with her as I was into humiliation.

'Of course you Englishmen are all the same about your homes,' she said, her voice becoming louder and louder, 'you depreciate them so as not to seem proud. Isn't there a minstrels' gallery at Manderley, and some very valuable portraits?' She turned to me by way of explanation. 'Mr de Winter is so modest he won't admit to it, but I believe that lovely home of his has been in his family's possession since the Conquest. They say that minstrels' gallery is a gem. I suppose your ancestors often entertained royalty at Manderley, Mr de Winter?'

This was more than I had hitherto endured, even from her, but the swift lash of his reply was unexpected. 'Not since Ethelred,' he said, 'the one who was called Unready. In fact, it was while staying with my family that the name was given him. He was invariably late for dinner.'

She deserved it, of course, and I waited for her change of face, but incredible as it may seem his words were lost on her, and I was left to writhe in her stead, feeling like a child that had been smacked.

'Is that really so?' she blundered. 'I'd no idea. My history is very shaky and the kings of England always muddled me. How interesting, though. I must write and tell my daughter; she's a great scholar.'

There was a pause, and I felt the colour flood into my face. I was too young, that was the trouble. Had I been older I would have caught his eye and smiled, her unbelievable behaviour making a bond between us; but as it was I was stricken into shame, and endured one of the frequent agonies of youth.

I think he realized my distress, for he leant forward in his chair and spoke to me, his voice gentle, asking if I would have more coffee, and when I refused and shook my head I felt his eyes were still on me, puzzled, reflective. He was pondering my exact relationship to her, and wondering whether he must bracket us together in futility.

'What do you think of Monte Carlo, or don't you think of it at all?' he said. This including of me in the conversation found me at my worst, the raw ex-schoolgirl, red-elbowed and lanky-haired, and I said something obvious and idiotic about the place being artificial, but before I could finish my halting sentence Mrs Van Hopper interrupted.

'She's spoilt, Mr de Winter, that's her trouble. Most girls would give their eyes for the chance of seeing Monte.'

'Wouldn't that rather defeat the purpose?' he said, smiling.

She shrugged her shoulders, blowing a great cloud of cigarette smoke into the air. I don't think she understood him for a moment. 'I'm faithful to Monte,' she told him; 'the English winter gets me down, and my constitution just won't stand it. What brings you here? You're not one of the regulars. Are you going to play "Chemy", or have you brought your golfclubs?'

'I have not made up my mind,' he said; 'I came away in rather a hurry.'

His own words must have jolted a memory, for his face clouded again and he frowned very slightly. She babbled on, impervious. 'Of course you miss the fogs at Manderley; it's quite another matter; the west country must be delightful in the spring.' He reached for the ash-tray, squashing his cigarette, and I noticed the subtle change in his eyes, the indefinable something that lingered there, momentarily, and I felt I had looked upon something personal to himself with which I had no concern.

'Yes,' he said shortly, 'Manderley was looking its best.'

A silence fell upon us during a moment or two, a silence that brought something of discomfort in its train, and stealing a glance at him I was reminded more than ever of my Gentleman Unknown who, cloaked and secret, walked a corridor by night. Mrs Van Hopper's voice pierced my dream like an electric bell.

'I suppose you know a crowd of people here, though I must say Monte is very dull this winter. One sees so few well-known faces. The Duke of Middlesex is here in his yacht, but I haven't been aboard yet.' She never had, to my knowledge. 'You know Nell Middlesex of course,' she went on. 'What a charmer she is. They always say that second child isn't his, but I don't believe it. People will say anything, won't they, when a woman is attractive? And she is so very lovely. Tell me, is it true the Caxton-Hyslop marriage is not a success?' She ran on, through a tangled fringe of gossip, never seeing that these names were alien to him, they meant nothing, and that as she prattled unaware he grew colder and more silent. Never for a moment did he interrupt or glance at his watch; it was as though he had set himself a standard of behaviour, since the original lapse when he had made a fool of her in front of me, and clung to it grimly rather than offend again. It was a page boy in the end who released him, with the news that a dress-maker awaited Mrs Van Hopper in the suite.

He got up at once, pushing back his chair. 'Don't let me keep you,' he said. 'Fashions change so quickly nowadays they may even have altered by the time you get upstairs.'

The sting did not touch her, she accepted it as a pleasantry. 'It's so delightful to have run into you like this, Mr de Winter,' she said, as we went towards the lift; 'now I've been brave enough to break the ice I hope I shall see something of you. You must come and have a drink some time in the suite. I may have one or two people coming in tomorrow evening. Why not join us?' I turned away so that I should not watch him search for an excuse.

'I'm so sorry,' he said, 'tomorrow I am probably driving to Sospel, I'm not sure when I shall get back.'

Reluctantly she left it, but we still hovered at the entrance to the lift.

'I hope they've given you a good room; the place is half empty, so if you are uncomfortable mind you make a fuss. Your valet has unpacked for you, I suppose?' This familiarity was excessive, even for her, and I caught a glimpse of his expression.

'I don't possess one,' he said quietly; 'perhaps you would like to do it for me?'

This time his shaft had found its mark, for she reddened, and laughed a little awkwardly.

'Why, I hardly think . . .' she began, and then suddenly, and unbelievably, she turned upon me, 'Perhaps you could make yourself useful to Mr de Winter, if he wants anything done. You're a capable child in many ways.'

There was a momentary pause, while I stood stricken, waiting for his answer. He looked down at us, mocking, faintly sardonic, a ghost of a smile on his lips.

'A charming suggestion,' he said, 'but I cling to the family motto. He travels the fastest who travels alone. Perhaps you have not heard of it.'

And without waiting for her answer he turned and left us.

'What a funny thing,' said Mrs Van Hopper, as we went upstairs in the lift. 'Do you suppose that sudden departure was a form of humour? Men do such extraordinary things. I remember a well-known writer once who used to dart down the Service staircase whenever he saw me coming. I suppose he had a penchant for me and wasn't sure of himself. However, I was younger then.'

The lift stopped with a jerk. We arrived at our floor. The page boy flung open the gates. 'By the way, dear,' she said, as we walked along the corridor, 'don't think I mean to be unkind, but you put yourself just a teeny bit forward this afternoon. Your efforts to monopolize the conversation quite embarrassed me, and I'm sure it did him. Men loathe that sort of thing.'

I said nothing. There seemed no possible reply. 'Oh, come, don't sulk,' she laughed, and shrugged her shoulders; 'after all, I am responsible for your behaviour here, and surely you can accept advice from a woman old enough to be your mother. *Eh bien, Blaize, je viens* . . .' and humming a tune she went into the bedroom where the dress-maker was waiting for her.

I knelt on the window-seat and looked out upon the afternoon. The sun shone very brightly still, and there was a gay high wind. In half an hour we should be sitting to our bridge, the windows tightly closed, the central heating turned to the full. I thought of the ash-trays I would have to clear, and how the squashed stubs, stained with lip-stick, would sprawl in company with discarded chocolate creams. Bridge does not come easily to a mind brought up on Snap and Happy Families; besides, it bored her friends to play with me.

I felt my youthful presence put a curb upon their conversation, much as a parlour-maid does until the arrival of dessert, and they could not fling themselves so easily into the melting pot of scandal and insinuation. Her men-friends would assume a sort of forced heartiness and ask me jocular questions about history or painting, guessing I had not long left school and that this would be my only form of conversation.

I sighed, and turned away from the window. The sun was so full of promise, and the sea was whipped white with a merry wind. I thought of that corner of Monaco which I had passed a day or two ago, and where a crooked house leant to a cobbled square. High up in the tumbled roof there was a window, narrow as a slit. It might have held a presence medieval; and, reaching to the desk for pencil and paper, I sketched in fancy with an absent mind a profile, pale and aquiline. A sombre eye, a high-bridged nose, a scornful upper lip. And I added a pointed beard and lace at the throat, as the painter had done, long ago in a different time.

Someone knocked at the door, and the lift-boy came in with a note in his hand. 'Madame is in the bedroom,' I told him but he shook his head and said it was for me. I opened it, and found a single sheet of note-paper inside, with a few words written in an unfamiliar hand.

'Forgive me. I was very rude this afternoon.' That was all. No signature, and no beginning. But my name was on the envelope, and spelt correctly, an unusual thing.

'Is there an answer?' asked the boy.

I looked up from the scrawled words. 'No,' I said. 'No, there isn't any answer.'

When he had gone I put the note away in my pocket, and turned once more to my pencil drawing, but for no known reason it did not please me any more; the face was stiff and lifeless, and the lace collar and the beard were like props in a charade.

4

THE MORNING AFTER the bridge party Mrs Van Hopper woke
with a sore throat and a temperature of a hundred and two. I rang
up her doctor, who came round at once and diagnosed the usual
influenza. 'You are to stay in bed until I allow you to get up,' he
told her; 'I don't like the sound of that heart of yours, and it won't
get better unless you keep perfectly quiet and still. I should prefer', he went on, turning to me, 'that Mrs Van Hopper had a
trained nurse. You can't possibly lift her. It will only be for a fortnight or so.'

I thought this rather absurd, and protested, but to my surprise
she agreed with him. I think she enjoyed the fuss it would create,
the sympathy of people, the visits and messages from friends, and
the arrival of flowers. Monte Carlo had begun to bore her,
and this little illness would make a distraction.

The nurse would give her injections, and a light massage, and
she would have a diet. I left her quite happy after the arrival of
the nurse, propped up on pillows with a falling temperature, her
best bed-jacket round her shoulders and be-ribboned boudoir
cap upon her head. Rather ashamed of my light heart, I telephoned her friends, putting off the small party she had arranged
for the evening, and went down to the restaurant for lunch, a
good half hour before our usual time. I expected the room to be
empty – nobody lunched generally before one o'clock. It was
empty, except for the table next to ours. This was a contingency
for which I was unprepared. I thought he had gone to Sospel. No
doubt he was lunching early because he hoped to avoid us at one
o'clock. I was already half-way across the room and could not go
back. I had not seen him since we disappeared in the lift the day
before, for wisely he had avoided dinner in the restaurant, possibly for the same reason that he lunched early now.

It was a situation for which I was ill-trained. I wished I was older, different. I went to our table, looking straight before me, and immediately paid the penalty of gaucherie by knocking over the vase of stiff anemones as I unfolded my napkin. The water soaked the cloth, and ran down on to my lap. The waiter was at the other end of the room, nor had he seen. In a second though my neighbour was by my side, dry napkin in hand.

'You can't sit at a wet tablecloth,' he said brusquely; 'it will put you off your food. Get out of the way.'

He began to mop the cloth, while the waiter, seeing the disturbance, came swiftly to the rescue.

'I don't mind,' I said, 'it doesn't matter a bit. I'm all alone.'

He said nothing, and then the waiter arrived and whipped away the vase and the sprawling flowers.

'Leave that,' he said suddenly, 'and lay another place at my table. Mademoiselle will have luncheon with me.'

I looked up in confusion. 'Oh, no,' I said, 'I couldn't possibly.'

'Why not?' he said.

I tried to think of an excuse. I knew he did not want to lunch with me. It was his form of courtesy. I should ruin his meal. I determined to be bold and speak the truth.

'Please,' I begged, 'don't be polite. It's very kind of you but I shall be quite all right if the waiter just wipes the cloth.'

'But I'm not being polite,' he insisted. 'I would like you to have luncheon with me. Even if you had not knocked over that vase so clumsily I should have asked you.' I suppose my face told him my doubt, for he smiled. 'You don't believe me,' he said; 'never mind, come and sit down. We needn't talk to each other unless we feel like it.'

We sat down, and he gave me the menu, leaving me to choose, and went on with his *hors d'œuvre* as though nothing had happened.

His quality of detachment was peculiar to himself, and I knew that we might continue thus, without speaking, throughout the meal and it would not matter. There would be no sense of strain. He would not ask me questions on history.

'What's happened to your friend?' he said. I told him about the influenza. 'I'm so sorry,' he said, and then, after pausing a moment, 'you got my note, I suppose. I felt very much ashamed of myself. My manners were atrocious. The only excuse I can make is that I've become boorish through living alone. That's why it's so kind of you to lunch with me today.'

'You weren't rude,' I said, 'at least, not the sort of rudeness she would understand. That curiosity of hers – she does not mean to be offensive, but she does it to everyone. That is, everyone of importance.'

'I ought to be flattered then,' he said; 'why should she consider me of any importance?'

I hesitated a moment before replying.

'I think because of Manderley,' I said.

He did not answer, and I was aware again of that feeling of discomfort, as though I had trespassed on forbidden ground. I wondered why it was that this home of his, known to so many people by hearsay, even to me, should so inevitably silence him, making as it were a barrier between him and others.

We ate for a while without talking, and I thought of a picture postcard I had bought once at a village shop, when on holiday as a child in the west country. It was the painting of a house, crudely done of course and highly coloured, but even those faults could not destroy the symmetry of the building, the wide stone steps before the terrace, the green lawns stretching to the sea. I paid twopence for the painting – half my weekly pocket money – and then asked the wrinkled shop woman what it was meant to be. She looked astonished at my ignorance.

'That's Manderley,' she said, and I remember coming out of the shop feeling rebuffed, yet hardly wiser than before.

Perhaps it was the memory of this postcard, lost long ago in some forgotten book, that made me sympathize with his defensive attitude. He resented Mrs Van Hopper and her like with their intruding questions. Maybe there was something inviolate about Manderley that made it a place apart; it would not bear discussion. I could imagine her tramping through the rooms, perhaps paying sixpence for admission, ripping the quietude with her sharp, staccato laugh. Our minds must have run in the same channel, for he began to talk about her.

'Your friend,' he began, 'she is very much older than you. Is she a relation? Have you known her long?' I saw he was still puzzled by us.

'She's not really a friend,' I told him, 'she's an employer. She's training me to be a thing called a companion, and she pays me ninety pounds a year.'

'I did not know one could buy companionship,' he said; 'it sounds a primitive idea. Rather like the Eastern slave market.'

'I looked up the word "companion" once in the dictionary,' I admitted, 'and it said "a companion is a friend of the bosom".'

'You haven't much in common with her,' he said.

He laughed, looking quite different, younger somehow and less detached. 'What do you do it for?' he asked me.

'Ninety pounds is a lot of money to me,' I said.

'Haven't you any family?'

'No – they're dead.'

'You have a very lovely and unusual name.'

'My father was a lovely and unusual person.'

'Tell me about him,' he said.

I looked at him over my glass of citronade. It was not easy to explain my father and usually I never talked about him. He was my secret property. Preserved for me alone, much as Manderley was preserved for my neighbour. I had no wish to introduce him casually over a table in a Monte Carlo restaurant.

There was a strange air of unreality about that luncheon, and looking back upon it now it is invested for me with a curious glamour. There was I, so much of a schoolgirl still, who only the day before had sat with Mrs Van Hopper, prim, silent, and subdued, and twenty-four hours afterwards my family history was mine no longer, I shared it with a man I did not know. For some reason I felt impelled to speak, because his eyes followed me in sympathy like the Gentleman Unknown.

My shyness fell away from me, loosening as it did so my reluctant tongue, and out they all came, the little secrets of childhood, the pleasures and the pains. It seemed to me as though he understood, from my poor description, something of the vibrant personality that had been my father's, and something too of the love my mother had for him; making it a vital, living force, with a spark of divinity about it, so much that when he died that desperate winter, struck down by pneumonia, she lingered behind him for five short weeks and stayed no more. I remember pausing, a little breathless, a little dazed. The restaurant was filled now with people who chatted and laughed to an orchestral background and a clatter of plates, and glancing at the clock above the door I saw that it was two o'clock. We had been sitting there an hour and a half, and the conversation had been mine alone.

I tumbled down into reality, hot-handed and self-conscious, with my face aflame, and began to stammer my apologies. He would not listen to me.

'I told you at the beginning of lunch you had a lovely and unusual name,' he said. 'I shall go further, if you will forgive me, and say that it becomes you as well as it became your father. I've enjoyed this hour with you more than I have enjoyed anything for a very long time. You've taken me out of myself, out of despondency and introspection, both of which have been my devils for a year.'

I looked at him, and believed he spoke the truth; he seemed less fettered than he had been before, more modern, more human; he was not hemmed in by shadows.

'You know,' he said, 'we've got a bond in common, you and I. We are both alone in the world. Oh, I've got a sister, though we don't see much of each other, and an ancient grandmother whom I pay duty visits to three times a year, but neither of them make for companionship. I shall have to congratulate Mrs Van Hopper. You're cheap at ninety pounds a year.'

'You forget', I said, 'you have a home and I have none.'

The moment I spoke I regretted my words, for the secret, inscrutable look came back in his eyes again, and once again I suffered the intolerable discomfort that floods one after lack of tact. He bent his head to light a cigarette, and did not reply immediately.

'An empty house can be as lonely as a full hotel,' he said at length. 'The trouble is that it is less impersonal.' He hesitated, and for a moment I thought he was going to talk of Manderley at last, but something held him back, some phobia that struggled to the surface of his mind and won supremacy, for he blew out his match and his flash of confidence at the same time.

'So the friend of the bosom has a holiday?' he said, on a level plane again, an easy camaraderie between us. 'What does she propose to do with it?'

I thought of the cobbled square in Monaco and the house with the narrow window. I could be off there by three o'clock with my sketchbook and pencil, and I told him as much, a little shyly perhaps, like all untalented persons with a pet hobby.

'I'll drive you there in the car,' he said, and would not listen to protests.

I remembered Mrs Van Hopper's warning of the night before about putting myself forward and was embarrassed that he might think my talk of Monaco was a subterfuge to win a lift. It was so blatantly the type of thing that she would do herself, and I did not want him to bracket us together. I had already risen in importance from my lunch with him, for as we got up from the table the little *maître d'hôtel* rushed forward to pull away my chair. He bowed and smiled – a total change from his usual attitude of indifference – picked up my handkerchief that had fallen on the floor, and hoped 'mademoiselle had enjoyed her lunch'. Even the page boy by the swing doors glanced at me with respect. My companion accepted it as natural, of course; he knew nothing of the ill-carved ham of yesterday. I found the change depressing, it made me despise myself. I remembered my father and his scorn of superficial snobbery.

'What are you thinking about?' We were walking along the corridor to the lounge, and looking up I saw his eyes fixed on me in curiosity.

'Has something annoyed you?' he said.

The attentions of the *maître d'hôtel* had opened up a train of thought, and as we drank coffee I told him about Blaize, the dress-maker. She had been so pleased when Mrs Van Hopper had bought three frocks, and I, taking her to the lift afterwards, had pictured her working upon them in her own small salon, behind the stuffy little shop, with a consumptive son wasting upon her sofa. I could see her, with tired eyes, threading needles, and the floor covered with snippets of material.

'Well?' he said smiling, 'wasn't your picture true?'

'I don't know,' I said, 'I never found out.' And I told him how

I had rung the bell for the lift, and as I had done so she had fumbled in her bag and gave me a note for a hundred francs. 'Here,' she had whispered, her tone intimate and unpleasant, 'I want you to accept this small commission in return for bringing your patron to my shop.' When I had refused, scarlet with embarrassment, she had shrugged her shoulders disagreeably. 'Just as you like,' she had said, 'but I assure you it's quite usual. Perhaps you would rather have a frock. Come along to the shop some time without Madame and I will fix you up without charging you a sou.' Somehow, I don't know why, I had been aware of that sick, unhealthy feeling I had experienced as a child when turning the pages of a forbidden book. The vision of the consumptive son faded, and in its stead arose the picture of myself had I been different, pocketing that greasy note with an understanding smile, and perhaps slipping round to Blaize's shop on this my free afternoon and coming away with a frock I had not paid for.

I expected him to laugh, it was a stupid story, I don't know why I told him, but he looked at me thoughtfully as he stirred his coffee.

'I think you've made a big mistake,' he said, after a moment.

'In refusing that hundred francs?' I asked, revolted.

'No – good heavens, what do you take me for? I think you've made a mistake in coming here, in joining forces with Mrs Van Hopper. You are not made for that sort of job. You're too young, for one thing, and too soft. Blaize and her commission, that's nothing. The first of many similar incidents from other Blaizes. You will either have to give in, and become a sort of Blaize yourself, or stay as you are and be broken. Who suggested you took on this thing in the first place?' It seemed natural for him to question me, nor did I mind. It was as though we had known one another for a long time, and had met again after a lapse of years.

'Have you ever thought about the future?' he asked me, 'and what this sort of thing will lead to? Supposing Mrs Van Hopper gets tired of her "friend of the bosom", what then?'

I smiled, and told him that I did not mind very much. There would be other Mrs Van Hoppers, and I was young, and confident, and strong. But even as he spoke I remembered those advertisements seen often in good class magazines where a friendly society demands succour for young women in reduced circumstances; I thought of the type of boarding-house that answers the advertisement and gives temporary shelter, and then I saw myself, useless sketchbook in hand, without qualifications of any kind, stammering replies to stern employment agents. Perhaps I should have accepted Blaize's ten per cent.

'How old are you?' he said, and when I told him he laughed, and got up from his chair. 'I know that age, it's a particularly obstinate one, and a thousand bogies won't make you fear the future. A pity we can't change over. Go upstairs and put your hat on, and I'll have the car brought round.'

As he watched me into the lift I thought of yesterday, Mrs Van Hopper's chattering tongue, and his cold courtesy. I had ill-judged him, he was neither hard nor sardonic, he was already my friend of many years, the brother I had never possessed. Mine was a happy mood that afternoon, and I remember it well. I can see the rippled sky, fluffy with cloud, and the white whipped sea. I can feel again the wind on my face, and hear my laugh, and his that echoed it. It was not the Monte Carlo I had known, or perhaps the truth was that it pleased me better. There was a glamour about it that had not been before. I must have looked upon it before with dull eyes. The harbour was a dancing thing, with fluttering paper boats, and the sailors on the quay were jovial, smiling fellows, merry as the wind. We passed the yacht, beloved of Mrs Van Hopper because of its ducal owner, and snapped our fingers at the glistening brass, and looked at one another and laughed again. I can remember as though I wore it still my comfortable, ill-fitting flannel suit, and how the skirt was lighter than the coat through harder wear. My shabby hat, too broad about the brim, and my low-heeled shoes, fastened with a single strap. A pair of gauntlet gloves clutched in a grubby hand. I had never looked more youthful, I had never felt so old. Mrs Van Hopper and her influenza did not exist for me. The bridge and the cocktail parties were forgotten, and with them my own humble status.

I was a person of importance, I was grown up at last. That girl who, tortured by shyness, would stand outside the sitting-room door twisting a handkerchief in her hands, while from within came that babble of confused chatter so unnerving to the intruder – she had gone with the wind that afternoon. She was a poor creature, and I thought of her with scorn if I considered her at all.

The wind was too high for sketching, it tore in cheerful gusts around the corner of my cobbled square, and back to the car we went and drove I know not where. The long road climbed the hills, and the car climbed with it, and we circled in the heights like a bird in the air. How different his car to Mrs Van Hopper's hireling for the season, a square old-fashioned Daimler that took us to Mentone on placid afternoons, when I, sitting on the little seat with my back to the driver, must crane my neck to see the view. This car had the wings of Mercury, I thought, for higher yet we climbed, and dangerously fast, and the danger pleased me because it was new to me, because I was young.

I remember laughing aloud, and the laugh being carried by the wind away from me; and looking at him, I realized he laughed no longer, he was once more silent and detached, the man of yesterday wrapped in his secret self.

I realized, too, that the car could climb no more, we had reached the summit, and below us stretched the way that we had come, precipitous and hollow. He stopped the car, and I could see that the edge of the road bordered a vertical slope that crumbled into vacancy, a fall of perhaps two thousand feet. We got out of the car and looked beneath us. This sobered me at last. I knew that but half the car's length had lain between us and the fall. The sea, like a crinkled chart, spread to the horizon, and lapped the sharp outline of the coast, while the houses were white shells in a rounded grotto, pricked here and there by a great orange sun. We knew another sunlight on our hill, and the silence made it harder, more austere. A change had come upon our afternoon; it was not the thing of gossamer it had been. The wind dropped, and it suddenly grew cold.

When I spoke my voice was far too casual, the silly, nervous voice of someone ill at ease. 'Do you know this place?' I said. 'Have you been here before?' He looked down at me without recognition, and I realized with a little stab of anxiety that he must have forgotten all about me, perhaps for some considerable time, and that he himself was so lost in the labyrinth of his own unquiet thoughts that I did not exist. He had the face of one who walks in his sleep, and for a wild moment the idea came to me that perhaps he was not normal, not altogether sane. There were people who had trances, I had surely heard of them, and they followed strange laws of which we could know nothing, they obeyed the tangled orders of their own subconscious minds. Perhaps he was one of them, and here we were within six feet of death.

'It's getting late, shall we go home?' I said, and my careless tone, my little ineffectual smile would scarcely have deceived a child.

I had misjudged him, of course, there was nothing wrong after all, for as soon as I spoke this second time he came clear of his dream and began to apologize. I had gone white, I suppose, and he had noticed it.

'That was an unforgivable thing for me to do,' he said, and taking my arm he pushed me back towards the car, and we climbed in again, and he slammed the door. 'Don't be frightened, the turn is far easier than it looks,' he said, and while I, sick and giddy, clung to the seat with both hands, he manoeuvred the car gently, very gently, until it faced the sloping road once more.

'Then you have been here before?' I said to him, my sense of strain departing, as the car crept away down the twisting narrow road.

'Yes,' he said, and then, after pausing a moment, 'but not for many years. I wanted to see if it had changed.'

'And has it?' I asked him.

'No,' he said. 'No, it has not changed.'

I wondered what had driven him to this retreat into the past, with me an unconscious witness of his mood. What gulf of years stretched between him and that other time, what deed of thought and action, what difference in temperament? I did not want to know. I wished I had not come.

Down the twisting road we went without a check, without a word, a great ridge of cloud stretched above the setting sun, and the air was cold and clean. Suddenly he began to talk about Manderley. He said nothing of his life there, no word about himself, but he told me how the sun set there, on a spring afternoon, leaving a glow upon the headland. The sea would look like slate, cold still from the long winter, and from the terrace you could hear the ripple of the coming tide washing in the little bay. The daffodils were in bloom, stirring in the evening breeze, golden heads cupped upon lean stalks, and however many you might pick there would be no thinning of the ranks, they were massed like an army, shoulder to shoulder. On a bank below the lawns, crocuses were planted, golden, pink, and mauve, but by this time they would be past their best, dropping and fading, like pallid snowdrops. The primrose was more vulgar, a homely pleasant creature who appeared in every cranny like a weed. Too early yet for bluebells, their heads were still hidden beneath last year's leaves, but when they came, dwarfing the more humble violet, they choked the very bracken in the woods, and with their colour made a challenge to the sky.

He never would have them in the house, he said. Thrust into vases they became dank and listless, and to see them at their best you must walk in the woods in the morning, about twelve o'clock, when the sun was overhead. They had a smoky, rather bitter smell, as though a wild sap ran in their stalks, pungent and juicy. People who plucked bluebells from the woods were vandals; he had forbidden it at Manderley. Sometimes, driving in the country, he had seen bicyclists with huge bunches strapped before them on the handles, the bloom already fading from the dying heads, the ravaged stalks straggling naked and unclean.

The primrose did not mind it quite so much; although a creature of the wilds it had a leaning towards civilization, and preened and smiled in a jam-jar in some cottage window without resentment, living quite a week if given water. No wild flowers came in the house at Manderley. He had special cultivated flowers, grown for the house alone, in the walled garden. A rose was one of the few flowers, he said, that looked better picked than growing. A bowl of roses in a drawing-room had a depth of colour and scent they had not possessed in the open. There was something rather blowzy about roses in full bloom, something shallow and raucous, like women with untidy hair. In the house they became mysterious and subtle. He had roses in the house at Manderley for eight months in the year. Did I like syringa, he asked me?

There was a tree on the edge of the lawn he could smell from his bedroom window. His sister, who was a hard, rather practical person, used to complain that there were too many scents at Manderley, they made her drunk. Perhaps she was right. He did not care. It was the only form of intoxication that appealed to him. His earliest recollection was of great branches of lilac, standing in white jars, and they filled the house with a wistful, poignant smell.

The little pathway down the valley to the bay had clumps of azalea and rhododendron planted to the left of it, and if you wandered down it on a May evening after dinner it was just as though the shrubs had sweated in the air. You could stoop down and pick a fallen petal, crush it between your fingers, and you had there, in the hollow of your hand, the essence of a thousand scents, unbearable and sweet. All from a curled and crumpled petal. And you came out of the valley, heady and rather dazed, to the hard white shingle of the beach and the still water. A curious, perhaps too sudden contrast . . .

As he spoke the car became one of many once again, dusk had fallen without my noticing it, and we were in the midst of light and sound in the streets of Monte Carlo. The clatter jagged on my nerves, and the lights were far too brilliant, far too yellow. It was a swift, unwelcome anticlimax.

Soon we would come to the hotel, and I felt for my gloves in the pocket of the car. I found them, and my fingers closed upon a book as well, whose slim covers told of poetry. I peered to read the title as the car slowed down before the door of the hotel. 'You can take it and read it if you like,' he said, his voice casual and indifferent now that the drive was over, and we were back again, and Manderley was many hundreds of miles distant.

I was glad, and held it tightly with my gloves. I felt I wanted some possession of his, now that the day was finished.

'Hop out,' he said. 'I must go and put the car away. I shan't see you in the restaurant this evening as I'm dining out. But thank you for today.'

I went up the hotel steps alone, with all the despondency of a child whose treat is over. My afternoon had spoilt me for the hours that still remained, and I thought how long they would seem until my bed-time, how empty too my supper all alone. Somehow I could not face the bright inquiries of the nurse upstairs, or the possibilities of Mrs Van Hopper's husky interrogation, so I sat down in the corner of the lounge behind a pillar and ordered tea.

The waiter appeared bored; seeing me alone there was no need for him to press, and anyway it was that dragging time of day, a few minutes after half past five, when the normal tea is finished and the hour for drinks remote.

Rather forlorn, more than a little dissatisfied, I leant back in my chair and took up the book of poems. The volume was well worn, well thumbed, falling open automatically at what must be a much-frequented page.

> I fled Him, down the nights and down the days;
> I fled Him, down the arches of the years;
> I fled Him, down the labyrinthine ways
> Of my own mind; and in the midst of tears
> I hid from Him, and under running laughter.
> Up vistaed slopes I sped
> And shot, precipited
> Adown Titanic glooms of chasmed fears,
> From those strong feet that followed, followed after.

I felt rather like someone peering through the keyhole of a locked door, and a little furtively I laid the book aside. What hound of heaven had driven him to the high hills this afternoon? I thought of his car, with half a length between it and that drop of two thousand feet, and the blank expression on his face. What footsteps echoed in his mind, what whispers, and what memories, and why, of all poems, must he keep this one in the pocket of his car? I wished he were less remote; and I anything but the creature that I was in my shabby coat and skirt, my broad-brimmed schoolgirl hat.

The sulky waiter brought my tea, and while I ate bread-and-butter dull as sawdust I thought of the pathway through the valley he had described to me this afternoon, the smell of the azaleas, and the white shingle of the bay. If he loved it all so much why did he seek the superficial froth of Monte Carlo? He had told Mrs Van Hopper he had made no plans, he came away in rather a hurry. And I pictured him running down that pathway in the valley with his own hound of heaven at his heels.

I picked up the book again, and this time it opened at the title-page, and I read the dedication. 'Max – from Rebecca. 17 May', written in a curious slanting hand. A little blob of ink marred the white page opposite, as though the writer, in impatience, had shaken her pen to make the ink flow freely. And then as it bubbled through the nib, it came a little thick, so that the name Rebecca stood out black and strong, the tall and sloping R dwarfing the other letters.

I shut the book with a snap, and put it away under my gloves; and stretching to a nearby chair, I took up an old copy of *L'Illustration* and turned the pages. There were some fine photographs of the chateaux of the Loire, and an article as well. I read it carefully, referring to the photographs, but when I finished I knew I had not understood a word. It was not Blois with its thin turrets and its spires that stared up at me from the printed page. It was the face of Mrs Van Hopper in the restaurant the day before, her small pig's eyes darting to the neighbouring table, her fork, heaped high with ravioli, pausing in mid-air.

'An appalling tragedy,' she was saying, 'the papers were full of it of course. They say he never talks about it, never mentions her name. She was drowned you know, in the bay near Manderley . . .'

5

I AM GLAD it cannot happen twice, the fever of first love. For it is a fever, and a burden, too, whatever the poets may say. They are not brave, the days when we are twenty-one. They are full of little cowardices, little fears without foundation, and one is so easily bruised, so swiftly wounded, one falls to the first barbed word. Today, wrapped in the complacent armour of approaching middle age, the infinitesimal pricks of day by day brush one lightly and are soon forgotten, but then – how a careless word would linger, becoming a fiery stigma, and how a look, a glance over a shoulder, branded themselves as things eternal. A denial heralded the thrice crowing of a cock, and an insincerity was like the kiss of Judas. The adult mind can lie with untroubled conscience and a gay composure, but in those days even a small deception scoured the tongue, lashing one against the stake itself.

'What have you been doing this morning?' I can hear her now, propped against her pillows, with all the small irritability of the patient who is not really ill, who has lain in bed too long, and I, reaching to the bedside drawer for the pack of cards, would feel the guilty flush form patches on my neck.

'I've been playing tennis with the professional,' I told her, the false words bringing me to panic, even as I spoke, for what if the professional himself should come up to the suite, then, that very afternoon, and bursting in upon her complain that I had missed my lesson now for many days?

'The trouble is with me laid up like this you haven't got enough to do,' she said, mashing her cigarette in a jar of cleansing cream, and taking the cards in her hand she mixed them in the deft, irritating shuffle of the inveterate player, shaking them in threes, snapping the backs.

'I don't know what you find to do with yourself all day,' she went on; 'you never have any sketches to show me, and when I do ask you to do some shopping for me you forget to buy my Taxol. All I can say is that I hope your tennis will improve; it will be useful to you later on. A poor player is a great bore. Do you still serve underhand?' She flipped the Queen of Spades into the pool, and the dark face stared up at me like Jezebel.

'Yes,' I said, stung by her question, thinking how just and appropriate her word. It described me well. I was underhand. I had not played tennis with the professional at all. I had not once played since she had lain in bed, and that was a little over a fortnight now. I wondered why it was I clung to this reserve, and why it was I did not tell her that every morning I drove with de Winter in his car, and lunched with him, too, at his table in the restaurant.

'You must come up to the net more; you will never play a good game until you do,' she continued, and I agreed, flinching at my own hypocrisy, covering the Queen with the weak-chinned Knave of Hearts.

I have forgotten much of Monte Carlo, of those morning drives, of where we went, even our conversation; but I have not forgotten how my fingers trembled, cramming on my hat, and how I ran along the corridor and down the stairs, too impatient to wait for the slow whining of the lift, and so outside, brushing the swing doors before the commissionaire could help me.

He would be there, in the driver's seat, reading a paper while he waited, and when he saw me he would smile, and toss it behind him in the back seat, and open the door, saying, 'Well, how is the friend-of-the-bosom this morning, and where does she want to go?' If he had driven round in circles it would not have mattered to me, for I was in that first flushed stage when to climb into the seat beside him, and lean forward to the windscreen hugging my knees, was almost too much to bear. I was like a little scrubby schoolboy with a passion for a sixth-form prefect, and he kinder, and far more inaccessible.

'There's a cold wind this morning, you had better put on my coat.'

I remember that, for I was young enough to win happiness in the wearing of his clothes, playing the schoolboy again who carries his hero's sweater and ties it about his throat choking with pride, and this borrowing of his coat, wearing it around my shoulders for even a few minutes at a time, was a triumph in itself, and made a glow about my morning.

Not for me the languor and the subtlety I had read about in books. The challenge and the chase. The sword-play, the swift glance, the stimulating smile. The art of provocation was unknown to me, and I would sit with his map upon my lap, the wind blowing my dull, lanky hair, happy in his silence yet eager for his words. Whether he talked or not made little difference to my mood. My only enemy was the clock on the dashboard, whose hands would move relentlessly to one o'clock. We drove east, we drove west, amidst the myriad villages that cling like limpets to the Mediterranean shore, and today I remember none of them.

All I remember is the feel of the leather seats, the texture of the map upon my knee, its frayed edges, its worn seams, and how one day, looking at the clock, I thought to myself, 'This moment now, at twenty past eleven, this must never be lost,' and I shut my eyes to make the experience more lasting. When I opened my eyes we were by a bend in the road, and a peasant girl in a black shawl waved to us; I can see her now, her dusty skirt, her gleaming, friendly smile, and in a second we had passed the bend and could see her no more. Already she belonged to the past, she was only a memory.

I wanted to go back again, to recapture the moment that had gone, and then it came to me that if we did it would not be the same, even the sun would be changed in the sky, casting another shadow, and the peasant girl would trudge past us along the road in a different way, not waving this time, perhaps not even seeing us. There was something chilling in the thought, something a little melancholy, and looking at the clock I saw that five more minutes had gone by. Soon we would have reached our time limit, and must return to the hotel.

'If only there could be an invention', I said impulsively, 'that bottled up a memory, like scent. And it never faded, and it never got stale. And then, when one wanted it the bottle could be uncorked, and it would be like living the moment all over again.'

I looked up at him, to see what he would say. He did not turn to me, he went on watching the road ahead.

'What particular moments in your young life do you wish uncorked?' he said. I could not tell from his voice whether he was teasing me or not. 'I'm not sure,' I began, and then blundered on, rather foolishly, not thinking of my words, 'I'd like to keep this moment and never forget it.'

'Is that meant to be a compliment to the day, or to my driving?' he said, and as he laughed, like a mocking brother, I became silent, overwhelmed suddenly by the great gulf between us, and how his very kindness to me widened it.

I knew then that I would never tell Mrs Van Hopper about these morning expeditions, for her smile would hurt me as his laugh had done. She would not be angry, nor would she be shocked; she would raise her eyebrows very faintly as though she did not altogether believe my story, and then with a tolerant shrug of the shoulder she would say, 'My dear child, it's extremely sweet and kind of him to take you driving; the only thing is – are you sure it does not bore him dreadfully?' And then she would send me out to buy Taxol, patting me on the shoulder. What degradation lay in being young, I thought, and fell to tearing my nails.

'I wish,' I said savagely, still mindful of his laugh and throwing discretion to the wind, 'I wish I was a woman of about thirty-six dressed in black satin with a string of pearls.'

'You would not be in this car with me if you were,' he said; 'and stop biting those nails, they are ugly enough already.'

'You'll think me impertinent and rude I dare say,' I went on, 'but I would like to know why you ask me to come out in the car, day after day. You are being kind, that's obvious, but why do you choose me for your charity?'

I sat up stiff and straight in my seat and with all the poor pomposity of youth.

'I ask you,' he said gravely, 'because you are not dressed in black satin, with a string of pearls, nor are you thirty-six.' His face was without expression, I could not tell whether he laughed inwardly or not.

'It's all very well,' I said; 'you know everything there is to know about me. There's not much, I admit, because I have not been alive for very long, and nothing much has happened to me, except people dying, but you – I know nothing more about you than I did the first day we met.'

'And what did you know then?' he asked.

'Why, that you lived at Manderley and – and that you had lost your wife.' There, I had said it at last, the word that had hovered on my tongue for days. Your wife. It came out with ease, without reluctance, as though the mere mention of her must be the most casual thing in all the world. Your wife. The word lingered in the air once I had uttered it, dancing before me, and because he received it silently, making no comment, the word magnified itself into something heinous and appalling, a forbidden word, unnatural to the tongue. And I could not call it back, it could never be unsaid. Once again I saw the inscription on the fly-leaf of that book of poems, and the curious slanting R. I felt sick at heart and cold. He would never forgive me, and this would be the end of our friendship.

I remember staring straight in front of me at the windscreen, seeing nothing of the flying road, my ears still tingling with that spoken word. The silence became minutes, and the minutes became miles, and everything is over now, I thought, I shall never drive with him again. Tomorrow he will go away. And Mrs Van Hopper will be up again. She and I will walk along the terrace as we did before. The porter will bring down his trunks, I shall catch a glimpse of them in the luggage lift, with new-plastered labels. The bustle and finality of departure. The sound of the car changing gear as it turned the corner, and then even that sound merging into the common traffic, and being lost, and so absorbed for ever.

I was so deep in my picture, I even saw the porter pocketing his tip and going back through the swing door of the hotel, saying something over his shoulder to the commissionaire, that I did not notice the slowing-down of the car, and it was only when we stopped, drawing up by the side of the road, that I brought myself back to the present once again. He sat motionless, looking without his hat and with his white scarf round his neck, more than ever like someone medieval who lived within a frame. He did not belong to the bright landscape, he should be standing on the steps of a gaunt cathedral, his cloak flung back, while a beggar at his feet scrambled for gold coins.

The friend had gone, with his kindliness and his easy *camaraderie*, and the brother too, who had mocked me for nibbling at my nails. This man was a stranger. I wondered why I was sitting beside him in the car.

Then he turned to me and spoke. 'A little while ago you talked about an invention,' he said, 'some scheme for capturing a memory. You would like, you told me, at a chosen moment to live the past again. I'm afraid I think rather differently from you. All memories are bitter, and I prefer to ignore them. Something happened a year ago that altered my whole life, and I want to forget every phase in my existence up to that time. Those days are finished. They are blotted out. I must begin living all over again. The first day we met, your Mrs Van Hopper asked me why I came to Monte Carlo. It put a stopper on those memories you would like to resurrect. It does not always work, of course; sometimes the scent is too strong for the bottle, and too strong for me. And then the devil in one, like a furtive peeping Tom, tries to draw the cork. I did that in the first drive we took together. When we climbed the hills and looked down over the precipice. I was there some years ago, with my wife. You asked me if it was still the same, if it had changed at all. It was just the same, but – I was thankful to realize – oddly impersonal. There was no suggestion of the other time. She and I had left no record. It may have been because you were with me. You have blotted out the past for me, you know, far more effectively than all the bright lights of Monte Carlo. But for you I should have left long ago, gone on to Italy, and Greece, and further still perhaps. You have spared me all those wanderings. Damn your puritanical little tight-lipped speech to me. Damn your idea of my kindness and my charity. I ask you to come with me because I want you and your company, and if you don't believe me you can leave the car now and find your own way home. Go on, open the door, and get out.'

I sat still, my hands in my lap, not knowing whether he meant it or not.

'Well,' he said, 'what are you going to do about it?'

Had I been a year or two younger I think I should have cried. Children's tears are very near the surface, and come at the first crisis. As it was I felt them prick behind my eyes, felt the ready colour flood my face, and catching a sudden glimpse of myself in the glass above the windscreen saw in full the sorry spectacle that I made, with troubled eyes and scarlet cheeks, lank hair flopping under broad felt hat.

'I want to go home,' I said, my voice perilously near to trembling, and without a word he started up the engine, let in the clutch, and turned the car round the way that we had come.

Swiftly we covered the ground, far too swiftly, I thought, far too easily, and the callous countryside watched us with indifference. We came to the bend in the road that I had wished to imprison as a memory, and the peasant girl was gone, and the colour was flat, and it was no more after all than any bend in any road passed by a hundred motorists. The glamour of it had gone with my happy mood, and at the thought of it my frozen face quivered into feeling, my adult pride was lost, and those despicable tears rejoicing at their conquest welled into my eyes and strayed upon my cheeks.

I could not check them, for they came unbidden, and had I reached in my pocket for a handkerchief he would have seen. I must let them fall untouched, and suffer the bitter salt upon my lips, plumbing the depths of humiliation. Whether he had turned his head to look at me I do not know, for I watched the road ahead with blurred and steady stare, but suddenly he put out his hand and took hold of mine, and kissed it, still saying nothing, and then he threw his handkerchief on my lap, which I was too ashamed to touch.

I thought of all those heroines of fiction who looked pretty when they cried, and what a contrast I must make with blotched and swollen face, and red rims to my eyes. It was a dismal finish to my morning, and the day that stretched ahead of me was long. I had to lunch with Mrs Van Hopper in her room because the nurse was going out, and afterwards she would make me play bezique with all the tireless energy of the convalescent. I knew I should stifle in that room. There was something sordid about the tumbled sheets, the sprawling blankets, and the thumped pillows, and that bedside table dusty with powder, spilt scent, and melting liquid rouge. Her bed would be littered with the separated sheets of the daily papers folded anyhow, while French novels with curling edges and the covers torn kept company with American magazines. The mashed stubs of cigarettes lay everywhere – in cleansing cream, in a dish of grapes, and on the floor beneath the bed. Visitors were lavish with their flowers, and the vases stood cheek-by-jowl in any fashion, hot-house exotics crammed beside mimosa, while a great beribboned casket crowned them all, with tier upon tier of crystallized fruit. Later her friends would come in for a drink, which I must mix for them, hating my task, shy and ill-at-ease in my corner hemmed in by their parrot chatter, and I would be a whipping boy again, blushing for her when, excited by her little crowd, she must sit up in bed and talk too loudly, laugh too long, reach to the portable gramophone and start a record, shrugging her large shoulders to the tune. I preferred her irritable and snappy, her hair done up in pins, scolding me for forgetting her Taxol. All this awaited me in the suite, while he, once he had left me at the hotel, would go away somewhere alone, towards the sea perhaps, feel the wind on his cheek, follow the sun; and it might happen that he would lose himself in those memories that I knew nothing of, that I could not share, he would wander down the years that were gone.

The gulf that lay between us was wider now than it had ever been, and he stood away from me, with his back turned, on the further shore. I felt young and small and very much alone, and now, in spite of my pride, I found his handkerchief and blew my nose, throwing my drab appearance to the winds. It could never matter.

'To hell with this,' he said suddenly, as though angry, as though bored, and he pulled me beside him, and put his arm round my shoulder, still looking straight ahead of him, his right hand on the wheel. He drove, I remember, even faster than before. 'I suppose you are young enough to be my daughter, and I don't know how to deal with you,' he said. The road narrowed then to a corner, and he had to swerve to avoid a dog. I thought he would release me, but he went on holding me beside him, and when the corner was passed, and the road came straight again he did not let me go. 'You can forget all I said to you this morning,' he said; 'that's all finished and done with. Don't let's ever think of it again. My family always call me Maxim, I'd like you to do the same. You've been formal with me long enough.' He felt for the brim of my hat, and took hold of it, throwing it over his shoulder to the back seat, and then bent down and kissed the top of my head. 'Promise me you will never wear black satin,' he said. I smiled then, and he laughed back at me, and the morning was gay again, the morning was a shining thing. Mrs Van Hopper and the afternoon did not matter a flip of the finger. It would pass so quickly, and there would be tonight, and another day tomorrow. I was cocksure, jubilant; at that moment I almost had the courage to claim equality. I saw myself strolling into Mrs Van Hopper's bedroom rather late for my bezique, and when questioned by her, yawning carelessly, saying, 'I forgot the time. I've been lunching with Maxim.'

I was still child enough to consider a Christian name like a plume in the hat, though from the very first he had called me by mine. The morning, for all its shadowed moments, had promoted me to a new level of friendship, I did not lag so far behind as I had thought. He had kissed me too, a natural business, comforting and quiet. Not dramatic as in books. Not embarrassing. It seemed to bring about an ease in our relationship, it made everything more simple. The gulf between us had been bridged after all. I was to call him Maxim. And that afternoon playing bezique with Mrs Van Hopper was not so tedious as it might have been, though my courage failed me and I said nothing of my morning. For when, gathering her cards together at the end, and reaching for the box, she said casually, 'Tell me, is Max de Winter still in the hotel?' I hesitated a moment, like a diver on the brink, then lost my nerve and my tutored self-possession, saying, 'Yes, I believe so – he comes into the restaurant for his meals.'

Someone has told her, I thought, someone has seen us together, the tennis professional has complained, the manager has sent a note, and I waited for her attack. But she went on putting the cards back into the box, yawning a little, while I straightened the tumbled bed. I gave her the bowl of powder, the rouge compact, and the lip-stick, and she put away the cards and took up

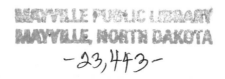

the hands glass from the table by her side. 'Attractive creature,' she said, 'but queer-tempered I should think, difficult to know. I thought he might have made some gesture of asking one to Manderley that day in the lounge, but he was very close.'

I said nothing. I watched her pick up the lip-stick and outline a bow upon her hard mouth. 'I never saw her,' she said, holding the glass away to see the effect, 'but I believe she was very lovely. Exquisitely turned out, and brilliant in every way. They used to give tremendous parties at Manderley. It was all very sudden and tragic, and I believe he adored her. I need the darker shade of powder with this brilliant red, my dear: fetch it, will you, and put this box back in the drawer?'

And we were busy then with powder, scent, and rouge, until the bell rang and her visitors came in. I handed them their drinks, dully, saying little; I changed the records on the gramophone, I threw away the stubs of cigarettes.

'Been doing any sketching lately, little lady?' The forced heartiness of an old banker, his monocle dangling on a string, and my bright smile of insincerity: 'No, not very lately; will you have another cigarette?'

It was not I that answered, I was not there at all. I was following a phantom in my mind, whose shadowy form had taken shape at last. Her features were blurred, her colouring indistinct, the setting of her eyes and the texture of her hair was still uncertain, still to be revealed.

She had beauty that endured, and a smile that was not forgotten. Somewhere her voice still lingered, and the memory of her words. There were places she had visited, and things that she had touched. Perhaps in cupboards there were clothes that she had worn, with the scent about them still. In my bedroom, under my pillow, I had a book that she had taken in her hands, and I could see her turning to that first white page, smiling as she wrote, and shaking the bent nib. Max from Rebecca. It must have been his birthday, and she had put it amongst her other presents on the breakfast table. And they had laughed together as he tore off the paper and string. She leant, perhaps, over his shoulder, while he read. Max. She called him Max. It was familiar, gay, and easy on the tongue. The family could call him Maxim if they liked. Grandmothers and aunts. And people like myself, quiet and dull and youthful, who did not matter. Max was her choice, the word was her possession; she had written it with so great a confidence on the fly-leaf of that book. That bold, slanting hand, stabbing the white paper, the symbol of herself, so certain, so assured.

How many times she must have written to him thus, in how many varied moods.

Little notes, scrawled on half-sheets of paper, and letters, when he was away, page after page, intimate, *their* news. Her voice, echoing through the house, and down the garden, careless and familiar like the writing in the book.

And I had to call him Maxim.

6

PACKING UP. THE nagging worry of departure. Lost keys, unwritten labels, tissue paper lying on the floor. I hate it all. Even now, when I have done so much of it, when I live, as the saying goes, in my boxes. Even today, when shutting drawers and flinging wide an hotel wardrobe, or the impersonal shelves of a furnished villa, is a methodical matter of routine, I am aware of sadness, of a sense of loss. Here, I say, we have lived, we have been happy. This has been ours, however brief the time. Though two nights only have been spent beneath a roof, yet we leave something of ourselves behind. Nothing material, not a hair-pin on a dressing-table, not an empty bottle of Aspirin tablets, not a handkerchief beneath a pillow, but something indefinable, a moment of our lives, a thought, a mood.

This house sheltered us, we spoke, we loved within those walls. That was yesterday. Today we pass on, we see it no more, and we are different, changed in some infinitesimal way. We can never be quite the same again. Even stopping for luncheon at a wayside inn, and going to a dark, unfamiliar room to wash my hands, the handle of the door unknown to me, the wallpaper peeling in strips, a funny little cracked mirror above the basin; for this moment, it is mine, it belongs to me. We know one another. This is the present. There is no past and no future. Here I am washing my hands, and the cracked mirror shows me to myself, suspended as it were, in time; this is me, this moment will not pass.

And then I open the door and go to the dining-room, where he is sitting waiting for me at a table, and I think how in that moment I have aged, passed on, how I have advanced one step towards an unknown destiny.

We smile, we choose our lunch, we speak of this and that, but

– I say to myself – I am not she who left him five minutes ago. She stayed behind. I am another woman, older, more mature . . .

I saw in a paper the other day that the Hôtel Côte d'Azur at Monte Carlo had gone to new management, and had a different name. The rooms have been redecorated, and the whole interior changed. Perhaps Mrs Van Hopper's suite on the first floor exists no more. Perhaps there is no trace of the small bedroom that was mine. I knew I should never go back, that day I knelt on the floor and fumbled with the awkward catch of her trunk.

The episode was finished, with the snapping of the lock. I glanced out of the window, and it was like turning the page of a photograph album. Those roof-tops and that sea were mine no more. They belonged to yesterday, to the past. The rooms already wore an empty air, stripped of our possessions, and there was something hungry about the suite, as though it wished us gone, and the new arrivals, who would come tomorrow, in our place. The heavy luggage stood ready strapped and locked in the corridor outside. The smaller stuff would be finished later. Waste-paper baskets groaned under litter. All her half-empty medicine bottles and discarded face-cream jars, with torn-up bills and letters. Drawers in tables gaped, the bureau was stripped bare.

She had flung a letter at me the morning before, as I poured out her coffee at breakfast. 'Helen is sailing for New York on Saturday. Little Nancy has a threatened appendix, and they've cabled her to go home. That's decided me. We're going too. I'm tired to death of Europe, and we can come back in the early fall. How d'you like the idea of seeing New York?'

The thought was worse than prison. Something of my misery must have shown in my face, for at first she looked astonished, then annoyed.

'What an odd, unsatisfactory child you are. I can't make you out. Don't you realize that at home girls in your position without any money can have the grandest fun? Plenty of boys and excitement. All in your own class. You can have your own little set of friends, and needn't be at my beck and call as much as you are here. I thought you didn't care for Monte?'

'I've got used to it,' I said lamely, wretchedly, my mind a conflict.

'Well, you'll just have to get used to New York, that's all. We're going to catch that boat of Helen's, and it means seeing about our passage at once. Go down to the reception office right away, and make that young clerk show some sign of efficiency. Your day will be so full that you won't have time to have any pangs about leaving Monte!' She laughed disagreeably, squashing her cigarette in the butter, and went to the telephone to ring up all her friends.

I could not face the office right away. I went into the bathroom and locked the door, and sat down on the cork mat, my head in my hands. It had happened at last, the business of going away. It was all over. Tomorrow evening I should be in the train, holding her jewel case and her rug, like a maid, and she in that monstrous new hat with the single quill, dwarfed in her fur-coat, sitting opposite me in the wagon-lit. We would wash and clean our teeth in that stuffy little compartment with the rattling doors, the splashed basin, the damp towel, the soap with a single hair on it, the carafe half-filled with water, the inevitable notice on the wall '*Sous le lavabo se trouve une vase*', while every rattle, every throb and jerk of the screaming train would tell me that the miles carried me away from him, sitting alone in the restaurant of the hotel, at the table I had known, reading a book, not minding, not thinking.

I should say good-bye to him in the lounge, perhaps, before we left. A furtive, scrambled farewell, because of her, and there would be a pause, and a smile, and words like 'Yes, of course, do write', and 'I've never thanked you properly for being so kind', and 'You must forward those snapshots', 'What about your address?' 'Well, I'll have to let you know.' And he would light a cigarette casually, asking a passing waiter for a light, while I thought, 'Four and a half more minutes to go. I shall never see him again.'

Because I was going, because it was over, there would suddenly be nothing more to say, we would be strangers, meeting for the last and only time, while my mind clamoured painfully, crying 'I love you so much. I'm terribly unhappy. This has never come to me before, and never will again.' My face would be set in a prim, conventional smile, my voice would be saying, look at that funny old man over there; I wonder who he is; he must be new here.' And we would waste the last moments laughing at a stranger, because we were already strangers to one another. 'I hope the snapshots come out well,' repeating oneself in desperation, and he 'Yes, that one of the square ought to be good; the light was just right.' Having both of us gone into all that at the time, having agreed upon it, and anyway I would not care if the result was fogged and black, because this was the last moment, the final good-bye had been attained.

'Well,' my dreadful smile stretching across my face, 'thanks most awfully once again, it's been so ripping . . .' using words I had never used before. Ripping: what did it mean? – God knows, I did not care; it was the sort of word that schoolgirls had for hockey, wildly inappropriate to those past weeks of misery and exultation. Then the doors of the lift would open upon Mrs Van Hopper and I would cross the lounge to meet her, and he would stroll back again to his corner and pick up a paper.

Sitting there, ridiculously, on the cork mat of the bathroom floor, I lived it all, and our journey too, and our arrival in New York. The shrill voice of Helen, a narrower edition of her mother, and Nancy, her horrid little child. The college boys that Mrs Van Hopper would have me know, and the young bank clerks, suitable to my station. 'Let's make Wednesday night a date.' 'D'you like Hot music?' Snub-nosed boys, with shiny faces. Having to be polite. And wanting to be alone with my own thoughts as I was now, locked behind the bathroom door . . .

She came and rattled on the door. 'What are you doing?'

'All right – I'm sorry, I'm coming now,' and I made a pretence of turning on the tap, of bustling about and folding a towel on a rail.

She glanced at me curiously as I opened the door. 'What a time you've been. You can't afford to dream this morning, you know, there's too much to be done.'

He would go back to Manderley, of course, in a few weeks; I felt certain of that. There would be a great pile of letters waiting for him in the hall, and mine amongst them, scribbled on the boat. A forced letter, trying to amuse, describing my fellow passengers. It would lie about inside his blotter, and he would answer it weeks later, one Sunday morning in a hurry, before lunch, having come across it when he paid some bills. And then no more. Nothing until the final degradation of the Christmas card. Manderley itself perhaps, against a frosted background. The message printed, saying 'A happy Christmas and a prosperous New Year from Maximilian de Winter.' Gold lettering. But to be kind he would have run his pen through the printed name and written in ink underneath 'from Maxim', as a sort of sop, and if there was space, a message, 'I hope you are enjoying New York.' A lick of the envelope, a stamp, and tossed in a pile of a hundred others.

'It's too bad you are leaving tomorrow,' said the reception clerk, telephone in hand; 'the Ballet starts next week, you know. Does Mrs Van Hopper know?' I dragged myself back from Christmas at Manderley to the realities of the wagon-lit.

Mrs Van Hopper lunched in the restaurant for the first time since her influenza, and I had a pain in the pit of my stomach as I followed her into the room. He had gone to Cannes for the day, that much I knew, for he had warned me the day before, but I kept thinking the waiter might commit an indiscretion and say: 'Will Mademoiselle be dining with Monsieur tonight as usual?' I felt a little sick whenever he came near the table, but he said nothing.

The day was spent in packing, and in the evening people came to say good-bye. We dined in the sitting-room, and she went to bed directly afterwards. Still I had not seen him. I went down to the lounge about half past nine on the pretext of getting luggage labels and he was not there. The odious reception clerk smiled when he saw me. 'If you are looking for Mr de Winter we had a message from Cannes to say he would not be back before midnight.'

'I want a packet of luggage labels,' I said, but I saw by his eye that he was not deceived. So there would be no last evening after all. The hour I had looked forward to all day must be spent by myself alone, in my own bedroom, gazing at my Revelation suit-case and the stout hold-all. Perhaps it was just as well, for I should have made a poor companion, and he must have read my face.

I know I cried that night, bitter youthful tears that could not come from me today. That kind of crying, deep into a pillow, does not happen after we are twenty-one. The throbbing head, the swollen eyes, the tight, contracted throat. And the wild anxiety in the morning to hide all traces from the world, sponging with cold water, dabbing eau-de-Cologne, the furtive dash of powder that is significant in itself. The panic, too, that one might cry again, the tears swelling without control, and a fatal trembling of the mouth lead one to disaster. I remember opening wide my window and leaning out, hoping the fresh morning air would blow away the tell-tale pink under the powder, and the sun had never seemed so bright, nor the day so full of promise. Monte Carlo was suddenly full of kindliness and charm, the one place in the world that held sincerity. I loved it. Affection overwhelmed me. I wanted to live there all my life. And I was leaving it today. This is the last time I brush my hair before the looking-glass, the last time I shall clean my teeth into the basin. Never again sleep in that bed. Never more turn off the switch of that electric light. There I was, padding about in a dressing-gown, making a slough of sentiment out of a commonplace hotel bedroom.

'You haven't started a cold, have you?' she said at breakfast.

'No,' I told her, 'I don't think so,' clutching at a straw, for this might serve as an excuse later, if I was over-pink about the eyes.

'I hate hanging about once everything is packed,' she grumbled; 'we ought to have decided on the earlier train. We could get it if we made the effort, and then have longer in Paris. Wire Helen not to meet us, but arrange another *rendezvous*. I wonder' – she glanced at her watch – 'I suppose they could change the reservations. Anyway it's worth trying. Go down to the office and see.'

'Yes,' I said, a dummy to her moods going into my bedroom and flinging off my dressing-gown, fastening my inevitable flannel skirt and stretching my home-made jumper over my head. My indifference to her turned to hatred. This was the end then, even my morning must be taken from me. No last half hour on the terrace, not even ten minutes perhaps to say good-bye. Because she had finished breakfast earlier than she expected, because she was bored. Well then, I would fling away restraint

and modesty, I would not be proud any more. I slammed the door
of the sitting-room and ran along the passage. I did not wait for
the lift, I climbed the stairs, three at a time, up to the third floor.
I knew the number of his room, 148, and I hammered at the door,
very flushed in the face and breathless.

'Come in,' he shouted, and I opened the door, repenting
already, my nerve failing me; for perhaps he had only just woken
up, having been late last night, and would be still in bed, tousled
in the head and irritable.

He was shaving by the open window, a camel-hair jacket over
his pyjamas, and I in my flannel suit and heavy shoes felt clumsy
and over-dressed. I was merely foolish, when I had felt myself
dramatic.

'What do you want?' he said. 'Is something the matter?'

'I've come to say good-bye,' I said, 'we're going this
morning.'

He stared at me, then put his razor down on the washstand.
'Shut the door,' he said.

I closed it behind me, and stood there, rather self-conscious,
my hands hanging by my side. 'What on earth are you talking
about?' he asked.

'It's true, we're leaving today. We were going by the later
train, and now she wants to catch the earlier one, and I was afraid
I shouldn't see you again. I felt I must see you before I left, to
thank you.'

They tumbled out, the idiotic words, just as I had imagined
them. I was stiff and awkward; in a moment I should say he had
been ripping.

'Why didn't you tell me about this before?' he said.

'She only decided yesterday. It was all done in a hurry. Her
daughter sails for New York on Saturday, and we are going with
her. We're joining her in Paris, and going through to
Cherbourg.'

'She's taking you with her to New York?'

'Yes, and I don't want to go. I shall hate it; I shall be miserable.'

'Why in heaven's name go with her then?'

'I have to, you know that. I work for a salary. I can't afford to
leave her.' He picked up his razor again, and took the soap off his

face. 'Sit down,' he said. 'I shan't be long. I'll dress in the bath-room, and be ready in five minutes.'

He took his clothes off the chair and threw them on the bath-room floor, and went inside, slamming the door. I sat down on the bed and began biting my nails. The situation was unreal, and I felt like a lay-figure. I wondered what he was thinking, what he was going to do. I glanced round the room, it was the room of any man, untidy and impersonal. Lots of shoes, more than ever were needed, and strings of ties. The dressing-table was bare, except for a large bottle of hair-wash and a pair of ivory hair-brushes. No photographs. No snapshots. Nothing like that. Instinctively I had looked for them, thinking there would be one photograph at least beside his bed, or in the middle of the mantel-piece. One large one, in a leather frame. There were only books though, and a box of cigarettes.

He was ready, as he had promised, in five minutes. 'Come down to the terrace while I eat my breakfast,' he said.

I looked at my watch. 'I haven't time,' I told him. 'I ought to be in the office now, changing the reservations.'

'Never mind about that, I've got to talk to you,' he said.

We walked down the corridor and he rang for the lift. He can't realize, I thought, that the early train leaves in about an hour and a half. Mrs Van Hopper will ring up the office, in a moment, and ask if I am there. We went down in the lift, not talking, and so out to the terrace, where the tables were laid for breakfast.

'What are you going to have?' he said.

'I've had mine already,' I told him, 'and I can only stay four minutes anyway.'

'Bring me coffee, a boiled egg, toast, marmalade, and a tanger-ine,' he said to the waiter. And he took an emery board out of his pocket and began filing his nails.

'So Mrs Van Hopper has had enough of Monte Carlo,' he said, 'and now she wants to go home. So do I. She to New York and I to Manderley. Which would you prefer? You can take your choice.'

'Don't make a joke about it; it's unfair,' I said; 'and I think I had better see about those tickets, and say good-bye now.'

'If you think I'm one of the people who try to be funny at

breakfast you're wrong,' he said. 'I'm invariably ill-tempered in the early morning. I repeat to you, the choice is open to you. Either you go to America with Mrs Van Hopper or you come home to Manderley with me.'

'Do you mean you want a secretary or something?'

'No, I'm asking you to marry me, you little fool.'

The waiter came with the breakfast, and I sat with my hands in my lap, watching while he put down the pot of coffee and the jug of milk.

'You don't understand,' I said, when the waiter had gone; 'I'm not the sort of person men marry.'

'What the devil do you mean?' he said, staring at me, laying down his spoon.

I watched a fly settle on the marmalade, and he brushed it away impatiently.

'I'm not sure,' I said slowly. 'I don't think I know how to explain. I don't belong to your sort of world for one thing.'

'What is my world?'

'Well – Manderley. You know what I mean.'

He picked up his spoon again and helped himself to marmalade.

'You are almost as ignorant as Mrs Van Hopper, and just as unintelligent. What do you know of Manderley? I'm the person to judge that, whether you would belong there or not. You think I ask you this on the spur of the moment, don't you? Because you say you don't want to go to New York. You think I ask you to marry me for the same reason you believed I drove you about in the car, yes, and gave you dinner that first evening. To be kind. Don't you?'

'Yes,' I said.

'One day,' he went on, spreading his toast thick, 'you may realize that philanthropy is not my strongest quality. At the moment I don't think you realize anything at all. You haven't answered my question. Are you going to marry me?'

I don't believe, even in my fiercest moments, I had considered this possibility. I had once, when driving with him and we had been silent for many miles, started a rambling story in my head about him being very ill, delirious I think, and sending for me and I having to nurse him. I had reached the point in my story where I was putting eau-de-Cologne on his head when we arrived at the hotel, and so it finished there. And another time I had imagined living in a lodge in the grounds of Manderley, and how he would visit me sometimes, and sit in front of the fire. This sudden talk of marriage bewildered me, even shocked me I think. It was as though the King asked one. It did not ring true. And he went on eating his marmalade as though everything were natural. In books men knelt to women, and it would be moonlight. Not at breakfast, not like this.

'My suggestion doesn't seem to have gone too well,' he said. 'I'm sorry. I rather thought you loved me. A fine blow to my conceit.'

'I do love you,' I said. 'I love you dreadfully. You've made me very unhappy and I've been crying all night because I thought I should never see you again.'

When I said this I remember he laughed, and stretched his hand to me across the breakfast table. 'Bless you for that,' he said; 'one day, when you reach that exalted age of thirty-six which you told me was your ambition, I'll remind you of this moment. And you won't believe me. It's a pity you have to grow up.'

I was ashamed already, and angry with him for laughing. So women did not make those confessions to men. I had a lot to learn.

'So that's settled, isn't it?' he said, going on with his toast and marmalade; 'instead of being companion to Mrs Van Hopper you become mine, and your duties will be almost exactly the same. I also like new library books, and flowers in the drawing-room, and bezique after dinner. And someone to pour out my tea. The only difference is that I don't take Taxol, I prefer Eno's, and you must never let me run out of my particular brand of toothpaste.'

I drummed with my fingers on the table, uncertain of myself and of him. Was he still laughing at me, was it all a joke? He looked up, and saw the anxiety on my face. 'I'm being rather a brute to you, aren't I?' he said; 'this isn't your idea of a proposal. We ought to be in a conservatory, you in a white frock with a rose in your hand, and a violin playing a waltz in the distance. And I should make violent love to you behind a palm tree. You would feel then you were getting your money's worth. Poor darling, what a shame. Never mind, I'll take you to Venice for our honeymoon and we'll hold hands in the gondola. But we won't stay too long, because I want to show you Manderley.'

He wanted to show me Manderley . . . And suddenly I realized that it would all happen; I would be his wife, we would walk in the garden together, we would stroll down that path in the valley to the shingle beach. I knew how I would stand on the steps after breakfast, looking at the day, throwing crumbs to the birds, and later wander out in a shady hat with long scissors in my hand, and cut flowers for the house. I knew now why I had bought that picture postcard as a child; it was a premonition, a blank step into the future.

He wanted to show me Manderley . . . My mind ran riot then, figures came before me and picture after picture – and all the while he ate his tangerine, giving me a piece now and then, and watching me. We would be in a crowd of people, and he would say, 'I don't think you have met my wife.' Mrs de Winter. I would be Mrs de Winter. I considered my name, and the signature on cheques, to tradesmen, and in letters asking people to dinner. I heard myself talking on the telephone: 'Why not come down to Manderley next week-end?' People, always a throng of people. 'Oh, but she's simply charming, you must meet her—' This about me, a whisper on the fringe of a crowd, and I would turn away, pretending I had not heard.

Going down to the lodge with a basket on my arm, grapes and peaches for the old lady who was sick. Her hands stretched out to me, 'The Lord bless you, Madam, for being so good,' and my saying, 'Just send up to the house for anything you want.' Mrs de Winter. I would be Mrs de Winter. I saw the polished table in the dining-room, and the long candles. Maxim sitting at the end. A party of twenty-four. I had a flower in my hair. Everyone looked towards me, holding up his glass. 'We must drink the health of the bride,' and Maxim saying afterwards, 'I have never seen you look so lovely.' Great cool rooms, filled with flowers. My bedroom, with a fire in the winter, someone knocking at the door. And a woman comes in, smiling; she is Maxim's sister, and she is saying, 'It's really wonderful how happy you have made him; everyone is so pleased, you are such a success.' Mrs de Winter. I would be Mrs de Winter.

'The rest of the tangerine is sour, I shouldn't eat it,' he said, and I stared at him, the words going slowly to my head, then looked down at the fruit on my plate. The quarter was hard and pale. He was right. The tangerine was very sour. I had a sharp, bitter taste in my mouth, and I had only just noticed it.

'Am I going to break the news to Mrs Van Hopper or are you?' he said.

He was folding up his napkin, pushing back his plate, and I wondered how it was he spoke so casually, as though the matter was of little consequence, a mere adjustment of plans. Whereas to me it was a bomb-shell, exploding in a thousand fragments.

'You tell her,' I said; 'she'll be so angry.'

We got up from the table, I excited and flushed, trembling already in anticipation. I wondered if he would tell the waiter, take my arm smilingly and say, 'You must congratulate us, Mademoiselle and I are going to be married.' And all the other waiters would hear, would bow to us, would smile, and we would pass into the lounge, a wave of excitement following us, a flutter of expectation. But he said nothing. He left the terrace without a word, and I followed him to the lift. We passed the reception desk and no one even looked at us. The clerk was busy with a sheaf of papers, he was talking over his shoulder to his junior. He does not know, I thought, that I am going to be Mrs de Winter. I am going to live at Manderley. Manderley will belong to me. We went up in the lift to the first floor, and so along the passage. He took my hand and swung it as we went along. 'Does forty-two seem very old to you?' he said.

'Oh, no,' I told him, quickly, too eagerly perhaps. 'I don't like young men.'

'You've never known any,' he said.

We came to the door of the suite. 'I think I had better deal with this alone,' he said; 'tell me something – do you mind how soon you marry me? You don't want a trousseau, do you, or any of that nonsense? Because the whole thing can be so easily arranged in a few days. Over a desk, with a licence, and then off in the car to Venice or anywhere you fancy.'

'Not in a church?' I asked. 'Not in white, with bridesmaids, and bells, and choir boys? What about your relations, and all your friends?'

'You forget,' he said, 'I had that sort of wedding before.'

We went on standing in front of the door of the suite, and I noticed that the daily paper was still thrust through the letter-box. We had been too busy to read it at breakfast.

'Well?' he said, 'what about it?'

'Of course,' I answered, 'I was thinking for the moment we would be married at home. Naturally I don't expect a church, or people, or anything like that.'

And I smiled at him. I made a cheerful face. 'Won't it be fun?' I said.

He had turned to the door though, and opened it, and we were inside the suite in the little entrance passage.

'Is that you?' called Mrs Van Hopper from the sitting-room. 'What in the name of Mike have you been doing? I've rung the office three times and they said they hadn't seen you.'

I was seized with a sudden desire to laugh, to cry, to do both, and I had a pain, too, at the pit of my stomach. I wished, for one wild moment, that none of this had happened, that I was alone somewhere, going for a walk, and whistling.

'I'm afraid it's all my fault,' he said, going into the sitting-room, shutting the door behind him, and I heard her exclamation of surprise.

Then I went into my bedroom and sat down by the open window. It was like waiting in the ante-room at a doctor's. I ought to turn over the pages of a magazine, look at photographs that did not matter and read articles I should never remember, until the nurse came, bright and efficient, all humanity washed away by years of disinfectant: 'It's all right, the operation was quite successful. There is no need to worry at all. I should go home and have some sleep.'

The walls of the suite were thick, I could hear no hum of voices. I wondered what he was saying to her, how he phrased his words. Perhaps he said, 'I fell in love with her, you know, the very first time we met. We've been seeing one another every day.' And she in answer, 'Why, Mr de Winter, it's quite the most

romantic thing I've ever heard.' Romantic, that was the word
I had tried to remember coming up in the lift. Yes, of course.
Romantic. That was what people would say. It was all very sudden and romantic. They suddenly decided to get married and
there it was. Such an adventure. I smiled to myself as I hugged
my knees on the window-seat, thinking how wonderful it was,
how happy I was going to be. I was to marry the man I loved.
I was to be Mrs de Winter. It was foolish to go on having that
pain in the pit of my stomach when I was so happy. Nerves of
course. Waiting like this; the doctor's ante-room. It would have
been better, after all, more natural surely to have gone into the
sitting-room hand in hand, laughing, smiling at one another and
for him to say 'We're going to be married, we're very much
in love.'

In love. He had not said anything yet about being in love. No
time perhaps. It was all so hurried at the breakfast table. Marmalade, and coffee, and that tangerine. No time. The tangerine was
very bitter. No, he had not said anything about being in love.
Just that we would be married. Short and definite, very original.
Original proposals were much better. More genuine. Not like
other people. Not like younger men who talked nonsense probably, not meaning half they said. Not like younger men being
very incoherent, very passionate, swearing impossibilities. Not
like him the first time, asking Rebecca ... I must not think of
that. Put it away. A thought forbidden, prompted by demons.
Get thee behind me, Satan. I must never think about that, never,
never, never. He loves me, he wants to show me Manderley.
Would they ever have done with their talking, would they ever
call me into the room?

There was the book of poems lying beside my bed. He had
forgotten he had ever lent them to me. They could not mean
much to him then. 'Go on,' whispered the demon, 'open the
title-page; that's what you want to do, isn't it? Open the title-
page.' Nonsense, I said, I'm only going to put the book with the
rest of the things. I yawned. I wandered to the table beside
the bed. I picked up the book. I caught my foot in the flex of the
bedside lamp, and stumbled, the book falling from my hands on
to the floor. It fell open, at the title-page. 'Max from Rebecca.'

She was dead, and one must not have thoughts about the dead. They slept in peace, the grass blew over their graves. How alive was her writing though, how full of force. Those curious, sloping letters. The blob of ink. Done yesterday. It was just as if it had been written yesterday. I took my nail scissors from the dressing-case and cut the page, looking over my shoulder like a criminal.

I cut the page right out of the book. I left no jagged edges, and the book looked white and clean when the page was gone. A new book, that had not been touched. I tore the page up in many little fragments and threw them into the waste-paper basket. Then I went and sat on the window-seat again. But I kept thinking of the torn scraps in the basket, and after a moment I had to get up and look in the basket once more. Even now the ink stood up on the fragments thick and black, the writing was not destroyed. I took a box of matches and set fire to the fragments. The flame had a lovely light, staining the paper, curling the edges, making the slanting writing impossible to distinguish. The fragments fluttered to grey ashes. The letter R was the last to go, it twisted in the flame, it curled outwards for a moment, becoming larger than ever. Then it crumpled too; the flame destroyed it. It was not ashes even, it was feathery dust ... I went and washed my hands in the basin. I felt better, much better. I had the clean new feeling that one has when the calendar is hung on the wall at the beginning of the year. January the 1st. I was aware of the same freshness, the same gay confidence. The door opened and he came into the room.

'All's well,' he said; 'shock made her speechless at first, but she's beginning to recover, so I'm going downstairs to the office, to make certain she will catch the first train. For a moment she wavered; I think she had hopes of acting witness at the wedding, but I was very firm. Go and talk to her.'

He said nothing about being glad, about being happy. He did not take my arm and go into the sitting-room with me. He smiled, and waved his hand, and went off down the corridor alone. I went to Mrs Van Hopper, uncertain, rather self-conscious, like a maid who has handed in her notice through a friend.

She was standing by the window, smoking a cigarette, an odd, dumpy little figure I should not see again, her coat stretched tight over her large breasts, her ridiculous hat perched sideways on her head.

'Well,' she said, her voice dry and hard, not the voice she would have used to him. 'I suppose I've got to hand it to you for a double-time worker. Still waters certainly run deep in your case. How did you manage it?'

I did not know what to answer. I did not like her smile. 'It was a lucky thing for you I had the influenza,' she said. 'I realize now how you spent your days, and why you were so forgetful. Tennis lessons my eye. You might have told me, you know.'

'I'm sorry,' I said.

She looked at me curiously, she ran her eyes over my figure. 'And he tells me he wants to marry you in a few days. Lucky again for you that you haven't a family to ask questions. Well, it's nothing to do with me any more, I wash my hands of the whole affair. I rather wonder what his friends will think, but I suppose that's up to him. You realize he's years older than you?'

'He's only forty-two,' I said, 'and I'm old for my age.'

She laughed, she dropped cigarette ash on the floor. 'You certainly are,' she said. She went on looking at me in a way she had never done before. Appraising me, running her eyes over my points like a judge at a cattle show. There was something inquisitive about her eyes, something unpleasant.

'Tell me,' she said, intimate, a friend to a friend, 'have you been doing anything you shouldn't?'

She was like Blaize, the dress-maker, who had offered me that ten per cent.

'I don't know what you mean,' I said.

She laughed, she shrugged her shoulders. 'Oh, well . . . never mind. But I always said English girls were dark horses, for all their hockey-playing attitude. So I'm supposed to travel to Paris alone, and leave you here while your beau gets a marriage licence? I notice he doesn't ask me to the wedding.'

'I don't think he wants anyone, and anyway you would have sailed,' I said.

'H'm, h'm,' she said. She took out her vanity case and began powdering her nose. 'I suppose you really do know your own mind,' she went on; 'after all, the whole thing has been very hurried, hasn't it? A matter of a few weeks. I don't suppose he's too easy, and you'll have to adapt yourself to his ways. You've led an extremely sheltered life up to now, you know, and you can't say that I've run you off your feet. You will have your work cut out as mistress of Manderley. To be perfectly frank, my dear, I simply can't see you doing it.'

Her words sounded like the echo of my own an hour before.

'You haven't the experience,' she continued, 'you don't know that milieu. You can scarcely string two sentences together at my bridge teas, what are you going to say to all his friends? The Manderley parties were famous when she was alive. Of course he's told you all about them?'

I hesitated, but she went on, thank heaven, not waiting for my answer.

'Naturally one wants you to be happy, and I grant you he's a very attractive creature but − well, I'm sorry; and personally I think you are making a big mistake − one you will bitterly regret.'

She put down the box of powder, and looked at me over her shoulder. Perhaps she was being sincere at last, but I did not want that sort of honesty. I did not say anything. I looked sullen, perhaps, for she shrugged her shoulders and wandered to the looking-glass, straightening her little mushroom hat. I was glad she was going, glad I should not see her again. I grudged the months I had spent with her, employed by her, taking her money, trotting in her wake like a shadow, drab and dumb. Of course I was inexperienced, of course I was idiotic, shy, and young. I knew all that. She did not have to tell me. I suppose her attitude was deliberate, and for some odd feminine reason she resented this marriage; her scale of values had received a shock.

Well, I would not care, I would forget her and her barbed words. A new confidence had been born in me when I burnt that page and scattered the fragments. The past would not exist for either of us; we were starting afresh, he and I. The past had blown away like the ashes in the waste-paper basket. I was going to be Mrs de Winter. I was going to live at Manderley.

Soon she would be gone, rattling alone in the wagon-lit

without me, and he and I would be together in the dining-room of the hotel, lunching at the same table, planning the future. The brink of a big adventure. Perhaps, once she had gone, he would talk to me at last, about loving me, about being happy. Up to now there had been no time, and anyway those things are not easily said, they must wait their moment. I looked up, and caught her reflection in the looking-glass. She was watching me, a little tolerant smile on her lips. I thought she was going to be generous after all, hold out her hand and wish me luck, give me encouragement and tell me that everything was going to be all right. But she went on smiling, twisting a stray hair into place beneath her hat.

'Of course,' she said, 'you know why he is marrying you, don't you? You haven't flattered yourself he's in love with you? The fact is that empty house got on his nerves to such an extent he nearly went off his head. He admitted as much before you came into the room. He just can't go on living there alone . . .'

7

WE CAME TO Manderley in early May, arriving, so Maxim said, with the first swallows and the bluebells. It would be the best moment, before the full flush of summer, and in the valley the azaleas would be prodigal of scent, and the blood-red rhododendrons in bloom. We motored, I remember, leaving London in the morning in a heavy shower of rain, coming to Manderley about five o'clock, in time for tea. I can see myself now, unsuitably dressed as usual, although a bride of seven weeks, in a tan-coloured stockinette frock, a small fur known as a stone marten round my neck, and over all a shapeless mackintosh, far too big for me and dragging to my ankles. It was, I thought, a gesture to the weather, and the length added inches to my height. I clutched a pair of gauntlet gloves in my hands, and carried a large leather handbag.

'This is London rain,' said Maxim when we left, 'you wait, the sun will be shining for you when we come to Manderley'; and he was right, for the clouds left us at Exeter, they rolled away behind us, leaving a great blue sky above our heads and a white road in front of us.

I was glad to see the sun, for in superstitious fashion I looked upon rain as an omen of ill-will, and the leaden skies of London had made me silent.

'Feeling better?' said Maxim, and I smiled at him, taking his hand, thinking how easy it was for him, going to his own home, wandering into the hall, picking up letters, ringing a bell for tea, and I wondered how much he guessed of my nervousness, and whether his question 'Feeling better?' meant that he understood. 'Never mind, we'll soon be there. I expect you want your tea,' he said, and he let go my hand because we had reached a bend in the road, and must slow down.

I knew then that he had mistaken my silence for fatigue, and it had not occurred to him I dreaded this arrival at Manderley as much as I had longed for it in theory. Now the moment was upon me I wished it delayed. I wanted to draw up at some wayside inn and stay there, in a coffee-room, by an impersonal fire. I wanted to be a traveller on the road, a bride in love with her husband. Not myself coming to Manderley for the first time, the wife of Maxim de Winter. We passed many friendly villages where the cottage windows had a kindly air. A woman, holding a baby in her arms, smiled at me from a doorway, while a man clanked across a road to a well, carrying a pail.

I wished we could have been one with them, perhaps their neighbours, and that Maxim could lean over a cottage gate in the evenings, smoking a pipe, proud of a very tall hollyhock he had grown himself; while I bustled in my kitchen, clean as a pin, laying the table for supper. There would be an alarm clock on the dresser ticking loudly, and a row of shining plates, while after supper Maxim would read his paper, boots on the fender, and I reach for a great pile of mending in the dresser drawer. Surely it would be peaceful and steady, that way of living, and easier, too, demanding no set standard?

'Only two miles further,' said Maxim; 'you see that great belt of trees on the brow of the hill there, sloping to the valley, with a scrap of sea beyond? That's Manderley, in there. Those are the woods.'

I forced a smile, and did not answer him, aware now of a stab of panic, an uneasy sickness that could not be controlled. Gone was my glad excitement, vanished my happy pride. I was like a child brought to her first school, or a little untrained maid who has never left home before, seeking a situation. Any measure of self-possession I had gained hitherto during the brief seven weeks of marriage, was like a rag now, fluttering before the wind; it seemed to me that even the most elementary knowledge of behaviour was unknown to me now, I should not know my right hand from my left, whether to stand or sit, what spoons and forks to use at dinner.

'I should shed that mackintosh,' he said, glancing down at me, 'it has not rained down here at all, and put your funny little fur straight. Poor lamb, I've bustled you down here like this, and you probably ought to have bought a lot of clothes in London.'

'It doesn't matter to me, as long as you don't mind,' I said.

'Most women think of nothing but clothes,' he said absently, and turning a corner we came to a cross-road, and the beginning of a high wall.

'Here we are,' he said, a new note of excitement in his voice, and I gripped the leather seat of the car with my two hands.

The road curved, and before us, on the left, were two high iron gates beside a lodge, open wide to the long drive beyond. As we drove through I saw faces peering through the dark window of the lodge, and a child ran round from the back, staring curiously. I shrank back against the seat, my heart beating quickly, knowing why the faces were at the window, and why the child stared.

They wanted to see what I was like. I could imagine them now, talking excitedly, laughing in the little kitchen. 'Only caught sight of the top of her hat,' they would say, 'she wouldn't show her face. Oh, well, we'll know by tomorrow. Word will come from the house.' Perhaps he guessed something of my shyness at last, for he took my hand, and kissed it, and laughed a little, even as he spoke.

'You mustn't mind if there's a certain amount of curiosity,' he said; 'everyone will want to know what you are like. They have probably talked of nothing else for weeks. You've only got to be yourself and they will all adore you. And you don't have to worry about the house, Mrs Danvers does everything. Just leave it all to her. She'll be stiff with you at first, I dare say, she's an extraordinary character, but you mustn't let it worry you. It's just her manner. See those shrubs? It's like a blue wall along here when the hydrangeas are in bloom.'

I did not answer him, for I was thinking of that self who long ago bought a picture postcard in a village shop, and came out into the bright sunlight twisting it in her hands, pleased with her purchase, thinking 'This will do for my album. "Manderley", what a lovely name.' And now I belonged here, this was my home. I would write letters to people saying, 'We shall be down at Manderley all the summer, you must come and see us,' and

I would walk along this drive, strange and unfamiliar to me now, with perfect knowledge, conscious of every twist and turn, marking and approving where the gardeners had worked, here a cutting back of the shrubs, there a lopping of a branch, calling at the lodge by the iron gates on some friendly errand, saying, 'Well, how's the leg today?' while the old woman, curious no longer, bade me welcome to her kitchen. I envied Maxim, careless and at ease, and the little smile on his lips which meant he was happy to be coming home.

It seemed remote to me, and far too distant, the time when I too should smile and be at ease, and I wished it could come quickly; that I could be old even, with grey hair and slow of step, having lived here many years – anything but the timid, foolish creature I felt myself to be.

The gates had shut to with a crash behind us, the dusty high-road was out of sight, and I became aware that this was not the drive I had imagined would be Manderley's, this was not a broad and spacious thing of gravel, flanked with neat turf at either side, kept smooth with rake and brush.

This drive twisted and turned as a serpent, scarce wider in places than a path, and above our heads was a great colonnade of trees, whose branches nodded and intermingled with one another, making an archway for us, like the roof of a church. Even the midday sun would not penetrate the interlacing of those green leaves, they were too thickly entwined, one with another, and only little flickering patches of warm light would come in intermittent waves to dapple the drive with gold. It was very silent, very still. On the high-road there had been a gay west wind blowing in my face, making the grass on the hedges dance in unison, but here there was no wind. Even the engine of the car had taken a new note, throbbing low, quieter than before. As the drive descended to the valley so the trees came in upon us, great beeches with lovely smooth white stems, lifting their myriad branches to one another, and other trees, trees I could not name, coming close, so close that I could touch them with my hands. On we went, over a little bridge that spanned a narrow stream, and still this drive that was no drive twisted and turned like an enchanted ribbon through the dark and silent woods, penetrating even deeper to the very heart surely of the forest itself, and still there was no clearing, no space to hold a house.

The length of it began to nag at my nerves; it must be this turn, I thought, or round that further bend; but as I leant forward in my seat I was for ever disappointed, there was no house, no field, no broad and friendly garden, nothing but the silence and deep woods. The lodge gates were a memory, and the high-road something belonging to another time, another world.

Suddenly I saw a clearing in the dark drive ahead, and a patch of sky, and in a moment the dark trees had thinned, the nameless shrubs had disappeared, and on either side of us was a wall of colour, blood-red, reaching far above our heads. We were amongst the rhododendrons. There was something bewildering, even shocking, about the suddenness of their discovery. The woods had not prepared me for them. They startled me with their crimson faces, massed one upon the other in incredible profusion, showing no leaf, no twig, nothing but the slaughterous red, luscious and fantastic, unlike any rhododendron plant I had seen before.

I glanced at Maxim. He was smiling. 'Like them?' he said.

I told him 'Yes,' a little breathlessly, uncertain whether I was speaking the truth or not, for to me a rhododendron was a homely, domestic thing, strictly conventional, mauve or pink in colour, standing one beside the other in a neat round bed. And these were monsters, rearing to the sky, massed like a battalion, too beautiful I thought, too powerful; they were not plants at all.

We were not far from the house now, I saw the drive broaden to the sweep I had expected, and with the blood-red wall still flanking us on either side, we turned the last corner, and so came to Manderley. Yes, there it was, the Manderley I had expected, the Manderley of my picture postcard long ago. A thing of grace and beauty, exquisite and faultless, lovelier even than I had ever dreamed, built in its hollow of smooth grassland and mossy lawns, the terraces sloping to the gardens, and the gardens to the sea. As we drove up to the wide stone steps and stopped before the open door, I saw through one of the mullioned windows that the hall was full of people, and I heard Maxim swear under his breath. 'Damn that woman,' he said; 'she knows perfectly well I did not want this sort of thing,' and he put on the brakes with a jerk.

'What's the matter?' I said. 'Who are all those people?'

'I'm afraid you will have to face it now,' he said, in irritation. 'Mrs Danvers has collected the whole damned staff in the house and on the estate to welcome us. It's all right, you won't have to say anything, I'll do it all.'

I fumbled for the handle of the door, feeling slightly sick, and cold now too from the long drive, and as I fumbled with the catch the butler came down the steps, followed by a footman, and he opened the door for me.

He was old, he had a kind face, and I smiled up at him, holding out my hand, but I don't think he could have seen, for he took the rug instead, and my small dressing-case, and turned to Maxim, helping me from the car at the same time.

'Well, here we are, Frith,' said Maxim, taking off his gloves. 'It was raining when we left London. You don't seem to have had it here. Everyone well?'

'Yes, sir, thank you, sir. No, we have had a dry month on the whole. Glad to see you home, and hope you have been keeping well. And Madam too.'

'Yes, we are both well, thank you, Frith. Rather tired from the drive, and wanting our tea. I didn't expect this business.' He jerked his head to the hall.

'Mrs Danvers' orders, sir,' said the man, his face expressionless.

'I might have guessed it,' said Maxim abruptly. 'Come on' – he turned to me – 'it won't take long, and then you shall have your tea.'

We went together up the flight of steps, Frith and the footman following with the rug and my mackintosh, and I was aware of a little pain at the pit of my stomach, and a nervous contraction in my throat.

I can close my eyes now, and look back on it, and see myself as I must have been, standing on the threshold of the house, a slim, awkward figure in my stockinette dress, clutching in my sticky hands a pair of gauntlet gloves. I can see the great stone hall, the wide doors open to the library, the Peter Lelys and the Vandykes on the walls, the exquisite staircase leading to the minstrels' gallery, and there, ranged one behind the other in the hall, overflowing to the stone passages beyond, and to the dining-room, a sea of faces, open-mouthed and curious, gazing at me as though they were the watching crowd about the block, and I the victim with my hands behind my back. Someone advanced from the sea of faces, someone tall and gaunt, dressed in deep black, whose prominent cheek-bones and great, hollow eyes gave her a skull's face, parchment-white, set on a skeleton's frame.

She came towards me, and I held out my hand, envying her for her dignity and her composure; but when she took my hand hers was limp and heavy, deathly cold, and it lay in mine like a lifeless thing.

'This is Mrs Danvers,' said Maxim, and she began to speak, still leaving that dead hand in mine, her hollow eyes never leaving my eyes, so that my own wavered and would not meet hers, and as they did so her hand moved in mine, the life returned to it, and I was aware of a sensation of discomfort and of shame.

I cannot remember her words now, but I know that she bade me welcome to Manderley, in the name of herself and the staff, a stiff, conventional speech rehearsed for the occasion, spoken in a voice as cold and lifeless as her hands had been. When she had finished she waited, as though for a reply, and I remember blush-ing scarlet, stammering some sort of thanks in return, and drop-ping both my gloves in my confusion. She stooped to pick them up, and as she handed them to me I saw a little smile of scorn upon her lips, and I guessed at once she considered me ill-bred. Something, in the expression of her face, gave me a feeling of unrest, and even when she had stepped back, and taken her place amongst the rest, I could see that black figure standing out alone, individual and apart, and for all her silence I knew her eye to be upon me. Maxim took my arm and made a little speech of thanks, perfectly easy and free from embarrassment, as though the making of it was no effort to him at all, and then he bore me off to the library to tea, closing the doors behind us, and we were alone again.

Two cocker spaniels came from the fireside to greet us. They pawed at Maxim, their long, silken ears strained back with affec-tion, their noses questing his hands, and then they left him and came to me, sniffing at my heels, rather uncertain, rather suspicious. One was the mother, blind in one eye, and soon she had enough of me, and took herself with a grunt to the fire again, but Jasper, the younger, put his nose into my hand, and laid a chin upon my knee, his eyes deep with meaning, his tail a-thump when I stroked his silken ears.

I felt better when I had taken my hat off, and my wretched little fur, and thrown them both beside my gloves and my bag on to the window-seat. It was a deep, comfortable room, with books lining the walls to the ceiling, the sort of room a man would move from never, did he live alone, solid chairs beside a great open fireplace, baskets for the two dogs in which I felt they never sat, for the hollows in the chairs had tell-tale marks. The long windows looked out upon the lawns, and beyond the lawns to the distant shimmer of the sea.

There was an old quiet smell about the room, as though the air in it was little changed, for all the sweet lilac scent and the roses brought to it throughout the early summer. Whatever air came to this room, whether from the garden or from the sea, would lose its first freshness, becoming part of the unchanging room itself, one with the books, musty and never read, one with the scrolled ceiling, the dark panelling, the heavy curtains.

It was an ancient mossy smell, the smell of a silent church where services are seldom held, where rusty lichen grows upon the stones and ivy tendrils creep to the very windows. A room for peace, a room for meditation.

Soon tea was brought to us, a stately little performance enacted by Frith and the young footman, in which I played no part until they had gone, and while Maxim glanced through his great pile of letters I played with two dripping crumpets, crumbled cake with my hands, and swallowed my scalding tea.

Now and again he looked up at me and smiled, and then returned to his letters, the accumulation of the last months I supposed, and I thought how little I knew of his life here at Manderley, of how it went day by day, of the people he knew, of his friends, men and women, of what bills he paid, what orders he gave about his household. The last weeks had gone so swiftly, and I – driving by his side through France and Italy – thought only of how I loved him, seeing Venice with his eyes, echoing his words, asking no questions of the past and future, content with the little glory of the living present.

For he was gayer than I had thought, more tender than I had dreamed, youthful and ardent in a hundred happy ways, not the Maxim I had first met, not the stranger who sat alone at the table in the restaurant, staring before him, wrapped in his secret self. My Maxim laughed and sang, threw stones into the water, took my hand, wore no frown between his eyes, carried no burden on his shoulder. I knew him as a lover, as a friend, and during those weeks I had forgotten that he had a life, orderly, methodical, a life which must be taken up again, continued as before, making vanished weeks a brief discarded holiday.

I watched him read his letters, saw him frown at one, smile at another, dismiss the next with no expression, and but for the grace of God I thought, my letter would be lying there, written from New York, and he would read it in the same indifferent fashion, puzzled at first perhaps by the signature, and then tossing it with a yawn to the pile of others in the basket, reaching for his cup of tea. The knowledge of this chilled me; how narrow a chance had stood between me and what might-have-been, for he would have sat here to his tea, as he sat now, continuing his home life as he would in any case, and perhaps he would not have thought of me much, not with regret anyway, while I, in New York, playing bridge with Mrs Van Hopper, would wait day after day for a letter that never came.

I leant back in my chair, glancing about the room, trying to instil into myself some measure of confidence, some genuine realization that I was here, at Manderley, the house of the picture postcard, the Manderley that was famous. I had to teach myself that all this was mine now, mine as much as his, the deep chair I was sitting in, that mass of books stretching to the ceiling, the pictures on the walls, the gardens, the woods, the Manderley I had read about, all of this was mine now because I was married to Maxim.

We should grow old here together, we should sit like this to our tea as old people, Maxim and I, with other dogs, the successors of these, and the library would wear the same ancient musty smell that it did now. It would know a period of glorious shabbiness and wear when the boys were young – our boys – for I saw them sprawling on the sofa with muddy boots, bringing with them always a litter of rods, and cricket bats, great clasp-knives, bows-and-arrows.

On the table there, polished now and plain, an ugly case would stand containing butterflies and moths, and another one with birds' eggs, wrapped in cotton wool. 'Not all this junk in here,' I would say, 'take them to the schoolroom, darlings,' and they would run off, shouting, calling to one another, but the little one staying behind, pottering on his own, quieter than the others.

My vision was disturbed by the opening of the door, and Frith came in with the footman to clear the tea. 'Mrs Danvers wondered, Madam, whether you would like to see your room,' he said to me, when the tea had been taken away.

Maxim glanced up from his letters. 'What sort of job have they made of the east wing?' he said.

'Very nice indeed, sir, it seems to me; the men made a mess when they were working, of course, and for a time Mrs Danvers was rather afraid it would not be finished by your return. But they cleared out last Monday. I should imagine you would be very comfortable there, sir; it's a lot lighter of course on that side of the house.'

'Have you been making alterations?' I asked.

'Oh, nothing much,' said Maxim briefly, 'only redecorating and painting the suite in the east wing, which I thought we would use for ours. As Frith says, it's much more cheerful on that side of the house, and it has a lovely view of the rose-garden. It was the visitors' wing when my mother was alive. I'll just finish these letters and then I'll come up and join you. Run along and make friends with Mrs Danvers; it's a good opportunity.'

I got up slowly, my old nervousness returning, and went out into the hall. I wished I could have waited for him, and then, taking his arm, seen the rooms together. I did not want to go alone, with Mrs Danvers. How vast the great hall looked now that it was empty. My feet rang on the flagged stones, echoing to the ceiling, and I felt guilty at the sound, as one does in church, self-conscious, aware of the same constraint. My feet made a stupid pitter-patter as I walked, and I thought that Frith, with his felt soles, must have thought me foolish.

'It's very big, isn't it?' I said, too brightly, too forced, a school-girl still, but he answered me in all solemnity.

'Yes, Madam, Manderley is a big place. Not so big as some, of course, but big enough. This was the old banqueting hall, in old days. It is used still on great occasions, such as a big dinner, or a ball. And the public are admitted here, you know, once a week.'

'Yes,' I said, still aware of my loud footsteps, feeling, as I fol-lowed him, that he considered me as he would one of the public visitors, and I behaved like a visitor too, glancing politely to right and left, taking in the weapons on the wall, and the pictures, touching the carved staircase with my hands.

A black figure stood waiting for me at the head of the stairs, the hollow eyes watching me intently from the white skull's face. I looked round for the solid Frith, but he had passed along the hall and into the further corridor.

I was alone now with Mrs Danvers. I went up the great stairs towards her, and she waited motionless, her hands folded before her, her eyes never leaving my face. I summoned a smile, which was not returned, nor did I blame her, for there was no purpose to the smile, it was a silly thing, bright and artificial. 'I hope I haven't kept you waiting,' I said.

'It's for you to make your own time, Madam,' she answered, 'I'm here to carry out your orders,' and then she turned, through the archway of the gallery, to the corridor beyond. We went along a broad, carpeted passage, and then turned left, through an oak door, and down a narrow flight of stairs and up a correspond-ing flight, and so to another door. This she flung open, standing aside to let me pass, and I came to a little ante-room, or boudoir, furnished with a sofa, chairs, and writing-desk, which opened out to a large double bedroom with wide windows and a bath-room beyond. I went at once to the window, and looked out. The rose-garden lay below, and the eastern part of the terrace, while beyond the rose-garden rose a smooth grass bank, stretch-ing to the near woods.

'You can't see the sea from here, then,' I said, turning to Mrs Danvers.

'No, not from this wing,' she answered; 'you can't even hear it, either. You would not know the sea was anywhere near, from this wing.'

She spoke in a peculiar way, as though something lay behind her words, and she laid an emphasis on the words 'this wing', as if suggesting that the suite where we stood now held some inferiority.

'I'm sorry about that; I like the sea,' I said.

She did not answer; she just went on staring at me, her hands folded before her.

'However, it's a very charming room,' I said, 'and I'm sure I shall be comfortable. I understand that it's been done up for our return.'

'Yes,' she said.

'What was it like before?' I asked.

'It had a mauve paper, and different hangings; Mr de Winter did not think it very cheerful. It was never much used, except for occasional visitors. But Mr de Winter gave special orders in his letters that you would have this room.'

'Then this was not his bedroom originally?' I said.

'No, Madam, he's never used the room in this wing before.'

'Oh,' I said, 'he didn't tell me that,' and I wandered to the dressing-table and began combing my hair. My things were already unpacked, my brushes and comb upon the tray. I was glad Maxim had given me a set of brushes, and that they were laid out there, upon the dressing-table, for Mrs Danvers to see. They were new, they had cost money, I need not be ashamed of them.

'Alice has unpacked for you and will look after you until your maid arrives,' said Mrs Danvers. I smiled at her again. I put down the brush upon the dressing-table.

'I don't have a maid,' I said awkwardly; 'I'm sure Alice, if she is the housemaid, will look after me all right.'

She wore the same expression that she had done on our first meeting, when I dropped my gloves so gauchely on the floor.

'I'm afraid that would not do for very long,' she said; 'it's usual, you know, for ladies in your position to have a personal maid.'

I flushed, and reached for my brush again. There was a sting

in her words I understood too well. 'If you think it necessary perhaps you would see about it for me,' I said, avoiding her eyes;
'some young girl perhaps, wanting to train.'

'If you wish,' she said. 'It's for you to say.'

There was silence between us. I wished she would go away.
I wondered why she must go on standing there, watching me,
her hands folded on her black dress.

'I suppose you have been at Manderley for many years,' I said,
making a fresh effort, 'longer than anyone else?'

'Not so long as Frith,' she said, and I thought how lifeless her
voice was, and cold, like her hand when it had lain in mine; 'Frith
was here when the old gentleman was living, when Mr de Winter
was a boy.'

'I see,' I said; 'so you did not come till after that?'

'No,' she said, 'not till after that.'

Once more, I glanced up at her and once more I met her eyes,
dark and sombre, in that white face of hers, instilling into me,
I knew not why, a strange feeling of disquiet, of foreboding.
I tried to smile, and could not; I found myself held by those eyes,
that had no light, no flicker of sympathy towards me.

'I came here when the first Mrs de Winter was a bride,' she
said, and her voice, which had hitherto, as I said, been dull and
toneless, was harsh now with unexpected animation, with life
and meaning, and there was a spot of colour on the gaunt
cheek-bones.

The change was so sudden that I was shocked, and a little
scared. I did not know what to do, or what to say. It was as though
she had spoken words that were forbidden, words that she had
hidden within herself for a long time and now would be repressed
no longer. Still her eyes never left my face; they looked upon me
with a curious mixture of pity and of scorn, until I felt myself to
be even younger and more untutored to the ways of life than I had
believed.

I could see she despised me, marking with all the snobbery of
her class that I was no great lady, that I was humble, shy, and
diffident. Yet there was something beside scorn in those eyes of
hers, something surely of positive dislike, or actual malice?

I had to say something, I could not go on sitting there, playing

with my hair-brush, letting her see how much I feared and mistrusted her.

'Mrs Danvers,' I heard myself saying, 'I hope we shall be
friends and come to understand one another. You must have
patience with me, you know, because this sort of life is new to
me, I've lived rather differently. And I do want to make a success
of it, and above all to make Mr de Winter happy. I know I can
leave all household arrangements to you, Mr de Winter said so,
and you must just run things as they have always been run; I shan't
want to make any changes.'

I stopped, a little breathless, still uncertain of myself and
whether I was saying the right thing, and when I looked up again
I saw that she had moved, and was standing with her hand on the
handle of the door.

'Very good,' she said; 'I hope I shall do everything to your
satisfaction. The house has been in my charge now for more than
a year, and Mr de Winter has never complained. It was very
different of course when the late Mrs de Winter was alive; there
was a lot of entertaining then, a lot of parties, and though I managed for her, she liked to supervise things herself.'

Once again I had the impression that she chose her words with
care, that she was feeling her way, as it were, into my mind, and
watching for the effect upon my face.

'I would rather leave it to you,' I repeated, 'much rather,' and
into her face came the same expression I had noticed before,
when first I had shaken hands with her in the hall, a look surely
of derision, of definite contempt. She knew that I would never
withstand her, and that I feared her too.

'Can I do anything more for you?' she said, and pretended to
glance round the room. 'No,' I said. 'No, I think I have everything. I shall be very comfortable here. You have made the room
so charming' – this last a final crawling sop to win her approval.
She shrugged her shoulders, and still she did not smile. 'I only
followed out Mr de Winter's instructions,' she said.

She hesitated by the doorway, her hand on the handle of the
open door. It was as though she still had something to say to me,
and could not decide upon the words, yet waited there, for me
to give her opportunity.

I wished she would go; she was like a shadow standing there, watching me, appraising me with her hollow eyes, set in that dead skull's face.

'If you find anything not to your liking you will tell me at once?' she asked.

'Yes,' I said. 'Yes, of course, Mrs Danvers,' but I knew this was not what she had meant to say, and silence fell between us once again.

'If Mr de Winter asks for his big wardrobe,' she said suddenly, 'you must tell him it was impossible to move. We tried, but we could not get it through these narrow doorways. These are smaller rooms than those in the west wing. If he doesn't like the arrangement of this suite he must tell me. It was difficult to know how to furnish these rooms.'

'Please don't worry, Mrs Danvers,' I said. 'I'm sure he will be pleased with everything. But I'm sorry it's given you so much trouble. I had no idea he was having rooms redecorated and furnished. He shouldn't have bothered. I'm sure I should have been just as happy and comfortable in the west wing.'

She looked at me curiously, and began twisting the handle of the door. 'Mr de Winter said you would prefer to be on this side,' she said, 'the rooms in the west wing are very old. The bedroom in the big suite is twice as large as this; a very beautiful room too, with a scrolled ceiling. The tapestry chairs are very valuable, and so is the carved mantelpiece. It's the most beautiful room in the house. And the windows look down across the lawns to the sea.'

I felt uncomfortable, a little shy. I did not know why she must speak with such an undercurrent of resentment, implying as she did at the same time that this room, where I found myself to be installed, was something inferior, not up to Manderley standard, a second-rate room, as it were, for a second-rate person.

'I suppose Mr de Winter keeps the most beautiful room to show to the public,' I said. She went on twisting the handle of the door, and then looked up at me again, watching my eyes, hesitating before replying, and when she spoke her voice was quieter even, and more toneless, than it had been before.

'The bedrooms are never shown to the public,' she said, 'only the hall and the gallery, and the room below.' She paused an instant, feeling me with her eyes. 'They used to live in the west wing and use those rooms when Mrs de Winter was alive. That big room, I was telling you about, that looked down to the sea, was Mrs de Winter's bedroom.'

Then I saw a shadow flit across her face, and she drew back against the wall, effacing herself, as a step sounded outside and Maxim came into the room.

'How is it?' he said to me. 'All right? Do you think you'll like it?'

He looked round with enthusiasm, pleased as a schoolboy. 'I always thought this a most attractive room,' he said. 'It was wasted all those years as a guest-room, but I always thought it had possibilities. You've made a great success of it, Mrs Danvers: I give you full marks.'

'Thank you, sir,' she said, her face expressionless, and then she turned, and went out of the room, closing the door softly behind her.

Maxim went and leant out of the window. 'I love the rose-garden,' he said; 'one of the first things I remember is walking after my mother, on very small, unsteady legs, while she picked off the dead heads of the roses. There's something peaceful and happy about this room, and it's quiet too. You could never tell you were within five minutes of the sea, from this room.'

'That's what Mrs Danvers said,' I told him.

He came away from the window, he prowled about the room, touching things, looking at the pictures, opening wardrobes, fingering my clothes, already unpacked.

'How did you get on with old Danvers?' he said abruptly.

I turned away, and began combing my hair again before the looking-glass. 'She seems just a little bit stiff,' I said, after a moment or two; 'perhaps she thought I was going to interfere with the running of the house.'

'I don't think she would mind your doing that,' he said. I looked up and saw him watching my reflection in the looking-glass, and then he turned away and went over to the window again, whistling quietly, under his breath, rocking backwards and forwards on his heels.

'Don't mind her,' he said; 'she's an extraordinary character in many ways, and possibly not very easy for another woman to get on with. You mustn't worry about it. If she really makes herself a nuisance we'll get rid of her. But she's efficient, you know, and will take all housekeeping worries off your hands. I dare say she's a bit of a bully to the staff. She doesn't dare bully me though. I'd have given her the sack long ago if she had tried.'

'I expect we shall get on very well when she knows me better,' I said quickly; 'after all, it's natural enough that she should resent me a bit at first.'

'Resent you? Why resent you? What the devil do you mean?' he said.

He turned from the window, frowning, an odd, half angry expression on his face. I wondered why he should mind, and wished I had said something else.

'I mean, it must be much easier for a housekeeper to look after a man alone,' I said. 'I dare say she had got into the way of doing it, and perhaps she was afraid I should be very overbearing.'

'Overbearing, my God ...' he began, 'if you think ...' and then he stopped, and came across to me, and kissed me on the top of my head.

'Let's forget about Mrs Danvers,' he said; 'she doesn't interest me very much, I'm afraid. Come along, and let me show you something of Manderley.'

I did not see Mrs Danvers again that evening, and we did not talk about her any more. I felt happier when I had dismissed her from my thoughts, less of an interloper, and as we wandered about the rooms downstairs, and looked at the pictures, and Maxim put his arm around my shoulder, I began to feel more like the self I wanted to become, the self I had pictured in my dreams, who made Manderley her home.

My footsteps no longer sounded foolish on the stone flags of the hall, for Maxim's nailed shoes made far more noise than mine, and the pattering feet of the two dogs was a comfortable, pleasing note.

I was glad, too, because it was the first evening and we had only been back a little while and the showing of the pictures had taken time, when Maxim, looking at the clock, said it was too late to change for dinner, so that I was spared the embarrassment of Alice, the maid, asking what I should wear, and of her helping me to dress, and myself walking down that long flight of stairs to the hall, cold, with bare shoulders, in a dress that Mrs Van Hopper had given me because it did not suit her daughter. I had dreaded the formality of dinner in that austere dining-room, and now, because of the little fact that we had not changed, it was quite all right, quite easy, just the same as when we had dined together in restaurants. I was comfortable in my stockinette dress, I laughed and talked about things we had seen in Italy and France, we even had the snapshots on the table, and Frith and the footman were impersonal people, as the waiters had been; they did not stare at me as Mrs Danvers had done.

We sat in the library after dinner, and presently the curtains were drawn, and more logs thrown on the fire; it was cool for May, I was thankful for the warmth that came from the steady burning logs.

It was new for us to sit together like this, after dinner, for in Italy we had wandered about, walked or driven, gone into little cafés, leant over bridges. Maxim made instinctively now for the chair on the left of the open fireplace, and stretched out his hand for the papers. He settled one of the broad cushions behind his head, and lit a cigarette. 'This is his routine,' I thought, 'this is what he always does: this has been his custom now for years.'

He did not look at me, he went on reading his paper, contented, comfortable, having assumed his way of living, the master of his house. And as I sat there, brooding, my chin in my hands, fondling the soft ears of one of the spaniels, it came to me that I was not the first one to lounge there in possession of the chair; someone had been before me, and surely left an imprint of her person on the cushions, and on the arm where her hand had rested. Another one had poured the coffee from that same silver coffee pot, had placed the cup to her lips, had bent down to the dog, even as I was doing.

Unconsciously, I shivered as though someone had opened the door behind me and let a draught into the room. I was sitting in Rebecca's chair, I was leaning against Rebecca's cushion, and the dog had come to me and laid his head upon my knee because that had been his custom, and he remembered, in the past, she had given sugar to him there.

8

I HAD NEVER realized, of course, that life at Manderley would be so orderly and planned. I remember now, looking back, how on that first morning Maxim was up and dressed and writing letters, even before breakfast, and when I got downstairs, rather after nine o'clock, a little flurried by the booming summons of the gong, I found he had nearly finished, he was already peeling his fruit.

He looked up at me and smiled. 'You mustn't mind,' he said; 'this is something you will have to get used to. I've no time to hang about at this hour of the day. Running a place like Manderley, you know, is a full-time job. The coffee and the hot dishes are on the sideboard. We always help ourselves at breakfast.' I said something about my clock being slow, about having been too long in the bath, but he did not listen, he was looking down at a letter, frowning at something.

How impressed I was, I remember well; impressed and a little overawed by the magnificence of the breakfast offered to us. There was tea, in a great silver urn, and coffee too, and on the heater, piping hot, dishes of scrambled eggs, of bacon, and another of fish. There was a little clutch of boiled eggs as well, in their own special heater, and porridge, in a silver porringer. On another sideboard was a ham, and a great piece of cold bacon. There were scones too, on the table, and toast, and various pots of jam, marmalade, and honey, while dessert dishes, piled high with fruit, stood at either end. It seemed strange to me that Maxim, who in Italy and France had eaten a *croissant* and fruit only, and drunk a cup of coffee, should sit down to this breakfast at home, enough for a dozen people, day after day probably, year after year, seeing nothing ridiculous about it, nothing wasteful.

I noticed he had eaten a small piece of fish. I took a boiled egg. And I wondered what happened to the rest, all those scrambled eggs, that crisp bacon, the porridge, the remains of the fish. Were there menials, I wondered, whom I should never know, never see, waiting behind kitchen doors for the gift of our breakfast? Or was it all thrown away, shovelled into dustbins? I would never know, of course, I would never dare to ask.

'Thank the Lord I haven't a great crowd of relations to inflict upon you,' said Maxim, 'a sister I very rarely see, and a grandmother who is nearly blind. Beatrice, by the way, asks herself over to lunch. I half expected she would. I suppose she wants to have a look at you.'

'Today?' I said, my spirits sinking to zero.

'Yes, according to the letter I got this morning. She won't stay long. You'll like her, I think. She's very direct, believes in speaking her mind. No humbug at all. If she doesn't like you she'll tell you so, to your face.'

I found this hardly comforting, and wondered if there was not some virtue in the quality of insincerity. Maxim got up from his chair, and lit a cigarette. 'I've a mass of things to see to this morning, do you think you can amuse yourself?' he said. 'I'd like to have taken you round the garden, but I must see Crawley, my agent. I've been away from things too long. He'll be in to lunch, too, by the way. You don't mind, do you? You will be all right?'

'Of course,' I said, 'I shall be quite happy.'

Then he picked up his letters, and went out of the room, and I remember thinking this was not how I imagined my first morning; I had seen us walking together, arms linked, to the sea, coming back rather late and tired and happy to a cold lunch, alone, and sitting afterwards under that chestnut tree I could see from the library window.

I lingered long over my first breakfast, spinning out the time, and it was not until I saw Frith come in and look at me, from behind the service screen, that I realized it was after ten o'clock. I sprang to my feet at once, feeling guilty, and apologized for sitting there so late, and he bowed, saying nothing, very polite, very correct, and I caught a flicker of surprise in his eyes. I wondered if I had said the wrong thing. Perhaps it did not do to apologize.

Perhaps it lowered me in his estimation. I wished I knew what to say, what to do. I wondered if he suspected, as Mrs Danvers had done, that poise, and grace, and assurance were not qualities inbred in me, but were things to be acquired, painfully perhaps, and slowly, costing me many bitter moments.

As it was, leaving the room, I stumbled, not looking where I was going, catching my foot on the step by the door, and Frith came forward to help me, picking up my handkerchief, while Robert, the young footman, who was standing behind the screen, turned away to hide his smile.

I heard the murmur of their voices as I crossed the hall, and one of them laughed – Robert, I supposed. Perhaps they were laughing about me. I went upstairs again, to the privacy of my bedroom, but when I opened the door I found the housemaids in there doing the room; one was sweeping the floor, the other dusting the dressing-table. They looked at me in surprise. I quickly went out again. It could not be right, then, for me to go to my room at that hour in the morning. It was not expected of me. It broke the household routine. I crept downstairs once more, silently, thankful of my slippers that made no sound on the stone flags, and so into the library, which was chilly, the windows flung wide open, the fire laid but not lit.

I shut the windows, and looked round for a box of matches. I could not find one. I wondered what I should do. I did not like to ring. But the library, so snug and warm last night with the burning logs, was like an ice-house now, in the early morning. There were matches upstairs in the bedroom, but I did not like to go for them because it would mean disturbing the housemaids at their work. I could not bear their moon faces staring at me again. I decided that when Frith and Robert had left the dining-room I would fetch the matches from the sideboard. I tiptoed out into the hall and listened. They were still clearing, I could hear the sound of voices, and the movement of trays. Presently all was silent, they must have gone through the service doors into the kitchen quarters, so I went across the hall and into the dining-room once more. Yes, there was a box of matches on the sideboard, as I expected. I crossed the room quickly and picked them up, and as I did so Frith came back into the room. I tried to cram the box furtively into my pocket, but I saw him glance at my hand in surprise.

'Did you require anything, Madam?' he said.

'Oh, Frith,' I said awkwardly, 'I could not find any matches.' He at once proffered me another box, handing me the cigarettes too, at the same time. This was another embarrassment, for I did not smoke.

'No, the fact is,' I said, 'I felt rather cool in the library, I suppose the weather seems chilly to me, after being abroad and I thought perhaps I would just put a match to the fire.'

'The fire in the library is not usually lit until the afternoon, Madam,' he said. 'Mrs de Winter always used the morning-room. There is a good fire in there. Of course if you should wish to have the fire in the library as well I will give orders for it to be lit.'

'Oh, no,' I said, 'I would not dream of it. I will go into the morning-room. Thank you, Frith.'

'You will find writing-paper, and pens, and ink, in there, Madam,' he said. 'Mrs de Winter always did all her correspondence and telephoning in the morning-room, after breakfast. The house telephone is also there, should you wish to speak to Mrs Danvers.'

'Thank you, Frith,' I said.

I turned away into the hall again, humming a little tune to give me an air of confidence. I could not tell him that I had never seen the morning-room, that Maxim had not shown it to me the night before. I knew he was standing in the entrance to the dining-room, watching me, as I went across the hall, and that I must make some show of knowing my way. There was a door to the left of the great staircase, and I went recklessly towards it, praying in my heart that it would take me to my goal, but when I came to it and opened it I saw that it was a garden room, a place for odds and ends: there was a table where flowers were done, there were basket chairs stacked against the wall, and a couple of mackintoshes too, hanging on a peg. I came out, a little defiantly, glancing across the hall, and saw Frith still standing there. I had not deceived him, though, not for a moment.

'You go through the drawing-room to the morning-room,

Madam,' he said, 'through the door there, on your right, this side of the staircase. You go straight through the double drawing-room, and turn to your left.'

'Thank you, Frith,' I said humbly, pretending no longer.

I went through the long drawing-room, as he had directed; a lovely room this, beautifully proportioned, looking out upon the lawns down to the sea. The public would see this room, I supposed, and Frith, if he showed them round, would know the history of the pictures on the wall, and the period of the furniture. It was beautiful of course, I knew that, and those chairs and tables probably without price, but for all that I had no wish to linger there; I could not see myself sitting ever in those chairs, standing before that carved mantelpiece, throwing books down on to the tables. It had all the formality of a room in a museum, where alcoves were roped off, and a guardian, in cloak and hat like the guides in the French chateaux, sat in a chair beside the door. I went through then, and turned to the left, and so on to the little morning-room I had not seen before.

I was glad to see the dogs there, sitting before the fire, and Jasper, the younger, came over to me at once, his tail wagging, and thrust his nose into my hand. The old one lifted her muzzle at my approach, and gazed in my direction with her blind eyes, but when she had sniffed the air a moment, and found I was not the one she sought, she turned her head away with a grunt, and looked steadily into the fire again. Then Jasper left me, too, and settled himself by the side of his companion, licking his side. This was their routine. They knew, even as Frith had known, that the library fire was not lit until the afternoon. They came to the morning-room from long custom. Somehow I guessed, before going to the window, that the room looked out upon the rhodo-dendrons. Yes, there they were, blood-red and luscious, as I had seen them the evening before, great bushes of them, massed beneath the open window, encroaching on to the sweep of the drive itself. There was a little clearing too, between the bushes, like a miniature lawn, the grass a smooth carpet of moss, and in the centre of this, the tiny statue of a naked faun, his pipes to his lips.

The crimson rhododendrons made his background, and the

clearing itself was like a little stage, where he would dance, and play his part. There was no musty smell about this room, as there had been in the library. There were no old well-worn chairs, no tables littered with magazines and papers, seldom if ever read, but left there from long custom, because Maxim's father, or even his grandfather perhaps, had wished it so.

This was a woman's room, graceful, fragile, the room of someone who had chosen every particle of furniture with great care, so that each chair, each vase, each small, infinitesimal thing should be in harmony with one another, and with her own personality. It was as though she who had arranged this room had said: 'This I will have, and this, and this,' taking piece by piece from the treasures in Manderley each object that pleased her best, ignoring the second-rate, the mediocre, laying her hand with sure certain instinct only upon the best. There was no intermingling of style, no confusing of period, and the result was perfection in a strange and startling way, not coldly formal like the drawing-room shown to the public, but vividly alive, having something of the same glow and brilliance that the rhododendrons had, massed there, beneath the window. And I noticed then that the rhododendrons, not content with forming their theatre on the little lawn outside the window, had been permitted to the room itself. Their great warm faces looked down upon me from the mantelpiece, they floated in a bowl upon the table by the sofa, they stood, lean and graceful, on the writing-desk beside the golden candlesticks.

The room was filled with them, even the walls took colour from them, becoming rich and glowing in the morning sun. They were the only flowers in the room, and I wondered if there was some purpose in it, whether the room had been arranged originally with this one end in view, for nowhere else in the house did the rhododendrons obtrude. There were flowers in the dining-room, flowers in the library, but orderly and trim, rather in the background, not like this, not in profusion. I went and sat down at the writing-desk, and I thought how strange it was that this room, so lovely and so rich in colour, should be, at the same time, so business-like and purposeful. Somehow I should have expected that a room furnished as this was in such exquisite taste, for all the exaggeration of the flowers, would be a place of decoration only, languorous and intimate.

But this writing-table, beautiful as it was, was no pretty toy where a woman would scribble little notes, nibbling the end of a pen, leaving it, day after day, in carelessness, the blotter a little askew. The pigeon-holes were docketed, 'letters unanswered', 'letters-to-keep', 'household', 'estate', 'menus', 'miscellaneous', 'addresses'; each ticket written in that same scrawling pointed hand that I knew already. And it shocked me, even startled me, to recognize it again, for I had not seen it since I had destroyed the page from the book of poems, and I had not thought to see it again.

I opened a drawer at hazard, and there was the writing once more, this time in an open leather book, whose heading 'Guests at Manderley' showed at once, divided into weeks and months, what visitors had come and gone, the rooms they had used, the food they had eaten. I turned over the pages and saw that the book was a complete record of a year, so that the hostess, glancing back, would know to the day, almost to the hour, what guest had passed what night under her roof, and where he had slept, and what she had given him to eat. There was note-paper also in the drawer, thick white sheets, for rough writing, and the note-paper of the house, with the crest, and the address, and visiting cards, ivory white, in little boxes.

I took one out and looked at it, unwrapped it from its thin tissue of paper. 'Mrs M. de Winter' it said, and in the corner 'Manderley'. I put it back in the box again, and shut the drawer, feeling guilty suddenly, and deceitful, as though I were staying in somebody else's house and my hostess had said to me, 'Yes, of course, write letters at my desk,' and I had unforgivably, in a stealthy manner, peeped at her correspondence. At any moment she might come back into the room and she would see me there, sitting before her open drawer, which I had no right to touch.

And when the telephone rang, suddenly, alarmingly, on the desk in front of me, my heart leapt and I started up in terror, thinking I had been discovered. I took the receiver off with trembling hands, and 'Who is it?' I said, 'who do you want?' There was a strange buzzing at the end of the line, and then a voice came, low and rather harsh, whether that of a woman or a man I could not tell, and 'Mrs de Winter?' it said, 'Mrs de Winter?'

'I'm afraid you have made a mistake,' I said; 'Mrs de Winter has been dead for over a year.' I sat there, waiting, staring stupidly into the mouthpiece, and it was not until the name was repeated again, the voice incredulous, slightly raised, that I became aware, with a rush of colour to my face, that I had blundered irretrievably, and could not take back my words. 'It's Mrs Danvers, Madam,' said the voice. 'I'm speaking to you on the house telephone.' My *faux pas* was so palpably obvious, so idiotic and unpardonable, that to ignore it would show me to be an even greater fool, if possible, than I was already.

'I'm sorry, Mrs Danvers,' I said, stammering, my words tumbling over one another; 'the telephone startled me, I didn't know what I was saying, I didn't realize the call was for me, and I never noticed I was speaking on the house telephone.'

'I'm sorry to have disturbed you, Madam,' she said; and she knows, I thought, she guesses I have been looking through the desk. 'I only wondered whether you wished to see me, and whether you approved of the menus for today.'

'Oh,' I said. 'Oh, I'm sure I do; that is, I'm sure I approve of the menus. Just order what you like, Mrs Danvers, you needn't bother to ask me.'

'It would be better, I think, if you read the list,' continued the voice; 'you will find the menu of the day on the blotter, beside you.'

I searched feverishly about me on the desk, and found at last a sheet of paper I had not noticed before. I glanced hurriedly through it: curried prawns, roast veal, asparagus, cold chocolate mousse – was this lunch or dinner? I could not see; lunch, I suppose.

'Yes, Mrs Danvers,' I said, 'very suitable, very nice indeed.'

'If you wish anything changed please say so,' she answered, 'and I will give orders at once. You will notice I have left a blank space beside the sauce, for you to mark your preference. I was not sure what sauce you are used to having served with the roast veal. Mrs de Winter was most particular about her sauces, and I always had to refer to her.'

'Oh,' I said. 'Oh, well . . . let me see, Mrs Danvers, I hardly know; I think we had better have what you usually have, whatever you think Mrs de Winter would have ordered.'

'You have no preference, Madam?'

'No,' I said. 'No, really, Mrs Danvers.'

'I rather think Mrs de Winter would have ordered a wine sauce, Madam.'

'We will have the same then, of course,' I said.

'I'm very sorry I disturbed you while you were writing, Madam.'

'You didn't disturb me at all,' I said; 'please don't apologize.'

'The post leaves at midday, and Robert will come for your letters, and stamp them himself,' she said; 'all you have to do is ring through to him, on the telephone, if you have anything urgent to be sent, and he will give orders for them to be taken in to the post-office immediately.'

'Thank you, Mrs Danvers,' I said. I listened for a moment, but she said no more, and then I heard a little click at the end of the telephone, which meant she had replaced the receiver. I did the same. Then I looked down again at the desk, and the note-paper, ready for use, upon the blotter. In front of me stared the ticketed pigeon-holes, and the words upon them 'letters unanswered', 'estate', 'miscellaneous', were like a reproach to me for my idleness. She who sat here before me had not wasted her time, as I was doing. She had reached out for the house telephone and given her orders for the day, swiftly, efficiently, and run her pencil perhaps through an item in the menu that had not pleased her. She had not said 'Yes, Mrs Danvers,' and 'Of course, Mrs Danvers,' as I had done. And then, when she had finished, she began her letters, five, six, seven perhaps to be answered, all written in that same curious, slanting hand I knew so well. She would tear off sheet after sheet of that smooth white paper, using it extravagantly, because of the long strokes she made when she wrote, and at the end of each of her personal letters she put her signature, 'Rebecca', that tall sloping R dwarfing its fellows.

I drummed with my fingers on the desk. The pigeon-holes were empty now. There were no 'letters unanswered' waiting to be dealt with, no bills to pay that I knew anything about. If I had anything urgent, Mrs Danvers said, I must telephone through to Robert and he would give orders for it to be taken to the post. I wondered how many urgent letters Rebecca used to write, and who they were written to. Dress-makers perhaps – 'I must have the white satin on Tuesday, without fail,' or to her hairdresser – 'I shall be coming up next Friday, and want an appointment at three o'clock with Monsieur Antoine himself. Shampoo, massage, set, and manicure.' No, letters of that type would be a waste of time. She would have a call put through to London. Frith would do it. Frith would say 'I am speaking for Mrs de Winter.' I went on drumming with my fingers on the desk. I could think of nobody to write to. Only Mrs Van Hopper. And there was something foolish, rather ironical, in the realization that here I was sitting at my own desk in my own home with nothing better to do than to write a letter to Mrs Van Hopper, a woman I disliked, whom I should never see again. I pulled a sheet of note-paper towards me. I took up the narrow, slender pen, with the bright pointed nib. 'Dear Mrs Van Hopper,' I began. And as I wrote, in halting, laboured fashion, saying I hoped the voyage had been good, that she had found her daughter better, that the weather in New York was fine and warm, I noticed for the first time how cramped and unformed was my own handwriting; without individuality, without style, uneducated even, the writing of an indifferent pupil taught in a second-rate school.

9

WHEN I HEARD the sound of the car in the drive I got up in sudden panic, glancing at the clock, for I knew that it meant Beatrice and her husband had arrived. It was only just gone twelve; they were much earlier than I expected. And Maxim was not yet back. I wondered if it would be possible to hide, to get out of the window, into the garden so that Frith, bringing them to the morning-room, would say, 'Madam must have gone out,' and it would seem quite natural, they would take it as a matter of course. The dogs looked up inquiringly as I ran to the window, and Jasper followed me, wagging his tail.

The window opened out on to the terrace and the little grass clearing beyond, but as I prepared to brush past the rhododendrons the sound of voices came close, and I backed again into the room. They were coming to the house by way of the garden, Frith having told them doubtless that I was in the morning-room. I went quickly into the big drawing-room, and made for a door near me on the left. It led into a long stone passage, and I ran along it, fully aware of my stupidity, despising myself for this sudden attack of nerves, but I knew I could not face these people, not for a moment anyway. The passage seemed to be taking me to the back regions, and as I turned a corner, coming upon another staircase, I met a servant I had not seen before, a scullery-maid perhaps; she carried a mop and pail in her hands. She stared at me in wonder, as though I were a vision, unexpected in this part of the house, and 'Good morning,' I said, in great confusion, making for the stairway, and 'Good morning, Madam,' she returned, her mouth open, her round eyes inquisitive as I climbed the stairs.

They would lead me, I supposed, to the bedrooms, and I could find my suite in the east wing, and sit up there a little while, until

I judged it nearly time for lunch, when good manners would compel me to come down again.

I must have lost my bearings, for passing through a door at the head of the stairs I came to a long corridor that I had not seen before, similar in some ways to the one in the east wing, but broader and darker – dark owing to the panelling of the walls.

I hesitated, then turned left, coming upon a broad landing and another staircase. It was very quiet and dark. No one was about. If there had been housemaids here, during the morning, they had finished their work by now and gone downstairs. There was no trace of their presence, no lingering dust smell of carpets lately swept, and I thought, as I stood there, wondering which way to turn, that the silence was unusual, holding something of the same oppression as an empty house does, when the owners have gone away.

I opened a door at hazard, and found a room in total darkness, no chink of light coming through the closed shutters, while I could see dimly, in the centre of the room, the outline of furniture swathed in white dust-sheets. The room smelt close and stale, the smell of a room seldom if ever used, whose ornaments are herded together in the centre of a bed and left there, covered with a sheet. It might be too that the curtain had not been drawn from the window since some preceding summer, and if one crossed there now and pulled them aside, opening the creaking shutters, a dead moth who had been imprisoned behind them for many months would fall to the carpet and lie there, beside a forgotten pin, and a dried leaf blown there before the windows were closed for the last time. I shut the door softly, and went uncertainly along the corridor, flanked on either side by doors, all of them closed, until I came to a little alcove, set in an outside wall, where a broad window gave me light at last. I looked out, and I saw below me the smooth grass lawns stretching to the sea, and the sea itself, bright green with white-tipped crests, whipped by a westerly wind and scudding from the shore.

It was closer than I had thought, much closer; it ran, surely, beneath that little knot of trees below the lawns, barely five minutes away, and if I listened now, my ear to the window, I could hear the surf breaking on the shores of some little bay I could not see. I knew then I had made the circuit of the house, and was standing in the corridor of the west wing. Yes, Mrs Danvers was right. You could hear the sea from here. You might imagine, in the winter, it would creep up on to those green lawns and threaten the house itself, for even now, because of the high wind, there was a mist upon the window-glass, as though someone had breathed upon it. A mist salt-laden, borne upwards from the sea. A hurrying cloud hid the sun for a moment as I watched, and the sea changed colour instantly, becoming black, and the white crests with them very pitiless suddenly, and cruel, not the gay sparkling sea I had looked on first.

Somehow I was glad my rooms were in the east wing. I preferred the rose-garden, after all, to the sound of the sea. I went back to the landing then, at the head of the stairs, and as I prepared to go down, one hand upon the banister, I heard the door behind me open, and it was Mrs Danvers. We stared at one another for a moment without speaking, and I could not be certain whether it was anger I read in her eyes or curiosity, for her face became a mask directly she saw me. Although she said nothing I felt guilty and ashamed, as though I had been caught trespassing, and I felt the tell-tale colour come up into my face.

'I lost my way,' I said, 'I was trying to find my room.'

'You have come to the opposite side of the house,' she said; 'this is the west wing.'

'Yes, I know,' I said.

'Did you go into any of the rooms?' she asked me.

'No,' I said. 'No, I just opened a door, I did not go in. Everything was dark, covered up in dust-sheets. I'm sorry. I did not mean to disturb anything. I expect you like to keep all this shut up.'

'If you wish to open up the rooms I will have it done,' she said; 'you have only to tell me. The rooms are all furnished, and can be used.'

'Oh, no,' I said. 'No. I did not mean you to think that.'

'Perhaps you would like me to show you all over the west wing?' she said.

I shook my head. 'No, I'd rather not,' I said. 'No, I must go downstairs.' I began to walk down the stairs, and she came with me, by my side, as though she were a warder, and I in custody.

'Any time, when you have nothing to do, you have only to ask me, and I will show you the rooms in the west wing,' she persisted, making me vaguely uncomfortable. I knew not why. Her insistence struck a chord in my memory, reminding me of a visit to a friend's house, as a child, when the daughter of the house, older than me, took my arm and whispered in my ear, 'I know where there is a book, locked in a cupboard, in my mother's bedroom. Shall we go and look at it?' I remembered her white, excited face, and her small, beady eyes, and the way she kept pinching my arm.

'I will have the dust-sheets removed, and then you can see the rooms as they looked when they were used,' said Mrs Danvers. 'I would have shown you this morning, but I believed you to be writing letters in the morning-room. You have only to telephone through to my room, you know, when you want me. It would only take a short while to have the rooms in readiness.'

We had come down the short flight of stairs, and she opened another door, standing aside for me to pass through, her dark eyes questing my face.

'It's very kind of you, Mrs Danvers,' I said. 'I will let you know some time.'

We passed out together on to the landing beyond, and I saw we were at the head of the main staircase now, behind the minstrels' gallery.

'I wonder how you came to miss your way?' she said, 'the door through the west wing is very different to this.'

'I did not come this way,' I said.

'Then you must have come up the back way, from the stone passage?' she said.

'Yes,' I said, not meeting her eyes. 'Yes, I came through a stone passage.'

She went on looking at me, as though she expected me to tell her why I left the morning-room in sudden panic, going through the back regions, and I felt suddenly that she knew, that she must have watched me, that she had seen me wandering perhaps in that west wing from the first, her eye to a crack in the door. 'Mrs Lacy, and Major Lacy, have been here some time,' she said. 'I heard their car drive up shortly after twelve.'

'Oh!' I said. 'I had not realized that.'

'Frith will have taken them to the morning-room,' she said: 'it must be getting on for half past twelve. You know your way now, don't you?'

'Yes, Mrs Danvers,' I said. And I went down the big stairway into the hall, knowing she was standing there above me, her eyes watching me.

I knew I must go back now, to the morning-room, and meet Maxim's sister and her husband. I could not hide in my bedroom now. As I went into the drawing-room I glanced back, over my shoulder, and I saw Mrs Danvers still standing there at the head of the stairs, like a black sentinel.

I stood for a moment outside the morning-room, with my hand on the door, listening to the hum of voices. Maxim had returned, then, while I had been upstairs, bringing his agent with him I supposed, for it sounded to me as if the room was full of people. I was aware of the same feeling of sick uncertainty I had experienced so often as a child, when summoned to shake hands with visitors, and turning the handle of the door I blundered in, to be met at once, it seemed, with a sea of faces and a general silence.

'Here she is at last,' said Maxim. 'Where have you been hiding? We were thinking of sending out a search party. Here is Beatrice, and this is Giles, and this is Frank Crawley. Look out, you nearly trod on the dog.'

Beatrice was tall, broad-shouldered, very handsome, very much like Maxim about the eyes and jaw, but not as smart as I had expected, much tweedier; the sort of person who would nurse dogs through distemper, know about horses, shoot well. She did not kiss me. She shook hands very firmly, looking me straight in the eyes, and then turned to Maxim. 'Quite different from what I expected. Doesn't answer to your description at all.'

Everyone laughed, and I joined in, not quite certain if the laugh was against me or not, wondering secretly what it was she had expected, and what had been Maxim's description.

And 'This is Giles,' said Maxim, prodding my arm, and Giles

stretched out an enormous paw and wrung my hand, squeezing the fingers limp, genial eyes smiling from behind horn-rimmed glasses.

'Frank Crawley,' said Maxim, and I turned to the agent, a colourless, rather thin man with a prominent Adam's apple, in whose eyes I read relief as he looked upon me. I wondered why, but I had no time to think of that, because Frith had come in, and was offering me sherry, and Beatrice was talking to me again. 'Maxim tells me you only got back last night. I had not realized that, or of course we would never have thrust ourselves upon you so soon. Well, what do you think of Manderley?'

'I've scarcely seen anything of it yet,' I answered; 'it's beautiful, of course.'

She was looking me up and down, as I had expected, but in a direct, straightforward fashion, not maliciously like Mrs Danvers, not with unfriendliness. She had a right to judge me, she was Maxim's sister, and Maxim himself came to my side now, putting his arm through mine, giving me confidence.

'You're looking better, old man,' she said to him, her head on one side, considering him; 'you've lost that fine-drawn look, thank goodness. I suppose we've got you to thank for that?' nodding at me.

'I'm always very fit,' said Maxim shortly, 'never had anything wrong with me in my life. You imagine everyone ill who doesn't look as fat as Giles.'

'Bosh,' said Beatrice; 'you know perfectly well you were a perfect wreck six months ago. Gave me the fright of my life when I came and saw you. I thought you were in for a breakdown. Giles, bear me out. Didn't Maxim look perfectly ghastly last time we came over, and didn't I say he was heading for a breakdown?'

'Well, I must say, old chap, you're looking a different person,' said Giles. 'Very good thing you went away. Doesn't he look well, Crawley?'

I could tell by the tightening of Maxim's muscles under my arm that he was trying to keep his temper. For some reason this talk about his health was not welcome to him, angered him even, and I thought it tactless of Beatrice to harp upon it in this way, making so big a point of it.

'Maxim's very sunburnt,' I said shyly; 'it hides a multitude of sins. You should have seen him in Venice having breakfast on the balcony, trying to get brown on purpose. He thinks it makes him better-looking.'

Everyone laughed, and Mr Crawley said, 'It must have been wonderful in Venice, Mrs de Winter, this time of year,' and 'Yes,' I said, 'we had really wonderful weather. Only one bad day, wasn't it, Maxim?' the conversation drawing away happily from his health, and so to Italy, safest of subjects, and the blessed topic of fine weather. Conversation was easy now, no longer an effort. Maxim and Giles and Beatrice were discussing the running of Maxim's car, and Mr Crawley was asking if it were true that there were no more gondolas in the canals now, only motor-boats. I don't think he would have cared at all had there been steamers at anchor in the Grand Canal, he was saying this to help me, it was his contribution to the little effort of steering the talk away from Maxim's health, and I was grateful to him, feeling him an ally, for all his dull appearance.

'Jasper wants exercise,' said Beatrice, stirring the dog with her foot; 'he's getting much too fat, and he's barely two years old. What do you feed him on, Maxim?'

'My dear Beatrice, he has exactly the same routine as your dogs,' said Maxim. 'Don't show off and make out you know more about animals than I do.'

'Dear old boy, how can you pretend to know what Jasper has been fed on when you've been away for a couple of months? Don't tell me Frith walks to the lodge gates with him twice a day. This dog hasn't had a run for weeks. I can tell by the condition of his coat.'

'I'd rather he looked colossal than half-starved like that half-wit dog of yours,' said Maxim.

'Not a very intelligent remark when Lion won two firsts at Cruft's last February,' said Beatrice.

The atmosphere was becoming rather strained again, I could tell by the narrow lines of Maxim's mouth, and I wondered if brothers and sisters always sparred like this, making it uncomfortable for those who listened. I wished that Frith would come in and announce lunch. Or would we be summoned by a booming gong? I did not know what happened at Manderley.

'How far away from us are you?' I asked, sitting down by
Beatrice; 'did you have to make a very early start?'

'We're fifty miles away, my dear, in the next county, the other
side of Trowchester. The hunting is so much better with us. You
must come over and stay, when Maxim can spare you. Giles will
mount you.'

'I'm afraid I don't hunt,' I confessed. 'I learnt to ride, as a
child, but very feebly; I don't remember much about it.'

'You must take it up again,' she said. 'You can't possibly live
in the country and not ride: you wouldn't know what to do with
yourself. Maxim says you paint. That's very nice, of course,
but there's no exercise in it, is there? All very well on a wet day
when there's nothing better to do.'

'My dear Beatrice, we are not all such fresh-air fiends as you,'
said Maxim.

'I wasn't talking to you, old boy. We all know you are perfectly
happy slopping about the Manderley gardens and never breaking
out of a slow walk.'

'I'm very fond of walking too,' I said swiftly. 'I'm sure I shall
never get tired of rambling about Manderley. And I can bathe
too, when it's warmer.'

'My dear, you are an optimist,' said Beatrice. 'I can hardly ever
remember bathing here. The water is far too cold, and the beach
is shingle.'

'I don't mind that,' I said. 'I love bathing. As long as the cur-
rents are not too strong. Is the bathing safe in the bay?'

Nobody answered, and I realized suddenly what I had said.
My heart thumped, and I felt my cheeks go flaming red. I bent
down to stroke Jasper's ear, in an agony of confusion. 'Jasper
could do with a swim, and get some of that fat off,' said Beatrice,
breaking the pause, 'but he'd find it a bit too much for him in the
bay, wouldn't you, Jasper? Good old Jasper. Nice old man.' We
patted the dog together, not looking at one another.

'I say, I'm getting infernally hungry. What on earth is happening to lunch?' said Maxim.

'It's only just on one now,' said Mr Crawley, 'according to the
clock on the mantelpiece.'

'That clock was always fast,' said Beatrice.

'It's kept perfect time now for months,' said Maxim.

At that moment the door opened and Frith announced that luncheon was served.

'I say, I must have a wash,' said Giles, looking at his hands.

We all got up and wandered through the drawing-room to the hall in great relief, Beatrice and I a little ahead of the men, she taking my arm.

'Dear old Frith,' she said, 'he always looks exactly the same, and makes me feel like a girl again. You know, don't mind me saying so, but you are even younger than I expected. Maxim told me your age, but you're an absolute child. Tell me, are you very much in love with him?'

I was not prepared for this question, and she must have seen the surprise in my face, for she laughed lightly, and squeezed my arm.

'Don't answer,' she said. 'I can see what you feel. I'm an inter-fering bore, aren't I? You mustn't mind me. I'm devoted to Maxim, you know, though we always bicker like cat and dog when we meet. I congratulate you again on his looks. We were all very worried about him this time last year, but of course you know the whole story.' We had come to the dining-room by now, and she said no more, for the servants were there and the others had joined us, but as I sat down, and unfolded my napkin, I wondered what Beatrice would say did she realize that I knew nothing of that preceding year, no details of the tragedy that had happened down there, in the bay, that Maxim kept these things to himself, that I questioned him never.

Lunch passed off better than I had dared to hope. There were few arguments, or perhaps Beatrice was exercising tact at last; at any rate she and Maxim chatted about matters concerning Manderley, her horses, the garden, mutual friends, and Frank Crawley, on my left, kept up an easy patter with me for which I was grateful, as it required no effort. Giles was more concerned with food than with the conversation, though now and again he remembered my existence and flung me a remark at hazard.

'Same cook I suppose, Maxim?' he said, when Robert had

offered him the cold soufflé for the second time. 'I always tell Bee, Manderley's the only place left in England where one can get decent cooking. I remember this soufflé of old.'

'I think we change cooks periodically,' said Maxim, 'but the standard of cooking remains the same. Mrs Danvers has all the recipes, she tells them what to do.'

'Amazing woman, that Mrs Danvers,' said Giles, turning to me; 'don't you think so?'

'Oh, yes,' I said. 'Mrs Danvers seems to be a wonderful person.'

'She's no oil painting though, is she?' said Giles, and he roared with laughter. Frank Crawley said nothing, and looking up I saw Beatrice was watching me. She turned away then, and began talking to Maxim.

'Do you play golf at all, Mrs de Winter?' said Mr Crawley.

'No, I'm afraid I don't,' I answered, glad that the subject had been changed again, that Mrs Danvers was forgotten, and even though I was no player, knew nothing of the game, I was prepared to listen to him as long as he pleased; there was something solid and safe and dull about golf, it could not bring us into any difficulties. We had cheese, and coffee, and I wondered whether I was supposed to make a move. I kept looking at Maxim, but he gave no sign, and then Giles embarked upon a story, rather difficult to follow, about digging a car out of a snow-drift – what had started the train of thought I could not tell – and I listened to him politely, nodding my head now and again and smiling, aware of Maxim becoming restive at his end of the table. At last he paused, and I caught Maxim's eye. He frowned very slightly and jerked his head towards the door.

I got up at once, shaking the table clumsily as I moved my chair, and upsetting Giles's glass of port. 'Oh, dear,' I said, hovering, wondering what to do, reaching ineffectively for my napkin, but 'All right, Frith will deal with it,' said Maxim, 'don't add to the confusion. Beatrice, take her out in the garden; she's scarcely seen the place yet.'

He looked tired, rather jaded. I began to wish none of them had come. They had spoilt our day anyway. It was too much of an effort, just as we returned. I felt tired too, tired and depressed.

Maxim had seemed almost irritable when he suggested we should go into the garden. What a fool I had been, upsetting that glass of port.

We went out on to the terrace and walked down on to the smooth green lawns.

'I think it's a pity you came back to Manderley so soon,' said Beatrice, 'it would have been far better to potter about in Italy for three or four months, and then come back in the middle of the summer. Done Maxim a power of good too, besides being easier from your point of view. I can't help feeling it's going to be rather a strain here for you at first.'

'Oh, I don't think so,' I said. 'I know I shall come to love Manderley.'

She did not answer, and we strolled backwards and forwards on the lawns.

'Tell me a bit about yourself,' she said at last; 'what was it you were doing in the south of France? Living with some appalling American woman, Maxim said.'

I explained about Mrs Van Hopper, and what had led to it, and she seemed sympathetic but a little vague, as though she was thinking of something else.

'Yes,' she said, when I paused, 'it all happened very suddenly, as you say. But of course we were all delighted, my dear, and I do hope you will be happy.'

'Thank you, Beatrice,' I said, 'thank you very much.'

I wondered why she said she hoped we would be happy, instead of saying she knew we would be so. She was kind, she was sincere, I liked her very much, but there was a tiny doubt in her voice that made me afraid.

'When Maxim wrote and told me,' she went on, taking my arm, 'and said he had discovered you in the south of France, and you were very young, very pretty, I must admit it gave me a bit of a shock. Of course we all expected a social butterfly, very modern and plastered with paint, the sort of girl you expected to meet in those sort of places. When you came into the morning-room before lunch you could have knocked me down with a feather.'

She laughed, and I laughed with her. But she did not say

whether or not she was disappointed in my appearance or relieved.

'Poor Maxim,' she said: 'he went through a ghastly time, and let's hope you have made him forget about it. Of course he adores Manderley.'

Part of me wanted her to continue her train of thought, to tell me more of the past, naturally and easily like this, and something else, way back in my mind, did not want to know, did not want to hear.

'We are not a bit alike, you know,' she said, 'our characters are poles apart. I show everything on my face: whether I like people or not, whether I am angry or pleased. There's no reserve about me. Maxim is entirely different. Very quiet, very reserved. You never know what's going on in that funny mind of his. I lose my temper on the slightest provocation, flare up, and then it's all over. Maxim loses his temper once or twice in a year, and when he does – my God – he *does* lose it. I don't suppose he ever will with you, I should think you are a placid little thing.'

She smiled, and pinched my arm, and I thought about being placid, how quiet and comfortable it sounded, someone with knitting on her lap, with calm unruffled brow. Someone who was never anxious, never tortured by doubt and indecision, someone who never stood as I did, hopeful, eager, frightened, tearing at bitten nails, uncertain which way to go, what star to follow.

'You won't mind me saying so, will you?' she went on, 'but I think you ought to do something to your hair. Why don't you have it waved? It's so very lanky, isn't it, like that? Must look awful under a hat. Why don't you sweep it back behind your ears?'

I did so obediently, and waited for her approval. She looked at me critically, her head on one side. 'No,' she said. 'No, I think that's worse. It's too severe, and doesn't suit you. No, all you need is a wave, just to pinch it up. I never have cared for that Joan of Arc business or whatever they call it. What does Maxim say? Does he think it suits you?'

'I don't know,' I said, 'he's never mentioned it.'

'Oh well,' she said, 'perhaps he likes it. Don't go by me. Tell me, did you get any clothes in London or Paris?'

'No,' I said, 'we had no time. Maxim was anxious to get home. And I can always send for catalogues.'

'I can tell by the way you dress that you don't care a hoot what you wear,' she said. I glanced at my flannel skirt apologetically.

'I do,' I said. 'I'm very fond of nice things. I've never had much money to spend on clothes up to now.'

'I wonder Maxim did not stay a week or so in London and get you something decent to wear,' she said. 'I must say, I think it's rather selfish of him. So unlike him too. He's generally so particular.'

'Is he?' I said; 'he's never seemed particular to me. I don't think he notices what I wear at all. I don't think he minds.'

'Oh,' she said. 'Oh, well, he must have changed then.'

She looked away from me, and whistled to Jasper, her hands in her pockets, and then stared up at the house above us.

'You're not using the west wing then,' she said.

'No,' I said. 'No, we have the suite in the east wing. It's all been done up.'

'Has it?' she said. 'I didn't know that. I wonder why.'

'It was Maxim's idea,' I said, 'he seems to prefer it.'

She said nothing, she went on looking at the windows, and whistling. 'How do you get on with Mrs Danvers?' she said suddenly.

I bent down, and began patting Jasper's head, and stroking his ears. 'I have not seen very much of her,' I said; 'she scares me a little. I've never seen anyone quite like her before.'

'I don't suppose you have,' said Beatrice.

Jasper looked up at me with great eyes, humble, rather self-conscious. I kissed the top of his silken head, and put my hand over his black nose.

'There's no need to be frightened of her,' said Beatrice; 'and don't let her see it, whatever you do. Of course I've never had anything to do with her, and I don't think I ever want to either. However, she's always been very civil to me.'

I went on patting Jasper's head.

'Did she seem friendly?' said Beatrice.

'No,' I said. 'No, not very.'

Beatrice began whistling again, and she rubbed Jasper's head with her foot. 'I shouldn't have more to do with her than you can help,' she said.

'No,' I said. 'She runs the house very efficiently, there's no need for me to interfere.'

'Oh, I don't suppose she'd mind that,' said Beatrice. That was what Maxim had said, the evening before, and I thought it odd that they should both have the same opinion. I should have imagined that interference was the one thing Mrs Danvers did not want.

'I dare say she will get over it in time,' said Beatrice, 'but it may make things rather unpleasant for you at first. Of course she's insanely jealous. I was afraid she would be.'

'Why?' I asked, looking up at her, 'why should she be jealous? Maxim does not seem to be particularly fond of her.'

'My dear child, it's not Maxim she's thinking of,' said Beatrice; 'I think she respects him and all that, but nothing more very much.

'No, you see,' – she paused, frowning a little, looking at me uncertainly – 'she resents your being here at all, that's the trouble.'

'Why?' I said, 'why should she resent me?'

'I thought you knew,' said Beatrice; 'I thought Maxim would have told you. She simply adored Rebecca.'

'Oh,' I said. 'Oh, I see.'

We both went on patting and stroking Jasper, who, unaccustomed to such attention, rolled over on his back in ecstasy.

'Here are the men,' said Beatrice, 'let's have some chairs out and sit under the chestnut. How fat Giles is getting, he looks quite repulsive beside Maxim. I suppose Frank will go back to the office. What a dull creature he is, never has anything interesting to say. Well, all of you. What have you been discussing? Pulling the world to bits, I suppose.' She laughed, and the others strolled towards us, and we stood about. Giles threw a twig for Jasper to retrieve. We all looked at Jasper. Mr Crawley looked at his watch. 'I must be off,' he said; 'thank you very much for lunch, Mrs de Winter.'

'You must come often,' I said, shaking hands.

I wondered if the others would go too. I was not sure

whether they had just come over for lunch or to spend the day. I hoped they would go. I wanted to be alone with Maxim again, and that it would be like we were in Italy. We all went and sat down under the chestnut tree. Robert brought out chairs and rugs. Giles lay down on his back and tipped his hat over his eyes. After a while he began to snore, his mouth open.

'Shut up, Giles,' said Beatrice. 'I'm not asleep,' he muttered, opening his eyes, and shutting them again. I thought him unattractive. I wondered why Beatrice had married him. She could never have been in love with him. Perhaps that was what she was thinking about me. I caught her eye upon me now and again, puzzled, reflective, as though she was saying to herself 'What on earth does Maxim see in her?' but kind at the same time, not unfriendly. They were talking about their grandmother.

'We must go over and see the old lady,' Maxim was saying, and 'She's getting gaga,' said Beatrice, 'drops food all down her chin, poor darling.'

I listened to them both, leaning against Maxim's arm, rubbing my chin on his sleeve. He stroked my hand absently, not thinking, talking to Beatrice.

'That's what I do to Jasper,' I thought. 'I'm being like Jasper now, leaning against him. He pats me now and again, when he remembers, and I'm pleased, I get closer to him for a moment. He likes me in the way I like Jasper.'

The wind had dropped. The afternoon was drowsy, peaceful. The grass had been new-mown; it smelt sweet and rich, like summer. A bee droned above Giles's head, and he flicked at it with his hat. Jasper sloped in to join us, too warm in the sun, his tongue lolling from his mouth. He flopped beside me, and began licking his side, his large eyes apologetic. The sun shone on the mullioned windows of the house, and I could see the green lawns and the terrace reflected in them. Smoke curled thinly from one of the near chimneys, and I wondered if the library fire had been lit, according to routine.

A thrush flew across the lawn to the magnolia tree outside the dining-room window. I could smell the faint, soft magnolia scent as I sat here, on the lawn. Everything was quiet and still. Very distant now came the washing of the sea in the bay below. The tide must have gone out. The bee droned over us again, pausing to taste the chestnut blossom above our heads. 'This is what I always imagined,' I thought, 'this is how I hoped it would be, living at Manderley.'

I wanted to go on sitting there, not talking, not listening to the others, keeping the moment precious for all time, because we were peaceful, all of us, we were content and drowsy even as the bee who droned above our heads. In a little while it would be different, there would come tomorrow, and the next day, and another year. And we would be changed perhaps, never sitting quite like this again. Some of us would go away, or suffer, or die; the future stretched away in front of us, unknown, unseen, not perhaps what we wanted, not what we planned. This moment was safe though, this could not be touched. Here we sat together, Maxim and I, hand-in-hand, and the past and the future mattered not at all. This was secure, this funny fragment of time he would never remember, never think about again. He would not hold it sacred; he was talking about cutting away some of the under-growth in the drive, and Beatrice agreed, interrupting with some suggestion of her own, and throwing a piece of grass at Giles at the same time. For them it was just after lunch, quarter past three on a haphazard afternoon, like any hour, like any day. They did not want to hold it close, imprisoned and secure, as I did. They were not afraid.

'Well, I suppose we ought to be off,' said Beatrice, brushing the grass from her skirt; 'I don't want to be late, we've got the Cartrights dining.'

'How is old Vera?' asked Maxim.

'Oh, same as ever, always talking about her health. He's getting very old. They're sure to ask all about you both.'

'Give them my love,' said Maxim.

We got up. Giles shook the dust off his hat. Maxim yawned and stretched. The sun went in. I looked up at the sky. It had changed already, a mackerel sky. Little clouds scurrying in formation, line upon line.

'Wind's backing,' said Maxim.

'I hope we don't run into rain,' said Giles.

'I'm afraid we've had the best of the day,' said Beatrice.

We wandered slowly towards the drive and the waiting car. 'You haven't seen what's been done to the east wing,' said Maxim.

'Come upstairs,' I suggested; 'it won't take a minute.'

We went into the hall, and up the big staircase, the men following behind.

It seemed strange that Beatrice had lived here for so many years. She had run down these same stairs as a little girl, with her nurse. She had been born here, bred here; she knew it all, she belonged here more than I should ever do. She must have many memories locked inside her heart. I wondered if she ever thought about the days that were gone, ever remembered the lanky pig-tailed child that she had been once, so different from the woman she had become, forty-five now, vigorous and settled in her ways, another person . . .

We came to the rooms, and Giles, stooping under the low doorway, said, 'How very jolly; this is a great improvement, isn't it, Bee?' and 'I say, old boy, you have spread yourself,' said Beatrice: 'new curtains, new beds, new everything. You remember, Giles, we had this room that time you were laid up with your leg? It was very dingy then. Of course Mother never had much idea of comfort. And then, you never put people here, did you, Maxim? Except when there was an overflow. The bachelors were always dumped here. Well, it's charming, I must say. Looks over the rose-garden too, which was always an advantage. May I powder my nose?'

The men went downstairs, and Beatrice peered in the mirror. 'Did old Danvers do all this for you?' she said.

'Yes,' I said. 'I think she's done it very well.'

'So she should, with her training,' said Beatrice. 'I wonder what on earth it cost. A pretty packet, I bet. Did you ask?'

'No, I'm afraid I did not,' I said.

'I don't suppose it worried Mrs Danvers,' said Beatrice. 'Do you mind if I use your comb? These are nice brushes. Wedding present?'

'Maxim gave them to me.'

'H'm. I like them. We must give you something of course. What do you want?'

'Oh, I don't really know. You mustn't bother,' I said.

'My dear, don't be absurd. I'm not one to grudge you a present, even though we weren't asked to your wedding!'

'I hope you did not mind about that. Maxim wanted it to be abroad.'

'Of course not. Very sensible of you both. After all, it wasn't as though ...' she stopped in the middle of her sentence, and dropped her bag. 'Damn, have I broken the catch? No, all is well. What was I saying? I can't remember. Oh, yes, wedding presents. We must think of something. You probably don't care for jewellery.'

I did not answer. 'It's so different from the ordinary young couple,' she said. 'The daughter of a friend of mine got married the other day, and of course they were started off in the usual way, with linen, and coffee sets, and dining-room chairs, and all that. I gave rather a nice standard lamp. Cost me a fiver at Harrods. If you do go up to London to buy clothes mind you go to my woman, Madame Carroux. She has damn good taste, and she doesn't rook you.'

She got up from the dressing-table, and pulled at her skirt.

'Do you suppose you will have a lot of people down?' she said.

'I don't know. Maxim hasn't said.'

'Funny old boy, one never quite knows with him. At one time one could not get a bed in the house, the place would be chock-a-block. I can't somehow see you ...' she stopped abruptly, and patted my arm. 'Oh, well,' she said, 'we'll see. It's a pity you don't ride or shoot, you miss such a lot. You don't sail by any chance, do you?'

'No,' I said.

'Thank God for that,' she said.

She went to the door, and I followed her down the corridor.

'Come and see us if you feel like it,' she said. 'I always expect people to ask themselves. Life is too short to send out invitations.'

'Thank you very much,' I said.

We came to the head of the stairs looking down upon the hall. The men were standing on the steps outside. 'Come on, Bee,' shouted Giles. 'I felt a spot of rain, so we've put on the cover. Maxim says the glass is falling.'

Beatrice took my hand, and bending down gave me a swift peck on my cheek. 'Good-bye,' she said; 'forgive me if I've asked you a lot of rude questions, my dear, and said all sorts of things I shouldn't. Tact never was my strong point, as Maxim will tell you. And, as I told you before, you're not a bit what I expected.' She looked at me direct, her lips pursed in a whistle, and then took a cigarette from her bag, and flashed her lighter.

'You see,' she said, snapping the top, and walking down the stairs, 'you are so very different from Rebecca.'

And we came out on to the steps and found the sun had gone behind a bank of cloud, a little thin rain was falling, and Robert was hurrying across the lawn to bring in the chairs.

10

WE WATCHED THE car disappear round the sweep of the drive, and then Maxim took my arm and said, 'Thank God that's that. Get a coat quickly, and come out. Damn the rain, I want a walk. I can't stand this sitting about.' He looked white and strained, and I wondered why the entertaining of Beatrice and Giles, his own sister and brother-in-law, should have tired him so.

'Wait while I run upstairs for my coat,' I said.

'There's a heap of mackintoshes in the flower room, get one of them,' he said impatiently, 'women are always half an hour when they go to their bedrooms. Robert, fetch a coat from the flower room, will you, for Mrs de Winter? There must be half a dozen raincoats hanging there left by people at one time or another.' He was already standing in the drive, and calling to Jasper, 'Come on, you lazy little beggar, and take some of that fat off.' Jasper ran round in circles, barking hysterically at the prospect of his walk. 'Shut up, you idiot,' said Maxim. 'What on earth is Robert doing?'

Robert came running out of the hall carrying a raincoat, and I struggled into it hurriedly, fumbling with the collar. It was too big, of course, and too long, but there was no time to change it, and we set off together across the lawn to the woods, Jasper running in front.

'I find a little of my family goes a very long way,' said Maxim. 'Beatrice is one of the best people in the world, but she invariably puts her foot in it.'

I was not sure where Beatrice had blundered, and thought it better not to ask. Perhaps he still resented the chat about his health before lunch.

'What did you think of her?' he went on.

'I liked her very much,' I said; 'she was very nice to me.'

'What did she talk to you about out here, after lunch?'

'Oh, I don't know. I think I did most of the talking. I was telling her about Mrs Van Hopper, and how you and I met, and all that. She said I was quite different from what she expected.'

'What the devil did she expect?'

'Someone much smarter, more sophisticated, I imagine. A social butterfly, she said.'

Maxim did not answer for a moment; he bent down, and threw a stick for Jasper. 'Beatrice can sometimes be infernally unintelligent,' he said.

We climbed the grass bank above the lawns, and plunged into the woods. The trees grew very close together, and it was dark. We trod upon broken twigs, and last year's leaves, and here and there the fresh green stubble of the young bracken, and the shoots of the bluebells soon to blossom. Jasper was silent now, his nose to the ground. I took Maxim's arm.

'Do you like my hair?' I said.

He stared down at me in astonishment. 'Your hair?' he said. 'Why on earth do you ask? Of course I like it. What's the matter with it?'

'Oh, nothing,' I said, 'I just wondered.'

'How funny you are,' he said.

We came to a clearing in the woods, and there were two paths, going in opposite directions. Jasper took the right-hand path without hesitation.

'Not that way,' called Maxim; 'come on, old chap.'

The dog looked back at us and stood there, wagging his tail, but did not return. 'Why does he want to go that way?' I asked.

'I suppose he's used to it,' said Maxim briefly; 'it leads to a small cove, where we used to keep a boat. Come on, Jasper, old man.'

We turned into the left-hand path, not saying anything, and presently I looked over my shoulder and saw that Jasper was following us.

'This brings us to the valley I told you about,' said Maxim, 'and you shall smell the azaleas. Never mind the rain, it will bring out the scent.'

He seemed all right again now, happy and cheerful, the

Maxim I knew and loved, and he began talking about Frank Crawley and what a good fellow he was, so thorough and reliable, and devoted to Manderley.

'This is better,' I thought; 'this is like it was in Italy', and I smiled up at him, squeezing his arm, relieved that the odd strained look on his face had passed away, and while I said 'Yes,' and 'Really?' and 'Fancy, darling,' my thoughts wandered back to Beatrice, wondering why her presence should have disturbed him, what she had done; and I thought too of all she had said about his temper, how he lost it, she told me, about once or twice a year.

She must know him, of course; she was his sister. But it was not what I had thought; it was not my idea of Maxim. I could see him moody, difficult, irritable perhaps, but not angry as she had inferred, not passionate. Perhaps she had exaggerated; people very often were wrong about their relatives.

'There,' said Maxim suddenly, 'take a look at that.'

We stood on a slope of a wooded hill, and the path wound away before us to a valley, by the side of a running stream. There were no dark trees here, no tangled undergrowth, but on either side of the narrow path stood azaleas and rhododendrons, not blood-coloured like the giants in the drive, but salmon, white, and gold, things of beauty and of grace, drooping their lovely, delicate heads in the soft summer rain.

The air was full of their scent, sweet and heady, and it seemed to me as though their very essence had mingled with the running waters of the stream, and become one with the falling rain and the dank rich moss beneath our feet. There was no sound here but the tumbling of the little stream, and the quiet rain. When Maxim spoke, his voice was hushed too, gentle and low, as if he had no wish to break upon the silence.

'We call it the Happy Valley,' he said.

We stood quite still, not speaking, looking down upon the clear white faces of the flowers closest to us, and Maxim stooped, and picked up a fallen petal and gave it to me. It was crushed and bruised, and turning brown at the curled edge, but as I rubbed it across my hand the scent rose to me, sweet and strong, vivid as the living tree from which it came.

Then the birds began. First a blackbird, his note clear and cool above the running stream, and after a moment he had answer from his fellow hidden in the woods behind us, and soon the still air about us was made turbulent with song, pursuing us as we wandered down into the valley, and the fragrance of the white petals followed us too. It was disturbing, like an enchanted place. I had not thought it could be as beautiful as this.

The sky, now overcast and sullen, so changed from the early afternoon, and the steady insistent rain could not disturb the soft quietude of the valley; the rain and the rivulet mingled with one another, and the liquid note of the blackbird fell upon the damp air in harmony with them both. I brushed the dripping heads of azaleas as I passed, so close they grew together, bordering the path. Little drops of water fell on to my hands from the soaked petals. There were petals at my feet too, brown and sodden, bearing their scent upon them still, and a richer, older scent as well, the smell of deep moss and bitter earth, the stems of bracken, and the twisted buried roots of trees. I held Maxim's hand and I had not spoken. The spell of the Happy Valley was upon me. This at last was the core of Manderley, the Manderley I would know and learn to love. The first drive was forgotten, the black, herded woods, the glaring rhododendrons, luscious and over-proud. And the vast house too, the silence of that echoing hall, the uneasy stillness of the west wing, wrapped in dust-sheets. There I was an interloper, wandering in rooms that did not know me, sitting at a desk and in a chair that were not mine. Here it was different. The Happy Valley knew no trespassers. We came to the end of the path, and the flowers formed an archway above our heads. We bent down, passing underneath, and when I stood straight again, brushing the raindrops from my hair, I saw that the valley was behind us, and the azaleas, and the trees, and, as Maxim had described to me that afternoon many weeks ago in Monte Carlo, we were standing in a little narrow cove, the shingle hard and white under our feet, and the sea was breaking on the shore beyond us.

Maxim smiled down at me, watching the bewilderment on my face.

'It's a shock, isn't it?' he said; 'no one ever expects it. The contrast is too sudden; it almost hurts.' He picked up a stone and flung it across the beach for Jasper. 'Fetch it, good man,' and Jasper streaked away in search of the stone, his long black ears flapping in the wind.

The enchantment was no more, the spell was broken. We were mortal again, two people playing on a beach. We threw more stones, went to the water's edge, flung ducks and drakes, and fished for driftwood. The tide had turned, and came lapping in the bay. The small rocks were covered, the seaweed washed on the stones. We rescued a big floating plank and carried it up the beach above high-water mark. Maxim turned to me, laughing, wiping the hair out of his eyes, and I unrolled the sleeves of my mackintosh caught by the sea spray. And then we looked round, and saw that Jasper had disappeared. We called and whistled, and he did not come. I looked anxiously towards the mouth of the cove where the waves were breaking upon the rocks.

'No,' said Maxim, 'we should have seen him, he can't have fallen. Jasper, you idiot, where are you? Jasper, Jasper?'

'Perhaps he's gone back to the Happy Valley?' I said.

'He was by that rock a minute ago, sniffing a dead sea-gull,' said Maxim.

We walked up the beach towards the valley once again. 'Jasper, Jasper?' called Maxim.

In the distance, beyond the rocks to the right of the beach, I heard a short, sharp bark. 'Hear that?' I said. 'He's climbed over this way.' I began to scramble up the slippery rocks in the direction of the bark.

'Come back,' said Maxim sharply; 'we don't want to go that way. The fool of a dog must look after himself.'

I hesitated, looked down from my rock. 'Perhaps he's fallen,' I said, 'poor little chap. Let me fetch him.' Jasper barked again, further away this time. 'Oh, listen,' I said, 'I must get him. It's quite safe, isn't it? The tide won't have cut him off?'

'He's all right,' said Maxim irritably; 'why not leave him? He knows his own way back.'

I pretended not to hear, and began scrambling over the rocks towards Jasper. Great jagged boulders screened the view, and I slipped and stumbled on the wet rocks, making my way as best

I could in Jasper's direction. It was heartless of Maxim to leave Jasper, I thought, and I could not understand it. Besides, the tide was coming in. I came up beside the big boulder that had hidden the view, and looked beyond it. And I saw, to my surprise, that I was looking down into another cove, similar to the one I had left, but wider and more rounded. A small stone breakwater had been thrown out across the cove for shelter, and behind it the bay formed a tiny natural harbour. There was a buoy anchored there, but no boat. The beach in the cove was white shingle, like the one behind me, but steeper, shelving suddenly to the sea. The woods came right down to the tangle of seaweed marking high water, encroaching almost to the rocks themselves, and at the fringe of the woods was a long low building, half cottage, half boat-house, built of the same stone as the breakwater.

There was a man on the beach, a fisherman perhaps, in long boots and a sou'wester, and Jasper was barking at him, running round him in circles, darting at his boots. The man took no notice; he was bending down, and scraping in the shingle. 'Jasper,' I shouted, 'Jasper, come here.'

The dog looked up, wagging his tail, but he did not obey me. He went on baiting the solitary figure on the beach.

I looked over my shoulder. There was still no sign of Maxim. I climbed down over the rocks to the beach below. My feet made a crunching noise across the shingle, and the man looked up at the sound. I saw then that he had the small slit eyes of an idiot, and the red, wet mouth. He smiled at me, showing toothless gums.

'G'day,' he said. 'Dirty, ain't it?'

'Good afternoon,' I said. 'No. I'm afraid it's not very nice weather.'

He watched me with interest, smiling all the while. 'Diggin' for shell,' he said. 'No shell here. Been diggin' since forenoon.'

'Oh,' I said, 'I'm sorry you can't find any.'

'That's right,' he said, 'no shell here.'

'Come on, Jasper,' I said, 'it's getting late. Come on, old boy.'

But Jasper was in an infuriating mood. Perhaps the wind and the sea had gone to his head, for he backed away from me, barking stupidly, and began racing round the beach after nothing at all. I saw he would never follow me, and I had no lead. I turned to the man, who had bent down again to his futile digging.

'Have you got any string?' I said.

'Eh?' he said.

'Have you got any string?' I repeated.

'No shell here,' he said, shaking his head. 'Been diggin' since forenoon.' He nodded his head at me, and wiped his pale blue watery eyes.

'I want something to tie the dog,' I said. 'He won't follow me.'

'Eh?' he said. And he smiled his poor idiot's smile.

'All right,' I said; 'it doesn't matter.'

He looked at me uncertainly, and then leant forward, and poked me in the chest.

'I know that dog,' he said; 'he comes fro' the house.'

'Yes,' I said. 'I want him to come back with me now.'

'He's not yourn,' he said.

'He's Mr de Winter's dog,' I said gently. 'I want to take him back to the house.'

'Eh?' he said.

I called Jasper once more, but he was chasing a feather blown by the wind. I wondered if there was any string in the boat-house, and I walked up the beach towards it. There must have been a garden once, but now the grass was long and overgrown, crowded with nettles. The windows were boarded up. No doubt the door was locked, and I lifted the latch without much hope. To my surprise it opened after the first stiffness, and I went inside, bending my head because of the low door. I expected to find the usual boat store, dirty and dusty with disuse, ropes and blocks and oars upon the floor. The dust was there, and the dirt too in places, but there were no ropes or blocks. The room was furnished, and ran the whole length of the cottage. There was a desk in the corner, a table, and chairs, and a bed-sofa pushed against the wall. There was a dresser too, with cups and plates. Bookshelves, the books inside them, and models of ships standing on the top of the shelves. For a moment I thought it must be inhabited – perhaps the poor man on the beach lived here – but I looked around me again and saw no sign of recent occupation. That rusted grate knew no fire, this dusty floor no footsteps, and the china there on the dresser was blue-spotted with the damp. There was a queer

musty smell about the place. Cobwebs spun threads upon the
ships' models, making their own ghostly rigging. No one lived
here. No one came here. The door had creaked on its hinges
when I opened it. The rain pattered on the roof with a hollow
sound, and tapped upon the boarded windows. The fabric of the
sofa-bed had been nibbled by mice or rats. I could see the jagged
holes, and the frayed edges. It was damp in the cottage, damp and
chill. Dark, and oppressive. I did not like it. I had no wish to stay
there. I hated the hollow sound of the rain pattering on the roof.
It seemed to echo in the room itself, and I heard the water dripping too into the rusted grate.

I looked about me for some string. There was nothing that
would serve my purpose, nothing at all. There was another door
at the end of the room, and I went to it, and opened it, a little
fearful now, a little afraid, for I had the odd, uneasy feeling that
I might come upon something unawares, that I had no wish to
see. Something that might harm me, that might be horrible.

It was nonsense of course, and I opened the door. It was only
a boat store after all. Here were the ropes and blocks I had
expected, two or three sails, fenders, a small punt, pots of paints,
all the litter and junk that goes with the using of boats. A ball of
twine lay on a shelf, a rusted clasp-knife beside it. This would be
all I needed for Jasper. I opened the knife, and cut a length of
twine, and came back into the room again. The rain still fell upon
the roof, and into the grate. I came out of the cottage hurriedly,
not looking behind me, trying not to see the torn sofa and the
mildewed china, the spun cobwebs on the model ships, and so
through the creaking gate and on to the white beach.

The man was not digging any more; he was watching me,
Jasper at his side.

'Come along, Jasper,' I said; 'come on, good dog.' I bent
down and this time he allowed me to touch him and pull hold of
his collar. 'I found some string in the cottage,' I said to the man.

He did not answer, and I tied the string loosely round Jasper's
collar.

'Good afternoon,' I said, tugging at Jasper.

The man nodded, staring at me with his narrow idiot's eyes.
'I saw'ee go in yonder,' he said.

'Yes,' I said; 'it's all right, Mr de Winter won't mind.'

'She don't go in there now,' he said.

'No,' I said, 'not now.'

'She's gone in the sea, ain't she?' he said; 'she won't come back no more?'

'No,' I said, 'she'll not come back.'

'I never said nothing, did I?' he said.

'No, of course not; don't worry,' I said.

He bent down again to his digging, muttering to himself. I went across the shingle and I saw Maxim waiting for me by the rocks, his hands in his pockets.

'I'm sorry,' I said. 'Jasper would not come. I had to get some string.'

He turned abruptly on his heel, and made towards the woods.

'Aren't we going back over the rocks?' I said.

'What's the point? We're here now,' he said briefly.

We went up past the cottage and struck into a path through the woods. 'I'm sorry I was such a time; it was Jasper's fault,' I said, 'he kept barking at the man. Who was he?'

'Only Ben,' said Maxim; 'he's quite harmless, poor devil. His old father used to be one of the keepers; they live near the home farm. Where did you get that piece of twine?'

'I found it in the cottage on the beach,' I said.

'Was the door open?' he asked.

'Yes, I pushed it open. I found the string in the other room, where the sails were, and a small boat.'

'Oh,' he said shortly. 'Oh, I see,' and then he added, after a moment or two: 'That cottage is supposed to be locked, the door has no business to be open.'

I said nothing; it was not my affair.

'Did Ben tell you the door was open?'

'No,' I said, 'he did not seem to understand anything I asked him.'

'He makes out he's worse than he is,' said Maxim. 'He can talk quite intelligibly if he wants to. He's probably been in and out of the cottage dozens of times, and did not want you to know.'

'I don't think so,' I answered; 'the place looked deserted, quite untouched. There was dust everywhere, and no footmarks. It was terribly damp. I'm afraid those books will be quite spoilt, and the chairs, and that sofa. There are rats there, too; they have eaten away some of the covers.'

Maxim did not reply. He walked at a tremendous pace, and the climb up from the beach was steep. It was very different from the Happy Valley. The trees were dark here and close together, there were no azaleas brushing the path. The rain dripped heavily from the thick branches. It splashed on my collar and trickled down my neck. I shivered; it was unpleasant, like a cold finger. My legs ached, after the unaccustomed scramble over the rocks. And Jasper lagged behind, weary from his wild scamper, his tongue hanging from his mouth.

'Come on, Jasper, for God's sake,' said Maxim. 'Make him walk up, pull at the twine or something, can't you? Beatrice was right. The dog is much too fat.'

'It's your fault,' I said, 'you walk so fast. We can't keep up with you.'

'If you had listened to me instead of rushing wildly over those rocks we would have been home by now,' said Maxim. 'Jasper knew his way back perfectly. I can't think what you wanted to go after him for.'

'I thought he might have fallen, and I was afraid of the tide,' I said.

'Is it likely I should have left the dog had there been any question of the tide?' said Maxim. 'I told you not to go on those rocks, and now you are grumbling because you are tired.'

'I'm not grumbling,' I said. 'Anyone, even if they had legs of iron, would be tired walking at this pace. I thought you would come with me when I went after Jasper anyway, instead of staying behind.'

'Why should I exhaust myself careering after the damn dog?' he said.

'It was no more exhausting careering after Jasper on the rocks than it was careering after the driftwood on the beach,' I answered. 'You just say that because you have not any other excuse.'

'My good child, what am I supposed to excuse myself about?'

'Oh, I don't know,' I said wearily; 'let's stop this.'

'Not at all, you began it. What do you mean by saying I was trying to find an excuse? Excuse for what?'

'Excuse for not having come with me over the rocks, I suppose,' I said.

'Well, and why do you think I did not want to cross to the other beach?'

'Oh, Maxim, how should I know? I'm not a thought-reader. I know you did not want to, that's all. I could see it in your face.'

'See what in my face?'

'I've already told you. I could see you did not want to go. Oh, do let's have an end to it. I'm sick to death of the subject.'

'All women say that when they've lost an argument. All right, I did not want to go to the other beach. Will that please you? I never go near the bloody place, or that God-damned cottage. And if you had my memories you would not want to go there either, or talk about it, or even think about it. There. You can digest that if you like, and I hope it satisfies you.'

His face was white, and his eyes strained and wretched with that dark lost look they had had when I first met him. I put out my hand to him, I took hold of his, holding it tight.

'Please, Maxim, please,' I said.

'What's the matter?' he said roughly.

'I don't want you to look like that,' I said. 'It hurts too much. Please, Maxim. Let's forget all we said. A futile silly argument. I'm sorry, darling. I'm sorry. Please let everything be all right.'

'We ought to have stayed in Italy,' he said. 'We ought never to have come back to Manderley. Oh, God, what a fool I was to come back.'

He brushed through the trees impatiently, striding even faster than before, and I had to run to keep pace with him, catching at my breath, tears very near the surface, dragging poor Jasper after me on the end of his string.

At last we came to the top of the path, and I saw its fellow branching left to the Happy Valley. We had climbed the path then that Jasper had wished to take at the beginning of the afternoon. I knew now why Jasper had turned to it. It led to the beach he knew best, and the cottage. It was his old routine.

We came out on to the lawns, and went across them to the house without a word. Maxim's face was hard, with no expression. He went straight into the hall and on to the library without looking at me. Frith was in the hall.

'We want tea at once,' said Maxim, and he shut the library door.

I fought to keep back my tears. Frith must not see them. He would think we had been quarrelling, and he would go to the servants' hall and say to them all, 'Mrs de Winter was crying in the hall just now. It looks as though things are not going very well.' I turned away, so that Frith should not see my face. He came towards me though, he began to help me off with my mackintosh.

'I'll put your raincoat away for you in the flower room, Madam,' he said.

'Thank you, Frith,' I replied, my face still away from him.

'Not a very pleasant afternoon for a walk, I fear, Madam.'

'No,' I said. 'No, it was not very nice.'

'Your handkerchief, Madam?' he said, picking up something that had fallen on the floor. 'Thank you,' I said, putting it in my pocket.

I was wondering whether to go upstairs or whether to follow Maxim to the library. Frith took the coat to the flower room. I stood there, hesitating, biting my nails. Frith came back again. He looked surprised to see me still there.

'There is a good fire in the library now, Madam.'

'Thank you, Frith,' I said.

I walked slowly across the hall to the library. I opened the door and went in. Maxim was sitting in his chair, Jasper at his feet, the old dog in her basket. Maxim was not reading the paper, though it lay on the arm of the chair beside him. I went and knelt down by his side and put my face close to his.

'Don't be angry with me any more,' I whispered.

He took my face in his hands, and looked down at me with his tired, strained eyes. 'I'm not angry with you,' he said.

'Yes,' I said. 'I've made you unhappy. It's the same as making you angry. You're all wounded and hurt and torn inside. I can't bear to see you like this. I love you so much.'

'Do you?' he said. 'Do you?' He held me very tight, and his eyes questioned me, dark and uncertain, the eyes of a child in pain, a child in fear.

'What is it, darling?' I said. 'Why do you look like that?'

I heard the door open before he could answer, and I sank back on my heels, pretending to reach for a log to throw on the fire, while Frith came into the room followed by Robert, and the ritual of our tea began.

The performance of the day before was repeated, the placing of the table, the laying of the snow-white cloth, the putting down of cakes and crumpets, the silver kettle of hot water placed on its little flame, while Jasper, wagging his tail, his ears stretched back in anticipation, watched my face. Five minutes must have passed before we were alone again, and when I looked at Maxim I saw the colour had come back into his face, the tired, lost look was gone, and he was reaching for a sandwich.

'Having all that crowd to lunch was the trouble,' he said. 'Poor old Beatrice always does rub me up the wrong way. We used to scrap like dogs as children. I'm so fond of her too, bless her. Such a relief though that they don't live too near. Which reminds me, we'll have to go over and see Granny some time. Pour out my tea, sweetheart, and forgive me for being a bear to you.'

It was over then. The episode was finished. We must not speak of it again. He smiled at me over his cup of tea, and then reached for the newspaper on the arm of his chair. The smile was my reward. Like a pat on the head to Jasper. Good dog then, lie down, don't worry me any more. I was Jasper again. I was back where I had been before. I took a piece of crumpet and divided it between the two dogs. I did not want it myself, I was not hungry. I felt very weary now, very tired in a dull, spent way. I looked at Maxim but he was reading his paper, he had folded it over to another page. My fingers were messy with the butter from the crumpet, and I felt in my pocket for a handkerchief. I drew it out, a tiny scrap of a thing, lace-edged. I stared at it, frowning, for it was not mine. I remembered then that Frith had picked it up from the stone floor of the hall. It must have fallen out of the pocket in the mackintosh. I turned it over in my hand. It was grubby; little bits of fluff from the pocket clung to it. It must have been in the mackintosh pocket for a long time. There was a monogram in the corner. A tall sloping R, with the letters de W interlaced. The R dwarfed the other letters, the tail of it ran down into the cambric, away from the laced edge. It was only a small handkerchief, quite a scrap of a thing. It had been rolled in a ball and put away in the pocket and forgotten.

I must have been the first person to put on that mackintosh since the handkerchief was used. She who had worn the coat then was tall, slim, broader than me about the shoulders, for I had found it big and overlong, and the sleeves had come below my wrist. Some of the buttons were missing. She had not bothered then to do it up. She had thrown it over her shoulders like a cape, or worn it loose, hanging open, her hands deep in the pockets.

There was a pink mark upon the handkerchief. The mark of lip-stick. She had rubbed her lips with the handkerchief, and then rolled it in a ball, and left it in the pocket. I wiped my fingers with the handkerchief, and as I did so I noticed that a dull scent clung about it still. A scent I recognized, a scent I knew. I shut my eyes and tried to remember. It was something elusive, something faint and fragrant that I could not name. I had breathed it before, touched it surely, that very afternoon.

And then I knew that the vanished scent upon the handkerchief was the same as the crushed white petals of the azaleas in the Happy Valley.

11

THE WEATHER WAS wet and cold for quite a week, as it often can be in the west country in the early summer, and we did not go down to the beach again. I could see the sea from the terrace, and the lawns. It looked grey and uninviting, great rollers sweeping in to the bay past the beacon on the headland. I pictured them surging into the little cove and breaking with a roar upon the rocks, then running swift and strong to the shelving beach. If I stood on the terrace and listened I could hear the murmur of the sea below me, low and sullen. A dull, persistent sound that never ceased. And the gulls flew inland too, driven by the weather. They hovered above the house in circles, wheeling and crying, flapping their spread wings. I began to understand why some people could not bear the clamour of the sea. It has a mournful harping note sometimes, and the very persistence of it, that eternal roll and thunder and hiss, plays a jagged tune upon the nerves. I was glad our rooms were in the east wing and I could lean out of my window and look down upon the rose-garden. For sometimes I could not sleep, and getting softly out of bed in the quiet night I would wander to the window, and lean there, my arms upon the sill, and the air would be very peaceful, very still.

I could not hear the restless sea, and because I could not hear it my thoughts would be peaceful too. They would not carry me down that steep path through the woods to the grey cove and the deserted cottage. I did not want to think about the cottage. I remembered it too often in the day. The memory of it nagged at me whenever I saw the sea from the terrace. For I would see once more the blue spots on the china, the spun webs on the little masts of those model ships, and the rat holes on the sofa-bed. I would remember the pattering of the rain on the roof. And I thought of Ben, too, with his narrow watery blue eyes, his sly idiot's smile. These things disturbed me, I was not happy about them. I wanted to forget them but at the same time I wanted to know why they disturbed me, why they made me uneasy and unhappy. Somewhere, at the back of my mind, there was a frightened furtive seed of curiosity that grew slowly and stealthily, for all my denial of it, and I knew all the doubt and anxiety of the child who has been told, 'these things are not discussed, they are forbidden'.

I could not forget the white, lost look in Maxim's eyes when we came up the path through the woods, and I could not forget his words. 'Oh, God, what a fool I was to come back.' It was all my fault, because I had gone down into the bay. I had opened up a road into the past again. And although Maxim had recovered, and was himself again, and we lived our lives together, sleeping, eating, walking, writing letters, driving to the village, working hour by hour through our day, I knew there was a barrier between us because of it.

He walked alone, on the other side, and I must not come to him. And I became nervous and fearful that some heedless word, some turn in a careless conversation should bring that expression back to his eyes again. I began to dread any mention of the sea, for the sea might lead to boats, to accidents, to drowning . . . Even Frank Crawley, who came to lunch one day, put me in a little fever of fear when he said something about the sailing races in Kerrith harbour, three miles away. I looked steadily at my plate, a stab of sickness in my heart at once, but Maxim went on talking quite naturally, he did not seem to mind, while I sat in a sweat of uncertainty wondering what would happen and where the conversation would lead us.

It was during cheese, Frith had left the room, and I remember getting up and going to the sideboard, and taking some more cheese, not wanting it, so as not to be at the table with them, listening; humming a little tune to myself so I could not hear. I was wrong of course, morbid, stupid; this was the hypersensitive behaviour of a neurotic, not the normal happy self I knew myself to be. But I could not help it. I did not know what to do. My shyness and gaucherie became worse, too, making me stolid and dumb when people came to the house. For we were called upon,

I remember, during those first weeks, by people who lived near us in the county, and the receiving of them, and the shaking hands, and the spinning out of the formal half hour became a worse ordeal than I first anticipated, because of this new fear of mine that they would talk about something that must not be discussed. The agony of those wheels on the drive, of that pealing bell, of my own first wild rush for flight to my own room. The scrambled dab of powder on my nose, the hasty comb through my hair, and then the inevitable knock on the door and the entrance of the cards on a silver salver.

'All right. I'll be down immediately.' The clap of my heels on the stairs and across the hall, the opening of the library door or, worse still, that long, cold, lifeless drawing-room, and the strange woman waiting there, or two of them perhaps, or a husband and a wife.

'How do you do? I'm sorry; Maxim is in the garden somewhere, Frith has gone to find him.'

'We felt we must come and pay our respects to the bride.'

A little laughter, a little flurry of chat, a pause, a glance round the room.

'Manderley is looking as charming as ever. Don't you love it?'

'Oh, yes, rather . . .' And in my shyness and anxiety to please, those schoolgirls' phrases would escape from me again, those words I never used except in moments like these, 'Oh, ripping'; and 'Oh, topping'; and 'absolutely'; and 'priceless'; even, I think, to one dowager who had carried a lorgnette 'cheerio'. My relief at Maxim's arrival would be tempered by the fear they might say something indiscreet, and I became dumb at once, a set smile on my lips, my hands in my lap. They would turn to Maxim then, talking of people and places I had not met or did not know, and now and again I would find their eyes upon me, doubtful, rather bewildered.

I could picture them saying to one another as they drove away, 'My dear, what a dull girl. She scarcely opened her mouth,' and then the sentence I had first heard upon Beatrice's lips, haunting me ever since, a sentence I read in every eye, on every tongue – 'She's so different from Rebecca.'

Sometimes I would glean little snatches of information to add

REBECCA   131

to my secret store. A word dropped here at random, a question, a passing phrase. And, if Maxim was not with me, the hearing of them would be a furtive, rather painful pleasure, guilty knowledge learnt in the dark.

I would return a call perhaps, for Maxim was punctilious in these matters and would not spare me, and if he did not come with me I must brave the formality alone, and there would be a pause in the conversation while I searched for something to say. 'Will you be entertaining much at Manderley, Mrs de Winter?' they would say, and my answer would come, 'I don't know, Maxim has not said much about it up to the present.' 'No, of course not, it's early yet. I believe the house was generally full of people in the old days.' Another pause. 'People from London, you know. There used to be tremendous parties.' 'Yes,' I would say. 'Yes, so I have heard.' A further pause, and then the lowered voice that is always used about the dead or in a place of worship, 'She was so tremendously popular, you know. Such a personality.' 'Yes,' I would say. 'Yes, of course.' And after a moment or so I would glance at my watch under cover of my glove, and say, 'I'm afraid I ought to be going; it must be after four.'

'Won't you stay for tea? We always have it at quarter past.'

'No – No, really, thanks most awfully. I promised Maxim . . .' my sentence would go trailing off into nothing, but the meaning would be understood. We would both rise to our feet, both of us knowing I was not deceived about her offer to tea nor she in my mention of a promise to Maxim. I had sometimes wondered what would happen if convention were denied, if, having got into the car and waved a hand to my hostess on the doorstep, I suddenly opened it again, and said, 'I don't think I'll go back after all. Let's go to your drawing-room again and sit down. I'll stay to dinner if you like, or stop the night.'

I used to wonder if convention and good county manners would brave the surprise, and whether a smile of welcome would be summoned to the frozen face, 'But of course! How very delightful of you to suggest it.' I used to wish I had the courage to try. But instead the door would slam, the car would go bowling away down the smooth gravel drive, and my late hostess would wander back to her room with a sigh of relief and become herself again. It was the wife of the bishop in the neighbouring cathedral town who said to me, 'Will your husband revive the Manderley fancy dress ball, do you suppose? Such a lovely sight always; I shall never forget it.'

I had to smile as though I knew all about it and say, 'We have not decided. There have been so many things to do and to discuss.'

'Yes, I suppose so. But I do hope it won't be dropped. You must use your influence with him. There was not one last year of course. But I remember two years ago, the bishop and I went, and it was quite enchanting. Manderley so lends itself to anything like that. The hall looked wonderful. They danced there, and had the music in the gallery; it was all so in keeping. A tremendous thing to organize, but everybody appreciated it so.'

'Yes,' I said. 'Yes, I must ask Maxim about it.'

I thought of the docketed pigeon-hole in the desk in the morning-room, I pictured the stack upon stack of invitation cards, the long list of names, the addresses, and I could see a woman sitting there at the desk and putting a V beside the names she wanted, and reaching for the invitation cards, dipping her pen in the ink, writing upon them swift and sure in that long, slanting hand.

'There was a garden party, too, we went to one summer,' said the bishop's wife. 'Everything always so beautifully done. The flowers at their best. A glorious day, I remember. Tea was served at little tables in the rose-garden; such an attractive original idea. Of course, she was so clever . . .'

She stopped, turning a little pink, fearing a loss of tact; but I agreed with her at once to save embarrassment, and I heard myself saying boldly, brazenly, 'Rebecca must have been a wonderful person.'

I could not believe that I had said the name at last. I waited, wondering what would happen. I had said the name. I had said the word Rebecca aloud. It was a tremendous relief. It was as though I had taken a purge and rid myself of an intolerable pain. Rebecca. I had said it aloud.

I wondered if the bishop's wife saw the flush on my face, but she went on smoothly with the conversation, and I listened to her greedily, like an eavesdropper at a shuttered window.

'You never met her then?' she asked, and when I shook my head she hesitated a moment, a little uncertain of her ground. 'We never knew her well personally, you know: the bishop was only inducted here four years ago, but of course she received us when we went to the ball and the garden party. We dined there, too, one winter. Yes, she was a very lovely creature. So full of life.'

'She seems to have been so good at everything too,' I said, my voice just careless enough to show I did not mind, while I played with the fringe of my glove. 'It's not often you get someone who is clever and beautiful and fond of sport.'

'No, I suppose you don't,' said the bishop's wife. 'She was certainly very gifted. I can see her now, standing at the foot of the stairs on the night of the ball, shaking hands with everybody, that cloud of dark hair against the very white skin, and her costume suited her so. Yes, she was very beautiful.'

'She ran the house herself, too,' I said, smiling, as if to say, 'I am quite at my ease, I often discuss her.' 'It must have taken a lot of time and thought. I'm afraid I leave it to the housekeeper.'

'Oh, well, we can't all do everything. And you are very young, aren't you? No doubt in time, when you have settled down. Besides, you have your own hobby, haven't you? Someone told me you were fond of sketching.'

'Oh, that,' I said. 'I don't know that I can count it for much.'

'It's a nice little talent to have,' said the bishop's wife; 'it's not everyone that can sketch. You must not drop it. Manderley must be full of pretty spots to sketch.'

'Yes,' I said. 'Yes, I suppose so,' depressed by her words, having a sudden vision of myself wandering across the lawns with a camp-stool and a box of pencils under one arm, and my 'little talent' as she described it, under the other. It sounded like a pet disease.

'Do you play any games? Do you ride, or shoot?' she asked.

'No,' I said, 'I don't do anything like that. I'm fond of walking,' I added, as a wretched anticlimax.

'The best exercise in the world,' she said briskly; 'the bishop and I walk a lot.' I wondered if he went round and round the cathedral, in his shovel hat and his gaiters, with her on his arm.

She began to talk about a walking holiday they had taken once, years ago, in the Pennines, how they had done an average of twenty miles a day, and I nodded my head, smiling politely, wondering about the Pennines, thinking they were something like the Andes, remembering, afterwards, they were that chain of hills marked with a furry line in the middle of a pink England on my school atlas. And he all the time in his hat and gaiters.

The inevitable pause, the glance at the watch unnecessary, as her drawing-room clock chimed four in shrill tones, and my rise from the chair. 'I'm so glad I found you in. I hope you will come and see us.'

'We should love to. The bishop is always so busy, alas. Please remember me to your husband, and be sure to ask him to revive the ball.'

'Yes, indeed I will.' Lying, pretending I knew all about it; and in the car going home I sat in my corner, biting my thumb nail, seeing the great hall at Manderley thronged with people in fancy dress, the chatter, hum, and laughter of the moving crowd, the musicians in the gallery, supper in the drawing-room probably, long buffet tables against the wall, and I could see Maxim standing at the front of the stairs, laughing, shaking hands, turning to someone who stood by his side, tall and slim, with dark hair, said the bishop's wife, dark hair against a white face, someone whose quick eyes saw to the comfort of her guests, who gave an order over her shoulder to a servant, someone who was never awkward, never without grace, who when she danced left a stab of perfume in the air like a white azalea.

'Will you be entertaining much at Manderley, Mrs de Winter?' I heard the voice again, suggestive, rather inquisitive, in the voice of that woman I had called upon who lived the other side of Kerrith, and I saw her eye too, dubious, considering, taking in my clothes from top to toe, wondering, with that swift downward glance given to all brides, if I was going to have a baby.

I did not want to see her again. I did not want to see any of them again. They only came to call at Manderley because they were curious and prying. They liked to criticize my looks, my manners, my figure, they liked to watch how Maxim and I behaved to each other, whether we seemed fond of one another, so that they could go back afterwards and discuss us, saying, 'Very different from the old days.' They came because they wanted to compare me to Rebecca ... I would not return these calls any more, I decided. I should tell Maxim so. I did not mind if they thought me rude and ungracious. It would give them more to criticize, more to discuss. They could say I was ill-bred. 'I'm not surprised,' they would say; 'after all, who was she?' And then a laugh and a shrug of the shoulder. 'My dear, don't you know? He picked her up in Monte Carlo or somewhere; she hadn't a penny. She was a companion to some old woman.' More laughter, more lifting of the eyebrows. 'Nonsense, not really? How extraordinary men are. Maxim, of all people, who was so fastidious. How could he, after Rebecca?'

I did not mind. I did not care. They could say what they liked. As the car turned in at the lodge gates I leant forward in my seat to smile at the woman who lived there. She was bending down, picking flowers in the front garden. She straightened up as she heard the car, but she did not see me smile. I waved, and she stared at me blankly. I don't think she knew who I was. I leant back in my seat again. The car went on down the drive.

When we turned at one of the narrow bends I saw a man walking along the drive a little distance ahead. It was the agent, Frank Crawley. He stopped when he heard the car, and the chauffeur slowed down. Frank Crawley took off his hat and smiled when he saw me in the car. He seemed glad to see me. I smiled back at him. It was nice of him to be glad to see me. I liked Frank Crawley. I did not find him dull or uninteresting as Beatrice had done. Perhaps it was because I was dull myself. We were both dull. We neither of us had a word to say for ourselves. Like to like.

I tapped on the glass and told the chauffeur to stop.

'I think I'll get out and walk with Mr Crawley,' I said.

He opened the door for me. 'Been paying calls, Mrs de Winter?' he said.

'Yes, Frank,' I said. I called him Frank because Maxim did, but he would always call me Mrs de Winter. He was that sort of person. Even if we had been thrown on a desert island together and lived there in intimacy for the rest of our lives, I should have been Mrs de Winter.

'I've been calling on the bishop,' I said, 'and I found the bishop out, but the bishop's lady was at home. She and the bishop are very fond of walking. Sometimes they do twenty miles a day, in the Pennines.'

'I don't know that part of the world,' said Frank Crawley; 'they say the country round is very fine. An uncle of mine used to live there.'

It was the sort of remark Frank Crawley always made. Safe, conventional, very correct.

'The bishop's wife wants to know when we are going to give a fancy dress ball at Manderley,' I said, watching him out of the tail of my eye. 'She came to the last one, she said, and enjoyed it very much. I did not know you have fancy dress dances here, Frank.'

He hesitated a moment before replying. He looked a little troubled. 'Oh, yes,' he said after a moment, 'the Manderley ball was generally an annual affair. Everyone in the county came. A lot of people from London too. Quite a big show.'

'It must have taken a lot of organization,' I said.

'Yes,' he said.

'I suppose', I said carelessly, 'Rebecca did most of it?'

I looked straight ahead of me along the drive, but I could see his face was turned towards me, as though he wished to read my expression.

'We all of us worked pretty hard,' he said quietly.

There was a funny reserve in his manner as he said this, a certain shyness that reminded me of my own. I wondered suddenly if he had been in love with Rebecca. His voice was the sort of voice I should have used in his circumstances, had this been so. The idea opened up a new field of possibilities. Frank Crawley being so shy, so dull, he would never have told anyone, least of all Rebecca.

'I'm afraid I should not be much use if we have a dance,' I said, 'I'm no earthly use at organizing anything.'

'There would be no need for you to do anything,' he said, 'you would just be your self and look decorative.'

'That's very polite of you, Frank,' I said, 'but I'm afraid I should not be able to do that very well either.'

'I think you would do it excellently,' he said. Dear Frank Crawley, how tactful he was and considerate. I almost believed him. But he did not deceive me really.

'Will you ask Maxim about the ball?' I said.

'Why don't you ask him?' he answered.

'No,' I said. 'No, I don't like to.'

We were silent then. We went on walking along the drive. Now that I had broken down my reluctance at saying Rebecca's name, first with the bishop's wife and now with Frank Crawley, the urge to continue was strong within me. It gave me a curious satisfaction, it acted upon me like a stimulant. I knew that in a moment or two I should have to say it again. 'I was down on one of the beaches the other day,' I said, 'the one with the breakwater. Jasper was being infuriating, he kept barking at the poor man with the idiot's eyes.'

'You must mean Ben,' said Frank, his voice quite easy now; 'he always potters about on the shore. He's quite a nice fellow, you need never be frightened of him. He would not hurt a fly.'

'Oh, I wasn't frightened,' I said. I waited a moment, humming a tune to give me confidence. 'I'm afraid that cottage place is going to rack and ruin,' I said lightly. 'I had to go in, to find a piece of string or something to tie up Jasper. The china is mouldy and the books are being ruined. Why isn't something done about it? It seems such a pity.'

I knew he would not answer at once. He bent down to tie up his shoe lace.

I pretended to examine a leaf on one of the shrubs. 'I think if Maxim wanted anything done he would tell me,' he said, still fumbling with his shoe.

'Are they all Rebecca's things?' I asked.

'Yes,' he said.

I threw the leaf away and picked another, turning it over in my hands.

'What did she use the cottage for?' I asked; 'it looked quite furnished. I thought from the outside it was just a boat-house.'

'It was a boat-house originally,' he said, his voice constrained again, difficult, the voice of someone who is uncomfortable about his subject. 'Then – then she converted it like that, had furniture put in, and china.'

I thought it funny the way he called her 'she'. He did not say Rebecca or Mrs de Winter, as I expected him to do.

'Did she use it a great deal?' I asked.

'Yes,' he said. 'Yes, she did. Moonlight picnics, and – and one thing and another.'

We were walking again side by side, I still humming my little tune. 'How jolly,' I said brightly. 'Moonlight picnics must be great fun. Did you ever go to them?'

'Once or twice,' he said. I pretended not to notice his manner, how quiet it had become, how reluctant to speak about these things.

'Why is the buoy there in the little harbour place?' I said.

'The boat used to be moored there,' he said.

'What boat?' I asked.

'Her boat,' he said.

A strange sort of excitement was upon me. I had to go on with my questions. He did not want to talk about it. I knew that, but although I was sorry for him and shocked at my own self I had to continue, I could not be silent.

'What happened to it?' I said. 'Was that the boat she was sailing when she was drowned?'

'Yes,' he said quietly, 'it capsized and sank. She was washed overboard.'

'What sort of size boat was it?' I asked.

'About three tons. It had a little cabin.'

'What made it capsize?' I said.

'It can be very squally in the bay,' he said.

I thought of that green sea, foam-flecked, that ran down channel beyond the headland. Did the wind come suddenly, I wondered, in a funnel from the beacon on the hill, and did the little boat heel to it, shivering, the white sail flat against a breaking sea?

'Could not someone have got out to her?' I said.

'Nobody saw the accident, nobody knew she had gone,' he said.

I was very careful not to look at him. He might have seen the surprise in my face. I had always thought it happened in a sailing race, that other boats were there, the boats from Kerrith, and that people were watching from the cliffs. I did not know she had been alone, quite alone, out there in the bay.

'They must have known up at the house!' I said.

'No,' he said. 'She often went out alone like that. She would come back any time of the night, and sleep at the cottage on the beach.'

'Was not she nervous?'

'Nervous?' he said; 'no, she was not nervous of anything.'

'Did – did Maxim mind her going off alone like that?'

He waited a minute, and then 'I don't know,' he said shortly. I had the impression he was being loyal to someone. Either to Maxim or to Rebecca, or perhaps even to himself. He was odd. I did not know what to make of it.

'She must have been drowned, then, trying to swim to shore, after the boat sank?' I said.

'Yes,' he said.

I knew how the little boat would quiver and plunge, the water gushing into the steering well, and how the sails would press her down, suddenly, horribly, in that gust of wind. It must have been very dark out there in the bay. The shore must have seemed very far away to anyone swimming there, in the water.

'How long afterwards was it that they found her?' I said.

'About two months,' he said.

Two months. I thought drowned people were found after two days. I thought they would be washed up close to the shore when the tide came.

'Where did they find her?' I asked.

'Near Edgecoombe, about forty miles up channel,' he said.

I had spent a holiday at Edgecoombe once, when I was seven. It was a big place, with a pier, and donkeys. I remembered riding a donkey along the sands.

'How did they know it was her – after two months, how could they tell?' I said. I wondered why he paused before each sentence, as though he weighed his words. Had he cared for her, then, had he minded so much?

'Maxim went up to Edgecoombe to identify her,' he said.

Suddenly I did not want to ask him any more. I felt sick at

myself, sick and disgusted. I was like a curious sightseer standing on the fringe of a crowd after someone had been knocked down. I was like a poor person in a tenement building, when someone had died, asking if I might see the body. I hated myself. My questions had been degrading, shameful. Frank Crawley must despise me.

'It was a terrible time for all of you,' I said rapidly. 'I don't suppose you like being reminded about it. I just wondered if there was anything one could do to the cottage, that's all. It seems such a pity, all the furniture being spoilt by the damp.'

He did not say anything. I felt hot and uncomfortable. He must have sensed that it was not concern for the empty cottage that had prompted me to all these questions, and now he was silent because he was shocked at me. Ours had been a comfortable, steady sort of friendship. I had felt him an ally. Perhaps I had destroyed all this, and he would never feel the same about me again.

'What a long drive this is,' I said; 'it always reminds me of the path in the forest in a Grimms' fairy tale, where the prince gets lost, you know. It's always longer than one expects, and the trees are so dark, and close.'

'Yes, it is rather exceptional,' he said.

I could tell by his manner he was still on his guard, as though waiting for a further question from me. There was an awkwardness between us that could not be ignored. Something had to be done about it, even if it covered me with shame.

'Frank,' I said desperately, 'I know what you are thinking. You can't understand why I asked all those questions just now. You think I'm morbid, and curious, in a rather beastly way. It's not that, I promise you. It's only that – that sometimes I feel myself at such a disadvantage. It's all very strange to me, living here at Manderley. Not the sort of life I've been brought up to. When I go returning these calls, as I did this afternoon, I know people are looking me up and down, wondering what sort of success I'm going to make of it. I can imagine them saying, "What on earth does Maxim see in her?" And then, Frank, I begin to wonder myself, and I begin to doubt, and I have a fearful haunting feeling that I should never have married Maxim, that we are not going to be happy. You see, I know that all the time, whenever I meet anyone new, they are all thinking the same thing – How different she is to Rebecca.'

I stopped breathless, already a little ashamed of my outburst, feeling that now at any rate I had burnt my boats for all time. He turned to me looking very concerned and troubled.

'Mrs de Winter, please don't think that,' he said. 'For my part I can't tell you how delighted I am that you have married Maxim. It will make all the difference to his life. I am positive that you will make a great success of it. From my point of view it's – it's very refreshing and charming to find someone like yourself who is not entirely – er—' he blushed, searching for a word 'not entirely *au fait*, shall we say, with ways at Manderley. And if people around here give you the impression that they are criticizing you, it's – well – it's most damnably offensive of them, that's all. I've never heard a word of criticism, and if I did I should take great care that it was never uttered again.'

'That's very sweet of you, Frank,' I said, 'and what you say helps enormously. I dare say I've been very stupid. I'm not good at meeting people, I've never had to do it, and all the time I keep remembering how – how it must have been at Manderley before, when there was someone there who was born and bred to it, did it all naturally and without effort. And I realize, every day, that things I lack, confidence, grace, beauty, intelligence, wit – Oh, all the qualities that mean most in a woman – she possessed. It doesn't help, Frank, it doesn't help.'

He said nothing. He went on looking anxious, and distressed. He pulled out his handkerchief and blew his nose. 'You must not say that,' he said.

'Why not? It's true,' I said.

'You have qualities that are just as important, far more so, in fact. It's perhaps cheek of me to say so, I don't know you very well. I'm a bachelor, I don't know very much about women, I lead a quiet sort of life down here at Manderley as you know, but I should say that kindness, and sincerity, and – if I may say so – modesty are worth far more to a man, to a husband, than all the wit and beauty in the world.'

He looked very agitated, and blew his nose again. I saw that

I had upset him far more than I had upset myself, and the realization of this calmed me and gave me a feeling of superiority. I wondered why he was making such a fuss. After all, I had not said very much. I had only confessed my sense of insecurity, following as I did upon Rebecca. And she must have had these qualities that he presented to me as mine. She must have been kind and sincere, with all her friends, her boundless popularity. I was not sure what he meant by modesty. It was a word I had never understood. I always imagined it had something to do with minding meeting people in a passage on the way to the bathroom ... Poor Frank. And Beatrice had called him a dull man, with never a word to say for himself.

'Well,' I said, rather embarrassed, 'well, I don't know about all that. I don't think I'm very kind, or particularly sincere, and as for being modest, I don't think I've ever had much of a chance to be anything else. It was not very modest, of course, being married hurriedly like that, down in Monte Carlo, and being alone there in that hotel, beforehand, but perhaps you don't count that?'

'My dear Mrs de Winter, you don't think I imagine for one moment that your meeting down there was not entirely above board?' he said in a low voice.

'No, of course not,' I said gravely. Dear Frank. I think I had shocked him. What a Frank-ish expression, too, 'above board'. It made one think immediately of the sort of things that would happen below board.

'I'm sure,' he began, and hesitated, his expression still troubled, 'I'm sure that Maxim would be very worried, very distressed, if he knew how you felt. I don't think he can have any idea of it.'

'You won't tell him?' I said hastily.

'No, naturally not, what do you take me for? But you see, Mrs de Winter, I know Maxim pretty well, and I've seen him through many ... moods. If he thought you were worrying about – well – about the past, it would distress him more than anything on earth. I can promise you that. He's looking very well, very fit, but Mrs Lacy was quite right the other day when she said he had been on the verge of a breakdown last year, though it was tactless of her to say so in front of him. That's why you are so good for him. You are fresh and young and – and sensible, you have nothing to do with all that time that has gone. Forget it, Mrs de Winter, forget it, as he has done, thank heaven, and the rest of us. We none of us want to bring back the past. Maxim least of all. And it's up to you, you know, to lead us away from it. Not to take us back there again.'

He was right, of course he was right. Dear good Frank, my friend, my ally. I had been selfish and hypersensitive, a martyr to my own inferiority complex. 'I ought to have told you all this before,' I said.

'I wish you had,' he said. 'I might have spared you some worry.'

'I feel happier,' I said, 'much happier. And I've got you for my friend whatever happens, haven't I, Frank?'

'Yes, indeed,' he said.

We were out of the dark wooded drive and into the light again. The rhododendrons were upon us. Their hour would soon be over. Already they looked a little overblown, a little faded. Next month the petals would fall one by one from the great faces, and the gardeners would come and sweep them away. Theirs was a brief beauty. Not lasting very long.

'Frank,' I said, 'before we put an end to this conversation, for ever let's say, will you promise to answer me one thing, quite truthfully?'

He paused, looking at me a little suspiciously. 'That's not quite fair,' he said, 'you might ask me something that I should not be able to answer, something quite impossible.'

'No,' I said, 'it's not that sort of question. It's not intimate or personal, or anything like that.'

'Very well, I'll do my best,' he said.

We came round the sweep of the drive and Manderley was before us, serene and peaceful in the hollow of the lawns, surprising me as it always did, with its perfect symmetry and grace, its great simplicity.

The sunlight flickered on the mullioned windows, and there was a soft rusted glow about the stone walls where the lichen clung. A thin column of smoke curled from the library chimney.

I bit my thumb nail, watching Frank out of the tail of my eye.

'Tell me,' I said, my voice casual, not caring a bit, 'tell me, was Rebecca very beautiful?'

Frank waited a moment. I could not see his face. He was look-ing away from me towards the house. 'Yes,' he said slowly, 'yes, I suppose she was the most beautiful creature I ever saw in my life.'

We went up the steps then to the hall, and I rang the bell for tea.

12

I DID NOT see much of Mrs Danvers. She kept very much to herself. She still rang the house telephone to the morning-room every day and submitted the menu to me as a matter of form, but that was the limit of our intercourse. She had engaged a maid for me, Clarice, the daughter of somebody on the estate, a nice quiet well-mannered girl, who, thank heaven, had never been in service before and had no alarming standards. I think she was the only person in the house who stood in awe of me. To her I was the mistress: I was Mrs de Winter. The possible gossip of the others could not affect her. She had been away for some time, brought up by an aunt fifteen miles away, and in a sense she was as new to Manderley as I was. I felt at ease with her. I did not mind saying 'Oh, Clarice, would you mend my stocking?'

The housemaid Alice had been so superior. I used to sneak my chemise and nightgowns out of my drawer and mend them myself rather than ask her to do them. I had seen her once, with one of my chemises over her arm, examining the plain material with its small edging of lace. I shall never forget her expression. She looked almost shocked, as though her own personal pride had received a blow. I had never thought about my underclothes before. As long as they were clean and neat I had not thought the material or the existence of lace mattered. Brides one read about had trousseaux, dozens of sets at a time, and I had never bothered. Alice's face taught me a lesson. I wrote quickly to a shop in London and asked for a catalogue of under-linen. By the time I had made my choice Alice was looking after me no longer and Clarice was installed instead. It seemed such a waste buying new underclothes for Clarice that I put the catalogue away in a drawer and never wrote to the shop after all.

I often wondered whether Alice told the others, and if my

underclothes became a topic of conversation in the servants' hall, something rather dreadful, to be discussed in low tones when the men were nowhere about. She was too superior for it to be made a joking question. Phrases like 'Chemise to you' would never be bandied between her and Frith, for instance.

No, my underclothes were more serious than that. More like a divorce case heard *in camera* ... At any rate I was glad when Alice surrendered me to Clarice. Clarice would never know real lace from false. It was considerate of Mrs Danvers to have engaged her. She must have thought we would be fit company, one for the other. Now that I knew the reason for Mrs Danvers' dislike and resentment it made things a little easier. I knew it was not just me personally she hated, but what I represented. She would have felt the same towards anyone who had taken Rebecca's place. At least that was what I understood from Beatrice the day she came to lunch.

'Did not you know?' she had said; 'she simply adored Rebecca.'

The words had shocked me at the time. Somehow I had not expected them. But when I thought it over I began to lose my first fear of Mrs Danvers. I began to be sorry for her. I could imagine what she must feel. It must hurt her every time she heard me called 'Mrs de Winter'. Every morning when she took up the house telephone and spoke to me, and I answered 'Yes, Mrs Danvers,' she must be thinking of another voice. When she passed through the rooms and saw traces of me about the place, a beret on a window-seat, a bag of knitting on a chair, she must think of another one, who had done these things before. Even as I did. I, who had never known Rebecca. Mrs Danvers knew how she walked and how she spoke. Mrs Danvers knew the colour of her eyes, her smile, the texture of her hair. I knew none of these things, I had never asked about them, but sometimes I felt Rebecca was as real to me as she was to Mrs Danvers.

Frank had told me to forget the past, and I wanted to forget it. But Frank did not have to sit in the morning-room as I did, every day, and touch the pen she had held between her fingers. He did not have to rest his hands on the blotter, and stare in front of him at her writing on the pigeon-holes. He did not have to look at the candlesticks on the mantelpiece, the clock, the vase in which the flowers stood, the pictures on the walls and remember, every day, that they belonged to her, she had chosen them, they were not mine at all. Frank did not have to sit at her place in the dining-room, hold the knife and fork that she had held, drink from her glass. He did not throw a coat over his shoulders which had been hers, nor find her handkerchief in the pocket. He did not notice, every day, as I did, the blind gaze of the old dog in its basket in the library, who lifted its head when it heard my foot-step, the footstep of a woman, and sniffing the air drooped its head again, because I was not the one she sought.

Little things, meaningless and stupid in themselves, but they were there for me to see, for me to hear, for me to feel. Dear God, I did not want to think about Rebecca. I wanted to be happy, to make Maxim happy, and I wanted us to be together. There was no other wish in my heart but that. I could not help it if she came to me in thoughts, in dreams. I could not help it if I felt like a guest in Manderley, my home, walking where she had trodden, resting where she had lain. I was like a guest, biding my time, waiting for the return of the hostess. Little sentences, little reproofs reminding me every hour, every day.

'Frith,' I said, coming into the library on a summer morning, my arms full of lilac, 'Frith, where can I find a tall vase for these? They are all too small in the flower room.'

'The white alabaster vase in the drawing-room was always used for the lilac, Madam.'

'Oh, wouldn't it be spoilt? It might get broken.'

'Mrs de Winter always used the alabaster vase, Madam.'

'Oh, oh, I see.'

Then the alabaster vase was brought for me, already filled with water, and as I put the sweet lilac in the vase and arranged the sprigs, one by one, the mauve warm scent filling the room, mingling with the smell of the new-mown lawn outside coming from the open window, I thought: 'Rebecca did this. She took the lilac, as I am doing, and put the sprigs one by one in the white vase. I'm not the first to do it. This is Rebecca's vase, this is Rebecca's lilac.' She must have wandered out into the garden as I did, in that floppy garden hat that I had seen once at the back

of the cupboard in the flower room, hidden under some old cushions, and crossed the lawn to the lilac bushes, whistling perhaps,
humming a tune, calling to the dogs to follow her, carrying in
her hands the scissors that I carried now.

'Frith, could you move that book-stand from the table in the
window, and I will put the lilac there?'

'Mrs de Winter always had the alabaster vase on the table
behind the sofa, Madam.'

'Oh, well . . .' I hesitated, the vase in my hands, Frith's face
impassive. He would obey me of course if I said I preferred to
put the vase on the smaller table by the window. He would move
the book-stand at once.

'All right,' I said, 'perhaps it would look better on the larger
table.' And the alabaster vase stood, as it had always done, on
the table behind the sofa . . .

Beatrice remembered her promise of a wedding present. A
large parcel arrived one morning, almost too large for Robert to
carry. I was sitting in the morning-room, having just read the
menu for the day. I have always had a childish love of parcels.
I snipped the string excitedly, and tore off the dark brown paper.
It looked like books. I was right. It was books. Four big volumes.
A History of Painting. And a sheet of note-paper in the first volume
saying 'I hope this is the sort of thing you like,' and signed 'Love
from Beatrice.' I could see her going into the shop in Wigmore
Street and buying them. Looking about her in her abrupt, rather
masculine way. 'I want a set of books for someone who is keen
on Art,' she would say, and the attendant would answer, 'Yes,
Madam, will you come this way.' She would finger the volumes
a little suspiciously. 'Yes, that's about the price. It's for a wedding
present. I want them to look good. Are these all about Art?' 'Yes,
this is the standard work on the subject,' the assistant would say.
And then Beatrice must have written her note, and paid her
cheque, and given the address 'Mrs de Winter, Manderley'.

It was nice of Beatrice. There was something rather sincere
and pathetic about her going off to a shop in London and buying
me these books because she knew I was fond of painting. She
imagined me, I expect, sitting down on a wet day and looking
solemnly at the illustrations, and perhaps getting a sheet of

drawing-paper and a paint-box and copying one of the pictures. Dear Beatrice. I had a sudden, stupid desire to cry. I gathered up the heavy volumes and looked round the morning-room for somewhere to put them. They were out of place in that fragile delicate room. Never mind, it was my room now, after all. I arranged them in a row on the top of the desk. They swayed dangerously, leaning one against the other. I stood back a bit, to watch the effect. Perhaps I moved too quickly, and it disturbed them. At any rate the foremost one fell, and the others slid after him. They upset a little china cupid who had hitherto stood alone on the desk except for the candlesticks. He fell to the ground, hitting the waste-paper basket as he did so, and broke into fragments. I glanced hurriedly at the door, like a guilty child. I knelt on the floor and swept up the pieces into my hand. I found an envelope to put them in. I hid the envelope at the back of one of the drawers in the desk. Then I took the books off to the library and found room for them on the shelves.

Maxim laughed when I showed them to him with pride.

'Dear old Bee,' he said, 'you must have had a success with her. She never opens a book if she can help it.'

'Did she say anything about – well – what she thought of me?' I asked.

'The day she came to lunch? No, I don't think so.'

'I thought she might have written or something.'

'Beatrice and I don't correspond unless there's a major event in the family. Writing letters is a waste of time,' said Maxim.

I supposed I was not a major event. Yet if I had been Beatrice, and had a brother, and the brother married, surely one would have said something, expressed an opinion, written two words? Unless of course one had taken a dislike to the wife, or thought her unsuitable. Then of course it would be different. Still, Beatrice had taken the trouble to go up to London and to buy the books for me. She would not have done that if she disliked me.

It was the following day I remember, when Frith, who had brought in the coffee after lunch to the library, waited a moment, hovering behind Maxim, and said,

'Could I speak to you, sir?' Maxim glanced up from his paper.

'Yes, Frith, what is it?' he said, rather surprised. Frith wore a stiff solemn expression, his lips pursed. I thought at once his wife had died.

'It's about Robert, sir. There has been a slight unpleasantness between him and Mrs Danvers. Robert is very upset.'

'Oh, Lord,' said Maxim, making a face at me. I bent down to fondle Jasper, my unfailing habit in moments of embarrassment.

'Yes, sir. It appears Mrs Danvers has accused Robert of secreting a valuable ornament from the morning-room. It is Robert's business to bring in the fresh flowers to the morning-room and place the vases. Mrs Danvers went in this morning after the flowers had been done, and noticed one of the ornaments was missing. It was there yesterday, she said. She accused Robert of either taking the ornament or breaking it and concealing the breakage. Robert denied both accusations most emphatically, and came to me nearly in tears, sir. You may have noticed he was not himself at lunch.'

'I wondered why he handed me the cutlets without giving me a plate,' murmured Maxim. 'I did not know Robert was so sensitive. Well, I suppose someone else did it. One of the maids.'

'No, sir. Mrs Danvers went into the room before the girl had done the room. Nobody had been there since Madam yesterday, and Robert first thing with the flowers. It makes it very unpleasant for Robert and myself, sir.'

'Yes, of course it does. Well you had better ask Mrs Danvers to come here and we'll get to the bottom of it. What ornament was it, anyway?'

'The china cupid, sir, that stands on the writing-table.'

'Oh! Oh, Lord. That's one of our treasures, isn't it? It will have to be found. Get hold of Mrs Danvers at once.'

'Very good, sir.'

Frith left the room and we were alone again. 'What a confounded nuisance,' said Maxim; 'that cupid is worth a hell of a lot. How I loathe servants' rows too. I wonder why they come to me about it. That's your job, sweetheart.'

I looked up from Jasper, my face red as fire. 'Darling,' I said, 'I meant to tell you before, but – but I forgot. The fact is I broke that cupid when I was in the morning-room yesterday.'

'You broke it? Well, why the devil didn't you say so when Frith was here?'

'I don't know. I didn't like to. I was afraid he would think me a fool.'

'He'll think you much more of a fool now You'll have to explain to him and Mrs Danvers.'

'Oh, no, please, Maxim, you tell them. Let me go upstairs.'

'Don't be a little idiot. Anyone would think you were afraid of them.'

'I am afraid of them. At least, not afraid, but . . .'

The door opened, and Frith ushered Mrs Danvers into the room. I looked nervously at Maxim. He shrugged his shoulders, half amused, half angry.

'It's all a mistake, Mrs Danvers. Apparently Mrs de Winter broke the cupid herself and forgot to say anything,' said Maxim.

They all looked at me. It was like being a child again. I was still aware of my guilty flush. 'I'm so sorry,' I said, watching Mrs Danvers, 'I never thought Robert would get into trouble.'

'Is it possible to repair the ornament, Madam?' said Mrs Danvers. She did not seem to be surprised that I was the culprit. She looked at me with her white skull's face and her dark eyes. I felt she had known it was me all along and had accused Robert to see if I would have the courage to confess.

'I'm afraid not,' I said, 'it's smashed in little pieces.'

'What did you do with the pieces?' said Maxim.

It was like being a prisoner, giving evidence. How paltry and mean my actions sounded, even to myself. 'I put them all into an envelope,' I said.

'Well, what did you do with the envelope?' said Maxim, lighting a cigarette, his tone a mixture of amusement and exasperation.

'I put it at the back of one of the drawers in the writing-desk,' I said.

'It looks as though Mrs de Winter thought you would put her in prison, doesn't it, Mrs Danvers?' said Maxim. 'Perhaps you would find the envelope and send the pieces up to London. If they are too far gone to mend it can't be helped. All right, Frith. Tell Robert to dry his tears.'

Mrs Danvers lingered when Frith had gone. 'I will apologize to Robert of course,' she said, 'but the evidence pointed so strongly to him. It did not occur to me that Mrs de Winter had broken the ornament herself. Perhaps, if such a thing should happen again, Mrs de Winter will tell me personally, and I will have the matter attended to? It would save everybody a lot of unpleasantness.'

'Naturally,' said Maxim impatiently, 'I can't think why she didn't do so yesterday. I was just going to tell her when you came into the room.'

'Perhaps Mrs de Winter was not aware of the value of the ornament?' said Mrs Danvers, turning her eyes upon me.

'Yes,' I said wretchedly. 'Yes, I was afraid it was valuable. That's why I swept the pieces up so carefully.'

'And hid them at the back of a drawer where no one would find them, eh?' said Maxim, with a laugh, and a shrug of the shoulders. 'Is not that the sort of thing the between-maid is supposed to do, Mrs Danvers?'

'The between-maid at Manderley would never be allowed to touch the valuable things in the morning-room, sir,' said Mrs Danvers.

'No, I can't see you letting her,' said Maxim.

'It's very unfortunate,' said Mrs Danvers, 'I don't think we have ever had any breakages in the morning-room before. We were always so particular. I've done the dusting in there myself since – last year. There was no one I could trust. When Mrs de Winter was alive we used to do the valuables together.'

'Yes, well – it can't be helped,' said Maxim. 'All right, Mrs Danvers.'

She went out of the room, and I sat on the window-seat, looking out of the window. Maxim picked up his paper again. Neither of us spoke.

'I'm awfully sorry, darling,' I said, after a moment, 'it was very careless of me. I can't think how it happened. I was just arranging those books on the desk, to see if they would stand, and the cupid slipped.'

'My sweet child, forget it. What does it matter?'

'It does matter. I ought to have been more careful. Mrs Danvers must be furious with me.'

'What the devil has she got to be furious about? It's not her bit of china.'

'No, but she takes such a pride in it all. It's so awful to think nothing in there has ever been broken before. It had to be me.'

'Better you than the luckless Robert.'

'I wish it had been Robert. Mrs Danvers will never forgive me.'

'Damn Mrs Danvers,' said Maxim, 'she's not God Almighty, is she? I can't understand you. What do you mean by saying you are afraid of her?'

'I did not mean afraid exactly. I don't see much of her. It's not that. I can't really explain.'

'You do such extraordinary things,' said Maxim; 'fancy not getting hold of her when you broke the thing and saying, "Here, Mrs Danvers, get this mended." She'd understand that. Instead of which you scrape up the remains in an envelope and hide 'em at the back of a drawer. Just like a between-maid, as I said, and not the mistress of a house.'

'I am like a between-maid,' I said slowly, 'I know I am, in lots of ways. That's why I have so much in common with Clarice. We are on the same sort of footing. And that's why she likes me. I went and saw her mother the other day. And do you know what she said? I asked her if she thought Clarice was happy with us, and she said, "Oh, yes, Mrs de Winter. Clarice seems quite happy. She says, 'It's not like being with a lady, Mum, it's like being with one of ourselves.'" Do you suppose she meant it as a compliment or not?'

'God knows,' said Maxim; 'remembering Clarice's mother, I should take it as a direct insult. Her cottage is generally a shambles and smells of boiled cabbage. At one time she had nine children under eleven, and she herself used to patter about in that patch of garden with no shoes and a stocking round her head. We nearly gave her notice to quit. Why Clarice looks as neat and clean as she does I can't imagine.'

'She's been living with an aunt,' I said, feeling rather subdued. 'I know my flannel skirt has a dirty mark down the front, but I've never walked barefoot with a stocking round my head.' I knew now why Clarice did not disdain my underclothes as Alice had done. 'Perhaps that's why I prefer calling on Clarice's mother to calling on people like the bishop's wife?' I went on. 'The bishop's wife never said I was like one of themselves.'

'If you wear that grubby skirt when you call on her I don't suppose she does,' said Maxim.

'Of course I didn't call on her in my old skirt, I wore a frock,' I said, 'and anyway I don't think much of people who just judge one by one's clothes.'

'I hardly think the bishop's wife cares twopence about clothes,' said Maxim, 'but she may have been rather surprised if you sat on the extreme edge of the chair and answered "Yes" and "No" like someone after a new job, which you did the only time we returned a call together.'

'I can't help being shy.'

'I know you can't, sweetheart. But you don't make an effort to conquer it.'

'I think that's very unfair,' I said. 'I try every day, every time I go out or meet anyone new. I'm always making efforts. You don't understand. It's all very well for you, you're used to that sort of thing. I've not been brought up to it.'

'Rot,' said Maxim; 'it's not a question of bringing up, as you put it. It's a matter of application. You don't think I like calling on people, do you? It bores me stiff. But it has to be done, in this part of the world.'

'We're not talking about boredom,' I said; 'there's nothing to be afraid of in being bored. If I was just bored it would be different. I hate people looking me up and down as though I were a prize cow.'

'Who looks you up and down?'

'All the people down here. Everybody.'

'What does it matter if they do? It gives them some interest in life.'

'Why must I be the one to supply the interest, and have all the criticism?'

'Because life at Manderley is the only thing that ever interests anybody down here.'

'What a slap in the eye I must be to them then.'

Maxim did not answer. He went on looking at his paper.

'What a slap in the eye I must be to them,' I repeated. And then, 'I suppose that's why you married me,' I said; 'you knew I was dull and quiet and inexperienced, so that there would never be any gossip about me.'

Maxim threw his paper on the ground and got up from his chair. 'What do you mean?' he said.

His face was dark and queer, and his voice was rough, not his voice at all.

'I – I don't know,' I said, leaning back against the window, 'I don't mean anything. Why do you look like that?'

'What do you know about any gossip down here?' he said.

'I don't,' I said, scared by the way he looked at me. 'I only said it because – because of something to say. Don't look at me like that. Maxim, what have I said? what's the matter?'

'Who's been talking to you,' he said slowly.

'No one. No one at all.'

'Why did you say what you did?'

'I tell you, I don't know. It just came to my head. I was angry, cross. I do hate calling on these people. I can't help it. And you criticized me for being shy. I didn't mean it. Really, Maxim, I didn't. Please believe me.'

'It was not a particularly attractive thing to say, was it?' he said.

'No,' I said. 'No, it was rude, hateful.'

He stared at me moodily, his hands in his pockets, rocking backwards and forwards on his heels. 'I wonder if I did a very selfish thing in marrying you,' he said. He spoke slowly, thoughtfully.

I felt very cold, rather sick. 'How do you mean?' I said.

'I'm not much of a companion to you, am I?' he said. 'There are too many years between us. You ought to have waited, and then married a boy of your own age. Not someone like myself, with half his life behind him.'

'That's ridiculous,' I said hurriedly, 'you know age doesn't mean anything in marriage. Of course we are companions.'

'Are we? I don't know,' he said.

I knelt up on the window-seat and put my arms round his

shoulders. 'Why do you say these things to me?' I said; 'you know I love you more than anything in the world. There has never been anyone but you. You are my father and my brother and my son. All those things.'

'It was my fault,' he said, not listening. 'I rushed you into it. I never gave you a chance to think it over.'

'I did not want to think it over,' I said, 'there was no other choice. You don't understand, Maxim. When one loves a person . . .'

'Are you happy here?' he said, looking away from me, out of the window, 'I wonder sometimes. You've got thinner. Lost your colour.'

'Of course I'm happy,' I said, 'I love Manderley. I love the garden, I love everything. I don't mind calling on people. I just said that to be tiresome. I'll call on people every day, if you want me to. I don't mind what I do. I've never for one moment regretted marrying you, surely you must know that?'

He patted my cheek in his terrible absent way, and bent down, and kissed the top of my head. 'Poor lamb, you don't have much fun, do you? I'm afraid I'm very difficult to live with.'

'You're not difficult,' I said eagerly, 'you are easy, very easy. Much easier than I thought you would be. I used to think it would be dreadful to be married, that one's husband would drink, or use awful language, or grumble if the toast was soft at breakfast, and be rather unattractive altogether, smell possibly. You don't do any of those things.'

'Good God, I hope not,' said Maxim, and he smiled.

I seized advantage of his smile, I smiled too, and took his hands and kissed them. 'How absurd to say we are not companions,' I said; 'why look how we sit here every evening, you with a book or a paper, and me with my knitting. Just like cups of tea. Just like old people, married for years and years. Of course we are companions. Of course we are happy. You talk as though you thought we had made a mistake? You don't mean it like that, do you, Maxim? You know our marriage is a success, a wonderful success?'

'If you say so, then it's all right,' he said.

'No, but you think it too, don't you, darling? It's not just me? We are happy, aren't we? Terribly happy?'

He did not answer. He went on staring out of the window while I held his hands. My throat felt dry and tight, and my eyes were burning. Oh, God, I thought, this is like two people in a play, in a moment the curtain will come down, we shall bow to the audience, and go off to our dressing-rooms. This can't be a real moment in the lives of Maxim and myself. I sat down on the window-seat, and let go of his hands. I heard myself speaking in a hard cool voice. 'If you don't think we are happy it would be much better if you would admit it. I don't want you to pretend anything. I'd much rather go away. Not live with you any more.' It was not really happening of course. It was the girl in the play talking, not me to Maxim. I pictured the type of girl who would play the part. Tall and slim, rather nervy.

'Well, why don't you answer me?' I said.

He took my face in his hands and looked at me, just as he had before, when Frith had come into the room with tea, the day we went to the beach.

'How can I answer you?' he said. 'I don't know the answer myself. If you say we are happy, let's leave it at that. It's something I know nothing about. I take your word for it. We are happy. All right then, that's agreed!' He kissed me again, and then walked away across the room. I went on sitting by the window, stiff and straight, my hands in my lap.

'You say all this because you are disappointed in me,' I said. 'I'm gauche and awkward, I dress badly, I'm shy with people. I warned you in Monte Carlo how it would be. You think I'm not right for Manderley.'

'Don't talk nonsense,' he said. 'I've never said you dressed badly or were gauche. It's your imagination. As for being shy, you'll get over that. I've told you so before.'

'We've argued in a circle,' I said, 'we've come right back to where we started. This all began because I broke the cupid in the morning-room. If I hadn't broken the cupid none of this would have happened. We'd have drunk our coffee, and gone out into the garden.'

'Oh, damn that infernal cupid,' said Maxim wearily. 'Do you really think I care whether it's in ten thousand pieces or not?'

'Was it very valuable?'

'Heaven knows. I suppose so. I've really forgotten.'

'Are all those things in the morning-room valuable?'

'Yes, I believe so.'

'Why were all the most valuable things put in the morning-room?'

'I don't know. I suppose because they looked well there.'

'Were they always there? When your mother was alive?'

'No. No, I don't think they were. They were scattered about the house. The chairs were in a lumber room I believe.'

'When was the morning-room furnished as it is now?'

'When I was married.'

'I suppose the cupid was put there then?'

'I suppose so.'

'Was that found in a lumber room?'

'No. No, I don't think it was. As a matter of fact I believe it was a wedding present. Rebecca knew a lot about china.'

I did not look at him. I began to polish my nails. He had said the word quite naturally, quite calmly. It had been no effort to him. After a minute I glanced at him swiftly. He was standing by the mantelpiece, his hands in his pockets. He was staring straight in front of him. He is thinking about Rebecca, I said to myself. He is thinking how strange it was that a wedding present to me should have been the cause of destroying a wedding present to Rebecca. He is thinking about the cupid. He is remembering who gave it to Rebecca. He is going over in his mind how the parcel came and how pleased she was. Rebecca knew a lot about china. Perhaps he came into the room, and she was kneeling on the floor, wrenching open the little crate in which the cupid was packed. She must have glanced up at him, and smiled. 'Look, Max,' she would have said, 'look what we've been sent.' And she then would have plunged her hand down into the shavings and brought out the cupid who stood on one foot, his bow in his hand. 'We'll have it in the morning-room,' she must have said, and he must have knelt down beside her, and they must have looked at the cupid together.

I went on polishing my nails. They were scrubby, like a schoolboy's nails. The cuticles grew up over the half moons. The thumb was bitten nearly to the quick. I looked at Maxim again. He was still standing in front of the fireplace.

'What are you thinking about?' I said.

My voice was steady and cool. Not like my heart, thumping inside me. Not like my mind, bitter and resentful. He lit a cigarette, surely the twenty-fifth that day, and we had only just finished lunch; he threw the match into the empty grate, he picked up the paper.

'Nothing very much, why?' he said.

'Oh, I don't know,' I said, 'you looked so serious, so far away.'

He whistled a tune absently, the cigarette twisting in his fingers. 'As a matter of fact I was wondering if they had chosen the Surrey side to play Middlesex at the Oval,' he said.

He sat down in the chair again and folded the paper. I looked out of the window. Presently Jasper came to me and climbed on my lap.

13

MAXIM HAD TO go up to London at the end of June to some public dinner. A man's dinner. Something to do with the county. He was away for two days and I was left alone. I dreaded his going. When I saw the car disappear round the sweep in the drive I felt exactly as though it were to be a final parting and I should never see him again. There would be an accident of course and later on in the afternoon, when I came back from my walk, I should find Frith white and frightened waiting for me with a message. The doctor would have rung up from some cottage hospital. 'You must be very brave,' he would say, 'I'm afraid you must be prepared for a great shock.'

And Frank would come, and we would go to the hospital together. Maxim would not recognize me. I went through the whole thing as I was sitting at lunch, I could see the crowd of local people clustering round the churchyard at the funeral, and myself leaning on Frank's arm. It was so real to me that I could scarcely eat any lunch, and I kept straining my ears to hear the telephone should it ring.

I sat out in the garden under the chestnut tree in the afternoon, with a book on my lap, but I scarcely read at all. When I saw Robert come across the lawn I knew it was the telephone and I felt physically sick. 'A message from the club, Madam, to say Mr de Winter arrived ten minutes ago.'

I shut up my book. 'Thank you, Robert. How quickly he got up.'

'Yes, Madam. A very good run.'

'Did he ask to speak to me, or leave any special message?'

'No, Madam. Just that he had arrived safely. It was the porter speaking.'

'All right, Robert. Thanks very much.'

The relief was tremendous. I did not feel sick any more. The pain had gone. It was like coming ashore after a channel crossing. I began to feel rather hungry, and when Robert had gone back into the house I crept into the dining-room through the long window and stole some biscuits from the sideboard. I had six of them. Bath Olivers. And then an apple as well. I had no idea I was so empty. I went and ate them in the woods, in case one of the servants should see me on the lawn from the windows, and then go and tell the cook that they did not think Mrs de Winter cared for the food prepared in the kitchen, as they had just seen her filling herself with fruit and biscuits. The cook would be offended, and perhaps go to Mrs Danvers.

Now that Maxim was safe in London, and I had eaten my biscuits, I felt very well and curiously happy. I was aware of a sense of freedom, as though I had no responsibilities at all. It was rather like a Saturday when one was a child. No lessons, and no prep. One could do as one liked. One put on an old skirt and a pair of sand-shoes and played Hares and Hounds on the common with the children who lived next door.

I had just the same feeling. I had not felt like this all the time I had been at Manderley. It must be because Maxim had gone to London.

I was rather shocked at myself. I could not understand it at all. I had not wanted him to go. And now this lightness of heart, this spring in my step, this childish feeling that I wanted to run across the lawn, and roll down the bank. I wiped the biscuit crumbs from my mouth and called to Jasper. Perhaps I was just feeling like this because it was a lovely day . . .

We went through the Happy Valley to the little cove. The azaleas were finished now, the petals lay brown and crinkled on the moss. The bluebells had not faded yet, they made a solid carpet in the woods above the valley, and the young bracken was shooting up, curling and green. The moss smelt rich and deep, and the bluebells were earthy, bitter. I lay down in the long grass beside the bluebells with my hands behind my head, and Jasper at my side. He looked down at me panting, his face foolish, saliva dripping from his tongue and his heavy jowl. There were pigeons somewhere in the trees above. It was very peaceful and quiet.

I wondered why it was that places are so much lovelier when one is alone. How commonplace and stupid it would be if I had a friend now, sitting beside me, someone I had known at school, who would say 'By the way, I saw old Hilda the other day. You remember her, the one who was so good at tennis. She's married, with two children.' And the bluebells beside us unnoticed, and the pigeons overhead unheard. I did not want anyone with me. Not even Maxim. If Maxim had been there I should not be lying as I was now, chewing a piece of grass, my eyes shut. I should have been watching him, watching his eyes, his expression. Wondering if he liked it, if he was bored. Wondering what he was thinking. Now I could relax, none of these things mattered. Maxim was in London. How lovely it was to be alone again. No, I did not mean that. It was disloyal, wicked. It was not what I meant. Maxim was my life and my world. I got up from the bluebells and called sharply to Jasper. We set off together down the valley to the beach. The tide was out, the sea very calm and remote. It looked like a great placid lake out there in the bay. I could not imagine it rough now, any more than I could imagine winter in summer. There was no wind, and the sun shone on the lapping water where it ran into the little pools in the rocks. Jasper scrambled up the rocks immediately, glancing back at me, one ear blown back against his head, giving him an odd rakish appearance.

'Not that way, Jasper,' I said.

He cared nothing for me of course. He loped off, deliberately disobedient. 'What a nuisance he is,' I said aloud, and I scrambled up the rocks after him, pretending to myself I did not want to go to the other beach. 'Oh, well,' I thought, 'it can't be helped. After all, Maxim is not with me. It's nothing to do with me.'

I splashed through the pools on the rocks, humming a tune. The cove looked different when the tide was out. Less formidable. There was only about three foot of water in the tiny harbour. A boat would just float there comfortably I supposed, at dead low water. The buoy was still there. It was painted white and green, I had not noticed that before. Perhaps because it had been raining the colouring was indistinct. There was no one on the beach. I walked across the shingle to the other side of the cove, and climbed the low stone wall of the jetty-arm. Jasper ran on ahead as though it was his custom. There was a ring in the wall and an iron ladder descending to the water. That's where the dinghy would be tied, I suppose, and one would climb to it from the ladder. The buoy was just opposite, about thirty feet away. There was something written on it. I craned my neck sideways to read the lettering. 'Je Reviens'. What a funny name. Not like a boat. Perhaps it had been a French boat though, a fishing boat. Fishing boats sometimes had names like that; 'Happy Return', 'I'm Here', those sort of names. 'Je Reviens' – 'I come back'. Yes, I suppose it was quite a good name for a boat. Only it had not been right for that particular boat which would never come back again.

It must be cold sailing out there in the bay, beyond the beacon away on the headland. The sea was calm in the bay, but even today, when it was so still, out there round the headland there was a ripple of white foam on the surface of the water where the tide was racing. A small boat would heel to the wind when she rounded the headland and came out of the landlocked bay. The sea would splash inboard perhaps, run down the deck. The person at the tiller would wipe spray out of her eyes and hair, glance up at the straining mast. I wondered what colour the boat had been. Green and white perhaps, like the buoy. Not very big, Frank had said, with a little cabin.

Jasper was sniffing at the iron ladder. 'Come away,' I said. 'I don't want to go in after you.' I went back along the harbour wall to the beach. The cottage did not seem so remote and sinister at the edge of the wood as it had done before. The sun made such a difference. No rain today, pattering on the roof. I walked slowly up the beach towards it. After all, it was only a cottage, with nobody living in it. There was nothing to be frightened of. Nothing at all. Any place seemed damp and sinister when it had been uninhabited for a certain time. Even new bungalows and places. Besides, they had moonlight picnics and things here. Week-end visitors probably used to come and bathe, and then go for a sail in the boat. I stood looking into the neglected garden choked with nettles. Someone ought to come and tidy it up. One of the gardeners. There was no need to leave it like this. I pushed the little gate and went to the door of the cottage. It was not entirely closed. I was certain I had closed it the last time. Jasper began growling, sniffing under the door.

'Don't, Jasper,' I said. He went on sniffing deeply, his nose thrust to the crack. I pushed the door open and looked inside. It was very dark. Like it had been before. Nothing was changed. The cobwebs still clung to the rigging of the model boats. The door into the boat-store at the end of the room was open though. Jasper growled again, and there was a sound of something falling. Jasper barked furiously, and darting between my legs into the room he tore to the open door of the store. I - followed him, heart beating, and then stood uncertainly in the middle of the room. 'Jasper, come back, don't be a fool,' I said. He stood in the doorway, still barking furiously, an hysterical note in his voice. Something was there then, inside the store. Not a rat. He would have gone for a rat. 'Jasper, Jasper. Come here,' I said. He would not come. I went slowly to the door of the store.

'Is there anybody there?' I said

No one answered. I bent down to Jasper, putting my hand on his collar, and looked round the edge of the door. Someone was sitting in the corner against the wall. Someone who, from his crouching position, was even more frightened than me. It was Ben. He was trying to hide behind one of the sails. 'What is the matter? Do you want something?' I said. He blinked at me stupidly, his mouth slightly open.

'I'm not doing nothing,' he said.

'Quiet, Jasper,' I scolded, putting my hand over his muzzle, and I took my belt off and ran it through his collar as a leash.

'What do you want, Ben?' I said, a little bolder this time.

He did not answer. He watched me with his sly idiot's eyes.

'I think you had better come out,' I said. 'Mr de Winter doesn't like people walking in and out of here.'

He shambled to his feet grinning furtively, wiping his nose with the back of his hand. The other hand he kept behind his back. 'What have you got, Ben?' I said. He obeyed me like a child, showing me the other hand. There was a fishing line in it. 'I'm not doing anything,' he repeated.

'Does that line belong here?' I asked.

'Eh?' he said.

'Listen, Ben,' I said. 'You can take that line if you want to, but you mustn't do it again. It's not honest, taking people's things.'

He said nothing. He blinked at me and wriggled.

'Come along,' I said firmly.

I went into the main room and he followed me. Jasper had stopped barking, and was now sniffing at Ben's heels. I did not want to stop any longer in the cottage. I walked quickly out into the sunshine, Ben shuffling behind me. Then I shut the door.

'You had better go home,' I said to Ben.

He held the fishing line clutched to his heart like a treasure. 'You won't put me to the asylum, will you?' he said.

I saw then that he was trembling with fright. His hands were shaking, and his eyes were fixed on mine in supplication, like a dumb thing.

'Of course not,' I said gently.

'I done nothing,' he repeated, 'I never told no one. I don't want to be put to the asylum.' A tear rolled down his dirty face.

'That's all right, Ben,' I said; 'no one will put you away. But you must not go to the cottage again.'

I turned away, and he came after me, pawing at my hand.

'Here,' he said. 'Here, I got something for you.'

He smiled foolishly, he beckoned with his finger, and turned towards the beach. I went with him, and he bent down and picked up a flat stone by a rock. There was a little heap of shells under the stone. He chose one, and presented it to me. 'That's yourn,' he said.

'Thank you; it's very pretty,' I said.

He grinned again, rubbing his ear, his fright forgotten. 'You've got angel's eyes,' he said.

I glanced down at the shell again, rather taken aback. I did not know what to say.

'You're not like the other one,' he said.

'Who do you mean?' I said. 'What other one?'

He shook his head. His eyes were sly again. He laid his finger against his nose. 'Tall and dark she was,' he said. 'She gave you the feeling of a snake. I seen her here with me own eyes. Be night she'd come. I seen her.' He paused, watching me intently. I did not say anything 'I looked in on her once,' he said, 'and she turned on me, she did. "You don't know me, do you?" she said. "You've never seen me here, and you won't again. If I catch you looking at me through the windows here I'll have you put to the asylum," she said. "You wouldn't like that would you? They're cruel to people in the asylum," she said. "I won't say nothing, M'am," I said. And I touched me cap, like this here.' He pulled at his sou'wester. 'She's gone now, ain't she?' he said anxiously.

'I don't know who you mean,' I said slowly; 'no one is going to put you in the asylum. Good afternoon, Ben.'

I turned away and walked up the beach to the path dragging Jasper by his belt. Poor wretch, he was potty, of course. He did not know what he was talking about. It was hardly likely that anyone would threaten him with the asylum. Maxim had said he was quite harmless, and so had Frank. Perhaps he had heard himself discussed once, amongst his own people, and the memory of it lingered, like an ugly picture in the mind of a child. He would have a child's mentality too, regarding likes and dislikes. He would take a fancy to a person for no reason, and be friendly one day perhaps and sullen the next. He had been friendly with me because I had said he could keep the fishing line. Tomorrow if I met him he might not know me. It was absurd to notice anything said by an idiot. I glanced back over my shoulder at the cove. The tide had begun to run and was swirling slowly round the arm of the harbour wall. Ben had disappeared over the rocks. The beach was deserted again. I could just see the stone chimney of the cottage through a gap in the dark trees. I had a sudden unaccountable desire to run. I pulled at Jasper's leash and panted up the steep narrow path through the woods, not looking back any more. Had I been offered all the treasures in the world I could not have turned and gone down to the cottage or the beach again. It was as though someone waited down there, in the little garden where the nettles grew. Someone who watched and listened.

Jasper barked as we ran together. He thought it was some new kind of game. He kept trying to bite the belt and worry it. I had not realized how closely the trees grew together here, their roots stretching across the path like tendrils ready to trip one. They ought to clear all this, I thought as I ran, catching my breath,

Maxim should get the men on to it. There is no sense or beauty in this undergrowth. That tangle of shrubs there should be cut down to bring light to the path. It was dark, much too dark. That naked eucalyptus tree stifled by brambles looked like the white bleached limb of a skeleton, and there was a black earthy stream running beneath it, choked with the muddied rains of years, trickling silently to the beach below. The birds did not sing here as they did in the valley. It was quiet in a different way. And even as I ran and panted up the path I could hear the wash of the sea as the tide crept into the cove. I understood why Maxim disliked the path and the cove. I disliked it too. I had been a fool to come this way. I should have stayed on the other beach, on the white shingle, and come home by the Happy Valley.

I was glad to come out on to the lawn and see the house there in the hollow, solid and secure. The woods were behind me. I would ask Robert to bring me my tea under the chestnut tree. I glanced at my watch. It was earlier than I thought, not yet four. I would have to wait a bit. It was not the routine at Manderley to have tea before half past. I was glad Frith was out. Robert would not make such a performance of bringing the tea out into the garden. As I wandered across the lawn to the terrace my eye was caught by a gleam of sunshine on something metal showing through the green of the rhododendron leaves at the turn in the drive. I shaded my eyes with my hand to see what it was. It looked like the radiator of a car. I wondered if someone had called. If they had though, they would have driven up to the house, not left their car concealed like that from the house, at the turn of the drive, by the shrubs. I went a little closer. Yes, it was a car all right. I could see the wings now and the hood. What a funny thing. Visitors never did that as a rule. And the tradesmen went round the back way by the old stables and the garage. It was not Frank's Morris. I knew that well. This was a long, low car, a sports car. I wondered what I had better do. If it was a caller Robert would have shown them into the library or the drawing-room. In the drawing-room they would be able to see me as I came across the lawn. I did not want to face a caller dressed like this. I should have to ask them to stay to tea. I hesitated, at the edge of the lawn. For no reason, perhaps because the sunlight flickered a moment on the glass, I looked up at the house, and as I did so I noticed with surprise that the shutters of one of the windows in the west wing had been opened up. Somebody stood by the window. A man. And then he must have caught sight of me because he drew back abruptly, and a figure behind him put up an arm and closed the shutters.

The arm belonged to Mrs Danvers. I recognized the black sleeve. I wondered for a minute if it was a public day and she was showing the rooms. It could not be so though because Frith always did that, and Frith was out. Besides, the rooms in the west wing were not shown to the public. I had not even been into them myself yet. No, I knew it was not a public day. The public never came on a Tuesday. Perhaps it was something to do with a repair in one of the rooms. It was odd though the way the man had been looking out and directly he saw me he whipped back into the room and the shutters were closed. And the car too, drawn up behind the rhododendrons, so that it could not be seen from the house. Still, that was up to Mrs Danvers. It was nothing to do with me. If she had friends she took to the west wing it was not exactly my affair. I had never known it happen before though. Odd that it should occur on the only day Maxim was from home.

I strolled rather self-consciously across the lawn to the house, aware that they might be watching me still from a chink in the shutters.

I went up the steps and through the big front door to the hall. There was no sign of a strange cap or stick, and no card on the salver. Evidently this was not an official visitor. Well, it was not my affair. I went into the flower room and washed my hands in the basin to save going upstairs. It would be awkward if I met them face to face on the stairs or somewhere. I remembered I had left my knitting in the morning-room before lunch, and I went along through the drawing-room to fetch it, the faithful Jasper at my heels. The morning-room door was open. And I noticed that my bag of knitting had been moved. I had left it on the divan, and it had been picked up and pushed behind a cushion. There was the imprint of a person on the fabric of the divan where my knitting had been before. Someone had sat down there recently, and picked up my knitting because it had been in the way. The chair by the desk had also been moved. It looked as though Mrs Danvers entertained her visitors in the morning-room when Maxim and I were out of the way. I felt rather uncomfortable. I would rather not know. Jasper was sniffing under the divan and wagging his tail. He was not suspicious of the visitor anyway. I took my bag of knitting and went out. As I did so the door in the large drawing-room that led to the stone passage and the back premises opened, and I heard voices. I darted back into the morning-room again, just in time. I had not been seen. I waited behind the door frowning at Jasper who stood in the doorway looking at me, his tongue hanging out, wagging his tail. The little wretch would give me away. I stood very still, holding my breath.

Then I heard Mrs Danvers speak. 'I expect she has gone to the library,' she said. 'She's come home early for some reason. If she has gone to the library you will be able to go through the hall without her seeing you. Wait here while I go and see.'

I knew they were talking about me. I began to feel more uncomfortable than ever. It was so furtive, the whole business. And I did not want to catch Mrs Danvers in the wrong. Then Jasper turned his head sharply towards the drawing-room. He trotted out, wagging his tail.

'Hullo, you little tyke,' I heard the man say. Jasper began to bark excitedly. I looked round desperately for somewhere to hide. Hopeless of course. And then I heard a footstep quite close to my ear, and the man came into the room. He did not see me at first because I was behind the door, but Jasper made a dive at me, still barking with delight.

The man wheeled round suddenly and saw me. I have never seen anyone look more astonished. I might have been the burglar and he the master of the house.

'I beg your pardon,' he said, looking me up and down.

He was a big, hefty fellow, good-looking in a rather flashy, sunburnt way. He had the hot, blue eyes usually associated with heavy drinking and loose living. His hair was reddish like his skin. In a few years he would run to fat, his neck bulging over the back of his collar. His mouth gave him away, it was too soft, too pink. I could smell the whisky in his breath from where I stood. He began to smile. The sort of smile he would give to every woman.

'I hope I haven't startled you,' he said.

I came out from behind the door looking no doubt as big a fool as I felt. 'No, of course not,' I said, 'I heard voices, I was not quite sure who it was. I did not expect any callers this afternoon.'

'What a shame,' he said heartily, 'it's too bad of me to butt in on you like this. I hope you'll forgive me. The fact is I just popped in to see old Danny, she's a very old friend of mine.'

'Oh, of course, it's quite all right,' I said.

'Dear old Danny,' he said, 'she's so anxious, bless her, not to disturb anyone. She didn't want to worry you.'

'Oh, it does not matter at all,' I said. I was watching Jasper who was jumping up and pawing at the man in delight.

'This little beggar hasn't forgotten me, has he?' he said. 'Grown into a jolly little beast. He was quite a youngster when I saw him last. He's too fat though. He needs more exercise.'

'I've just taken him for a long walk,' I said.

'Have you really? How sporting of you,' he said. He went on patting Jasper and smiling at me in a familiar way. Then he pulled out his cigarette case. 'Have one?' he said.

'I don't smoke,' I told him.

'Don't you really?' He took one himself and lighted it.

I never minded those things, but it seemed odd to me, in somebody else's room. It was surely rather bad manners? Not polite to me.

'How's old Max?' he said.

I was surprised at his tone. It sounded as though he knew him well. It was queer, to hear Maxim talked of as Max. No one called him that.

'He's very well, thank you,' I said. 'He's gone up to London.'

'And left the bride all alone? Why, that's too bad. Isn't he afraid someone will come and carry you off?'

He laughed, opening his mouth. I did not like his laugh. There was something offensive about it. I did not like him, either. Just then Mrs Danvers came into the room. She turned her eyes upon me and I felt quite cold. Oh, God, I thought, how she must hate me.

'Hullo, Danny, there you are,' said the man; 'all your

precautions were in vain. The mistress of the house was hiding behind the door.' And he laughed again. Mrs Danvers did not say anything. She just went on looking at me. 'Well, aren't you going to introduce me?' he said; 'after all it's the usual thing to do, isn't it, to pay one's respect to a bride?'

'This is Mr Favell, Madam,' said Mrs Danvers. She spoke quietly, rather unwillingly. I don't think she wanted to introduce him to me.

'How do you do,' I said, and then, with an effort to be polite, 'Won't you stay to tea?'

He looked very amused. He turned to Mrs Danvers.

'Now isn't that a charming invitation?' he said. 'I've been asked to stay to tea? By heaven, Danny, I've a good mind to.'

I saw her flash a look of warning at him. I felt very uneasy. It was all wrong, this situation. It ought not to be happening at all.

'Well, perhaps you're right,' he said; 'it would have been a lot of fun, all the same. I suppose I had better be going, hadn't I? Come and have a look at my car.' He still spoke in a familiar rather offensive way. I did not want to go and look at his car. I felt very awkward and embarrassed. 'Come on,' he said, 'it's a jolly good little car. Much faster than anything poor old Max ever has.'

I could not think of an excuse. The whole business was so forced and stupid. I did not like it. And why did Mrs Danvers have to stand there looking at me with that smouldering look in her eyes?

'Where is the car?' I said feebly.

'Round the bend in the drive. I didn't drive to the door, I was afraid of disturbing you. I had some idea you probably rested in the afternoon.'

I said nothing. The lie was too obvious. We all walked out through the drawing-room and into the hall. I saw him glance over his shoulder and wink at Mrs Danvers. She did not wink in return. I hardly expected she would. She looked very hard and grim. Jasper frolicked out on to the drive. He seemed delighted with the sudden appearance of this visitor whom he appeared to know so well.

'I left my cap in the car, I believe,' said the man, pretending to glance round the hall. 'As a matter of fact, I didn't come in this way. I slipped round and bearded Danny in her den. Coming out to see the car too?'

He looked inquiringly at Mrs Danvers. She hesitated, watching me out of the tail of her eye.

'No,' she said. 'No, I don't think I'll come out now. Good-bye, Mr Jack.'

He seized her hand and shook it heartily. 'Good-bye, Danny: take care of yourself. You know where to get in touch with me always. It's done me a power of good to see you again.' He walked out on to the drive, Jasper dancing at his heels, and I followed him slowly, feeling very uncomfortable still.

'Dear old Manderley,' he said, looking up at the windows. 'The place hasn't changed much. I suppose Danny sees to that. What a wonderful woman she is, eh?'

'Yes, she's very efficient,' I said.

'And what do you think of it all? Like being buried down here?'

'I'm very fond of Manderley,' I said stiffly.

'Weren't you living somewhere down in the south of France when Max met you? Monte, wasn't it? I used to know Monte well.'

'Yes, I was in Monte Carlo,' I said.

We had come to his car now. A green sports thing, typical of its owner.

'What do you think of it?' he said.

'Very nice,' I said, politely.

'Come for a run to the lodge gates?' he said.

'No, I don't think I will,' I said. 'I'm rather tired.'

'You don't think it would look too good for the mistress of Manderley to be seen driving with someone like me, is that it?' he said, and he laughed, shaking his head at me.

'Oh, no,' I said, turning rather red. 'No, really.'

He went on looking me up and down in his amused way with those familiar, unpleasant blue eyes. I felt like a barmaid.

'Oh, well,' he said, 'we mustn't lead the bride astray, must we, Jasper? It wouldn't do at all.' He reached for his cap, and an enormous pair of motoring gloves. He threw his cigarette away on the drive.

'Good-bye,' he said, holding out his hand; 'it's been a lot of fun meeting you.'

'Good-bye,' I said.

'By the way,' he said carelessly, 'it would be very sporting and grand of you if you did not mention this little visit of mine to Max? He doesn't exactly approve of me, I'm afraid; I don't know why, and it might get poor old Danny into trouble.'

'No,' I said awkwardly. 'No, all right.'

'That's very sporting of you. Sure you won't change your mind and come for a run?'

'No, I don't think I will, if you don't mind.'

'Bye-bye, then. Perhaps I'll come and look you up one day. Get down, Jasper, you devil, you'll scratch my paint. I say, I call it a damn shame Max going up to London and leaving you alone like this!'

'I don't mind. I like being alone,' I said.

'Do you, by Jove? What an extraordinary thing. It's all wrong, you know. Against nature. How long have you been married? Three months, isn't it?'

'About that,' I said.

'I say, I wish I'd got a bride of three months waiting for me at home! I'm a poor lonesome bachelor.' He laughed again, and pulled his cap down over his eyes. 'Fare you well,' he said, starting up the engine, and the car shot down the drive snorting explosive fury from the exhaust, while Jasper stood looking after it, his ears drooping, his tail between his legs.

'Oh, come on, Jasper,' I said, 'don't be so idiotic.' I walked slowly back to the house. Mrs Danvers had disappeared. I stood in the hall and rang the bell. Nothing happened for about five minutes. I rang again. Presently Alice appeared, her face rather aggrieved. 'Yes, Madam?' she said.

'Oh, Alice,' I said, 'isn't Robert there? I rather fancied my tea out under the chestnut tree.'

'Robert went to the post this afternoon, and isn't back yet, Madam,' said Alice. 'Mrs Danvers gave him to understand you would be late for tea. Frith is out too of course. If you want your tea now I can get it for you. I don't think it's quite half past four yet.'

'Oh, it doesn't matter, Alice. I'll wait till Robert comes back,' I said. I supposed when Maxim was away things automatically became slack. I had never known Frith and Robert to be out at the same time. It was Frith's day of course. And Mrs Danvers had sent Robert to the post. And I myself was understood to have gone for a long walk. That man Favell had chosen his time well to pay his call on Mrs Danvers. It was almost too well chosen. There was something not right about it, I was certain of that. And then he had asked me not to say anything to Maxim. It was all very awkward. I did not want to get Mrs Danvers into trouble or make any sort of scene. More important still I did not want to worry Maxim.

I wondered who he was, this man Favell. He had called Maxim 'Max'. No one ever called him Max. I had seen it written once, on the fly-leaf of a book, the letters thin and slanting, curiously pointed, the tail of the M very definite, very long. I thought there was only one person who had ever called him Max . . .

As I stood there in the hall, undecided about my tea, wondering what to do, the thought suddenly came to me that perhaps Mrs Danvers was dishonest, that all this time she was engaged in some business behind Maxim's back, and coming back early as I had today I had discovered her and this man, an accomplice, who had then bluffed his way out by pretending to be familiar with the house and with Maxim. I wondered what they had been doing in the west wing. Why had they closed the shutters when they saw me on the lawn? I was filled with vague disquiet. Frith and Robert had been away. The maids were generally in their bedrooms changing during the afternoon. Mrs Danvers would have the run of the place. Supposing this man was a thief, and Mrs Danvers was in his pay? There were valuable things in the west wing. I had a sudden rather terrifying impulse to creep upstairs now to the west wing and go into those rooms and see for myself.

Robert was not yet back. I would just have time before tea. I hesitated, glancing at the gallery. The house seemed very still and quiet. The servants were all in their own quarters beyond the kitchen. Jasper lapped noisily at his drinking bowl below the stairs, the sound echoing in the great stone hall. I began to walk upstairs. My heart was beating in a queer excited way.

14

I FOUND MYSELF in the corridor where I had stood that first morning. I had not been there since, nor had I wished to go. The sun streamed in from the window in the alcove and made gold patterns on the dark panelling.

There was no sound at all. I was aware of the same musty, unused smell that had been before. I was uncertain which way to go. The plan of the rooms was not familiar to me. I remembered then that last time Mrs Danvers had come out of a door here, just behind me, and it seemed to me that the position of the room would make it the one I wanted, whose windows looked out upon the lawns to the sea. I turned the handle of the door and went inside. It was dark of course, because of the shutters. I felt for the electric light switch on the wall and turned it on. I was standing in a little ante-room, a dressing-room I judged, with big wardrobes round the wall, and at the end of this room was another door, open, leading to a larger room. I went through to this room, and turned on the light. My first impression was one of shock because the room was fully furnished, as though in use.

I had expected to see chairs and tables swathed in dust-sheets, and dust-sheets too over the great double bed against the wall. Nothing was covered up. There were brushes and combs on the dressing-table, scent, and powder. The bed was made up, I saw the gleam of white linen on the pillow-case, and the tip of a blanket beneath the quilted coverlet. There were flowers on the dressing-table and on the table beside the bed. Flowers too on the carved mantelpiece. A satin dressing-gown lay on a chair, and a pair of bedroom slippers beneath. For one desperate moment I thought that something had happened to my brain, that I was seeing back into Time, and looking upon the room as it used to be, before she died ... In a minute Rebecca herself would come back into the room, sit down before the looking-glass at her dressing-table, humming a tune, reach for her comb and run it through her hair. If she sat there I should see her reflection in the glass and she would see me too, standing like this by the door. Nothing happened. I went on standing there, waiting for something to happen. It was the clock ticking on the wall that brought me to reality again. The hands stood at twenty-five past four. My watch said the same. There was something sane and comforting about the ticking of the clock. It reminded me of the present, and that tea would soon be ready for me on the lawn. I walked slowly into the middle of the room. No, it was not used. It was not lived in any more. Even the flowers could not destroy the musty smell. The curtains were drawn and the shutters were closed. Rebecca would never come back to the room again. Even if Mrs Danvers did put the flowers on the mantelpiece and the sheets upon the bed, they would not bring her back. She was dead. She had been dead now for a year. She lay buried in the crypt of the church with all the other dead de Winters.

I could hear the sound of the sea very plainly. I went to the window and swung back the shutter. Yes, I was standing at the same window where Favell and Mrs Danvers had stood, half an hour ago. The long shaft of daylight made the electric light look false and yellow. I opened the shutter a little more. The daylight cast a white beam upon the bed. It shone upon the nighdress-case, lying on the pillow. It shone on the glass top of the dressing-table, on the brushes, and on the scent bottles.

The daylight gave an even greater air of reality to the room. When the shutter was closed and it had been lit by electricity the room had more the appearance of a setting on the stage. The scene set between performances. The curtain having fallen for the night, the evening over, and the first act set for tomorrow's matinée. But the daylight made the room vivid and alive. I forgot the musty smell and the drawn curtains of the other windows. I was a guest again. An uninvited guest. I had strolled into my hostess's bedroom by mistake. Those were her brushes on the dressing-table, that was her dressing-gown and slippers laid out upon the chair.

I realized for the first time since I had come into the room that my legs were trembling, weak as straw. I sat down on the stool by the dressing-table. My heart no longer beat in a strange excited way. It felt as heavy as lead. I looked about me in the room with a sort of dumb stupidity. Yes, it was a beautiful room. Mrs Danvers had not exaggerated that first evening. It was the most beautiful room in the house. That exquisite mantelpiece, the ceiling, the carved bedstead, and the curtain hangings, even the clock on the wall and the candlesticks up on the dressing-table beside me, all were things I would have loved and almost worshipped had they been mine. They were not mine though. They belonged to somebody else. I put out my hand and touched the brushes. One was more worn than its fellow. I understood it well. There was always one brush that had the greater use. Often you forgot to use the other, and when they were taken to be washed there was one that was still quite clean and untouched. How white and thin my face looked in the glass, my hair hanging lank and straight. Did I always look like this? Surely I had more colour as a rule? The reflection stared back at me, sallow and plain.

I got up from the stool and went and touched the dressing-gown on the chair. I picked up the slippers and held them in my hand. I was aware of a growing sense of horror, of horror turning to despair. I touched the quilt on the bed, traced with my fingers the monogram on the nightdress-case, R de W, interwoven and interlaced. The letters were corded and strong against the golden satin material. The nightdress was inside the case, thin as gossamer, apricot in colour. I touched it, drew it out from the case, put it against my face. It was cold, quite cold. But there was a dim mustiness about it still where the scent had been. The scent of the white azaleas. I folded it, and put it back into the case, and as I did so I noticed with a sick dull aching in my heart that there were creases in the nightdress, the texture was ruffled, it had not been touched or laundered since it was last worn.

On a sudden impulse I moved away from the bed and went back to the little ante-room where I had seen the wardrobes. I opened one of them. It was as I thought. The wardrobe was full of clothes. There were evening dresses here, I caught the shimmer of silver over the top of the white bags that enfolded them. There was a piece of gold brocade. There, next to it, was velvet, wine-coloured and soft. There was a train of white satin, dripping on the floor of the wardrobe. Peeping out from a piece of tissue paper on a shelf above was an ostrich feather fan.

The wardrobe smelt stuffy, queer. The azalea scent, so fragrant and delicate in the air, had turned stale inside the wardrobe, tarnishing the silver dresses and the brocade, and the breath of it wafted towards me now from the open doors, faded and old. I shut the doors. I went back into the bedroom once again. The gleam of light from the shutter still shone white and clear on the golden coverlet of the bed, picking out clearly and distinctly the tall sloping R of the monogram.

Then I heard a step behind me and turning round I saw Mrs Danvers. I shall never forget the expression on her face. Triumphant, gloating, excited in a strange unhealthy way. I felt very frightened.

'Is anything the matter, Madam?' she said.

I tried to smile at her, and could not. I tried to speak.

'Are you feeling unwell?' she said, coming nearer to me, speaking very softly. I backed away from her. I believe if she had come any closer to me I should have fainted. I felt her breath on my face.

'I'm all right, Mrs Danvers,' I said, after a moment, 'I did not expect to see you. The fact is, I was looking up at the windows from the lawn. I noticed one of the shutters was not quite closed. I came up to see if I could fasten it.'

'I will fasten it,' she said, and she went silently across the room and clamped back the shutter. The daylight had gone. The room looked unreal again in the false yellow light. Unreal and ghastly.

Mrs Danvers came back and stood beside me. She smiled, and her manner, instead of being still and unbending as it usually was, became startlingly familiar, fawning even.

'Why did you tell me the shutter was open?' she asked. 'I closed it before I left the room. You opened it yourself, didn't you, now? You wanted to see the room. Why have you never asked me to show it to you before? I was ready to show it to you every day. You had only to ask me.'

I wanted to run away, but I could not move. I went on watching her eyes.

'Now you are here, let me show you everything,' she said, her voice ingratiating and sweet as honey, horrible, false. 'I know you want to see it all, you've wanted to for a long time, and you were too shy to ask. It's a lovely room, isn't it? The loveliest room you have ever seen.'

She took hold of my arm, and walked me towards the bed. I could not resist her, I was like a dumb thing. The touch of her hand made me shudder. And her voice was low and intimate, a voice I hated and feared.

'That was her bed. It's a beautiful bed, isn't it? I keep the golden coverlet on it always, it was her favourite. Here is her nightdress inside the case. You've been touching it, haven't you? This was the nightdress she was wearing for the last time, before she died. Would you like to touch it again?' She took the night-dress from the case and held it before me. 'Feel it, hold it,' she said, 'how soft and light it is, isn't it? I haven't washed it since she wore it for the last time. I put it out like this, and the dressing-gown and slippers, just as I put them out for her the night she never came back, the night she was drowned.' She folded up the nightgown and put it back in the case. 'I did everything for her, you know,' she said, taking my arm again, leading me to the dressing-gown and slippers. 'We tried maid after maid but not one of them suited. "You maid me better than anyone, Danny," she used to say, "I won't have anyone but you." Look, this is her dressing-gown. She was much taller than you, you can see by the length. Put it up against you. It comes down to your ankles. She had a beautiful figure. These are her slippers. "Throw me my slips, Danny," she used to say. She had little feet for her height. Put your hands inside the slippers. They are quite small and narrow, aren't they?'

She forced the slippers over my hands, smiling all the while, watching my eyes. 'You never would have thought she was so tall, would you?' she said, 'these slippers would fit a tiny foot. She was so slim too. You would forget her height, until she stood beside you. She was every bit as tall as me. But lying there in bed she looked quite a slip of a thing, with her mass of dark hair, standing out from her face like a halo.'

She put the slippers back on the floor, and laid the dressing-gown on the chair. 'You've seen her brushes, haven't you?' she said, taking me to the dressing-table; 'there they are, just as she used them, unwashed and untouched. I used to brush her hair for her every evening. "Come on, Danny, hair-drill," she would say, and I'd stand behind her by the stool here, and brush away for twenty minutes at a time. She only wore it short the last few years, you know. It came down below the waist, when she was first married. Mr de Winter used to brush it for her then. I've come into this room time and time again and seen him, in his shirt sleeves, with the two brushes in his hand. "Harder, Max, harder," she would say, laughing up at him, and he would do as she told him. They would be dressing for dinner, you see, and the house filled with guests. "Here, I shall be late," he would say, throwing the brushes to me, and laughing back at her. He was always laughing and gay then.' She paused, her hand still resting on my arm.

'Everyone was angry with her when she cut her hair,' she said, 'but she did not care. "It's nothing to do with anyone but myself," she would say. And of course short hair was much easier for riding and sailing. She was painted on horseback, you know. A famous artist did it. The picture hung in the Academy. Did you ever see it?'

I shook my head. 'No,' I said. 'No.'

'I understood it was the picture of the year,' she went on, 'but Mr de Winter did not care for it, and would not have it at Manderley. I don't think he considered it did her justice. You would like to see her clothes, wouldn't you?' She did not wait for my answer. She led me to the little ante-room and opened the wardrobes, one by one.

'I keep her furs in here,' she said, 'the moths have not got to them yet, and I doubt if they ever will. I'm too careful. Feel that sable wrap. That was a Christmas present from Mr de Winter. She told me the cost once, but I've forgotten it now. This chinchilla she wore in the evenings mostly. Round her shoulders, very often, when the evenings were cold. This wardrobe here is full of her evening clothes. You opened it, didn't you? The latch is not quite closed. I believe Mr de Winter liked her to wear silver mostly. But of course she could wear anything, stand any colour.

She looked beautiful in this velvet. Put it against your face. It's soft, isn't it? You can feel it, can't you? The scent is still fresh, isn't it? You could almost imagine she had only just taken it off. I would always know when she had been before me in a room. There would be a little whiff of her scent in the room. These are her underclothes, in this drawer. This pink set here she had never worn. She was wearing slacks of course and a shirt when she died. They were torn from her body in the water though. There was nothing on the body when it was found, all those weeks afterwards.'

Her fingers tightened on my arm. She bent down to me, her skull's face close, her dark eyes searching mine. 'The rocks had battered her to bits, you know,' she whispered, 'her beautiful face unrecognizable, and both arms gone. Mr de Winter identified her. He went up to Edgecoombe to do it. He went quite alone. He was very ill at the time but he would go. No one could stop him. Not even Mr Crawley.'

She paused, her eyes never leaving my face. 'I shall always blame myself for the accident,' she said, 'it was my fault for being out that evening. I had gone into Kerrith for the afternoon and stayed there late, as Mrs de Winter was up in London and not expected back until much later. That's why I did not hurry back. When I came in, about half past nine, I heard she had returned just before seven, had her dinner, and then went out again. Down to the beach of course. I felt worried then. It was blowing from the south-west. She would never have gone if I'd been in. She always listened to me. "I wouldn't go out this evening, it's not fit," I should have said, and she would have answered me "All right, Danny, you old fuss-pot." And we would have sat up here talking no doubt, she telling me all she had done in London, like she always did.'

My arm was bruised and numb from the pressure of her fingers. I could see how tightly the skin was stretched across her face, showing the cheek-bones. There were little patches of yellow beneath her ears.

'Mr de Winter had been dining with Mr Crawley down at his house,' she went on. 'I don't know what time he got back, I dare say it was after eleven. But it began to blow quite hard just before midnight, and she had not come back. I went downstairs, but there were no lights under the library door. I came upstairs again and knocked on the dressing-room door. Mr de Winter answered at once, "Who is it, what do you want?" he said. I told him I was worried about Mrs de Winter not being back. He waited a moment, and then he came and opened the door in his dressing-gown. "She's spending the night down at the cottage I expect," he said. "I should go to bed if I were you. She won't come back here to sleep if it goes on like this." He looked tired, and I did not like to disturb him. After all, she spent many nights at the cottage, and had sailed in every sort of weather. She might not even have gone for a sail, but just wanted the night at the cottage as a change after London. I said good night to Mr de Winter and went back to my room. I did not sleep though. I kept wondering what she was doing.'

She paused again. I did not want to hear any more. I wanted to get away from her, away from the room.

'I sat on my bed until half past five,' she said, 'then I couldn't wait there any longer. I got up and put on my coat and went down through the woods to the beach. It was getting light, but there was still a misty sort of rain falling, although the wind had dropped. When I got to the beach I saw the buoy there in the water and the dinghy, but the boat had gone . . .' It seemed to me that I could see the cove in the grey morning light, feel the thin drizzle on my face, and peering through the mist could make out, shadowy and indistinct, the low dark outline of the buoy.

Mrs Danvers loosened the pressure on my arm. Her hand fell back again to her side. Her voice lost all expression, became the hard mechanical voice of every day.

'One of the life-buoys was washed up at Kerrith in the afternoon,' she said, 'and another was found the next day by some crabbers on the rocks below the headland. Bits and pieces of rigging too would come in with the tide.' She turned away from me, and closed the chest of drawers. She straightened one of the pictures on the wall. She picked up a piece of fluff from the carpet. I stood watching her, not knowing what to do.

'You know now', she said, 'why Mr de Winter does not use these rooms any more. Listen to the sea.'

Even with the windows closed and the shutters fastened I could hear it; a low sullen murmur as the waves broke on the white shingle in the cove. The tide would be coming in fast now and running up the beach nearly to the stone cottage.

'He has not used these rooms since the night she was drowned,' she said. 'He had his things moved out from the dressing-room. We made up one of the rooms at the end of the corridor. I don't think he slept much even there. He used to sit in the armchair. There would be cigarette ash all round it in the morning. And in the daytime Frith would hear him in the library pacing up and down. Up and down, up and down.'

I too could see the ash on the floor beside the chair. I too could hear his footsteps; one, two, one, two, backwards and forwards across the library . . . Mrs Danvers closed the door softly between the bedroom and the ante-room where we were standing, and put out the light. I could not see the bed any more, nor the night-dress-case upon the pillow, nor the dressing-table, nor the slippers by the chair. She crossed the ante-room and put her hand on the knob of the door and stood waiting for me to follow her.

'I come to the rooms and dust them myself every day,' she said. 'If you want to come again you have only to tell me. Ring me on the house telephone. I shall understand. I don't allow the maids up here. No one ever comes but me.'

Her manner was fawning again, intimate and unpleasant. The smile on her face was a false, unnatural thing. 'Sometimes when Mr de Winter is away, and you feel lonely, you might like to come up to these rooms and sit here. You have only to tell me. They are such beautiful rooms. You would not think she had gone now for so long, would you, not by the way the rooms are kept? You would think she had just gone out for a little while and would be back in the evening.'

I forced a smile. I could not speak. My throat felt dry and tight.

'It's not only this room,' she said. 'It's in many rooms in the house. In the morning-room, in the hall, even in the little flower room. I feel her everywhere. You do too, don't you?'

She stared at me curiously. Her voice dropped to a whisper. 'Sometimes, when I walk along the corridor here, I fancy I hear her just behind me. That quick, light footstep. I could not mistake it anywhere. And in the minstrels' gallery above the hall. I've seen her leaning there, in the evenings in the old days, looking down at the hall below and calling to the dogs. I can fancy her there now from time to time. It's almost as though I catch the sound of her dress sweeping the stairs as she comes down to dinner.' She paused. She went on looking at me, watching my eyes. 'Do you think she can see us, talking to one another now?' she said slowly. 'Do you think the dead come back and watch the living?'

I swallowed. I dug my nails into my hands.

'I don't know,' I said. 'I don't know.' My voice sounded high-pitched and unnatural. Not my voice at all.

'Sometimes I wonder,' she whispered. 'Sometimes I wonder if she comes back here to Manderley and watches you and Mr de Winter together.'

We stood there by the door, staring at one another. I could not take my eyes away from hers. How dark and sombre they were in the white skull's face of hers, how malevolent, how full of hatred. Then she opened the door into the corridor. 'Robert is back now,' she said. 'He came back a quarter of an hour ago. He has orders to take your tea out under the chestnut tree.'

She stepped aside for me to pass. I stumbled out on to the corridor, not looking where I was going. I did not speak to her, I went down the stairs blindly, and turned the corner and pushed through the door that led to my own rooms in the east wing. I shut the door of my room and turned the key, and put the key in my pocket.

Then I lay down on my bed and closed my eyes. I felt deadly sick.

15

MAXIM RANG UP the next morning to say he would be back about seven. Frith took the message. Maxim did not ask to speak to me himself. I heard the telephone ring while I was at breakfast and I thought perhaps Frith would come into the dining-room and say 'Mr de Winter on the telephone, Madam.' I had put down my napkin and had risen to my feet. And then Frith came back into the dining-room and gave me the message.

He saw me push back my chair and go to the door. 'Mr de Winter has rung off, Madam,' he said, 'there was no message. Just that he would be back about seven.'

I sat down in my chair again and picked up my napkin. Frith must have thought me eager and stupid rushing across the dining-room.

'All right, Frith. Thank you,' I said.

I went on eating my eggs and bacon, Jasper at my feet, the old dog in her basket in the corner. I wondered what I should do with my day. I had slept badly; perhaps because I was alone in the room. I had been restless, waking up often, and when I glanced at my clock I saw the hands had scarcely moved. When I did fall asleep I had varied, wandering dreams. We were walking through woods, Maxim and I, and he was always just a little ahead of me. I could not keep up with him. Nor could I see his face. Just his figure, striding away in front of me all the time. I must have cried while I slept, for when I woke in the morning the pillow was damp. My eyes were heavy too, when I looked in the glass. I looked plain, unattractive. I rubbed a little rouge on my cheeks in a wretched attempt to give myself colour. But it made me worse. It gave me a false clown look. Perhaps I did not know the best way to put it on. I noticed Robert staring at me as I crossed the hall and went into breakfast.

About ten o'clock as I was crumbling some pieces for the birds on the terrace the telephone rang again. This time it was for me. Frith came and said Mrs Lacy wanted to speak to me.

'Good morning, Beatrice,' I said.

'Well, my dear, how are you?' she said, her telephone voice typical of herself, brisk, rather masculine, standing no nonsense, and then not waiting for my answer. 'I thought of motoring over this afternoon and looking up Gran. I'm lunching with people about twenty miles from you. Shall I come and pick you up and we'll go together? It's time you met the old lady, you know.'

'I'd like to very much, Beatrice,' I said.

'Splendid. Very well, then. I'll come along for you about half past three. Giles saw Maxim at the dinner. Poor food, he said, but excellent wine. All right, my dear, see you later.'

The click of the receiver, and she was gone. I wandered back into the garden. I was glad she had rung up and suggested the plan of going over to see the grandmother. It made something to look forward to, and broke the monotony of the day. The hours had seemed so long until seven o'clock. I did not feel in my holiday mood today, and I had no wish to go off with Jasper to the Happy Valley and come to the cove and throw stones in the water. The sense of freedom had departed, and the childish desire to run across the lawns in sand-shoes. I went and sat down with a book and *The Times* and my knitting in the rose-garden, domestic as a matron, yawning in the warm sun while the bees hummed amongst the flowers.

I tried to concentrate on the bald newspaper columns, and later to lose myself in the racy plot of the novel in my hands. I did not want to think of yesterday afternoon and Mrs Danvers. I tried to forget that she was in the house at this moment, perhaps looking down on me from one of the windows. And now and again, when I looked up from my book or glanced across the garden, I had the feeling I was not alone.

There were so many windows in Manderley, so many rooms that were never used by Maxim and myself that were empty now; dust-sheeted, silent, rooms that had been occupied in the old days when his father and his grandfather had been alive, when there had been much entertaining, many servants. It would be easy for

Mrs Danvers to open those doors softly and close them again, and then steal quietly across the shrouded room and look down upon me from behind the drawn curtains.

I should not know. Even if I turned in my chair and looked up at the windows I would not see her. I remembered a game I had played as a child that my friends next-door had called 'Grandmother's Steps' and myself 'Old Witch'. You had to stand at the end of the garden with your back turned to the rest, and one by one they crept nearer to you, advancing in short furtive fashion. Every few minutes you turned to look at them, and if you saw one of them moving the offender had to retire to the back line and begin again. But there was always one a little bolder than the rest, who came up very close, whose movement was impossible to detect, and as you waited there, your back turned, counting the regulation Ten, you knew, with a fatal terrifying certainty, that before long, before even the Ten was counted, this bold player would pounce upon you from behind, unheralded, unseen, with a scream of triumph. I felt as tense and expectant as I did then. I was playing 'Old Witch' with Mrs Danvers.

Lunch was a welcome break to the long morning. The calm efficiency of Frith, and Robert's rather foolish face, helped me more than my book and my newspaper had done. And at half past three, punctual to the moment, I heard the sound of Beatrice's car round the sweep of the drive and pull up at the steps before the house. I ran out to meet her, ready dressed, my gloves in my hand. 'Well, my dear, here I am, what a splendid day, isn't it?' She slammed the door of the car and came up the steps to meet me. She gave me a hard swift kiss, brushing me somewhere near the ear.

'You don't look well,' she said immediately, looking me up and down, 'much too thin in the face and no colour. What's wrong with you?'

'Nothing,' I said humbly, knowing the fault of my face too well. 'I'm not a person who ever has much colour.'

'Oh, bosh,' she replied, 'you looked quite different when I saw you before.'

'I expect the brown of Italy has worn off,' I said, getting into the car.

'H'mph,' she said shortly, 'you're as bad as Maxim. Can't stand any criticism about your health. Slam the door hard or it doesn't shut.' We started off down the drive, swerving at the corner, going rather too fast. 'You're not by any chance starting an infant, are you?' she said, turning her hawk-brown eyes upon me.

'No,' I said awkwardly. 'No, I don't think so.'

'No morning sickness or anything like that?'

'No.'

'Oh, well – of course it doesn't always follow. I never turned a hair when Roger was born. Felt as fit as a fiddle the whole nine months. I played golf the day before he arrived. There's nothing to be embarrassed about in the facts of nature, you know. If you have any suspicions you had better tell me.'

'No, really, Beatrice,' I said, 'there's nothing to tell.'

'I must say I do hope you will produce a son and heir before long. It would be so terribly good for Maxim. I hope you are doing nothing to prevent it.'

'Of course not,' I said. What an extraordinary conversation.

'Oh, don't be shocked,' she said, 'you must never mind what I say. After all, brides of today are up to everything. It's a damn nuisance if you want to hunt and you land yourself with an infant your first season. Quite enough to break a marriage up if you are both keen. Wouldn't matter in your case. Babies needn't interfere with sketching. How is the sketching, by the way?'

'I'm afraid I don't seem to do much,' I said.

'Oh, really? Nice weather, too, for sitting out of doors. You only need a camp-stool and a box of pencils, don't you? Tell me, were you interested in those books I sent you?'

'Yes, of course,' I said. 'It was a lovely present, Beatrice.'

She looked pleased. 'Glad you liked them,' she said.

The car sped along. She kept her foot permanently on the accelerator, and took every corner at an acute angle. Two motorists we passed looked out of their windows outraged as she swept by, and one pedestrian in a lane waved his stick at her. I felt rather hot for her. She did not seem to notice though. I crouched lower in my seat.

'Roger goes up to Oxford next term,' she said, 'heaven knows what he'll do with himself. Awful waste of time I think, and so

does Giles, but we couldn't think what else to do with him. Of
course he's just like Giles and myself. Thinks of nothing but
horses. What on earth does this car in front think it's doing? Why
don't you put out your hand, my good man? Really, some of
these people on the road today ought to be shot.'

We swerved into a main road, narrowly avoiding the car ahead
of us. 'Had any people down to stay?' she asked.

'No, we've been very quiet,' I said.

'Much better, too,' she said, 'awful bore, I always think, those
big parties. You won't find it alarming if you come to stay with
us. Very nice lot of people all round, and we all know one another
frightfully well. We dine in one another's houses, and have our
bridge, and don't bother with outsiders. You do play bridge,
don't you?'

'I'm not very good, Beatrice.'

'Oh, we shan't mind that. As long as you can play. I've no
patience with people who won't learn. What on earth can one
do with them between tea and dinner in the winter, and after
dinner? One can't just sit and talk.'

I wondered why. However, it was simpler not to say anything.

'It's quite amusing now Roger is a reasonable age,' she went
on, 'because he brings his friends to stay, and we have really good
fun. You ought to have been with us last Christmas. We had charades. My dear, it was the greatest fun. Giles was in his element.
He adores dressing-up, you know, and after a glass or two of
champagne he's the funniest thing you've ever seen. We often say
he's missed his vocation and ought to have been on the stage.'
I thought of Giles, and his large moon face, his horn spectacles.
I felt the sight of him being funny after champagne would embar-
rass me. 'He and another man, a great friend of ours, Dickie
Marsh, dressed up as women and sang a duet. What exactly it had
to do with the word in the charade nobody knew, but it did not
matter. We all roared.'

I smiled politely. 'Fancy, how funny,' I said.

I saw them all rocking from side to side in Beatrice's drawing-
room. All these friends who knew one another so well. Roger
would look like Giles. Beatrice was laughing again at the
memory. 'Poor Giles,' she said. 'I shall never forget his face when

Dick squirted the soda syphon down his back. We were all in fits.'

I had an uneasy feeling we might be asked to spend the approaching Christmas with Beatrice. Perhaps I could have influenza.

'Of course our acting was never very ambitious,' she said. 'It was just a lot of fun amongst ourselves. At Manderley now, there is scope for a really fine show. I remember a pageant they had there, some years ago. People from London came down to do it. Of course that type of thing needs terrific organization.'

'Yes,' I said.

She was silent for a while, and drove without speaking.

'How is Maxim?' she said, after a moment.

'Very well, thanks,' I said.

'Quite cheerful and happy?'

'Oh, yes. Yes, rather.'

A narrow village street engaged her attention. I wondered whether I should tell her about Mrs Danvers. About the man Favell. I did not want her to make a blunder though, and perhaps tell Maxim.

'Beatrice,' I said, deciding upon it, 'have you ever heard of someone called Favell? Jack Favell?'

'Jack Favell,' she repeated. 'Yes, I do know the name. Wait a minute. Jack Favell. Of course. An awful bounder. I met him once, ages ago.'

'He came to Manderley yesterday to see Mrs Danvers,' I said.

'Really? Oh, well, perhaps he would . . .'

'Why?' I said.

'I rather think he was Rebecca's cousin,' she said.

I was very surprised. That man her relation? It was not my idea of the sort of cousin Rebecca would have. Jack Favell her cousin. 'Oh,' I said. 'Oh, I hadn't realized that.'

'He probably used to go to Manderley a lot,' said Beatrice. 'I don't know. I couldn't tell you. I was very seldom there.' Her manner was abrupt. It gave me the impression she did not want to pursue the subject.

'I did not take to him much,' I said.

'No,' said Beatrice. 'I don't blame you.'

I waited, but she did not say any more. I thought it wiser not to tell her how Favell had asked me to keep the visit a secret. It might lead to some complication. Besides, we were just coming to our destination. A pair of white gates and a smooth gravel drive.

'Don't forget the old lady is nearly blind,' said Beatrice, 'and she's not very bright these days. I telephoned to the nurse that we were coming, so everything will be all right.'

The house was large, red-bricked, and gabled. Late Victorian I supposed. Not an attractive house. I could tell in a glance it was the sort of house that was aggressively well-kept by a big staff. And all for one old lady who was nearly blind.

A trim parlour-maid opened the door.

'Good afternoon, Norah, how are you?' said Beatrice.

'Very well, thank you, Madam. I hope you are keeping well?'

'Oh, yes, we are all flourishing. How has the old lady been, Norah?'

'Rather mixed, Madam. She has one good day, and then a bad. She's not too bad in herself, you know. She will be pleased to see you I'm sure.' She glanced curiously at me.

'This is Mrs Maxim,' said Beatrice.

'Yes, Madam. How do you do,' said Norah.

We went through a narrow hall and a drawing-room crowded with furniture to a veranda facing a square clipped lawn. There were many bright geraniums in stone vases on the steps of the veranda. In the corner was a bath chair. Beatrice's grandmother was sitting there, propped up with pillows and surrounded by shawls. When we came close to her I saw that she had a strong, rather uncanny, resemblance to Maxim. That was what Maxim would look like, if he was very old, if he was blind. The nurse by her side got up from her chair and put a mark in the book she was reading aloud. She smiled at Beatrice.

'How are you, Mrs Lacy?' she said.

Beatrice shook hands with her and introduced me. 'The old lady looks all right,' she said. 'I don't know how she does it, at eighty-six. Here we are, Gran,' she said, raising her voice, 'arrived safe and sound.'

The grandmother looked in our direction. 'Dear Bee,' she said, 'how sweet of you to come and visit me. We're so dull here, nothing for you to do.'

Beatrice leant over her and kissed her. 'I've brought Maxim's wife over to see you,' she said, 'she wanted to come and see you before, but she and Maxim have been so busy.'

Beatrice prodded me in the back. 'Kiss her,' she murmured. I too bent down and kissed her on the cheek.

The grandmother touched my face with her fingers. 'You nice thing,' she said, 'so good of you to come. I'm very pleased to see you, dear. You ought to have brought Maxim with you.'

'Maxim is in London,' I said, 'he's coming back tonight.'

'You might bring him next time,' she said. 'Sit down, dear, in this chair, where I can see you. And Bee, come the other side. How is dear Roger? He's a naughty boy, he doesn't come and see me.'

'He shall come during August,' shouted Beatrice; 'he's leaving Eton, you know, he's going up to Oxford.'

'Oh, dear, he'll be quite a young man, I shan't know him.'

'He's taller than Giles now,' said Beatrice.

She went on, telling her about Giles, and Roger, and the horses, and the dogs. The nurse brought out some knitting, and clicked her needles sharply. She turned to me, very bright, very cheerful.

'How are you liking Manderley, Mrs de Winter?'

'Very much, thank you,' I said.

'It's a beautiful spot, isn't it?' she said, the needles jabbing one another. 'Of course we don't get over there now, she's not up to it. I am sorry, I used to love our days at Manderley.'

'You must come over yourself some time,' I said.

'Thank you, I should love to. Mr de Winter is well, I suppose?'

'Yes, very well.'

'You spent your honeymoon in Italy, didn't you? We were so pleased with the picture postcard Mr de Winter sent.'

I wondered whether she used 'we' in the royal sense, or if she meant that Maxim's grandmother and herself were one.

'Did he send one? I can't remember.'

'Oh, yes, it was quite an excitement. We love anything like that. We keep a scrap-book you know, and paste anything to do with the family inside it. Anything pleasant, that is.'

'How nice,' I said.

I caught snatches of Beatrice's conversation on the other side. 'We had to put old Marksman down,' she was saying. 'You remember old Marksman? The best hunter I ever had.'

'Oh, dear, not old Marksman?' said her grandmother.

'Yes, poor old man. Got blind in both eyes, you know.'

'Poor Marksman,' echoed the old lady.

I thought perhaps it was not very tactful to talk about blindness, and I glanced at the nurse. She was still busy clicking her needles.

'Do you hunt, Mrs de Winter?' she said.

'No, I'm afraid I don't,' I said.

'Perhaps you will come to it. We are all very fond of hunting in this part of the world.'

'Yes.'

'Mrs de Winter is very keen on art,' said Beatrice to the nurse. 'I tell her there are heaps of spots in Manderley that would make very jolly pictures.'

'Oh rather,' agreed the nurse, pausing a moment from the fury of knitting. 'What a nice hobby. I had a friend who was a wonder with her pencil. We went to Provence together one Easter and she did such pretty sketches.'

'How nice,' I said.

'We're talking about sketching,' shouted Beatrice to her grandmother, 'you did not know we had an artist in the family, did you?'

'Who's an artist?' said the old lady. 'I don't know any.'

'Your new granddaughter,' said Beatrice: 'you ask her what I gave her for a wedding present.'

I smiled, waiting to be asked. The old lady turned her head in my direction. 'What's Bee talking about?' she said. 'I did not know you were an artist. We've never had any artists in the family.'

'Beatrice was joking,' I said: 'of course I'm not an artist really. I like drawing as a hobby. I've never had any lessons. Beatrice gave me some lovely books as a present.'

'Oh,' she said, rather bewildered. 'Beatrice gave you some books, did she? Rather like taking coals to Newcastle, wasn't it? There are so many books in the library at Manderley.' She laughed heartily. We all joined in her joke. I hoped the subject would be left at that, but Beatrice had to harp on it. 'You don't understand, Gran,' she said. 'They weren't ordinary books. They were volumes on art. Four of 'em.'

The nurse leant forward to add her tribute. 'Mrs Lacy is trying to explain that Mrs de Winter is very fond of sketching as a hobby. So she gave her four fine volumes all about painting as a wedding present.'

'What a funny thing to do,' said the grandmother. 'I don't think much of books for a wedding present. Nobody ever gave me any books when I was married. I should never have read them if they had.'

She laughed again. Beatrice looked rather offended. I smiled at her to show my sympathy. I don't think she saw. The nurse resumed her knitting.

'I want my tea,' said the old lady querulously, 'isn't it half past four yet? Why doesn't Norah bring the tea?'

'What? Hungry again after our big lunch?' said the nurse, rising to her feet and smiling brightly at her charge.

I felt rather exhausted, and wondered, rather shocked at my callous thought, why old people were sometimes such a strain. Worse than young children or puppies because one had to be polite. I sat with my hands in my lap ready to agree with what anybody said. The nurse was thumping the pillows and arranging the shawls.

Maxim's grandmother suffered her in patience. She closed her eyes as though she too were tired. She looked more like Maxim than ever. I knew how she must have looked when she was young, tall, and handsome, going round to the stables at Manderley with sugar in her pockets, holding her trailing skirt out of the mud. I pictured the nipped-in waist, the high collar, I heard her ordering the carriage for two o'clock. That was all finished now for her, all gone. Her husband had been dead for forty years, her son for fifteen. She had to live in this bright, red gabled house with the nurse until it was time for her to die. I thought how little we know about the feelings of old people. Children we understand, their fears and hopes and make-believe. I was a child yesterday. I had not forgotten. But Maxim's grandmother, sitting there in her shawl with her poor blind eyes, what did she feel, what was she thinking? Did she know that Beatrice was yawning and glancing at her watch? Did she guess that we had come to visit her because we felt it right, it was a duty, so that when she got home afterwards Beatrice would be able to say, 'Well, that clears my conscience for three months'?

Did she ever think about Manderley? Did she remember sitting at the dining-room table, where I sat? Did she too have tea under the chestnut tree? Or was it all forgotten and laid aside, and was there nothing left behind that calm, pale face of hers but little aches and little strange discomforts, a blurred thankfulness when the sun shone, a tremor when the wind blew cold?

I wished that I could lay my hands upon her face and take the years away. I wished I could see her young, as she was once, with colour in her cheeks and chestnut hair, alert and active as Beatrice by her side, talking as she did about hunting, hounds, and horses. Not sitting there with her eyes closed while the nurse thumped the pillows behind her head.

'We've got a treat today, you know,' said the nurse, 'water-cress sandwiches for tea. We love water-cress, don't we?'

'Is it water-cress day?' said Maxim's grandmother, raising her head from the pillows, and looking towards the door. 'You did not tell me that. Why does not Norah bring in the tea?'

'I wouldn't have your job, Sister, for a thousand a day,' said Beatrice *sotto voce* to the nurse.

'Oh, I'm used to it, Mrs Lacy,' smiled the nurse; 'it's very comfortable here, you know. Of course we have our bad days but they might be a great deal worse. She's very easy, not like some patients. The staff are obliging too, that's really the main thing. Here comes Norah.'

The parlour-maid brought out a little gate-legged table and a snowy cloth.

'What a time you've been, Norah,' grumbled the old lady.

'It's only just turned the half hour, Madam,' said Norah in a special voice, bright and cheerful like the nurse. I wondered if Maxim's grandmother realized that people spoke to her in this way. I wondered when they had done so for the first time, and if she had noticed then. Perhaps she had said to herself, 'They think

I'm getting old, how very ridiculous', and then little by little she had become accustomed to it, and now it was as though they had always done so, it was part of her background. But the young woman with the chestnut hair and the narrow waist who gave sugar to the horses, where was she?

We drew our chairs to the gate-legged table and began to eat the water-cress sandwiches. The nurse prepared special ones for the old lady.

'There, now, isn't that a treat?' she said.

I saw a slow smile pass over the calm, placid face. 'I like water-cress day,' she said.

The tea was scalding, much too hot to drink. The nurse drank hers in tiny sips.

'Boiling water today,' she said, nodding at Beatrice. 'I have such trouble about it. They will let the tea stew. I've told them time and time again about it. They will not listen.'

'Oh, they're all the same,' said Beatrice. 'I've given it up as a bad job.' The old lady stirred hers with a spoon, her eyes very far and distant. I wished I knew what she was thinking about.

'Did you have fine weather in Italy?' said the nurse.

'Yes, it was very warm,' I said.

Beatrice turned to her grandmother. 'They had lovely weather in Italy for their honeymoon, she says. Maxim got quite sunburnt.'

'Why isn't Maxim here today?' said the old lady.

'We told you, darling, Maxim had to go to London,' said Beatrice impatiently. 'Some dinner, you know. Giles went too.'

'Oh, I see. Why did you say Maxim was in Italy?'

'He was in Italy, Gran. In April. They're back at Manderley now.' She glanced at the nurse, shrugging her shoulders.

'Mr and Mrs de Winter are in Manderley now,' repeated the nurse.

'It's been lovely there this month,' I said, drawing nearer to Maxim's grandmother. 'The roses are in bloom now. I wish I had brought you some.'

'Yes, I like roses,' she said vaguely, and then peering closer at me with her dim blue eyes. 'Are you staying at Manderley too?'

I swallowed. There was a slight pause. Then Beatrice broke in

with her loud, impatient voice, 'Gran, darling, you know perfectly well she lives there now. She and Maxim are married.'

I noticed the nurse put down her cup of tea and glance swiftly
at the old lady. She had relaxed against the pillows, plucking at
her shawl, and her mouth began to tremble. 'You talk too much,
all of you. I don't understand.' Then she looked across at me, a
frown on her face, and began shaking her head. 'Who are you, my
dear, I haven't seen you before? I don't know your face. I don't
remember you at Manderley. Bee, who is this child? Why did
not Maxim bring Rebecca? I'm so fond of Rebecca. Where is
dear Rebecca?'

There was a long pause, a moment of agony. I felt my cheeks
grow scarlet. The nurse got to her feet very quickly and went to
the bath chair.

'I want Rebecca,' repeated the old lady, 'what have you done
with Rebecca?' Beatrice rose clumsily from the table, shaking the
cups and saucers. She too had turned very red, and her mouth
twitched.

'I think you'd better go, Mrs Lacy,' said the nurse, rather pink
and flustered. 'She's looking a little tired, and when she wanders
like this it sometimes lasts a few hours. She does get excited like
this from time to time. It's very unfortunate it should happen
today. I'm sure you will understand, Mrs de Winter?' She turned
apologetically to me.

'Of course,' I said quickly, 'it's much better we should go.'

Beatrice and I groped for our bags and gloves. The nurse
had turned to her patient again. 'Now, what's all this about?
Do you want your nice water-cress sandwich that I've cut for
you?'

'Where is Rebecca? Why did not Maxim come and bring
Rebecca?' replied the thin, querulous voice.

We went through the drawing-room to the hall and let ourselves out of the front door. Beatrice started up the car without
a word. We drove down the smooth gravel drive and out of the
white gates.

I stared straight in front of me down the road. I did not mind
for myself. I should not have cared if I had been alone. I minded
for Beatrice.

The whole thing had been so wretched and awkward for Beatrice.

She spoke to me when we turned out of the village 'My dear,' she began, 'I'm so dreadfully sorry. I don't know what to say.'

'Don't be absurd, Beatrice,' I said hurriedly, 'it doesn't matter a bit. It's absolutely all right.'

'I had no idea she would do that,' said Beatrice. 'I would never have dreamt of taking you to see her. I'm so frightfully sorry.'

'There's nothing to be sorry about. Please don't say any more.'

'I can't make it out. She knew all about you. I wrote and told her, and so did Maxim. She was so interested in the wedding abroad.'

'You forget how old she is,' I said. 'Why should she remember that? She doesn't connect me with Maxim. She only connects him with Rebecca.' We went on driving in silence. It was a relief to be in the car again. I did not mind the jerky motion and the swaying corners.

'I'd forgotten she was so fond of Rebecca,' said Beatrice slowly, 'I was a fool not to expect something like this. I don't believe she ever took it in properly about the accident. Oh, Lord, what a ghastly afternoon. What on earth will you think of me?'

'Please, Beatrice, don't. I tell you I don't mind.'

'Rebecca made a great fuss of her always. And she used to have the old lady over to Manderley. Poor darling Gran was much more alert then. She used to rock with laughter at whatever Rebecca said. Of course she was always very amusing, and the old lady loved that. She had an amazing gift, Rebecca I mean, of being attractive to people; men, women, children, dogs. I suppose the old lady has never forgotten her. My dear, you won't thank me for this afternoon.'

'I don't mind, I don't mind,' I repeated mechanically. If only Beatrice could leave the subject alone. It did not interest me. What did it matter after all? What did anything matter?

'Giles will be very upset,' said Beatrice. 'He will blame me for taking you over. "What an idiotic thing to do, Bee." I can hear him saying it. I shall get into a fine row.'

'Don't say anything about it,' I said. 'I would much rather it was forgotten. The story will only get repeated and exaggerated.'

'Giles will know something is wrong from my face. I never have been able to hide anything from him.'

I was silent. I knew how the story would be tossed about in their immediate circle of friends. I could imagine the little crowd at Sunday lunch. The round eyes, the eager ears, and the gasps and exclamations—

'My Lord, how awful, what on earth did you do?' and then, 'How did she take it? How terribly embarrassing for everyone!'

The only thing that mattered to me was that Maxim should never come to hear of it. One day I might tell Frank Crawley, but not yet, not for quite a while.

It was not long before we came to the high-road at the top of the hill. In the distance I could see the first grey roofs of Kerrith, while to the right, in a hollow, lay the deep woods of Manderley and the sea beyond.

'Are you in a frightful hurry to get home?' said Beatrice.

'No,' I said. 'I don't think so. Why?'

'Would you think me a perfect pig if I dropped you at the lodge gates? If I drive like hell now I shall just be in time to meet Giles by the London train, and it will save him taking the station taxi.'

'Of course,' I said. 'I can walk down the drive.'

'Thanks awfully,' she said gratefully.

I felt the afternoon had been too much for her. She wanted to be alone again, and did not want to face another belated tea at Manderley.

I got out of the car at the lodge gates and we kissed goodbye.

'Put on some weight next time I see you,' she said; 'it doesn't suit you to be so thin. Give Maxim my love, and forgive me for today.' She vanished in a cloud of dust and I turned in down the drive.

I wondered if it had altered much since Maxim's grandmother had driven down it in her carriage. She had ridden here as a young woman, she had smiled at the woman at the lodge as I did now. And in her day the lodge-keeper's wife had curtseyed, sweeping the path with her full wide skirt. This woman nodded to me briefly, and then called to her little boy, who was grubbing with some kittens at the back. Maxim's grandmother had bowed her head to avoid the sweeping branches of the trees, and the horse had trotted down the twisting drive where I now walked. The drive had been wider then, and smoother too, better kept. The woods did not encroach upon it.

I did not think of her as she was now, lying against those pillows, with that shawl around her. I saw her when she was young, and when Manderley was her home. I saw her wandering in the gardens with a small boy, Maxim's father, clattering behind her on his hobby horse. He would wear a stiff Norfolk jacket and a round white collar. Picnics to the cove would be an expedition, a treat that was not indulged in very often. There would be a photograph somewhere, in an old album – all the family sitting very straight and rigid round a tablecloth set upon the beach, the servants in the background beside a huge lunch-basket. And I saw Maxim's grandmother when she was older too, a few years ago. Walking on the terrace at Manderley, leaning on a stick. And someone walked beside her, laughing, holding her arm. Someone tall and slim and very beautiful, who had a gift, Beatrice said, of being attractive to people. Easy to like, I supposed, easy to love.

When I came to the end of the long drive at last I saw that Maxim's car was standing in front of the house. My heart lifted, I ran quickly into the hall. His hat and gloves were lying on the table. I went towards the library, and as I came near I heard the sound of voices, one raised louder than the other, Maxim's voice. The door was shut. I hesitated a moment before going in.

'You can write and tell him from me to keep away from Manderley in future, do you hear? Never mind who told me, that's of no importance. I happen to know his car was seen here yesterday afternoon. If you want to meet him you can meet him outside Manderley. I won't have him inside the gates, do you understand? Remember, I'm warning you for the last time.'

I slipped away from the door to the stairs. I heard the door of the library open. I ran swiftly up the stairs and hid in the gallery. Mrs Danvers came out of the library, shutting the door behind her. I crouched against the wall of the gallery so that I should not be seen. I had caught one glimpse of her face. It was grey with anger, distorted, horrible.

She passed up the stairs swiftly and silently and disappeared through the door leading to the west wing.

I waited a moment. Then I went slowly downstairs to the library. I opened the door and went in. Maxim was standing by the window, some letters in his hand. His back was turned to me. For a moment I thought of creeping out again, and going upstairs to my room and sitting there. He must have heard me though, for he swung round impatiently.

'Who is it now?' he said.

I smiled, holding out my hands. 'Hullo!' I said.

'Oh, it's you . . .'

I could tell in a glance that something had made him very angry. His mouth was hard, his nostrils white and pinched. 'What have you been doing with yourself?' he said. He kissed the top of my head and put his arm round my shoulder. I felt as if a very long time had passed since he had left me yesterday.

'I've been to see your grandmother,' I said. 'Beatrice drove me over this afternoon.'

'How was the old lady?'

'All right.'

'What's happened to Bee?'

'She had to get back to meet Giles.'

We sat down together on the window-seat. I took his hand in mine. 'I hated you being away, I've missed you terribly,' I said.

'Have you?' he said.

We did not say anything for a bit. I just held his hand.

'Was it hot up in London?' I said.

'Yes, pretty awful. I always hate the place.'

I wondered if he would tell me what had happened just now in the library with Mrs Danvers. I wondered who had told him about Favell.

'Are you worried about something?' I said.

'I've had a long day,' he said, 'that drive twice in twenty-four hours is too much for anyone.'

He got up and wandered away, lighting a cigarette. I knew then that he was not going to tell me about Mrs Danvers.

'I'm tired too,' I said slowly, 'it's been a funny sort of day.'

16

IT WAS ONE Sunday, I remember, when we had an invasion of visitors during the afternoon, that the subject of the fancy dress ball was first brought up. Frank Crawley had come over to lunch, and we were all three of us looking forward to a peaceful afternoon under the chestnut tree when we heard the fatal sound of a car rounding the sweep in the drive. It was too late to warn Frith, the car itself came upon us standing on the terrace with cushions and papers under our arms.

We had to come forward and welcome the unexpected guests. As often happens in such cases, these were not to be the only visitors. Another car arrived about half an hour afterwards, followed by three local people who had walked from Kerrith, and we found ourselves, with the peace stripped from our day, entertaining group after group of dreary acquaintances, doing the regulation walk in the grounds, the tour of the rose-garden, the stroll across the lawns, and the formal inspection of the Happy Valley.

They stayed for tea of course, and instead of a lazy nibbling of cucumber sandwiches under the chestnut tree, we had the paraphernalia of a stiff tea in the drawing-room, which I always loathed. Frith in his element of course, directing Robert with a lift of his eyebrows, and myself rather hot and flustered with a monstrous silver tea-pot and kettle that I never knew how to manage. I found it very difficult to gauge the exact moment when it became imperative to dilute the tea with the boiling water, and more difficult still to concentrate on the small talk that was going on at my side.

Frank Crawley was invaluable at a moment like this. He took the cups from me and handed them to people, and when my answers seemed more than usually vague owing to my concentration on the silver tea-pot he quietly and unobtrusively put in his small wedge to the conversation, relieving me of responsibility. Maxim was always at the other end of the room, showing a book to a bore, or pointing out a picture, playing the perfect host in his own inimitable way, and the business of tea was a side-issue that did not matter to him. His own cup of tea grew cold, left on a side table behind some flowers, and I, steaming behind my kettle, and Frank gallantly juggling with scones and angel cake, were left to minister to the common wants of the herd. It was Lady Crowan, a tiresome gushing woman who lived in Kerrith, who introduced the matter. There was one of those pauses in conversation that happen in every tea-party, and I saw Frank's lips about to form the inevitable and idiotic remark about an angel passing overhead, when Lady Crowan, balancing a piece of cake on the edge of her saucer, looked up at Maxim who happened to be beside her.

'Oh, Mr de Winter,' she said, 'there is something I've been wanting to ask you for ages. Now tell me, is there any chance of you reviving the Manderley fancy dress ball?' She put her head on one side as she spoke, flashing her too prominent teeth in what she supposed was a smile. I lowered my head instantly, and became very busy with the emptying of my own tea-cup, screening myself behind the cosy.

It was a moment or two before Maxim replied, and when he did his voice was quite calm and matter-of-fact. 'I haven't thought about it,' he said, 'and I don't think anyone else has.'

'Oh, but I assure you we have all thought of it so much,' continued Lady Crowan. 'It used to make the summer for all of us in this part of the world. You have no idea of the pleasure it used to give. Can't I persuade you to think about it again?'

'Well, I don't know,' said Maxim drily. 'It was all rather a business to organize. You had better ask Frank Crawley, he'd have to do it.'

'Oh, Mr Crawley, do be on my side,' she persisted, and one or two of the others joined in. 'It would be a most popular move, you know, we all miss the Manderley gaiety.'

I heard Frank's quiet voice beside me. 'I don't mind organizing the ball if Maxim has no objection to giving it. It's up to him and Mrs de Winter. It's nothing to do with me.'

Of course I was bombarded at once. Lady Crowan moved her chair so that the cosy no longer hid me from view. 'Now, Mrs de Winter, you get round your husband. You are the person he will listen to. He should give the ball in your honour as the bride.'

'Yes, of course,' said somebody else, a man. 'We missed the fun of the wedding, you know; it's a shame to deprive us of all excitement. Hands up for the Manderley fancy dress ball. There you see, de Winter? Carried unanimously.' There was much laughter and clapping of hands.

Maxim lit a cigarette and his eyes met mine over the tea-pot.

'What do you think about it?' he said.

'I don't know,' I said uncertainly. 'I don't mind.'

'Of course she longs to have a ball in her honour,' gushed Lady Crowan. 'What girl wouldn't? You'd look sweet, Mrs de Winter, dressed as a little Dresden shepherdess, your hair tucked under a big three-cornered hat.'

I thought of my clumsy hands and feet and the slope of my shoulders. A fine Dresden shepherdess I should make! What an idiot the woman was. I was not surprised when nobody agreed with her, and once more I was grateful to Frank for turning the conversation away from me.

'As a matter of fact, Maxim, someone was talking about it the other day. "I suppose we shall be having some sort of celebration for the bride, shan't we, Mr Crawley?" he said. "I wish Mr de Winter would give a ball again. It was rare fun for all of us." It was Tucker at the Home farm,' he added, to Lady Crowan. 'Of course they do adore a show of any kind. I don't know, I told him. Mr de Winter hasn't said anything to me.'

'There you are,' said Lady Crowan triumphantly to the drawing-room in general. 'What did I say? Your own people are asking for a ball. If you don't care for us, surely you care about them.'

Maxim still watched me doubtfully over the tea-pot. It occurred to me that perhaps he thought I could not face it, that being shy, as he knew only too well, I should find myself unable to cope. I did not want him to think that. I did not want him to feel I should let him down.

'I think it would be rather fun,' I said.

Maxim turned away, shrugging his shoulders. 'That settles it of course,' he said. 'All right, Frank, you will have to go ahead with the arrangements. Better get Mrs Danvers to help you. She will remember the form.'

'That amazing Mrs Danvers is still with you then?' said Lady Crowan.

'Yes,' said Maxim shortly, 'have some more cake, will you? Or have you finished? Then let's all go into the garden.'

We wandered out on to the terrace, everyone discussing the prospect of the ball and suitable dates, and then, greatly to my relief, the car parties decided it was time to take their departure, and the walkers went too, on being offered a lift. I went back into the drawing-room and had another cup of tea which I thoroughly enjoyed now that the burden of entertaining had been taken from me, and Frank came too, and we crumbled up the remains of the scones and ate them, feeling like conspirators.

Maxim was throwing sticks for Jasper on the lawn. I wondered if it was the same in every home, this feeling of exuberance when visitors had gone. We did not say anything about the ball for a little while, and then, when I had finished my cup of tea and wiped my sticky fingers on a handkerchief, I said to Frank: 'What do you truthfully think about this fancy dress business?'

Frank hesitated, half glancing out of the window at Maxim on the lawn. 'I don't know,' he said. 'Maxim did not seem to object, did he? I thought he took the suggestion very well.'

'It was difficult for him to do anything else,' I said. 'What a tiresome person Lady Crowan is. Do you really believe all the people round here are talking and dreaming of nothing but a fancy dress ball at Manderley?'

'I think they would all enjoy a show of some sort,' said Frank. 'We're very conventional down here, you know, about these things. I don't honestly think Lady Crowan was exaggerating when she said something should be done in your honour. After all, Mrs de Winter, you are a bride.'

How pompous and stupid it sounded. I wished Frank would not always be so terribly correct.

'I'm not a bride,' I said. 'I did not even have a proper wedding.

No white dress or orange blossom or trailing bridesmaids. I don't want any silly dance given in my honour.'

'It's a very fine sight, Manderley *en fête*,' said Frank. 'You'll enjoy it, you see. You won't have to do anything alarming. You just receive the guests and there's nothing in that. Perhaps you'll give me a dance?'

Dear Frank. I loved his little solemn air of gallantry.

'You shall have as many dances as you like,' I said. 'I shan't dance with anyone except you and Maxim.'

'Oh, but that would not look right at all,' said Frank seriously. 'People would be very offended. You must dance with the people who ask you.'

I turned away to hide my smile. It was a joy to me the way he never knew when his leg had been pulled.

'Do you think Lady Crowan's suggestion about the Dresden shepherdess was a good one?' I said slyly.

He considered me solemnly without the trace of a smile. 'Yes, I do,' he said. 'I think you'd look very well indeed.'

I burst into laughter. 'Oh, Frank, dear, I do love you,' I said, and he turned rather pink, a little shocked I think at my impulsive words, and a little hurt too that I was laughing at him.

'I don't see that I've said anything funny,' he said stiffly.

Maxim came in at the window, Jasper dancing at his heels. 'What's all the excitement about?' he said.

'Frank is being so gallant,' I said. 'He thinks Lady Crowan's idea of my dressing up as a Dresden shepherdess is nothing to laugh at.'

'Lady Crowan is a damned nuisance,' said Maxim. 'If she had to write out all the invitations and organize the affair she would not be so enthusiastic. It's always been the same though. The locals look upon Manderley as if it was a pavilion on the end of a pier, and expect us to put up a turn for their benefit. I suppose we shall have to ask the whole county.'

'I've got the records in the office,' said Frank. 'It won't really entail much work. Licking the stamps is the longest job.'

'We'll give that to you to do,' said Maxim, smiling at me.

'Oh, we'll do that in the office,' said Frank. 'Mrs de Winter need not bother her head about anything at all.' I wondered what they would say if I suddenly announced my intention of running the whole affair. Laugh, I supposed, and then begin talking of something else. I was glad, of course, to be relieved of responsibility, but it rather added to my sense of humility to feel that I was not even capable of licking stamps. I thought of the writing-desk in the morning-room, the docketed pigeon-holes all marked in ink by that slanting pointed hand.

'What will you wear?' I said to Maxim.

'I never dress up,' said Maxim. 'It's the one perquisite allowed to the host, isn't it, Frank?'

'I can't really go as a Dresden shepherdess,' I said, 'what on earth shall I do? I'm not much good at dressing-up.'

'Put a ribbon round your hair and be Alice-in-Wonderland,' said Maxim lightly; 'you look like it now, with your finger in your mouth.'

'Don't be so rude,' I said. 'I know my hair is straight, but it isn't as straight as that. I tell you what, I'll give you and Frank the surprise of your lives, and you won't know me.'

'As long as you don't black your face and pretend to be a monkey I don't mind what you do,' said Maxim.

'All right, that's a bargain,' I said. 'I'll keep my costume a secret to the last minute, and you won't know anything about it. Come on, Jasper, we don't care what they say, do we?' I heard Maxim laughing as I went out into the garden, and he said something to Frank which I did not catch.

I wished he would not always treat me as a child, rather spoilt, rather irresponsible, someone to be petted from time to time when the mood came upon him but more often forgotten, more often patted on the shoulder and told to run away and play. I wished something would happen to make me look wiser, more mature. Was it always going to be like this? He away ahead of me, with his own moods that I did not share, his secret troubles that I did not know? Would we never be together, he a man and I a woman, standing shoulder to shoulder, hand-in-hand, with no gulf between us? I did not want to be a child. I wanted to be his wife, his mother. I wanted to be old.

I stood on the terrace, biting my nails, looking down towards the sea, and as I stood there I wondered for the twentieth time that day whether it was by Maxim's orders that those rooms in the west wing were kept furnished and untouched. I wondered if he went, as Mrs Danvers did, and touched the brushes on the dressing-table, opened the wardrobe doors, and put his hands amongst the clothes.

'Come on, Jasper,' I shouted, 'run, run with me, come on, can't you?' and I tore across the grass, savagely, angrily, the bitter tears behind my eyes, with Jasper leaping at my heels and barking hysterically.

The news soon spread about the fancy dress ball. My little maid Clarice, her eyes shining with excitement, talked of nothing else. I gathered from her that the servants in general were delighted. 'Mr Frith says it will be like old times,' said Clarice eagerly. 'I heard him saying so to Alice in the passage this morning. What will you wear, Madam?'

'I don't know, Clarice, I can't think,' I said.

'Mother said I was to be sure and tell her,' said Clarice. 'She remembers the last ball they gave at Manderley, and she has never forgotten it. Will you be hiring a costume from London, do you think?'

'I haven't made up my mind, Clarice,' I said. 'But I tell you what. When I do decide, I shall tell you and nobody else. It will be a dead secret between us both.'

'Oh, Madam, how exciting,' breathed Clarice. 'I don't know how I am going to wait for the day.'

I was curious to know Mrs Danvers' reaction to the news. Since that afternoon I dreaded even the sound of her voice down the house telephone, and by using Robert as mediator between us I was spared this last ordeal. I could not forget the expression of her face when she left the library after that interview with Maxim. I thanked God she had not seen me crouching in the gallery. And I wondered too, if she thought that it was I who had told Maxim about Favell's visit to the house. If so, she would hate me more than ever. I shuddered now when I remembered the touch of her hand on my arm, and that dreadful soft, intimate pitch of her voice close to my ear. I did not want to remember anything about that afternoon. That was why I did not speak to her, not even on the house telephone.

The preparations went on for the ball. Everything seemed to be done down at the estate office. Maxim and Frank were down there every morning. As Frank had said, I did not have to bother my head about anything. I don't think I licked one stamp. I began to get in a panic about my costume. It seemed so feeble not to be able to think of anything, and I kept remembering all the people who would come, from Kerrith and round about, the bishop's wife who had enjoyed herself so much, the last time, Beatrice and Giles, that tiresome Lady Crowan, and many more people I did not know and who had never seen me, they would every one of them have some criticism to offer, some curiosity to know what sort of effort I should make. At last, in desperation, I remembered the books that Beatrice had given me for a wedding present, and I sat down in the library one morning turning over the pages as a last hope, passing from illustration to illustration in a sort of frenzy. Nothing seemed suitable, they were all so elaborate and pretentious, those gorgeous costumes of velvet and silk in the reproductions given of Rubens, Rembrandt and others. I got hold of a piece of paper and a pencil and copied one or two of them, but they did not please me, and I threw the sketches into the waste-paper basket in disgust, thinking no more about them.

In the evening, when I was changing for dinner, there was a knock at my bedroom door. I called 'Come in,' thinking it was Clarice. The door opened and it was not Clarice. It was Mrs Danvers. She held a piece of paper in her hand. 'I hope you will forgive me disturbing you,' she said, 'but I was not sure whether you meant to throw these drawings away. All the waste-paper baskets are always brought to me to check, at the end of the day, in case of mislaying anything of value. Robert told me this was thrown into the library basket.'

I had turned quite cold all over at the sight of her, and at first I could not find my voice. She held out the paper for me to see. It was the rough drawing I had done during the morning.

'No, Mrs Danvers,' I said, after a moment, 'it doesn't matter throwing that away. It was only a rough sketch. I don't want it.'

'Very good,' she said, 'I thought it better to inquire from you personally to save any misunderstanding.'

'Yes,' I said. 'Yes, of course.' I thought she would turn and go, but she went on standing there by the door.

'So you have not decided yet what you will wear?' she said. There was a hint of derision in her voice, a trace of odd satisfaction. I supposed she had heard of my efforts through Clarice in some way.

'No,' I said. 'No, I haven't decided.'

She continued watching me, her hand on the handle of the door.

'I wonder you don't copy one of the pictures in the gallery,' she said.

I pretended to file my nails. They were too short and too brittle, but the action gave me something to do and I did not have to look at her.

'Yes, I might think about that,' I said. I wondered privately why such an idea had never come to me before. It was an obvious and very good solution to my difficulty. I did not want her to know this though. I went on filing my nails.

'All the pictures in the gallery would make good costumes,' said Mrs Danvers, 'especially that one of the young lady in white, with her hat in her hand. I wonder Mr de Winter does not make it a period ball, everyone dressed more or less the same, to be in keeping. I never think it looks right to see a clown dancing with a lady in powder and patches.'

'Some people enjoy the variety,' I said. 'They think it makes it all the more amusing.'

'I don't like it myself,' said Mrs Danvers. Her voice was surprisingly normal and friendly, and I wondered why it was she had taken the trouble to come up with my discarded sketch herself. Did she want to be friends with me at last? Or did she realize that it had not been me at all who had told Maxim about Favell, and this was her way of thanking me for my silence?

'Has not Mr de Winter suggested a costume for you?' she said.

'No,' I said, after a moment's hesitation. 'No, I want to surprise him and Mr Crawley. I don't want them to know anything about it.'

'It's not for me to make a suggestion, I know,' she said, 'but when you do decide, I should advise you to have your dress made in London. There is no one down here can do that sort of thing well. Voce, in Bond Street, is a good place I know.'

'I must remember that,' I said.

'Yes,' she said, and then, as she opened the door, 'I should study the pictures in the gallery, Madam, if I were you, especially the one I mentioned. And you need not think I will give you away. I won't say a word to anyone.'

'Thank you, Mrs Danvers,' I said. She shut the door very gently behind her. I went on with my dressing, puzzled at her attitude, so different from our last encounter, and wondering whether I had the unpleasant Favell to thank for it.

Rebecca's cousin. Why should Maxim dislike Rebecca's cousin? Why had he forbidden him to come to Manderley? Beatrice had called him a bounder. She had not said much about him. And the more I considered him the more I agreed with her. Those hot blue eyes, that loose mouth, and the careless familiar laugh. Some people would consider him attractive. Girls in sweet shops giggling behind the counter, and girls who gave one pro-grammes in a cinema. I knew how he would look at them, smil-ing, and half whistling a tune under his breath. The sort of look and the type of whistle that would make one feel uncomfortable. I wondered how well he knew Manderley. He seemed quite at home, and Jasper certainly recognized him, but these two facts did not fit in with Maxim's words to Mrs Danvers. And I could not connect him with my idea of Rebecca. Rebecca, with her beauty, her charm, her breeding, why did she have a cousin like Jack Favell? It was wrong, out of all proportion. I decided he must be the skeleton in the family cupboard, and Rebecca with her generosity had taken pity on him from time to time and invited him to Manderley, perhaps when Maxim was from home, know-ing his dislike. There had been some argument about it probably, Rebecca defending him, and ever after this perhaps a slight awk-wardness whenever his name was mentioned.

As I sat down to dinner in the dining-room in my accustomed place, with Maxim at the head of the table, I pictured Rebecca sitting where I sat now, picking up her fork for the fish, and then the telephone ringing and Frith coming into the room and saying 'Mr Favell on the phone, Madam, wishing to speak to you,' and

Rebecca would get up from her chair with a quick glance at Maxim, who would not say anything, who would go on eating his fish. And when she came back, having finished her conversation, and sat down in her place again, Rebecca would begin talking about something different, in a gay, careless way, to cover up the little cloud between them. At first Maxim would be glum, answering in monosyllables, but little by little she would win his humour back again, telling him some story of her day, about someone she had seen in Kerrith, and when they had finished the next course he would be laughing again, looking at her and smiling, putting out his hand to her across the table.

'What the devil are you thinking about?' said Maxim.

I started, the colour flooding my face, for in that brief moment, sixty seconds in time perhaps, I had so identified myself with Rebecca that my own dull self did not exist, had never come to Manderley. I had gone back in thought and in person to the days that were gone.

'Do you know you were going through the most extraordinary antics instead of eating your fish?' said Maxim. 'First you listened, as though you heard the telephone, and then your lips moved, and you threw half a glance at me. And you shook your head, and smiled, and shrugged your shoulders. All in about a second. Are you practising your appearance for the fancy dress ball?' He looked across at me, laughing, and I wondered what he would say if he really knew my thoughts, my heart, and my mind, and that for one second he had been the Maxim of another year, and I had been Rebecca. 'You look like a little criminal,' he said, 'what is it?'

'Nothing,' I said quickly, 'I wasn't doing anything.'

'Tell me what you were thinking?'

'Why should I? You never tell me what you are thinking about.'

'I don't think you've ever asked me, have you?'

'Yes, I did once.'

'I don't remember.'

'We were in the library.'

'Very probably. What did I say?'

'You told me you were wondering who had been chosen to play for Surrey against Middlesex.'

Maxim laughed again. 'What a disappointment to you. What did you hope I was thinking?'

'Something very different.'

'What sort of thing?'

'Oh, I don't know.'

'No, I don't suppose you do. If I told you I was thinking about Surrey and Middlesex I was thinking about Surrey and Middlesex. Men are simpler than you imagine, my sweet child. But what goes on in the twisted tortuous minds of women would baffle anyone. Do you know, you did not look a bit like yourself just now? You had quite a different expression on your face.'

'I did? What sort of expression?'

'I don't know that I can explain. You looked older suddenly, deceitful. It was rather unpleasant.'

'I did not mean to.'

'No, I don't suppose you did.'

I drank some water, watching him over the rim of my glass.

'Don't you want me to look older?' I said.

'No.'

'Why not?'

'Because it would not suit you.'

'One day I shall. It can't be helped. I shall have grey hair, and lines and things.'

'I don't mind that.'

'What do you mind then?'

'I don't want you to look like you did just now. You had a twist to your mouth and a flash of knowledge in your eyes. Not the right sort of knowledge.'

I felt very curious, rather excited. 'What do you mean, Maxim? What isn't the right sort of knowledge?'

He did not answer for a moment. Frith had come back into the room and was changing the plates. Maxim waited until Frith had gone behind the screen and through the service door before speaking again.

'When I met you first you had a certain expression on your face,' he said slowly, 'and you have it still. I'm not going to define it, I don't know how to. But it was one of the reasons why I married you. A moment ago, when you were going through that curious little performance, the expression had gone. Something else had taken its place.'

'What sort of thing? Explain to me, Maxim,' I said eagerly.

He considered me a moment, his eyebrows raised, whistling softly. 'Listen, my sweet. When you were a little girl, were you ever forbidden to read certain books, and did your father put those books under lock and key?'

'Yes,' I said.

'Well, then. A husband is not so very different from a father after all. There is a certain type of knowledge I prefer you not to have. It's better kept under lock and key. So that's that. And now eat up your peaches, and don't ask me any more questions, or I shall put you in the corner.'

'I wish you would not treat me as if I was six,' I said.

'How do you want to be treated?'

'Like other men treat their wives.'

'Knock you about, you mean?'

'Don't be absurd. Why must you make a joke of everything?'

'I'm not joking. I'm very serious.'

'No, you're not. I can tell by your eyes. You're playing with me all the time, just as if I was a silly little girl.'

'Alice-in-Wonderland. That was a good idea of mine. Have you bought your sash and your hair-ribbon yet?'

'I warn you. You'll get the surprise of your life when you do see me in my fancy dress.'

'I'm sure I shall. Get on with your peach and don't talk with your mouth full. I've got a lot of letters to write after dinner.' He did not wait for me to finish. He got up and strolled about the room, and asked Frith to bring the coffee in the library. I sat still, sullenly, being as slow as I could, hoping to keep things back and irritate him, but Frith took no notice of me and my peach, he brought the coffee at once and Maxim went off to the library by himself.

When I had finished I went upstairs to the minstrels' gallery to have a look at the pictures. I knew them well of course by now, but had never studied them with a view to reproducing one of them as a fancy dress. Mrs Danvers was right of course. What an idiot I had been not to think of it before. I always loved the girl in white, with a hat in her hand. It was a Raeburn, and the portrait was of Caroline de Winter, a sister of Maxim's great-great grandfather. She married a great Whig politician, and was a famous London beauty for many years, but this portrait was painted before that, when she was still unmarried. The white dress should be easy to copy. Those puffed sleeves, the flounce, and the little bodice. The hat might be rather difficult, and I should have to wear a wig. My straight hair would never curl in that way. Perhaps that Voce place in London that Mrs Danvers had told me about would do the whole thing. I would send them a sketch of the portrait and tell them to copy it faithfully, sending my measurements.

What a relief it was to have decided at last! Quite a weight off my mind. I began almost to look forward to the ball. Perhaps I should enjoy it after all, almost as much as little Clarice.

I wrote to the shop in the morning, enclosing a sketch of the portrait, and I had a very favourable reply, full of honour at my esteemed order, and saying the work would be put in hand right away, and they would manage the wig as well.

Clarice could hardly contain herself for excitement, and I, too, began to get party fever as the great day approached. Giles and Beatrice were coming for the night, but nobody else, thank heaven, although a lot of people were expected to dinner first. I had imagined we should have to hold a large house-party for the occasion, but Maxim decided against it. 'Having the dance alone is quite enough effort,' he said; and I wondered whether he did it for my sake alone, or whether a large crowd of people really bored him as he said. I had heard so much of the Manderley parties in the old days, with people sleeping in bathrooms and on sofas because of the squash. And here we were alone in the vast house, with only Beatrice and Giles to count as guests.

The house began to wear a new, expectant air. Men came to lay the floor for dancing in the great hall, and in the drawing-room some of the furniture was moved so that the long buffet tables could be placed against the wall. Lights were put up on the terrace, and in the rose-garden too, wherever one walked there would be some sign of preparation for the ball. Workmen from the estate were everywhere, and Frank came to lunch nearly every day. The servants talked of nothing else, and Frith stalked about as though the whole of the evening would depend on him alone. Robert rather lost his head, and kept forgetting things, napkins at lunch, and handing vegetables. He wore a harassed expression, like someone who has got to catch a train. The dogs were miserable. Jasper trailed about the hall with his tail between his legs, and nipped every workman on sight. He used to stand on the terrace, barking idiotically, and then dash madly to one corner of the lawn and eat grass in a sort of frenzy. Mrs Danvers never obtruded herself; but I was aware of her continually. It was her voice I heard in the drawing-room when they came to put the tables, it was she who gave directions for the laying of the floor in the hall. Whenever I came upon the scene she had always just disappeared; I would catch a glimpse of her skirt brushing the door, or hear the sound of her footsteps on the stairs. I was a lay-figure, no use to man or beast. I used to stand about doing nothing except get in the way. 'Excuse me, Madam,' I would hear a man say, just behind me, and he would pass, with a smile of apology, carrying two chairs on his back, his face dripping with perspiration.

'I'm awfully sorry,' I would say, getting quickly to one side, and then as a cover to my idleness, 'Can I help you? What about putting those chairs in the library?' The man would look bewildered. 'Mrs Danvers' orders, Madam, was that we were to take the chairs round to the back, to be out of the way.'

'Oh,' I said, 'yes, of course. How silly of me. Take them round to the back, as she said.' And I would walk quickly away murmuring something about finding a piece of paper and a pencil, in a vain attempt to delude the man into thinking I was busy, while he went on across the hall, looking rather astonished, and I would feel I had not deceived him for a moment.

The great day dawned misty and overcast, but the glass was high and we had no fears. The mist was a good sign. It cleared about eleven, as Maxim had foretold, and we had a glorious still summer's day without a cloud in the blue sky. All the morning the gardeners were bringing flowers into the house, the last of the white lilac, and great lupins and delphiniums, five foot high, roses in hundreds, and every sort of lily.

Mrs Danvers showed herself at last; quietly, calmly, she told the gardeners where to put the flowers, and she herself arranged them, stacking the vases with quick, deft fingers. I watched her in fascination, the way she did vase after vase, carrying them herself through the flower room to the drawing-room and the various corners of the house, massing them in just the right numbers and profusion, putting colour where colour was needed, leaving the walls bare where severity paid.

Maxim and I had lunch with Frank at his bachelor establishment next-door to the office to be out of the way. We were all three in the rather hearty, cheerful humour of people after a funeral. We made pointless jokes about nothing at all, our minds eternally on the thought of the next few hours. I felt very much the same as I did the morning I was married. The same stifled feeling that I had gone too far now to turn back.

The evening had got to be endured. Thank heaven Messrs Voce had sent my dress in time. It looked perfect, in its folds of tissue paper. And the wig was a triumph. I had tried it on after breakfast, and was amazed at the transformation. I looked quite attractive, quite different altogether. Not me at all. Someone much more interesting, more vivid and alive. Maxim and Frank kept asking me about my costume.

'You won't know me,' I told them, 'you will both get the shock of your lives.'

'You are not going to dress up as a clown, are you?' said Maxim gloomily. 'No frightful attempt to be funny?'

'No, nothing like that,' I said, full of importance.

'I wish you had kept to Alice-in-Wonderland,' he said.

'Or Joan of Arc with your hair,' said Frank shyly.

'I never thought of that,' I said blankly, and Frank went rather pink. 'I'm sure we shall like whatever you wear,' he said in his most pompous Frank-ish voice.

'Don't encourage her, Frank,' said Maxim. 'She's so full of her precious disguise already there's no holding her. Bee will put you in your place, that's one comfort. She'll soon tell you if she doesn't like your dress. Dear old Bee always looks just wrong on these occasions, bless her. I remember her once as Madame Pompadour and she tripped up going in to supper and her wig came adrift. "I can't stand this damned thing," she said, in that blunt voice of hers, and chucked it on a chair and went through the rest of the evening with her own cropped hair. You can imagine what it looked like, against a pale blue satin crinoline, or whatever the dress was. Poor Giles did not cope that year. He came as a cook, and sat about in the bar all night looking perfectly miserable. I think he felt Bee had let him down.'

'No, it wasn't that,' said Frank, 'he'd lost his front teeth trying out a new mare, don't you remember, and he was so shy about it he wouldn't open his mouth.'

'Oh, was that it? Poor Giles. He generally enjoys dressing-up.'

'Beatrice says he loves playing charades,' I said. 'She told me they always have charades at Christmas.'

'I know,' said Maxim, 'that's why I've never spent Christmas with her.'

'Have some more asparagus, Mrs de Winter, and another potato?'

'No, really, Frank, I'm not hungry, thank you.'

'Nerves,' said Maxim, shaking his head. 'Never mind, this time tomorrow it will all be over.'

'I sincerely hope so,' said Frank seriously. 'I was going to give orders that all cars should stand by for 5 a.m.'

I began to laugh weakly, the tears coming into my eyes. 'Oh dear,' I said, 'let's send wires to everybody not to come.'

'Come on, be brave and face it,' said Maxim. 'We need not give another one for years. Frank, I have an uneasy feeling we ought to be going up to the house. What do you think?'

Frank agreed, and I followed them unwillingly, reluctant to leave the cramped, rather uncomfortable little dining-room that was so typical of Frank's bachelor establishment, and which seemed to me today the embodiment of peace and quietude. When we came to the house we found that the band had arrived, and were standing about in the hall rather pink in the face and self-conscious, while Frith, more important than ever, offered refreshments. The band were to be our guests for the night, and after we had welcomed them and exchanged a few slightly obvious jokes proper to the occasion, the band were borne off to their quarters to be followed by a tour of the grounds.

The afternoon dragged, like the last hour before a journey when one is packed up and keyed to departure, and I wandered from room to room almost as lost as Jasper, who trailed reproachfully at my heels.

There was nothing I could do to help, and it would have been wiser on my part to have kept clear of the house altogether and taken the dog and myself for a long walk. By the time I decided upon this it was too late, Maxim and Frank were demanding tea, and when tea was over Beatrice and Giles arrived. The evening had come upon us all too soon.

'This is like old times,' said Beatrice, kissing Maxim, and looking about her. 'Congratulations to you for remembering every detail. The flowers are exquisite,' she added, turning to me. 'Did you do them?'

'No,' I said, rather ashamed, 'Mrs Danvers is responsible for everything.'

'Oh. Well, after all . . .' Beatrice did not finish her sentence, she accepted a light for her cigarette from Frank, and once it was lit she appeared to have forgotten what she was going to say.

'Have you got Mitchell's to do the catering as usual?' asked Giles.

'Yes,' said Maxim. 'I don't think anything has been altered, has it, Frank? We had all the records down at the office. Nothing has been forgotten, and I don't think we have left anyone out.'

'What a relief to find only ourselves,' said Beatrice. 'I remember once arriving about this time, and there were about twenty-five people in the place already. All going to stop the night.'

'What's everyone going to wear? I suppose Maxim, as always, refuses to play?'

'As always,' said Maxim.

'Such a mistake I think. The whole thing would go with much more swing if you did.'

'Have you ever known a ball at Manderley not to go with a swing?'

'No, my dear boy, the organization is too good. But I do think the host ought to give the lead himself.'

'I think it's quite enough if the hostess makes the effort,' said Maxim. 'Why should I make myself hot and uncomfortable and a damn fool into the bargain?'

'Oh, but that's absurd. There's no need to look a fool. With your appearance, my dear Maxim, you could get away with any costume. You don't have to worry about your figure like poor Giles.'

'What is Giles going to wear tonight?' I asked, 'or is it a dead secret?'

'No, rather not,' beamed Giles; 'as a matter of fact it's a pretty good effort. I got our local tailor to rig it up. I'm coming as an Arabian sheik.'

'Good God,' said Maxim.

'It's not at all bad,' said Beatrice warmly. 'He stains his face of course, and leaves off his glasses. The head-dress is authentic. We borrowed it off a friend who used to live in the East, and the rest the tailor copied from some paper. Giles looks very well in it.'

'What are you going to be, Mrs Lacy?' said Frank.

'Oh, I'm afraid I haven't coped much,' said Beatrice, 'I've got some sort of Eastern get-up to go with Giles, but I don't pretend it's genuine. Strings of beads, you know, and a veil over my face.'

'It sounds very nice,' I said politely.

'Oh, it's not bad. Comfortable to wear, that's one blessing. I shall take off the veil if I get too hot. What are you wearing?'

'Don't ask her,' said Maxim. 'She won't tell any of us. There has never been such a secret. I believe she even wrote to London for it.'

'My dear,' said Beatrice, rather impressed, 'don't say you have gone a bust and will put us all to shame? Mine is only home-made, you know.'

'Don't worry,' I said, laughing, 'it's quite simple really. But Maxim would tease me, and I've promised to give him the surprise of his life.'

'Quite right too,' said Giles. 'Maxim is too superior altogether. The fact is he's jealous. Wishes he was dressing-up like the rest of us, and doesn't like to say so.'

'Heaven forbid,' said Maxim.

'What are you doing, Crawley?' asked Giles.

Frank looked rather apologetic. 'I've been so busy I'm afraid I've left things to the last moment. I hunted up an old pair of trousers last night, and a striped football jersey, and thought of putting a patch over one eye and coming as a pirate.'

'Why on earth didn't you write to us and borrow a costume?' said Beatrice. 'There's one of a Dutchman that Roger had last winter in Switzerland. It would have suited you excellently.'

'I refuse to allow my agent to walk about as a Dutchman,' said Maxim. 'He'd never get rents out of anybody again. Let him stick to his pirate. It might frighten some of them.'

'Anything less like a pirate,' murmured Beatrice in my ear.

I pretended not to hear. Poor Frank, she was always rather down on him.

'How long will it take me to paint my face?' asked Giles.

'Two hours at least,' said Beatrice. 'I should begin thinking about it if I were you. How many shall we be at dinner?'

'Sixteen,' said Maxim, 'counting ourselves. No strangers. You know them all.'

'I'm beginning to get dress fever already,' said Beatrice. 'What fun it all is. I'm so glad you decided to do this again, Maxim.'

'You've got her to thank for it,' said Maxim, nodding at me.

'Oh, it's not true,' I said. 'It was all the fault of Lady Crowan.'

'Nonsense,' said Maxim, smiling at me, 'you know you're as excited as a child at its first party.'

'I'm not.'

'I'm longing to see your dress,' said Beatrice.

'It's nothing out of the way. Really it's not,' I insisted.

'Mrs de Winter says we shan't know her,' said Frank.

Everybody looked at me and smiled. I felt pleased and flushed and rather happy. People were being nice. They were all so friendly. It was suddenly fun, the thought of the dance, and that I was to be the hostess.

The dance was being given for me, in my honour, because I was the bride. I sat on the table in the library, swinging my legs, while the rest of them stood round, and I had a longing to go upstairs and put on my dress, try the wig in front of the looking-glass, turn this way and that before the long mirror on the wall. It was new this sudden unexpected sensation of being important, of having Giles, and Beatrice, and Frank and Maxim all looking at me and talking about my dress. All wondering what I was going to wear. I thought of the soft white dress in its folds of tissue paper, and how it would hide my flat dull figure, my rather sloping shoulders. I thought of my own lank hair covered by the sleek and gleaming curls.

'What's the time?' I said carelessly, yawning a little, pretending I did not care. 'I wonder if we ought to think about going upstairs . . .?'

As we crossed the great hall on the way to our rooms I realized for the first time how the house lent itself to the occasion, and how beautiful the rooms were looking. Even the drawing-room, formal and cold to my consideration when we were alone, was a blaze of colour now, flowers in every corner, red roses in silver bowls on the white cloth of the supper table, the long windows open to the terrace, where, as soon as it was dusk, the fairy lights would shine. The band had stacked their instruments ready in the minstrels' gallery above the hall, and the hall itself wore a strange, waiting air; there was a warmth about it I had never known before, due to the night itself, so still and clear, to the flowers beneath the pictures, to our own laughter as we hovered on the wide stone stairs.

The old austerity had gone. Manderley had come alive in a fashion I would not have believed possible. It was not the still quiet Manderley I knew. There was a certain significance about it now that had not been before. A reckless air, rather triumphant, rather pleasing. It was as if the house remembered other days, long, long ago, when the hall was a banqueting hall indeed, with weapons and tapestry hanging upon the walls, and men sat at a long narrow table in the centre laughing louder than we laughed now, calling for wine, for song, throwing great pieces of meat upon the flags to the slumbering dogs. Later, in other years, it would still be gay, but with a certain grace and dignity, and Caroline de Winter, whom I should present tonight, would walk down the wide stone stairs in her white dress to dance the minuet. I wished we could sweep away the years and see her. I wished we did not have to degrade the house with our modern jig-tunes, so out-of-place and unromantic. They would not suit Manderley.

I found myself in sudden agreement with Mrs Danvers. We should have made it a period ball, not the hotchpotch of humanity it was bound to be, with Giles, poor fellow, well-meaning and hearty in his guise of Arabian sheik. I found Clarice waiting for me in my bedroom, her round face scarlet with excitement. We giggled at one another like schoolgirls, and I bade her lock my door. There was much sound of tissue paper, rustling and mysterious. We spoke to one another softly like conspirators, we walked on tiptoe. I felt like a child again on the eve of Christmas. This padding to and fro in my room with bare feet, the little furtive bursts of laughter, the stifled exclamations, reminded me of hanging up my stocking long ago. Maxim was safe in his dressing-room, and the way through was barred against him. Clarice alone was my ally and favoured friend. The dress fitted perfectly. I stood still, hardly able to restrain my impatience while Clarice hooked me up with fumbling fingers.

'It's handsome, Madam,' she kept saying, leaning back on her heels to look at me. 'It's a dress fit for the Queen of England.'

'What about under the left shoulder there,' I said, anxiously. 'That strap of mine, is it going to show?'

'No, Madam, nothing shows.'

'How is it? How do I look?' I did not wait for her answer, I twisted and turned in front of the mirror, I frowned, I smiled. I felt different already, no longer hampered by my appearance. My own dull personality was submerged at last. 'Give me the wig,' I said excitedly, 'careful, don't crush it, the curls mustn't be flat. They are supposed to stand out from the face.' Clarice stood behind my shoulder, I saw her round face beyond mine in the reflection of the looking-glass, her eyes shining, her mouth a little open. I brushed my own hair sleek behind my ears. I took hold of the soft gleaming curls with trembling fingers, laughing under my breath, looking up at Clarice.

'Oh, Clarice,' I said, 'what will Mr de Winter say?'

I covered my own mousy hair with the curled wig, trying to hide my triumph, trying to hide my smile. Somebody came and hammered on the door.

'Who's there?' I called in panic. 'You can't come in.'

'It's me, my dear, don't alarm yourself,' said Beatrice, 'how far have you got? I want to look at you.'

'No, no,' I said, 'you can't come in, I'm not ready.'

The flustered Clarice stood beside me, her hand full of hair-pins, while I took them from her one by one, controlling the curls that had become fluffed in the box.

'I'll come down when I am ready,' I called. 'Go on down, all of you. Don't wait for me. Tell Maxim he can't come in.'

'Maxim's down,' she said. 'He came along to us. He said he hammered on your bathroom door and you never answered. Don't be too long, my dear, we are all so intrigued. Are you sure you don't want any help?'

'No,' I shouted impatiently, losing my head, 'go away, go on down.'

Why did she have to come and bother just at this moment? It fussed me, I did not know what I was doing. I jabbed with a hair-pin, flattening it against a curl. I heard no more from Beatrice, she must have gone along the passage. I wondered if she was happy in her Eastern robes and if Giles had succeeded in painting his face. How absurd it was, the whole thing. Why did we do it, I wonder, why were we such children?

I did not recognize the face that stared at me in the glass. The eyes were larger surely, the mouth narrower, the skin white and clear? The curls stood away from the head in a little cloud. I watched this self that was not me at all and then smiled; a new, slow smile.

'Oh, Clarice!' I said. 'Oh, Clarice!' I took the skirt of my dress in my hands and curtseyed to her, the flounces sweeping the ground. She giggled excitedly, rather embarrassed, flushed though, very pleased. I paraded up and down in front of my glass watching my reflection.

'Unlock the door,' I said. 'I'm going down. Run ahead and see if they are there.' She obeyed me, still giggling, and I lifted my skirts off the ground and followed her along the corridor.

She looked back at me and beckoned. 'They've gone down,' she whispered, 'Mr de Winter, and Major and Mrs Lacy. Mr Crawley has just come. They are all standing in the hall.' I peered through the archway at the head of the big staircase, and looked down on the hall below.

Yes, there they were. Giles, in his white Arab dress, laughing loudly, showing the knife at his side; Beatrice swathed in an extraordinary green garment and hung about the neck with trailing beads; poor Frank self-conscious and slightly foolish in his striped jersey and sea-boots; Maxim, the only normal one of the party, in his evening clothes.

'I don't know what she's doing,' he said, 'she's been up in her bedroom for hours. What's the time, Frank? The dinner crowd will be upon us before we know where we are.'

The band were changed, and in the gallery already. One of the men was tuning his fiddle. He played a scale softly, and then plucked at a string. The light shone on the picture of Caroline de Winter.

Yes, the dress had been copied exactly from my sketch of the portrait. The puffed sleeve, the sash and the ribbon, the wide floppy hat I held in my hand. And my curls were her curls, they stood out from my face as hers did in the picture. I don't think I have ever felt so excited before, so happy and so proud. I waved my hand at the man with the fiddle, and then put my finger to my lips for silence. He smiled and bowed. He came across the gallery to the archway where I stood.

'Make the drummer announce me,' I whispered, 'make him beat the drum, you know how they do, and then call out Miss Caroline de Winter. I want to surprise them below.' He nodded his head, he understood. My heart fluttered absurdly, and my cheeks were burning. What fun it was, what mad ridiculous childish fun! I smiled at Clarice still crouching on the corridor. I picked up my skirt in my hands. Then the sound of the drum echoed in the great hall, startling me for a moment, who had waited for it, who knew that it would come. I saw them look up surprised and bewildered from the hall below.

'Miss Caroline de Winter,' shouted the drummer.

I came forward to the head of the stairs and stood there, smiling, my hat in my hand, like the girl in the picture. I waited for the clapping and laughter that would follow as I walked slowly down the stairs. Nobody clapped, nobody moved.

They all stared at me like dumb things. Beatrice uttered a little cry and put her hand to her mouth. I went on smiling, I put one hand on the banister.

'How do you do, Mr de Winter,' I said.

Maxim had not moved. He stared up at me, his glass in his hand. There was no colour in his face. It was ashen white. I saw Frank go to him as though he would speak, but Maxim shook him off. I hesitated, one foot already on the stairs. Something was wrong, they had not understood. Why was Maxim looking like that? Why did they all stand like dummies, like people in a trance?

Then Maxim moved forward to the stairs, his eyes never leaving my face.

'What the hell do you think you are doing?' he asked. His eyes blazed in anger. His face was still ashen white.

I could not move, I went on standing there, my hand on the banister.

'It's the picture,' I said, terrified at his eyes, at his voice. 'It's the picture, the one in the gallery.'

There was a long silence. We went on staring at each other. Nobody moved in the hall. I swallowed, my hand moved to my throat. 'What is it?' I said. 'What have I done?'

If only they would not stare at me like that with dull blank faces. If only somebody would say something. When Maxim spoke again I did not recognize his voice. It was still and quiet, icy cold, not a voice I knew.

'Go and change,' he said, 'it does not matter what you put on. Find an ordinary evening frock, anything will do. Go now, before anybody comes.'

I could not speak, I went on staring at him. His eyes were the only living things in the white mask of his face.

'What are you standing there for?' he said, his voice harsh and queer. 'Didn't you hear what I said?'

I turned and ran blindly through the archway to the corridors beyond. I caught a glimpse of the astonished face of the drummer who had announced me. I brushed past him, stumbling, not looking where I went. Tears blinded my eyes. I did not know what was happening. Clarice had gone. The corridor was deserted. I looked about me stunned and stupid like a haunted thing. Then I saw that the door leading to the west wing was open wide, and that someone was standing there.

It was Mrs Danvers. I shall never forget the expression on her face, loathsome, triumphant. The face of an exulting devil. She stood there, smiling at me.

And then I ran from her, down the long narrow passage to my own room, tripping, stumbling over the flounces of my dress.

17

CLARICE WAS WAITING for me in my bedroom. She looked pale and scared. As soon as she saw me she burst into tears. I did not say anything. I began tearing at the hooks of my dress, ripping the stuff. I could not manage them properly, and Clarice came to help me, still crying noisily.

'It's all right, Clarice, it's not your fault,' I said, and she shook her head, the tears still running down her cheeks.

'Your lovely dress, Madam,' she said, 'your lovely white dress.'

'It doesn't matter,' I said. 'Can't you find the hook? There it is, at the back. And another one somewhere, just below.'

She fumbled with the hooks, her hands trembling, making worse trouble with it than I did myself, and all the time catching at her breath.

'What will you wear instead, Madam?' she said.

'I don't know,' I said, 'I don't know.' She had managed to unfasten the hooks, and I struggled out of the dress. 'I think I'd rather like to be alone, Clarice,' I said, 'would you be a dear and leave me? Don't worry, I shall manage all right. Forget what's happened. I want you to enjoy the party.'

'Can't I press out a dress for you, Madam?' she said, looking up at me with swollen streaming eyes. 'It won't take me a moment.'

'No,' I said, 'don't bother, I'd rather you went, and Clarice . . .'

'Yes, Madam?'

'Don't – don't say anything about what's just happened.'

'No, Madam.' She burst into another torrent of weeping.

'Don't let the others see you like that,' I said. 'Go to your bedroom and do something to your face. There's nothing to cry about, nothing at all.' Somebody knocked on the door. Clarice threw me a quick frightened glance.

'Who is it?' I said. The door opened and Beatrice came into the room. She came to me at once, a strange, rather ludicrous figure in her Eastern drapery, the bangles jangling on her wrists.

'My dear,' she said, 'my dear,' and held out her hands to me.

Clarice slipped out of the room. I felt tired suddenly, and unable to cope. I went and sat down on the bed. I put my hand up to my head and took off the curled wig. Beatrice stood watching me.

'Are you all right?' she said. 'You look very white.'

'It's the light,' I said. 'It never gives one any colour.'

'Sit down for a few minutes and you'll be all right,' she said; 'wait, I'll get a glass of water.'

She went into the bathroom, her bangles jangling with her every movement, and then she came back, the glass of water in her hands.

I drank some to please her, not wanting it a bit. It tasted warm from the tap; she had not let it run.

'Of course I knew at once it was just a terrible mistake,' she said. 'You could not possibly have known, why should you?'

'Known what?' I said.

'Why, the dress, you poor dear, the picture you copied of the girl in the gallery. It was what Rebecca did at the last fancy dress ball at Manderley. Identical. The same picture, the same dress. You stood there on the stairs, and for one ghastly moment I thought . . .'

She did not go on with her sentence, she patted me on the shoulder.

'You poor child, how wretchedly unfortunate, how were you to know?'

'I ought to have known,' I said stupidly, staring at her, too stunned to understand. 'I ought to have known.'

'Nonsense, how could you know? It was not the sort of thing that could possibly enter any of our heads. Only it was such a shock, you see. We none of us expected it, and Maxim . . .'

'Yes, Maxim?' I said.

'He thinks, you see, it was deliberate on your part. You had some bet that you would startle him, didn't you? Some foolish joke. And of course, he doesn't understand. It was such a frightful

shock for him. I told him at once you could not have done such
a thing, and that it was sheer appalling luck that you had chosen
that particular picture.'

'I ought to have known,' I repeated again. 'It's all my fault,
I ought to have seen. I ought to have known.'

'No, no. Don't worry, you'll be able to explain the whole
thing to him quietly. Everything will be quite all right. The first
lot of people were arriving just as I came upstairs to you. They
are having drinks. Everything's all right. I've told Frank and Giles
to make up a story about your dress not fitting, and you are very
disappointed.'

I did not say anything. I went on sitting on the bed with my
hands in my lap.

'What can you wear instead?' said Beatrice, going to my wardrobe and flinging open the doors. 'Here. What's this blue? It
looks charming. Put this on. Nobody will mind. Quick. I'll
help you.'

'No,' I said. 'No, I'm not coming down.'

Beatrice stared at me in great distress, my blue frock over
her arm.

'But, my dear, you must,' she said in dismay. 'You can't possibly not appear.'

'No, Beatrice, I'm not coming down. I can't face them, not
after what's happened.'

'But nobody will know about the dress,' she said. 'Frank and
Giles will never breathe a word. We've got the story all arranged.
The shop sent the wrong dress, and it did not fit, so you are wearing an ordinary evening dress instead. Everyone will think it perfectly natural. It won't make any difference to the evening.'

'You don't understand,' I said. 'I don't care about the dress.
It's not that at all. It's what has happened, what I did. I can't come
down now, Beatrice, I can't.'

'But, my dear, Giles and Frank understand perfectly. They are
full of sympathy. And Maxim too. It was just the first shock . . .
I'll try and get him alone a minute, I'll explain the whole thing.'

'No!' I said. 'No!'

She put my blue frock down beside me on the bed. 'Everyone
will be arriving,' she said, very worried, very upset. 'It will look

so extraordinary if you don't come down. I can't say you've suddenly got a headache.'

'Why not?' I said wearily. 'What does it matter? Make anything up. Nobody will mind, they don't any of them know me.'

'Come now, my dear,' she said, patting my hand, 'try and
make the effort. Put on this charming blue. Think of Maxim. You
must come down for his sake.'

'I'm thinking about Maxim all the time,' I said.

'Well, then, surely . . .?'

'No,' I said, tearing at my nails, rocking backwards and forwards on the bed. 'I can't, I can't.'

Somebody else knocked on the door. 'Oh, dear, who on earth
is that?' said Beatrice, walking to the door. 'What is it?'

She opened the door. Giles was standing just outside. 'Everyone has turned up. Maxim sent me up to find out what's happening,' he said.

'She says she won't come down,' said Beatrice. 'What on earth
are we going to say?'

I caught sight of Giles peering at me through the open door.

'Oh, Lord, what a frightful mix-up,' he whispered. He turned
away embarrassed when he noticed that I had seen him.

'What shall I say to Maxim?' he asked Beatrice. 'It's five past
eight now.'

'Say she's feeling rather faint, but will try and come down
later. Tell them not to wait dinner. I'll be down directly, I'll make
it all right.'

'Yes, right you are.' He half glanced in my direction again,
sympathetic but rather curious, wondering why I sat there on the
bed, and his voice was low, as it might be after an accident, when
people are waiting for the doctor.

'Is there anything else I can do?' he said.

'No,' said Beatrice, 'go down now, I'll follow in a minute.'

He obeyed her, shuffling away in his Arabian robes. This is the
sort of moment, I thought, that I shall laugh at years afterwards,
that I shall say 'Do you remember how Giles was dressed as an
Arab, and Beatrice had a veil over her face, and jangling bangles
on her wrist?' And time will mellow it, make it a moment for
laughter. But now it was not funny, now I did not laugh. It was

not the future, it was the present. It was too vivid and too real. I sat on the bed, plucking at the eiderdown, pulling a little feather out of a slit in one corner.

'Would you like some brandy?' said Beatrice, making a last effort. 'I know it's only Dutch courage, but it sometimes works wonders.'

'No,' I said. 'No, I don't want anything.'

'I shall have to go down. Giles says they are waiting dinner. Are you sure it's all right for me to leave you?'

'Yes. And thank you, Beatrice.'

'Oh, my dear, don't thank me. I wish I could do something.' She stooped swiftly to my looking-glass and dabbed her face with powder. 'God, what a sight I look,' she said, 'this damn veil is crooked I know. However it can't be helped.' She rustled out of the room, closing the door behind her. I felt I had forfeited her sympathy by my refusal to go down. I had shown the white feather. She had not understood. She belonged to another breed of men and women, another race than I. They had guts, the women of her race. They were not like me. If it had been Beatrice who had done this thing instead of me she would have put on her other dress and gone down again to welcome her guests. She would have stood by Giles's side, and shaken hands with people, a smile on her face. I could not do that. I had not the pride, I had not the guts. I was badly bred.

I kept seeing Maxim's eyes blazing in his white face, and behind him Giles, and Beatrice and Frank standing like dummies, staring at me.

I got up from my bed and went and looked out of the window. The gardeners were going round to the lights in the rose-garden, testing them to see if they all worked. The sky was pale, with a few salmon clouds of evening streaking to the west. When it was dusk the lamps would all be lit. There were tables and chairs in the rose-garden, for the couples who wanted to sit out. I could smell the roses from my window. The men were talking to one another and laughing. 'There's one here gone,' I heard a voice call out; 'can you get me another small bulb? One of the blue ones, Bill.' He fixed the light into position. He whistled a popular tune of the moment with easy confidence, and I thought how tonight perhaps the band would play the same tune in the minstrels' gallery above the hall. 'That's got it,' said the man, switching the light on and off, 'they're all right here. No others gone. We'd better have a look at those on the terrace.' They went off round the corner of the house, still whistling the song. I wished I could be the man. Later in the evening he would stand with his friend in the drive and watch the cars drive up to the house, his hands in his pockets, his cap on the back of his head. He would stand in a crowd with other people from the estate, and then drink cider at the long table arranged for them in one corner of the terrace. 'Like the old days, isn't it?' he would say. But his friend would shake his head, puffing at his pipe. 'This new one's not like our Mrs de Winter, she's different altogether.' And a woman next them in the crowd would agree, other people too, all saying 'That's right,' and nodding their heads.

'Where is she tonight? She's not been on the terrace once.'

'I can't say, I'm sure. I've not seen her.'

'Mrs de Winter used to be here, there, and everywhere.'

'Aye, that's right.'

And the woman would turn to her neighbours nodding mysteriously.

'They say she's not appearing tonight at all.'

'Go on.'

'That's right. One of the servants from the house told me Mrs de Winter hasn't come down from her room all evening.'

'What's wrong with the maid, is she bad?'

'No, sulky I reckon. They say her dress didn't please her.'

A squeal of laughter and a murmur from the little crowd.

'Did you ever hear of such a thing? It's a shame for Mr de Winter.'

'I wouldn't stand for it, not from a chit like her.'

'Maybe it's not true at all.'

'It's true all right. They're full of it up at the house.' One to the other. This one to the next. A smile, a wink, a shrug of the shoulder. One group, and then another group. And then spreading to the guests who walked on the terrace and strolled across the lawns. The couple who in three hours' time would sit in those chairs beneath me in the rose-garden.

'Do you suppose it's true what I heard?'

'What did you hear?'

'Why, that there's nothing wrong with her at all, they've had a colossal row, and she won't appear!'

'I say!' A lift of the eyebrows, a long whistle.

'I know. Well, it does look rather odd, don't you think? What I mean is, people don't suddenly for no reason have violent head-aches. I call the whole thing jolly fishy.'

'I thought he looked a bit grim.'

'So did I.'

'Of course I have heard before the marriage is not a wild success.'

'Oh, really?'

'H'm. Several people have said so. They say he's beginning to realize he's made a big mistake. She's nothing to look at, you know.'

'No, I've heard there's nothing much to her. Who was she?'

'Oh, no one at all. Some pick-up in the south of France, a nursery gov., or something.'

'Good Lord!'

'I know. And when you think of Rebecca . . .'

I went on staring at the empty chairs. The salmon sky had turned to grey. Above my head was the evening star. In the woods beyond the rose-garden the birds were making their last little rustling noises before nightfall. A lone gull flew across the sky. I went away from the window, back to the bed again. I picked up the white dress I had left on the floor and put it back in the box with the tissue paper. I put the wig back in its box too. Then I looked in one of my cupboards for the little portable iron I used to have in Monte Carlo for Mrs Van Hopper's dresses. It was lying at the back of a shelf with some woollen jumpers I had not worn for a long time. The iron was one of those universal kinds that go on any voltage and I fitted it to the plug in the wall. I began to iron the blue dress that Beatrice had taken from the wardrobe, slowly, methodically, as I used to iron Mrs Van Hopper's dresses in Monte Carlo.

When I had finished I laid the dress ready on the bed. Then I cleaned the make-up off my face that I had put on for the fancy dress. I combed my hair, and washed my hands. I put on the blue dress and the shoes that went with it. I might have been my old self again, going down to the lounge of the hotel with Mrs Van Hopper. I opened the door of my room and went along the corridor. Everything was still and silent. There might not have been a party at all. I tiptoed to the end of the passage and turned the corner. The door to the west wing was closed. There was no sound of anything at all. When I came to the archway by the gallery and the staircase I heard the murmur and hum of conversation coming from the dining-room. They were still having dinner. The great hall was deserted. There was nobody in the gallery either. The band must be having their dinner too. I did not know what arrangements had been made for them. Frank had done it – Frank or Mrs Danvers.

From where I stood I could see the picture of Caroline de Winter facing me in the gallery. I could see the curls framing her face, and I could see the smile on her lips. I remembered the bishop's wife who had said to me that day I called, 'I shall never forget her, dressed all in white, with that cloud of dark hair.' I ought to have remembered that, I ought to have known. How queer the instruments looked in the gallery, the little stands for the music, the big drum. One of the men had left his handkerchief on a chair. I leant over the rail and looked down at the hall below. Soon it would be filled with people, like the bishop's wife had said, and Maxim would stand at the bottom of the stairs shaking hands with them as they came into the hall. The sound of their voices would echo to the ceiling, and then the band would play from the gallery where I was leaning now, the man with the violin smiling, swaying to the music.

It would not be quiet like this any more. A board creaked in the gallery. I swung round, looking at the gallery behind me. There was nobody there. The gallery was empty, just as it had been before. A current of air blew in my face though, somebody must have left a window open in one of the passages. The hum of voices continued in the dining-room. I wondered why the board creaked when I had not moved at all. The warmth of the night perhaps, a swelling somewhere in the old wood. The draught still blew in my face though. A piece of music on one of the stands fluttered to the floor. I looked towards the archway above the stairs. The draught was coming from there. I went beneath the arch again, and when I came out on to the long corridor I saw that the door to the west wing had blown open and swung back against the wall. It was dark in the west passage, none of the lights had been turned on. I could feel the wind blowing on my face from an open window. I fumbled for a switch on the wall and could not find one. I could see the window in an angle of the passage, the curtain blowing softly, backwards and forwards. The grey evening light cast queer shadows on the floor. The sound of the sea came to me through the open window, the soft hissing sound of the ebb-tide leaving the shingle.

I did not go and shut the window. I stood there shivering a moment in my thin dress, listening to the sea as it sighed and left the shore. Then I turned quickly and shut the door of the west wing behind me, and came out again through the archway by the stairs.

The murmur of voices had swollen now and was louder than before. The door of the dining-room was open. They were coming out of dinner. I could see Robert standing by the open door, and there was a scraping of chairs, a babble of conversation, and laughter.

I walked slowly down the stairs to meet them.

When I look back at my first party at Manderley, my first and my last, I can remember little isolated things standing alone out of the vast blank canvas of the evening. The background was hazy, a sea of dim faces none of whom I knew, and there was the slow drone of the band harping out a waltz that never finished, that went on and on. The same couples swung by in rotation, with the same fixed smiles, and to me, standing with Maxim at the bottom of the stairs to welcome the late-comers, these dancing couples seemed like marionettes twisting and turning on a piece of string, held by some invisible hand.

There was a woman, I never knew her name, never saw her again, but she wore a salmon-coloured gown hooped in crinoline form, a vague gesture to some past century but whether seventeenth, eighteenth, or nineteenth I could not tell, and every time she passed me it coincided with a sweeping bar of the waltz to which she dipped and swayed, smiling as she did so in my direction. It happened again and again until it became automatic, a matter of routine, like those promenades on board ship when we meet the same people bent on exercise like ourselves, and know with deadly certainty that we will pass them by the bridge.

I can see her now, the prominent teeth, the gay spot of rouge placed high upon her cheek-bones, and her smile, vacant, happy, enjoying her evening. Later I saw her by the supper table, her keen eyes searching the food, and she heaped a plate high with salmon and lobster mayonnaise and went off into a corner. There was Lady Crowan too, monstrous in purple, disguised as I know not what romantic figure of the past, it might have been Marie Antoinette or Nell Gwynne for all I knew, or a strange erotic combination of the two, and she kept exclaiming in excited high-pitch tones, a little higher than usual because of the champagne she had consumed, 'You all have me to thank for this, not the de Winters at all.'

I remember Robert dropping a tray of ices, and the expression of Frith's face when he saw Robert was the culprit and not one of the minions hired for the occasion. I wanted to go to Robert and stand beside him and say 'I know how you feel. I understand. I've done worse than you tonight.' I can feel now the stiff, set smile on my face that did not match the misery in my eyes. I can see Beatrice, dear friendly tactless Beatrice, watching me from her partner's arms, nodding encouragement, the bangles jangling on her wrists, the veil slipping continually from her overheated forehead. I can picture myself once more whirled round the room in a desperate dance with Giles, who with doglike sympathy and kind heart would take no refusal, but must steer me through the stamping crowd as he would one of his own horses at a meet. 'That's a jolly pretty dress you're wearing,' I can hear him say, 'it makes all these people look damn silly,' and I blessed him for his pathetic simple gesture of understanding and sincerity, thinking, dear Giles, that I was disappointed in my dress, that I was worrying about my appearance, that I cared.

It was Frank who brought me a plate of chicken and ham that

I could not eat, and Frank who stood by my elbow with a glass of champagne I would not drink.

'I wish you would,' he said quietly, 'I think you need it,' and I took three sips of it to please him. The black patch over his eye gave him a pale odd appearance, it made him look older, different. There seemed to be lines on his face I had not seen before.

He moved amongst the guests like another host, seeing to their comfort, that they were supplied with drink, and food, and cigarettes, and he danced too in solemn painstaking fashion, walking his partners round the room with a set face. He did not wear his pirate costume with abandon, and there was something rather tragic about the side-whiskers he had fluffed under the scarlet handkerchief on his head. I thought of him standing before the looking-glass in his bare bachelor bedroom curling them round his fingers. Poor Frank. Dear Frank. I never asked, I never knew, how much he hated the last fancy dress ball given at Manderley.

The band played on, and the swaying couples twisted like bobbing marionettes, to and fro, to and fro, across the great hall and back again, and it was not I who watched them at all, not someone with feelings, made of flesh and blood, but a dummy-stick of a person in my stead, a prop who wore a smile screwed to its face. The figure who stood beside it was wooden too. His face was a mask, his smile was not his own. The eyes were not the eyes of the man I loved, the man I knew. They looked through me and beyond me, cold, expressionless, to some place of pain and torture I could not enter, to some private, inward hell I could not share.

He never spoke to me. He never touched me. We stood beside one another, the host and the hostess, and we were not together. I watched his courtesy to his guests. He flung a word to one, a jest to another, a smile to a third, a call over his shoulder to a fourth, and no one but myself could know that every utterance he made, every movement, was automatic and the work of a machine. We were like two performers in a play, but we were divided, we were not acting with one another. We had to endure it alone, we had to put up this show, this miserable, sham performance, for the sake of all these people I did not know and did not want to see again.

'I hear your wife's frock never turned up in time,' said some-one with a mottled face and a sailor's pig-tail, and he laughed, and dug Maxim in the ribs. 'Damn shame, what? I should sue the shop for fraud. Same thing happened to my wife's cousin once.'

'Yes, it was unfortunate,' said Maxim.

'I tell you what,' said the sailor, turning to me, 'you ought to say you are a forget-me-not. They're blue aren't they? Jolly little flowers, forget-me-nots. That's right, isn't it, de Winter? Tell your wife she must call herself a "forget-me-not".' He swept away, roaring with laughter, his partner in his arms. 'Pretty good idea, what? A forget-me-not.' Then Frank again hovering just behind me, another glass in his hand, lemonade this time. 'No, Frank, I'm not thirsty.'

'Why don't you dance? Or come and sit down a moment; there's a corner in the terrace.'

'No, I'm better standing. I don't want to sit down.'

'Can't I get you something, a sandwich, a peach?'

'No, I don't want anything.'

There was the salmon lady again; she forgot to smile at me this time. She was flushed after her supper. She kept looking up into her partner's face. He was very tall, very thin, he had a chin like a fiddle.

The Destiny waltz, the Blue Danube, the Merry Widow, one-two-three, one-two-three, round-and-round, one-two-three, one-two-three, round-and-round. The salmon lady, a green lady, Beatrice again, her veil pushed back off her forehead; Giles, his face streaming with perspiration, and that sailor once more, with another partner; they stopped beside me, I did not know her; she was dressed as a Tudor woman, any Tudor woman; she wore a ruffle round her throat and a black velvet dress.

'When are you coming to see us?' she said, as though we were old friends, and I answered, 'Soon of course; we were talking about it the other day,' wondering why I found it so easy to lie suddenly, no effort at all. 'Such a delightful party; I do congratu-late you,' she said, and 'Thank you very much,' I said. 'It's fun, isn't it?'

'I hear they sent you the wrong dress?'

'Yes; absurd, wasn't it?'

'These shops are all the same. No depending on them. But you look delightfully fresh in that pale blue. Much more comfortable than this hot velvet. Don't forget, you must both come and dine at the Palace soon.'

'We should love to.'

What did she mean, where, what palace? Were we entertaining royalty? She swept on to the Blue Danube in the arms of the sailor, her velvet frock brushing the ground like a carpet-sweeper, and it was not until long afterwards, in the middle of some night, when I could not sleep, that I remembered the Tudor woman was the bishop's wife who liked walking in the Pennines.

What was the time? I did not know. The evening dragged on, hour after hour; the same faces and the same tunes. Now and again the bridge people crept out of the library like hermits to watch the dancers, and then returned again. Beatrice, her draperies trailing behind her, whispered in my ear.

'Why don't you sit down? You look like death.'

'I'm all right.'

Giles, the make-up running on his face, poor fellow, and stifling in his Arab blanket, came up to me and said, 'Come and watch the fireworks on the terrace.'

I remember standing on the terrace and staring up at the sky as the foolish rockets burst and fell. There was little Clarice in a corner with some boy off the estate; she was smiling happily, squealing with delight as a squib spluttered at her feet. She had forgotten her tears.

'Hullo, this will be a big 'un.' Giles, his large face upturned, his mouth open. 'Here she comes. Bravo, jolly fine show.'

The slow hiss of the rocket as it sped into the air, the burst of the explosion, the stream of little emerald stars. A murmur of approval from the crowd, cries of delight, and a clapping of hands.

The salmon lady well to the front, her face eager with expectation, a remark for every star that fell. 'Oh, what a beauty . . . look at that one now; I say, how pretty . . . Oh, that one didn't burst . . . take care, it's coming our way . . . what are those men doing over there?' ... Even the hermits left their lair and came to join the dancers on the terrace. The lawns were black with people. The bursting stars shone on their upturned faces.

Again and again the rockets sped into the air like arrows, and the sky became crimson and gold. Manderley stood out like an enchanted house, every window aflame, the grey walls coloured by the falling stars. A house bewitched, carved out of the dark woods. And when the last rocket burst and the cheering died away, the night that had been fine before seemed dull and heavy in contrast, the sky became a pall. The little groups on the lawns and in the drive broke up and scattered. The guests crowded the long windows in the terrace back to the drawing-room again. It was anticlimax, the aftermath had come. We stood about with blank faces. Someone gave me a glass of champagne. I heard the sound of cars starting up in the drive.

'They're beginning to go,' I thought. 'Thank God, they're beginning to go.' The salmon lady was having some more supper. It would take time yet to clear the hall. I saw Frank make a signal to the band. I stood in the doorway between the drawing-room and the hall beside a man I did not know.

'What a wonderful party it's been,' he said.

'Yes,' I said.

'I've enjoyed every minute of it,' he said.

'I'm so glad,' I said.

'Molly was wild with fury at missing it,' he said.

'Was she?' I said.

The band began to play Auld Lang Syne. The man seized my hand and started swinging it up and down. 'Here,' he said, 'come on, some of you.' Somebody else swung my other hand, and more people joined us. We stood in a great circle singing at the top of our voices. The man who had enjoyed his evening and said Molly would be wild at missing it was dressed as a Chinese mandarin, and his false nails got caught up in his sleeve as we swung our hands up and down. He roared with laughter. We all laughed. 'Should auld acquaintance be forgot,' we sang.

The hilarious gaiety changed swiftly at the closing bars, and the drummer rattled his sticks in the inevitable prelude to God Save the King. The smiles left our faces as though wiped clean by a sponge. The Mandarin sprang to attention, his hands stiff to his sides. I remember wondering vaguely if he was in the Army. How queer he looked with his long poker face, and his drooping Mandarin moustache. I caught the salmon lady's eye. God Save the King had taken her unawares, she was still holding a plate heaped with chicken in aspic. She held it stiffly out in front of her like a church collection. All animation had gone from her face. As the last note of God Save the King died away she relaxed again, and attacked her chicken in a sort of frenzy, chattering over her shoulder to her partner. Somebody came and wrung me by the hand.

'Don't forget, you're dining with us on the fourteenth of next month.'

'Oh, are we?' I stared at him blankly.

'Yes, we've got your sister-in-law to promise too.'

'Oh. Oh, what fun.'

'Eight-thirty, and black tie. So looking forward to seeing you.'

'Yes. Yes, rather.'

People began to form up in queues to say good-bye. Maxim was at the other side of the room. I put on my smile again, which had worn thin after Auld Lang Syne.

'The best evening I've spent for a long time.'

'I'm so glad.'

'Many thanks for a grand party.'

'I'm so glad.'

'Here we are, you see, staying to the bitter end.'

'Yes, I'm so glad.'

Was there no other sentence in the English language? I bowed and smiled like a dummy, my eyes searching for Maxim above their heads. He was caught up in a knot of people by the library. Beatrice too was surrounded, and Giles had led a team of stragglers to the buffet table in the drawing-room. Frank was out in the drive seeing that people got their cars. I was hemmed in by strangers.

'Good-bye, and thanks tremendously.'

'I'm so glad.'

The great hall began to empty. Already it wore that drab deserted air of a vanished evening and the dawn of a tired day.

There was a grey light on the terrace, I could see the shapes of the blown firework stands taking form on the lawns.

'Good-bye; a wonderful party.'

'I'm so glad.'

Maxim had gone out to join Frank in the drive. Beatrice came up to me, pulling off her jangling bracelets. 'I can't stand these things a moment longer. Heavens, I'm dead beat. I don't believe I've missed a dance. Anyway, it was a tremendous success.'

'Was it?' I said.

'My dear, hadn't you better go to bed? You look worn out. You've been standing nearly all the evening Where are the men?'

'Out on the drive.'

'I shall have some coffee, and eggs and bacon. What about you?'

'No, Beatrice, I don't think I will.'

'You looked very charming in your blue. Everyone said so. And nobody had an inkling about – about the other things, so you mustn't worry.'

'No.'

'If I were you I should have a good long lie tomorrow morning. Don't attempt to get up. Have your breakfast in bed.'

'Yes, perhaps.'

'I'll tell Maxim you've gone up, shall I?'

'Please, Beatrice.'

'All right, my dear. Sleep well.' She kissed me swiftly, patting my shoulder at the same time, and then went off to find Giles in the supper room. I walked slowly up the stairs, one step at a time. The band had turned the lights off in the gallery, and had gone down to have eggs and bacon too. Pieces of music lay about the floor. One chair had been upturned. There was an ash-tray full of the stubs of their cigarettes. The aftermath of the party. I went along the corridor to my room. It was getting lighter every moment, and the birds had started singing. I did not have to turn on the light to undress. A little chill wind blew in from the open window. It was rather cold. Many people must have used the rose-garden during the evening, for all the chairs were moved, and dragged from their places. There was a tray of empty glasses on one of the tables. Someone had left a bag behind on a chair.

I pulled the curtain to darken the room, but the grey morning light found its way through the gaps at the side.

I got into bed, my legs very weary, a niggling pain in the small of my back. I lay back and closed my eyes, thankful for the cool white comfort of clean sheets. I wished my mind would rest like my body, relax, and pass to sleep. Not hum round in the way it did, jigging to music, whirling in a sea of faces. I pressed my hands over my eyes but they would not go.

I wondered how long Maxim would be. The bed beside me looked stark and cold. Soon there would be no shadows in the room at all, the walls and the ceiling and the floor would be white with the morning. The birds would sing their songs, louder, gayer, less subdued. The sun would make a yellow pattern on the curtain. My little bedside clock ticked out the minutes one by one. The hand moved round the dial. I lay on my side watching it. It came to the hour and passed it again. It started afresh on its journey. But Maxim did not come.

18

I THINK I fell asleep a little after seven. It was broad daylight, I remember, there was no longer any pretence that the drawn curtains hid the sun. The light streamed in at the open window and made patterns on the wall. I heard the men below in the rose-garden clearing away the tables and the chairs, and taking down the chain of fairy lights. Maxim's bed was still bare and empty. I lay across my bed, my arms over my eyes, a strange, mad position and the least likely to bring sleep, but I drifted to the border-line of the unconscious and slipped over it at last. When I awoke it was past eleven, and Clarice must have come in and brought me my tea without my hearing her, for there was a tray by my side, and a stone-cold tea-pot, and my clothes had been tidied, my blue frock put away in the wardrobe.

I drank my cold tea, still blurred and stupid from my short heavy sleep, and stared at the blank wall in front of me. Maxim's empty bed brought me to realization with a queer shock to my heart, and the full anguish of the night before was upon me once again. He had not come to bed at all. His pyjamas lay folded on the turned-down sheet untouched. I wondered what Clarice had thought when she came into the room with my tea. Had she noticed? Would she have gone out and told the other servants, and would they all discuss it over their breakfast? I wondered why I minded that, and why the thought of the servants talking about it in the kitchen should cause me such distress. It must be that I had a small mean mind, a conventional, petty hatred of gossip.

That was why I had come down last night in my blue dress and had not stayed hidden in my room. There was nothing brave or fine about it, it was a wretched tribute to convention. I had not come down for Maxim's sake, for Beatrice's, for the sake of Manderley. I had come down because I did not want the people at the ball to think I had quarrelled with Maxim. I didn't want them to go home and say, 'Of course you know they don't get on. I hear he's not at all happy.' I had come for my own sake, my own poor personal pride. As I sipped my cold tea I thought with a tired bitter feeling of despair that I would be content to live in one corner of Manderley and Maxim in the other so long as the outside world should never know. If he had no more tenderness for me, never kissed me again, did not speak to me except on matters of necessity, I believed I could bear it if I were certain that nobody knew of this but our two selves. If we could bribe servants not to tell, play our part before relations, before Beatrice, and then when we were alone sit apart in our separate rooms, leading our separate lives.

It seemed to me, as I sat there in bed, staring at the wall, at the sunlight coming in at the window, at Maxim's empty bed, that there was nothing quite so shaming, so degrading as a marriage that had failed. Failed after three months, as mine had done. For I had no illusions left now, I no longer made any effort to pretend. Last night had shown me too well. My marriage was a failure. All the things that people would say about it if they knew, were true. We did not get on. We were not companions. We were not suited to one another. I was too young for Maxim, too inexperienced, and, more important still, I was not of his world. The fact that I loved him in a sick, hurt, desperate way, like a child or a dog, did not matter. It was not the sort of love he needed. He wanted something else that I could not give him, something he had had before. I thought of the youthful almost hysterical excitement and conceit with which I had gone into this marriage, imagining I would bring happiness to Maxim, who had known much greater happiness before. Even Mrs Van Hopper, with her cheap views and common outlook, had known I was making a mistake. 'I'm afraid you will regret it,' she said. 'I believe you are making a big mistake.'

I would not listen to her, I thought her hard and cruel. But she was right. She was right in everything. That last mean thrust thrown at me before she said good-bye, 'You don't flatter yourself he's in love with you, do you? He's lonely, he can't bear that great empty house,' was the sanest, most truthful statement she had

ever made in her life. Maxim was not in love with me, he had
never loved me. Our honeymoon in Italy had meant nothing at
all to him, nor our living here together. What I had thought was
love for me, for myself as a person, was not love. It was just that
he was a man, and I was his wife and was young, and he was
lonely. He did not belong to me at all, he belonged to Rebecca.
He still thought about Rebecca. He would never love me because
of Rebecca. She was in the house still, as Mrs Danvers had said;
she was in that room in the west wing, she was in the library, in
the morning-room, in the gallery above the hall. Even in the little
flower room, where her mackintosh still hung. And in the garden, and in the woods, and down in the stone cottage on the
beach. Her footsteps sounded in the corridors, her scent lingered
on the stairs. The servants obeyed her orders still, the food we ate
was the food she liked. Her favourite flowers filled the rooms.
Her clothes were in the wardrobes in her room, her brushes were
on the table, her shoes beneath the chair, her nightdress on her
bed. Rebecca was still mistress of Manderley. Rebecca was still
Mrs de Winter. I had no business here at all. I had come blunder-
ing like a poor fool on ground that was preserved. 'Where is
Rebecca?' Maxim's grandmother had cried. 'I want Rebecca.
What have you done with Rebecca?' She did not know me, she
did not care about me. Why should she? I was a stranger to her.
I did not belong to Maxim or to Manderley. And Beatrice at our
first meeting, looking me up and down, frank, direct, 'You're so
very different from Rebecca.' Frank, reserved, embarrassed
when I spoke of her, hating those questions I had poured upon
him, even as I had hated them myself, and then answering that
final one as we came towards the house, his voice grave and quiet.
'Yes, she was the most beautiful creature I have ever seen.'

Rebecca, always Rebecca. Wherever I walked in Manderley,
wherever I sat, even in my thoughts and in my dreams, I met
Rebecca. I knew her figure now, the long slim legs, the small and
narrow feet. Her shoulders, broader than mine, the capable clever
hands. Hands that could steer a boat, could hold a horse. Hands
that arranged flowers, made the models of ships, and wrote 'Max
from Rebecca' on the fly-leaf of a book. I knew her face too,
small and oval, the clear white skin, the cloud of dark hair. I knew

the scent she wore, I could guess her laughter and her smile. If I heard it, even among a thousand others, I should recognize her voice. Rebecca, always Rebecca. I should never be rid of Rebecca.

Perhaps I haunted her as she haunted me; she looked down on me from the gallery as Mrs Danvers had said, she sat beside me when I wrote my letters at her desk. That mackintosh I wore, that handkerchief I used. They were hers. Perhaps she knew and had seen me take them. Jasper had been her dog, and he ran at my heels now. The roses were hers and I cut them. Did she resent me and fear me as I resented her? Did she want Maxim alone in the house again? I could fight the living but I could not fight the dead. If there was some woman in London that Maxim loved, someone he wrote to, visited, dined with, slept with, I could fight with her. We would stand on common ground. I should not be afraid. Anger and jealousy were things that could be conquered. One day the woman would grow old or tired or different, and Maxim would not love her any more. But Rebecca would never grow old. Rebecca would always be the same. And her I could not fight. She was too strong for me.

I got out of bed and pulled the curtains. The sun streamed into the room. The men had cleared the mess away from the rose-garden. I wondered if people were talking about the ball in the way they do the day after a party.

'Did you think it quite up to their usual standard?'

'Oh, I think so.'

'The band dragged a bit, I thought.'

'The supper was damn good.'

'Fireworks weren't bad.'

'Bee Lacy is beginning to look old.'

'Who wouldn't in that get-up?'

'I thought he looked rather ill.'

'He always does.'

'What did you think of the bride?'

'Not much. Rather dull.'

'I wonder if it's a success.'

'Yes, I wonder . . .'

Then I noticed for the first time there was a note under my

door. I went and picked it up. I recognized the square hand of
Beatrice. She had scribbled it in pencil after breakfast.

> I knocked at your door but had no answer so gather you've
> taken my advice and are sleeping off last night. Giles is
> anxious to get back early as they have rung up from home
> to say he's wanted to take somebody's place in a cricket
> match, and it starts at two. How he is going to see the ball
> after all the champagne he put away last night heaven only
> knows! I'm feeling a bit weak in the legs, but slept like a
> top. Frith says Maxim was down to an early breakfast, and
> there's now no sign of him! So please give him our love,
> and many thanks to you both for our evening, which we
> thoroughly enjoyed. Don't think any more about the dress.
> [This last was heavily underlined] Yours affectionately, Bee.
> [And a postscript] You must both come over and see us soon.

She had scribbled nine-thirty a.m. at the top of the paper, and
it was now nearly half past eleven. They had been gone about
two hours. They would be home by now, Beatrice with her suit-
case unpacked, going out into her garden and taking up her ordinary routine, and Giles preparing for his match, renewing the
whipping on his bat.

In the afternoon Beatrice would change into a cool frock and
a shady hat and watch Giles play cricket. They would have tea
afterwards in a tent, Giles very hot and red in the face, Beatrice
laughing and talking to her friends. 'Yes, we went over for the
dance at Manderley; it was great fun. I wonder Giles was able to
run a yard.' Smiling at Giles, patting him on the back. They were
both middle-aged and unromantic. They had been married for
twenty years and had a grown-up son who was going to Oxford.
They were very happy. Their marriage was a success. It had not
failed after three months as mine had done.

I could not go on sitting in my bedroom any longer. The
maids would want to come and do the room. Perhaps Clarice
would not have noticed about Maxim's bed after all. I rumpled
it, to make it look as though he had slept there. I did not want
the housemaids to know, if Clarice had not told them.

I had a bath and dressed, and went downstairs. The men had taken up the floor already in the hall and the flowers had been carried away. The music stands were gone from the gallery. The band must have caught an early train. The gardeners were sweeping the lawns and the drive clear of the spent fireworks. Soon, there would be no trace left of the fancy dress ball at Manderley. How long the preparations had seemed, and how short and swift the clearance now.

I remembered the salmon lady standing by the drawing-room door with her plate of chicken, and it seemed to me a thing I must have fancied, or something that had happened very long ago. Robert was polishing the table in the dining-room. He was normal again, stolid, dull, not the fey excited creature of the past few weeks.

'Good morning, Robert,' I said.

'Good morning, Madam.'

'Have you seen Mr de Winter anywhere?'

'He went out soon after breakfast, Madam, before Major and Mrs Lacy were down. He has not been in since.'

'You don't know where he went?'

'No, Madam, I could not say.'

I wandered back again into the hall. I went through the drawing-room to the morning-room. Jasper rushed at me and licked my hands in a frenzy of delight as if I had been away for a long time. He had spent the evening on Clarice's bed and I had not seen him since tea-time yesterday. Perhaps the hours had been as long for him as they had for me.

I picked up the telephone and asked for the number of the estate office. Perhaps Maxim was with Frank. I felt I must speak to him, even if it was only for two minutes. I must explain to him that I had not meant to do what I had done last night. Even if I never spoke to him again, I must tell him that. The clerk answered the telephone, and told me that Maxim was not there.

'Mr Crawley is here, Mrs de Winter,' said the clerk; 'would you speak to him?' I would have refused, but he gave me no chance, and before I could put down the receiver I heard Frank's voice.

'Is anything the matter?' It was a funny way to begin a

conversation. The thought flashed through my mind. He did not say good-morning, or did you sleep well? Why did he ask if something was the matter?

'Frank, it's me,' I said; 'where's Maxim?'

'I don't know, I haven't seen him. He's not been in this morning.'

'Not been to the office?'

'No.'

'Oh! Oh, well, it doesn't matter.'

'Did you see him at breakfast?' Frank said.

'No, I did not get up.'

'How did he sleep?'

I hesitated, Frank was the only person I did not mind knowing. 'He did not come to bed last night.'

There was silence at the other end of the line, as though Frank was thinking hard for an answer.

'Oh,' he said at last, very slowly. 'Oh, I see,' and then, after a minute, 'I was afraid something like that would happen.'

'Frank,' I said desperately, 'what did he say last night when everyone had gone? What did you all do?'

'I had a sandwich with Giles and Mrs Lacy,' said Frank. 'Maxim did not come. He made some excuse and went into the library. I came back home almost at once. Perhaps Mrs Lacy can tell you.'

'She's gone,' I said, 'they went after breakfast. She sent up a note. She had not seen Maxim, she said.'

'Oh,' said Frank. I did not like it. I did not like the way he said it. It was sharp, ominous.

'Where do you think he's gone?' I said.

'I don't know,' said Frank; 'perhaps he's gone for a walk.' It was the sort of voice doctors used to relatives at a nursing-home when they came to inquire.

'Frank, I must see him,' I said. 'I've got to explain about last night.'

Frank did not answer. I could picture his anxious face, the lines on his forehead.

'Maxim thinks I did it on purpose,' I said, my voice breaking in spite of myself, and the tears that had blinded me last night and I had not shed came coursing down my cheeks sixteen hours too late. 'Maxim thinks I did it as a joke, a beastly damnable joke!'

'No,' said Frank. 'No.'

'He does, I tell you. You didn't see his eyes, as I did. You didn't stand beside him all the evening, watching him, as I did. He didn't speak to me, Frank. He never looked at me again. We stood there together the whole evening and we never spoke to one another.'

'There was no chance,' said Frank. 'All those people. Of course I saw, don't you think I know Maxim well enough for that? Look here . . .'

'I don't blame him,' I interrupted. 'If he believes I played that vile hideous joke he has a right to think what he likes of me, and never talk to me again, never see me again.'

'You mustn't talk like that,' said Frank. 'You don't know what you're saying. Let me come up and see you. I think I can explain.'

What was the use of Frank coming to see me, and us sitting in the morning-room together, Frank smoothing me down, Frank being tactful, Frank being kind? I did not want kindness from anybody now. It was too late.

'No,' I said. 'No, I don't want to go over it and over it again. It's happened, it can't be altered now. Perhaps it's a good thing; it's made me realize something I ought to have known before, that I ought to have suspected when I married Maxim.'

'What do you mean?' said Frank.

His voice was sharp, queer. I wondered why it should matter to him about Maxim not loving me. Why did he not want me to know?

'About him and Rebecca,' I said, and as I said her name it sounded strange and sour like a forbidden word, a relief to me no longer, not a pleasure, but hot and shaming as a sin confessed.

Frank did not answer for a moment. I heard him draw in his breath at the other end of the wire.

'What do you mean?' he said again, shorter and sharper than before. 'What do you mean?'

'He doesn't love me, he loves Rebecca,' I said. 'He's never forgotten her, he thinks about her still, night and day. He's never loved me, Frank. It's always Rebecca, Rebecca, Rebecca.'

I heard Frank give a startled cry but I did not care how much

I shocked him now. 'Now you know how I feel,' I said, 'now you understand.'

'Look here,' he said; 'I've got to come and see you, I've got to, do you hear? It's vitally important; I can't talk to you down the telephone. Mrs de Winter? Mrs de Winter?'

I slammed down the receiver, and got up from the writing-desk. I did not want to see Frank. He could not help me over this. No one could help me but myself. My face was red and blotchy from crying. I walked about the room biting the corner of my handkerchief, tearing at the edge.

The feeling was strong within me that I should never see Maxim again. It was certainty, born of some strange instinct. He had gone away and would not come back. I knew in my heart that Frank believed this too and would not admit it to me on the telephone. He did not want to frighten me. If I rang him up again at the office now I should find that he had gone. The clerk would say, 'Mr Crawley has just gone out, Mrs de Winter', and I could see Frank, hatless, climbing into his small, shabby Morris, driving off in search of Maxim.

I went and stared out of the window at the little clearing where the satyr played his pipes. The rhododendrons were all over now. They would not bloom again for another year. The tall shrubs looked dark and drab now that the colour had gone. A fog was rolling up from the sea, and I could not see the woods beyond the bank. It was very hot, very oppressive. I could imagine our guests of last night saying to one another, 'What a good thing this fog kept off for yesterday, we should never have seen the fireworks.' I went out of the morning-room and through the drawing-room to the terrace. The sun had gone in now behind a wall of mist. It was as though a blight had fallen upon Manderley taking the sky away and the light of the day. One of the gardeners passed me with a barrow full of bits of paper, and litter, and the skins of fruit left on the lawns by the people last night.

'Good morning,' I said.

'Good morning, Madam.'

'I'm afraid the ball last night has made a lot of work for you,' I said.

'That's all right, Madam,' he said. 'I think everyone enjoyed themselves good and hearty, and that's the main thing, isn't it?'

'Yes, I suppose so,' I said.

He looked across the lawns to the clearing in the woods where the valley sloped to the sea. The dark trees loomed thin and indistinct.

'It's coming up very thick,' he said.

'Yes,' I said.

'A good thing it wasn't like this last night,' he said.

'Yes,' I said.

He waited a moment, and then he touched his cap and went off trundling his barrow. I went across the lawns to the edge of the woods. The mist in the trees had turned to moisture and dripped upon my bare head like a thin rain. Jasper stood by my feet dejected, his tail downcast, his pink tongue hanging from his mouth. The clammy oppression of the day made him listless and heavy. I could hear the sea from where I stood, sullen and slow, as it broke in the coves below the woods. The white fog rolled on past me towards the house smelling of damp salt and seaweed. I put my hand on Jasper's coat. It was wringing wet. When I looked back at the house I could not see the chimneys or the contour of the walls, I could only see the vague substance of the house, the windows in the west wing, and the flower tubs on the terrace. The shutter had been pulled aside from the window of the large bedroom in the west wing, and someone was standing there, looking down upon the lawns. The figure was shadowy and indistinct and for one moment of shock and fear I believed it to be Maxim. Then the figure moved, I saw the arm reach up to fold the shutter, and I knew it was Mrs Danvers. She had been watching me as I stood at the edge of the woods bathed in that white wall of fog. She had seen me walk slowly from the terrace to the lawns. She may have listened to my conversation with Frank on the telephone from the connecting line in her own room. She would know that Maxim had not been with me last night. She would have heard my voice, known about my tears. She knew the part I had played through the long hours, standing by Maxim's side in my blue dress at the bottom of the stairs, and that he had not looked at me nor spoken to me. She knew because she had meant it to happen. This was her triumph, hers and Rebecca's.

I thought of her as I had seen her last night, watching me through the open door to the west wing, and that diabolical smile on her white skull's face, and I remembered that she was a living breathing woman like myself, she was made of flesh and blood. She was not dead, like Rebecca. I could speak to her, but I could not speak to Rebecca.

I walked back across the lawns on sudden impulse to the house. I went through the hall and up the great stairs, I turned in under the archway by the gallery, I passed through the door to the west wing, and so along the dark silent corridor to Rebecca's room. I turned the handle of the door and went inside.

Mrs Danvers was still standing by the window, and the shutter was folded back.

'Mrs Danvers,' I said. 'Mrs Danvers.' She turned to look at me, and I saw her eyes were red and swollen with crying, even as mine were, and there were dark shadows in her white face.

'What is it?' she said, and her voice was thick and muffled from the tears she had shed, even as mine had been.

I had not expected to find her so. I had pictured her smiling as she had smiled last night, cruel and evil. Now she was none of these things, she was an old woman who was ill and tired.

I hesitated, my hand still on the knob of the open door, and I did not know what to say to her now or what to do.

She went on staring at me with those red, swollen eyes and I could not answer her. 'I left the menu on the desk as usual,' she said. 'Do you want something changed?' Her words gave me courage, and I left the door and came to the middle of the room.

'Mrs Danvers,' I said. 'I have not come to talk about the menu. You know that, don't you?'

She did not answer me. Her left hand opened and shut.

'You've done what you wanted, haven't you?' I said, 'you meant this to happen, didn't you? Are you pleased now? Are you happy?'

She turned her head away, and looked out of the window as she had done when I first came into the room. 'Why did you ever come here?' she said. 'Nobody wanted you at Manderley. We were all right until you came. Why did you not stay where you were out in France?'

'You seem to forget I love Mr de Winter,' I said.

'If you loved him you would never have married him,' she said.

I did not know what to say. The situation was mad, unreal. She kept talking in that choked muffled way with her head turned from me.

'I thought I hated you but I don't now,' she said; 'it seems to have spent itself, all the feeling I had.'

'Why should you hate me?' I asked; 'what have I ever done to you that you should hate me?'

'You tried to take Mrs de Winter's place,' she said.

Still she would not look at me. She stood there sullen, her head turned from me. 'I had nothing changed,' I said. 'Manderley went on as it had always been. I gave no orders, I left everything to you. I would have been friends with you, if you had let me, but you set yourself against me from the first. I saw it in your face, the moment I shook hands with you.'

She did not answer, and her hand kept opening and shutting against her dress. 'Many people marry twice, men and women,' I said. 'There are thousands of second marriages taking place every day. You talk as though my marrying Mr de Winter was a crime, a sacrilege against the dead. Haven't we as much right to be happy as anyone else?'

'Mr de Winter is not happy,' she said, turning to look at me at last; 'any fool can see that. You have only to look at his eyes. He's still in hell, and he's looked like that ever since she died.'

'It's not true,' I said. 'It's not true. He was happy when we were in France together; he was younger, much younger, and laughing and gay.'

'Well, he's a man, isn't he?' she said. 'No man denies himself on a honeymoon, does he? Mr de Winter's not forty-six yet.'

She laughed contemptuously, and shrugged her shoulders.

'How dare you speak to me like that? How dare you?' I said.

I was not afraid of her any more. I went up to her, shook her by the arm. 'You made me wear that dress last night,' I said, 'I should never have thought of it but for you. You did it because you wanted to hurt Mr de Winter, you wanted to make him suffer. Hasn't he suffered enough without your playing that vile hideous joke upon him? Do you think his agony and pain will bring Mrs de Winter back again?'

She shook herself clear of me, the angry colour flooded her dead white face. 'What do I care for his suffering?' she said, 'he's never cared about mine. How do you think I've liked it, watching you sit in her place, walk in her footsteps, touch the things that were hers? What do you think it's meant to me all these months knowing that you wrote at her desk in the morning-room, using the very pen that she used, speaking down the house telephone, where she used to speak every morning of her life to me, ever since she first came to Manderley? What do you think it meant to me to hear Frith and Robert and the rest of the servants talking about you as "Mrs de Winter"? "Mrs de Winter has gone out for a walk." "Mrs de Winter wants the car this afternoon at three o'clock." "Mrs de Winter won't be in to tea till five o'clock." And all the while my Mrs de Winter, my lady with her smile and her lovely face and brave ways, the real Mrs de Winter, lying dead and cold and forgotten in the church crypt. If he suffers then he deserves to suffer, marrying a young girl like you not ten months afterwards. Well, he's paying for it now, isn't he? I've seen his face, I've seen his eyes. He's made his own hell and there's no one but himself to thank for it. He knows she sees him, he knows she comes by night and watches him. And she doesn't come kindly, not she, not my lady. She was never one to stand mute and still and be wronged. "I'll see them in hell, Danny," she'd say, "I'll see them in hell first." "That's right, my dear," I'd tell her, "no one will put upon you. You were born into this world to take what you could out of it," and she did, she didn't care, she wasn't afraid. She had all the courage and spirit of a boy, had my Mrs de Winter. She ought to have been a boy, I often told her that. I had the care of her as a child. You knew that, didn't you?'

'No!' I said, 'no. Mrs Danvers, what's the use of all this? I don't want to hear any more, I don't want to know. Haven't I got feelings as well as you? Can't you understand what it means to me, to hear her mentioned, to stand here and listen while you tell me about her?'

She did not hear me, she went on raving like a mad woman, a fanatic, her long fingers twisting and tearing the black stuff of her dress.

'She was lovely then,' she said. 'Lovely as a picture; men turning to stare at her when she passed, and she not twelve years old. She knew then, she used to wink at me like the little devil she was. "I'm going to be a beauty, aren't I, Danny?" she said, and "We'll see about that, my love, we'll see about that," I told her. She had all the knowledge then of a grown person; she'd enter into conversation with men and women as clever and full of tricks as someone of eighteen. She twisted her father round her little finger, and she'd have done the same with her mother, had she lived. Spirit, you couldn't beat my lady for spirit. She drove a four-in-hand on her fourteenth birthday, and her cousin, Mr Jack, got up on the box beside her and tried to take the reins from her hands. They fought it out there together, for three minutes, like a couple of wild cats, and the horses galloping to glory. She won though, my lady won. She cracked her whip over his head and down he came, head-over-heels, cursing and laughing. They were a pair, I tell you, she and Mr Jack. They sent him in the Navy, but he wouldn't stand the discipline, and I don't blame him. He had too much spirit to obey orders, like my lady.'

I watched her, fascinated, horrified; a queer ecstatic smile was on her lips, making her older than ever, making her skull's face vivid and real. 'No one got the better of her, never, never,' she said. 'She did what she liked, she lived as she liked. She had the strength of a little lion too. I remember her at sixteen getting up on one of her father's horses, a big brute of an animal too, that the groom said was too hot for her to ride. She stuck to him, all right. I can see her now, with her hair flying out behind her, slashing at him, drawing blood, digging the spurs into his side, and when she got off his back he was trembling all over, full of froth and blood. "That will teach him, won't it, Danny?" she said, and walked off to wash her hands as cool as you please. And that's how she went at life, when she grew up. I saw her, I was with her. She cared for nothing and for no one. And then she was beaten in the end. But it wasn't a man, it wasn't a woman. The sea got her. The sea was too strong for her. The sea got her in the end.'

She broke off, her mouth working strangely, and dragging at the corners. She began to cry noisily, harshly, her mouth open and her eyes dry.

'Mrs Danvers,' I said. 'Mrs Danvers.' I stood before her helplessly, not knowing what to do. I mistrusted her no longer, I was afraid of her no more, but the sight of her sobbing there, dry-eyed, made me shudder, made me ill. 'Mrs Danvers,' I said, 'you're not well, you ought to be in bed. Why don't you go to your room and rest? Why don't you go to bed?'

She turned on me fiercely. 'Leave me alone, can't you?' she said. 'What's it to do with you if I show my grief? I'm not ashamed of it, I don't shut myself up in my room to cry. I don't walk up and down, up and down, in my room like Mr de Winter, with the door locked on me.'

'What do you mean?' I said. 'Mr de Winter does not do that.'

'He did,' she said, 'after she died. Up and down, up and down in the library. I heard him. I watched him too, through the key-hole, more than once. Backwards and forwards, like an animal in a cage.'

'I don't want to hear,' I said. 'I don't want to know.'

'And then you say you made him happy on his honeymoon,' she said; 'made him happy – you, a young ignorant girl, young enough to be his daughter. What do you know about life? What do you know about men? You come here and think you can take Mrs de Winter's place. You. You take my lady's place. Why, even the servants laughed at you when you came to Manderley. Even the little scullery-maid you met in the back passage there on your first morning. I wonder what Mr de Winter thought when he got you back here at Manderley, after his precious honeymoon was over. I wonder what he thought when he saw you sitting at the dining-room table for the first time.'

'You'd better stop this, Mrs Danvers,' I said; 'you'd better go to your room.'

'Go to my room,' she mimicked, 'go to my room. The mistress of the house thinks I had better go to my room. And after that, what then? You'll go running to Mr de Winter and saying, "Mrs Danvers has been unkind to me, Mrs Danvers has been

rude." You'll go running to him like you did before when Mr
Jack came to see me.'

'I never told him,' I said.

'That's a lie,' she said. 'Who else told him, if you didn't? No
one else was here. Frith and Robert were out, and none of the
other servants knew. I made up my mind then I'd teach you a
lesson, and him too. Let him suffer, I say. What do I care? What's
his suffering to me? Why shouldn't I see Mr Jack here at Manderley? He's the only link I have left now with Mrs de Winter. "I'll
not have him here," he said. "I'm warning you, it's the last time."
He's not forgotten to be jealous, has he?'

I remembered crouching in the gallery when the library door
was open. I remembered Maxim's voice raised in anger, using
the words that Mrs Danvers had just repeated. Jealous, Maxim
jealous . . .

'He was jealous while she lived, and now he's jealous when
she's dead,' said Mrs Danvers. 'He forbids Mr Jack the house now
like he did then. That shows you he's not forgotten her, doesn't
it? Of course he was jealous. So was I. So was everyone who knew
her. She didn't care. She only laughed. "I shall live as I please,
Danny," she told me, "and the whole world won't stop me." A
man had only to look at her once and be mad about her. I've seen
them here, staying in the house, men she'd meet up in London
and bring for week-ends. She would take them bathing from the
boat, she would have a picnic supper at her cottage in the cove.
They made love to her of course; who would not? She laughed,
she would come back and tell me what they had said, and what
they'd done. She did not mind, it was like a game to her. Like a
game. Who wouldn't be jealous? They were all jealous, all mad
for her. Mr de Winter, Mr Jack, Mr Crawley, everyone who
knew her, everyone who came to Manderley.'

'I don't want to know,' I said. 'I don't want to know.'

Mrs Danvers came close to me, she put her face near to mine.
'It's no use, is it?' she said. 'You'll never get the better of her.
She's still mistress here, even if she is dead. She's the real Mrs de
Winter, not you. It's you that's the shadow and the ghost. It's
you that's forgotten and not wanted and pushed aside. Well, why
don't you leave Manderley to her? Why don't you go?'

I backed away from her towards the window, my old fear and horror rising up in me again. She took my arm and held it like a vice.

'Why don't you go?' she said. 'We none of us want you. He doesn't want you, he never did. He can't forget her. He wants to be alone in the house again, with her. It's you that ought to be lying there in the church crypt, not her. It's you who ought to be dead, not Mrs de Winter.'

She pushed me towards the open window. I could see the terrace below me grey and indistinct in the white wall of fog. 'Look down there,' she said. 'It's easy, isn't it? Why don't you jump? It wouldn't hurt, not to break your neck. It's a quick, kind way. It's not like drowning. Why don't you try it? Why don't you go?'

The fog filled the open window, damp and clammy, it stung my eyes, it clung to my nostrils. I held on to the window-sill with my hands.

'Don't be afraid,' said Mrs Danvers. 'I won't push you. I won't stand by you. You can jump of your own accord. What's the use of your staying here at Manderley? You're not happy. Mr de Winter doesn't love you. There's not much for you to live for, is there? Why don't you jump now and have done with it? Then you won't be unhappy any more.'

I could see the flower tubs on the terrace and the blue of the hydrangeas clumped and solid. The paved stones were smooth and grey. They were not jagged and uneven. It was the fog that made them look so far away. They were not far really, the window was not so very high.

'Why don't you jump?' whispered Mrs Danvers. 'Why don't you try?'

The fog came thicker than before and the terrace was hidden from me. I could not see the flower tubs any more, nor the smooth paved stones. There was nothing but the white mist about me, smelling of sea-weed dank and chill. The only reality was the window-sill beneath my hands and the grip of Mrs Danvers on my left arm. If I jumped I should not see the stones rise up to meet me, the fog would hide them from me. The pain would be sharp and sudden as she said. The fall would break my neck. It would not be slow, like drowning. It would soon be over.

And Maxim did not love me. Maxim wanted to be alone again, with Rebecca.

'Go on,' whispered Mrs Danvers. 'Go on, don't be afraid.'

I shut my eyes. I was giddy from staring down at the terrace, and my fingers ached from holding to the ledge. The mist entered my nostrils and lay upon my lips rank and sour. It was stifling, like a blanket, like an anaesthetic. I was beginning to forget about being unhappy, and about loving Maxim. I was beginning to forget Rebecca. Soon I would not have to think about Rebecca any more . . .

As I relaxed my hands and sighed, the white mist and the silence that was part of it was shattered suddenly, was rent in two by an explosion that shook the window where we stood. The glass shivered in its frame. I opened my eyes. I stared at Mrs Danvers. The burst was followed by another, and yet a third and fourth. The sound of the explosions stung the air and the birds rose unseen from the woods around the house and made an echo with their clamour.

'What is it?' I said stupidly. 'What has happened?'

Mrs Danvers relaxed her grip upon my arm. She stared out of the window into the fog. 'It's the rockets,' she said; 'there must be a ship gone ashore there in the bay.'

We listened, staring into the white fog together. And then we heard the sound of footsteps running on the terrace beneath us.

19

IT WAS MAXIM. I could not see him but I could hear his voice. He was shouting for Frith as he ran. I heard Frith answer from the hall and come out on the terrace. Their figures loomed out of the mist beneath us.

'She's ashore all right,' said Maxim. 'I was watching her from the headland and I saw her come right into the bay, and head for the reef. They'll never shift her, not with these tides. She must have mistaken the bay for Kerrith harbour. It's like a wall out there, in the bay. Tell them in the house to stand by with food and drink in case these fellows want anything, and ring through to the office to Mr Crawley and tell him what's happened. I'm going back to the cove to see if I can do anything. Get me some cigarettes, will you?'

Mrs Danvers drew back from the window. Her face was expressionless once more, the cold white mask that I knew.

'We had better go down,' she said, 'Frith will be looking for me to make arrangements. Mr de Winter may bring the men back to the house as he said. Be careful of your hands, I'm going to shut the window.' I stepped back into the room still dazed and stupid, not sure of myself or of her. I watched her close the window and fasten the shutters, and draw the curtains in their place.

'It's a good thing there is no sea running,' she said, 'there wouldn't have been much chance for them then. But on a day like this there's no danger. The owners will lose their ship, though, if she's run on the reef as Mr de Winter said.'

She glanced round the room to make certain that nothing was disarranged or out of place. She straightened the cover on the double bed. Then she went to the door and held it open for me. 'I will tell them in the kitchen to serve cold lunch in the dining-room after all,' she said, 'and then it won't matter what time you come for it. Mr de Winter may not want to rush back at one o'clock if he's busy down there in the cove.'

I stared at her blankly and then passed out of the open door, stiff and wooden like a dummy.

'When you see Mr de Winter, Madam, will you tell him it will be quite all right if he wants to bring the men back from the ship? There will be a hot meal ready for them any time.'

'Yes,' I said. 'Yes, Mrs Danvers.'

She turned her back on me and went along the corridor to the service staircase, a weird gaunt figure in her black dress, the skirt just sweeping the ground like the full, wide skirts of thirty years ago. Then she turned the corner of the corridor and disappeared.

I walked slowly along the passage to the door by the archway, my mind still blunt and slow as though I had just woken from a long sleep. I pushed through the door and went down the stairs with no set purpose before me. Frith was crossing the hall towards the dining-room. When he saw me he stopped, and waited until I came down into the hall.

'Mr de Winter was in a few moments ago, Madam,' he said. 'He took some cigarettes, and then went back again to the beach. It appears there is a ship gone ashore.'

'Yes,' I said.

'Did you hear the rockets, Madam?' said Frith.

'Yes, I heard the rockets,' I said.

'I was in the pantry with Robert, and we both thought at first that one of the gardeners had let off a firework left over from last night,' said Frith, 'and I said to Robert, "What do they want to do that for in this weather? Why don't they keep them for the kiddies on Saturday night?" And then the next one came, and then the third. "That's not fireworks," says Robert, "that's a ship in distress." "I believe you're right," I said, and I went out to the hall and there was Mr de Winter calling me from the terrace.'

'Yes,' I said.

'Well, it's hardly to be wondered at in this fog, Madam. That's what I said to Robert just now. It's difficult to find your way on the road, let alone on the water.'

'Yes,' I said.

'If you want to catch Mr de Winter he went straight across the lawn only two minutes ago,' said Frith.

'Thank you, Frith,' I said.

I went out on the terrace. I could see the trees taking shape beyond the lawns. The fog was lifting, it was rising in little clouds to the sky above. It whirled above my head in wreaths of smoke. I looked up at the windows above my head. They were tightly closed, and the shutters were fastened. They looked as though they would never open, never be thrown wide.

It was by the large window in the centre that I had stood five minutes before. How high it seemed above my head, how lofty and remote. The stones were hard and solid under my feet. I looked down at my feet and then up again to the shuttered window, and as I did so I became aware suddenly that my head was swimming and I felt hot. A little trickle of perspiration ran down the back of my neck. Black dots jumped about in the air in front of me. I went into the hall again and sat down on a chair. My hands were quite wet. I sat very still, holding my knees.

'Frith,' I called, 'Frith, are you in the dining-room?'

'Yes, Madam?' He came out at once, and crossed the hall towards me.

'Don't think me very odd, Frith, but I rather think I'd like a small glass of brandy.'

'Certainly, Madam.'

I went on holding my knees and sitting very still. He came back with a liqueur glass on a silver salver.

'Do you feel a trifle unwell, Madam?' said Frith. 'Would you like me to call Clarice?'

'No, I'll be all right, Frith,' I said. 'I felt a bit hot, that's all.'

'It's a very warm morning, Madam. Very warm indeed. Oppressive, one might almost say.'

'Yes, Frith. Very oppressive.'

I drank the brandy and put the glass back on the silver salver.

'Perhaps the sound of those rockets alarmed you,' said Frith; 'they went off so very sudden.'

'Yes, they did,' I said.

'And what with the hot morning and standing about all last night, you are not perhaps feeling quite like yourself, Madam,' said Frith.

'No, perhaps not,' I said.

'Will you lie down for half an hour? It's quite cool in the library.'

'No. No, I think I'll go out in a moment or two. Don't bother, Frith.'

'No. Very good, Madam.'

He went away and left me alone in the hall. It was quiet sitting there, quiet and cool. All trace of the party had been cleared away. It might never have happened. The hall was as it had always been, grey and silent and austere, with the portraits and the weapons on the wall. I could scarcely believe that last night I had stood there in my blue dress at the bottom of the stairs, shaking hands with five hundred people. I could not believe that there had been music-stands in the minstrels' gallery, and a band playing there, a man with a fiddle, a man with a drum. I got up and went out on to the terrace again.

The fog was rising, lifting to the tops of the trees. I could see the woods at the end of the lawns. Above my head a pale sun tried to penetrate the heavy sky. It was hotter than ever. Oppressive, as Frith had said. A bee hummed by me in search of scent, bumbling, noisy, and then creeping inside a flower was suddenly silent. On the grass banks above the lawns the gardener started his mowing machine. A startled linnet fled from the whirring blades towards the rose-garden. The gardener bent to the handles of the machine and walked slowly along the bank scattering the short-tipped grass and the pin-point daisy-heads. The smell of the sweet warm grass came towards me on the air, and the sun shone down upon me full and strong from out of the white mist. I whistled for Jasper but he did not come. Perhaps he had followed Maxim when he went down to the beach. I glanced at my watch. It was after half past twelve, nearly twenty to one. This time yesterday Maxim and I were standing with Frank in the little garden in front of his house, waiting for his housekeeper to serve lunch.

Twenty-four hours ago. They were teasing me, baiting me

about my dress. 'You'll both get the surprise of your lives,'
I had said.

I felt sick with shame at the memory of my words. And then
I realized for the first time that Maxim had not gone away as I had
feared. The voice I had heard on the terrace was calm and practical. The voice I knew. Not the voice of last night when I stood
at the head of the stairs. Maxim had not gone away. He was down
there in the cove somewhere. He was himself, normal and sane.
He had just been for a walk, as Frank had said. He had been on
the headland, he had seen the ship closing in towards the shore.
All my fears were without foundation. Maxim was safe. Maxim
was all right. I had just experienced something that was degrading
and horrible and mad, something that I did not fully understand
even now, that I had no wish to remember, that I wanted to bury
for evermore, deep in the shadows of my mind with old forgotten
terrors of childhood; but even this did not matter as long as
Maxim was all right.

Then I, too, went down the steep twisting path through the
dark woods to the beach below.

The fog had almost gone, and when I came to the cove I could
see the ship at once, lying about two miles off-shore with her
bows pointed towards the cliffs. I went along the breakwater and
stood at the end of it, leaning against the rounded wall. There
was a crowd of people on the cliffs already who must have walked
along the coast-guard path from Kerrith. The cliffs and the headland were part of Manderley, but the public had always used the
right-of-way along the cliffs. Some of them were scrambling
down the cliff face to get a closer view of the stranded ship. She
lay at an awkward angle, her stern tilted, and there were a number
of rowing-boats already pulling round her. The life-boat was
standing off. I saw someone stand up in her and shout through a
megaphone. I could not hear what he was saying. It was still misty
out in the bay, and I could not see the horizon. Another motor-
boat chugged into the light with some men aboard. The
motor-boat was dark grey. I could see someone in uniform. That
would be the harbour-master from Kerrith, and the Lloyd's agent
with him. Another motor-boat followed, a party of holiday-
makers from Kerrith aboard. They circled round and round the

stranded steamer chatting excitedly. I could hear their voices echoing across the still water.

I left the breakwater and the cove and climbed up the path over the cliffs towards the rest of the people. I did not see Maxim anywhere. Frank was there, talking to one of the coast-guards. I hung back when I saw him, momentarily embarrassed. Barely an hour ago I had been crying to him, down the telephone. I was not sure what I ought to do. He saw me at once and waved his hand. I went over to him and the coast-guard. The coast-guard knew me.

'Come to see the fun, Mrs de Winter?' he said smiling. 'I'm afraid it will be a hard job. The tugs may shift her, but I doubt it. She's hard and fast where she is on that ledge.'

'What will they do?' I said.

'They'll send a diver down directly to see if she's broken her back,' he replied. 'There's the fellow there in the red stocking cap. Like to see through these glasses?'

I took his glasses and looked at the ship. I could see a group of men staring over her stern. One of them was pointing at something. The man in the life-boat was still shouting through the megaphone.

The harbour-master from Kerrith had joined the group of men in the stern of the stranded ship. The diver in his stocking cap was sitting in the grey motor-boat belonging to the harbour-master.

The pleasure-boat was still circling round the ship. A woman was standing up taking a snapshot. A group of gulls had settled on the water and were crying foolishly, hoping for scraps.

I gave the glasses back to the coast-guard.

'Nothing seems to be happening,' I said.

'They'll send him down directly,' said the coast-guard. 'They'll argue a bit first, like all foreigners. Here come the tugs.'

'They'll never do it,' said Frank. 'Look at the angle she's lying at. It's much shallower there than I thought.'

'That reef runs out quite a way,' said the coast-guard; 'you don't notice it in the ordinary way, going over that piece of water in a small boat. But a ship with her depth would touch all right.'

'I was down in the first cove by the valley when they fired the rockets,' said Frank. 'I could scarcely see three yards in front of me where I was. And then the things went off out of the blue.'

I thought how alike people were in a moment of common interest. Frank was Frith all over again, giving his version of the story, as though it mattered, as though we cared. I knew that he had gone down to the beach to look for Maxim. I knew that he had been frightened, as I had been. And now all this was forgotten and put aside: our conversation down the telephone, our mutual anxiety, his insistence that he must see me. All because a ship had gone ashore in the fog.

A small boy came running up to us. 'Will the sailors be drowned?' he asked.

'Not them. They're all right, sonny,' said the coast-guard. 'The sea's as flat as the back of my hand. No one's going to be hurt this time.'

'If it had happened last night we should never have heard them,' said Frank. 'We must have let off more than fifty rockets at our show, beside all the smaller things.'

'We'd have heard all right,' said the coast-guard. 'We'd have seen the flash and known the direction. There's the diver, Mrs de Winter. See him putting on his helmet?'

'I want to see the diver,' said the small boy.

'There he is,' said Frank, bending and pointing – 'that chap there putting on the helmet. They're going to lower him into the water.'

'Won't he be drowned?' said the child.

'Divers don't drown,' said the coast-guard. 'They have air pumped into them all the time. Watch him disappear. There he goes.'

The surface of the water was disturbed a minute and then was clear again. 'He's gone,' said the small boy.

'Where's Maxim?' I said.

'He's taken one of the crew into Kerrith,' said Frank; 'the fellow lost his head and jumped for it apparently when the ship struck. We found him clinging on to one of the rocks here under the cliff. He was soaked to the skin of course and shaking like a jelly. Couldn't speak a word of English, of course. Maxim went down to him, and found him bleeding like a pig from a scratch on the rocks. He spoke to him in German. Then he hailed one of the motor-boats from Kerrith that was hanging around like a hungry shark, and he's gone off with him to get him bandaged by a doctor. If he's lucky he'll just catch old Phillips sitting down to lunch.'

'When did he go?' I said.

'He went just before you turned up,' said Frank, 'about five minutes ago. I wonder you didn't see the boat. He was sitting in the stern with this German fellow.'

'He must have gone while I was climbing up the cliff,' I said.

'Maxim is splendid at anything like this,' said Frank. 'He always gives a hand if he can. You'll find he will invite the whole crew back to Manderley, and feed them, and give them beds into the bargain.'

'That's right,' said the coast-guard. 'He'd give the coat off his back for any of his own people, I know that. I wish there was more like him in the county.'

'Yes, we could do with them,' said Frank.

We went on staring at the ship. The tugs were standing off still, but the life-boat had turned and gone back towards Kerrith.

'It's not their turn today,' said the coast-guard.

'No,' said Frank, 'and I don't think it's a job for the tugs either. It's the ship-breaker who's going to make money this time.'

The gulls wheeled overhead, mewing like hungry cats; some of them settled on the ledges of the cliff, while others, bolder, rode the surface of the water beside the ship.

The coast-guard took off his cap and mopped his forehead.

'Seems kind of airless, doesn't it?' he said.

'Yes,' I said.

The pleasure-boat with the camera people went chugging off towards Kerrith. 'They've got fed up,' said the coast-guard.

'I don't blame them,' said Frank. 'I don't suppose anything will happen for hours. The diver will have to make his report before they try to shift her.'

'That's right,' said the coast-guard.

'I don't think there's much sense in hanging about here,' said Frank; 'we can't do anything. I want my lunch.'

I did not say anything. He hesitated. I felt his eyes upon me.

'What are you going to do?' he said.

'I think I shall stay here a bit,' I said. 'I can have lunch any time. It's cold. It doesn't matter. I want to see what the diver's going to do.' Somehow I could not face Frank just at the moment. I wanted to be alone, or with someone I did not know, like the coast-guard.

'You won't see anything,' said Frank; 'there won't be anything to see. Why not come back and have some lunch with me?'

'No,' I said. 'No, really . . .'

'Oh, well,' said Frank, 'you know where to find me if you do want me. I shall be at the office all the afternoon.'

'All right,' I said.

He nodded to the coast-guard and went off down the cliff towards the cove. I wondered if I had offended him. I could not help it. All these things would be settled some day, one day. So much seemed to have happened since I spoke to him on the tele-phone, and I did not want to think about anything any more. I just wanted to sit there on the cliff and stare at the ship.

'He's a good sort, Mr Crawley,' said the coast-guard.

'Yes,' I said.

'He'd give his right hand for Mr de Winter too,' he said.

'Yes, I think he would,' I said.

The small boy was still hopping around on the grass in front of us.

'When's the diver coming up again?' he said.

'Not yet, sonny,' said the coast-guard.

A woman in a pink striped frock and a hair-net came across the grass towards us. 'Charlie? Charlie? Where are you?' she called.

'Here's your mother coming to give you what-for,' said the coast-guard.

'I've seen the diver, Mum,' shouted the boy.

The woman nodded to us and smiled. She did not know me. She was a holiday-maker from Kerrith. 'The excitement all seems to be over doesn't it?' she said; 'they are saying down on the cliff there the ship will be there for days.'

'They're waiting for the diver's report,' said the coast-guard.

'I don't know how they get them to go down under the water like that,' said the woman; 'they ought to pay them well.'

'They do that,' said the coast-guard.

'I want to be a diver, Mum,' said the small boy.

'You must ask your Daddy, dear,' said the woman, laughing at us. 'It's a lovely spot up here, isn't it?' she said to me. 'We brought a picnic lunch, never thinking it would turn foggy and we'd have a wreck into the bargain. We were just thinking of going back to Kerrith when the rockets went off under our noses, it seemed. I nearly jumped out of my skin. "Why, whatever's that?" I said to my husband. "That's a distress signal," he said; "let's stop and see the fun." There's no dragging him away; he's as bad as my little boy. I don't see anything in it myself.'

'No, there's not much to see now,' said the coast-guard.

'Those are nice-looking woods over there; I suppose they're private,' said the woman.

The coast-guard coughed awkwardly, and glanced at me. I began eating a piece of grass and looked away.

'Yes, that's all private in there,' he said.

'My husband says all these big estates will be chopped up in time and bungalows built,' said the woman. 'I wouldn't mind a nice little bungalow up here facing the sea. I don't know that I'd care for this part of the world in the winter though.'

'No, it's very quiet here winter times,' said the coast-guard.

I went on chewing my piece of grass. The little boy kept running round in circles. The coast-guard looked at his watch. 'Well, I must be getting on,' he said; 'good afternoon!' He saluted me, and turned back along the path towards Kerrith. 'Come on, Charlie, come and find Daddy,' said the woman.

She nodded to me in friendly fashion, and sauntered off to the edge of the cliff, the little boy running at her heels. A thin man in khaki shorts and a striped blazer waved to her. They sat down by a clump of gorse bushes and the woman began to undo paper packages.

I wished I could lose my own identity and join them. Eat hard-boiled eggs and potted meat sandwiches, laugh rather loudly, enter their conversation, and then wander back with them during the afternoon to Kerrith and paddle on the beach, run races across the stretch of sand, and so to their lodgings and have shrimps for tea. Instead of which I must go back alone through the woods to Manderley and wait for Maxim. And I did not know what we should say to one another, how he would look at me, what would be his voice. I went on sitting there on the cliff. I was not hungry. I did not think about lunch.

More people came and wandered over the cliffs to look at the ship. It made an excitement for the afternoon. There was nobody I knew. They were all holiday-makers from Kerrith. The sea was glassy calm. The gulls no longer wheeled overhead, they had settled on the water a little distance from the ship. More pleasure-boats appeared during the afternoon. It must be a field day for Kerrith boat-men. The diver came up and then went down again. One of the tugs steamed away while the other still stood by. The harbour-master went back in his grey motor-boat, taking some men with him, and the diver who had come to the surface for the second time. The crew of the ship leant against the side throwing scraps to the gulls, while visitors in pleasure-boats rowed slowly round the ship. Nothing happened at all. It was dead low water now, and the ship was heeled at an angle, the propeller showing clean. Little ridges of white cloud formed in the western sky and the sun became pallid. It was still very hot. The woman in the pink striped frock with the little boy got up and wandered off along the path towards Kerrith, the man in the shorts following with the picnic basket.

I glanced at my watch. It was after three o'clock. I got up and went down the hill to the cove. It was quiet and deserted as always. The shingle was dark and grey. The water in the little harbour was glassy like a mirror. My feet made a queer crunching noise as I crossed the shingle. The ridges of white cloud now covered all the sky above my head, and the sun was hidden. When I came to the further side of the cove I saw Ben crouching by a little pool between two rocks scraping winkles into his hand. My shadow fell upon the water as I passed, and he looked up and saw me.

'G' day,' he said, his mouth opening in a grin.

'Good afternoon,' I said.

He scrambled to his feet and opened a dirty handkerchief he had filled with winkles.

'You eat winkles?' he said.

I did not want to hurt his feelings. 'Thank you,' I said.

He emptied about a dozen winkles into my hand, and I put them in the two pockets of my skirt. 'They'm all right with bread-an'-butter,' he said, 'you must boil 'em first.'

'Yes, all right,' I said.

He stood there grinning at me. 'Seen the steamer?' he said.

'Yes,' I said, 'she's gone ashore, hasn't she?'

'Eh?' he said.

'She's run aground,' I repeated. 'I expect she's got a hole in her bottom.'

His face went blank and foolish. 'Aye,' he said, 'she's down there all right. She'll not come back again.'

'Perhaps the tugs will get her off when the tide makes,' I said.

He did not answer. He was staring out towards the stranded ship. I could see her broadside on from here, the red underwater section showing against the black of the top-sides, and the single funnel leaning rakishly towards the cliffs beyond. The crew were still leaning over her side feeding the gulls and staring into the water. The rowing-boats were pulling back to Kerrith.

'She's a Dutchman, ain't she?' said Ben.

'I don't know,' I said. 'German or Dutch.'

'She'll break up there where she's to,' he said.

'I'm afraid so,' I said.

He grinned again, and wiped his nose with the back of his hand.

'She'll break up bit by bit,' he said, 'she'll not sink like a stone like the little 'un.' He chuckled to himself, picking his nose. I did not say anything. 'The fishes have eaten her up by now, haven't they?' he said.

'Who?' I said.

He jerked his thumb towards the sea. 'Her,' he said, 'the other one.'

'Fishes don't eat steamers, Ben,' I said.

'Eh?' he said. He stared at me, foolish and blank once more.

'I must go home now,' I said; 'good afternoon.'

I left him and walked towards the path through the woods. I did not look at the cottage. I was aware of it on my right hand; grey and quiet. I went straight to the path and up through the trees. I paused to rest half-way and looking through the trees I could still see the stranded ship leaning towards the shore. The pleasure-boats had all gone. Even the crew had disappeared below. The ridges of cloud covered the whole sky. A little wind sprang from nowhere and blew into my face. A leaf fell onto my hand from the tree above. I shivered for no reason. Then the wind went again, it was hot and sultry as before. The ship looked desolate there upon her side, with no one on her decks, and her thin black funnel pointing to the shore. The sea was so calm that when it broke upon the shingle in the cove it was like a whisper, hushed and still. I turned once more to the steep path through the woods, my legs reluctant, my head heavy, a strange sense of foreboding in my heart.

The house looked very peaceful as I came upon it from the woods and crossed the lawns. It seemed sheltered and protected, more beautiful than I had ever seen it. Standing there, looking down upon it from the banks, I realized, perhaps for the first time, with a funny feeling of bewilderment and pride that it was my home, I belonged there, and Manderley belonged to me. The trees and the grass and the flower tubs on the terrace were reflected in the mullioned windows. A thin column of smoke rose in the air from one of the chimneys. The new-cut grass on the lawn smelt sweet as hay. A blackbird was singing on the chestnut tree. A yellow butterfly winged his foolish way before me to the terrace.

I went into the hall and through to the dining-room. My place was still laid, but Maxim's had been cleared away. The cold meat and salad awaited me on the sideboard. I hesitated, and then rang the dining-room bell. Robert came in from behind the screen.

'Has Mr de Winter been in?' I said.

'Yes, Madam,' said Robert; 'he came in just after two, and had a quick lunch, and then went out again. He asked for you and Frith said he thought you must have gone down to see the ship.'

'Did he say when he would be back again?' I asked.

'No, Madam.'

'Perhaps he went to the beach another way,' I said; 'I may have missed him.'

'Yes, Madam,' said Robert.

I looked at the cold meat and the salad. I felt empty but not hungry. I did not want cold meat now. 'Will you be taking lunch?' said Robert.

'No,' I said. 'No, you might bring me some tea, Robert, in the library. Nothing like cakes or scones. Just tea and bread-and-butter.'

'Yes, Madam.'

I went and sat on the window-seat in the library. It seemed funny without Jasper. He must have gone with Maxim. The old dog lay asleep in her basket. I picked up *The Times* and turned the pages without reading it. It was queer this feeling of marking time, like sitting in a waiting-room at a dentist's. I knew I should never settle to my knitting or to a book. I was waiting for something to happen, something unforeseen. The horror of my morning and the stranded ship and not having any lunch had all combined to give birth to a latent sense of excitement at the back of my mind that I did not understand. It was as though I had entered into a new phase of my life and nothing would be quite the same again. The girl who had dressed for the fancy dress ball the night before had been left behind. It had all happened a very long time ago. This self who sat on the window-seat was new, was different . . . Robert brought in my tea, and I ate my bread-and-butter hungrily. He had brought scones as well, and some sandwiches, and an angel cake. He must have thought it derogatory to bring bread-and-butter alone, nor was it Manderley routine. I was glad of the scones and the angel cake. I remembered I had only had cold tea at half past eleven, and no breakfast. Just after I had drunk my third cup Robert came in again.

'Mr de Winter is not back yet is he, Madam?' he said.

'No,' I said. 'Why? Does someone want him?'

'Yes, Madam,' said Robert, 'it's Captain Searle, the harbour-master of Kerrith, on the telephone. He wants to know if he can come up and see Mr de Winter personally.'

'I don't know what to say,' I said. 'He may not be back for ages.'

'No, Madam.'

'You'd better tell him to ring again at five o'clock,' I said.

Robert went out of the room and came back again in a few minutes.

'Captain Searle would like to see you, if it would be convenient, Madam,' said Robert. 'He says the matter is rather urgent. He tried to get Mr Crawley, but there was no reply.'

'Yes, of course I must see him if it's urgent,' I said. 'Tell him to come along at once if he likes. Has he got a car?'

'Yes, I believe so, Madam.'

Robert went out of the room. I wondered what I should say to Captain Searle. His business must be something to do with the stranded ship. I could not understand what concern it was of Maxim's. It would have been different if the ship had gone ashore in the cove. That was Manderley property. They might have to ask Maxim's permission to blast away rocks or whatever it was that was done to move a ship. But the open bay and the ledge of rock under the water did not belong to Maxim. Captain Searle would waste his time talking to me about it all.

He must have got into his car right away after talking to Robert because in less than quarter of an hour he was shown into the room.

He was still in his uniform as I had seen him through the glasses in the early afternoon. I got up from the window-seat and shook hands with him. 'I'm sorry my husband isn't back yet, Captain Searle,' I said; 'he must have gone down to the cliffs again, and he went into Kerrith before that. I haven't seen him all day.'

'Yes, I heard he'd been to Kerrith but I missed him there,' said the harbour-master. 'He must have walked back across the cliffs when I was in my boat. And I can't get hold of Mr Crawley either.'

'I'm afraid the ship has disorganized everybody,' I said. 'I was out on the cliffs and went without my lunch, and I know Mr Crawley was there earlier on. What will happen to her? Will tugs get her off, do you think?'

Captain Searle made a great circle with his hands. 'There's a hole that deep in her bottom,' he said, 'she'll not see Hamburg again. Never mind the ship. Her owner and Lloyd's agent will settle that between them. No, Mrs de Winter, it's not the ship that's brought me here. Indirectly of course she's the cause of my coming. The fact is, I've got some news for Mr de Winter, and I hardly know how to break it to him.' He looked at me very straight with his bright blue eyes.

'What sort of news, Captain Searle?'

He brought a large white handkerchief out of his pocket and blew his nose. 'Well, Mrs de Winter, it's not very pleasant for me to tell you either. The last thing I want to do is to cause distress or pain to you and your husband. We're all very fond of Mr de Winter in Kerrith, you know, and the family has always done a lot of good. It's hard on him and hard on you that we can't let the past lie quiet. But I don't see how we can under the circumstances.' He paused, and put his handkerchief back in his pocket. He lowered his voice, although we were alone in the room.

'We sent the diver down to inspect the ship's bottom,' he said, 'and while he was down there he made a discovery. It appears he found the hole in the ship's bottom and was working round to the other side to see what further damage there was when he came across the hull of a little sailing boat, lying on her side, quite intact and not broken up at all. He's a local man, of course, and he recognized the boat at once. It was the little boat belonging to the late Mrs de Winter.'

My first feeling was one of thankfulness that Maxim was not there to hear. This fresh blow coming swiftly upon my masquerade of the night before was ironic, and rather horrible.

'I'm so sorry,' I said slowly, 'it's not the sort of thing one expected would happen. Is it necessary to tell Mr de Winter? Couldn't the boat be left there, as it is? It's not doing any harm, is it?'

'It would be left, Mrs de Winter, in the ordinary way. I'm the last man in the world to want to disturb it. And I'd give anything, as I said before, to spare Mr de Winter's feelings. But that wasn't all, Mrs de Winter. My man poked round the little boat and he made another, more important discovery. The cabin door was tightly closed, it was not stove in, and the portlights were closed too. He broke one of the ports with a stone from the sea bed, and looked into the cabin. It was full of water, the sea must have come through some hole in the bottom, there seemed no damage elsewhere. And then he got the fright of his life, Mrs de Winter.'

Captain Searle paused, he looked over his shoulder as though one of the servants might hear him. 'There was a body in there, lying on the cabin floor,' he said quietly. 'It was dissolved of course, there was no flesh on it. But it was a body all right. He saw the head and the limbs. He came up to the surface then and reported it direct to me. And now you understand, Mrs de Winter, why I've got to see your husband.'

I stared at him, bewildered at first, then shocked, then rather sick.

'She was supposed to be sailing alone?' I whispered, 'there must have been someone with her then, all the time, and no one ever knew?'

'It looks like it,' said the harbour-master.

'Who could it have been?' I said. 'Surely relatives would know if anyone had been missing? There was so much about it at the time, it was all in the papers. Why should one of them be in the cabin and Mrs de Winter herself be picked up many miles away, months afterwards?'

Captain Searle shook his head. 'I can't tell any more than you,' he said. 'All we know is that the body is there, and it has got to be reported. There'll be publicity, I'm afraid, Mrs de Winter. I don't know how we're going to avoid it. It's very hard on you and Mr de Winter. Here you are, settled down quietly, wanting to be happy, and this has to happen.'

I knew now the reason for my sense of foreboding. It was not the stranded ship that was sinister, nor the crying gulls, nor the thin black funnel pointing to the shore. It was the stillness of the black water, and the unknown things that lay beneath. It was the diver going down into those cool quiet depths and stumbling upon Rebecca's boat, and Rebecca's dead companion. He had touched the boat, had looked into the cabin, and all the while I sat on the cliffs and had not known.

'If only we did not have to tell him,' I said. 'If only we could keep the whole thing from him.'

'You know I would if it were possible, Mrs de Winter,' said the harbour-master, 'but my personal feelings have to go, in a matter like this. I've got to do my duty. I've got to report that body.' He broke off short as the door opened, and Maxim came into the room.

'Hullo,' he said, 'what's happening? I didn't know you were here, Captain Searle? Is anything the matter?'

I could not stand it any longer. I went out of the room like the coward I was and shut the door behind me. I had not even glanced at Maxim's face. I had the vague impression that he looked tired, untidy, hatless.

I went and stood in the hall by the front door. Jasper was drinking noisily from his bowl. He wagged his tail when he saw me and went on drinking. Then he loped towards me, and stood up, pawing at my dress. I kissed the top of his head and went and sat on the terrace. The moment of crisis had come, and I must face it. My old fears, my diffidence, my shyness, my hopeless sense of inferiority, must be conquered now and thrust aside. If I failed now I should fail for ever. There would never be another chance. I prayed for courage in a blind despairing way, and dug my nails into my hands. I sat there for five minutes staring at the green lawns and the flower tubs on the terrace. I heard the sound of a car starting up in the drive. It must be Captain Searle. He had broken his news to Maxim and had gone. I got up from the terrace and went slowly through the hall to the library. I kept turning over in my pockets the winkles that Ben had given me. I clutched them tight in my hands.

Maxim was standing by the window. His back was turned to me. I waited by the door. Still he did not turn round. I took my hands out of my pockets and went and stood beside him. I reached out for his hand and laid it against my cheek. He did not say anything. He went on standing there.

'I'm so sorry,' I whispered, 'so terribly, terribly sorry.' He did not answer. His hand was icy cold. I kissed the back of it, and then the fingers, one by one. 'I don't want you to bear this alone,' I said. 'I want to share it with you. I've grown up, Maxim, in twenty-four hours. I'll never be a child again.'

He put his arm round me and pulled me to him very close. My reserve was broken, and my shyness too. I stood there with my face against his shoulder. 'You've forgiven me, haven't you?' I said.

He spoke to me at last. 'Forgiven you?' he said. 'What have I got to forgive you for?'

'Last night,' I said; 'you thought I did it on purpose.'

'Ah, that,' he said. 'I'd forgotten. I was angry with you, wasn't I?'

'Yes,' I said.

He did not say any more. He went on holding me close to his shoulder. 'Maxim,' I said, 'can't we start all over again? Can't we begin from today, and face things together? I don't want you to love me, I won't ask impossible things. I'll be your friend and your companion, a sort of boy. I don't ever want more than that.'

He took my face between his hands and looked at me. For the first time I saw how thin his face was, how lined and drawn. And there were great shadows beneath his eyes.

'How much do you love me?' he said.

I could not answer. I could only stare back at him, at his dark tortured eyes, and his pale drawn face.

'It's too late, my darling, too late,' he said. 'We've lost our little chance of happiness.'

'No, Maxim. No,' I said.

'Yes,' he said. 'It's all over now. The thing has happened.'

'What thing?' I said.

'The thing I've always foreseen. The thing I've dreamt about, day after day, night after night. We're not meant for happiness, you and I.' He sat down on the window-seat, and I knelt in front of him, my hands on his shoulders.

'What are you trying to tell me?' I said.

He put his hands over mine and looked into my face. 'Rebecca has won,' he said.

I stared at him, my heart beating strangely, my hands suddenly cold beneath his hands.

'Her shadow between us all the time,' he said. 'Her damned shadow keeping us from one another. How could I hold you like this, my darling, my little love, with the fear always in my heart that this would happen? I remembered her eyes as she looked at me before she died. I remembered that slow treacherous smile. She knew this would happen even then. She knew she would win in the end.'

'Maxim,' I whispered, 'what are you saying, what are you trying to tell me?'

'Her boat,' he said, 'they've found it. The diver found it this afternoon.'

'Yes,' I said. 'I know. Captain Searle came to tell me. You are thinking about the body, aren't you, the body the diver found in the cabin?'

'Yes,' he said.

'It means she was not alone,' I said. 'It means there was somebody sailing with Rebecca at the time. And you have to find out who it was. That's it, isn't it, Maxim?'

'No,' he said. 'No, you don't understand.'

'I want to share this with you, darling,' I said. 'I want to help you.'

'There was no one with Rebecca, she was alone,' he said.

I knelt there watching his face, watching his eyes.

'It's Rebecca's body lying there on the cabin floor,' he said.

'No,' I said. 'No.'

'The woman buried in the crypt is not Rebecca,' he said. 'It's the body of some unknown woman, unclaimed, belonging nowhere. There never was an accident. Rebecca was not drowned at all. I killed her. I shot Rebecca in the cottage in the cove. I carried her body to the cabin, and took the boat out that night and sunk it there, where they found it today. It's Rebecca who's lying dead there on the cabin floor. Will you look into my eyes and tell me that you love me now?'

20

IT WAS VERY quiet in the library. The only sound was that of Jasper licking his foot. He must have caught a thorn in his pads, for he kept biting and sucking at the skin. Then I heard the watch on Maxim's wrist ticking close to my ear. The little normal sounds of every day. And for no reason the stupid proverb of my schooldays ran through my mind, 'Time and Tide wait for no man.' The words repeated themselves over and over again. 'Time and Tide wait for no man.' These were the only sounds then, the ticking of Maxim's watch and Jasper licking his foot on the floor beside me.

When people suffer a great shock, like death, or the loss of a limb, I believe they don't feel it just at first. If your hand is taken from you you don't know, for a few minutes, that your hand is gone. You go on feeling the fingers. You stretch and beat them on the air, one by one, and all the time there is nothing there, no hand, no fingers. I knelt there by Maxim's side, my body against his body, my hands upon his shoulders, and I was aware of no feeling at all, no pain and no fear, there was no horror in my heart. I thought how I must take the thorn out of Jasper's foot and I wondered if Robert would come in and clear the tea-things. It seemed strange to me that I should think of these things, Jasper's foot, Maxim's watch, Robert and the tea-things. I was shocked at my lack of emotion and this queer cold absence of distress. Little by little the feeling will come back to me, I said to myself, little by little I shall understand. What he has told me and all that has happened will tumble into place like pieces of a jig-saw puzzle. They will fit themselves into a pattern. At the moment I am nothing, I have no heart, and no mind, and no senses, I am just a wooden thing in Maxim's arms. Then he began to kiss me. He had not kissed me like this before. I put my hands behind his head and shut my eyes.

'I love you so much,' he whispered. 'So much.'

This is what I have wanted him to say every day and every night, I thought, and now he is saying it at last. This is what I imagined in Monte Carlo, in Italy, here in Manderley. He is saying it now. I opened my eyes and looked at a little patch of curtain above his head. He went on kissing me, hungry, desperate, murmuring my name. I kept on looking at the patch of curtain, and saw where the sun had faded it, making it lighter than the piece above. 'How calm I am,' I thought. 'How cool. Here I am looking at the piece of curtain, and Maxim is kissing me. For the first time he is telling me he loves me.'

Then he stopped suddenly, he pushed me away from him, and got up from the window-seat. 'You see, I was right,' he said. 'It's too late. You don't love me now. Why should you?' He went and stood over by the mantelpiece. 'We'll forget that,' he said, 'it won't happen again.'

Realization flooded me at once, and my heart jumped in quick and sudden panic. 'It's not too late,' I said swiftly, getting up from the floor and going to him, putting my arms about him; 'you're not to say that, you don't understand. I love you more than anything in the world. But when you kissed me just now I felt stunned and shaken. I could not feel anything. I could not grasp anything. It was just as though I had no more feeling left in me at all.'

'You don't love me,' he said, 'that's why you did not feel anything. I know. I understand. It's come too late for you, hasn't it?'

'No,' I said.

'This ought to have happened four months ago,' he said. 'I should have known. Women are not like men.'

'I want you to kiss me again,' I said; 'please, Maxim.'

'No,' he said, 'it's no use now.'

'We can't lose each other now,' I said. 'We've got to be together always, with no secrets, no shadows. Please, darling, please.'

'There's no time,' he said. 'We may only have a few hours, a few days. How can we be together now that this has happened? I've told you they've found the boat. They've found Rebecca.'

I stared at him stupidly, not understanding 'What will they do?' I said.

'They'll identify her body,' he said, 'there's everything to tell them, there in the cabin. The clothes she had, the shoes, the rings on her fingers. They'll identify her body; and then they will remember the other one, the woman buried up there, in the crypt.'

'What are you going to do?' I whispered.

'I don't know,' he said. 'I don't know.'

The feeling was coming back to me, little by little, as I knew it would. My hands were cold no longer. They were clammy, warm. I felt a wave of colour come into my face, my throat. My cheeks were burning hot. I thought of Captain Searle, the diver, the Lloyd's agent, all those men on the stranded ship leaning against the side, staring down into the water. I thought of the shopkeepers in Kerrith, of errand boys whistling in the street, of the vicar walking out of church, of Lady Crowan cutting roses in her garden, of the woman in the pink dress and her little boy on the cliffs. Soon they would know. In a few hours. By breakfast time tomorrow. 'They've found Mrs de Winter's boat, and they say there is a body in the cabin.' A body in the cabin. Rebecca was lying there on the cabin floor. She was not in the crypt at all. Some other woman was lying in the crypt. Maxim had killed Rebecca. Rebecca had not been drowned at all. Maxim had killed her. He had shot her in the cottage in the woods. He had carried her body to the boat, and sunk the boat there in the bay. That grey, silent cottage, with the rain pattering on the roof. The jig-saw pieces came tumbling thick and fast upon me. Disjointed pictures flashed one by one through my bewildered mind. Maxim sitting in the car beside me in the south of France. 'Something happened nearly a year ago that altered my whole life. I had to begin living all over again ...' Maxim's silence, Maxim's moods. The way he never talked about Rebecca. The way he never mentioned her name. Maxim's dislike of the cove, the stone cottage. 'If you had my memories you would not go there either.' The way he climbed the path through the woods not looking behind him. Maxim pacing up and down the library after Rebecca died. Up and down. Up and down. 'I came away in rather a hurry,' he said to Mrs Van Hopper, a line, thin as gossamer, between his brows. 'They say he can't get over his wife's death.' The fancy dress dance last night, and I coming down to the head of the stairs, in Rebecca's dress. 'I killed Rebecca,' Maxim had said. 'I shot Rebecca in the cottage in the woods.' And the diver had found her lying there, on the cabin floor . . .

'What are we going to do?' I said. 'What are we going to say?'

Maxim did not answer. He stood there by the mantelpiece, his eyes wide and staring, looking in front of him, not seeing anything.

'Does anyone know?' I said, 'anyone at all?'

He shook his head. 'No,' he said.

'No one but you and me?' I asked.

'No one but you and me,' he said.

'Frank,' I said suddenly, 'are you sure Frank does not know?'

'How could he?' said Maxim. 'There was nobody there but myself. It was dark . . .' He stopped. He sat down on a chair, he put his hand up to his forehead. I went and knelt beside him. He sat very still a moment. I took his hands away from his face and looked into his eyes. 'I love you,' I whispered, 'I love you. Will you believe me now?' He kissed my face and my hands. He held my hands very tightly like a child who would gain confidence.

'I thought I should go mad,' he said, 'sitting here, day after day, waiting for something to happen. Sitting down at the desk there, answering those terrible letters of sympathy. The notices in the papers, the interviews, all the little aftermath of death. Eating and drinking, trying to be normal, trying to be sane. Frith, the servants, Mrs Danvers. Mrs Danvers, who I had not the courage to turn away, because with her knowledge of Rebecca she might have suspected, she might have guessed . . . Frank, always by my side, discreet, sympathetic. "Why don't you get away?" he used to say, "I can manage here. You ought to get away." And Giles, and Bee, poor dear tactless Bee. "You're looking frightfully ill, can't you go and see a doctor?" I had to face them all, these people, knowing every word I uttered was a lie.'

I went on holding his hands very tight. I leant close to him, quite close. 'I nearly told you, once,' he said, 'that day Jasper ran to the cove, and you went to the cottage for some string. We were sitting here, like this, and then Frith and Robert came in with the tea.'

'Yes,' I said. 'I remember. Why didn't you tell me? The time we've wasted when we might have been together. All these weeks and days.'

'You were so aloof,' he said, 'always wandering into the garden with Jasper, going off on your own. You never came to me like this.'

'Why didn't you tell me?' I whispered. 'Why didn't you tell me?'

'I thought you were unhappy, bored,' he said. 'I'm so much older than you. You seemed to have more to say to Frank than you ever had to me. You were funny with me, awkward, shy.'

'How could I come to you when I knew you were thinking about Rebecca?' I said. 'How could I ask you to love me when I knew you loved Rebecca still?'

He pulled me close to him and searched my eyes.

'What are you talking about? What do you mean?' he said.

I knelt up straight beside him. 'Whenever you touched me I thought you were comparing me to Rebecca,' I said. 'Whenever you spoke to me or looked at me, walked with me in the garden, sat down to dinner, I felt you were saying to yourself, "This I did with Rebecca, and this, and this."' He stared at me bewildered as though he did not understand.

'It was true, wasn't it?' I said.

'Oh, my God,' he said. He pushed me away, he got up and began walking up and down the room, clasping his hands.

'What is it? What's the matter?' I said.

He whipped round and looked at me as I sat there huddled on the floor. 'You thought I loved Rebecca?' he said. 'You thought I killed her, loving her? I hated her, I tell you. Our marriage was a farce from the very first. She was vicious, damnable, rotten through and through. We never loved each other, never had one moment of happiness together. Rebecca was incapable of love, of tenderness, of decency. She was not even normal.'

I sat on the floor, clasping my knees, staring at him.

'She was clever of course,' he said. 'Damnably clever. No one would guess meeting her that she was not the kindest, most

generous, most gifted person in the world. She knew exactly
what to say to different people, how to match her mood to theirs.
Had she met you, she would have walked off into the garden with
you, arm-in-arm, calling to Jasper, chatting about flowers, music,
painting, whatever she knew to be your particular hobby; and
you would have been taken in, like the rest. You would have sat
at her feet and worshipped her.'

Up and down he walked, up and down across the library floor.

'When I married her I was told I was the luckiest man in the
world,' he said. 'She was so lovely, so accomplished, so amusing.
Even Gran, the most difficult person to please in those days,
adored her from the first. "She's got the three things that matter
in a wife," she told me: "breeding, brains, and beauty." And
I believed her, or forced myself to believe her. But all the time
I had a seed of doubt at the back of my mind. There was something about her eyes . . .'

The jig-saw pieces came together piece by piece, the real
Rebecca took shape and form before me, stepping from her
shadow world like a living figure from a picture frame. Rebecca
slashing at her horse; Rebecca seizing life with her two hands;
Rebecca, triumphant, leaning down from the minstrels' gallery
with a smile on her lips.

Once more I saw myself standing on the beach beside poor
startled Ben. 'You're kind,' he said, 'not like the other one. You
won't put me to the asylum, will you?' There was someone who
walked through the woods by night, someone tall and slim. She
gave you the feeling of a snake . . .

Maxim was talking though. Maxim was walking up and down
the library floor. 'I found her out at once,' he was saying, 'five
days after we were married. You remember that time I drove
you in the car, to the hills above Monte Carlo? I wanted to stand
there again, to remember. She sat there, laughing, her black
hair blowing in the wind; she told me about herself; told me
things I shall never repeat to a living soul. I knew then what I had
done, what I had married. Beauty, brains, and breeding. Oh, my
God!'

He broke off abruptly. He went and stood by the window,
looking out upon the lawns. He began to laugh. He stood there

laughing. I could not bear it, it made me frightened, ill. I could not stand it.

'Maxim!' I cried. 'Maxim!'

He lit a cigarette, and stood there smoking, not saying anything. Then he turned away again, and paced up and down the room once more. 'I nearly killed her then,' he said. 'It would have been so easy. One false step, one slip. You remember the precipice. I frightened you, didn't I? You thought I was mad. Perhaps I was. Perhaps I am. It doesn't make for sanity, does it, living with the devil.'

I sat there watching him, up and down, up and down.

'She made a bargain with me up there, on the side of the precipice,' he said. '"I'll run your house for you," she told me, "I'll look after your precious Manderley for you, make it the most famous show-place in all the country, if you like. And people will visit us, and envy us, and talk about us; they'll say we are the luckiest, happiest, handsomest couple in all England. What a leg-pull, Max!" she said, "what a God-damn triumph!" She sat there on the hillside, laughing, tearing a flower to bits in her hands.'

Maxim threw his cigarette away, a quarter smoked, into the empty grate.

'I did not kill her,' he said. 'I watched her, I said nothing, I let her laugh. We got into the car together and drove away. And she knew I would do as she suggested: come here to Manderley, throw the place open, entertain, have our marriage spoken of as the success of the century. She knew I would sacrifice pride, honour, personal feelings, every damned quality on earth, rather than stand before our little world after a week of marriage and have them know the things about her that she had told me then. She knew I would never stand in a divorce court and give her away, have fingers pointing at us, mud flung at us in the newspapers, all the people who belong down here whispering when my name was mentioned, all the trippers from Kerrith trooping to the lodge gates, peering into the grounds and saying, "That's where he lives, in there. That's Manderley. That's the place that belongs to the chap who had that divorce case we read about. Do you remember what the judge said about his wife . . . ?"'

He came and stood before me. He held out his hands. 'You

despise me, don't you?' he said. 'You can't understand my shame, and loathing and disgust?'

I did not say anything. I held his hands against my heart. I did not care about his shame. None of the things that he had told me mattered to me at all. I clung to one thing only, and repeated it to myself, over and over again. Maxim did not love Rebecca. He had never loved her, never, never. They had never known one moment's happiness together. Maxim was talking and I listened to him, but his words meant nothing to me. I did not really care. 'I thought about Manderley too much,' he said. 'I put Manderley first, before anything else. And it does not prosper, that sort of love. They don't preach about it in the churches. Christ said nothing about stones, and bricks, and walls, the love that a man can bear for his plot of earth, his soil, his little kingdom. It does not come into the Christian creed.'

'My darling,' I said, 'my Maxim, my love.' I laid his hands against my face, I put my lips against them.

'Do you understand?' he said, 'do you, do you?'

'Yes,' I said, 'my sweet, my love.' But I looked away from him so he should not see my face. What did it matter whether I understood him or not? My heart was light like a feather floating in the air. He had never loved Rebecca.

'I don't want to look back on those years,' he said slowly. 'I don't want even to tell you about them. The shame and the degradation. The lie we lived, she and I. The shabby, sordid farce we played together. Before friends, before relations, even before the servants, before faithful, trusting creatures like old Frith. They all believed in her down here, they all admired her, they never knew how she laughed at them behind their backs, jeered at them, mimicked them. I can remember days when the place was full for some show or other, a garden party, a pageant, and she walked about with a smile like an angel on her face, her arm through mine, giving prizes afterwards to a little troop of children; and then the day afterwards she would be up at dawn driving to London, streaking to that flat of hers by the river like an animal to its hole in the ditch, coming back here at the end of the week, after five unspeakable days. Oh, I kept to my side of the bargain all right. I never gave her away. Her blasted taste made

Manderley the thing it is today. The gardens, the shrubs, even the azaleas in the Happy Valley; do you think they existed when my father was alive? God, the place was a wilderness; lovely, yes, wild and lonely with a beauty of its own, yes, but crying out for skill and care and the money that he would never give to it, that I would not have thought of giving to it – but for Rebecca. Half the stuff you see here in the rooms was never here originally. The drawing-room as it is today, the morning-room – that's all Rebecca. Those chairs that Frith points out so proudly to the visitors on the public day, and that panel of tapestry – Rebecca again. Oh, some of the things were here admittedly, stored away in back rooms – my father knew nothing about furniture or pictures – but the majority was bought by Rebecca. The beauty of Manderley that you see today, the Manderley that people talk about and photograph and paint, it's all due to her, to Rebecca.'

I did not say anything. I held him close. I wanted him to go on talking like this, that his bitterness might loosen and come away, carrying with it all the pent-up hatred and disgust and muck of the lost years.

'And so we lived,' he said, 'month after month, year after year. I accepted everything – because of Manderley. What she did in London did not touch me – because it did not hurt Manderley. And she was careful those first years; there was never a murmur about her, never a whisper. Then little by little she began to grow careless. You know how a man starts drinking? He goes easy at first, just a little at a time, a bad bout perhaps every five months or so. And then the period between grows less and less. Soon it's every month, every fortnight, every few days. There's no margin of safety left and all his secret cunning goes. It was like that with Rebecca. She began to ask her friends down here. She would have one or two of them and mix them up at a week-end party so that at first I was not quite sure, not quite certain. She would have picnics down at her cottage in the cove. I came back once, having been away shooting in Scotland, and found her there, with half a dozen of them; people I had never seen before. I warned her, and she shrugged her shoulders. "What the hell's it got to do with you?" she said. I told her she could see her friends in London, but Manderley was mine. She must stick to that part of the bargain. She smiled, she did not say anything. Then she started on Frank, poor shy faithful Frank. He came to me one day and said he wanted to leave Manderley and take another job. We argued for two hours, here in the library, and then I understood. He broke down and told me. She never left him alone, he said, she was always going down to his house, trying to get him to the cottage. Dear, wretched Frank, who had not understood, who had always thought we were the normal happy married couple we pretended to be.

'I accused Rebecca of this, and she flared up at once, cursing me, using every filthy word in her particular vocabulary. We had a sickening, loathsome scene. She went up to London after that and stayed there for a month. When she came back again she was quiet at first; I thought she had learnt her lesson. Bee and Giles came for a week-end, and I realized then what I had sometimes suspected before, that Bee did not like Rebecca. I believe, in her funny abrupt, downright way she saw through her, guessed something was wrong. It was a tricky, nervy sort of week-end. Giles went out sailing with Rebecca, Bee and I lazed on the lawn. And when they came back I could tell by Giles's rather hearty jovial manner and by a look in Rebecca's eye that she had started on him, as she had done on Frank. I saw Bee watching Giles at dinner, who laughed louder than usual, talked a little too much. And all the while Rebecca sitting there at the head of the table, looking like an angel.'

They were all fitting into place, the jig-saw pieces. The odd strained shapes that I had tried to piece together with my fumbling fingers and they had never fitted. Frank's odd manner when I spoke about Rebecca. Beatrice, and her rather diffident negative attitude. The silence that I had always taken for sympathy and regret was a silence born of shame and embarrassment. It seemed incredible to me now that I had never understood. I wondered how many people there were in the world who suffered, and continued to suffer, because they could not break out from their own web of shyness and reserve, and in their blindness and folly built up a great distorted wall in front of them that hid the truth. This was what I had done. I had built up false pictures in my mind and sat before them. I had never had the courage to demand the truth. Had I made one step forward out of my own shyness, Maxim would have told me these things four months, five months ago.

'That was the last week-end Bee and Giles ever spent at Manderley,' said Maxim. 'I never asked them alone again. They came officially, to garden parties, and dances. Bee never said a word to me or I to her. But I think she guessed my life, I think she knew. Even as Frank did. Rebecca grew cunning again. Her behaviour was faultless, outwardly. But if I happened to be away when she was here at Manderley I could never be certain what might happen. There had been Frank, and Giles. She might get hold of one of the workmen on the estate, someone from Kerrith, anyone . . . And then the bomb would have to fall. The gossip, the publicity I dreaded.'

It seemed to me I stood again by the cottage in the woods, and I heard the drip-drip of the rain upon the roof. I saw the dust on the model ships, the rat holes on the divan. I saw Ben with his poor staring idiot's eyes. 'You'll not put me to the asylum, will you?' And I thought of the dark steep path through the woods, and how, if a woman stood there behind the trees, her evening dress would rustle in the thin night breeze.

'She had a cousin,' said Maxim slowly, 'a fellow who had been abroad, and was living in England again. He took to coming here, if ever I was away. Frank used to see him. A fellow called Jack Favell.'

'I know him,' I said; 'he came here the day you went to London.'

'You saw him too?' said Maxim. 'Why didn't you tell me? I heard it from Frank, who saw his car turn in at the lodge gates.'

'I did not like to,' I said, 'I thought it would remind you of Rebecca.'

'Remind me?' whispered Maxim. 'Oh, God, as if I needed reminding.'

He stared in front of him, breaking off from his story, and I wondered if he was thinking, as I was, of that flooded cabin beneath the waters in the bay.

'She used to have this fellow Favell down to the cottage,' said Maxim, 'she would tell the servants she was going to sail, and would not be back before the morning. Then she would spend the night down there with him. Once again I warned her. I said if I found him here, anywhere on the estate, I'd shoot him. He had a black, filthy record ... The very thought of him walking about the woods in Manderley, in places like the Happy Valley, made me mad. I told her I would not stand for it. She shrugged her shoulders. She forgot to blaspheme. And I noticed she was looking paler than usual, nervy, rather haggard. I wondered then what the hell would happen to her when she began to look old, feel old. Things drifted on. Nothing very much happened. Then one day she went up to London, and came back again the same day, which she did not do as a rule. I did not expect her. I dined that night with Frank at his house, we had a lot of work on at the time.' He was speaking now in short, jerky sentences. I had his hands very tightly between my two hands.

'I came back after dinner, about half past ten, and I saw her scarf and gloves lying on a chair in the hall. I wondered what the devil she had come back for. I went into the morning-room, but she was not there. I guessed she had gone off there then, down to the cove. And I knew then I could not stand this life of lies and filth and deceit any longer. The thing had got to be settled, one way or the other. I thought I'd take a gun and frighten the fellow, frighten them both. I went down right away to the cottage. The servants never knew I had come back to the house at all. I slipped out into the garden and through the woods. I saw the light in the cottage window, and I went straight in. To my surprise Rebecca was alone. She was lying on the divan with an ash-tray full of cigarette stubs beside her. She looked ill, queer.

'I began at once about Favell and she listened to me without a word. "We've lived this life of degradation long enough, you and I," I said. "This is the end, do you understand? What you do in London does not concern me. You can live with Favell there, or with anyone you like. But not here. Not at Manderley."

'She said nothing for a moment. She stared at me, and then she smiled. "Suppose it suits me better to live here, what then?" she said.

'"You know the conditions," I said. "I've kept my part of our dirty, damnable bargain, haven't I? But you've cheated. You think you can treat my house and my home like your own sink in London. I've stood enough, but my God, Rebecca, this is your last chance."

'I remember she squashed out her cigarette in the tub by the divan, and then she got up, and stretched herself, her arms above her head.

'"You're right, Max," she said. "It's time I turned over a new leaf."

'She looked very pale, very thin. She began walking up and down the room, her hands in the pockets of her trousers. She looked like a boy in her sailing kit, a boy with a face like a Botticelli angel.

'"Have you ever thought", she said, "how damned hard it would be for you to make a case against me? In a court of law, I mean. If you wanted to divorce me. Do you realize that you've never had one shred of proof against me, from the very first? All your friends, even the servants, believe our marriage to be a success."

'"What about Frank?" I said. "What about Beatrice?"

'She threw back her head and laughed. "What sort of a story could Frank tell against mine?" she said. "Don't you know me well enough for that? As for Beatrice, wouldn't it be the easiest thing in the world for her to stand in a witness-box as the ordinary jealous woman whose husband once lost his head and made a fool of himself? Oh, no, Max, you'd have a hell of a time trying to prove anything against me."

'She stood watching me, rocking on her heels, her hands in her pockets and a smile on her face. "Do you realize that I could get Danny, as my personal maid, to swear anything I asked her to swear, in a court of law? And that the rest of the servants, in blind ignorance, would follow her example and swear too? They think we live together at Manderley as husband and wife, don't they? And so does everyone, your friends, all our little world. Well, how are you going to prove that we don't?"

'She sat down on the edge of the table, swinging her legs, watching me.

'"Haven't we acted the parts of a loving husband and wife rather too well?" she said. I remember watching that foot of hers in its striped sandal swinging backwards and forwards, and my eyes and brain began to burn in a strange quick way.

'"We could make you look very foolish, Danny and I," she said softly. "We could make you look so foolish that no one would believe you, Max, nobody at all." Still that foot of hers, swinging to and fro, that damned foot in its blue and white striped sandal.

'Suddenly she slipped off the table and stood in front of me, smiling still, her hands in her pockets.

'"If I had a child, Max," she said, "neither you, nor anyone in the world, would ever prove that it was not yours. It would grow up here in Manderley, bearing your name. There would be nothing you could do. And when you died Manderley would be his. You could not prevent it. The property's entailed. You would like an heir, wouldn't you, for your beloved Manderley? You would enjoy it, wouldn't you, seeing my son lying in his pram under the chestnut tree, playing leap-frog on the lawn, catching butterflies in the Happy Valley? It would give you the biggest thrill of your life, wouldn't it, Max, to watch my son grow bigger day by day, and to know that when you died, all this would be his?"

'She waited a minute, rocking on her heels, and then she lit a cigarette and went and stood by the window. She began to laugh. She went on laughing. I thought she would never stop. "God, how funny," she said, "how supremely, wonderfully funny! Well, you heard me say I was going to turn over a new leaf, didn't you? Now you know the reason. They'll be happy, won't they, all these smug locals, all your blasted tenants? 'It's what we've always hoped for, Mrs de Winter,' they will say. I'll be the perfect mother, Max, like I've been the perfect wife. And none of them will ever guess, none of them will ever know."

'She turned round and faced me, smiling, one hand in her pocket, the other holding her cigarette. When I killed her she was smiling still. I fired at her heart. The bullet passed right through. She did not fall at once. She stood there, looking at me, that slow smile on her face, her eyes wide open . . .'

Maxim's voice had sunk low, so low that it was like a whisper. The hand that I held between my own was cold. I did not look at him. I watched Jasper's sleeping body on the carpet beside me, the little thump of his tail, now and then, upon the floor.

'I'd forgotten,' said Maxim, and his voice was slow now, tired, without expression, 'that when you shot a person there was so much blood.'

There was a hole there on the carpet beneath Jasper's tail. The burnt hole from a cigarette. I wondered how long it had been there. Some people said ash was good for the carpets.

'I had to get water from the cove,' said Maxim. 'I had to keep going backwards and forwards to the cove for water. Even by the fireplace, where she had not been, there was a stain. It was all round where she lay on the floor. It began to blow too. There was no catch on the window. The window kept banging backwards and forwards, while I knelt there on the floor with that dishcloth, and the bucket beside me.'

And the rain on the roof, I thought, he does not remember the rain on the roof. It pattered thin and light and very fast.

'I carried her out to the boat,' he said; 'it must have been half past eleven by then, nearly twelve. It was quite dark. There was no moon. The wind was squally, from the west. I carried her down to the cabin and left her there. Then I had to get under way, with the dinghy astern, and beat out of the little harbour against the tide. The wind was with me, but it came in puffs, and I was in the lee there, under cover of the headland. I remember I got the mainsail jammed half-way up the mast. I had not done it, you see, for a long time. I never went out with Rebecca.

'And I thought of the tide, how swift it ran and strong into the little cove. The wind blew down from the headland like a funnel. I got the boat out into the bay. I got her out there, beyond the beacon, and I tried to go about, to clear the ridge of rocks. The little jib fluttered. I could not sheet it in. A puff of wind came and the sheet tore out of my hands, went twisting round the mast. The sail thundered and shook. It cracked like a whip above my head. I could not remember what one had to do. I could not remember. I tried to reach that sheet and it blew above me in the air. Another blast of wind came straight ahead. We began to drift sideways, closer to the ridge. It was dark, so damned dark I couldn't see anything on the black, slippery deck. Somehow

I blundered down into the cabin. I had a spike with me. If I didn't do it now it would be too late. We were getting so near to the ridge, and in six or seven minutes, drifting like this, we should be out of deep water. I opened the sea-cocks. The water began to come in. I drove the spike into the bottom boards. One of the planks split right across. I took the spike out and began to drive in another plank. The water came up over my feet. I left Rebecca lying on the floor. I fastened both the scuttles. I bolted the door. When I came up on deck I saw we were within twenty yards of the ridge. I threw some of the loose stuff on the deck into the water. There was a life-buoy, a pair of sweeps, a coil of rope. I climbed into the dinghy. I pulled away, and lay back on the paddles, and watched. The boat was drifting still. She was sinking too. Sinking by the head. The jib was still shaking and cracking like a whip. I thought someone must hear it, someone walking the cliffs late at night, some fisherman from Kerrith away beyond me in the bay, whose boat I could not see. The boat was smaller, like a black shadow on the water. The mast began to shiver, began to crack. Suddenly she heeled right over and as she went the mast broke in two, split right down the centre. The life-buoy and the sweeps floated away from me on the water. The boat was not there any more. I remember staring at the place where she had been. Then I pulled back to the cove. It started raining.'

Maxim waited. He stared in front of him still. Then he looked at me, sitting beside him on the floor.

'That's all,' he said, 'there's no more to tell. I left the dinghy on the buoy, as she would have done. I went back and looked at the cottage. The floor was wet with the salt water. She might have done it herself. I walked up the path through the woods. I went into the house. Up the stairs to the dressing-room. I remember undressing. It began to blow and rain very hard. I was sitting there, on the bed, when Mrs Danvers knocked on the door. I went and opened it, in my dressing-gown, and spoke to her. She was worried about Rebecca. I told her to go back to bed. I shut the door again. I went back and sat by the window in my dressing-gown, watching the rain, listening to the sea as it broke there, in the cove.'

We sat there together without saying anything. I went on

holding his cold hands. I wondered why Robert did not come to clear the tea.

'She sank too close in,' said Maxim. 'I meant to take her right out in the bay. They would never have found her there. She was too close in.'

'It was the ship,' I said; 'it would not have happened but for the ship. No one would have known.'

'She was too close in,' said Maxim.

We were silent again. I began to feel very tired.

'I knew it would happen one day,' said Maxim, 'even when I went up to Edgecoombe and identified that body as hers. I knew it meant nothing, nothing at all. It was only a question of waiting, of marking time. Rebecca would win in the end. Finding you has not made any difference has it? Loving you does not alter things at all. Rebecca knew she would win in the end. I saw her smile, when she died.'

'Rebecca is dead,' I said. 'That's what we've got to remember. Rebecca is dead. She can't speak, she can't bear witness. She can't harm you any more.'

'There's her body,' he said, 'the diver has seen it. It's lying there, on the cabin floor.'

'We've got to explain it,' I said. 'We've got to think out a way to explain it. It's got to be the body of someone you don't know. Someone you've never seen before.'

'Her things will be there still,' he said. 'The rings on her fingers. Even if her clothes have rotted in the water there will be something there to tell them. It's not like a body lost at sea, battered against rocks. The cabin is untouched. She must be lying there on the floor as I left her. The boat has been there, all these months. No one has moved anything. There is the boat, lying on the sea bed where she sank.'

'A body rots in water, doesn't it?' I whispered; 'even if it's lying there, undisturbed, the water rots it, doesn't it?'

'I don't know,' he said. 'I don't know.'

'How will you find out? how will you know?' I said.

'The diver is going down again at five-thirty tomorrow morning,' said Maxim. 'Searle has made all the arrangements. They are going to try to raise the boat. No one will be about. I'm going with them. He's sending his boat to pick me up in the cove. Five-thirty tomorrow morning.'

'And then?' I said, 'if they get it up, what then?'

'Searle's going to have his big lighter anchored there, just out in the deep water. If the boat's wood has not rotted, if it still holds together, his crane will be able to lift it on to the lighter. They'll go back to Kerrith then. Searle says he will moor the lighter at the head of that disused creek half-way up Kerrith harbour. It drives out very easily. It's mud there at low water and the trippers can't row up there. We shall have the place to ourselves. He says we'll have to let the water drain out of the boat, leaving the cabin bare. He's going to get hold of a doctor.'

'What will he do?' I said. 'What will the doctor do?'

'I don't know,' he said.

'If they find out it's Rebecca you must say the other body was a mistake,' I said. 'You must say that the body in the crypt was a mistake, a ghastly mistake. You must say that when you went to Edgecoombe you were ill, you did not know what you were doing. You were not sure, even then. You could not tell. It was a mistake, just a mistake. You will say that, won't you?'

'Yes,' he said. 'Yes.'

'They can't prove anything against you,' I said. 'Nobody saw you that night. You had gone to bed. They can't prove anything. No one knows but you and I. No one at all. Not even Frank. We are the only two people in the world to know, Maxim. You and I.'

'Yes,' he said. 'Yes.'

'They will think the boat capsized and sank when she was in the cabin,' I said; 'they will think she went below for a rope, for something, and while she was there the wind came from the headland, and the boat heeled over, and Rebecca was trapped. They'll think that, won't they?'

'I don't know,' he said. 'I don't know.'

Suddenly the telephone began ringing in the little room behind the library.

21

MAXIM WENT INTO the little room and shut the door. Robert came in a few minutes afterwards to clear away the tea. I stood up, my back turned to him so that he should not see my face. I wondered when they would begin to know, on the estate, in the servants' hall, in Kerrith itself. I wondered how long it took for news to trickle through.

I could hear the murmur of Maxim's voice in the little room beyond. I had a sick expectant feeling at the pit of my stomach. The sound of the telephone ringing seemed to have woken every nerve in my body. I had sat there on the floor beside Maxim in a sort of dream, his hand in mine, my face against his shoulder. I had listened to his story, and part of me went with him like a shadow in his tracks. I too had killed Rebecca, I too had sunk the boat there in the bay. I had listened beside him to the wind and water. I had waited for Mrs Danvers' knocking on the door. All this I had suffered with him, all this and more beside. But the rest of me sat there on the carpet, unmoved and detached, thinking and caring for one thing only, repeating a phrase over and over again, 'He did not love Rebecca, he did not love Rebecca.' Now, at the ringing of the telephone, these two selves merged and became one again. I was the self that I had always been, I was not changed. But something new had come upon me that had not been before. My heart, for all its anxiety and doubt, was light and free. I knew then that I was no longer afraid of Rebecca. I did not hate her any more. Now that I knew her to have been evil and vicious and rotten I did not hate her any more. She could not hurt me. I could go to the morning-room and sit down at her desk and touch her pen and look at her writing on the pigeon-holes, and I should not mind. I could go to her room in the west wing, stand by the window even as I had done this morning, and

I should not be afraid. Rebecca's power had dissolved into the air, like the mist had done. She would never haunt me again. She would never stand behind me on the stairs, sit beside me in the dining-room, lean down from the gallery and watch me standing in the hall. Maxim had never loved her. I did not hate her any more. Her body had come back, her boat had been found with its queer prophetic name, *Je Reviens*, but I was free of her for ever.

I was free now to be with Maxim, to touch him, and hold him, and love him. I would never be a child again. It would not be I, I, I any longer; it would be we, it would be us. We would be together. We would face this trouble together, he and I. Captain Searle, and the diver, and Frank, and Mrs Danvers, and Beatrice, and the men and women of Kerrith reading their newspapers, could not break us now. Our happiness had not come too late. I was not young any more. I was not shy. I was not afraid. I would fight for Maxim. I would lie and perjure and swear, I would blaspheme and pray. Rebecca had not won. Rebecca had lost.

Robert had taken away the tea and Maxim came back into the room.

'It was Colonel Julyan,' he said; 'he's just been talking to Searle. He's coming out with us to the boat tomorrow. Searle has told him.'

'Why Colonel Julyan, why?' I said.

'He's the magistrate for Kerrith. He has to be present.'

'What did he say?'

'He asked me if I had any idea whose body it could be.'

'What did you say?'

'I said I did not know. I said we believed Rebecca to be alone. I said I did not know of any friend.'

'Did he say anything after that?'

'Yes.'

'What did he say?'

'He asked me if I thought it possible that I made a mistake when I went up to Edgecoombe?'

'He said that? He said that already?'

'Yes.'

'And you?'

'I said it might be possible. I did not know.'

'He'll be with you then tomorrow when you look at the boat? He, and Captain Searle, and a doctor.'

'Inspector Welch too.'

'Inspector Welch?'

'Yes.'

'Why? Why Inspector Welch?'

'It's the custom, when a body has been found.'

I did not say anything. We stared at one another. I felt the little pain come again at the pit of my stomach.

'They may not be able to raise the boat,' I said.

'No,' he said.

'They couldn't do anything then about the body, could they?' I said.

'I don't know,' he said.

He glanced out of the window. The sky was white and over-cast as it had been when I came away from the cliffs. There was no wind though. It was still and quiet.

'I thought it might blow from the south-west about an hour ago but the wind has died away again,' he said.

'Yes,' I said.

'It will be a flat calm tomorrow for the diver,' he said.

The telephone began ringing again from the little room. There was something sickening about the shrill urgent summons of the bell. Maxim and I looked at one another. Then he went into the room to answer it, shutting the door behind him as he had done before. The queer nagging pain had not left me yet. It returned again in greater force with the ringing of the bell. The feel of it took me back across the years to my childhood. This was the pain I had known when I was very small and the maroons had sounded in the streets of London, and I had sat, shivering, not understanding, under a little cupboard beneath the stairs. It was the same feeling, the same pain.

Maxim came back into the library. 'It's begun,' he said slowly.

'What do you mean? What's happened?' I said, grown sud-denly cold.

'It was a reporter,' he said, 'the fellow from the *County Chron-icle*. Was it true, he said, that the boat belonging to the late Mrs de Winter had been found.'

'What did you say?'

'I said yes, a boat had been found, but that was all we know. It might not be her boat at all.'

'Was that all he said?'

'No. He asked if I could confirm the rumour that a body had been found in the cabin.'

'No!'

'Yes. Someone must have been talking. Not Searle, I know that. The diver, one of his friends. You can't stop these people. The whole story will be all over Kerrith by breakfast time tomorrow.'

'What did you say, about the body?'

'I said I did not know. I had no statement to make. And I should be obliged if he did not ring me up again.'

'You will irritate them. You will have them against you.'

'I can't help that. I don't make statements to newspapers. I won't have those fellows ringing up and asking questions.'

'We might want them on our side,' I said.

'If it comes to fighting, I'll fight alone,' he said. 'I don't want a newspaper behind me.'

'The reporter will ring up someone else,' I said. 'He will get on to Colonel Julyan or Captain Searle.'

'He won't get much change out of them,' said Maxim.

'If only we could do something,' I said, 'all these hours ahead of us, and we sit here, idle, waiting for tomorrow morning.'

'There's nothing we can do,' said Maxim.

We went on sitting in the library. Maxim picked up a book but I know he did not read. Now and again I saw him lift his head and listen, as though he heard the telephone again. But it did not ring again. No one disturbed us. We dressed for dinner as usual. It seemed incredible to me that this time last night I had been putting on my white dress, sitting before the mirror at my dressing-table, arranging the curled wig. It was like an old forgotten nightmare, something remembered months afterwards with doubt and disbelief. We had dinner. Frith served us, returned from his afternoon. His face was solemn, expressionless. I wondered if he had been in Kerrith, if he had heard anything.

After dinner we went back again to the library. We did not

talk much. I sat on the floor at Maxim's feet, my head against his knees. He ran his fingers through my hair. Different from his old abstracted way. It was not like stroking Jasper any more. I felt his finger tips on the scalp of my head. Sometimes he kissed me. Sometimes he said things to me. There were no shadows between us any more, and when we were silent it was because the silence came to us of our own asking. I wondered how it was I could be so happy when our little world about us was so black. It was a strange sort of happiness. Not what I had dreamt about or expected. It was not the sort of happiness I had imagined in the lonely hours. There was nothing feverish or urgent about this. It was a quiet, still happiness. The library windows were open wide, and when we did not talk or touch one another we looked out at the dark dull sky.

It must have rained in the night, for when I woke the next morning, just after seven, and got up, and looked out of the window, I saw the roses in the garden below were folded and drooping, and the grass banks leading to the woods were wet and silver. There was a little smell in the air of mist and damp, the smell that comes with the first fall of the leaf. I wondered if autumn would come upon us two months before her time. Maxim had not woken me when he got up at five. He must have crept from his bed and gone through the bathroom to his dressing-room without a sound. He would be down there now, in the bay, with Colonel Julyan, and Captain Searle, and the men from the lighter. The lighter would be there, the crane and the chain, and Rebecca's boat coming to the surface. I thought about it calmly, coolly, without feeling. I pictured them all down there in the bay, and the little dark hull of the boat rising slowly to the surface, sodden, dripping, the grass-green sea-weed and shells clinging to her sides. When they lifted her on to the lighter the water would stream from her sides, back into the sea again. The wood of the little boat would look soft and grey, pulpy in places. She would smell of mud and rust, and that dark weed that grows deep beneath the sea beside rocks that are never uncovered. Perhaps the name-board still hung upon her stern. *Je Reviens.* The lettering green and faded. The nails rusted through. And Rebecca herself was there, lying on the cabin floor.

I got up and had my bath and dressed, and went down to breakfast at nine o'clock as usual. There were a lot of letters on my plate. Letters from people thanking us for the dance. I skimmed through them, I did not read them all. Frith wanted to know whether to keep the breakfast hot for Maxim. I told him I did not know when he would be back. He had to go out very early, I said. Frith did not say anything. He looked very solemn, very grave. I wondered again if he knew.

After breakfast I took my letters along to the morning-room. The room smelt fusty, the windows had not been opened. I flung them wide, letting in the cool fresh air. The flowers on the mantelpiece were drooping, many of them dead. The petals lay on the floor. I rang the bell, and Maud, the under-housemaid, came into the room.

'This room has not been touched this morning,' I said, 'even the windows were shut. And the flowers are dead. Will you please take them away?'

She looked nervous and apologetic. 'I'm very sorry, Madam,' she said. She went to the mantelpiece and took the vases.

'Don't let it happen again,' I said.

'No, Madam,' she said. She went out of the room, taking the flowers with her. I had not thought it would be so easy to be severe. I wondered why it had seemed hard for me before. The menu for the day lay on the writing-desk. Cold salmon and mayonnaise, cutlets in aspic, galantine of chicken, soufflé. I recognized them all from the buffet-supper of the night of the ball. We were evidently still living on the remains. This must be the cold lunch that was put out in the dining-room yesterday and I had not eaten. The staff were taking things easily, it seemed. I put a pencil through the list and rang for Robert. 'Tell Mrs Danvers to order something hot,' I said. 'If there's still a lot of cold stuff to finish we don't want it in the dining-room.'

'Very good, Madam,' he said.

I followed him out of the room and went to the little flower room for my scissors. Then I went into the rose-garden and cut some young buds. The chill had worn away from the air. It was going to be as hot and airless as yesterday had been. I wondered if they were still down in the bay or whether they had gone back to the creek in Kerrith harbour. Presently I should hear. Presently Maxim would come back and tell me. Whatever happened I must be calm and quiet. Whatever happened I must not be afraid. I cut my roses and took them back into the morning-room. The carpet had been dusted, and the fallen petals removed. I began to arrange the flowers in the vases that Robert had filled with water. When I had nearly finished there was a knock on the door.

'Come in,' I said.

It was Mrs Danvers. She had the menu list in her hand. She looked pale and tired. There were great rings round her eyes.

'Good morning, Mrs Danvers,' I said.

'I don't understand', she began, 'why you sent the menu out and the message by Robert. Why did you do it?'

I looked across at her, a rose in my hand.

'Those cutlets and that salmon were sent in yesterday,' I said. 'I saw them on the side-board. I should prefer something hot today. If they won't eat the cold in the kitchen you had better throw the stuff away. So much waste goes on in this house anyway that a little more won't make any difference.'

She stared at me. She did not say anything. I put the rose in the vase with the others.

'Don't tell me you can't think of anything to give us, Mrs Danvers,' I said. 'You must have menus for all occasions in your room.'

'I'm not used to having messages sent to me by Robert,' she said. 'If Mrs de Winter wanted anything changed she would ring me personally on the house telephone.'

'I'm afraid it does not concern me very much what Mrs de Winter used to do,' I said. 'I am Mrs de Winter now, you know. And if I choose to send a message by Robert I shall do so.'

Just then Robert came into the room. 'The *County Chronicle* on the telephone, Madam,' he said.

'Tell the *County Chronicle* I'm not at home,' I said.

'Yes, Madam,' he said. He went out of the room.

'Well, Mrs Danvers, is there anything else?' I said.

She went on staring at me. Still she did not say anything. 'If you have nothing else to say you had better go and tell the cook about the hot lunch,' I said. 'I'm rather busy.'

'Why did the *County Chronicle* want to speak to you?' she said.

'I haven't the slightest idea, Mrs Danvers,' I said.

'Is it true,' she said slowly, 'the story Frith brought back with him from Kerrith last night, that Mrs de Winter's boat has been found?'

'Is there such a story?' I said. 'I'm afraid I don't know anything about it.'

'Captain Searle, the Kerrith harbour-master, called here yesterday, didn't he?' she said. 'Robert told me, Robert showed him in. Frith says the story in Kerrith is that the diver who went down about the ship there in the bay found Mrs de Winter's boat.'

'Perhaps so,' I said. 'You had better wait until Mr de Winter himself comes in and ask him about it.'

'Why was Mr de Winter up so early?' she asked.

'That was Mr de Winter's business,' I said.

She went on staring at me. 'Frith said the story goes that there was a body in the cabin of the little boat,' she said. 'Why should there be a body there? Mrs de Winter always sailed alone.'

'It's no use asking me, Mrs Danvers,' I said. 'I don't know any more than you do.'

'Don't you?' she said slowly. She kept on looking at me. I turned away, I put the vase back on the table by the window.

'I will give the orders about the lunch,' she said. She waited a moment. I did not say anything. Then she went out of the room. She can't frighten me any more, I thought. She has lost her power with Rebecca. Whatever she said or did now it could not matter to me or hurt me. I knew she was my enemy and I did not mind. But if she should learn the truth about the body in the boat and become Maxim's enemy too – what then? I sat down in the chair. I put the scissors on the table. I did not feel like doing any more roses. I kept wondering what Maxim was doing. I wondered why the reporter from the *County Chronicle* had rung us up again. The old sick feeling came back inside me. I went and leant out of the window. It was very hot. There was thunder in the air. The gardeners began to mow the grass again. I could see one of the men with his machine walk backwards and forwards on the top of the bank. I could not go on sitting in the morning-room. I left my scissors and my roses and went out on to the terrace. I began to walk up and down. Jasper padded after me, wondering why I did not take him for a walk. I went on walking up and down the terrace. About half past eleven Frith came out to me from the hall.

'Mr de Winter on the telephone, Madam,' he said.

I went through the library to the little room beyond. My hands were shaking as I lifted the receiver.

'Is that you?' he said. 'It's Maxim. I'm speaking from the office. I'm with Frank.'

'Yes?' I said.

There was a pause. 'I shall be bringing Frank and Colonel Julyan back to lunch at one o'clock,' he said.

'Yes,' I said.

I waited. I waited for him to go on. 'They were able to raise the boat,' he said. 'I've just got back from the creek.'

'Yes,' I said.

'Searle was there, and Colonel Julyan, and Frank, and the others,' he said. I wondered if Frank was standing beside him at the telephone, and if that was the reason he was so cool, so distant.

'All right then,' he said; 'expect us about one o'clock.'

I put back the receiver. He had not told me anything. I still did not know what had happened. I went back again to the terrace, telling Frith first that we should be four to lunch instead of two.

An hour dragged past, slow, interminable. I went upstairs and changed into a thinner frock. I came down again. I went and sat in the drawing-room and waited. At five minutes to one I heard the sound of a car in the drive, and then voices in the hall. I patted my hair in front of the looking-glass. My face was very white. I pinched some colour into my cheeks and stood up waiting for them to come into the room. Maxim came in, and Frank, and Colonel Julyan. I remembered seeing Colonel Julyan at the ball dressed as Cromwell. He looked shrunken now, different. A smaller man altogether.

'How do you do?' he said. He spoke quietly, gravely, like a doctor.

'Ask Frith to bring the sherry,' said Maxim. 'I'm going to wash.'

'I'll have a wash too,' said Frank. Before I rang the bell Frith appeared with the sherry. Colonel Julyan did not have any. I took some to give me something to hold. Colonel Julyan came and stood beside me by the window.

'This is a most distressing thing, Mrs de Winter,' he said gently. 'I do feel for you and your husband most acutely.'

'Thank you,' I said. I began to sip my sherry. Then I put the glass back again on the table. I was afraid he would notice that my hand was shaking.

'What makes it so difficult was the fact of your husband identifying that first body, over a year ago,' he said.

'I don't quite understand,' I said.

'You did not hear, then, what we found this morning?' he said.

'I knew there was a body. The diver found a body,' I said.

'Yes,' he said. And then, half glancing over his shoulder towards the hall, 'I'm afraid it was her, without a doubt,' he said, lowering his voice. 'I can't go into details with you, but the evidence was sufficient for your husband and Doctor Phillips to identify.'

He stopped suddenly, and moved away from me. Maxim and Frank had come back into the room.

'Lunch is ready; shall we go in?' said Maxim.

I led the way into the hall, my heart like a stone, heavy, numb. Colonel Julyan sat on my right, Frank on my left. I did not look at Maxim. Frith and Robert began to hand the first course. We all talked about the weather. 'I see in *The Times* they had it well over eighty in London yesterday,' said Colonel Julyan.

'Really?' I said.

'Yes. Must be frightful for the poor devils who can't get away.'

'Yes, frightful,' I said.

'Paris can be hotter than London,' said Frank. 'I remember staying a week-end in Paris in the middle of August, and it was quite impossible to sleep. There was not a breath of air in the whole city. The temperature was over ninety.'

'Of course the French always sleep with their windows shut, don't they?' said Colonel Julyan.

'I don't know,' said Frank. 'I was staying in a hotel. The people were mostly Americans.'

'You know France of course, Mrs de Winter?' said Colonel Julyan.

'Not so very well,' I said.

'Oh, I had the idea you had lived many years out there.'

'No,' I said.

'She was staying in Monte Carlo when I met her,' said Maxim. 'You don't call that France, do you?'

'No, I suppose not,' said Colonel Julyan; 'it must be very cosmopolitan. The coast is pretty though, isn't it?'

'Very pretty,' I said.

'Not so rugged as this, eh? Still, I know which I'd rather have. Give me England every time, when it comes to settling down. You know where you are over here.'

'I dare say the French feel that about France,' said Maxim.

'Oh, no doubt,' said Colonel Julyan.

We went on eating awhile in silence. Frith stood behind my chair. We were all thinking of one thing, but because of Frith we had to keep up our little performance. I suppose Frith was thinking about it too, and I thought how much easier it would be if we cast aside convention and let him join in with us, if he had anything to say. Robert came with the drinks. Our plates were changed. The second course was handed. Mrs Danvers had not forgotten my wish for hot food. I took something out of a casserole covered in mushroom sauce.

'I think everyone enjoyed your wonderful party the other night,' said Colonel Julyan.

'I'm so glad,' I said.

'Does an immense amount of good locally, that sort of thing,' he said.

'Yes, I suppose it does,' I said.

'It's a universal instinct of the human species, isn't it, that desire to dress up in some sort of disguise?' said Frank.

'I must be very inhuman, then,' said Maxim.

'It's natural, I suppose,' said Colonel Julyan, 'for all of us to wish to look different. We are all children in some ways.'

I wondered how much pleasure it had given him to disguise himself as Cromwell. I had not seen much of him at the ball. He had spent most of the evening in the morning-room, playing bridge.

'You don't play golf, do you, Mrs de Winter?' said Colonel Julyan.

'No, I'm afraid I don't,' I said.

'You ought to take it up,' he said. 'My eldest girl is very keen, and she can't find young people to play with her. I gave her a small car for her birthday, and she drives herself over to the north coast nearly every day. It gives her something to do.'

'How nice,' I said.

'She ought to have been the boy,' he said. 'My lad is different altogether. No earthly use at games. Always writing poetry. I suppose he'll grow out of it.'

'Oh, rather,' said Frank. 'I used to write poetry myself when I was his age. Awful nonsense too. I never write any now.'

'Good heavens, I should hope not,' said Maxim.

'I don't know where my boy gets it from,' said Colonel Julyan; 'certainly not from his mother or from me.'

There was another long silence. Colonel Julyan had a second dip into the casserole. 'Mrs Lacy looked very well the other night,' he said.

'Yes,' I said.

'Her dress came adrift as usual,' said Maxim.

'Those Eastern garments must be the devil to manage,' said Colonel Julyan, 'and yet they say, you know, they are far more comfortable and far cooler than anything you ladies wear in England.'

'Really?' I said.

'Yes, so they say. It seems all that loose drapery throws off the hot rays of the sun.'

'How curious,' said Frank; 'you'd think it would have just the opposite effect.'

'No, apparently not,' said Colonel Julyan.

'Do you know the East, sir?' said Frank.

'I know the Far East,' said Colonel Julyan. 'I was in China for five years. Then Singapore.'

'Isn't that where they make the curry?' I said.

'Yes, they gave us very good curry in Singapore,' he said.

'I'm fond of curry,' said Frank.

'Ah, it's not curry at all in England, it's hash,' said Colonel Julyan.

The plates were cleared away. A soufflé was handed, and a bowl of fruit salad. 'I suppose you are coming to the end of your raspberries,' said Colonel Julyan. 'It's been a wonderful summer for them, hasn't it? We've put down pots and pots of jam.'

'I never think raspberry jam is a great success,' said Frank; 'there are always so many pips.'

'You must come and try some of ours,' said Colonel Julyan. 'I don't think we have a great lot of pips.'

'We're going to have a mass of apples this year at Manderley,' said Frank. 'I was saying to Maxim a few days ago we ought to have a record season. We shall be able to send a lot up to London.'

'Do you really find it pays?' said Colonel Julyan; 'by the time you've paid your men for the extra labour, and then the packing, and carting, do you make any sort of profit worth while?'

'Oh, Lord, yes,' said Frank.

'How interesting. I must tell my wife,' said Colonel Julyan.

The soufflé and the fruit salad did not take long to finish. Robert appeared with cheese and biscuits, and a few minutes later Frith came with the coffee and cigarettes. Then they both went out of the room and shut the door. We drank our coffee in silence. I gazed steadily at my plate.

'I was saying to your wife before luncheon, de Winter,' began Colonel Julyan, resuming his first quiet confidential tone, 'that the awkward part of this whole distressing business is the fact that you identified that original body.'

'Yes, quite,' said Maxim.

'I think the mistake was very natural under the circumstances,' said Frank quickly. 'The authorities wrote to Maxim, asking him to go up to Edgecoombe, presupposing before he arrived there that the body was hers. And Maxim was not well at the time. I wanted to go with him, but he insisted on going alone. He was not in a fit state to undertake anything of the sort.'

'That's nonsense,' said Maxim. 'I was perfectly well.'

'Well, it's no use going into all that now,' said Colonel Julyan. 'You made that first identification, and now the only thing to do is to admit the error. There seems to be no doubt about it this time.'

'No,' said Maxim.

'I wish you could be spared the formality and the publicity of an inquest,' said Colonel Julyan, 'but I'm afraid that's quite impossible.'

'Naturally,' said Maxim.

'I don't think it need take very long,' said Colonel Julyan. 'It's just a case of you re-affirming identification, and then getting Tabb, who you say converted the boat when your wife brought her from France, just to give his piece of evidence that the boat was seaworthy and in good order when he last had her in his yard. It's just red-tape, you know. But it has to be done. No, what bothers me is the wretched publicity of the affair. So sad and unpleasant for you and your wife.'

'That's quite all right,' said Maxim. 'We understand.'

'So unfortunate that wretched ship going ashore there,' said Colonel Julyan; 'but for that the whole matter would have rested in peace.'

'Yes,' said Maxim.

'The only consolation is that now we know poor Mrs de Winter's death must have been swift and sudden, not the dreadful slow lingering affair we all believed it to be. There can have been no question of trying to swim.'

'None,' said Maxim.

'She must have gone down for something, and then the door jammed, and a squall caught the boat without anyone at the helm,' said Colonel Julyan. 'A dreadful thing.'

'Yes,' said Maxim.

'That seems to be the solution, don't you think, Crawley?' said Colonel Julyan, turning to Frank.

'Oh, yes, undoubtedly,' said Frank.

I glanced up, and I saw Frank looking at Maxim. He looked away again immediately but not before I had seen and understood the expression in his eyes. Frank knew. And Maxim did not know that he knew. I went on stirring my coffee. My hand was hot, damp.

'I suppose sooner or later we all make a mistake in judgement,' said Colonel Julyan, 'and then we are for it. Mrs de Winter must have known how the wind comes down like a funnel in that bay, and that it was not safe to leave the helm of a small boat like that. She must have sailed alone over that spot scores of times. And then the moment came, she took a chance – and the chance killed her. It's a lesson to all of us.'

'Accidents happen so easily,' said Frank, 'even to the most experienced people. Think of the number killed out hunting every season.'

'Oh, I know. But then it's the horse falling generally that lets you down. If Mrs de Winter had not left the helm of her boat the accident would never have happened. An extraordinary thing to do. I must have watched her many times in the handicap race on Saturdays from Kerrith, and I never saw her make an elementary mistake. It's the sort of thing a novice would do. In that particular place too, just by the ridge.'

'It was very squally that night,' said Frank; 'something may have happened to the gear. Something may have jammed. And then she slipped down for a knife.'

'Of course. Of course. Well, we shall never know. And I don't suppose we should be any the better for it if we did. As I said before, I wish I could stop this inquest but I can't. I'm trying to arrange it for Tuesday morning, and it will be as short as possible. Just a formal matter. But I'm afraid we shan't be able to keep the reporters out of it.'

There was another silence. I judged the time had come to push back my chair.

'Shall we go into the garden?' I said.

We all stood up, and then I led the way to the terrace. Colonel Julyan patted Jasper.

'He's grown into a nice-looking dog,' he said.

'Yes,' I said.

'They make nice pets,' he said.

'Yes,' I said.

We stood about for a minute. Then he glanced at his watch.

'Thank you for your most excellent lunch,' he said. 'I have rather a busy afternoon in front of me, and I hope you will excuse me dashing away.'

'Of course,' I said.

'I'm so very sorry this should have happened. You have all my sympathy. I consider it's almost harder for you than for your husband. However, once the inquest is over you must both forget all about it.'

'Yes,' I said, 'yes, we must try to.'

'My car is here in the drive. I wonder whether Crawley would like a lift. Crawley? I can drop you at your office if it's any use.'

'Thank you, sir,' said Frank.

He came and took my hand. 'I shall be seeing you again,' he said.

'Yes,' I said.

I did not look at him. I was afraid he would understand my eyes. I did not want him to know that I knew. Maxim walked with them to the car. When they had gone he came back to me on the terrace. He took my arm. We stood looking down at the green lawns towards the sea and the beacon on the headland.

'It's going to be all right,' he said. 'I'm quite calm, quite confident. You saw how Julyan was at lunch, and Frank. There won't be any difficulty at the inquest. It's going to be all right.'

I did not say anything. I held his arm tightly.

'There was never any question of the body being someone unknown,' he said. 'What we saw was enough for Doctor Phillips even to make the identification alone without me. It was straightforward, simple. There was no trace of what I'd done. The bullet had not touched the bone.'

A butterfly sped past us on the terrace, silly and inconsequent.

'You heard what they said,' he went on; 'they think she was trapped there, in the cabin. The jury will believe that at the inquest too. Phillips will tell them so.' He paused. Still I did not speak.

'I only mind for you,' he said. 'I don't regret anything else. If it had to come all over again I should not do anything different. I'm glad I killed Rebecca. I shall never have any remorse for that, never, never. But you. I can't forget what it has done to you. I was looking at you, thinking of nothing else all through lunch. It's gone for ever, that funny, young, lost look that I loved. It won't come back again. I killed that too, when I told you about Rebecca ... It's gone, in twenty-four hours. You are so much older ...'

22

THAT EVENING, WHEN Frith brought in the local paper, there were great headlines right across the top of the page. He brought the paper and laid it down on the table. Maxim was not there; he had gone up early to change for dinner. Frith stood a moment, waiting for me to say something, and it seemed to me stupid and insulting to ignore a matter that must mean so much to everyone in the house.

'This is a very dreadful thing, Frith,' I said.

'Yes, Madam; we are all most distressed outside,' he said.

'It's so sad for Mr de Winter,' I said, 'having to go through it all again.'

'Yes, Madam. Very sad. Such a shocking experience, Madam, having to identify the second body having seen the first. I suppose there is no doubt then, that the remains in the boat are genuinely those of the late Mrs de Winter?'

'I'm afraid not, Frith. No doubt at all.'

'It seems so odd to us, Madam, that she should have let herself be trapped like that in the cabin. She was so experienced in a boat.'

'Yes, Frith. That's what we all feel. But accidents will happen. And how it happened I don't suppose any of us will ever know.'

'I suppose not, Madam. But it's a great shock, all the same. We are most distressed about it outside. And coming suddenly just after the party. It doesn't seem right somehow, does it?'

'No, Frith.'

'It seems there is to be an inquest, Madam?'

'Yes. A formality, you know.'

'Of course, Madam. I wonder if any of us will be required to give evidence?'

'I don't think so.'

'I shall be only too pleased to do anything that might help the family; Mr de Winter knows that.'

'Yes, Frith. I'm sure he does.'

'I've told them outside not to discuss the matter, but it's very difficult to keep an eye on them, especially the girls. I can deal with Robert, of course. I'm afraid the news has been a great shock to Mrs Danvers.'

'Yes, Frith. I rather expected it would.'

'She went up to her room straight after lunch, and has not come down again. Alice took her a cup of tea and the paper a few minutes ago. She said Mrs Danvers looked very ill indeed.'

'It would be better really if she stayed where she is,' I said. 'It's no use her getting up and seeing to things if she is ill. Perhaps Alice would tell her that. I can very well manage the ordering. The cook and I between us.'

'Yes, Madam. I don't think she is physically ill, Madam; it's just the shock of Mrs de Winter being found. She was very devoted to Mrs de Winter.'

'Yes,' I said. 'Yes, I know.'

Frith went out of the room after that, and I glanced quickly at the paper before Maxim came down. There was a great column, all down the front page, and an awful blurred photograph of Maxim that must have been taken at least fifteen years ago. It was dreadful, seeing it there on the front page staring at me. And the little line about myself at the bottom, saying whom Maxim had married as his second wife, and how we had just given the fancy dress ball at Manderley. It sounded so crude and callous, in the dark print of the newspaper. Rebecca, whom they described as beautiful, talented, and loved by all who knew her, having been drowned a year ago, and then Maxim marrying again the following spring, bringing his bride straight to Manderley (so it said) and giving the big fancy dress ball in her honour. And then the following morning the body of his first wife being found, trapped in the cabin of her sailing boat, at the bottom of the bay.

It was true of course, though sprinkled with the little inaccuracies that added to the story, making it strong meat for the hundreds of readers who wanted value for their pennies. Maxim sounded vile in it, a sort of satyr. Bringing back his 'young bride', as it described me, to Manderley, and giving the dance, as though we wanted to display ourselves before the world.

I hid the paper under the cushion of the chair so that Maxim should not see it. But I could not keep the morning editions from him. The story was in our London papers too. There was a picture of Manderley, and the story underneath. Manderley was news, and so was Maxim. They talked about him as Max de Winter. It sounded racy, horrible. Each paper made great play of the fact that Rebecca's body had been found the day after the fancy dress ball, as though there was something deliberate about it. Both papers used the same word, 'ironic'. Yes, I suppose it was ironic. It made a good story. I watched Maxim at the breakfast table getting whiter and whiter as he read the papers, one after the other, and then the local one as well. He did not say anything. He just looked across at me, and I stretched out my hand to him. 'Damn them,' he whispered, 'damn them, damn them.'

I thought of all the things they could say, if they knew the truth. Not one column, but five or six. Placards in London. Newsboys shouting in the streets, outside the underground stations. That frightful word of six letters, in the middle of the placard, large and black.

Frank came up after breakfast. He looked pale and tired, as though he had not slept. 'I've told the exchange to put all calls for Manderley through to the office,' he said to Maxim. 'It doesn't matter who it is. If reporters ring up I can deal with them. And anyone else too. I don't want either of you to be worried at all. We've had several calls already from locals. I gave the same answer to each. Mr and Mrs de Winter were grateful for all sympathetic inquiries, and they hoped their friends would understand that they were not receiving calls during the next few days. Mrs Lacy rang up about eight-thirty. Wanted to come over at once.'

'Oh, my God . . .' began Maxim.

'It's all right, I prevented her. I told her quite truthfully that I did not think she would do any good coming over. That you did not want to see anyone but Mrs de Winter. She wanted to know when they were holding the inquest, but I told her it had not been settled. I don't know that we can stop her from coming to that, if she finds it in the papers.'

'Those blasted reporters,' said Maxim.

'I know,' said Frank; 'we all want to wring their necks, but you've got to see their point of view. It's their bread-and-butter; they've got to do the job for their paper. If they don't get a story the editor probably sacks them. If the editor does not produce a saleable edition the proprietor sacks him. And if the paper doesn't sell, the proprietor loses all his money. You won't have to see them or speak to them, Maxim. I'm going to do all that for you. All you have to concentrate on is your statement at the inquest.'

'I know what to say,' said Maxim.

'Of course you do, but don't forget old Horridge is the Coroner. He's a sticky sort of chap, goes into details that are quite irrelevant, just to show the jury how thorough he is at his job. You must not let him rattle you.'

'Why the devil should I be rattled? I have nothing to be rattled about.'

'Of course not. But I've attended these coroner's inquests before, and it's so easy to get nervy and irritable. You don't want to put the fellow's back up.'

'Frank's right,' I said. 'I know just what he means. The swifter and smoother the whole thing goes the easier it will be for everyone. Then once the wretched thing is over we shall forget all about it, and so will everyone else, won't they, Frank?'

'Yes, of course,' said Frank.

I still avoided his eye, but I was more convinced than ever that he knew the truth. He had always known it. From the very first. I remembered the first time I met him, that first day of mine at Manderley, when he, and Beatrice, and Giles had all been at lunch, and Beatrice had been tactless about Maxim's health. I remembered Frank, his quiet turning of the subject, the way he had come to Maxim's aid in his quiet unobtrusive manner if there was ever any question of difficulty. That strange reluctance of his to talk about Rebecca, his stiff, funny, pompous way of making conversation whenever we had approached anything like intimacy. I understood it all. Frank knew, but Maxim did not know that he knew. And Frank did not want Maxim to know that he knew. And we all stood there, looking at one another, keeping up these little barriers between us.

We were not bothered with the telephone again. All the calls were put through to the office. It was just a question of waiting now. Waiting until the Tuesday.

I saw nothing of Mrs Danvers. The menu was sent through as usual, and I did not change it. I asked little Clarice about her. She said she was going about her work as usual but she was not speaking to anybody. She had all her meals alone in her sitting-room.

Clarice was wide-eyed, evidently curious, but she did not ask me any questions, and I was not going to discuss it with her. No doubt they talked of nothing else, out in the kitchen, and on the estate too, in the lodge, on the farms. I supposed all Kerrith was full of it. We stayed in Manderley, in the gardens close to the house. We did not even walk in the woods. The weather had not broken yet. It was still hot, oppressive. The air was full of thunder, and there was rain behind the white dull sky, but it did not fall. I could feel it, and smell it, pent up there, behind the clouds. The inquest was to be on the Tuesday afternoon at two o'clock.

We had lunch at a quarter to one. Frank came. Thank heaven Beatrice had telephoned that she could not get over. The boy Roger had arrived home with measles; they were all in quarantine. I could not help blessing the measles. I don't think Maxim could have borne it, with Beatrice sitting here, staying in the house, sincere, anxious, and affectionate, but asking questions all the time. Forever asking questions.

Lunch was a hurried, nervous meal. We none of us talked very much. I had that nagging pain again. I did not want anything to eat. I could not swallow. It was a relief when the farce of the meal was over, and I heard Maxim go out on to the drive and start up the car. The sound of the engine steadied me. It meant we had to go, we had to be doing something. Not just sitting at Manderley. Frank followed us in his own car. I had my hand on Maxim's knee all the way as he drove. He seemed quite calm. Not nervous in any way. It was like going with someone to a nursing-home, someone who was to have an operation. And not knowing what would happen. Whether the operation would be successful. My hands were very cold. My heart was beating in a funny, jerky way.

And all the time that little nagging pain beneath my heart. The inquest was to be held at Lanyon, the market town six miles the other side of Kerrith. We had to park the cars in the big cobbled square by the market-place. Doctor Phillips' car was there already, and also Colonel Julyan's. Other cars too. I saw a passer-by stare curiously at Maxim, and then nudge her companion's arm.

'I think I shall stay here,' I said. 'I don't think I'll come in with you after all.'

'I did not want you to come,' said Maxim. 'I was against it from the first. You'd much better have stayed at Manderley.'

'No,' I said. 'No, I'll be all right here, sitting in the car.'

Frank came and looked in at the window. 'Isn't Mrs de Winter coming?' he said.

'No,' said Maxim. 'She wants to stay in the car.'

'I think she's right,' said Frank; 'there's no earthly reason why she should be present at all. We shan't be long.'

'It's all right,' I said.

'I'll keep a seat for you,' said Frank, 'in case you should change your mind.'

They went off together and left me sitting there. It was early-closing day. The shops looked drab and dull. There were not many people about. Lanyon was not much of a holiday centre anyway; it was too far inland. I sat looking at the silent shops. The minutes went by. I wondered what they were doing, the Coroner, Frank, Maxim, Colonel Julyan. I got out of the car and began walking up and down the market square. I went and looked in a shop window. Then I walked up and down again. I saw a policeman watching me curiously. I turned up a side-street to avoid him.

Somehow, in spite of myself, I found I was coming to the building where the inquest was being held. There had been little publicity about the actual time, and because of this there was no crowd waiting, as I had feared and expected. The place seemed deserted. I went up the steps and stood just inside the door.

A policeman appeared from nowhere. 'Do you want anything?' he said.

'No,' I said. 'No.'

'You can't wait here,' he said.

'I'm sorry,' I said. I went back towards the steps into the street.

'Excuse me, Madam,' he said, 'aren't you Mrs de Winter?'

'Yes,' I said.

'Of course that's different,' he said; 'you can wait here if you like. Would you like to take a seat just inside this room?'

'Thank you,' I said.

He showed me into a little bare room with a desk in it. It was like a waiting-room at a station. I sat there, with my hands on my lap. Five minutes passed. Nothing happened. It was worse than being outside, than sitting in the car. I got up and went into the passage. The policeman was still standing there.

'How long will they be?' I said.

'I'll go and inquire if you like,' he said.

He disappeared along the passage. In a moment he came back again. 'I don't think they will be very much longer,' he said. 'Mr de Winter has just given his evidence. Captain Searle, and the diver, and Doctor Phillips have already given theirs. There's only one more to speak. Mr Tabb, the boat-builder from Kerrith.'

'Then it's nearly over,' I said.

'I expect so, Madam,' he said. Then he said, on a sudden thought, 'Would you like to hear the remaining evidence? There is a seat there, just inside the door. If you slip in now nobody will notice you.'

'Yes,' I said. 'Yes, I think I will.'

It was nearly over. Maxim had finished giving his evidence. I did not mind hearing the rest. It was Maxim I had not wanted to hear. I had been nervous of listening to his evidence. That was why I had not gone with him and Frank in the first place. Now it did not matter. His part of it was over.

I followed the policeman, and he opened a door at the end of the passage. I slipped in, I sat down just by the door. I kept my head low so that I did not have to look at anybody. The room was smaller than I had imagined. Rather hot and stuffy. I had pictured a great bare room with benches, like a church. Maxim and Frank were sitting down at the other end. The Coroner was a thin, elderly man in pince-nez. There were people there I did not know. I glanced at them out of the tail of my eye. My heart gave a jump suddenly as I recognized Mrs Danvers. She was sit-ting right at the back. And Favell was beside her. Jack Favell, Rebecca's cousin. He was leaning forward, his chin in his hands, his eyes fixed on the Coroner, Mr Horridge. I had not expected him to be there. I wondered if Maxim had seen him. James Tabb, the boat-builder, was standing up now and the Coroner was ask-ing him a question.

'Yes, sir,' answered Tabb, 'I converted Mrs de Winter's little boat. She was a French fishing boat originally, and Mrs de Winter bought her for next to nothing over in Brittany, and had her shipped over. She gave me the job of converting her and doing her up like a little yacht.'

'Was the boat in a fit state to put to sea?' said the Coroner.

'She was when I fitted her out in April of last year,' said Tabb. 'Mrs de Winter laid her up as usual at my yard in the October, and then in March I had word from her to fit her up as usual, which I did. That would be Mrs de Winter's fourth season with the boat since I did the conversion job for her.'

'Had the boat ever been known to capsize before?' asked the Coroner.

'No, sir. I should soon have heard of it from Mrs de Winter had there been any question of it. She was delighted with the boat in every way, according to what she said to me.'

'I suppose great care was needed to handle the boat?' said the Coroner.

'Well, sir, everyone has to have their wits about them, when they go sailing boats, I won't deny it. But Mrs de Winter's boat wasn't one of those cranky little craft that you can't leave for a moment, like some of the boats you see in Kerrith. She was a stout seaworthy boat, and could stand a lot of wind. Mrs de Winter had sailed her in worse weather than she ever found that night. Why, it was only blowing in fits and starts at the time. That's what I've said all along. I couldn't understand Mrs de Winter's boat being lost on a night like that.'

'But surely, if Mrs de Winter went below for a coat, as is sup-posed, and a sudden puff of wind was to come down from that headland, it would be enough to capsize the boat?' asked the Coroner.

James Tabb shook his head. 'No,' he said stubbornly, 'I don't see that it would.'

'Well, I'm afraid that is what must have happened,' said the Coroner. 'I don't think Mr de Winter or any of us suggest that your workmanship was to blame for the accident at all. You fitted the boat out at the beginning of the season, you reported her sound and seaworthy, and that's all I want to know. Unfortunately the late Mrs de Winter relaxed her watchfulness for a moment and she lost her life, the boat sinking with her aboard. Such accidents have happened before. I repeat again we are not blaming you.'

'Excuse me, sir,' said the boat-builder, 'but there is a little bit more to it than that. And if you would allow me I should like to make a further statement.'

'Very well, go on,' said the Coroner.

'It's like this, sir. After the accident last year a lot of people in Kerrith made unpleasantness about my work. Some said I had let Mrs de Winter start the season in a leaky, rotten boat. I lost two or three orders because of it. It was very unfair, but the boat had sunk, and there was nothing I could say to clear myself. Then that steamer went ashore, as we all know, and Mrs de Winter's little boat was found, and brought to the surface. Captain Searle himself gave me permission yesterday to go and look at her, and I did. I wanted to satisfy myself that the work I had put in to her was sound, in spite of the fact that she had been waterlogged for twelve months or more.'

'Well, that was very natural,' said the Coroner, 'and I hope you were satisfied.'

'Yes, sir, I was. There was nothing wrong with that boat as regards the work I did to her. I examined every corner of her there on the lighter up the pill where Captain Searle had put her. She had sunk on sandy bottom. I asked the diver about that, and he told me so. She had not touched the ridge at all. The ridge was a clear five feet away. She was lying on sand, and there wasn't the mark of a rock on her.'

He paused. The Coroner looked at him expectantly.

'Well?' he said, 'is that all you want to say?'

'No, sir,' said Tabb emphatically, 'it's not. What I want to know is this. Who drove the holes in her planking? Rocks didn't do it. The nearest rock was five feet away. Besides, they weren't the sort of marks made by a rock. They were holes. Done with a spike.'

I did not look at him. I was looking at the floor. There was oil-cloth laid on the boards. Green oil-cloth. I looked at it.

I wondered why the Coroner did not say something. Why did the pause last so long? When he spoke at last his voice sounded rather far away.

'What do you mean?' he said, 'what sort of holes?'

'There were three of them altogether,' said the boat-builder, 'one right for'ard, by her chain locker, on her starboard planking, below the water-line. The other two close together amidships, underneath her floor boards in the bottom. The ballast had been shifted too. It was lying loose. And that's not all. The sea-cocks had been turned on.'

'The sea-cocks? What are they?' asked the Coroner.

'The fitting that plugs the pipes leading from a washbasin or lavatory, sir. Mrs de Winter had a little place fitted up right aft. And there was a sink for'ard, where the washing-up was done. There was a sea-cock there, and another in the lavatory. These are always kept tight closed when you're under way, otherwise the water would flow in. When I examined the boat yesterday both sea-cocks were turned full on.'

It was hot, much too hot. Why didn't they open a window? We should be suffocated if we sat here with the air like this, and there were so many people, all breathing the same air, so many people.

'With those holes in her planking, sir, and the sea-cocks not closed, it wouldn't take long for a small boat like her to sink. Not much more than ten minutes, I should say. Those holes weren't there when the boat left my yard. I was proud of my work and so was Mrs de Winter. It's my opinion, sir, that the boat never capsized at all. She was deliberately scuttled.'

I must try and get out of the door. I must try and go back to the waiting-room again. There was no air left in this place, and the person next to me was pressing close, close . . . Someone in front of me was standing up, and they were talking, too, they were all talking. I did not know what was happening. I could not see

anything. It was hot, so very hot. The Coroner was asking everybody to be silent. And he said something about 'Mr de Winter'.
I could not see. That woman's hat was in front of me. Maxim was
standing up now. I could not look at him. I must not look at him.
I felt like this once before. When was it? I don't know. I don't
remember. Oh, yes, with Mrs Danvers. The time Mrs Danvers
stood with me by the window. Mrs Danvers was in this place
now, listening to the Coroner. Maxim was standing up over
there. The heat was coming up at me from the floor, rising in
slow waves. It reached my hands, wet and slippery, it touched my
neck, my chin, my face.

'Mr de Winter, you heard the statement from James Tabb,
who had the care of Mrs de Winter's boat? Do you know anything of these holes driven in the planking?'

'Nothing whatever.'

'Can you think of any reason why they should be there?'

'No, of course not.'

'It's the first time you have heard them mentioned?'

'Yes.'

'It's a shock to you, of course?'

'It was shock enough to learn that I made a mistake in identification over twelve months ago, and now I learn that my late
wife was not only drowned in the cabin of her boat, but that holes
were bored in the boat with the deliberate intent of letting in the
water so that the boat should sink. Does it surprise you that
I should be shocked?'

No, Maxim. No. You will put his back up. You heard what
Frank said. You must not put his back up. Not that voice. Not
that angry voice, Maxim. He won't understand. Please, darling,
please. Oh, God, don't let Maxim lose his temper. Don't let him
lose his temper.

'Mr de Winter, I want you to believe that we all feel very
deeply for you in this matter. No doubt you have suffered a shock,
a very severe shock, in learning that your late wife was drowned
in her own cabin, and not at sea as you supposed. And I am
inquiring into the matter for you. I want, for your sake, to find
out exactly how and why she died. I don't conduct this inquiry
for my own amusement.'

'That's rather obvious, isn't it?'

'I hope that it is. James Tabb has just told us that the boat which contained the remains of the late Mrs de Winter had three holes hammered through her bottom. And that the sea-cocks were open. Do you doubt his statement?'

'Of course not. He's a boat-builder, he knows what he is talking about.'

'Who looked after Mrs de Winter's boat?'

'She looked after it herself.'

'She employed no hand?'

'No, nobody at all.'

'The boat was moored in the private harbour belonging to Manderley?'

'Yes.'

'Any stranger who tried to tamper with the boat would be seen? There is no access to the harbour by public footpath?'

'No, none at all.'

'The harbour is quiet, is it not, and surrounded by trees?'

'Yes.'

'A trespasser might not be noticed?'

'Possibly not.'

'Yet James Tabb has told us, and we have no reason to disbelieve him, that a boat with those holes drilled in her bottom and the sea-cocks open could not float for more than ten or fifteen minutes.'

'Quite.'

'Therefore we can put aside the idea that the boat was tampered with maliciously before Mrs de Winter went for her evening sail. Had that been the case the boat would have sunk at her moorings.'

'No doubt.'

'Therefore we must assume that whoever took the boat out that night drove in the planking and opened the sea-cocks.'

'I suppose so.'

'You have told us already that the door of the cabin was shut, the port-holes closed, and your wife's remains were on the floor. This was in your statement, and in Doctor Phillips', and in Captain Searle's?'

'Yes.'

'And now added to this is the information that a spike was driven through the bottom, and the sea-cocks were open. Does not this strike you, Mr de Winter, as being very strange?'

'Certainly.'

'You have no suggestion to make?'

'No, none at all.'

'Mr de Winter, painful as it may be, it is my duty to ask you a very personal question.'

'Yes.'

'Were relations between you and the late Mrs de Winter perfectly happy?'

They had to come of course, those black spots in front of my eyes, dancing, flickering, stabbing the hazy air, and it was hot, so hot, with all these people, all these faces, and no open window; the door, from being near to me, was farther away than I had thought, and all the time the ground coming up to meet me.

And then, out of the queer mist around me, Maxim's voice, clear and strong. 'Will someone take my wife outside? She is going to faint.'

23

I WAS SITTING in the little room again. The room like a waiting-room at the station. The policeman was there, bending over me, giving me a glass of water, and someone's hand was on my arm, Frank's hand. I sat quite still, the floor, the walls, the figures of Frank and the policeman taking solid shape before me.

'I'm so sorry,' I said, 'such a stupid thing to do. It was so hot in that room, so very hot.'

'It gets very airless in there,' said the policeman, 'there's been complaints about it often, but nothing's ever done. We've had ladies fainting in there before.'

'Are you feeling better, Mrs de Winter?' said Frank.

'Yes. Yes, much better. I shall be all right again. Don't wait with me.'

'I'm going to take you back to Manderley.'

'No.'

'Yes. Maxim has asked me to.'

'No. You ought to stay with him.'

'Maxim told me to take you back to Manderley.'

He put his arm through mine and helped me to get up. 'Can you walk as far as the car or shall I bring it round?'

'I can walk. But I'd much rather stay. I want to wait for Maxim.'

'Maxim may be a long time.'

Why did he say that? What did he mean? Why didn't he look at me? He took my arm and walked with me along the passage to the door, and so down the steps into the street. Maxim may be a long time . . .

We did not speak. We came to the little Morris car belonging to Frank. He opened the door, and helped me in. Then he got in himself and started up the engine. We drove away from the cobbled market-place, through the empty town, and out on to the road to Kerrith.

'Why will they be a long time? What are they going to do?'

'They may have to go over the evidence again.' Frank looked straight in front of him along the hard white road.

'They've had all the evidence,' I said. 'There's nothing more anyone can say.'

'You never know,' said Frank, 'the Coroner may put his questions in a different way. Tabb has altered the whole business. The Coroner will have to approach it now from another angle.'

'What angle? How do you mean?'

'You heard the evidence? You heard what Tabb said about the boat? They won't believe in an accident any more.'

'It's absurd, Frank, it's ridiculous. They should not listen to Tabb. How can he tell, after all these months, how holes came to be in a boat? What are they trying to prove?'

'I don't know.'

'That Coroner will go on and on harping at Maxim, making him lose his temper, making him say things he doesn't mean. He will ask question after question, Frank, and Maxim won't stand it, I know he won't stand it.'

Frank did not answer. He was driving very fast. For the first time since I had known him he was at a loss for the usual conventional phrase. That meant he was worried, very worried. And usually he was such a slow careful driver, stopping dead at every cross-roads, peering to right and left, blowing his horn at every bend in the road.

'That man was there,' I said, 'that man who came once to Manderley to see Mrs Danvers.'

'You mean Favell?' asked Frank. 'Yes, I saw him.'

'He was sitting there, with Mrs Danvers.'

'Yes, I know.'

'Why was he there? What right had he to go to the inquest?'

'He was her cousin.'

'It's not right that he and Mrs Danvers should sit there, listening to that evidence. I don't trust them, Frank.'

'No.'

'They might do something; they might make mischief.'

Again Frank did not answer. I realized that his loyalty to Maxim was such that he would not let himself be drawn into a discussion, even with me. He did not know how much I knew. Nor could I tell for certainty how much he knew. We were allies, we travelled the same road, but we could not look at one another. We neither of us dared risk a confession. We were turning in now at the lodge gates, and down the long twisting narrow drive to the house. I noticed for the first time how the hydrangeas were coming into bloom, their blue heads thrusting themselves from the green foliage behind. For all their beauty there was something sombre about them, funereal; they were like the wreaths, stiff and artificial, that you see beneath glass cases in a foreign churchyard. There they were, all the way along the drive, on either side of us, blue, monotonous, like spectators lined up in a street to watch us pass.

We came to the house at last and rounded the great sweep before the steps. 'Will you be all right now?' said Frank. 'You can lie down, can't you?'

'Yes,' I said, 'yes, perhaps.'

'I shall go back to Lanyon,' he said, 'Maxim may want me.'

He did not say anything more. He got quickly back into the car again and drove away. Maxim might want him. Why did he say Maxim might want him? Perhaps the Coroner was going to question Frank as well. Ask him about that evening, over twelve months ago, when Maxim had dined with Frank. He would want to know the exact time that Maxim left his house. He would want to know if anybody saw Maxim when he returned to the house. Whether the servants knew that he was there. Whether anybody could prove that Maxim went straight up to bed and undressed. Mrs Danvers might be questioned. They might ask Mrs Danvers to give evidence. And Maxim beginning to lose his temper, beginning to go white . . .

I went into the hall. I went upstairs to my room, and lay down upon my bed, even as Frank had suggested. I put my hands over my eyes. I kept seeing that room and all the faces. The lined, painstaking, aggravating face of the Coroner, the gold pince-nez on his nose.

'I don't conduct this inquiry for my own amusement.' His

slow, careful mind, easily offended. What were they all saying now? What was happening? Suppose in a little while Frank came back to Manderley alone?

I did not know what happened. I did not know what people did. I remembered pictures of men in the papers, leaving places like that, and being taken away. Suppose Maxim was taken away? They would not let me go to him. They would not let me see him. I should have to stay here at Manderley day after day, night after night, waiting, as I was waiting now. People like Colonel Julyan being kind. People saying 'You must not be alone. You must come to us.' The telephone, the newspapers, the telephone again. 'No, Mrs de Winter can't see anyone. Mrs de Winter has no story to give the *County Chronicle*.' And another day. And another day. Weeks that would be blurred and non-existent. Frank at last taking me to see Maxim. He would look thin, queer, like people in hospital . . .

Other women had been through this. Women I had read about in papers. They sent letters to the Home Secretary and it was not any good. The Home Secretary always said that justice must take its course. Friends sent petitions too, everybody signed them, but the Home Secretary could never do anything. And the ordinary people who read about it in the papers said why should the fellow get off, he murdered his wife, didn't he? What about the poor, murdered wife? This sentimental business about abolishing the death penalty simply encourages crime. This fellow ought to have thought about that before he killed his wife. It's too late now. He will have to hang for it, like any other murderer. And serve him right too. Let it be a warning to others.

I remember seeing a picture on the back of a paper once, of a little crowd collected outside a prison gate, and just after nine o'clock a policeman came and pinned a notice on the gate for the people to read. The notice said something about the sentence being carried out. 'Sentence of death was carried out this morning at nine o'clock. The Governor, the Prison Doctor, and the Sheriff of the County were present.' Hanging was quick. Hanging did not hurt. It broke your neck at once. No, it did not. Someone said once it did not always work. Someone who had known the Governor of a prison. They put that bag over your head, and you stand on the little platform, and then the floor gives way beneath you. It takes exactly three minutes to go from the cell to the moment you are hanged. No, fifty seconds, someone said. No, that's absurd. It could not be fifty seconds. There's a little flight of steps down the side of the shed, down to the pit. The doctor goes down there to look. They die instantly. No, they don't. The body moves for some time, the neck is not always broken. Yes, but even so they don't feel anything. Someone said they did. Someone who had a brother who was a prison doctor said it was not generally known, because it would be such a scandal, but they did not always die at once. Their eyes were open, they stay open for quite a long time.

God, don't let me go on thinking about this. Let me think about something else. About other things. About Mrs Van Hopper in America. She must be staying with her daughter now. They had that house on Long Island in the summer. I expect they played a lot of bridge. They went to the races. Mrs Van Hopper was fond of the races. I wonder if she still wears that little yellow hat. It was too small for her. Much too small on that big face. Mrs Van Hopper sitting about in the garden of that house on Long Island, with novels, and magazines, and papers on her lap. Mrs Van Hopper putting up her lorgnette and calling to her daughter. 'Look at this, Helen. They say Max de Winter murdered his first wife. I always did think there was something peculiar about him. I warned that fool of a girl she was making a mistake, but she wouldn't listen to me. Well, she's cooked her goose now all right. I suppose they'll make her a big offer to go on the pictures.'

Something was touching my hand. It was Jasper. It was Jasper, thrusting his cold damp nose in my hands. He had followed me up from the hall. Why did dogs make one want to cry? There was something so quiet and hopeless about their sympathy. Jasper, knowing something was wrong, as dogs always do. Trunks being packed. Cars being brought to the door. Dogs standing with drooping tails, dejected eyes. Wandering back to their baskets in the hall when the sound of the car dies away . . .

I must have fallen asleep because I woke suddenly with a start, and heard that first crack of thunder in the air. I sat up. The clock said five. I got up and went to the window. There was not a breath of wind. The leaves hung listless on the trees, waiting. The sky was slatey grey. The jagged lightning split the sky. Another rumble in the distance. No rain fell. I went out into the corridor and listened. I could not hear anything. I went to the head of the stairs. There was no sign of anybody. The hall was dark because of the menace of thunder overhead. I went down and stood on the terrace. There was another burst of thunder. One spot of rain fell on my hand. One spot. No more. It was very dark. I could see the sea beyond the dip in the valley like a black lake. Another spot fell on my hands, and another crack of thunder came. One of the housemaids began shutting the windows in the rooms upstairs. Robert appeared and shut the windows of the drawing-room behind me.

'The gentlemen are not back yet, are they, Robert?' I asked.

'No, Madam, not yet. I thought you were with them, Madam.'

'No. No, I've been back some time.'

'Will you have tea, Madam?'

'No, no, I'll wait.'

'It looks as though the weather was going to break at last, Madam.'

'Yes.'

No rain fell. Nothing since those two drops on my hand. I went back and sat in the library. At half past five Robert came into the room.

'The car has just driven up to the door now, Madam,' he said.

'Which car?' I said.

'Mr de Winter's car, Madam,' he said.

'Is Mr de Winter driving it himself?'

'Yes, Madam.'

I tried to get up but my legs were things of straw, they would not bear me. I stood leaning against the sofa. My throat was very dry. After a minute Maxim came into the room. He stood just inside the door.

He looked very tired, old. There were lines at the corner of his mouth I had never noticed before.

'It's all over,' he said.

I waited. Still I could not speak or move towards him.

'Suicide,' he said, 'without sufficient evidence to show the state of mind of the deceased. They were all at sea of course, they did not know what they were doing.'

I sat down on the sofa. 'Suicide,' I said, 'but the motive? Where was the motive?'

'God knows,' he said. 'They did not seem to think a motive was necessary. Old Horridge, peering at me, wanting to know if Rebecca had any money troubles. Money troubles. God in heaven.'

He went and stood by the window, looking out at the green lawns. 'It's going to rain,' he said. 'Thank God it's going to rain at last.'

'What happened?' I said, 'what did the Coroner say? Why have you been there all this time?'

'He went over and over the same ground again,' said Maxim. 'Little details about the boat that no one cared about a damn. Were the sea-cocks hard to turn on? Where exactly was the first hole in relation to the second? What was ballast? What effect upon the stability of the boat would the shifting of the ballast have? Could a woman do this unaided? Did the cabin door shut firmly? What pressure of water was necessary to burst open the door? I thought I should go mad. I kept my temper though. Seeing you there, by the door, made me remember what I had to do. If you had not fainted like that, I should never have done it. It brought me up with a jerk. I knew exactly what I was going to say. I faced Horridge all the time. I never took my eyes off his thin, pernickety, little face and those gold-rimmed pince-nez. I shall remember that face of his to my dying day. I'm tired, darling; so tired I can't see, or hear or feel anything.'

He sat down on the window-seat. He leant forward, his head in his hands. I went and sat beside him. In a few minutes Frith came in, followed by Robert carrying the table for tea. The solemn ritual went forward as it always did, day after day, the leaves of the table pulled out, the legs adjusted, the laying of the snowy cloth, the putting down of the silver tea-pot and the kettle with the little flame beneath. Scones, sandwiches, three different sorts of cake. Jasper sat close to the table, his tail thumping now and again upon the floor, his eyes fixed expectantly on me. It's funny,

I thought, how the routine of life goes on, whatever happens, we do the same things, go through the little performance of eating, sleeping, washing. No crisis can break through the crust of habit. I poured out Maxim's tea, I took it to him on the window-seat, gave him his scone, and buttered one for myself.

'Where's Frank?' I asked.

'He had to go and see the vicar. I would have gone too but I wanted to come straight back to you. I kept thinking of you, waiting here, all by yourself, not knowing what was going to happen.'

'Why the vicar?' I said.

'Something has to happen this evening,' he said. 'Something at the church.'

I stared at him blankly. Then I understood. They were going to bury Rebecca. They were going to bring Rebecca back from the mortuary.

'It's fixed for six-thirty,' he said. 'No one knows but Frank, and Colonel Julyan, and the vicar, and myself. There won't be anyone hanging about. This was arranged yesterday. The verdict doesn't make any difference.'

'What time must you go?'

'I'm meeting them there at the church at twenty-five past six.'

I did not say anything. I went on drinking my tea. Maxim put his sandwich down untasted. 'It's still very hot, isn't it,' he said.

'It's the storm,' I said. 'It won't break. Only little spots at a time. It's there in the air. It won't break.'

'It was thundering when I left Lanyon,' he said, 'the sky was like ink over my head. Why in the name of God doesn't it rain?'

The birds were hushed in the trees. It was still very dark.

'I wish you did not have to go out again,' I said.

He did not answer. He looked tired, so deathly tired.

'We'll talk over things this evening when I get back,' he said presently. 'We've got so much to do together, haven't we? We've got to begin all over again. I've been the worst sort of husband for you.'

'No!' I said. 'No!'

'We'll start again, once this thing is behind us. We can do it, you and I. It's not like being alone. The past can't hurt us if we are together. You'll have children too.' After a while he glanced at his watch. 'It's ten past six,' he said, 'I shall have to be going. It won't take long, not more than half an hour. We've got to go down to the crypt.'

I held his hand. 'I'll come with you. I shan't mind. Let me come with you.'

'No,' he said. 'No, I don't want you to come.'

Then he went out of the room. I heard the sound of the car starting up in the drive. Presently the sound died away, and I knew he had gone.

Robert came to clear away the tea. It was like any other day. The routine was unchanged. I wondered if it would have been so had Maxim not come back from Lanyon. I wondered if Robert would have stood there, that wooden expression on his young sheep's face, brushing the crumbs from the snow-white cloth, picking up the table, carrying it from the room.

It seemed very quiet in the library when he had gone. I began to think of them down at the church, going through that door and down the flight of stairs to the crypt. I had never been there. I had only seen the door. I wondered what a crypt was like, if there were coffins standing there. Maxim's father and mother. I wondered what would happen to the coffin of that other woman who had been put there by mistake. I wondered who she was, poor unclaimed soul, washed up by the wind and tide. Now another coffin would stand there. Rebecca would lie there in the crypt as well. Was the vicar reading the burial service there, with Maxim, and Frank, and Colonel Julyan standing by his side? Ashes to ashes. Dust to dust. It seemed to me that Rebecca had no reality any more. She had crumbled away when they had found her on the cabin floor. It was not Rebecca who was lying in the crypt, it was dust. Only dust.

Just after seven the rain began to fall. Gently at first, a light pattering in the trees, and so thin I could not see it. Then louder and faster, a driving torrent falling slantways from the slate sky, like water from a sluice. I left the windows open wide. I stood in front of them and breathed the cold clean air. The rain splashed into my face and on my hands. I could not see beyond the lawns, the falling rain came thick and fast. I heard it sputtering in the gutter-pipes above the window, and splashing on the stones of the terrace. There was no more thunder. The rain smelt of moss and earth and of the black bark of trees.

I did not hear Frith come in at the door. I was standing by the window, watching the rain. I did not see him until he was beside me.

'Excuse me, Madam,' he said, 'do you know if Mr de Winter will be long?'

'No,' I said, 'not very long.'

'There's a gentleman to see him, Madam,' said Frith after a moment's hesitation. 'I'm not quite sure what I ought to say. He's very insistent about seeing Mr de Winter.'

'Who is it?' I said. 'Is it anyone you know?'

Frith looked uncomfortable. 'Yes, Madam,' he said, 'it's a gentleman who used to come here frequently at one time, when Mrs de Winter was alive. A gentleman called Mr Favell.'

I knelt on the window-seat and shut the window. The rain was coming in on the cushions. Then I turned round and looked at Frith.

'I think perhaps I had better see Mr Favell,' I said.

'Very good, Madam.'

I went and stood over on the rug beside the empty fireplace. It was just possible that I should be able to get rid of Favell before Maxim came back. I did not know what I was going to say to him, but I was not frightened.

In a few moments Frith returned and showed Favell into the library. He looked much the same as before but a little rougher if possible, a little more untidy. He was the sort of man who invariably went hatless, his hair was bleached from the sun of the last days and his skin was deeply tanned. His eyes were rather bloodshot. I wondered if he had been drinking.

'I'm afraid Maxim is not here,' I said. 'I don't know when he will be back. Wouldn't it be better if you made an appointment to see him at the office in the morning?'

'Waiting doesn't worry me,' said Favell, 'and I don't think I shall have to wait very long, you know. I had a look in the dining-room as I came along, and I see Max's place is laid for dinner all right.'

'Our plans have been changed,' I said. 'It's quite possible Maxim won't be home at all this evening.'

'He's run off, has he?' said Favell, with a half-smile I did not like. 'I wonder if you really mean it. Of course under the circumstances it's the wisest thing he can do. Gossip is an unpleasant thing to some people. It's more pleasant to avoid it, isn't it?'

'I don't know what you mean,' I said.

'Don't you?' he said. 'Oh, come, you don't expect me to believe that, do you? Tell me, are you feeling better? Too bad fainting like that at the inquest this afternoon. I would have come and helped you out but I saw you had one knight-errant already. I bet Frank Crawley enjoyed himself. Did you let him drive you home? You wouldn't let me drive you five yards when I offered to.'

'What do you want to see Maxim about?' I asked.

Favell leant forward to the table and helped himself to a cigarette. 'You don't mind my smoking, I suppose?' he said, 'it won't make you sick, will it? One never knows with brides.'

He watched me over his lighter. 'You've grown up a bit since I saw you last, haven't you?' he said. 'I wonder what you have been doing. Leading Frank Crawley up the garden-path?' He blew a cloud of smoke in the air. 'I say, do you mind asking old Frith to get me a whisky-and-soda?'

I did not say anything. I went and rang the bell. He sat down on the edge of the sofa, swinging his legs, that half-smile on his lips. Robert answered the bell. 'A whisky-and-soda for Mr Favell,' I said.

'Well, Robert?' said Favell, 'haven't seen you for a very long time. Still breaking the hearts of the girls in Kerrith?'

Robert flushed. He glanced at me, horribly embarrassed.

'All right, old chap, I won't give you away. Run along and get me a double whisky, and jump on it.'

Robert disappeared. Favell laughed, dropping ash all over the floor.

'I took Robert out once on his half-day,' he said. 'Rebecca bet me a fiver I wouldn't ask him. I won my fiver all right. Spent one of the funniest evenings of my life. Did I laugh? Oh, boy! Robert on the razzle takes a lot of beating, I tell you. I must say he's got a good eye for a girl. He picked the prettiest of the bunch we saw that night.'

Robert came back again with the whisky-and-soda on a tray. He still looked very red, very uncomfortable. Favell watched him with a smile as he poured out his drink, and then he began to laugh, leaning back on the arm of the sofa. He whistled the bar of a song, watching Robert all the while.

'That was the one, wasn't it?' he said, 'that was the tune? Do you still like ginger hair, Robert?'

Robert gave him a flat weak smile. He looked miserable. Favell laughed louder still. Robert turned and went out of the room.

'Poor kid,' said Favell. 'I don't suppose he's been on the loose since. That old ass Frith keeps him on a leading string.'

He began drinking his whisky-and-soda, glancing round the room, looking at me every now and again, and smiling.

'I don't think I shall mind very much if Max doesn't get back to dinner,' he said. 'What say you?'

I did not answer. I stood by the fireplace, my hands behind my back. 'You wouldn't waste that place at the dining-room table, would you?' he said. He looked at me, smiling still, his head on one side.

'Mr Favell,' I said, 'I don't want to be rude, but as a matter of fact I'm very tired. I've had a long and fairly exhausting day. If you can't tell me what you want to see Maxim about it's not much good your sitting here. You had far better do as I suggest, and go round to the estate office in the morning.'

He slid off the arm of the sofa and came towards me, his glass in his hand. 'No, no,' he said. 'No, no, don't be a brute. I've had an exhausting day too. Don't run away and leave me, I'm quite harmless, really I am. I suppose Max has been telling tales about me to you?'

I did not answer. 'You think I'm the big, bad wolf, don't you?' he said, 'but I'm not, you know. I'm a perfectly ordinary, harmless bloke. And I think you are behaving splendidly over all this, perfectly splendidly. I take off my hat to you, I really do.' This last speech of his was very slurred and thick. I wished I had never told Frith I would see him.

'You come down here to Manderley,' he said, waving his arm

vaguely, 'you take on all this place, meet hundreds of people you've never seen before, you put up with old Max and his moods, you don't give a fig for anyone, you just go your own way. I call it a damn good effort, and I don't care who hears me say so. A damn good effort.' He swayed a little as he stood. He steadied himself, and put the empty glass down on the table. 'This business has been a shock to me, you know,' he said. 'A bloody awful shock. Rebecca was my cousin. I was damn fond of her.'

'Yes,' I said. 'I'm very sorry for you.'

'We were brought up together,' he went on. 'Always tremendous pals. Liked the same things, the same people. Laughed at the same jokes. I suppose I was fonder of Rebecca than anyone else in the world. And she was fond of me. All this has been a bloody shock.'

'Yes,' I said. 'Yes, of course.'

'And what is Max going to do about it, that's what I want to know? Does he think he can sit back quietly now that sham inquest is over? Tell me that?' He was not smiling any more. He bent towards me.

'I'm going to see justice is done to Rebecca,' he said, his voice growing louder. 'Suicide ... God Almighty, that doddering old fool of a Coroner got the jury to say suicide. You and I know it wasn't suicide, don't we?' He leant closer to me still. 'Don't we?' he said slowly.

The door opened and Maxim came into the room, with Frank just behind him. Maxim stood quite still, with the door open, staring at Favell. 'What the hell are you doing here?' he said.

Favell turned round, his hands in his pockets. He waited a moment, and then he began to smile. 'As a matter of fact, Max, old chap, I came to congratulate you on the inquest this afternoon.'

'Do you mind leaving the house?' said Max, 'or do you want Crawley and me to chuck you out?'

'Steady a moment, steady a moment,' said Favell. He lit another cigarette, and sat down once more on the arm of the sofa.

'You don't want Frith to hear what I'm going to say, do you?' he said. 'Well, he will, if you don't shut that door.'

Maxim did not move. I saw Frank close the door very quietly.

'Now, listen here, Max,' said Favell, 'you've come very well out of this affair, haven't you? Better than you ever expected. Oh, yes, I was in the court this afternoon, and I dare say you saw me. I was there from start to finish. I saw your wife faint, at a rather critical moment, and I don't blame her. It was touch and go, then, wasn't it, Max, what way the inquiry would go? And luckily for you it went the way it did. You hadn't squared those thick-headed fellows who were acting jury, had you? It looked damn like it to me.'

Maxim made a move towards Favell, but Favell held up his hand.

'Wait a bit, can't you?' he said. 'I haven't finished yet. You realize, don't you, Max, old man, that I can make things damned unpleasant for you if I choose. Not only unpleasant, but shall I say dangerous?'

I sat down on the chair beside the fireplace. I held the arms of the chair very tight. Frank came over and stood behind the chair. Still Maxim did not move. He never took his eyes off Favell.

'Oh, yes?' he said, 'in what way can you make things dangerous?'

'Look here, Max,' said Favell, 'I suppose there are no secrets between you and your wife and from the look of things Crawley there just makes the happy trio. I can speak plainly then, and I will. You all know about Rebecca and me. We were lovers, weren't we? I've never denied it, and I never will. Very well then. Up to the present I believed, like every other fool, that Rebecca was drowned sailing in the bay, and that her body was picked up at Edgecoombe weeks afterwards. It was a shock to me then, a bloody shock. But I said to myself, That's the sort of death Rebecca would choose, she'd go out like she lived, fighting.' He paused, he sat there on the edge of the sofa, looking at all of us in turn. 'Then I pick up the evening paper a few days ago and I read that Rebecca's boat had been stumbled on by the local diver and that there was a body in the cabin. I couldn't understand it. Who the hell would Rebecca have as a sailing companion? It didn't make sense. I came down here, and put up at a pub just outside Kerrith. I got in touch with Mrs Danvers. She told me then that the body in the cabin was Rebecca's. Even so I thought like everyone else that the first body was a mistake and Rebecca had somehow got shut in the cabin when she went to fetch a coat. Well, I attended that inquest today, as you know. And everything went smoothly, didn't it, until Tabb gave his evidence? But after that? Well, Max, old man, what have you got to say about those holes in the floor boards, and those sea-cocks turned full on?'

'Do you think,' said Maxim slowly, 'that after those hours of talk this afternoon I am going into it again – with you? You heard the evidence, and you heard the verdict. It satisfied the Coroner, and it must satisfy you.'

'Suicide, eh?' said Favell. 'Rebecca committing suicide. The sort of thing she would do, wasn't it? Listen; you never knew I had this note, did you? I kept it, because it was the last thing she ever wrote to me. I'll read it to you. I think it will interest you.'

He took a piece of paper out of his pocket. I recognized that thin, pointed, slanting hand.

I tried to ring you from the flat, but could get no answer [*he read*]. I'm going down to Manders right away. I shall be at the cottage this evening, and if you get this in time will you get the car and follow me. I'll spend the night at the cottage, and leave the door open for you. I've got something to tell you and I want to see you as soon as possible. Rebecca.

He put the note back in his pocket. 'That's not the sort of note you write when you're going to commit suicide, is it?' he said. 'It was waiting for me at my flat when I got back about four in the morning. I had no idea Rebecca was to be in London that day or I should have got in touch with her. It happened, by a vile stroke of fortune, I was on a party that night. When I read the note at four in the morning I decided it was too late to go crashing down on a six-hour run to Manderley. I went to bed, determined to put a call through later in the day. I did. About twelve o'clock. And I heard Rebecca had been drowned!'

He sat there, staring at Maxim. None of us spoke.

'Supposing the Coroner this afternoon had read that note, it would have made it a little bit more tricky for you, wouldn't it, Max, old man?' said Favell.

'Well,' said Maxim, 'why didn't you get up and give it to him?'

'Steady, old boy, steady. No need to get rattled. I don't want to smash you, Max. God knows you've never been a friend to me, but I don't bear malice about it. All married men with lovely wives are jealous, aren't they? And some of 'em just can't help playing Othello. They're made that way. I don't blame them. I'm sorry for them. I'm a bit of a Socialist in my way, you know, and I can't think why fellows can't share their women instead of killing them. What difference does it make? You can get your fun just the same. A lovely woman isn't like a motor tyre, she doesn't wear out. The more you use her the better she goes. Now, Max, I've laid all my cards on the table. Why can't we come to some agreement? I'm not a rich man. I'm too fond of gambling for that. But what gets me down is never having any capital to fall back upon. Now if I had a settlement of two or three thousand a year for life I could jog along comfortably. And I'd never trouble you again. I swear before God I would not.'

'I've asked you before to leave the house,' said Maxim. 'I'm not going to ask you again. There's the door behind me. You can open it yourself.'

'Half a minute, Maxim,' said Frank; 'it's not quite so easy as all that.' He turned to Favell. 'I see what you're driving at. It happens, very unfortunately, that you could, as you say, twist things round and make it difficult for Maxim. I don't think he sees it as clearly as I do. What is the exact amount you propose Maxim should settle on you?'

I saw Maxim go very white, and a little pulse began to show on his forehead. 'Don't interfere with this, Frank,' he said, 'this is my affair entirely. I'm not going to give way to blackmail.'

'I don't suppose your wife wants to be pointed out as Mrs de Winter, the widow of a murderer, of a fellow who was hanged,' said Favell. He laughed, and glanced towards me.

'You think you can frighten me, don't you, Favell?' said Maxim. 'Well, you are wrong. I'm not afraid of anything you can do. There is the telephone, in the next room. Shall I ring up

Colonel Julyan and ask him to come over? He's the magistrate. He'll be interested in your story.'

Favell stared at him, and laughed.

'Good bluff,' he said, 'but it won't work. You wouldn't dare ring up old Julyan. I've got enough evidence to hang you, Max, old man.'

Maxim walked slowly across the room and passed through to the little room beyond. I heard the click of the telephone.

'Stop him!' I said to Frank. 'Stop him, for God's sake.'

Frank glanced at my face, he went swiftly towards the door.

I heard Maxim's voice, very cool, very calm. 'I want Kerrith 17,' he said.

Favell was watching the door, his face curiously intense.

'Leave me alone,' I heard Maxim say to Frank. And then, two minutes afterwards. 'Is that Colonel Julyan speaking? It's de Winter here. Yes. Yes, I know. I wonder if you could possibly come over here at once. Yes, to Manderley. It's rather urgent. I can't explain why on the telephone, but you shall hear everything directly you come. I'm very sorry to have to drag you out. Yes. Thank you very much. Good-bye.'

He came back again into the room. 'Julyan is coming right away,' he said. He crossed over and threw open the windows. It was still raining very hard. He stood there, with his back to us, breathing the cold air.

'Maxim,' said Frank quietly. 'Maxim.'

He did not answer. Favell laughed, and helped himself to another cigarette. 'If you want to hang yourself, old fellow, it's all the same to me,' he said. He picked up a paper from the table and flung himself down on the sofa, crossed his legs, and began to turn over the pages. Frank hesitated, glancing from me to Maxim. Then he came beside me.

'Can't you do something?' I whispered. 'Go out and meet Colonel Julyan, prevent him from coming, say it was all a mistake?'

Maxim spoke from the window without turning round.

'Frank is not to leave this room,' he said. 'I'm going to manage this thing alone. Colonel Julyan will be here in exactly ten minutes.'

We none of us said anything. Favell went on reading his paper. There was no sound but the steady falling rain. It fell without a break, steady, straight, and monotonous. I felt helpless, without strength. There was nothing I could do. Nothing that Frank could do. In a book or in a play I would have found a revolver, and we should have shot Favell, hidden his body in a cupboard. There was no revolver. There was no cupboard. We were ordinary people. These things did not happen. I could not go to Maxim now and beg him on my knees to give Favell the money. I had to sit there, with my hands in my lap, watching the rain, watching Maxim with his back turned to me, standing by the window.

It was raining too hard to hear the car. The sound of the rain covered all other sounds. We did not know Colonel Julyan had arrived until the door opened, and Frith showed him into the room.

Maxim swung round from the window. 'Good evening,' he said. 'We meet again. You've made very good time.'

'Yes,' said Colonel Julyan, 'you said it was urgent, so I came at once. Luckily, my man had left the car handy. What an evening.'

He glanced at Favell uncertainly, and then came over and shook hands with me, nodding to Maxim. 'A good thing the rain has come,' he said. 'It's been hanging about too long. I hope you're feeling better.'

I murmured something, I don't know what, and he stood there looking from one to the other of us, rubbing his hands.

'I think you realize,' Maxim said, 'that I haven't brought you out on an evening like this for a social half-hour before dinner. This is Jack Favell, my late wife's first cousin. I don't know if you have ever met.'

Colonel Julyan nodded. 'Your face seems familiar. I've probably met you here in the old days.'

'Quite,' said Maxim. 'Go ahead, Favell.'

Favell got up from the sofa and chucked the paper back on the table. The ten minutes seemed to have sobered him. He walked quite steadily. He was not smiling any longer. I had the impression that he was not entirely pleased with the turn in the events, and he was ill-prepared for the encounter with Colonel Julyan.

He began speaking in a loud, rather domineering voice. 'Look here, Colonel Julyan,' he said, 'there's no sense in beating about the bush. The reason why I'm here is that I'm not satisfied with the verdict given at the inquest this afternoon.'

'Oh?' said Colonel Julyan, 'isn't that for de Winter to say, not you?'

'No, I don't think it is,' said Favell. 'I have a right to speak, not only as Rebecca's cousin, but as her prospective husband, had she lived.'

Colonel Julyan looked rather taken aback. 'Oh,' he said. 'Oh, I see. That's rather different. Is this true, de Winter?'

Maxim shrugged his shoulders. 'It's the first I've heard of it,' he said.

Colonel Julyan looked from one to the other doubtfully. 'Look here, Favell,' he said, 'what exactly is your trouble?'

Favell stared at him a moment. I could see he was planning something in his mind, and he was still not sober enough to carry it through. He put his hand slowly in his waistcoat pocket and brought out Rebecca's note. 'This note was written a few hours before Rebecca was supposed to have set out on that suicidal sail. Here it is. I want you to read it, and say whether you think a woman who wrote that note had made up her mind to kill herself.'

Colonel Julyan took a pair of spectacles from a case in his pocket and read the note. Then he handed it back to Favell. 'No,' he said, 'on the face of it, no. But I don't know what the note refers to. Perhaps you do. Or perhaps de Winter does?'

Maxim did not say anything. Favell twisted the piece of paper in his fingers, considering Colonel Julyan all the while. 'My cousin made a definite appointment in that note, didn't she?' he said. 'She deliberately asked me to drive down to Manderley that night because she had something to tell me. What it actually was I don't suppose we shall ever know, but that's beside the point. She made the appointment, and she was to spend the night in the cottage on purpose to see me alone. The mere fact of her going for a sail never surprised me. It was the sort of thing she did, for an hour or so, after a long day in London. But to plug holes in the cabin and deliberately drown herself, the hysterical impulsive

freak of a neurotic girl – oh, no, Colonel Julyan, by Christ no!'
The colour had flooded into his face, and the last words were
shouted. His manner was not helpful to him, and I could see by
the thin line of Colonel Julyan's mouth that he had not taken to
Favell.

'My dear fellow,' he said, 'it's not the slightest use your losing
your temper with me. I'm not the Coroner who conducted the
inquiry this afternoon, nor am I a member of the jury who gave
the verdict. I'm merely the magistrate of the district. Naturally
I want to help you all I can, and de Winter, too. You say you
refuse to believe your cousin committed suicide. On the other
hand you heard, as we all did, the evidence of the boat-builder.
The sea-cocks were open, the holes were there. Very well. Suppose we get to the point. What do you suggest really happened?'

Favell turned his head and looked slowly towards Maxim. He
was still twisting the note between his fingers. 'Rebecca never
opened those sea-cocks, nor split the holes in the planking.
Rebecca never committed suicide. You've asked for my opinion,
and by God you shall have it. Rebecca was murdered. And if you
want to know who the murderer is, why there he stands, by the
window there, with that God-damned superior smile on his face.
He couldn't even wait could he, until the year was out, before
marrying the first girl he set eyes on? There he is, there's your
murderer for you, Mr Maximilian de Winter. Take a good long
look at him. He'd look well hanging, wouldn't he?'

And Favell began to laugh, the laugh of a drunkard, high-
pitched, forced, and foolish, and all the while twisting Rebecca's
note between his fingers.

24

THANK GOD FOR Favell's laugh. Thank God for his pointing finger, his flushed face, his staring bloodshot eyes. Thank God for the way he stood there swaying on his two feet. Because it made Colonel Julyan antagonistic, it put him on our side. I saw the disgust on his face, the quick movement of his lips. Colonel Julyan did not believe him. Colonel Julyan was on our side.

'The man's drunk,' he said quickly. 'He doesn't know what he's saying.'

'Drunk, am I?' shouted Favell. 'Oh, no, my fine friend. You may be a magistrate and a colonel into the bargain, but it won't cut any ice with me. I've got the law on my side for a change, and I'm going to use it. There are other magistrates in this bloody county besides you. Fellows with brains in their heads, who understand the meaning of justice. Not soldiers who got the sack years ago for incompetence and walk about with a string of putty medals on their chest. Max de Winter murdered Rebecca and I'm going to prove it.'

'Wait a minute, Mr Favell,' said Colonel Julyan quietly, 'you were present at the inquiry this afternoon, weren't you? I remember you now. I saw you sitting there. If you felt so deeply about the injustice of the verdict why didn't you say so then, to the jury, to the Coroner himself? Why didn't you produce that letter in court?'

Favell stared at him, and laughed. 'Why?' he said, 'because I did not choose to, that's why. I preferred to come and tackle de Winter personally.'

'That's why I rang you up,' said Maxim, coming forward from the window; 'we've already heard Favell's accusations. I asked him the same question. Why didn't he tell his suspicions to the Coroner? He said he was not a rich man, and that if I cared to settle two or three thousand on him for life he would never worry me again. Frank was here, and my wife. They both heard him. Ask them.'

'It's perfectly true, sir,' said Frank. 'It's blackmail, pure and simple.'

'Yes, of course,' said Colonel Julyan, 'the trouble is that blackmail is not very pure, nor is it particularly simple. It can make a lot of unpleasantness for a great many people, even if the blackmailer finds himself in jail at the end of it. Sometimes innocent people find themselves in jail as well. We want to avoid that, in this case. I don't know whether you are sufficiently sober, Favell, to answer my questions, and if you keep off irrelevant personalities we may get through with the business quicker. You have just made a serious accusation against de Winter. Have you any proof to back that accusation?'

'Proof?' said Favell. 'What the hell do you want with proof? Aren't those holes in the boat proof enough?'

'Certainly not,' said Colonel Julyan, 'unless you can bring a witness who saw him do it. Where's your witness?'

'Witness be damned,' said Favell. 'Of course de Winter did it. Who else would kill Rebecca?'

'Kerrith has a large population,' said Colonel Julyan. 'Why not go from door to door making inquiries? I might have done it myself. You appear to have no more proof against de Winter there than you would have against me.'

'Oh, I see,' said Favell, 'you're going to hold his hand through this. You're going to back de Winter. You won't let him down because you've dined with him, and he's dined with you. He's a big name down here. He's the owner of Manderley. You poor bloody little snob.'

'Take care, Favell, take care.'

'You think you can get the better of me, don't you? You think I've got no case to bring to a court of law. I'll get my proof for you all right. I tell you de Winter killed Rebecca because of me. He knew I was her lover; he was jealous, madly jealous. He knew she was waiting for me at the cottage on the beach, and he went down that night and killed her. Then he put her body in the boat and sank her.'

'Quite a clever story, Favell, in its way, but I repeat again you have no proof. Produce your witness who saw it happen and I might begin to take you seriously. I know that cottage on the beach. A sort of picnic place, isn't it? Mrs de Winter used to keep the gear there for the boat. It would help your story if you could turn it into a bungalow with fifty replicas alongside of it. There would be a chance then that one of the inhabitants might have seen the whole affair.'

'Hold on,' said Favell slowly, 'hold on ... There is a chance de Winter might have been seen that night. Quite a good chance too. It's worth finding out. What would you say if I did produce a witness?'

Colonel Julyan shrugged his shoulders. I saw Frank glance inquiringly at Maxim. Maxim did not say anything. He was watching Favell. I suddenly knew what Favell meant. I knew who he was talking about. And in a flash of fear and horror I knew that he was right. There had been a witness that night. Little sentences came back to me. Words I had not understood, phrases I believed to be the fragments of a poor idiot's mind. 'She's down there isn't she? She won't come back again.' 'I didn't tell no one.' 'They'll find her there, won't they? The fishes have eaten her, haven't they?' 'She'll not come back no more.' Ben knew. Ben had seen. Ben, with his queer crazed brain, had been a witness all the time. He had been hiding in the woods that night. He had seen Maxim take the boat from the moorings, and pull back in the dinghy, alone. I knew all the colour was draining away from my face. I leant back against the cushion of the chair.

'There's a local half-wit who spends his time on the beach,' said Favell. 'He was always hanging about, when I used to come down and meet Rebecca. I've often seen him. He used to sleep in the woods, or on the beach when the nights were hot. The fellow's cracked, he would never have come forward on his own. But I could make him talk if he did see anything that night. And there's a bloody big chance he did.'

'Who is this? What's he talking about?' said Colonel Julyan.

'He must mean Ben,' said Frank, with another glance at Maxim. 'He's the son of one of our tenants. But the man's not responsible for what he says or does. He's been an idiot since birth.'

'What the hell does that matter?' said Favell. 'He's got eyes, hasn't he? He knows what he sees. He's only got to answer yes or no. You're getting windy now, aren't you? Not so mighty confident?'

'Can we get hold of this fellow and question him?' asked Colonel Julyan.

'Of course,' said Maxim. 'Tell Robert to cut down to his mother's cottage, Frank, and bring him back.'

Frank hesitated. I saw him glance at me out of the tail of his eye.

'Go on, for God's sake,' said Maxim. 'We want to end this thing, don't we?' Frank went out of the room. I began to feel the old nagging pain beneath my heart.

In a few minutes Frank came back again into the room.

'Robert's taken my car,' he said. 'If Ben is at home he won't be more than ten minutes.'

'The rain will keep him at home all right,' said Favell; 'he'll be there. And I think you will find I shall be able to make him talk.' He laughed, and looked at Maxim. His face was still very flushed. Excitement had made him sweat; there were beads of perspiration on his forehead. I noticed how his neck bulged over the back of his collar, and how low his ears were set on his head. Those florid good looks would not last him very long. Already he was out of condition, puffy. He helped himself to another cigarette. 'You're like a little trade union here at Manderley, aren't you?' he said; 'no one going to give anyone else away. Even the local magistrate is on the same racket. We must exempt the bride of course. A wife doesn't give evidence against her husband. Crawley of course has been squared. He knows he would lose his job if he told the truth. And if I guess rightly there's a spice of malice in his soul towards me too. You didn't have much success with Rebecca, did you, Crawley? That garden-path wasn't quite long enough, eh? It's a bit easier this time, isn't it. The bride will be grateful for your fraternal arm every time she faints. When she hears the judge sentence her husband to death that arm of yours will come in very handy.'

It happened very quickly. Too quick for me to see how Maxim did it. But I saw Favell stagger and fall against the arm of the sofa, and down on to the floor. And Maxim was standing just beside him. I felt rather sick. There was something degrading in the fact that Maxim had hit Favell. I wished I had not known. I wished I had not been there to see. Colonel Julyan did not say anything. He looked very grim. He turned his back on them and came and stood beside me.

'I think you had better go upstairs,' he said quietly.

I shook my head. 'No,' I whispered. 'No.'

'That fellow is in a state capable of saying anything,' he said. 'What you have just seen was not very attractive, was it? Your husband was right of course, but it's a pity you saw it.'

I did not answer. I was watching Favell who was getting slowly to his feet. He sat down heavily on the sofa and put his handkerchief to his face.

'Get me a drink,' he said, 'get me a drink.'

Maxim looked at Frank. Frank went out of the room. None of us spoke. In a moment Frank came back with the whisky-and-soda on a tray. He mixed some in a glass and gave it to Favell. Favell drank it greedily, like an animal. There was something sensual and horrible the way he put his mouth to the glass. His lips folded upon the glass in a peculiar way. There was a dark red patch on his jaw where Maxim had hit him. Maxim had turned his back on him again and had returned to the window. I glanced at Colonel Julyan and saw that he was looking at Maxim. His gaze was curious, intent. My heart began beating very quickly. Why did Colonel Julyan look at Maxim in that way?

Did it mean that he was beginning to wonder, to suspect?

Maxim did not see. He was watching the rain. It fell straight and steady as before. The sound filled the room. Favell finished his whisky-and-soda and put the glass back on the table beside the sofa. He was breathing heavily. He did not look at any of us. He was staring straight in front of him at the floor.

The telephone began ringing in the little room. It struck a shrill, discordant note. Frank went to answer it.

He came back at once and looked at Colonel Julyan. 'It's your daughter,' he said; 'they want to know if they are to keep dinner back.'

Colonel Julyan waved his hand impatiently. 'Tell them to

start,' he said, 'tell them I don't know when I shall be back.' He glanced at his watch. 'Fancy ringing up,' he muttered; 'what a moment to choose.'

Frank went back into the little room to give the message. I thought of the daughter at the other end of the telephone. It would be the one who played golf. I could imagine her calling to her sister, 'Dad says we're to start. What on earth can he be doing? The steak will be like leather.' Their little household disorganized because of us. Their evening routine upset. All these foolish inconsequent threads hanging upon one another, because Maxim had killed Rebecca. I looked at Frank. His face was pale and set.

'I heard Robert coming back with the car,' he said to Colonel Julyan. 'The window in there looks on to the drive.'

He went out of the library to the hall. Favell had lifted his head when he spoke. Then he got to his feet once more and stood looking towards the door. There was a queer ugly smile on his face.

The door opened, and Frank came in. He turned and spoke to someone in the hall outside.

'All right, Ben,' he said quietly, 'Mr de Winter wants to give you some cigarettes. There's nothing to be frightened of.'

Ben stepped awkwardly into the room. He had his sou'wester in his hands. He looked odd and naked without his hat. I realized for the first time that his head was shaved all over, and he had no hair. He looked different, dreadful.

The light seemed to daze him. He glanced foolishly round the room, blinking his small eyes. He caught sight of me, and I gave him a weak, rather tremulous smile. I don't know if he recognized me or not. He just blinked his eyes. Then Favell walked slowly towards him and stood in front of him.

'Hullo,' he said; 'how's life treated you since we last met?'

Ben stared at him. There was no recognition on his face. He did not answer.

'Well?' said Favell, 'you know who I am, don't you?'

Ben went on twisting his sou'wester. 'Eh?' he said.

'Have a cigarette,' said Favell, handing him the box. Ben glanced at Maxim and Frank.

'All right,' said Maxim, 'take as many as you like.'

Ben took four and stuck two behind each ear. Then he stood twisting his cap again.

'You know who I am don't you?' repeated Favell.

Still Ben did not answer. Colonel Julyan walked across to him. 'You shall go home in a few moments, Ben,' he said. 'No one is going to hurt you. We just want you to answer one or two questions. You know Mr Favell, don't you?'

This time Ben shook his head. 'I never seen 'un,' he said.

'Don't be a bloody fool,' said Favell roughly; 'you know you've seen me. You've seen me go to the cottage on the beach, Mrs de Winter's cottage. You've seen me there, haven't you?'

'No,' said Ben. 'I never seen no one.'

'You damned half-witted liar,' said Favell, 'are you going to stand there and say you never saw me, last year, walk through those woods with Mrs de Winter, and go into the cottage? Didn't we catch you once, peering at us from the window?'

'Eh?' said Ben.

'A convincing witness,' said Colonel Julyan sarcastically.

Favell swung round on him. 'It's a put-up job,' he said. 'Someone has got at this idiot and bribed him too. I tell you he's seen me scores of times. Here. Will this make you remember?' He fumbled in his hip-pocket and brought out a note-case. He flourished a pound note in front of Ben. 'Now do you remember me?' he said.

Ben shook his head. 'I never seen 'un,' he said, and then he took hold of Frank's arm. 'Has he come here to take me to the asylum?' he said.

'No,' said Frank. 'No, of course not, Ben.'

'I don't want to go to the asylum,' said Ben. 'They'm cruel to folk in there. I want to stay home. I done nothing.'

'That's all right, Ben,' said Colonel Julyan. 'No one's going to put you in the asylum. Are you quite sure you've never seen this man before?'

'No,' said Ben. 'I've never seen 'un.'

'You remember Mrs de Winter, don't you?' said Colonel Julyan.

Ben glanced doubtfully towards me.

'No,' said Colonel Julyan gently, 'not this lady. The other lady, who used to go to the cottage.'

'Eh?' said Ben.

'You remember the lady who had the boat?'

Ben blinked his eyes. 'She's gone,' he said.

'Yes, we know that,' said Colonel Julyan. 'She used to sail the boat, didn't she? Were you on the beach when she sailed the boat the last time? One evening, over twelve months ago. When she didn't come back again?'

Ben twisted his sou'wester. He glanced at Frank, and then at Maxim.

'Eh?' he said.

'You were there, weren't you?' said Favell, leaning forward. 'You saw Mrs de Winter come down to the cottage, and presently you saw Mr de Winter too. He went into the cottage after her. What happened then? Go on. What happened?'

Ben shrank back against the wall. 'I seen nothing,' he said. 'I want to stay home. I'm not going to the asylum. I never seen you. Never before. I never seen you and she in the woods.' He began to blubber like a child.

'You crazy little rat,' said Favell slowly, 'you bloody crazy little rat.'

Ben was wiping his eyes with the sleeve of his coat.

'Your witness does not seem to have helped you,' said Colonel Julyan. 'The performance has been rather a waste of time, hasn't it? Do you want to ask him anything else?'

'It's a plot,' shouted Favell. 'A plot against me. You're all in it, every one of you. Someone's paid this half-wit, I tell you. Paid him to tell his string of dirty lies.'

'I think Ben might be allowed to go home,' said Colonel Julyan.

'All right, Ben,' said Maxim. 'Robert shall take you back. And no one will put you in the asylum, don't be afraid. Tell Robert to find him something in the kitchen,' he added to Frank. 'Some cold meat, whatever he fancies.'

'Payment for services rendered, eh?' said Favell. 'He's done a good day's work for you, Max, hasn't he?'

Frank took Ben out of the room. Colonel Julyan glanced at

Maxim. 'The fellow appeared to be scared stiff,' he said; 'he was shaking like a leaf. I was watching him. He's never been ill-treated, has he?'

'No,' said Maxim, 'he's perfectly harmless, and I've always let him have the run of the place.'

'He's been frightened at some time,' said Colonel Julyan. 'He was showing the whites of his eyes, just like a dog does when you're going to whip him.'

'Well, why didn't you?' said Favell. 'He'd have remembered me all right if you'd whipped him. Oh, no, he's going to be given a good supper for his work tonight. Ben's not going to be whipped.'

'He has not helped your case, has he?' said Colonel Julyan quietly; 'we're still where we were. You can't produce one shred of evidence against de Winter and you know it. The very motive you gave won't stand the test. In a court of law, Favell, you wouldn't have a leg to stand on. You say you were Mrs de Winter's prospective husband, and that you held clandestine meetings with her in that cottage on the beach. Even the poor idiot we have just had in this room swears he never saw you. You can't even prove your own story, can you?'

'Can't I?' said Favell. I saw him smile. He came across to the fireplace and rang the bell.

'What are you doing?' said Colonel Julyan.

'Wait a moment and you'll see,' said Favell.

I guessed already what was going to happen. Frith answered the bell.

'Ask Mrs Danvers to come here,' said Favell.

Frith glanced at Maxim. Maxim nodded shortly.

Frith went out of the room. 'Isn't Mrs Danvers the house-keeper?' said Colonel Julyan.

'She was also Rebecca's personal friend,' said Favell. 'She was with her for years before she married and practically brought her up. You are going to find Danny a very different sort of witness to Ben.'

Frank came back into the room. 'Packed Ben off to bed?' said Favell. 'Given him his supper and told him he was a good boy? This time it won't be quite so easy for the trade union.'

'Mrs Danvers is coming down,' said Colonel Julyan. 'Favell seems to think he will get something out of her.'

Frank glanced quickly at Maxim. Colonel Julyan saw the glance. I saw his lips tighten. I did not like it. No, I did not like it. I began biting my nails.

We all waited, watching the door. And Mrs Danvers came into the room. Perhaps it was because I had generally seen her alone, and beside me she had seemed tall and gaunt, but she looked shrunken now in size, more wizened, and I noticed she had to look up to Favell and to Frank and Maxim. She stood by the door, her hands folded in front of her, looking from one to the other of us.

'Good evening, Mrs Danvers,' said Colonel Julyan.

'Good evening, sir,' she said.

Her voice was that old, dead, mechanical one I had heard so often.

'First of all, Mrs Danvers, I want to ask you a question,' said Colonel Julyan, 'and the question is this. Were you aware of the relationship between the late Mrs de Winter and Mr Favell here?'

'They were first cousins,' said Mrs Danvers.

'I was not referring to blood-relationship, Mrs Danvers,' said Colonel Julyan. 'I mean something closer than that.'

'I'm afraid I don't understand, sir,' said Mrs Danvers.

'Oh, come off it, Danny,' said Favell; 'you know damn well what he's driving at. I've told Colonel Julyan already, but he doesn't seem to believe me. Rebecca and I had lived together off and on for years, hadn't we? She was in love with me, wasn't she?'

To my surprise Mrs Danvers considered him a moment without speaking, and there was something of scorn in the glance she gave him.

'She was not,' she said.

'Listen here, you old fool . . .' began Favell, but Mrs Danvers cut him short.

'She was not in love with you, or with Mr de Winter. She was not in love with anyone. She despised all men. She was above all that.'

Favell flushed angrily. 'Listen here. Didn't she come down the path through the woods to meet me, night after night? Didn't you wait up for her? Didn't she spend the week-ends with me in London?'

'Well?' said Mrs Danvers, with sudden passion, 'and what if she did? She had a right to amuse herself, hadn't she. Love-making was a game with her, only a game. She told me so. She did it because it made her laugh. It made her laugh, I tell you. She laughed at you like she did at the rest. I've known her come back and sit upstairs in her bed and rock with laughter at the lot of you.'

There was something horrible in the sudden torrent of words, something horrible and unexpected. It revolted me, even though I knew. Maxim had gone very white. Favell stared at her blankly, as though he had not understood. Colonel Julyan tugged at his small moustache. No one said anything for a few minutes. And there was no sound but that inevitable falling rain. Then Mrs Danvers began to cry. She cried like she had done that morning in the bedroom. I could not look at her. I had to turn away. No one said anything. There were just the two sounds in the room, the falling rain and Mrs Danvers crying. It made me want to scream. I wanted to run out of the room and scream and scream.

No one moved towards her, to say anything, or to help her. She went on crying. Then at last, it seemed eternity, she began to control herself. Little by little the crying ceased. She stood quite still, her face working, her hands clutching the black stuff of her frock. At last she was silent again. Then Colonel Julyan spoke, quietly, slowly.

'Mrs Danvers,' he said, 'can you think of any reason, however remote, why Mrs de Winter should have taken her own life?'

Mrs Danvers swallowed. She went on clutching at her frock. She shook her head. 'No,' she said. 'No.'

'There, you see?' Favell said swiftly. 'It's impossible. She knows that as well as I do. I've told you already.'

'Be quiet, will you?' said Colonel Julyan. 'Give Mrs Danvers time to think. We all of us agree that on the face of it the thing's absurd, out of the question. I'm not disputing the truth or vera-city of that note of yours. It's plain for us to see. She wrote you that note some time during those hours she spent in London. There was something she wanted to tell you. It's just possible that if we knew what that something was we might have the answer to the whole appalling problem. Let Mrs Danvers read the note. She may be able to throw light on it.' Favell shrugged his shoulders. He felt in his pocket for the note and threw it on the floor at Mrs Danvers' feet. She stooped and picked it up. We watched her lips move as she read the words. She read it twice. Then she shook her head. 'It's no use,' she said. 'I don't know what she meant. If there was something important she had to tell Mr Jack she would have told me first.'

'You never saw her that night?'

'No, I was out. I was spending the afternoon and evening in Kerrith. I shall never forgive myself for that. Never till my dying day.'

'Then you know of nothing on her mind, you can't suggest a solution, Mrs Danvers? Those words *"I have something to tell you"* do not convey anything to you at all?'

'No,' she answered. 'No, sir, nothing at all.'

'Does anybody know how she spent that day in London?'

Nobody answered. Maxim shook his head. Favell swore under his breath. 'Look here, she left that note at my flat at three in the afternoon,' he said. 'The porter saw her. She must have driven down here straight after that, and gone like the wind too.'

'Mrs de Winter had a hair appointment from twelve until one thirty,' said Mrs Danvers. 'I remember that, because I had to telephone through to London from here earlier in the week and book it for her. I remember doing it. Twelve to one thirty. She always lunched at her club after a hair appointment so that she could leave the pins in her hair. It's almost certain she lunched there that day.'

'Say it took her half-an-hour to have lunch; what was she doing from two until three? We ought to verify that,' said Colonel Julyan.

'Oh, Christ Jesus, who the hell cares what she was doing?' shouted Favell. 'She didn't kill herself, that's the only thing that matters, isn't it?'

'I've got her engagement diary locked in my room,' said Mrs Danvers slowly. 'I kept all those things. Mr de Winter never asked me for them. It's just possible she may have noted down her appointments for that day. She was methodical in that way. She used to put everything down and then tick the items off with a cross. If you think it would be helpful I'll go and fetch the diary.'

'Well, de Winter?' said Colonel Julyan, 'what do you say? Do you mind us seeing this diary?'

'Of course not,' said Maxim. 'Why on earth should I?'

Once again I saw Colonel Julyan give him that swift, curious glance. And this time Frank noticed it. I saw Frank look at Maxim too. And then back again to me. This time it was I who got up and went towards the window. It seemed to me that it was no longer raining quite so hard. The fury was spent. The rain that was falling now had a quieter, softer note. The grey light of evening had come into the sky. The lawns were dark and drenched with the heavy rain, and the trees had a shrouded humped appearance. I could hear the housemaid overhead drawing the curtains for the night, shutting down the windows that had not been closed already. The little routine of the day going on inevitably as it had always done. The curtains drawn, shoes taken down to be cleaned, the towel laid out on the chair in the bathroom, and the water run for my bath. Beds turned down, slippers put beneath a chair. And here were we in the library, none of us speaking, knowing in our hearts that Maxim was standing trial here for his life.

I turned round when I heard the soft closing of the door. It was Mrs Danvers. She had come back again with the diary in her hand.

'I was right,' she said quietly. 'She had marked down the engagements as I said she would. Here they are on the date she died.'

She opened the diary, a small, red leather book. She gave it to Colonel Julyan. Once more he brought his spectacles from his case. There was a long pause while he glanced down the page. It seemed to me then that there was something about that particular moment, while he looked at the page of the diary, and we stood waiting, that frightened me more than anything that had happened that evening.

I dug my nails in my hands. I could not look at Maxim. Surely Colonel Julyan must hear my heart beating and thumping in my breast?

'Ah!' he said. His finger was in the middle of the page. Something is going to happen, I thought, something terrible is going to happen. 'Yes,' he said, 'yes, here it is. Hair at twelve, as Mrs Danvers said. And a cross beside it. She kept her appointment, then. Lunch at the club, and a cross beside that. What have we here, though? Baker, two o'clock. Who was Baker?' He looked at Maxim. Maxim shook his head. Then at Mrs Danvers.

'Baker?' repeated Mrs Danvers. 'She knew no one called Baker. I've never heard the name before.'

'Well, here it is,' said Colonel Julyan, handing her the diary. 'You can see for yourself, Baker. And she's put a great cross beside it as though she wanted to break the pencil. She evidently saw this Baker, whoever he may have been.'

Mrs Danvers was staring at the name written in the diary, and the black cross beside it. 'Baker,' she said. 'Baker.'

'I believe if we knew who Baker was we'd be getting to the bottom of the whole business,' said Colonel Julyan. 'She wasn't in the hands of money-lenders, was she?'

Mrs Danvers looked at him with scorn. 'Mrs de Winter?' she said.

'Well, blackmailers perhaps?' said Colonel Julyan, with a glance at Favell.

Mrs Danvers shook her head. 'Baker,' she repeated. 'Baker.'

'She had no enemy, no one who had ever threatened her, no one she was afraid of?'

'Mrs de Winter afraid?' said Mrs Danvers. 'She was afraid of nothing and no one. There was only one thing ever worried her, and that was the idea of getting old, of illness, of dying in her bed. She has said to me a score of times, "When I go, Danny, I want to go quickly, like the snuffing out of a candle." That used to be the only thing that consoled me, after she died. They say drowning is painless, don't they?'

She looked searchingly at Colonel Julyan. He did not answer. He hesitated, tugging at his moustache. I saw him throw another glance at Maxim.

'What the hell's the use of all this?' said Favell, coming forward. 'We're streaking away from the point the whole bloody time. Who cares about this Baker fellow? What's he got to do with it? It was probably some damn merchant who sold stockings, or face-cream. If he had been anyone important Danny here would know him. Rebecca had no secrets from Danny.'

But I was watching Mrs Danvers. She had the book in her hands and was turning the leaves. Suddenly she gave an exclamation.

'There's something here,' she said, 'right at the back among the telephone numbers. Baker. And there's a number beside it: 0488. But there is no exchange.'

'Brilliant Danny,' said Favell: 'becoming quite a sleuth in your old age, aren't you? But you're just twelve months too late. If you'd done this a year ago there might have been some use in it.'

'That's his number all right,' said Colonel Julyan, '0488, and the name Baker beside it. Why didn't she put the exchange?'

'Try every exchange in London,' jeered Favell. 'It will take you through the night but we don't mind. Max doesn't care if his telephone bill is a hundred pounds, do you, Max? You want to play for time, and so should I, if I were in your shoes.'

'There is a mark beside the number but it might mean anything,' said Colonel Julyan; 'take a look at it, Mrs Danvers. Could it possibly be an M?'

Mrs Danvers took the diary in her hands again. 'It might be,' she said doubtfully. 'It's not like her usual M but she may have scribbled it in a hurry. Yes, it might be M.'

'Mayfair 0488,' said Favell; 'what a genius, what a brain!'

'Well?' said Maxim, lighting his first cigarette, 'something had better be done about it. Frank? Go through and ask the exchange for Mayfair 0488.'

The nagging pain was strong beneath my heart. I stood quite still, my hands by my side. Maxim did not look at me.

'Go on, Frank,' he said. 'What are you waiting for?'

Frank went through to the little room beyond. We waited while he called the exchange. In a moment he was back again. 'They're going to ring me,' he said quietly. Colonel Julyan clasped his hands behind his back and began walking up and down the room. No one said anything. After about four minutes the telephone rang shrill and insistent, that irritating, monotonous note of a long-distance call. Frank went through to answer it. 'Is that Mayfair 0488?' he said. 'Can you tell me if anyone of the name of Baker lives there? Oh, I see. I'm so sorry. Yes, I must have got the wrong number. Thank you very much.'

The little click as he replaced the receiver. Then he came back into the room. 'Someone called Lady Eastleigh lives at Mayfair 0488. It's an address in Grosvenor Street. They've never heard of Baker.'

Favell gave a great cackle of laughter. 'The butcher, the baker, the candlestick-maker, they all jumped out of a rotten potato,' he said. 'Carry on, detective Number One, what's the next exchange on the list?'

'Try Museum,' said Mrs Danvers.

Frank glanced at Maxim. 'Go ahead,' said Maxim.

The farce was repeated all over again. Colonel Julyan repeated his walk up and down the room. Another five minutes went by, and the telephone rang again. Frank went to answer it. He left the door wide open, I could see him lean down to the table where the telephone stood, and bend to the mouth-piece.

'Hullo? Is that Museum 0488? Can you tell me if anyone of the name of Baker lives there? Oh; who is that speaking? A night porter. Yes. Yes, I understand. Not offices. No, no of course. Can you give me the address? Yes, it's rather important.' He paused. He called to us over his shoulder. 'I think we've got him,' he said.

Oh, God, don't let it be true. Don't let Baker be found. Please God make Baker be dead. I knew who Baker was. I had known all along. I watched Frank through the door, I watched him lean forward suddenly, reach for a pencil and a piece of paper. 'Hullo? Yes, I'm still here. Could you spell it? Thank you. Thank you very much. Good night.' He came back into the room, the piece of paper in his hands. Frank who loved Maxim, who did not know that the piece of paper he held was the one shred of evidence that was worth a damn in the whole nightmare of our evening, and that by producing it he could destroy Maxim as well and truly as though he had a dagger in his hand and stabbed him in the back.

'It was the night porter from an address in Bloomsbury,' he said. 'There are no residents there at all. The place is used during the day as a doctor's consulting rooms. Apparently Baker's given up practice, and left six months ago. But we can get hold of him all right. The night porter gave me his address. I wrote it down on this piece of paper.'

25

IT WAS THEN that Maxim looked at me. He looked at me for the first time that evening. And in his eyes I read a message of farewell. It was as though he leant against the side of a ship, and I stood below him on the quay. There would be other people touching his shoulder, and touching mine, but we would not see them. Nor would we speak or call to one another, for the wind and the distance would carry away the sound of our voices. But I should see his eyes and he would see mine before the ship drew away from the side of the quay. Favell, Mrs Danvers, Colonel Julyan, Frank with the slip of paper in his hands, they were all forgotten at this moment. It was ours, inviolate, a fraction of time suspended between two seconds. And then he turned away and held out his hand to Frank.

'Well done,' he said. 'What's the address?'

'Somewhere near Barnet, north of London,' said Frank, giving him the paper. 'But it's not on the telephone. We can't ring him up.'

'Satisfactory work, Crawley,' said Colonel Julyan, 'and from you too, Mrs Danvers. Can you throw any light on the matter now?'

Mrs Danvers shook her head. 'Mrs de Winter never needed a doctor. Like all strong people she despised them. We only had Doctor Phillips from Kerrith here once, that time she sprained her wrist. I've never heard her speak of this Doctor Baker, she never mentioned his name to me.'

'I tell you the fellow was a face-cream mixer,' said Favell. 'What the hell does it matter who he was? If there was anything to it Danny would know. I tell you it's some fool fellow who had discovered a new way of bleaching the hair or whitening the skin, and Rebecca had probably got the address from her hairdresser that morning and went along after lunch out of curiosity.'

'No,' said Frank. 'I think you're wrong there. Baker wasn't a quack. The night porter at Museum 0488 told me he was a very well-known woman's specialist.'

'H'm,' said Colonel Julyan, pulling at his moustache, 'there must have been something wrong with her after all. It seems very curious that she did not say a word to anybody, not even to you, Mrs Danvers.'

'She was too thin,' said Favell. 'I told her about it, but she only laughed. Said it suited her. Banting I suppose, like all these women. Perhaps she went to this chap Baker for a diet sheet.'

'Do you think that's possible, Mrs Danvers?' asked Colonel Julyan.

Mrs Danvers shook her head slowly. She seemed dazed, bewildered by this sudden news about Baker. 'I can't understand it,' she said. 'I don't know what it means. Baker. A Doctor Baker. Why didn't she tell me? Why did she keep it from me? She told me everything.'

'Perhaps she didn't want to worry you,' said Colonel Julyan. No doubt she made an appointment with him, and saw him, and then when she came down that night she was going to have told you all about it.'

'And the note to Mr Jack,' said Mrs Danvers suddenly. 'That note to Mr Jack, "*I have something to tell you. I must see you*"; she was going to tell him too?'

'That's true,' said Favell slowly. 'We were forgetting the note.' Once more he pulled it out of his pocket and read it to us aloud. '"*I've got something to tell you, and I want to see you as soon as possible. Rebecca.*"'

'Of course, there's no doubt about it,' said Colonel Julyan, turning to Maxim. 'I wouldn't mind betting a thousand pounds on it. She was going to tell Favell the result of that interview with this Doctor Baker.'

'I believe you're right after all,' said Favell. 'The note and that appointment seem to hang together. But what the hell was it all about, that's what I want to know? What was the matter with her?'

The truth screamed in their faces and they did not see. They all

stood there, staring at one another, and they did not understand.
I dared not look at them. I dared not move lest I betray my knowledge. Maxim said nothing. He had gone back to the window
and was looking out into the garden that was hushed and dark
and still. The rain had ceased at last, but the spots fell from the
dripping leaves and from the gutter above the window.

'It ought to be quite easy to verify,' said Frank. 'Here is the
doctor's present address. I can write him a letter and ask him if
he remembers an appointment last year with Mrs de Winter.'

'I don't know if he would take any notice of it,' said Colonel
Julyan, 'there is so much of this etiquette in the medical profession. Every case is confidential, you know. The only way to get
anything out of him would be to get de Winter to see him
privately and explain the circumstances. What do you say, de
Winter?'

Maxim turned round from the window. 'I'm ready to do
whatever you care to suggest,' he said quietly.

'Anything for time, eh?' said Favell; 'a lot can be done in
twenty-four hours, can't it? Trains can be caught, ships can sail,
aeroplanes can fly.'

I saw Mrs Danvers look sharply from Favell to Maxim, and
I realized then, for the first time, that Mrs Danvers had not
known about Favell's accusation. At last she was beginning to
understand. I could tell from the expression on her face. There
was doubt written on it, then wonder and hatred mixed, and then
conviction. Once again those lean long hands of hers clutched
convulsively at her dress, and she passed her tongue over her lips.
She went on staring at Maxim. She never took her eyes away from
Maxim. It's too late, I thought, she can't do anything to us now,
the harm is done. It does not matter what she says to us now, or
what she does. The harm is done. She can't hurt us any more.
Maxim did not notice her, or if he did he gave no sign. He was
talking to Colonel Julyan.

'What do you suggest?' he said. 'Shall I go up in the morning,
drive to this address at Barnet? I can wire Baker to expect me.'

'He's not going alone,' said Favell, with a short laugh. 'I have
a right to insist on that, haven't I? Send him up with Inspector
Welch and I won't object.'

If only Mrs Danvers would take her eyes away from Maxim. Frank had seen her now. He was watching her, puzzled, anxious. I saw him glance once more at the slip of paper in his hands, on which he had written Doctor Baker's address. Then he too glanced at Maxim. I believe then that some faint idea of the truth began to force itself to his conscience, for he went very white and put the paper down on the table.

'I don't think there is any necessity to bring Inspector Welch into the affair – yet,' said Colonel Julyan. His voice was different, harder. I did not like the way he used the word 'yet'. Why must he use it at all? I did not like it. 'If I go with de Winter, and stay with him the whole time, and bring him back, will that satisfy you?' he said.

Favell looked at Maxim, and then at Colonel Julyan. The expression on his face was ugly, calculating, and there was something of triumph too in his light blue eyes. 'Yes,' he said slowly, 'yes, I suppose so. But for safety's sake do you mind if I come with you too?'

'No,' said Colonel Julyan, 'unfortunately I think you have the right to ask that. But if you do come, I have the right to insist on your being sober.'

'You needn't worry about that,' said Favell, beginning to smile; 'I'll be sober all right. Sober as the judge will be when he sentences Max in three months' time. I rather think this Doctor Baker is going to prove my case, after all.'

He looked around at each one of us and began to laugh. I think he too had understood at last the significance of that visit to the doctor.

'Well,' he said, 'what time are we going to start in the morning?'

Colonel Julyan looked at Maxim. 'How early can you be ready?'

'Any time you say,' said Maxim.

'Nine o'clock?'

'Nine o'clock,' said Maxim.

'How do we know he won't do a bolt in the night?' said Favell. 'He's only to cut round to the garage and get his car.'

'Is my word enough for you?' said Maxim, turning to Colonel

Julyan. And for the first time Colonel Julyan hesitated. I saw him glance at Frank. And a flush came over Maxim's face. I saw the little pulse beating on his forehead. 'Mrs Danvers,' he said slowly, 'when Mrs de Winter and I go to bed tonight will you come up yourself and lock the door on the outside? And call us yourself, at seven in the morning?'

'Yes, sir,' said Mrs Danvers. Still she kept her eyes on him, still her hands clutched at her dress.

'Very well, then,' said Colonel Julyan brusquely. 'I don't think there is anything else we need discuss, tonight. I shall be here sharp at nine in the morning. You will have room for me in your car, de Winter?'

'Yes,' said Maxim.

'And Favell will follow us in his?'

'Right on your tail, my dear fellow, right on your tail,' said Favell.

Colonel Julyan came up to me and took my hand. 'Good night,' he said. 'You know how I feel for you in all this, there's no need for me to tell you. Get your husband to bed early, if you can. It's going to be a long day.' He held my hand a minute and then he turned away. It was curious how he avoided my eye. He looked at my chin. Frank held the door for him as he went out. Favell leant forward and filled his case with cigarettes from the box on the table.

'I suppose I'm not going to be asked to stop to dinner?' he said.

Nobody answered. He lit one of the cigarettes, and blew a cloud of smoke into the air. 'It means a quiet evening at the pub on the high-road then,' he said, 'and the barmaid has a squint. What a hell of a night I'm going to spend! Never mind, I'm looking forward to tomorrow. Good night, Danny old lady, don't forget to turn the key on Mr de Winter, will you?'

He came over to me and held out his hand.

Like a foolish child I put my hands behind my back. He laughed, and bowed.

'It's just too bad, isn't it?' he said. 'A nasty man like me coming and spoiling all your fun. Don't worry, it will be a great thrill for you when the yellow Press gets going with your life story, and you see the headlines "From Monte Carlo to Manderley. Experiences of murderer's girl-bride," written across the top. Better luck next time.'

He strolled across the room to the door, waving his hand to Maxim by the window. 'So long, old man,' he said, 'pleasant dreams. Make the most of your night behind that locked door.' He turned and laughed at me, and then he went out of the room. Mrs Danvers followed him. Maxim and I were alone. He went on standing by the window. He did not come to me. Jasper came trotting in from the hall. He had been shut outside all the evening. He came fussing up to me, biting the edge of my skirt.

'I'm coming with you in the morning,' I said to Maxim. 'I'm coming up to London with you in the car.'

He did not answer for a moment. He went on looking out of the window. Then 'Yes,' he said, his voice without expression. 'Yes, we must go on being together.'

Frank came back into the room. He stood in the entrance, his hand on the door. 'They've gone,' he said, 'Favell and Colonel Julyan, I watched them go.'

'All right, Frank,' said Maxim.

'Is there anything I can do?' said Frank, 'anything at all? Wire to anyone, arrange anything? I'll stay up all night if only there's anything I can do. I'll get that wire off to Baker of course.'

'Don't worry,' said Maxim, 'there's nothing for you to do – yet. There may be plenty – after tomorrow. We can go into all that when the time comes. Tonight we want to be together. You understand, don't you?'

'Yes,' said Frank. 'Yes, of course.'

He waited a moment, his hand on the door. 'Good night,' he said.

'Good night,' said Maxim.

When he had gone, and shut the door behind him, Maxim came over to me where I was standing by the fireplace. I held out my arms to him and he came to me like a child. I put my arms round him and held him. We did not say anything for a long time. I held him and comforted him as though he were Jasper. As though Jasper had hurt himself in some way and he had come to me to take his pain away.

'We can sit together,' he said, 'driving up in the car.'

'Yes,' I said.

'Julyan won't mind,' he said.

'No,' I said.

'We shall have tomorrow night too,' he said. 'They won't do anything at once, not for twenty-four hours perhaps.'

'No,' I said.

'They aren't so strict now,' he said. 'They let one see people. And it all takes such a long time. If I can I shall try and get hold of Hastings. He's the best. Hastings or Birkett. Hastings used to know my father.'

'Yes,' I said.

'I shall have to tell him the truth,' he said. 'It makes it easier for them. They know where they are.'

'Yes,' I said.

The door opened and Frith came into the room. I pushed Maxim away, I stood up straight and conventional, patting my hair into place.

'Will you be changing, Madam, or shall I serve dinner at once?'

'No, Frith, we won't be changing, not tonight,' I said.

'Very good, Madam,' he said.

He left the door open. Robert came in and began drawing the curtains. He arranged the cushions, straightened the sofa, tidied the books and papers on the table. He took away the whisky-and-soda and the dirty ash-trays. I had seen him do these things as a ritual every evening I had spent at Manderley, but tonight they seemed to take on a special significance, as though the memory of them would last for ever and I would say, long after, in some other time, 'I remember this moment.'

Then Frith came in and told us that dinner was served.

I remember every detail of that evening. I remember the ice-cold consommé in the cups, and the fillets of sole, and the hot shoulder of lamb.

I remember the burnt sugar sweet, the sharp savoury that followed.

We had new candles in the silver candlesticks, they looked white and slim and very tall. The curtains had been drawn here too against the dull grey evening. It seemed strange to be sitting in the dining-room and not look out on to the lawns. It was like the beginning of autumn.

It was while we were drinking our coffee in the library that the telephone rang. This time it was I who answered it. I heard Beatrice speaking at the other end. 'Is that you?' she said, 'I've been trying to get through all the evening. Twice it was engaged.'

'I'm so sorry,' I said, 'so very sorry.'

'We had the evening papers about two hours ago,' she said, 'and the verdict was a frightful shock to both Giles and myself. What does Maxim say about it?'

'I think it was a shock to everybody,' I said.

'But, my dear, the thing is preposterous. Why on earth should Rebecca have committed suicide? The most unlikely person in the world. There must have been a blunder somewhere.'

'I don't know,' I said.

'What does Maxim say? Where is he?' she said.

'People have been here,' I said – 'Colonel Julyan, and others. Maxim is very tired. We're going up to London tomorrow.'

'What on earth for?'

'Something to do with the verdict. I can't very well explain.'

'You ought to get it quashed,' she said. 'It's ridiculous, quite ridiculous. And so bad for Maxim, all this frightful publicity. It's going to reflect on him.'

'Yes,' I said.

'Surely Colonel Julyan can do something?' she said. 'He's a magistrate. What are magistrates for? Old Horridge from Lanyon must have been off his head. What was her motive supposed to be? It's the most idiotic thing I've ever heard in my life. Someone ought to get hold of Tabb. How can he tell whether those holes in the boat were made deliberately or not? Giles said of course it must have been the rocks.'

'They seemed to think not,' I said.

'If only I could have been there,' she said. 'I should have insisted on speaking. No one seems to have made any effort. Is Maxim very upset?'

'He's tired,' I said, 'more tired than anything else.'

'I wish I could come up to London and join you,' she said,

'but I don't see how I can. Roger has a temperature of 103, poor old boy, and the nurse we've got in is a perfect idiot, he loathes her. I can't possibly leave him.'

'Of course not,' I said. 'You mustn't attempt it.'

'Whereabouts in London will you be?'

'I don't know,' I said. 'It's all rather vague.'

'Tell Maxim he must try and do something to get that verdict altered. It's so bad for the family. I'm telling everybody here it's absolutely wicked. Rebecca would never have killed herself, she wasn't the type. I've got a good mind to write to the Coroner myself.'

'It's too late,' I said. 'Much better leave it. It won't do any good.'

'The stupidity of it gets my goat,' she said. 'Giles and I think it much more likely that if those holes weren't done by the rocks they were done deliberately, by some tramp or other. A Communist perhaps. There are heaps of them about. Just the sort of thing a Communist would do.'

Maxim called to me from the library. 'Can't you get rid of her? What on earth is she talking about?'

'Beatrice,' I said desperately, 'I'll try and ring you up from London.'

'Is it any good my tackling Dick Godolphin?' she said. 'He's your M.P. I know him very well, much better than Maxim does. He was at Oxford with Giles. Ask Maxim whether he would like me to telephone Dick and see if he can do anything to quash the verdict? Ask Maxim what he thinks of this Communist idea.'

'It's no use,' I said. 'It can't do any good. Please, Beatrice, don't try and do anything. It will make it worse, much worse. Rebecca may have had some motive we don't know anything about. And I don't think Communists go ramming holes in boats, what would be the use? Please, Beatrice, leave it alone.'

Oh, thank God she had not been with us today. Thank God for that at least. Something was buzzing in the telephone. I heard Beatrice shouting, 'Hullo, hullo, don't cut us off, exchange,' and then there was a click, and silence.

I went back into the library, limp and exhausted. In a few minutes the telephone began ringing again. I did not do anything. I let it ring. I went and sat down at Maxim's feet. It went on ringing. I did not move. Presently it stopped, as though cut suddenly in exasperation. The clock on the mantelpiece struck ten o'clock. Maxim put his arms round me and lifted me against him. We began to kiss one another, feverishly, desperately, like guilty lovers who have not kissed before.

26

WHEN I AWOKE the next morning, just after six o'clock, and got up and went to the window there was a foggy dew upon the grass like frost, and the trees were shrouded in a white mist. There was a chill in the air and a little, fresh wind, and the cold, quiet smell of autumn.

As I knelt by the window looking down on to the rose-garden where the flowers themselves drooped upon their stalks, the petals brown and dragging after last night's rain, the happenings of the day before seemed remote and unreal. Here at Manderley a new day was starting, the things of the garden were not concerned with our troubles. A blackbird ran across the rose-garden to the lawns in swift, short rushes, stopping now and again to stab at the earth with his yellow beak. A thrush, too, went about his business, and two stout little wagtails, following one another, and a little cluster of twittering sparrows. A gull poised himself high in the air, silent and alone, and then spread his wings wide and swooped beyond the lawns to the woods and the Happy Valley. These things continued, our worries and anxieties had no power to alter them. Soon the gardeners would be astir, brushing the first leaves from the lawns and the paths, raking the gravel in the drive. Pails would clank in the courtyard behind the house, the hose would be turned on the car, the little scullery-maid would begin to chatter through the open door to the men in the yard. There would be the crisp, hot smell of bacon. The house-maids would open up the house, throw wide the windows, draw back the curtains.

The dogs would crawl from their baskets, yawn and stretch themselves, wander out on to the terrace and blink at the first struggles of the pale sun coming through the mist. Robert would lay the table for breakfast, bring in those piping scones, the clutch of eggs, the glass dishes of honey, jam, and marmalade, the bowl of peaches, the cluster of purple grapes with the bloom upon them still, hot from the greenhouses.

Maids sweeping in the morning-room, the drawing-room, the fresh clean air pouring into the long open windows. Smoke curling from the chimneys, and little by little the autumn mist fading away and the trees and the banks and the woods taking shape, the glimmer of the sea showing with the sun upon it below the valley, the beacon standing tall and straight upon the headland.

The peace of Manderley. The quietude and the grace. Whoever lived within its walls, whatever trouble there was and strife, however much uneasiness and pain, no matter what tears were shed, what sorrows borne, the peace of Manderley could not be broken or the loveliness destroyed. The flowers that died would bloom again another year, the same birds build their nests, the same trees blossom. The old quiet moss smell would linger in the air, and bees would come, and crickets, and herons build their nests in the deep dark woods. The butterflies would dance their merry jig across the lawns, and spiders spin foggy webs, and small startled rabbits who had no business to come trespassing poke their faces through the crowded shrubs. There would be lilac and honeysuckle still, and the white magnolia buds unfolding slow and tight beneath the dining-room window. No one would ever hurt Manderley. It would lie always in a hollow like an enchanted thing, guarded by the woods, safe, secure, while the sea broke and ran and came again in the little shingle bays below.

Maxim slept on and I did not wake him. The day ahead of us would be a weary thing and long. High-roads, and telegraph poles, and the monotony of passing traffic, the slow crawl into London. We did not know what we should find at the end of our journey. The future was unknown. Somewhere to the north of London lived a man called Baker who had never heard of us, but he held our future in the hollow of his hand. Soon he too would be waking, stretching, yawning, going about the business of his day. I got up, and went into the bathroom, and began to run my bath. These actions held for me the same significance as Robert and his clearing of the library had the night before. I had done these things before mechanically, but now I was aware as I dropped my sponge into the water, as I spread my towel on the chair from the hot rail, as I lay back and let the water run over my body. Every moment was a precious thing, having in it the essence of finality. When I went back to the bedroom and began to dress I heard a soft footstep come and pause outside the door, and the key turn quietly in the lock. There was silence a moment, and then the footsteps went away. It was Mrs Danvers.

She had not forgotten. I had heard the same sound the night before after we had come up from the library. She had not knocked upon the door, she had not made herself known; there was just the sound of footsteps and the turning of the key in the lock. It brought me to reality and the facing of the immediate future.

I finished dressing, and went and turned on Maxim's bath. Presently Clarice came with our tea. I woke Maxim. He stared at me at first like a puzzled child, and then he held out his arms. We drank our tea. He got up and went to his bath and I began putting things methodically in my suitcase. It might be that we should have to stay in London.

I packed the brushes Maxim had given me, a nightdress, my dressing-gown and slippers, and another dress too and a pair of shoes. My dressing-case looked unfamiliar as I dragged it from the back of a wardrobe. It seemed so long since I had used it, and yet it was only four months ago. It still had the Customs mark upon it they had chalked at Calais. In one of the pockets was a concert ticket from the casino in Monte Carlo. I crumpled it and threw it into the waste-paper basket. It might have belonged to another age, another world. My bedroom began to take on the appearance of all rooms when the owner goes away. The dressing-table was bare without my brushes. There was tissue paper lying on the floor, and an old label. The beds where we had slept had a terrible emptiness about them. The towels lay crumpled on the bathroom floor. The wardrobe doors gaped open. I put on my hat so that I should not have to come up again, and I took my bag and my gloves and my suit-case. I glanced round the room to see if there was anything I had forgotten. The mist was breaking, the sun was forcing its way through and throwing patterns on the carpet. When I was half-way down the passage I had a curious, inexplicable feeling that I must go back and look in my room again. I went without reason, and stood a moment looking at the gaping wardrobe and the empty bed, and the tray of tea upon the table. I stared at them, impressing them for ever on my mind, wondering why they had the power to touch me, to sadden me, as though they were children that did not want me to go away.

Then I turned and went downstairs to breakfast. It was cold in the dining-room, the sun not yet on the windows, and I was grateful for the scalding bitter coffee and heartening bacon. Maxim and I ate in silence. Now and again he glanced at the clock. I heard Robert put the suit-cases in the hall with the rug, and presently there was the sound of the car being brought to the door.

I went out and stood on the terrace. The rain had cleared the air, and the grass smelt fresh and sweet. When the sun was higher it would be a lovely day. I thought how we might have wandered in the valley before lunch, and then sat out afterwards under the chestnut tree with books and papers. I closed my eyes a minute and felt the warmth of the sun on my face and on my hands.

I heard Maxim calling to me from the house. I went back, and Frith helped me into my coat. I heard the sound of another car. It was Frank.

'Colonel Julyan is waiting at the lodge gates,' he said. 'He did not think it worth while to drive up to the house.'

'No,' said Maxim.

'I'll stand by in the office all day and wait for you to telephone,' said Frank. 'After you've seen Baker you may find you want me, up in London.'

'Yes,' said Maxim. 'Yes, perhaps.'

'It's just nine now,' said Frank. 'You're up to time. It's going to be fine too. You should have a good run.'

'Yes.'

'I hope you won't get over-tired, Mrs de Winter,' he said to me. 'It's going to be a long day for you.'

'I shall be all right,' I said. I looked at Jasper who was standing by my feet with ears drooping and sad reproachful eyes.

'Take Jasper back with you to the office,' I said. 'He looks so miserable.'

'Yes,' he said. 'Yes, I will.'

'We'd better be off,' said Maxim. 'Old Julyan will be getting impatient. All right, Frank.'

I climbed in the car beside Maxim. Frank slammed the door.

'You will telephone, won't you?' he said.

'Yes, of course,' said Maxim.

I looked back at the house. Frith was standing at the top of the steps, and Robert just behind. My eyes filled with tears for no reason. I turned away and groped with my bag on the floor of the car so that nobody should see. Then Maxim started up the car and we swept round and into the drive and the house was hidden.

We stopped at the lodge gates and picked up Colonel Julyan. He got in at the back. He looked doubtful when he saw me.

'It's going to be a long day,' he said. 'I don't think you should have attempted it. I would have taken care of your husband you know.'

'I wanted to come,' I said.

He did not say any more about it. He settled himself in the corner. 'It's fine, that's one thing,' he said.

'Yes,' said Maxim.

'That fellow Favell said he would pick us up at the cross-roads. If he's not there don't attempt to wait, we'd do much better without him. I hope the damned fellow has overslept himself.'

When we came to the cross-roads though I saw the long green body of his car, and my heart sank. I had thought he might not be on time. Favell was sitting at the wheel, hatless, a cigarette in his mouth. He grinned when he saw us, and waved us on. I settled down in my seat for the journey ahead, one hand on Maxim's knee. The hours passed, and the miles were covered. I watched the road ahead in a kind of stupor. Colonel Julyan slept at the back from time to time. I turned occasionally and saw his head loll against the cushions, and his mouth open. The green car kept close beside us. Sometimes it shot ahead; sometimes it dropped behind. But we never lost it. At one we stopped for lunch at one of those inevitable old-fashioned hotels in the main street of a county town. Colonel Julyan waded through the whole set lunch, starting with soup and fish, and going on to roast beef and Yorkshire pudding. Maxim and I had cold ham and coffee.

I half expected Favell to wander into the dining-room and join us, but when we came out to the car again I saw his car had been drawn up outside a café on the opposite side of the road. He must have seen us from the window, for three minutes after we had started he was on our tail again.

We came to the suburbs of London about three o'clock. It was then that I began to feel tired, the noise and the traffic blocks started a humming in my head. It was warm in London too. The streets had that worn dusty look of August, and the leaves hung listless on dull trees. Our storm must have been local, there had been no rain here.

People were walking about in cotton frocks and the men were hatless. There was a smell of waste-paper, and orange-peel, and feet, and burnt dried grass. Buses lumbered slowly, and taxis crawled. I felt as though my coat and skirt were sticking to me, and my stockings pricked my skin.

Colonel Julyan sat up and looked out through his window. 'They've had no rain here,' he said.

'No,' said Maxim.

'Looks as though the place needed it, too.'

'Yes.'

'We haven't succeeded in shaking Favell off. He's still on our tail.'

'Yes.'

Shopping centres on the outskirts seemed congested. Tired women with crying babies in prams stared into windows, hawkers shouted, small boys hung on to the backs of lorries. There were too many people, too much noise. The very air was irritable and exhausted and spent.

The drive through London seemed endless, and by the time we had drawn clear again and were out beyond Hampstead there was a sound in my head like the beating of a drum, and my eyes were burning.

I wondered how tired Maxim was. He was pale, and there were shadows under his eyes, but he did not say anything. Colonel

Julyan kept yawning at the back. He opened his mouth very wide and yawned aloud, sighing heavily afterwards. He would do this every few minutes. I felt a senseless stupid irritation come over me, and I did not know how to prevent myself from turning round and screaming to him to stop.

Once we had passed Hampstead he drew out a large-scale map from his coat-pocket and began directing Maxim to Barnet. The way was clear and there were sign-posts to tell us, but he kept pointing out every turn and twist in the road, and if there was any hesitation on Maxim's part Colonel Julyan would turn down the window and call for information from a passer-by.

When we came to Barnet itself he made Maxim stop every few minutes. 'Can you tell us where a house called Roselands is? It belongs to a Doctor Baker, who's retired, and come to live there lately,' and the passer-by would stand frowning a moment, obviously at sea, ignorance written plain upon his face.

'Doctor Baker? I don't know a Doctor Baker. There used to be a house called Rose Cottage near the church, but a Mrs Wilson lives there.'

'No, it's Roselands we want, Doctor Baker's house,' said Colonel Julyan, and then we would go on and stop again in front of a nurse and a pram. 'Can you tell us where Roselands is?'

'I'm sorry. I'm afraid I've only just come to live here.'

'You don't know a Doctor Baker?'

'Doctor Davidson. I know Doctor Davidson.'

'No, it's Doctor Baker we want.'

I glanced up at Maxim. He was looking very tired. His mouth was set hard. Behind us crawled Favell, his green car covered in dust.

It was a postman who pointed out the house in the end. A square house, ivy covered, with no name on the gate, which we had already passed twice. Mechanically I reached for my bag and dabbed my face with the end of the powder puff. Maxim drew up outside at the side of the road. He did not take the car into the short drive. We sat silently for a few minutes.

'Well, here we are,' said Colonel Julyan, 'and it's exactly twelve minutes past five. We shall catch them in the middle of their tea. Better wait for a bit.'

Maxim lit a cigarette, and then stretched out his hand to me. He did not speak. I heard Colonel Julyan crinkling his map.

'We could have come right across without touching London,' he said, 'saved us forty minutes I dare say. We made good time the first two hundred miles. It was from Chiswick on we took the time.'

An errand boy passed us whistling on his bicycle. A motor-coach stopped at the corner and two women got out. Somewhere a church clock chimed the quarter. I could see Favell leaning back in his car behind us and smoking a cigarette. I seemed to have no feeling in me at all. I just sat and watched the little things that did not matter. The two women from the bus walk along the road. The errand boy disappears round the corner. A sparrow hops about in the middle of the road pecking at dirt.

'This fellow Baker can't be much of a gardener,' said Colonel Julyan. 'Look at those shrubs tumbling over his wall. They ought to have been pruned right back.' He folded up the map and put it back in his pocket. 'Funny sort of place to choose to retire in,' he said. 'Close to the main road and overlooked by other houses. Shouldn't care about it myself. I dare say it was quite pretty once before they started building. No doubt there's a good golf-course somewhere handy.'

He was silent for a while, then he opened the door and stood out in the road. 'Well, de Winter,' he said, 'what do you think about it?'

'I'm ready,' said Maxim.

We got out of the car. Favell strolled up to meet us.

'What were you all waiting for, cold feet?' he said.

Nobody answered him. We walked up the drive to the front door, a strange incongruous little party. I caught sight of a tennis lawn beyond the house, and I heard the thud of balls. A boy's voice shouted 'Forty-fifteen, not thirty all. Don't you remember hitting it out, you silly ass?'

'They must have finished tea,' said Colonel Julyan.

He hesitated a moment, glancing at Maxim. Then he rang the bell.

It tinkled somewhere in the back premises. There was a long

pause. A very young maid opened the door to us. She looked startled at the sight of so many of us.

'Doctor Baker?' said Colonel Julyan.

'Yes, sir, will you come in?'

She opened the door on the left of the hall as we went in. It would be the drawing-room, not used much in the summer. There was a portrait of a very plain dark woman on the wall. I wondered if it was Mrs Baker. The chintz covers on the chairs and on the sofa were new and shiny. On the mantelpiece were photographs of two schoolboys with round, smiling faces. There was a very large wireless in the corner of the room by the window. Cords trailed from it, and bits of aerial. Favell examined the portrait on the wall. Colonel Julyan went and stood by the empty fireplace. Maxim and I looked out of the window. I could see a deck-chair under a tree, and the back of a woman's head. The tennis court must be round the corner. I could hear the boys shouting to each other. A very old Scotch terrier was scratching himself in the middle of the path. We waited there for about five minutes. It was as though I was living the life of some other person and had come to this house to call for a subscription to a charity. It was unlike anything I had ever known. I had no feeling, no pain.

Then the door opened and a man came into the room. He was medium height, rather long in the face, with a keen chin. His hair was sandy, turning grey. He wore flannels, and a dark blue blazer.

'Forgive me for keeping you waiting,' he said, looking a little surprised, as the maid had done, to see so many of us. 'I had to run up and wash. I was playing tennis when the bell rang. Won't you sit down?' He turned to me. I sat down in the nearest chair and waited.

'You must think this a very unorthodox invasion, Doctor Baker,' said Colonel Julyan, 'and I apologize very humbly for disturbing you like this. My name is Julyan. This is Mr de Winter, Mrs de Winter, and Mr Favell. You may have seen Mr de Winter's name in the papers recently.'

'Oh,' said Doctor Baker, 'yes, yes, I suppose I have. Some inquest or other, wasn't it? My wife was reading all about it.'

'The jury brought in a verdict of suicide,' said Favell coming forward, 'which I say is absolutely out of the question. Mrs de Winter was my cousin, I knew her intimately. She would never have done such a thing, and what's more she had no motive. What we want to know is what the devil she came to see you about the very day she died?'

'You had better leave this to Julyan and myself,' said Maxim quietly. 'Doctor Baker has not the faintest idea what you are driving at.'

He turned to the doctor who was standing between them with a line between his brows, and his first polite smile frozen on his lips. 'My late wife's cousin is not satisfied with the verdict,' said Maxim, 'and we've driven up to see you today because we found your name, and the telephone number of your old consulting rooms, in my wife's engagement diary. She seems to have made an appointment with you, and kept it, at two o'clock on the last day she ever spent in London. Could you possibly verify this for us?'

Doctor Baker was listening with great interest, but when Maxim had finished he shook his head. 'I'm most awfully sorry,' he said, 'but I think you've made a mistake. I should have remembered the name de Winter. I've never attended a Mrs de Winter in my life.'

Colonel Julyan brought out his note-case and gave him the page he had torn from the engagement diary. 'Here it is, written down,' he said, 'Baker, two o'clock. And a big cross beside it, to show that the appointment was kept. And here is the telephone address. Museum 0488.'

Doctor Baker stared at the piece of paper. 'That's very odd, very odd indeed. Yes, the number is quite correct as you say.'

'Could she have come to see you and given a false name?' said Colonel Julyan.

'Why, yes, that's possible. She may have done that. It's rather unusual of course. I've never encouraged that sort of thing. It doesn't do us any good in the profession if people think they can treat us like that.'

'Would you have any record of the visit in your files?' said

Colonel Julyan. 'I know it's not etiquette to ask, but the circumstances are very unusual. We do feel her appointment with you must have some bearing on the case and her subsequent – suicide.'

'Murder,' said Favell.

Doctor Baker raised his eyebrows, and looked inquiringly at Maxim. 'I'd no idea there was any question of that,' he said quietly. 'Of course I understand, and I'll do anything in my power to help you. If you will excuse me a few minutes I will go and look up my files. There should be a record of every appointment booked throughout the year, and a description of the case. Please help yourself to cigarettes. It's too early to offer you sherry, I suppose?'

Colonel Julyan and Maxim shook their heads. I thought Favell was going to say something but Doctor Baker had left the room before he had a chance.

'Seems a decent sort of fellow,' said Colonel Julyan.

'Why didn't he offer us whisky-and-soda?' said Favell. 'Keeps it locked up, I suppose. I didn't think much of him. I don't believe he's going to help us now.'

Maxim did not say anything. I could hear the sound of the tennis balls from the court. The Scotch terrier was barking. A woman's voice shouted to him to be quiet. The summer holidays. Baker playing with his boys. We had interrupted their routine. A high-pitched, gold clock in a glass case ticked very fast on the mantelpiece. There was a postcard of the Lake of Geneva leaning against it. The Bakers had friends in Switzerland.

Doctor Baker came back into the room with a large book and a file-case in his hands. He carried them over to the table. 'I've brought the collection for last year,' he said. 'I haven't been through them yet since we moved. I only gave up practice six months ago you know.' He opened the book and began turning the pages. I watched him fascinated. He would find it of course. It was only a question of moments now, of seconds. 'The seventh, eighth, tenth,' he murmured, 'nothing here. The twelfth did you say? At two o'clock? Ah!'

We none of us moved. We all watched his face.

'I saw a Mrs Danvers on the twelfth at two o'clock,' he said.

'Danny? What on earth . . .' began Favell, but Maxim cut him short.

'She gave a wrong name, of course,' he said. 'That was obvious from the first. Do you remember the visit now, Doctor Baker?'

But Doctor Baker was already searching his files. I saw his fingers delve into the pocket marked with D. He found it almost at once. He glanced down rapidly at his handwriting. 'Yes,' he said slowly. 'Yes, Mrs Danvers. I remember now.'

'Tall, slim, dark, very handsome?' said Colonel Julyan quietly.

'Yes,' said Doctor Baker. 'Yes.'

He read through the files, and then replaced them in the case. 'Of course,' he said, glancing at Maxim, 'this is unprofessional you know? We treat patients as though they were in the confessional. But your wife is dead, and I quite understand the circumstances are exceptional. You want to know if I can suggest any motive why your wife should have taken her life? I think I can. The woman who called herself Mrs Danvers was very seriously ill.'

He paused. He looked at every one of us in turn.

'I remember her perfectly well,' he said, and he turned back to the files again. 'She came to me for the first time a week previously to the date you mentioned. She complained of certain symptoms, and I took some X-rays of her. The second visit was to find out the result of those X-rays. The photographs are not here, but I have the details written down. I remember her standing in my consulting room and holding out her hand for the photographs. "I want to know the truth," she said; "I don't want soft words and a bedside manner. If I'm for it, you can tell me right away."' He paused, he glanced down at the files once again.

I waited, waited. Why couldn't he get done with it and finish and let us go? Why must we sit there, waiting, our eyes upon his face.

'Well,' he said, 'she asked for the truth, and I let her have it. Some patients are better for it. Shirking the point does them no good. This Mrs Danvers, or Mrs de Winter rather, was not the type to accept a lie. You must have known that. She stood it very well. She did not flinch. She said she had suspected it for some time. Then she paid my fee and went out. I never saw her again.'

He shut up the box with a snap, and closed the book. 'The pain was slight as yet, but the growth was deep-rooted,' he said, 'and in three or four months' time she would have been under morphia. An operation would have been no earthly use at all. I told her that. The thing had got too firm a hold. There is nothing anyone can do in a case like that, except give morphia, and wait.'

No one said a word. The little clock ticked on the mantelpiece, and the boys played tennis in the garden. An aeroplane hummed overhead.

'Outwardly of course she was a perfectly healthy woman,' he said – 'rather too thin, I remember, rather pale; but then that's the fashion nowadays, pity though it is. It's nothing to go upon with a patient. No, the pain would increase week by week, and as I told you, in four or five months' time she would have had to be kept under morphia. The X-rays showed a certain malformation of the uterus, I remember, which meant she could never have had a child; but that was quite apart, it had nothing to do with the disease.'

I remember hearing Colonel Julyan speak, saying something about Doctor Baker being very kind to have taken so much trouble. 'You have told us all we want to know,' he said, 'and if we could possibly have a copy of the memoranda in your file it might be very useful.'

'Of course,' said Doctor Baker. 'Of course.'

Everyone was standing up. I got up from my chair too, I shook hands with Doctor Baker. We all shook hands with him. We followed him out into the hall. A woman looked out of the room on the other side of the hall and darted back when she saw us. Someone was running a bath upstairs, the water ran loudly. The Scotch terrier came in from the garden and began sniffing at my heels.

'Shall I send the report to you or to Mr de Winter?' said Doctor Baker.

'We may not need it at all,' said Colonel Julyan. 'I rather think it won't be necessary. Either de Winter or I will write. Here is my card.'

'I'm so glad to have been of use,' said Doctor Baker; 'it never entered my head for a moment that Mrs de Winter and Mrs Danvers could be the same person.'

'No, naturally,' said Colonel Julyan.

'You'll be returning to London, I suppose?'

'Yes. Yes, I imagine so.'

'Your best way then is to turn sharp left by that pillar-box, and then right by the church. After that it's a straight road.'

'Thank you. Thank you very much.'

We came out on to the drive and went towards the cars. Doctor Baker pulled the Scotch terrier inside the house. I heard the door shut. A man with one leg and a barrel-organ began playing 'Roses in Picardy', at the end of the road.

27

WE WENT AND stood by the car. No one said anything for a few minutes. Colonel Julyan handed round his cigarette case. Favell looked grey, rather shaken. I noticed his hands were trembling as he held the match. The man with the barrel-organ ceased playing for a moment and hobbled towards us, his cap in his hand. Maxim gave him two shillings. Then he went back to the barrel-organ and started another tune. The church clock struck six o'clock. Favell began to speak. His voice was diffident, careless, but his face was still grey. He did not look at any of us, he kept glancing down at his cigarette and turning it over in his fingers. 'This cancer business,' he said; 'does anybody know if it's contagious?'

No one answered him. Colonel Julyan shrugged his shoulders.

'I never had the remotest idea,' said Favell jerkily. 'She kept it a secret from everyone, even Danny. What a God-damned appalling thing, eh? Not the sort of thing one would ever connect with Rebecca. Do you fellows feel like a drink? I'm all out over this, and I don't mind admitting it. Cancer! Oh, my God!'

He leant up against the side of the car and shaded his eyes with his hands. 'Tell that bloody fellow with the barrel-organ to clear out,' he said. 'I can't stand that God-damned row.'

'Wouldn't it be simpler if we went ourselves?' said Maxim. 'Can you manage your own car, or do you want Julyan to drive it for you?'

'Give me a minute,' muttered Favell. 'I'll be all right. You don't understand. This thing has been a damned unholy shock to me.'

'Pull yourself together, man, for heaven's sake,' said Colonel Julyan. 'If you want a drink go back to the house and ask Baker. He knows how to treat for shock, I dare say. Don't make an exhibition of yourself in the street.'

'Oh, you're all right, you're fine,' said Favell, standing straight and looking at Colonel Julyan and Maxim. 'You've got nothing to worry about any more. Max is on a good wicket now, isn't he? You've got your motive, and Baker will supply it in black and white free of cost, whenever you send the word. You can dine at Manderley once a week on the strength of it and feel proud of yourself. No doubt Max will ask you to be godfather to his first child.'

'Shall we get into the car and go?' said Colonel Julyan to Maxim. 'We can make our plans going along.'

Maxim held open the door of the car, and Colonel Julyan climbed in. I sat down in my seat in the front. Favell still leant against the car and did not move. 'I should advise you to get straight back to your flat and go to bed,' said Colonel Julyan shortly, 'and drive slowly, or you will find yourself in jail for manslaughter. I may as well warn you now, as I shall not be seeing you again, that as a magistrate I have certain powers that will prove effective if you ever turn up in Kerrith or the district. Blackmail is not much of a profession, Mr Favell. And we know how to deal with it in our part of the world, strange though it may seem to you.'

Favell was watching Maxim. He had lost the grey colour now, and the old unpleasant smile was forming on his lips. 'Yes, it's been a stroke of luck for you, Max, hasn't it?' he said slowly; 'you think you've won, don't you? The law can get you yet, and so can I, in a different way . . .'

Maxim switched on the engine. 'Have you anything else you want to say?' he said; 'because if you have you had better say it now.'

'No,' said Favell. 'No, I won't keep you. You can go.' He stepped back on to the pavement, the smile still on his lips. The car slid forward. As we turned the corner I looked back and saw him standing there, watching us, and he waved his hand and he was laughing.

We drove on for a while in silence. Then Colonel Julyan spoke. 'He can't do anything,' he said. 'That smile and that wave were part of his bluff. They're all alike, those fellows. He hasn't a thread of a case to bring now. Baker's evidence would squash it.

Maxim did not answer. I glanced sideways at his face but it
told me nothing. 'I always felt the solution would lie in Baker,'
said Colonel Julyan; 'the furtive business of that appointment,
and the way she never even told Mrs Danvers. She had her suspicions, you see. She knew something was wrong. A dreadful thing,
of course. Very dreadful. Enough to send a young and lovely
woman right off her head.'

We drove on along the straight main road. Telegraph poles,
motor-coaches, open sports cars, little semi-detached villas with
new gardens, they flashed past making patterns in my mind
I should always remember.

'I suppose you never had any idea of this, de Winter?' said
Colonel Julyan.

'No,' said Maxim. 'No.'

'Of course some people have a morbid dread of it,' said
Colonel Julyan. 'Women especially. That must have been the
case with your wife. She had courage for every other thing
but that. She could not face pain. Well, she was spared that at
any rate.'

'Yes,' said Maxim.

'I don't think it would do any harm if I quietly let it be known
down in Kerrith and in the county that a London doctor has supplied us with a motive,' said Colonel Julyan. 'Just in case there
should be any gossip. You never can tell, you know. People are
odd, sometimes. If they knew about Mrs de Winter it might
make it a lot easier for you.'

'Yes,' said Maxim, 'yes, I understand.'

'It's curious and very irritating,' said Colonel Julyan slowly,
'how long stories spread in country districts. I never know why
they should, but unfortunately they do. Not that I anticipate any
trouble over this, but it's as well to be prepared. People are
inclined to say the wildest things if they are given half a chance.'

'Yes,' said Maxim.

'You and Crawley of course can squash any nonsense in Manderley or the estate, and I can deal with it effectively in Kerrith.
I shall say a word to my girl too. She sees a lot of the younger
people, who very often are the worst offenders in story-telling.
I don't suppose the newspapers will worry you any more, that's

one good thing. You'll find they will drop the whole affair in a day or two.'

'Yes,' said Maxim.

We drove on through the northern suburbs and came once more to Finchley and Hampstead.

'Half past six,' said Colonel Julyan; 'what do you propose doing? I've got a sister living in St John's Wood, and feel inclined to take her unawares and ask for dinner, and then catch the last train from Paddington. I know she doesn't go away for another week. I'm sure she would be delighted to see you both as well.'

Maxim hesitated, and glanced at me. 'It's very kind of you,' he said, 'but I think we had better be independent. I must ring up Frank, and one thing and another. I dare say we shall have a quiet meal somewhere and start off again afterwards, spending the night at a pub on the way, I rather think that's what we shall do.'

'Of course,' said Colonel Julyan, 'I quite understand. Could you throw me out at my sister's? It's one of those turnings off the Avenue Road.'

When we came to the house Maxim drew up a little way ahead of the gate. 'It's impossible to thank you,' he said, 'for all you've done today. You know what I feel about it without my telling you.'

'My dear fellow,' said Colonel Julyan, 'I've been only too glad. If only we'd known what Baker knew of course there would have been none of this at all. However, never mind about that now. You must put the whole thing behind you as a very unpleasant and unfortunate episode. I'm pretty sure you won't have any more trouble from Favell. If you do, I count on you to tell me at once. I shall know how to deal with him.' He climbed out of the car, collecting his coat and his map. 'I should feel inclined,' he said, not looking directly at us, 'to get away for a bit. Take a short holiday. Go abroad, perhaps.'

We did not say anything. Colonel Julyan was fumbling with his map. 'Switzerland is very nice this time of year,' he said. 'I remember we went once for the girl's holidays, and thoroughly enjoyed ourselves. The walks are delightful.' He hesitated, cleared his throat. 'It is just faintly possible certain little difficulties might arise,' he said, 'not from Favell, but from one or two people in the district. One never knows quite what Tabb has been saying, and repeating, and so on. Absurd of course. But you know the old saying? Out of sight, out of mind. If people aren't there to be talked about the talk dies. It's the way of the world.'

He stood for a moment, counting his belongings. 'I've got everything, I think. Map, glasses, stick, coat. Everything complete. Well, good-bye, both of you. Don't get over-tired. It's been a long day.'

He turned in at the gate and went up the steps. I saw a woman come to the window and smile and wave her hand. We drove away down the road and turned the corner. I leant back in my seat and closed my eyes. Now that we were alone again and the strain was over, the sensation was one of almost unbearable relief. It was like the bursting of an abscess. Maxim did not speak. I felt his hand cover mine. We drove on through the traffic and I saw none of it. I heard the rumble of the buses, the hooting of taxis, that inevitable, tireless London roar, but I was not part of it. I rested in some other place that was cool and quiet and still. Nothing could touch us any more. We had come through our crisis.

When Maxim stopped the car I opened my eyes and sat up. We were opposite one of those numerous little restaurants in a narrow street in Soho. I looked about me, dazed and stupid.

'You're tired,' said Maxim briefly. 'Empty and tired and fit for nothing. You'll be better when you've had something to eat. So shall I. We'll go in here and order dinner right away. I can telephone to Frank too.'

We got out of the car. There was no one in the restaurant but the *maître d'hôtel* and a waiter and a girl behind a desk. It was dark and cool. We went to a table right in the corner. Maxim began ordering the food. 'Favell was right about wanting a drink,' he said. 'I want one too and so do you. You're going to have some brandy.'

The *maître d'hotel* was fat and smiling. He produced long thin rolls in paper envelopes. They were very hard, very crisp. I began to eat one ravenously. My brandy-and-soda was soft, warming, curiously comforting.

'When we've had dinner we'll drive slowly, very quietly,' said Maxim. 'It will be cool, too, in the evening. We'll find somewhere on the road we can put up for the night. Then we can get along to Manderley in the morning.'

'Yes,' I said.

'You didn't want to dine with Julyan's sister and go down by the late train?'

'No.'

Maxim finished his drink. His eyes looked large and they were ringed with the shadows. They seemed very dark against the pallor of his face.

'How much of the truth', he said, 'do you think Julyan guessed?'

I watched him over the rim of my glass. I did not say anything.

'He knew,' said Maxim slowly, 'of course he knew.'

'If he did,' I said, 'he will never say anything. Never, never.'

'No,' said Maxim. 'No.'

He ordered another drink from the *maître d'hôtel*. We sat silent and peaceful in our dark corner.

'I believe', said Maxim, 'that Rebecca lied to me on purpose. The last supreme bluff. She wanted me to kill her. She foresaw the whole thing. That's why she laughed. That's why she stood there laughing when she died.'

I did not say anything. I went on drinking my brandy-and-soda. It was all over. It was all settled. It did not matter any more. There was no need for Maxim to look white and troubled.

'It was her last practical joke,' said Maxim, 'the best of them all. And I'm not sure if she hasn't won, even now.'

'What do you mean? How can she have won?' I said.

'I don't know,' he said. 'I don't know.' He swallowed his second drink. Then he got up from the table. 'I'm going to ring up Frank,' he said.

I sat there in my corner, and presently the waiter brought me my fish. It was lobster. Very hot and good. I had another brandy-and-soda, too. It was pleasant and comfortable sitting there and nothing mattered very much. I smiled at the waiter. I asked for some more bread in French for no reason. It was quiet and happy and friendly in the restaurant. Maxim and I were together.

Everything was over. Everything was settled. Rebecca was dead. Rebecca could not hurt us. She had played her last joke as Maxim had said. She could do no more to us now. In ten minutes Maxim came back again.

'Well,' I said, my own voice sounding far away, 'how was Frank?'

'Frank was all right,' said Maxim. 'He was at the office, been waiting there for me to telephone him ever since four o'clock. I told him what had happened. He sounded glad, relieved.'

'Yes,' I said.

'Something rather odd though,' said Maxim slowly, a line between his brows. 'He thinks Mrs Danvers has cleared out. She's gone, disappeared. She said nothing to anyone, but apparently she'd been packing up all day, stripping her room of things, and the fellow from the station came for her boxes at about four o'clock. Frith telephoned down to Frank about it, and Frank told Frith to ask Mrs Danvers to come down to him at the office. He waited, and she never came. About ten minutes before I rang up, Frith telephoned to Frank again and said there had been a long-distance call for Mrs Danvers which he had switched through to her room, and she had answered. This must have been about ten past six. At a quarter to seven he knocked on the door and found her room empty. Her bedroom too. They looked for her and could not find her. They think she's gone. She must have gone straight out of the house and through the woods. She never passed the lodge gates.'

'Isn't it a good thing?' I said. 'It saves us a lot of trouble. We should have had to send her away, anyway. I believe she guessed, too. There was an expression on her face last night. I kept thinking of it, coming up in the car.'

'I don't like it,' said Maxim. 'I don't like it.'

'She can't do anything,' I argued. 'If she's gone, so much the better. It was Favell who telephoned of course. He must have told her about Baker. He would tell her what Colonel Julyan said. Colonel Julyan said if there was any attempt at blackmail we were to tell him. They won't dare do it. They can't. It's too dangerous.'

'I'm not thinking of blackmail,' said Maxim.

'What else can they do?' I said. 'We've got to do what Colonel

Julyan said. We've got to forget it. We must not think about it any more. It's all over, darling, it's finished. We ought to go down on our knees and thank God that it's finished.'

Maxim did not answer. He was staring in front of him at nothing.

'Your lobster will be cold,' I said; 'eat it, darling. It will do you good, you want something inside you. You're tired.' I was using the words he had used to me. I felt better and stronger. It was I now who was taking care of him. He was tired, pale. I had got over my weakness and fatigue and now he was the one to suffer from reaction. It was just because he was empty, because he was tired. There was nothing to worry about at all. Mrs Danvers had gone. We should praise God for that, too. Everything had been made so easy for us, so very easy. 'Eat up your fish,' I said.

It was going to be very different in the future. I was not going to be nervous and shy with the servants any more. With Mrs Danvers gone I should learn bit by bit to control the house. I would go and interview the cook in the kitchen. They would like me, respect me. Soon it would be as though Mrs Danvers had never had command. I would learn more about the estate, too. I should ask Frank to explain things to me. I was sure Frank liked me. I liked him, too. I would go into things, and learn how they were managed. What they did at the farm. How the work in the grounds was planned. I might take to gardening myself, and in time have one or two things altered. That little square lawn outside the morning-room with the statue of the satyr. I did not like it. We would give the satyr away. There were heaps of things that I could do, little by little. People would come and stay and I should not mind. There would be the interest of seeing to their rooms, having flowers and books put, arranging the food. We would have children. Surely we would have children.

'Have you finished?' said Maxim suddenly. 'I don't think I want any more. Only coffee. Black, very strong, please, and the bill,' he added to the *maître d'hôtel*.

I wondered why we must go so soon. It was comfortable in the restaurant, and there was nothing to take us away. I liked sitting there, with my head against the sofa back, planning the future idly in a hazy pleasant way. I could have gone on sitting there for a long while.

I followed Maxim out of the restaurant, stumbling a little, and yawning. 'Listen,' he said, when we were on the pavement, 'do you think you could sleep in the car if I wrapped you up with the rug, and tucked you down in the back. There's the cushion there, and my coat as well.'

'I thought we were going to put up somewhere for the night?' I said blankly. 'One of those hotels one passes on the road.'

'I know,' he said, 'but I have this feeling I must get down tonight. Can't you possibly sleep in the back of the car?'

'Yes,' I said doubtfully. 'Yes, I suppose so.'

'If we start now, it's a quarter to eight, we ought to be there by half past two,' he said. 'There won't be much traffic on the road.'

'You'll be so tired,' I said. 'So terribly tired.'

'No,' he shook his head. 'I shall be all right. I want to get home. Something's wrong. I know it is. I want to get home.'

His face was anxious, strange. He pulled open the door and began arranging the rugs and the cushion at the back of the car.

'What can be wrong?' I said. 'It seems so odd to worry now, when everything's over. I can't understand you.'

He did not answer. I climbed into the back of the car and lay down with my legs tucked under me. He covered me with the rug. It was very comfortable. Much better than I imagined. I settled the pillow under my head.

'Are you all right?' he said; 'are you sure you don't mind?'

'No,' I said, smiling. 'I'm all right. I shall sleep. I don't want to stay anywhere on the road. It's much better to do this and get home. We'll be at Manderley long before sunrise.'

He got in in front and switched on the engine. I shut my eyes. The car drew away and I felt the slight jolting of the springs under my body. I pressed my face against the cushion. The motion of the car was rhythmic, steady, and the pulse of my mind beat with it. A hundred images came to me when I closed my eyes, things seen, things known, and things forgotten. They were jumbled together in a senseless pattern. The quill of Mrs Van Hopper's hat, the hard straight-backed chairs in Frank's dining-room, the wide window in the west wing at Manderley, the salmon-coloured frock of the smiling lady at the fancy dress ball, a peasant girl in a road near Monte Carlo.

Sometimes I saw Jasper chasing butterflies across the lawns; sometimes I saw Doctor Baker's Scotch terrier scratching his ear beside a deck-chair. There was the postman who had pointed out the house to us today, and there was Clarice's mother wiping a chair for me in the back parlour. Ben smiled at me, holding winkles in his hands, and the bishop's wife asked me if I would stay to tea. I could feel the cold comfort of my sheets in my own bed, and the gritty shingle in the cove. I could smell the bracken in the woods, the wet moss, and the dead azalea petals. I fell into a strange broken sleep, waking now and again to the reality of my narrow cramped position and the sight of Maxim's back in front of me. The dusk had turned to darkness. There were the lights of passing cars upon the road. There were villages with drawn curtains and little lights behind them. And I would move, and turn upon my back, and sleep again.

I saw the staircase at Manderley, and Mrs Danvers standing at the top in her black dress, waiting for me to go to her. As I climbed the stairs she backed under the archway and disappeared. I looked for her and I could not find her. Then her face looked at me through a hollow door and I cried out and she had gone again.

'What's the time?' I called. 'What's the time?'

Maxim turned round to me, his face pale and ghostly in the darkness of the car. 'It's half past eleven,' he said. 'We're over halfway already. Try and sleep again.'

'I'm thirsty,' I said.

He stopped at the next town. The man at the garage said his wife had not gone to bed and she would make us some tea. We got out of the car and stood inside the garage. I stamped up and down to bring the blood back to my hands and feet. Maxim smoked a cigarette. It was cold. A bitter wind blew in through the open garage door, and rattled the corrugated roof. I shivered, and buttoned up my coat.

'Yes, it's nippy tonight,' said the garage man, as he wound the petrol pump. 'The weather seemed to break this afternoon. It's the last of the heat waves for this summer. We shall be thinking of fires soon.'

'It was hot in London,' I said.

'Was it?' he said. 'Well, they always have the extremes up there, don't they? We get the first of the bad weather down here. It will blow hard on the coast before morning.'

His wife brought us the tea. It tasted of bitter wood, but it was hot. I drank it greedily, thankfully. Already Maxim was glancing at his watch.

'We ought to be going,' he said. 'It's ten minutes to twelve.' I left the shelter of the garage reluctantly. The cold wind blew in my face. The stars raced across the sky. There were threads of cloud too. 'Yes,' said the garage man, 'summer's over for this year.'

We climbed back into the car. I settled myself once more under the rug. The car went on. I shut my eyes. There was the man with the wooden leg winding his barrel-organ, and the tune of 'Roses in Picardy' hummed in my head against the jolting of the car. Frith and Robert carried the tea into the library. The woman at the lodge nodded to me abruptly, and called her child into the house. I saw the model boats in the cottage in the cove, and the feathery dust. I saw the cobwebs stretching from the little masts. I heard the rain upon the roof and the sound of the sea. I wanted to get to the Happy Valley and it was not there. There were woods about me, there was no Happy Valley. Only the dark trees and the young bracken. The owls hooted. The moon was shining in the windows of Manderley. There were nettles in the garden, ten foot, twenty foot high.

'Maxim!' I cried. 'Maxim!'

'Yes,' he said. 'It's all right, I'm here.'

'I had a dream,' I said. 'A dream.'

'What was it?' he said.

'I don't know. I don't know.'

Back again into the moving unquiet depths. I was writing letters in the morning-room. I was sending out invitations. I wrote them all myself with a thick black pen. But when I looked down to see what I had written it was not my small square handwriting at all, it was long, and slanting, with curious pointed strokes.

I pushed the cards away from the blotter and hid them. I got up and went to the looking-glass. A face stared back at me that was not my own. It was very pale, very lovely, framed in a cloud of dark hair. The eyes narrowed and smiled. The lips parted. The face in the glass stared back at me and laughed. And I saw then that she was sitting on a chair before the dressing-table in her bed-room, and Maxim was brushing her hair. He held her hair in his hands, and as he brushed it he wound it slowly into a thick rope. It twisted like a snake, and he took hold of it with both hands and smiled at Rebecca and put it round his neck.

'No,' I screamed. 'No, no. We must go to Switzerland. Col-onel Julyan said we must go to Switzerland.'

I felt Maxim's hand upon my face. 'What is it?' he said. 'What's the matter?'

I sat up and pushed my hair away from my face.

'I can't sleep,' I said. 'It's no use.'

'You've been sleeping,' he said. 'You've slept for two hours. It's quarter past two. We're four miles the other side of Lanyon.'

It was even colder than before. I shuddered in the darkness of the car.

'I'll come beside you,' I said. 'We shall be back by three.'

I climbed over and sat beside him, staring in front of me through the wind screen. I put my hand on his knee. My teeth were chattering.

'You're cold,' he said.

'Yes,' I said.

The hills rose in front of us, and dipped, and rose again. It was quite dark. The stars had gone.

'What time did you say it was?' I asked.

'Twenty past two,' he said.

'It's funny,' I said. 'It looks almost as though the dawn was breaking over there, beyond those hills. It can't be though, it's too early.'

'It's the wrong direction,' he said, 'you're looking west.'

'I know,' I said. 'It's funny, isn't it?'

He did not answer and I went on watching the sky. It seemed to get lighter even as I stared. Like the first red streak of sunrise. Little by little it spread across the sky.

'It's in winter you see the northern lights, isn't it?' I said. 'Not in summer?'

'That's not the northern lights,' he said. 'That's Manderley.'

I glanced at him and saw his face. I saw his eyes.

'Maxim,' I said. 'Maxim, what is it?'

He drove faster, much faster. We topped the hill before us and saw Lanyon lying in a hollow at our feet. There to the left of us was the silver streak of the river, widening to the estuary at Kerrith six miles away. The road to Manderley lay ahead. There was no moon. The sky above our heads was inky black. But the sky on the horizon was not dark at all. It was shot with crimson, like a splash of blood. And the ashes blew towards us with the salt wind from the sea.

ABOUT THE INTRODUCER

LUCY HUGHES-HALLET is the author of *Cleopatra: Histories, Dreams and Distortions*, *Heroes: Saviours, Traitors and Supermen* and *The Pike: Gabriele D'Annunzio, Poet, Seducer and Preacher of War*.

CHINUA ACHEBE
The African Trilogy
Things Fall Apart

AESCHYLUS
The Oresteia

ISABEL ALLENDE
The House of the Spirits

MARTIN AMIS
London Fields

THE ARABIAN NIGHTS

ISAAC ASIMOV
Foundation
Foundation and Empire
Second Foundation
(in 1 vol.)

MARGARET ATWOOD
The Handmaid's Tale

JOHN JAMES AUDUBON
The Audubon Reader

AUGUSTINE
The Confessions

JANE AUSTEN
Emma
Mansfield Park
Northanger Abbey
Persuasion
Pride and Prejudice
Sanditon and Other Stories
Sense and Sensibility

JAMES BALDWIN
Giovanni's Room
Go Tell It on the Mountain

HONORÉ DE BALZAC
Cousin Bette
Eugénie Grandet
Old Goriot

MIKLOS BANFFY
The Transylvanian Trilogy
(in 2 vols)

JOHN BANVILLE
The Book of Evidence
The Sea (in 1 vol.)

JULIAN BARNES
Flaubert's Parrot
A History of the World in
10½ Chapters (in 1 vol.)

GIORGIO BASSANI
The Garden of the Finzi-Continis

SIMONE DE BEAUVOIR
The Second Sex

SAMUEL BECKETT
Molloy, Malone Dies,
The Unnamable

SAUL BELLOW
The Adventures of Augie March

HECTOR BERLIOZ
The Memoirs of Hector Berlioz

THE BIBLE
(King James Version)
The Old Testament
The New Testament

WILLIAM BLAKE
Poems and Prophecies

GIOVANNI BOCCACCIO
Decameron

JORGE LUIS BORGES
Ficciones

JAMES BOSWELL
The Life of Samuel Johnson
The Journal of a Tour to
the Hebrides

RAY BRADBURY
The Stories of Ray Bradbury

JEAN ANTHELME
BRILLAT-SAVARIN
The Physiology of Taste

ANNE BRONTË
Agnes Grey and The Tenant of
Wildfell Hall

CHARLOTTE BRONTË
Jane Eyre
Villette
Shirley and The Professor

EMILY BRONTË
Wuthering Heights

MIKHAIL BULGAKOV
The Master and Margarita

EDMUND BURKE
Reflections on the Revolution in
France and Other Writings

SAMUEL BUTLER
The Way of all Flesh

A. S. BYATT
Possession

JAMES M. CAIN
The Postman Always Rings Twice
Double Indemnity
Mildred Pierce
Selected Stories
(in 1 vol. US only)

ITALO CALVINO
If on a winter's night a traveler

ALBERT CAMUS
The Outsider (UK)
The Stranger (US)
The Plague, The Fall,
Exile and the Kingdom,
and Selected Essays (in 1 vol.)

GIACOMO CASANOVA
History of My Life

WILLA CATHER
Death Comes for the
Archbishop (US only)
My Ántonia
O Pioneers!

BENVENUTO CELLINI
The Autobiography of
Benvenuto Cellini

MIGUEL DE CERVANTES
Don Quixote

RAYMOND CHANDLER
The novels (in 2 vols)
Collected Stories

GEOFFREY CHAUCER
Canterbury Tales

ANTON CHEKHOV
The Complete Short Novels
My Life and Other Stories
The Steppe and Other Stories

G. K. CHESTERTON
The Everyman Chesterton

KATE CHOPIN
The Awakening

CARL VON CLAUSEWITZ
On War

S. T. COLERIDGE
Poems

WILKIE COLLINS
The Moonstone
The Woman in White

CONFUCIUS
The Analects

JOSEPH CONRAD
Heart of Darkness
Lord Jim
Nostromo
The Secret Agent
Typhoon and Other Stories
Under Western Eyes
Victory

JULIO CORTÁZAR
Hopscotch
Blow-Up and Other Stories
We Love Glenda So Much and
Other Tales
(in 1 vol.)

THOMAS CRANMER
The Book of Common Prayer
(UK only)

ROALD DAHL
Collected Stories

DANTE ALIGHIERI
The Divine Comedy

CHARLES DARWIN
The Origin of Species
The Voyage of the Beagle
(in 1 vol.)

DANIEL DEFOE
Moll Flanders
Robinson Crusoe

CHARLES DICKENS
Barnaby Rudge
Bleak House
A Christmas Carol and
Other Christmas Books
David Copperfield
Dombey and Son
Great Expectations
Hard Times
Little Dorrit
Martin Chuzzlewit
The Mystery of Edwin Drood
Nicholas Nickleby
The Old Curiosity Shop
Oliver Twist
Our Mutual Friend
The Pickwick Papers
A Tale of Two Cities

DENIS DIDEROT
Memoirs of a Nun

JOAN DIDION
We Tell Ourselves Stories in Order
to Live (US only)

JOHN DONNE
The Complete English Poems

FYODOR DOSTOEVSKY
The Adolescent
The Brothers Karamazov
Crime and Punishment
Demons
The Double and The Gambler
The Idiot
Notes from Underground

ARTHUR CONAN DOYLE
The Hound of the Baskervilles
Study in Scarlet
The Sign of Four
(in 1 vol.)

W. E. B. DU BOIS
The Souls of Black Folk
(US only)

ALEXANDRE DUMAS
The Count of Monte Cristo
The Three Musketeers

DAPHNE DU MAURIER
Rebecca

UMBERTO ECO
The Name of the Rose

GEORGE ELIOT
Adam Bede
Daniel Deronda
Middlemarch
The Mill on the Floss
Silas Marner

JOHN EVELYN
The Diary of John Evelyn
(UK only)

J. G. FARRELL
The Siege of Krishnapur
and Troubles

WILLIAM FAULKNER
The Sound and the Fury
(UK only)

HENRY FIELDING
Joseph Andrews and Shamela
(UK only)
Tom Jones

F. SCOTT FITZGERALD
The Great Gatsby
This Side of Paradise
(UK only)

PENELOPE FITZGERALD
The Bookshop
The Gate of Angels
The Blue Flower (in 1 vol.)
Offshore
Human Voices
The Beginning of Spring
(in 1 vol.)

GUSTAVE FLAUBERT
Madame Bovary

FORD MADOX FORD
The Good Soldier
Parade's End

RICHARD FORD
The Bascombe Novels

E. M. FORSTER
Howards End
A Passage to India
A Room with a View,
Where Angels Fear to Tread
(in 1 vol., US only)

ANNE FRANK
The Diary of a Young Girl
(US only)

BENJAMIN FRANKLIN
The Autobiography
and Other Writings

GEORGE MACDONALD
FRASER
Flashman
Flash for Freedom!
Flashman in the Great Game
(in 1 vol.)

MAVIS GALLANT
The Collected Stories

ELIZABETH GASKELL
Mary Barton

EDWARD GIBBON
The Decline and Fall of the
Roman Empire
Vols 1 to 3: The Western Empire
Vols 4 to 6: The Eastern Empire

KAHLIL GIBRAN
The Collected Works

J. W. VON GOETHE
Selected Works

NIKOLAI GOGOL
The Collected Tales
Dead Souls

IVAN GONCHAROV
Oblomov

GÜNTER GRASS
The Tin Drum

GRAHAM GREENE
Brighton Rock
The Human Factor

DASHIELL HAMMETT
The Maltese Falcon
The Thin Man
Red Harvest
(in 1 vol.)
The Dain Curse,
The Glass Key,
and Selected Stories

THOMAS HARDY
Far From the Madding Crowd
Jude the Obscure
The Mayor of Casterbridge
The Return of the Native
Tess of the d'Urbervilles
The Woodlanders

JAROSLAV HAŠEK
The Good Soldier Švejk

NATHANIEL HAWTHORNE
The Scarlet Letter

JOSEPH HELLER
Catch-22

ERNEST HEMINGWAY
A Farewell to Arms
The Collected Stories
(UK only)

GEORGE HERBERT
The Complete English Works

HERODOTUS
The Histories

MICHAEL HERR
Dispatches (US only)

PATRICIA HIGHSMITH
The Talented Mr. Ripley
Ripley Under Ground
Ripley's Game
(in 1 vol.)

HINDU SCRIPTURES
(tr. R. C. Zaehner)

JAMES HOGG
Confessions of a Justified Sinner

HOMER
The Iliad
The Odyssey

VICTOR HUGO
The Hunchback of Notre-Dame
Les Misérables

ALDOUS HUXLEY
Brave New World

KAZUO ISHIGURO
The Remains of the Day

HENRY JAMES
The Ambassadors
The Awkward Age
The Bostonians
The Golden Bowl
The Portrait of a Lady
The Princess Casamassima
Washington Square
The Wings of the Dove
Collected Stories (in 2 vols)

SAMUEL JOHNSON
A Journey to the Western
Islands of Scotland

JAMES JOYCE
Dubliners
A Portrait of the Artist as
a Young Man
Ulysses

FRANZ KAFKA
Collected Stories
The Castle
The Trial

JOHN KEATS
The Poems

SØREN KIERKEGAARD
Fear and Trembling and
The Book on Adler

MAXINE HONG KINGSTON
The Woman Warrior and
China Men
(US only)

RUDYARD KIPLING
Collected Stories
Kim

THE KORAN
(tr. Marmaduke Pickthall)

GIUSEPPE TOMASI DI
LAMPEDUSA
The Leopard

WILLIAM LANGLAND
Piers Plowman
with (anon.) Sir Gawain and the
Green Knight, Pearl, Sir Orfeo
(UK only)

D. H. LAWRENCE
Collected Stories
The Rainbow
Sons and Lovers
Women in Love

MIKHAIL LERMONTOV
A Hero of Our Time

DORIS LESSING
Stories

PRIMO LEVI
If This is a Man and The Truce
(UK only)
The Periodic Table

THE MABINOGION

NICCOLÒ MACHIAVELLI
The Prince

NAGUIB MAHFOUZ
The Cairo Trilogy
Three Novels of Ancient Egypt

THOMAS MANN
Buddenbrooks
Collected Stories (UK only)
Death in Venice and Other Stories
(US only)
Doctor Faustus
Joseph and His Brothers
The Magic Mountain

KATHERINE MANSFIELD
The Garden Party and Other
Stories

ALESSANDRO MANZONI
The Betrothed

MARCUS AURELIUS
Meditations

GABRIEL GARCÍA MÁRQUEZ
The General in His Labyrinth
Love in the Time of Cholera
One Hundred Years of Solitude

ANDREW MARVELL
The Complete Poems

W. SOMERSET MAUGHAM
Collected Stories
Of Human Bondage
The Skeptical Romancer (US only)

CORMAC McCARTHY
The Border Trilogy

IAN McEWAN
Atonement

HERMAN MELVILLE
The Complete Shorter Fiction
Moby-Dick

JOHN STUART MILL
On Liberty and Utilitarianism

JOHN MILTON
The Complete English Poems

YUKIO MISHIMA
The Temple of the
Golden Pavilion

MARY WORTLEY MONTAGU
Letters

MICHEL DE MONTAIGNE
The Complete Works

THOMAS MORE
Utopia

TONI MORRISON
Beloved
Song of Solomon

JOHN MUIR
Selected Writings

ALICE MUNRO
Carried Away: A Selection of
Stories

MURASAKI SHIKIBU
The Tale of Genji

IRIS MURDOCH
The Sea, The Sea
A Severed Head
(in 1 vol.)

VLADIMIR NABOKOV
Lolita
Pale Fire
Pnin
Speak, Memory

V. S. NAIPAUL
Collected Short Fiction (US only)
A House for Mr Biswas

R. K. NARAYAN
Swami and Friends
The Bachelor of Arts
The Dark Room
The English Teacher
(in 1 vol.)
Mr Sampath – The Printer of
Malgudi
The Financial Expert
Waiting for the Mahatma
(in 1 vol.)

IRÈNE NÉMIROVSKY
David Golder
The Ball
Snow in Autumn
The Courilof Affair
(in 1 vol.)

FLANN O'BRIEN
The Complete Novels

FRANK O'CONNOR
The Best of Frank O'Connor

MICHAEL ONDAATJE
The English Patient

GEORGE ORWELL
Animal Farm
Nineteen Eighty-Four
Essays
Burmese Days, Keep the Aspidistra
Flying, Coming Up for Air
(in 1 vol.)

OVID
The Metamorphoses

THOMAS PAINE
Rights of Man
and Common Sense

ORHAN PAMUK
My Name is Red
Snow

BORIS PASTERNAK
Doctor Zhivago

SYLVIA PLATH
The Bell Jar (US only)

PLATO
The Republic
Symposium and Phaedrus

EDGAR ALLAN POE
The Complete Stories

MARCO POLO
The Travels of Marco Polo

MARCEL PROUST
In Search of Lost Time
(in 4 vols, UK only)

PHILIP PULLMAN
His Dark Materials

ALEXANDER PUSHKIN
The Collected Stories

FRANÇOIS RABELAIS
Gargantua and Pantagruel

JOSEPH ROTH
The Radetzky March

JEAN-JACQUES
ROUSSEAU
Confessions
The Social Contract and
the Discourses

SALMAN RUSHDIE
Midnight's Children

JOHN RUSKIN
Praeterita and Dilecta

PAUL SCOTT
The Raj Quartet (in 2 vols)

WALTER SCOTT
Rob Roy

WILLIAM SHAKESPEARE
Comedies Vols 1 and 2
Histories Vols 1 and 2
Romances
Sonnets and Narrative Poems
Tragedies Vols 1 and 2

MARY SHELLEY
Frankenstein

ADAM SMITH
The Wealth of Nations

ALEXANDER SOLZHENITSYN
One Day in the Life of
Ivan Denisovich

SOPHOCLES
The Theban Plays

MURIEL SPARK
The Prime of Miss Jean Brodie,
The Girls of Slender Means, The
Driver's Seat, The Only Problem
(in 1 vol.)

CHRISTINA STEAD
The Man Who Loved Children

JOHN STEINBECK
The Grapes of Wrath

STENDHAL
The Charterhouse of Parma
Scarlet and Black

LAURENCE STERNE
Tristram Shandy

ROBERT LOUIS STEVENSON
The Master of Ballantrae and
Weir of Hermiston
Dr Jekyll and Mr Hyde
and Other Stories

BRAM STOKER
Dracula

HARRIET BEECHER STOWE
Uncle Tom's Cabin

ITALO SVEVO
Zeno's Conscience

GRAHAM SWIFT
Waterland

JONATHAN SWIFT
Gulliver's Travels

TACITUS
Annals and Histories

JUNICHIRŌ TANIZAKI
The Makioka Sisters

W. M. THACKERAY
Vanity Fair

HENRY DAVID THOREAU
Walden

ALEXIS DE TOCQUEVILLE
Democracy in America

LEO TOLSTOY
Collected Shorter Fiction (in 2 vols)
Anna Karenina
Childhood, Boyhood and Youth
The Cossacks
War and Peace

ANTHONY TROLLOPE
Barchester Towers
Can You Forgive Her?
Doctor Thorne
The Duke's Children
The Eustace Diamonds
Framley Parsonage
The Last Chronicle of Barset
Phineas Finn
The Small House at Allington
The Warden

IVAN TURGENEV
Fathers and Children
First Love and Other Stories
A Sportsman's Notebook

MARK TWAIN
Tom Sawyer
and Huckleberry Finn

JOHN UPDIKE
The Complete Henry Bech
Rabbit Angstrom

GIORGIO VASARI
Lives of the Painters, Sculptors and
Architects (in 2 vols)

JULES VERNE
Journey to the Centre of the Earth
Twenty Thousand Leagues under
the Sea
Round the World in Eighty Days

VIRGIL
The Aeneid

VOLTAIRE
Candide and Other Stories

HORACE WALPOLE
Selected Letters

EVELYN WAUGH
(US only)
Black Mischief, Scoop, The Loved
One, The Ordeal of Gilbert
Pinfold (in 1 vol.)
Brideshead Revisited
Decline and Fall
A Handful of Dust

EVELYN WAUGH (cont.)
The Sword of Honour Trilogy
Waugh Abroad: Collected Travel
Writing
The Complete Short Stories

H. G. WELLS
The Time Machine,
The Invisible Man,
The War of the Worlds
(in 1 vol., US only)

EDITH WHARTON
The Age of Innocence
The Custom of the Country
Ethan Frome, Summer,
Bunner Sisters
(in 1 vol.)
The House of Mirth
The Reef

PATRICK WHITE
Voss

OSCAR WILDE
Plays, Prose Writings and Poems

P. G. WODEHOUSE
The Best of Wodehouse

MARY WOLLSTONECRAFT
A Vindication of the Rights of
Woman

VIRGINIA WOOLF
To the Lighthouse
Mrs Dalloway

WILLIAM WORDSWORTH
Selected Poems (UK only)

RICHARD YATES
Revolutionary Road
The Easter Parade
Eleven Kinds of Loneliness
(in 1 vol.)

W. B. YEATS
The Poems (UK only)

ÉMILE ZOLA
Germinal

This book is set in BEMBO which was cut
by the punch-cutter Francesco Griffo
for the Venetian printer-publisher
Aldus Manutius in early 1495
and first used in a pamphlet
by a young scholar
named Pietro
Bembo.

GEORGE BALANCHINE was born in 1904, and in 1913 began his dance training in St. Petersburg at the Imperial Theater School. In 1924 he left Russia and joined Serge Diaghilev's Ballets Russes in Monte Carlo, where he served as *maître de ballet*. After Diaghilev's death in 1929, he was guest ballet master of the Royal Danish Ballet, staged dances for London shows, and in Paris formed a company, Les Ballets 1933. At the end of 1933, he accepted Lincoln Kirstein's invitation to come to the United States to establish a ballet school and company. The great institutions that resulted were the School of American Ballet and the New York City Ballet, which Balanchine headed as artistic director and ballet master until his death in 1983.

CHOREOGRAPHY
BY GEORGE BALANCHINE

CHOREOGRAPHY
by
GEORGE BALANCHINE

A Catalogue of Works

An Eakins Press Foundation Book
VIKING

VIKING

Viking Penguin Inc., 40 West 23rd Street, New York, New York 10010, U.S.A.
Penguin Books Ltd, Harmondsworth, Middlesex, England
Penguin Books Australia Ltd, Ringwood, Victoria, Australia
Penguin Books Canada Limited, 2801 John Street, Markham, Ontario, Canada L3R 1B4
Penguin Books (N.Z.) Ltd, 182–190 Wairau Road, Auckland 10, New Zealand

This edition first published in 1984 by Viking Penguin Inc.
Published simultaneously in Canada

This edition, with new and additional material, is a reduced reproduction
by lithography of the original publication by the Eakins Press Foundation.
The book was set in Monotype Dante and
was originally printed in a limited edition by letterpress
at the Stamperia Valdonega in Verona, Italy.

Lyre by Pavel Tchelitchew from *Orpheus and Eurydice*, 1936
Epigraphs from an interview with Balanchine, 1978
Portrait by Tanaquil Le Clercq, 1952

LIBRARY OF CONGRESS CATALOGING IN PUBLICATION DATA

Choreography by George Balanchine.
1. Balanchine, George.   2. Ballet—Catalogs.   3. Choreography.
GV1785.B32C49   1984   792.8'2'0924 [B]   83-40475
ISBN 0-670-22008-6

Printed in the United States of America

The eye of man hath not heard,
the ear of man hath not seen,
man's hand is not able to taste,
his tongue to conceive,
nor his heart to report,
what my dream was.

WILLIAM SHAKESPEARE

Eye hath not seen, nor ear heard,
neither have entered into the heart of man,
the things which God hath prepared
for them that love him.

SAINT PAUL

CONTENTS

PREFACE   11

INTRODUCTION   15

CHRONOLOGY   23

CHRONOLOGICAL TITLE LIST   43

CATALOGUE   51

    CATALOGUE OF WORKS
      1920-1924 Russia   53
      1925-1929 Europe, with Serge Diaghilev   67
      1930-1933 Paris, Copenhagen, Monte Carlo, London   94
      1934-1945 America, with Lincoln Kirstein   117
      1946-1948 Ballet Society   170
      1948-1964 New York City Ballet—City Center   180
      1964-1982 New York City Ballet—New York State Theater   243

    SOURCE NOTES   289

APPENDIXES   295
    COMPANY ITINERARIES   297
    FESTIVALS DIRECTED   311
    ROLES PERFORMED   319

BIBLIOGRAPHY   331

ADDENDA   347

INDEXES   363
    TITLES BY CATEGORY   365
    KEY TO COMPANIES   373
    GENERAL INDEX   379

ACKNOWLEDGMENTS   421

A printed listing of the works of George Balanchine may be set along-side the Köchel catalogue of Mozart: the works of choreographer and composer share many qualities.

Balanchine has been extremely prolific. For over fifty years his invention has been uninterrupted. There has been hardly a season since he was a boy of eighteen when he has not brought out something new in the nature of dancing.

A catalogue is not a visualization, yet even a list demonstrates the extraordinary variety and inclusiveness of Balanchine's musical support and his unprecedented use of musical literature since the seventeenth century. A trained musician, he has been able to have always at his fingertips the quality of structure and sonority that fills his needs at a certain moment of development or necessity.

If he is to be compared with anyone in his time in the frame of his own talents, visual or plastic or musical, these must be Picasso and Stravinsky. Painting and musical composition, however, have had their universal acceptance for more than five hundred years, while classic academic dance, which issued from court-shows in the seventeenth century and court theaters in the nineteenth, has only in our own century begun to compete on an equal level of popularity with the repertories of opera and orchestra.

He has specialized in pièces d'occasion, creating musical celebrations. Certain events summon or suggest appropriate answers. He has operated on the order of public official as well as very private experimenter. He has been profligate in stage production when patronage was available, and parsimonious when decoration would have been superfluous or patronage was absent.

Balanchine issued from a school which inherited an imperial tradition. He left Russia at a time when the Soviet Union froze taste and attempted to stabilize artistic expression as a lowest common denominator. Entering the Diaghilev company in London at the age of twenty, he was plunged into an ambience of extreme artistic license for which he had prepared himself by student experiments even before leaving Leningrad. When Diaghilev died, five years later, Balanchine attempted to continue the formula of elegant improvisation with whatever means were at hand. Russia was closed, the Soviet schools were no longer a source for recruitment, and the efforts of European impresarios proved haphazard and without institutional stability.

Balanchine decided to come to the United States as if the decision was almost a foregone conclusion, although there were other possibilities which might have been attractive had he not already had the experience of the Diaghilev years. When he came to America late in 1933 he founded a school which would commence teaching American dancers, toward forming an eventual American company. The School of American Ballet was conceived to be a national service school like the Imperial School in St. Petersburg, which held parity with the military and naval academies.

The first company Balanchine organized was called the American Ballet. Balanchine's present company, founded in 1948, bears the name of the town that is its home, New York City, the cultural capital of the nation. The name of the school has remained the same. It is now a national service institution with students from forty states and more than a dozen nations. The city built Balanchine the theater he required. National foundations, recognizing their importance, gave his school and the New York City Ballet the support they needed.

His imperial ambitions as a servant of social democracy seem to have been fulfilled according to a logical schedule and a simple history. Reading the catalogue of his work, however, one may deduce some of the difficulties in the path, and along the way. The conditions of theatrical production, the size of companies, the presence or absence of patronage or money, the requirements of seasonal circumstance, all determine the state of repertory at a given moment. Just as certain ballets were abandoned and the effort ploughed under, so certain expenditures in nerve and work have served to braid sinew toward further strength. Many ballets are no longer performed, yet parallels and portions can be recognized as resurrected in subsequent dances.

The present adoption of classic dance throughout the country continues to appear a mystery to those who have come to its performances relatively lately. In one form or another, however, formal stage dance has been available to be seen in America for more than six decades. But now, in large measure due to Balanchine's insistence on a rigorous profile and authoritarian practice, classic ballet is less confused with other forms of dance, and its training has advanced toward high professional criteria and performance. It is granted the status of peak virtuosity — as hard to attain and as quick to be recognized as the violin, the piano or the Olympic categories.

One aspect of 'modernism' has been its effort to annihilate history, to create an art without precedent, to renovate sensibility, to canonize the New. We have had more than a half-century of newness, and suddenly it has aged. The classic ballet, born in the seventeenth century, combines historical legitimacy with contemporary manner. Its gestures are courtly, yet respond in accent, celerity and syncopation to the colloquial cadence of the day. Balanchine has defined the 'modern' direction of classic ballet.

Our century has licensed extremes of chaos and violence on the grandest scale known to man. The reflections in literature, music and the plastic arts of two world wars scarred the whole structure of the imaginative process. The fragmentary, the night-marish, the mad, exploited to their capacity of excess, have become mechanical, repetitive, dead-end.

The essence of ballet, on the other hand, is order. What one sees in Balanchine's ballets are structures of naked order, executed by celebrants who have no other aim than to show an aspect of order in their own persons, testifying to an impersonal purity and a personal interest.

There has undoubtedly occurred what must be called an unfocussed but active revival of religious interest in the West, seeking unfamiliar access to an absolute. It is not too much to consider a well-performed ballet a rite, executed and followed with intense devotion, that shares in some sort of moral figuration. The response of the audience to good dancing is a release of body and breath, a thanksgiving that is selfless, generous, complete, and leaves the spectator corroborated in the hope that, despite the world and its horrors, here somehow is a paradigm of perfection.

The consideration of last things, millennial factors, the approach of another century, wars and the rumor of war, surround us. We have a sense that the times we live in are extremely frail, that frailty is the single cohering net that connects. Nothing is more frail or transient than a ballet. Every action is evanescent, and after its enactment it is gone for good, or until a next time, when the same conditions obtain. Human bodies are frail. The design the dancers thread is also frail, and to a degree entirely imaginary. It can be learned, but never completely documented.

The whole operation of a ballet company is a microcosm of a civil condition. The frailty of its operation is that of any artistic or cultural institution in a civilization that prefers to spend its bounty on armament and consumer goods. However, a ballet company, existing in the interstices of the community, almost vaunts its hardy frailty. In an infinitesimal way, each good performance clears a small area of menace, and for the moment reminds us of the possible which, if it is not perfection, approaches it.

In this process of asserting the importance of the classic dance, Balanchine acts as a public servant of order. He is a maker and teacher. The twentieth century has specialized in the metrics of time and space. Nobody before has ever danced as fast as a Balanchine dancer; no one has ever had such markedly separate structures of steps to dance. No dancers before have been obliged to analyze with their feet the kinds of musical composition that Balanchine has set for them. Only a dancer dancing can say for him, what he says to them.

LINCOLN KIRSTEIN

*'I believe that if some Michelangelo were alive today—so it
occurred to me, looking at the frescoes in the Sistine Chapel—
the only thing that his genius would admit and recognize
is choreography. And this is now coming to life again . . . .
The only form of theatre art that makes its cornerstone
the problems of beauty and nothing more is the ballet,
just as the only goal that Michelangelo pursued was
the beauty of the perceived.'*

IGOR STRAVINSKY (1911)

On the basis of the ballets listed in this catalogue of works it is possible
to read the above words as a prophecy, fulfilled in the choreography
created by George Balanchine. In 1911, Balanchine was seven years old.
His first formal choreography was made in 1920, nine years later. *Apollo*,
to Stravinsky's music in 1928, became a catalytic moment that in addition
to commencing a partnership and creating a masterpiece marked a
new development and direction for classic dance in the twentieth
century. Balanchine's choreography renews and perpetuates ideals of
human skill and civilization that find their origin in the sources of
Euterpe and Terpsichore. He joins in one unbroken line, through dance,
the very earliest and very latest in human art.

Choreography by George Balanchine is a first chronological listing, giving
first-performance details, note of major revisions, a record of stagings,
and other information in a condensed form for each work Balanchine
has created since his student days through June, 1982. Research has
included archival study as well as correspondence and interviews with
associates and dancers in the United States, Canada, Mexico, South
America, England, Denmark, France, Germany, Austria, Monaco,
Spain, Italy, and the Soviet Union. Balanchine's own participation in
the effort has been invaluable.

Unlike the works of a musical composer, whose creations have the
permanence of written form, or those of a painter or sculptor, works of
dance are perpetuated through a tradition of staging that relies essentially not on notation, words, or even images preserved on film, but on
one dancer teaching another. Dance is living art. While certain works

survive and are perpetuated in repertory or in stagings at different times by different companies, even when remounted by the choreographer himself they often evolve, develop, and undergo revision, in detail if not in essentials.

The entries in *Choreography by George Balanchine* are based on records of premieres; ensuing performances by dancers who have danced roles throughout the life of a ballet, often in sustained repertory, cannot be documented within the scope of the book. Nor can the book reflect the essential contributions of the administrative and technical staffs whose continued dedication over the years has provided the structure upon which a ballet company depends for its existence. Credit cannot be given here to individual patrons whose generosity has made continuity of production possible. Photographic illustration is beyond the intention of the *Catalogue*.

Basic to Balanchine's accomplishment is the School of American Ballet; a special volume commemorating its fiftieth anniversary will give recognition to those teachers and directors who have nurtured generations of students. They have become the dancers for whom his choreography is designed.

Within the table of *Contents* headings designate and divide the choreographer's production, reflecting his principal locations, associations and milieu: Russia, Europe with Diaghilev, Europe after Diaghilev, the United States and early companies, followed by the formation of Ballet Society, culminating in the New York City Ballet.

The schematic *Chronology* is designed to provide the reader with a comprehensive overview and context of works year by year, giving the names of composers, relating the geographical location and Balanchine's company associations, and noting important events related to the progress of his undertakings. It is intended as a chronology of work, providing neither biography nor critical assessment.

The *Chronology* cannot suggest Balanchine's larger responsibilities, which have made the mounting of ballets possible. The choreographing and production of new works involves conception, selection and often commissioning of music, direction and approval of scenic and costume design, rehearsals and changes up to the moment of premiere, and adjustment and revision after. Balanchine's supervision and main-tenance of the repertory of the New York City Ballet has been accompanied by his organization and administration of the Company and the School: Although not commented upon in the *Chronology* or *Catalogue*, these factors play a constant and essential role in the creation of the listed works.

A *Chronological Title List* of numbered entries precedes the *Catalogue*. Entry numbers, rather than page numbers, are the primary reference indicators of the book and are used in the *Indexes*. Titles are given in the language of the premiere performance, with the exception of works first performed in Russia, which are given their most common Western title. Later or variant names of works appear in parentheses following the title; when a work enters the repertory of a later company under a different (or translated) name, that is given as title, with the original name following in parentheses. Subtitles of works are retained when given in printed programs, and are supplied to identify works other than ballets. The *Chronological Title List* is supplemented by an alphabetical listing of *Titles by Category*, given as one of the indexes; the categories are Ballet, Ballet for Opera, Opera, Opera-Ballet, Staged Choral Works, Operetta, Concert Works, Musical Theater, Theater, Circus, Film, and Television.

Each catalogue entry presents information under the subheadings MUSIC, PRODUCTION, PREMIERE, and CAST, and where appropriate, a NOTE, REVISIONS, STAGINGS, TELEVISION, and at the end, cross references in italics. Due to difficulty of access, and often fragmentary nature, notated scores and films of ballets have not been listed.

Subsequent mountings of a ballet that has entered the repertory of more than one of the companies directed by Balanchine, or entered the repertory of a company directed by him after having first been performed by another company, are given separate entries. Full information is included in the first entry; the later mountings appear in chronological sequence, with the principal entry number starred in the italic cross references, which also link different works choreographed to the same music. This serves to indicate the repeated and varying use of certain scores, and the importance of works that have remained in the repertory of different companies with which Balanchine has been associated, as for instance *Apollo*, which has entries in 1928 [84, Diaghilev's Ballets Russes], 1937 [176, American Ballet], 1941 [198, American Ballet Caravan], and 1951 [284, New York City Ballet]. For works which continued from the Ballet Society repertory directly into that of the New York City Ballet, no second entry is given.

Student performances are included only in cases where they are unique (such as *Circus Polka*, 1945 [230]), not when they are precedent to professional performances (such as *Serenade*, 1934 [141]).

Ballets choreographed for operas are principally short divertissements that appear as interludes, and have been given abbreviated entries, including all available information on the dance passages but not providing production information for the opera; full entries are given only for operas directed or staged by Balanchine.

Each work is treated as it appeared at the time of its creation and premiere, as a creative venture with an identity and existence of its own apart from its reception or survival. The long life in repertory of such well-known or key ballets as *Apollo, Serenade* and *Ballet Imperial* (*Tschaikovsky Piano Concerto No. 2*) is suggested by their several entries and detailed treatment; however, the entry gives no indication of how many performances the ballet received or whether it continues in repertory. The length of an entry is no indication of a ballet's significance or importance: *Kammermusik No. 2* [408], for example, receives a very short entry, while *House of Flowers* [305], because of its large cast and elaborate production, has a long entry.

Each entry begins with the subheading MUSIC, giving composer, title, date, and note of commission when applicable. The variation in duration of performance is extreme, from a few minutes to a full evening. For certain ballets, such as *Agon* [316] and *The Four Temperaments* [236], Balanchine commissioned scores; for others, such as *Jewels* [358], he is responsible not only for the selection of music but its sequence; and in other instances, such as *Union Jack* [401], he has commissioned the orchestration of existing music. For the purposes of his conceptions, he has also combined selections made from a number of works of the same composer, as in *A Midsummer Night's Dream* [340]. Readers unfamiliar with any specific work can form some idea of length by studying the MUSIC entry, together with other entry information.

Information concerning scenic design, costumes, décor, lighting, and executors is given under the subheading PRODUCTION. Listings under PREMIERE provide the date of the first performance, the name of the performing company, the theater or place of performance, and the names of the conductor and principal soloists.

Listings of CAST follow the original printed program. In addition to providing the names of principal dancers they frequently indicate roles,

scenes, or the movements of the music, suggesting the structure of
the work. When the cast listing does not refer to form or content,
principal dancers and soloists are distinguished from supporting dancers
and corps de ballet by the use of semicolons. Dancers' names have in
most instances been standardized to the form most commonly used
(for example, Geva rather than Gevergeyeva); in cases where the name
given in the program is a variant, there is a bracketed reference (as in
the case of Sylvia Giselle [Gisella Caccialanza]). The names of roles are
given throughout in English. When a synopsis of action is given under
CAST, it is taken from the printed program or musical score.

The NOTES within the entries are intended to provide minimal but
essential information not given under other subheadings. Although the
primary subject matter and content of all Balanchine ballets may be
described as dance itself, for those ballets that feature a subject, locale
or plot, in actuality or by suggestion, annotation has been provided.
Further description of many of the works may be found in sources
provided in the Bibliography.

Under REVISIONS, principal alterations of works are detailed. Major
remountings within the repertory of companies directed by Balanchine
are given under NEW PRODUCTIONS. When a work has had a completely
new interpretation, but retains the same music and title, there is a
listing of OTHER VERSIONS.

The names of professional companies which have staged each work
appear under STAGINGS, with the year of first performance. Ballets
requested (and even set), but never performed, are not included.
Restagings and revivals have not been included. When a company
changes its name or merges with another company, repertory often
carries over and no new first performance date is given; the exception is
the New York City Ballet and its predecessor companies (excluding
Ballet Society). Guest performances and performances by temporary
companies are generally not included. Company names are often
simplified; the Key to Companies Staging Balanchine Works, preceding the
General Index, provides information on the company name at the time
of staging and subsequently, as well as clarification of geographic
location, dates of existence, or note of disbanding.

Television versions of ballets are listed under the subheading
TELEVISION, with date and broadcasting channel; geographic locations
are given for foreign and little-known American channels, with the

names of such major program series as The Bell Telephone Hour and Dance in America. Full information on televised and filmed rehearsals and performances, including casts, production information, critical comments, and bibliographies of reviews, forms part of the project archive.

Following the *Catalogue* are *Source Notes*, which give sources of published and archival information, and especially information obtained from individuals, used to clarify or correct programs and to construct entries for works for which programs do not exist or have not been located. A number of persons closely associated with Balanchine who have generously provided valuable information are credited in the *Source Notes*.

The *Company Itineraries* provide context for Balanchine's work. Information on seasons and tours has been limited to American companies directed by him beginning in 1934. While his earlier travels after leaving Russia, and then with Diaghilev's Ballets Russes and after are partially indicated in the *Chronology*, the earlier and less well known periods of his career remain open to further study.

Festivals Directed by Balanchine lists the works of each performance (including works by choreographers other than Balanchine) for five principal festivals conceived by him and produced under his direction: the Stravinsky Festival, 1937; the Stravinsky Festival, 1972; the Ravel Festival, 1976; the Tschaikovsky Festival, 1981; and the Stravinsky Centennial Celebration, 1982.

Roles Performed by Balanchine is a list of all known roles performed from the choreographer's student days until the present.

The *Bibliography* includes all writings known to have been published by Balanchine, arranged chronologically, and a selection of books relating to him, arranged alphabetically. While not complete, the list has been chosen to provide an initial guide for further study. For the general reader, five titles can be described as principal reference works: *Balanchine's Complete Stories of the Great Ballets* (with Francis Mason; Doubleday, 1977); *The New York City Ballet*, by Anatole Chujoy (Knopf, 1953); *Thirty Years: Lincoln Kirstein's The New York City Ballet* (Knopf, 1978); *Repertory in Review: Forty Years of the New York City Ballet*, by Nancy Reynolds (Dial, 1977); and *Balanchine: A Biography*, by Bernard Taper (Macmillan, 1974).

The *General Index* provides reference by entry number to all names and titles of works in the *Catalogue*. Supplementary indexes list *Titles by Category* and provide a *Key to Companies Staging Balanchine Works*.

★

Choreography by George Balanchine—a work of scholarship—should also be understood to be a book of a million dreams come true. Each entry signifies a separate creation, a work of art with a life of its own. The procession of ballets traces a steady, inspired journey, a pilgrimage holding its course from continent to continent, maintaining its direction and identity in the face of opposition, establishing in its progress centers of creativity, overcoming circumstance by the magic of vision and faith in form, through training and utilizing successive generations of dancers. Absorbing into classic discipline the irrepressible vitality of the vernacular, proving the universality of native character, persisting in every medium of theatrical production open to ballet, a moral imagination found recognition and support. All this seriousness dares joy, tragedy, exuberance, delight, renewed in every performance.

George Balanchine is a cultural avatar whose work and standards have affirmed in the United States the nation's own best dreams and ideals. The compilers of the book, like the myriad uncounted members of audiences, offer thanks for the gift and heritage given us. This printed list is testament and tribute.

LESLIE GEORGE KATZ   NANCY LASSALLE   HARVEY SIMMONDS

For this edition, minor corrections have been made in the text and Addenda have been added following p. 346, which reflect information available through February 1984. Although the compilers could not know it at the time, *Variations for Piano and Orchestra*, the last entry in the Catalogue, was Balanchine's final work. But his ballets and his company go on, so the entries under Bibliography, Itineraries, and Stagings have increased greatly since the book was originally published.

The ballets for which new information is included have been marked with a plus sign (+) in the original index, starting on p. 379. A separate index for stagings since July 1982 will be found on p. 361 of the Addenda.

21

CHRONOLOGY OF WORK

1904-1924
Russia

1904   Georgi Melitonovich Balanchivadze is born in St. Petersburg on January 22.

1913   Enters ballet section of Imperial Theater School, St. Petersburg.

1915   While still a student, first appears on stage at Maryinsky Theater; dances in school performances, and acts in plays.

1917   Schooling interrupted by Revolution for more than a year.

1918   Resumes studies at Petrograd Theater (Ballet) School. – Performs in repertory maintained at State Theater of Opera and Ballet (formerly Maryinsky); performs with fellow students for workers' clubs, army units and educational institutions.

1919   Creates first choreography, for Ballet School concerts [1-3]. – Studies piano and other instruments at Petrograd Conservatory of Music, directed by Alexander Glazounov. – Begins to compose music.

1921   Graduates with honors from Petrograd Theater (Ballet) School [4-5]. – Enters ballet company of State Theater of Opera and Ballet. – Sees and is influenced by performances of Kasyan Goleizovsky's Chamber Ballet. – Obtains score of Stravinsky's *Pulcinella* [35].

1922   Choreographs works for Petrograd Theater School graduation performances and continues to perform with State Theater of Opera and Ballet [6-13]. – With Pëtr Gusev, Vladimir Dimitriev, Yuri Slonimsky, and others, organizes company called Young Ballet, performing in Petrograd, nearby resorts and Moscow. – Fëdor Lopukhov, artistic director of State Theater of Opera and Ballet, invites Young Ballet to participate in his independent production, *Dance Symphony.*

1923   Creates works for official debut of Young Ballet. – Performs as pianist and dancer in cabarets, cinemas and at Svobodny Theater, and works with FEKS company (The Fabricators of Eccentricities, Inc.). – Is named ballet master of Maly Opera Theater in Petrograd. [14-29]

1924   Choreographs works for what will be final performances of Young Ballet [30-35]. – With Dimitriev forms troupe of dancers, singers and musicians to tour Germany. – Departs from Russia as head of troupe which, as Principal Dancers of the Russian State Ballet, performs in Berlin and tours Rhineland towns. – At end of tour, company decides not to return to Soviet Union and goes to London. – Performs at popular music hall; seen by Anton Dolin and Boris Kochno. – In Paris, group auditions for Serge Diaghilev. – Diaghilev engages dancers, who join his Ballets Russes in London, and changes name Georgi Balanchivadze to Georges Balanchine.

1925-1929
Europe, with Serge Diaghilev

1925   Goes to Monte Carlo, where Ballets Russes is based. – Assigned by Diaghilev to choreograph ballets for productions of Opéra de Monte-Carlo [38-42, 44-47, 49], which employs dancers from Ballets Russes between touring seasons. – For Opéra, choreographs world premiere of *L'Enfant et les Sortilèges* (Ravel) [48]. – As first assignment for Ballets Russes, revises Léonide Massine's choreography of *Le Chant du Rossignol* (Stravinsky) [52], given premiere in Paris. – For London premiere choreographs *Barabau* (Rieti) [53], his first original ballet for Diaghilev. – While creating new works, rehearses Ballets Russes repertory and dances with company, which performs in Barcelona, London, Paris, Antwerp, and Berlin.

1926   Choreographs for Opéra de Monte-Carlo [54-60], and for Diaghilev creates *La Pastorale* (Auric) [62] and *Jack in the Box* (Satie) [63]. – Goes to Rome to work with Lord Berners on *The Triumph of Neptune* [64], which has its premiere in London. – Revises divertissement from *The Sleeping Beauty* (Tschaikovsky) [65], among many changes he makes to repertory pieces of Ballets Russes as *maître de ballet*. – Company presents seasons in Paris and London, and on tour in Berlin, Ostend and Le Touquet.

1927   Provides choreography for productions of Opéra de Monte-Carlo [66-71], and for Ballets Russes choreographs *La Chatte* (Sauguet) [72]. – For Nikita Balieff's traveling Russian cabaret choreographs *Grotesque Espagnol* (Albéniz) and *Sarcasm* (Prokofiev) [73, 74], his first works to be seen in America. – Ballets Russes gives seasons in Paris and London, and tours in France, Italy, Germany, Austria, Switzerland, and Spain.

1928 Creates dances for Opéra de Monte-Carlo productions [76-82]. – For South American tour of Anna Pavlova's company, choreographs *Aleko* (Rachmaninoff) and *Polka Grotesque* (music unknown) [83]. – For Ballets Russes, creates *Apollon Musagète* [84], his first original ballet to Stravinsky's music, which receives premiere in Paris. – First performance of *The Gods Go A-Begging* (Handel) [85] given in London. – Ballets Russes gives seasons in Paris and London, tours Great Britain, and performs in Antwerp, Liège, Brussels, Lausanne, and Ostend.

1929 Sets ballets for Opéra de Monte-Carlo [86-90, 92], and for Diaghilev choreographs *Le Bal* (Rieti) [93]. – Ballets Russes performs in Berlin, Cologne and London. – Choreographs Cole Porter's song 'What Is This Thing Called Love?' for 1929 Cochran Revue in London [91]. – For Ballets Russes premiere in Paris, creates *Le Fils Prodigue* (Prokofiev) [94], last ballet to be commissioned and presented by Diaghilev. – Performs with Ballets Russes in Ostend and Vichy. – In London, choreographs dance sequence to music by Moussorgsky for *Dark Red Roses* [97], first feature-length talking movie made in England. – Diaghilev dies in Venice August 19, and his Ballets Russes ceases to exist. – For small group formed by Dolin in London, Balanchine choreographs *Pas de Deux* (da Costa) [95]. – In Paris, at invitation of Jacques Rouché, director of Paris Opéra, conceives and begins to choreograph ballet to *Les Créatures de Prométhée* (Beethoven) [96], which, due to illness, is completed by Serge Lifar.

1930-1933
Paris, London, Copenhagen, Monte Carlo

1930 In Paris, creates *Aubade* (Poulenc) [98] for company formed by Vera Nemtchinova. – In London, choreographs seven numbers (music by Berners, Sauguet and others) for *Charles B. Cochran's 1930 Revue* [99]. – In Copenhagen as guest ballet master of Royal Danish Ballet for five months, stages and rechoreographs six ballets by Fokine and

Massine [101-106]; presents two all-Balanchine programs for several performances.

1931   Returning to London, gathers small company sometimes billed as '16 Delightful Balanchine Girls 16' to perform numbers he stages for Sir Oswald Stoll's Variety Shows [107], to music by Liszt, Glinka, Mendelssohn, Rimsky-Korsakov, and others. – At same time, stages dances for *Charles B. Cochran's 1931 Revue* [108]. – In Paris, makes ballets for production of Offenbach's comic opera *Orphée aux Enfers* [109], with group of dancers called Les Ballets Russes de Georges Balanchine. – René Blum invites Balanchine to become ballet master of new company to be based in Monte Carlo.

1932   While organizing and rehearsing first season of Ballets Russes de Monte-Carlo, choreographs ballets for eighteen opera productions of the Opéra de Monte-Carlo [111-128]. – For the new company creates four ballets, *Cotillon* (Chabrier), *La Concurrence* (Auric), *Le Bourgeois Gentilhomme* (Richard Strauss), and *Suites de Danse* (Glinka) [129-132]. – Disagreements over policy with Blum's partner, Colonel Vasily de Basil, lead to departure from company.

1933   In Paris, forms Les Ballets 1933 with Kochno. – For brief seasons in Paris and London, creates completely new repertory of six works [134-139]; four are to be included in repertories of his future companies: *Mozartiana* (his first major work to Tschaikovsky), *Les Songes* (Milhaud), *Les Sept Péchés Capitaux* (*The Seven Deadly Sins*, Weill/Brecht), and *L'Errante* (Schubert). – The others are *Fastes* (Sauguet) and *Les Valses de Beethoven*. – Les Ballets 1933 disbands. – Lincoln Kirstein meets Balanchine in London and invites him to the United States to establish a ballet school and company. – He accepts, canceling second engagement with Royal Danish Ballet. – On October 17, Balanchine arrives in New York with Dimitriev.

1934-1945
America, with Lincoln Kirstein

1934   School of American Ballet opens at 637 Madison Avenue in New York City on January 2, with Balanchine, Dimitriev and Kirstein as officers, Balanchine, Pierre Vladimiroff and Dorothie Littlefield as faculty, and Edward M. M. Warburg as first patron. – In March, Balanchine begins choreographing *Serenade* (Tschaikovsky) for students, who first perform it with stagings of *Mozartiana* and *Dreams* (a revision of *Les Songes*) at Woodland, the Warburg estate near White Plains. – In Hartford, Connecticut, non-professional Producing Company of the School of American Ballet, predecessor of American Ballet, presents programs that include *Mozartiana* and three new ballets: *Serenade, Alma Mater* (Swift), and *Transcendence* (Liszt). – Balanchine, Kirstein and Warburg establish American Ballet, with dancers from the School.

1935 In New York City, American Ballet has first professional season, with official premieres of *Serenade, Alma Mater, Reminiscence* (Godard), and *Transcendence*, and American premieres of *Errante* and *Dreams* [141-146]. – After performances in Philadelphia, New York and White Plains, company begins projected United States tour in Greenwich, Connecticut, which ends one week later in Scranton, Pennsylvania. – Edward Johnson, general manager of Metropolitan Opera, engages Balanchine as ballet master, and American Ballet (to be called American Ballet Ensemble) as resident ballet company. – Choreographs ballets for seven opera productions [150-156], and in first of several programs combining independent ballets with opera, presents *Reminiscence* with Humperdinck's *Hansel and Gretel*.

1936 For Metropolitan Opera season, sets ballets for seven operas [158-161, 163, 167, 168]. – With William Dollar, choreographs *Concerto* [165]; creates the ballet *The Bat* (Johann Strauss the Younger) [169]. – Directs and choreographs the opera *Orpheus and Eurydice* (Gluck) [170] in a production designed by Pavel Tchelitchew. – Stages first ballets for a Broadway musical, six pieces for *Ziegfeld Follies: 1936 Edition* (Duke) [162]. – Creates *Serenata: Magic* (Mozart) [164] for Hartford Festival. For Broadway, choreographs *Slaughter on Tenth Avenue* and other ballets for *On Your Toes* (Rodgers and Hart) [166].

1937 Choreographs opera ballets [171, 173, 174, 179], and stages and choreographs *Le Coq d'Or* (Rimsky-Korsakov) [172], for Metropolitan Opera. – Prepares his first Stravinsky Festival, presented at Metropolitan Opera House for two evenings by American Ballet: Revives *Apollon Musagète* for its first performance in America, creates

The Card Party, his and Kirstein's first commission to Stravinsky, and choreographs *Le Baiser de la Fée* [176-178]. – Sets dances for *Babes in Arms* (Rodgers and Hart) [175]. – Engaged by Samuel Goldwyn for first Hollywood assignment, creates dances with members of American Ballet for *Goldwyn Follies* (Gershwin) [185]. – Choreographs opera ballets for winter/spring Metropolitan Opera season [179-181].

1938   Metropolitan Opera terminates engagement of American Ballet after spring season. – Dancers continue to work with Balanchine in musical comedy and with Ballet Caravan, a touring company founded by Kirstein in 1936. – For Broadway, choreographs *I Married an Angel* and *The Boys from Syracuse* (Rodgers and Hart), and *Great Lady* (Loewe) [182-184]. – Plans for Balanchine company to be sponsored by Broadway producers Dwight Deere Wiman and J. H. Del Bondio lead to rehearsals, but not to production.

1939   Balanchine becomes a United States citizen. – In Hollywood, directs dances for film version of *On Your Toes* [186], and later directs dances for film *I Was an Adventuress* [191].

1940   In New York, stages *Le Baiser de la Fée*, *Poker Game* (*The Card Party*), and *Serenade* for Ballet Russe de Monte Carlo. – Choreographs dances for Broadway musicals *Keep Off the Grass* (McHugh) and *Louisiana Purchase* (Berlin), and stages entire production of *Cabin in the Sky* (Duke) [187, 188, 190]. – School of American Ballet is incorporated as non-profit institution with Kirstein as President and Director, and Balanchine as Chairman of Faculty.

1941   For de Basil's current company, Original Ballet Russe, choreographs *Balustrade* (to Stravinsky's Violin Concerto) [192], first ballet created in America for company not his own. – With Kirstein, establishes American Ballet Caravan, formed with dancers from American Ballet, Ballet Caravan and School of American Ballet, for five-month good-will tour of Latin America arranged by Nelson A. Rockefeller, Coordinator of Inter-American Affairs. – Choreographs new ballets for tour: *Ballet Imperial* (Tschaikovsky) and *Concerto Barocco* (Bach; first conceived for School of American Ballet students); *Divertimento* (Rossini–Britten) and *Fantasia Brasileira* (Mignone) are choreographed in South America during tour [194-196, 200]. – Also stages *Serenata* (*Serenade*), *Alma Errante* (*Errante*),

Apolo Musageta (Apollon Musagète), and *El Murciélago (The Bat)*
[**193, 197-199**]. – Tour opens in Rio de Janeiro, and continues in
Argentina, Chile, Peru, Colombia, and Venezuela. – Company is
disbanded at end of engagement. – In New York, stages dances for
Broadway musical *The Lady Comes Across* (Duke/Latouche) [**201**].

1942   Choreographs *The Ballet of the Elephants* [**202**] to Stravinsky's *Circus
Polka*, written at Balanchine's request for Ringling Brothers and
Barnum & Bailey Circus, Madison Square Garden, with cast of
fifty elephants and fifty women. – In Argentina as guest director
of ballet of Teatro Colón in Buenos Aires, creates choreography for
opera *Mârouf* (Rabaud) [**204**], stages *Apollon Musagète* in new production designed by Tchelitchew, and choreographs *Concierto de Mozart*
[**205**]. – In New York, for recently formed New Opera Company,
choreographs *Rosalinda (Die Fledermaus*, Johann Strauss the Younger)
[**206**], choreographs for opera productions [**207-211**], and stages *Ballet
Imperial*, using members of former American Ballet Caravan. – In
Hollywood, choreographs Harold Arlen and Johnny Mercer's
'That Old Black Magic' for film *Star Spangled Rhythm* [**213**].

1943   In first association with Ballet Theatre, founded in 1939, stages
Apollo and *The Wanderer (Errante)*, and assists David Lichine in
revising Fokine's last ballet, *Helen of Troy* (Offenbach) [**214**]. – With
Leopold Stokowski and Robert Edmond Jones, collaborates on
production of *The Crucifixion of Christ* [**215**], a modern miracle play
set to Bach's *St. Matthew Passion*, using students from School of
American Ballet. – Stages dances for New Opera Company
production of *The Merry Widow* (Lehár) [**216**], and for Broadway
musical comedy *What's Up* (Loewe) [**217**]. – Plans resident company
in New York to give performances on Sunday evenings, but project
does not materialize. – Stages *Concerto Barocco* for American
Concert Ballet, company formed by members of former American
Ballet Caravan.

1944   Choreographs ballet sequences for Broadway musical comedy
Dream with Music (Warnick) [**218**]. – In Los Angeles, stages dances
for operetta *Song of Norway* [**219**] to music by Edvard Grieg, using
ensemble from Ballet Russe de Monte Carlo. – Begins two-year
association with that company as resident choreographer; first
original work for company is *Danses Concertantes* (Stravinsky) [**220**];

stages new version of *Le Bourgeois Gentilhomme* (Richard Strauss) [221]. – To honor his twenty-fifth year as choreographer, Chicago Public Library mounts exhibition. – Choreographs *Waltz Academy* (Rieti) [222], first original work for Ballet Theatre.

1945 Devises movement sequences for role of Ariel in Broadway production of Shakespeare's *The Tempest* [224], directed by Margaret Webster. – *Dance Index*, the magazine founded by Kirstein in 1942, devotes February-March issue to a study of Balanchine's work, including his own 'Notes on Choreography.' – Ballet Russe de Monte Carlo celebrates Balanchine's twenty-fifth year as choreographer with two full evenings of his work; for the occasion he creates *Pas de Deux* (Tschaikovsky) [225], and stages *Ballet Imperial* and *Mozartiana*. – In Mexico City, with former American Ballet Caravan members and advanced students of School of American Ballet, choreographs ballets for productions of the Ópera Nacional, Palacio de Bellas Artes [226-228], and stages ballets, including *Concerto Barocco* and *Apollo*. – Choreographs dances for Broadway musical *Mr. Strauss Goes to Boston* (Johann Strauss the Younger– Stolz) [229]. – Choreographs *Circus Polka* (Stravinsky), *Élégie* (Stravinsky) and *Symphonie Concertante* (Mozart) [230, 245, 241] for Carnegie Hall performance with students of School of American Ballet for *Adventure in Ballet*, Kirstein's first enterprise in ballet following his return from wartime service.

1946-1948
Ballet Society

1946 For Ballet Russe de Monte Carlo, choreographs *The Night Shadow* (Rieti) [232], stages *Le Baiser de la Fée*, and collaborates with Alexandra Danilova in a version of *Raymonda* (Glazounov) [233] after Petipa. – In Hollywood, begins choreography for film titled *The Life and Loves of Pavlova*, canceled after two months. – Stages traditional Maryinsky Act II death scene for Ballet Theatre revival of *Giselle* (Adam) [234]. – With Kirstein, organizes Ballet Society, Inc., a subscription-supported company to advance lyric theater. – For first performance, at Central High School of Needle Trades, Balanchine rechoreographs *L'Enfant et les Sortilèges* (Ravel) [235] for

American premiere, and creates *The Four Temperaments* (Hindemith) [236] to score he commissioned from composer in 1940. – Balanchine and Kirstein commission *Orpheus* from Stravinsky; Balanchine goes to Hollywood to work with composer.

1947 For second series of Ballet Society performances, at Hunter College Playhouse, choreographs *Renard* (Stravinsky) [237] and *Divertimento* (Haieff) [238]. – Stages dances for Broadway production of operetta *The Chocolate Soldier* (Oscar Straus) [239]. – During six months as guest ballet master of Paris Opéra, mounts *Serenade*, *Le Baiser de la Fée* and *Apollon Musagète*, and to recently rediscovered Bizet First Symphony creates *Le Palais de Cristal* [240], retitled *Symphony in C* for American premiere in 1948. – In Hollywood, continues work on *Orpheus* with Stravinsky. – During first series of Ballet Society performances at City Center of Music and Drama in New York, presents *Symphonie Concertante* (Mozart) [241]. – Choreographs *Theme and Variations* (Tschaikovsky) [242] for Ballet Theatre.

1948-1964
New York City Ballet: City Center

1948 Choreographs *The Triumph of Bacchus and Ariadne* (Rieti) [243] for second series of Ballet Society performances at City Center. – Ballet Society gives American premiere of *Symphony in C* [244]. – Ballet Society presents *Élégie* (Stravinsky) [245] and the Stravinsky–Balanchine–Noguchi *Orpheus* [246] at City Center of Music and Drama, in what prove to be its final performances. – Following the premiere of *Orpheus*, Morton Baum, Chairman of Executive Committee of City Center, invites Kirstein and Balanchine to found permanent company, to be called New York City Ballet, with residency at City Center; Ballet Society, Inc., continues as sponsor for special projects. – In addition to presenting independent repertory, Company is to provide opera ballets for New York City Opera productions; ballet evenings are to be Mondays and Tuesdays. – In Monte Carlo, for Grand Ballet du Marquis de Cuevas, stages *Night Shadow* and *Concerto Barocco*, and choreographs *Pas de Trois Classique* (Minkus) [247], given its premiere in London. – While preparing inaugural season of New York City Ballet,

Balanchine choreographs dances for Broadway musical *Where's Charley?* (Loesser) [249] and ballets for New York City Opera [248, 251-253, 255, 256]. – New York City Ballet and *Where's Charley?* open October 11. – For first performance, New York City Ballet presents *Concerto Barocco, Orpheus* and *Symphony in C*; second performance consists of *Serenade, The Four Temperaments* and *Orpheus.* – Directs movements for actors in Broadway production of Giraudoux's play *The Madwoman of Chaillot* [257].

1949   New York City Ballet presents first independent season, and provides New York City Opera ballets [258, 260]. – Company is to give regular repertory seasons each year at City Center, and later at New York State Theater (detailed in *Company Itineraries,* page 297). – For Ballet Theatre, adapts Petipa's choreography for *Princess Aurora* [259] and *Don Quixote* and *Swan Lake (Black Swan) Pas de Deux* [262], and stages *Theme and Variations* and *Apollo.* – Balanchine's first original production for television, *Cinderella* [261], to music by Tschaikovsky, is telecast by CBS. – Stages Fokine's choreography of *La Mort du Cygne* (Saint-Saëns) [263] for performance at Holland Festival in Amsterdam. – For New York City Ballet, choreographs Stravinsky's *Firebird* [264] and *Bourrée Fantasque* (Chabrier) [265].

1950   Revives Prokofiev's *Prodigal Son* [267] for New York City Ballet, and appears several times in role of the Father. – Choreographs *Pas de Deux Romantique* (Weber) [268], and with Jerome Robbins creates *Jones Beach* (Andriessen) [269]. – In London, stages *Ballet Imperial* for Sadler's Wells Ballet at invitation of Ninette de Valois. – New York City Ballet presents six-week season at Royal Opera House, Covent Garden, London, and makes three-week tour of England in first of frequent foreign tours (detailed in *Company Itineraries,* page 297). – Choreographs Haydn's *Trumpet Concerto* [270] for touring company of Sadler's Wells Ballet. – For New York City Ballet, stages *The Fairy's Kiss (Le Baiser de la Fée)* (Stravinsky) and choreographs *Mazurka from 'A Life for the Tsar'* (Glinka) and *Sylvia: Pas de Deux* (Delibes) [271-273].

1951   Engaged by Samuel Goldwyn to choreograph dances for film *Hans Christian Andersen,* but schedule conflicts with New York City Ballet season prevent participation. – Is principal choreographer for *Music and Dance* [274], presented by National Orchestral Society at

Carnegie Hall, performed by members of New York City Ballet and students from School of American Ballet. – For New York City Ballet, stages *The Card Game* (Stravinsky) and *Pas de Trois* (Minkus), and choreographs Ravel's *La Valse* and Mendelssohn's *Capriccio Brillant* [275-277, 279]. – Designs pavane to music by David Diamond for Dwight Deere Wiman's Broadway production of Shakespeare's *Romeo and Juliet* [278]. – New York City Ballet presents first American season outside New York at Civic Opera House, Chicago. – Stages dances for Broadway musical comedy *Courtin' Time* (Lawrence/Walker) [280]. – New York City Ballet dances *La Valse* on first color television program, broadcast by CBS. – For New York City Ballet, choreographs *À la Françaix* (Françaix) and *Tyl Ulenspiegel* (Richard Strauss), stages *Apollon Musagète* under title *Apollo, Leader of the Muses*, and presents his own version of Act II of the Petipa/Ivanov *Swan Lake* [282-285].

1952   For New York City Ballet, choreographs *Caracole* [286] to Mozart's Divertimento No. 15, and *Bayou* (Thomson) [287]. – In Milan, stages *Ballet Imperial* for ballet company of La Scala. – New York City Ballet forms exchange program with San Francisco Ballet, which stages *Serenade*. – For New York City Ballet, choreographs *Scotch Symphony* (Mendelssohn), *Metamorphoses* (Hindemith), *Harlequinade Pas de Deux* (Drigo), and *Concertino* (Françaix) [288-290, 292]. – As Christmas program for television, stages abridged treatment of *Coppélia* (Delibes), titled *One, Yuletide Square* [291].

1953   Choreographs *Valse Fantaisie* (Glinka) [293] for New York City Ballet. – Company performs in Washington, D.C., on eve of inauguration of President Dwight D. Eisenhower. – Publication of Anatole Chujoy's book *The New York City Ballet* (Knopf). – Choreographs *The Countess Becomes the Maid* [294] to music by Johann Strauss the Younger for telecast on Kate Smith Hour. – Directs American premiere of Stravinsky's opera *The Rake's Progress* [295] for Metropolitan Opera. – Arranges *Cotillion Promenade* [296] for five hundred couples at Negro Debutante Ball, 369th Armory, in Harlem, New York City. – Stages opera ballets for La Scala in Milan, and in Florence [297-300]. – New York City Ballet performs in Colorado and California on first of continuing tours throughout United States (detailed in *Company Itineraries*, page 297).

1954 Appears on cover of *Time* magazine. – Choreographs *Opus 34*
(Schoenberg) [301] while preparing *The Nutcracker* (Tschaikovsky)
[302], New York City Ballet's first full-length ballet and most
elaborate production, using children from School of American
Ballet. – Publication of Balanchine's *Complete Stories of the Great
Ballets*, edited by Francis Mason (Doubleday). – Choreographs
Western Symphony (Kay) [303]; *Ivesiana* [304] is given premiere four
months after death of composer Charles Ives. – Stages dances for
Broadway musical *House of Flowers* (Arlen) [305], but withdraws
prior to New York opening.

1955 For New York City Ballet, choreographs *Roma* (Bizet) [306] and
Pas de Trois (Glinka) [307]. – Stages ballet masque for American
Shakespeare Festival production of *The Tempest* [308] in Stratford,
Connecticut. – Choreographs *Pas de Dix* (Glazounov) [309] and
Jeux d'Enfants (Bizet) [310] for New York City Ballet.

1956 Stage director of NBC Opera Theatre color telecast of *The Magic
Flute* (Mozart) [311]. – School of American Ballet moves to new
classrooms at 2291 Broadway. – For New York City Ballet, choreographs *Allegro Brillante* (Tschaikovsky) [312]. – Choreographs
A Musical Joke (Mozart) [313] and *Divertimento No. 15* (Mozart) [314]
for bicentennial Mozart Festival produced by American
Shakespeare Festival in Stratford, Connecticut. – Stages *Apollon
Musagète* and *Serenade* for Royal Danish Ballet during absence of five
months from United States and New York City Ballet.

1957 Company goes to Montreal for first formal filming of ballets from
repertory, made for Canadian Broadcasting Company: *Pas de Dix*
and *Serenade* are among initial works made into kinescopes for
telecasts; others are filmed during subsequent visits. – Conceives
and choreographs *Square Dance* (Vivaldi–Corelli) [315] for New York
City Ballet. – Working closely with Stravinsky, creates *Agon* [316]
to third commission from Stravinsky by Balanchine and Kirstein.

1958 Immediately following *Agon*, presents *Gounod Symphony* [317] and
Stars and Stripes (Sousa-Kay) [318]. – New York City Ballet makes
five-month tour of Japan, Australia and Philippines, sponsored by
United States Department of State and American National Theatre
and Academy (ANTA). – Choreographs dance passages for
American Shakespeare Festival productions of *A Midsummer Night's*

Dream [319] and *The Winter's Tale* [320]. – Choreographs *Waltz-Scherzo* (Tschaikovsky) [321] and restages *The Seven Deadly Sins* (Weill/Brecht) [322] for New York City Ballet. – Designs production of *The Nutcracker* especially for CBS Christmas telecast; performs role of Drosselmeyer.

1959   Choreographs *Native Dancers* (Rieti) [323] for New York City Ballet. – Company performs *Stars and Stripes* at inauguration celebration of Governor Rockefeller in Albany. – In Paris, stages *Gounod Symphony* for Opéra Ballet. – Choreographs *Part II* of *Episodes* [324] to music by Webern; at his invitation, *Part I* is choreographed by Martha Graham. – Invited by Kirstein, Imperial Gagaku troupe of dancers and singers from Japan performs on regular programs of New York City Ballet. – For American Shakespeare Festival, stages dances for productions of *Romeo and Juliet* [325] and *The Merry Wives of Windsor* [326]. – Under W. McNeil Lowry, Director of the Program in Humanities and the Arts, the Ford Foundation awards grant to Ballet Society enabling School of American Ballet to survey American ballet instruction and to establish first national scholarship fund. – Through Department of State, Balanchine arranges to give his ballets to state-supported national companies in Europe; first companies to benefit are La Scala, Netherlands Ballet and Royal Swedish Ballet.

1960   For New York City Ballet, revives and restages *Night Shadow* (later called *La Sonnambula*, Rieti), creates *Panamerica* (Latin American composers), stages *Theme and Variations* (Tschaikovsky), and choreographs *Pas de Deux* (Tschaikovsky) [328-331]; creates *The Figure in the Carpet* (Handel) [332] in honor of Fourth International Congress of Iranian Art and Archeology. – Gives first of continuing School of American Ballet seminars for regional teachers, a four-day program. – *Theme and Variations* performed by American Ballet Theatre during first visit by an American ballet company to Russia. – *Symphony in C* and *The Four Temperaments* performed in People's Republic of China by Royal Swedish Ballet. – New York City Ballet performs series of Saturday matinees for underprivileged New York City children, sponsored by Ballet Society. – Balanchine presides at Ballet Society national convocation of ballet company directors. – For Company, choreographs *Variations from Don Sebastian* (later called *Donizetti Variations*), *Monumentum pro Gesualdo* (Stravinsky), *Liebeslieder Walzer* (Brahms), and *Ragtime (I)* (Stravinsky) [333-336].

1961 For New York City Ballet, choreographs *Modern Jazz: Variants* (Schuller) [337], and *Electronics* (Gassmann-Sala) [338] to electronic tape. – Atlanta Civic Ballet presents *Serenade*, first result of Balanchine's offer to make works available to United States regional companies able to stage them. – Assists in efforts to form company that becomes Pennsylvania Ballet. – For New York City Ballet, choreographs *Valses et Variations* (*Raymonda Variations*, Glazounov) [339].

1962 Choreographs *A Midsummer Night's Dream* (Mendelssohn) [340], his first wholly original full-length ballet. – Under auspices of New York State Council on the Arts, New York City Ballet makes first of continuing tours to upstate New York; also gives lecture-demonstrations in twelve cities. – In Germany, stages and choreographs *Eugen Onegin* (Tschaikovsky) [341] for Hamburg State Opera, at invitation of its director, Rolf Liebermann. – Working with Stravinsky, choreographs *Noah and the Flood* [342], composed for television. – Returns to Hamburg with dancers of New York City Ballet to participate with Stravinsky in celebrations of composer's eightieth birthday; *Agon*, *Orpheus* and *Apollo* are performed. – Participates in planning Saratoga Performing Arts Center at Saratoga Springs, New York. – Company performs in Germany and Austria, and Balanchine makes first return to Russia, as Company makes its initial tour of Soviet Union, visiting Moscow, Leningrad, Kiev, Tbilisi, and Baku.

1963 Publication of Bernard Taper's biography *Balanchine* (Macmillan). – In Washington, D. C., New York City Ballet dances *Stars and Stripes* at Second Anniversary Inaugural Celebration of Kennedy administration. – For Company, choreographs *Bugaku* (Mayuzumi) [343] and *Movements for Piano and Orchestra* (Stravinsky) [344]. – New York City Ballet begins lecture-demonstrations in New York City schools. – Directs and choreographs Gluck's *Orpheus und Eurydike* [345] for Hamburg State Opera. – For Company, choreographs *Meditation* (Tschaikovsky) [346]. – Stages *Concerto Barocco*, *Scotch Symphony*, *The Four Temperaments*, and *Bourrée Fantasque* for Paris Opéra Ballet. – Ford Foundation makes first of a series of grants to support New York City Ballet, and first of two grants to School of American Ballet.

1964-1982
New York City Ballet: New York State Theater

1964   Last performance of New York City Ballet at City Center; choreographs *Tarantella* (Gottschalk-Kay) [347]. – Company participates in gala opening of New York State Theater at Lincoln Center for the Performing Arts, designed by Philip Johnson in consultation with Balanchine and Kirstein. – *Clarinade* (Gould) [348] is first work choreographed for Company in new permanent home. – Establishes costume shop for New York City Ballet under direction of Barbara Karinska. – Founds James A. Doolittle–George Balanchine Ballet of Los Angeles, intended to become permanent West Coast company closely associated with New York City Ballet; company will disband after two years. – For large-scale stage of New York State Theater, restages *The Nutcracker* with new scenery and costumes; mounts *Ballet Imperial* (*Tschaikovsky Piano Concerto No. 2*) [349] for its first New York City Ballet production.

1965   For New York City Ballet, choreographs *Pas de Deux and Divertissement* (Delibes) [350] and *Harlequinade* (Drigo) [351]; creates full-length ballet *Don Quixote* (Nabokov) [352] and performs title role at preview performance. – First annual School of American Ballet Workshop performance.

1966   New York City Ballet has first subscription season; subscription plan significantly enlarges audience attending on regular basis. – Choreographs *Variations* (Stravinsky) [353] and *Brahms–Schoenberg Quartet* [354]. – For *A Festival of Stravinsky: His Heritage and His Legacy*, directed by Lucas Foss at Philharmonic Hall, choreographs *Élégie* [355] and *Ragtime (II)* [356]. – New York City Ballet's production of *A Midsummer Night's Dream* becomes first feature-length ballet film made in United States; filming is under Balanchine's direction and supervision. – First New York City Ballet season at new permanent summer home, Saratoga Performing Arts Center, Saratoga Springs, New York, where it is to give seasons each July. – In Stockholm, supervises final rehearsals for Royal Swedish Ballet all-Balanchine evening.

1967   For New York City Ballet, choreographs *Trois Valses Romantiques* (Chabrier), the full-length, plotless *Jewels* (Fauré, Stravinsky, Tschaikovsky), and *Glinkiana* [357-359].

1968   For New York City Ballet, creates *Metastaseis & Pithoprakta* (Xenakis) [360], and restages *Slaughter on Tenth Avenue* [361], originally created for *On Your Toes* in 1936. – Produces and directs stage movements for Company performance of *Requiem Canticles* (Stravinsky) [362], presented once, in memory of Martin Luther King, Jr. – For Ed Sullivan Show on television, choreographs *Diana and Actaeon Pas de Deux* (Pugni) [363]. – Choreographs *La Source* (Delibes) [364] for New York City Ballet.

1969   For Hamburg State Opera, stages and choreographs first production outside Russia of Glinka's opera *Ruslan und Ludmilla* [365]. – Agrees to allow his ballets to be staged by West Berlin Ballet Ensemble, to work with young choreographers there, and to encourage exchanges between Berlin and New York City Ballet. – For New York City Ballet, stages second section of *Glinkiana*, *Valse Fantaisie* [366], as separate ballet. – Between New York and Saratoga seasons, New York City Ballet participates in Diaghilev Festival held in Monte Carlo to commemorate fortieth anniversary of last season of Ballets Russes and sixtieth anniversary of founding of that company, performing *Apollo* and *Prodigal Son*. – School of American Ballet moves to its own specially designed quarters in Juilliard School of Music building at Lincoln Center for the Performing Arts. – In Switzerland, stages four-act production of Ivanov/Petipa *Le Lac des Cygnes* (Tschaikovsky) [367] for Ballet du Grand Théâtre of Geneva. – In West Berlin, rehearses Berlin Opera Ballet in *Episodes, Symphony in C* and *Apollon Musagète* in preparation for its first all-Balanchine evening. – Becomes artistic advisor of ballet school and company of Grand Théâtre, Geneva, which presents its first all-Balanchine evening. – Kirstein becomes Chairman of the Board and Balanchine a Vice President of Dance Theatre of Harlem, the black classical ballet company and school newly founded by former New York City Ballet principal Arthur Mitchell. – National Endowment for the Arts makes first of a series of grants to New York City Ballet.

1970   For New York City Ballet, creates *Who Cares?* (Gershwin) [368] and choreographs full *Tschaikovsky Suite No. 3* [369], incorporating choreography of the 1947 *Theme and Variations* as fourth movement. – Receives Handel Medallion, New York City's highest cultural award. – New York State Council on the Arts makes first of a series of grants for New York City Ballet production and administration costs.

1971 Dance Theatre of Harlem appears with New York City Ballet in single performance of *Concerto for Jazz Band and Orchestra* (Liebermann) [370], choreographed by Balanchine and Mitchell. – Choreographs *PAMTGG* [371] to music based on radio and television airline commercial. – Ballet du Grand Théâtre in Geneva presents performances of *Divertimento No. 15, Episodes, Theme and Variations,* and *Who Cares?,* with guest artists from New York City Ballet.

1972 Under auspices of New York State Council on the Arts, Governor Rockefeller presents New York State Award to Balanchine honoring his unique contribution to development of dance and dance audiences in New York. – Conceives and directs eight-day festival to celebrate the music of Stravinsky, who had died in 1971, honoring ninetieth anniversary of composer's birth. – Thirty-one ballets to Stravinsky compositions are presented, twenty-two of which are newly created by seven choreographers. – Ten new ballets and stagings are by Balanchine: *Sonata, Symphony in Three Movements, Violin Concerto, Danses Concertantes* (revised from first presentation in 1944), *Divertimento from 'Le Baiser de la Fée,' Scherzo à la Russe, Duo Concertant, Pulcinella, Choral Variations on Bach's 'Vom Himmel Hoch,'* and a staging of *Symphony of Psalms* [372-381]. – In *Pulcinella,* choreographed in collaboration with Robbins, Balanchine and Robbins dance as masked beggars. – In Munich, New York City Ballet represents United States in cultural presentations at Olympic Games. – Company makes second Russian tour, followed by first engagement in Poland.

1973 *Tschaikovsky Concerto No. 2* [382, originally created in 1941 as *Ballet Imperial*] is given first performance by New York City Ballet in revised form. – In West Berlin, stages Act II *Polovtsian Dances* (based on Fokine's choreography) for Berlin Opera production of Borodin's *Prince Igor* [383]. – In Paris, rehearses ballet sequences for Paris Opéra production of Gluck's *Orfeo ed Euridice,* and *Symphony in C* for

Paris Opéra Ballet. – Choreographs *Cortège Hongrois* [384] for Melissa Hayden on her retirement from New York City Ballet. – Goes to Berlin with eighty-one members of New York City Ballet for RM Productions filming of fifteen Balanchine ballets. – Publication of Kirstein's *The New York City Ballet* (Knopf) marks Company's twenty-fifth anniversary year.

1974   For Company, creates *Variations pour une Porte et un Soupir* (Henry) [386] to *musique concrète* recorded on tape. – For Saratoga Springs premiere, Balanchine and Danilova recreate full-length production of *Coppélia* (Delibes) [387] from Petipa choreography. – Stages polonaise for Metropolitan Opera production of *Boris Godunov* (Moussorgsky) [388].

1975   Conceives and supervises New York City Ballet Ravel Festival in honor of the composer and France. – During two-week period, twenty ballets are presented to Ravel's music; sixteen are new works by four choreographers, eight by Balanchine. – These are *Sonatine, L'Enfant et les Sortilèges* (his third version of the opera-ballet), *Shéhérazade, Le Tombeau de Couperin, Pavane, Tzigane, Gaspard de la Nuit,* and *Rapsodie Espagnole* [389-396]. – France awards Balanchine Order of the Légion d'Honneur. – Choreographs *Walpurgisnacht Ballet* in Paris Opéra production of *Faust* (Gounod) [397]. – In Saratoga Springs, *The Steadfast Tin Soldier* (Bizet) [398] receives premiere during Company's summer season. – In Chicago, choreographs dance sequences for Chicago Lyric Opera production of *Orfeo ed Euridice* (Gluck) [399].

1976   *Chaconne* [400], based on choreography for 1963 Hamburg State Opera production of Gluck's *Orfeo ed Euridice,* is presented by New York City Ballet as independent ballet. – Creates *Union Jack* [401] to British military, music-hall and folk music arranged by Hershy Kay as New York City Ballet tribute to United States Bicentennial. – In Paris, as part of French salute to Bicentennial, New York City Ballet gives series of performances featuring ballets from Stravinsky repertory. – Choreographs dances for School of American Ballet students in Juilliard American Opera Center production of *Le Roi Malgré Lui* (Chabrier) [403]. – Revival of *The Seven Deadly Sins* is rehearsed by New York City Ballet, but canceled due to musicians' strike.

1977 Publication of Nancy Reynolds' *Repertory in Review: Forty Years of the New York City Ballet* (Dial). – Choreographs *Étude for Piano* (Scriabin) [405] for first Spoleto Festival U. S. A. in Charleston, South Carolina. – Creates *Vienna Waltzes* (Johann Strauss the Younger, Lehár, Richard Strauss) [406] for New York City Ballet. – Balanchine and members of Company travel to Nashville, Tennessee, to film under his direction first of series of five programs devoted to his ballets for Dance in America on public television. – In Montreal, under his supervision, Canadian Broadcasting System films *Bugaku* and *Chaconne*.

1978 Creates for Company *Ballo della Regina* (Verdi) [407] and *Kammermusik No. 2* (Hindemith) [408]. – *Coppélia* is televised as New York City Ballet's first appearance on Live from Lincoln Center series. – School of American Ballet becomes first professional dance academy to receive a major grant from National Endowment for the Arts and, in 1980, first to receive a Challenge Grant. – Supervises production of *Tricolore* (Auric) [409], which, with *Stars and Stripes* and *Union Jack*, forms an 'Entente Cordiale.' – In appreciation of his contribution to Royal Danish Ballet, is named Knight of the Order of Dannebrog, First Class. – First annual Kennedy Center Honors are presented by President Jimmy Carter to Marian Anderson, Fred Astaire, George Balanchine, Richard Rodgers, and Arthur Rubinstein.

1979 Choreographs *Le Bourgeois Gentilhomme* (Richard Strauss) [410] as first Balanchine ballet presented by New York City Opera together with an opera performance, and assists with pantomime scenes in *Dido and Aeneas* (Purcell) [411]. – In London, rehearses Royal Ballet production of *Liebeslieder Walzer*. – New York City Ballet, in cooperation with Board of Education, presents first annual Young People's Matinee at New York State Theater for New York City public-school children.

1980 For New York City Ballet, choreographs Fauré's *Ballade* [412] and stages *Walpurgisnacht Ballet* (Gounod) [413] to music from *Faust*, earlier choreographed for Paris Opéra. – *Le Bourgeois Gentilhomme* (Richard Strauss) [414] enters New York City Ballet repertory. – Creates for Company *Robert Schumann's 'Davidsbündlertänze'* [415]. – Receives first National Gold Medal Award of National Society of

Arts and Letters. – New York City Ballet performs in festivals honoring Stravinsky Centennial in Berlin and Paris.

1981   For special production designed for television, using New York City Ballet dancers, creates fourth realization of Ravel's *L'Enfant et les Sortilèges* [416]. – Organizes and presents two-week Tschaikovsky Festival for New York City Ballet. – Included are twelve new works by six choreographers, of which Balanchine choreographs two and sections of two others. – These are *Mozartiana*, *Hungarian Gypsy Airs*, *Garland Dance* from *The Sleeping Beauty* for *Tempo di Valse*, and *Adagio Lamentoso* from *Symphony No. 6—Pathétique* [417-420].

1982   Plans acoustical improvements for New York State Theater. – To celebrate one-hundredth anniversary of Stravinsky's birth, conceives and supervises Stravinsky Centennial Celebration by New York City Ballet. – Between June 10 and June 18, twenty-five ballets and staged choral works set to Stravinsky's music by six choreographers are performed. — Of ten new works, Balanchine choreographs *Tango* and *Élégie*, and costages *Noah and the Flood* and *Perséphone* [421-424]. – Following official closing of Centennial Celebration rechoreographs, as solo for a ballerina, Stravinsky's *Variations for Orchestra* [425].

1983   Peter Martins appointed Co-chairman of Faculty, School of American Ballet. – Revival of *On Your Toes* [166], with additional choreography by Martins. – In March, Balanchine *in absentia* presented with Medal of Freedom by President Ronald Reagan. – On March 16, Balanchine named Ballet Master Emeritus of the New York City Ballet, Martins and Jerome Robbins become Ballet Masters-in-Chief. – Balanchine dies on April 30, New York City. – Buried in Sag Harbor, L. I., May 3.

CHRONOLOGICAL TITLE LIST

1920

1 La Nuit (Romance)
2 Schön Rosmarin
3 [Concert Works]

1921

4 Poème
5 [Foxtrots]

1922

6 Waltz
7 Waltz and Adagio
8 Romanza
9 Waltz
10 Valse Triste
11 Matelotte
12 Orientalia
13 Hungarian Gypsy Dance

1923

14 Valse Caprice
15 Columbine's Veil
   (Der Schleier der Pierrette)
16 La Mort du Cygne
17 Adagio
18 Spanish Dance
19 Marche Funèbre
20 Waltz
21 Extase
22 Pas de Deux
23 Polka
24 Le Coq d'Or
25 Enigma
26 Caesar and Cleopatra
27 Eugene the Unfortunate
   (The Broken Brow)

28 Chorus Reading
29 [Cabaret Entertainment]
30 Étude
31 Oriental Dance
32 Elegy

1924

33 Pas de Deux
34 Invitation to the Dance
35 Le Bœuf sur le Toit and Pulcinella

1925

36 Pizzicato Polka
37 Valse Caprice
38 Carmen
39 Thaïs
40 Manon
41 Le Hulla
42 Le Démon
43 Hopac
44 Fay-Yen-Fah
45 Faust
46 Hérodiade
47 Un Début
48 L'Enfant et les Sortilèges
49 La Damnation de Faust
50 Étude
51 Polka Mélancolique
52 Le Chant du Rossignol
53 Barabau

1926

54 Boris Godunov
55 Judith
56 L'Hirondelle (La Rondine)
57 Lakmé

43

58   Les Contes d'Hoffmann
59   Jeanne d'Arc
60   Hamlet
61   Romeo and Juliet
62   La Pastorale
63   Jack in the Box
64   The Triumph of Neptune

1927
65   Aurora's Wedding:
     Ariadne and Her Brothers
66   Samson et Dalila
67   La Traviata
68   Turandot
69   La Damnation de Faust
70   Ivan le Terrible
71   Obéron
72   La Chatte
73   Grotesque Espagnol
74   Sarcasm
75   Swan Lake

1928
76   Mireille
77   Les Maîtres Chanteurs (Die
     Meistersinger von Nürnberg)
78   Venise
79   Sior Todéro Brontolon
80   Un Bal Masqué
     (Un Ballo in Maschera)
81   Don Juan (Don Giovanni)
82   La Fille d'Abdoubarahah
83   Aleko and Polka Grotesque
84   Apollon Musagète
85   The Gods Go A-Begging

1929
86   Roméo et Juliette

87   La Gioconda
88   Rigoletto
89   La Femme Nue
90   Martha
91   Wake Up and Dream!
92   La Croisade des Dames
     (Die Verschworenen)
93   Le Bal
94   Le Fils Prodigue
95   Pas de Deux (Moods)
96   Les Créatures de Prométhée
97   Dark Red Roses

1930
98   Aubade
99   Charles B. Cochran's 1930 Revue
100   [Duet and Trio]
101   Den Trekantede Hat
      (Le Tricorne)
102   Schéhérazade
103   Legetøjsbutiken
      (La Boutique Fantasque)
104   Fyrst Igor (Prince Igor)
105   Rosendrømmen
      (Le Spectre de la Rose)

1931
106   Josef-Legende
      (La Légende de Joseph)
107   Dances for Sir Oswald Stoll's
      Variety Shows
108   Charles B. Cochran's 1931 Revue
109   Orphée aux Enfers

1932
110   Les Amours du Poète
111   Tannhäuser
112   Les Contes d'Hoffmann

113   Le Prophète
114   Une Nuit à Venise
115   Lakmé
116   Samson et Dalila
117   Faust
118   Patrie
119   Hérodiade
120   Turandot
121   Rigoletto
122   Manon
123   La Traviata
124   Roméo et Juliette
125   Fay-Yen-Fah
126   Aïda
127   Carmen
128   La Périchole
129   Cotillon
130   La Concurrence
131   Le Bourgeois Gentilhomme
132   Suites de Danse
133   Numéro les Canotiers

1933

134   Mozartiana
135   Les Songes
136   Les Sept Péchés Capitaux
137   Fastes
138   L'Errante
139   Les Valses de Beethoven
140   Dans l'Élysée

1935

141   Serenade
142   Alma Mater
143   Errante
144   Reminiscence
145   Dreams

146   Transcendence
147   [Solo]
148   Jeanne d'Arc
149   Mozartiana
150   La Traviata
151   Faust
152   Aïda
153   Lakmé
154   Tannhäuser
155   Carmen
156   Rigoletto
157   [Pas de Deux]

1936

158   Mignon
159   Manon
160   La Juive
161   La Rondine
162   Ziegfeld Follies: 1936 Edition
163   Die Meistersinger von Nürnberg
164   Serenata: 'Magic'
165   Concerto (Classic Ballet)
166   On Your Toes
167   The Bartered Bride
168   Lucia di Lammermoor
169   The Bat
170   Orpheus and Eurydice
      (Orfeo ed Euridice)
171   Samson et Dalila

1937

172   Le Coq d'Or
173   Caponsacchi
174   La Gioconda
175   Babes in Arms
176   Apollon Musagète
177   The Card Party

178   Le Baiser de la Fée
179   Mârouf
180   Roméo et Juliette

1938
181   Don Giovanni
182   I Married an Angel
183   The Boys from Syracuse
184   Great Lady
185   Goldwyn Follies

1939
186   On Your Toes

1940
187   Keep Off the Grass
188   Louisiana Purchase
189   Pas de Deux—Blues
190   Cabin in the Sky
191   I Was an Adventuress

1941
192   Balustrade
193   Serenata (Serenade)
194   Ballet Imperial
195   Concerto Barocco
196   Divertimento
197   Alma Errante (Errante)
198   Apolo Musageta
       (Apollon Musagète)
199   El Murciélago (The Bat)
200   Fantasia Brasileira

1942
201   The Lady Comes Across
202   The Ballet of the Elephants
203   Pas de Trois for Piano
       and Two Dancers

204   Maruf (Mârouf)
205   Concierto de Mozart
206   Rosalinda
207   The Opera Cloak
208   The Fair at Sorochinsk
209   La Vie Parisienne
210   The Queen of Spades
       (Pique Dame)
211   Macbeth
212   [Solo]
213   Star Spangled Rhythm

1943
214   Helen of Troy
215   The Crucifixion of Christ
216   The Merry Widow
217   What's Up

1944
218   Dream with Music
219   Song of Norway
220   Danses Concertantes
221   Le Bourgeois Gentilhomme
222   Waltz Academy
223   Sentimental Colloquy

1945
224   The Tempest
225   Pas de Deux (Grand Adagio)
226   Aïda
227   Fausto (Faust)
228   Sansón y Dalila
       (Samson et Dalila)
229   Mr. Strauss Goes to Boston
230   Circus Polka

1946
231   Resurgence

232 The Night Shadow

233 Raymonda

234 Giselle: Act II Grave Scene

235 The Spellbound Child
(L'Enfant et les Sortilèges)

236 The Four Temperaments

1947

237 Renard

238 Divertimento

239 The Chocolate Soldier

240 Le Palais de Cristal

241 Symphonie Concertante

242 Theme and Variations

1948

243 The Triumph of Bacchus
and Ariadne

244 Symphony in C

245 Élégie

246 Orpheus

247 Pas de Trois Classique

248 Carmen

249 Where's Charley?

250 Concerto Barocco

251 The Marriage of Figaro
(Le Nozze di Figaro)

252 La Traviata

253 Don Giovanni

254 Serenade

255 Aïda

256 Eugen Onegin

257 The Madwoman of Chaillot
(La Folle de Chaillot)

1949

258 Troubled Island

259 Princess Aurora

260 The Tales of Hoffmann
(Les Contes d'Hoffmann)

261 Cinderella

262 Don Quixote and Swan Lake
(Black Swan) Pas de Deux

263 La Mort du Cygne

264 Firebird

265 Bourrée Fantasque

266 [Pas de Deux]

1950

267 Prodigal Son

268 Pas de Deux Romantique

269 Jones Beach

270 Trumpet Concerto

271 The Fairy's Kiss
(Le Baiser de la Fée)

272 Mazurka from 'A Life
for the Tsar'

273 Sylvia: Pas de Deux

1951

274 Music and Dance

275 The Card Game

276 Pas de Trois

277 La Valse

278 Romeo and Juliet

279 Capriccio Brillant

280 Courtin' Time

281 The Sleeping Beauty: Variation
from Aurora's Wedding

282 À la Françaix

283 Tyl Ulenspiegel

284 Apollo, Leader of the Muses

285 Swan Lake

1952

286 Caracole

287   Bayou
288   Scotch Symphony
289   Metamorphoses
290   Harlequinade Pas de Deux
291   One, Yuletide Square
292   Concertino

1953

293   Valse Fantaisie
294   The Countess Becomes
      the Maid
295   The Rake's Progress
296   [Cotillion Promenade]
297   La Favorita
298   Boris Godunov
299   Adriana Lecouvreur
300   Amahl and the Night Visitors

1954

301   Opus 34
302   The Nutcracker
303   Western Symphony
304   Ivesiana
305   House of Flowers

1955

306   Roma
307   Pas de Trois
308   The Tempest
309   Pas de Dix
310   Jeux d'Enfants

1956

311   The Magic Flute
312   Allegro Brillante
313   A Musical Joke
314   Divertimento No. 15

1957

315   Square Dance
316   Agon

1958

317   Gounod Symphony
318   Stars and Stripes
319   A Midsummer Night's Dream
320   The Winter's Tale
321   Waltz-Scherzo
322   The Seven Deadly Sins

1959

323   Native Dancers
324   Episodes
325   Romeo and Juliet
326   The Merry Wives of Windsor
327   The Warrior

1960

328   Night Shadow
329   Panamerica
330   Theme and Variations
331   Pas de Deux
      (Tschaikovsky Pas de Deux)
332   The Figure in the Carpet
333   Variations from Don Sebastian
      (Donizetti Variations)
334   Monumentum pro Gesualdo
335   Liebeslieder Walzer
336   Ragtime (I)

1961

337   Modern Jazz: Variants
338   Electronics
339   Valses et Variations
      (Raymonda Variations)

1962

340 A Midsummer Night's Dream
341 Eugen Onegin
342 Noah and the Flood

1963

343 Bugaku
344 Movements for Piano
     and Orchestra
345 Orpheus und Eurydike
     (Orfeo ed Euridice)
346 Meditation

1964

347 Tarantella
348 Clarinade
349 Ballet Imperial

1965

350 Pas de Deux and Divertissement
351 Harlequinade
352 Don Quixote

1966

353 Variations
354 Brahms – Schoenberg Quartet
355 Élégie
356 Ragtime (II)

1967

357 Trois Valses Romantiques
358 Jewels
359 Glinkiana

1968

360 Metastaseis & Pithoprakta
361 Slaughter on Tenth Avenue

362 Requiem Canticles
363 Diana and Actaeon Pas de Deux
364 La Source

1969

365 Ruslan und Ludmilla
366 Valse Fantaisie
367 Le Lac des Cygnes

1970

368 Who Cares?
369 Suite No. 3
     (Tschaikovsky Suite No. 3)

1971

370 Concerto for Jazz Band
     and Orchestra
371 PAMTGG

1972

372 Sonata
373 Symphony in Three Movements
374 Violin Concerto
     (Stravinsky Violin Concerto)
375 Danses Concertantes
376 Divertimento from 'Le Baiser
     de la Fée'
377 Scherzo à la Russe
378 Duo Concertant
379 Pulcinella
380 Choral Variations on Bach's
     'Vom Himmel Hoch'
381 Symphony of Psalms

1973

382 Tschaikovsky Piano Concerto
     No. 2
383 Fürst Igor (Prince Igor)

384 Cortège Hongrois
385 Begin the Beguine

1974

386 Variations pour une Porte
     et un Soupir
387 Coppélia
388 Boris Godunov

1975

389 Sonatine
390 L'Enfant et les Sortilèges
391 Shéhérazade
392 Le Tombeau de Couperin
393 Pavane
394 Tzigane
395 Gaspard de la Nuit
396 Rapsodie Espagnole
397 Faust
398 The Steadfast Tin Soldier
399 Orfeo ed Euridice

1976

400 Chaconne
401 Union Jack
402 Pal Joey
403 The Reluctant King
     (Le Roi Malgré Lui)

1977

404 The Sleeping Beauty:
     Aurora's Solo, Vision Scene
405 Étude for Piano
406 Vienna Waltzes

1978

407 Ballo della Regina
408 Kammermusik No. 2
409 Tricolore

1979

410 Le Bourgeois Gentilhomme
411 Dido and Aeneas

1980

412 Ballade
413 Walpurgisnacht Ballet
414 Le Bourgeois Gentilhomme
415 Robert Schumann's
     'Davidsbündlertänze'

1981

416 The Spellbound Child/
     L'Enfant et les Sortilèges
417 Mozartiana
418 Tempo di Valse: Garland Dance
     from The Sleeping Beauty
419 Hungarian Gypsy Airs
420 Symphony No. 6—Pathétique:
     Fourth Movement, Adagio
     Lamentoso

1982

421 Tango
422 Noah and the Flood
423 Élégie
424 Perséphone
425 Variations for Orchestra

CATALOGUE

1920

1 LA NUIT (later called ROMANCE)

Music: By Anton Rubinstein (Romance in E-flat, Op. 44, no. 1, for voice and piano, danced to piano and violin).

Premiere: 1920?, concert at Petrograd Theater (Ballet) School.

Cast: Olga Mungalova (or possibly Lydia Ivanova), George Balanchine.

Note: Balanchine remembers this as the first work he choreographed, although the date of its premiere has not been established. Mikhail Mikhailov, a contemporary of Balanchine's at the official ballet school in St. Petersburg/Petrograd, suggests in *My Life in Ballet* that it may have been created as early as 1917-18. Mungalova's unpublished memoirs describe her performance of this dance with Balanchine at the ballet school in the summer of 1920. She danced it with Pëtr Gusev at the school graduation performance of 1920 or 1921. As *Romance*, the ballet was presented on June 1, 1923, at the first performance of the Young Ballet, the company created by Balanchine, Gusev, Vladimir Dimitriev, Boris Erbshtein, and Yuri Slonimsky; it was also in the repertory of the Principal Dancers of the Russian State Ballet, the small troupe led by Balanchine and Dimitriev on tour in Germany during the summer of 1924. The work was performed for many years in the Soviet Union after Balanchine's departure.

2 SCHÖN ROSMARIN

Music: By Fritz Kreisler (from *Alt Wiener Tanzweisen*, 1911).

Premiere: April 4, 1920, Petrograd Theater (Ballet) School graduation performance, State Theater of Opera and Ballet (formerly Maryinsky).

Cast: O. Barysheva, D. Kirsanov.

Note: Also performed by the Principal Dancers of the Russian State Ballet in 1924 on their summer tour of Germany and in London that October at the Empire Theatre.

See 22

3 [CONCERT WORKS]

As a young man, Balanchine frequently created, as he says, 'informal little things,' performed once or twice and then forgotten. Among these were compositions to music by Nicolai Medtner and to excerpts from *Salome* by Richard Strauss. He also remembers making 'something new' to Chopin (or to the 'Chopin' section of Schumann's *Carnaval*) for a 'soirée.' Alexandra Danilova remembers a solo waltz done for her, possibly to Johann Strauss (she performed a Strauss waltz September 4 and 9, 1923, at the Svobodny Theater, Petrograd). She also recalls a solo to Scriabin (not the *Étude* pas de deux [30]). There is a possibility that Balanchine choreographed a pas de deux called *Dutch Dance* to the music of Grieg, but both he and Danilova think it equally possible that this dance, which appears on the programs for London performances of the Principal Dancers of the Russian State Ballet in 1924, might have been from Albert Lortzing's opera *Zar und Zimmermann*, with choreography by Pavel Petrov or Andrei Lopukhov. In published interviews, Balanchine has mentioned other early works: a ballet for eight boys in the Fokine style, done while he was still a student (*Dance Magazine*, June 1954, p. 148), a ballet to Stravinsky's *Ragtime* in 1922 (New York City Center: *Playbill* 1:10, December 2, 1957), and concert dances to music by Schumann (*Washington Post*, October 12, 1980).

See *110, 336, 356*

1921

4 POÈME

MUSIC: By Zdeněk Fibich.

PRODUCTION: Costumes by George Balanchine.

PREMIERE: Concert at the Petrograd Theater (Ballet) School some time prior to Balanchine's graduation on April 4, 1921.

CAST: Alexandra Danilova?, George Balanchine.

NOTE: The woman's costume, a light blue tunic, was unusual for the time: the standard costume was the tutu. It is not certain that Danilova danced the first performance of this work, but both the late Marietta Frangopoulo, Curator of the Museum of the Leningrad Academic Choreographic School, and the late Vera Kostrovitskaya, Senior Instructor of Classical Ballet and a slightly younger colleague of Balanchine's at the ballet school, have described Danilova in this ballet. She and Mikhail Dudko danced it at the Donon Restaurant, Petrograd, in 1923, and it was also included on the first Evening of the Young Ballet, June 1, 1923. The ballet continued to be performed for many years in the Soviet Union. The Soviet dance historian Vera Krasovskaya danced it at a school concert about 1932.

5 [FOXTROTS]

By 1921, the Bolsheviks had signed treaties with a number of European and Asian countries, renouncing claims to various border territories, guaranteeing mutual non-aggression in some cases, and resuming trade relations. Perhaps the most important of these was the Anglo-Soviet trade agreement of March 16, 1921, in which Lenin opened the ports of Petrograd to trade with the West. In celebration of this (or, perhaps, another similar treaty), a giant party was held; for entertainment there were actors, German music, and a foxtrot composed for the crowd by Balanchine.

A review in *Krasnaya gazeta*, May 20, 1924, mentions a foxtrot performed by the Young Ballet as part of a demonstration concert. This is almost certainly not the work composed for the public party; Pëtr Gusev suggests it may have been a solo created by Balanchine for Nicholas Efimov.

1922

6 WALTZ

MUSIC: By Riccardo Drigo.

PREMIERE: April 9, 1922, Petrograd Theater (Ballet) School graduation performance, State Theater of Opera and Ballet (formerly Maryinsky).

CAST: Anna Vorobieva.

NOTE: A Drigo *Waltz* was performed by Alexandra Danilova as a member of the Principal Dancers of the Russian State Ballet on the summer tour of Germany in 1924. It may have been this composition, but more probably was the waltz from Petipa's short ballet *The Lovely Pearl* (Drigo), which was in the repertory of the Young Ballet.

7 WALTZ AND ADAGIO

MUSIC: By George Balanchine.

PREMIERE: April 9, 1922, Petrograd Theater (Ballet) School graduation performance, State Theater of Opera and Ballet (formerly Maryinsky) [?].

CAST: Olga Mungalova, Pëtr Gusev.

NOTE: Information about the premiere was supplied by Gusev, a contemporary of Balanchine's at ballet school in St. Petersburg/Petrograd, in an unpublished interview with Poel Karp; however, the work does not appear on the printed program. A performance by Alexandra Danilova and Balanchine was reviewed on June 11, 1922, and the work is known to have been performed on the first Evening of the Young Ballet, June 1, 1923, probably by Gusev and Mungalova, who performed in the Young Ballet's first concert and often danced together.

8 ROMANZA

MUSIC: Music by George Balanchine. Lyrics by Evgeny Mravinsky.

PREMIERE: 1922, Pavlovsk?

CAST: Olga Mungalova, Pëtr Gusev.

NOTE: This work was created by Balanchine after his graduation in 1921; he thinks it was perhaps first performed at the summer resort of Pavlovsk, near Petrograd, with himself as the piano accompanist.

9 WALTZ

PREMIERE: August 15, 1922, resort at Sestroretsk, near Petrograd.

CAST: Alexandra Danilova, George Balanchine.

NOTE: Neither Balanchine nor Danilova remembers the music.

10 VALSE TRISTE

MUSIC: By Jean Sibelius (*Valse Triste* from incidental music for *Kuolema*, Op. 44, 1903).

PRODUCTION: Costume by Boris Erbshtein.

PREMIERE: August 15, 1922, resort at Sestroretsk, near Petrograd.

CAST: Lydia Ivanova.

NOTE: Also performed by Tamara Geva and Alexandra Danilova on the tour of Germany and during the London engagement of the Principal Dancers of the Russian State Ballet, in the summer and fall of 1924.

11 MATELOTTE (also called SAILOR'S HORNPIPE)

MUSIC: Traditional hornpipe music, arranged by Zuev.

PREMIERE: 1922?

CAST: Unavailable (a woman and two men).

NOTE: This little dance may have been given its first performance on August 15, 1922, at the resort at Sestroretsk, near Petrograd; Balanchine, Lydia Ivanova and Alexandra Danilova are known to have participated in a concert there on that date. The dance was included on the first Evening of the Young Ballet, June 1, 1923, at the Duma, Petrograd, when the musical arrangement of Zuev was first credited. It was apparently performed many times in the Soviet Union, but no casting for Soviet performances has been found. The work was in the repertory of the Principal Dancers of the Russian State Ballet in 1924, both for the summer German tour and the October performances at the Empire Theatre in London, where it was danced by Balanchine, Danilova and Nicholas Efimov.

12 ORIENTALIA

MUSIC: By César Cui (Op. 50, no. 9, 1912).

PREMIERE: Season of 1922-23.

CAST: *Young Oriental Dancer*, Nina Mlodzinskaya; *Blind Old Beggar*, George Balanchine.

NOTE: Yuri Slonimsky, in *Balanchine: The Early Years*, notes that this dance was choreographed when Balanchine had already received recognition in Petrograd. Mikhailov dates it 1922-23. There is record of a performance at the Hôtel d'Europe, Petrograd, on June 2, 1923, with Tamara Geva and Rostislav Slavianinov. The work was probably danced by the Principal Dancers of the Russian State Ballet on the 1924 tour of Germany, although newspaper announcements are unclear.

13 HUNGARIAN GYPSY DANCE

MUSIC: By Johannes Brahms.

PREMIERE: Season of 1922-23.

CAST: Tamara K. Leshevich, Rostislav Slavianinov.

NOTE: Balanchine thinks this work was first performed at Pavlovsk; he is quite sure the premiere was not on the formal stage of the State Theater of Opera and Ballet (formerly Maryinsky). Mikhailov gives 1922-23 as the premiere date. The Principal Dancers of the Russian State Ballet performed the work in 1924 during the summer German tour and the October performances at the Empire Theatre in London, where it was danced by Tamara Geva both with Balanchine and with Nicholas Efimov.

1923

14 VALSE CAPRICE

MUSIC: By Anton Rubinstein (Op. 118).

PREMIERE: April 2, 1923, Muzykalnaya Komediĩâ, Petrograd.

CAST: Xenia Maklezova, D. I. Beeness.

NOTE: First performed at the Thirty-fifth Year Jubilee benefit for I. A. Smolyakov. In 1925, Balanchine rechoreographed Serafima Astafieva's solo for Alicia Markova to this music.

See 37

15 COLUMBINE'S VEIL (DER SCHLEIER DER PIERRETTE)
Pantomime with Dances

MUSIC: By Ernst von Dohnanyi (produced 1910). Scenario by Arthur Schnitzler.

PRODUCTION: Directed by N. A. Shcherbakov. Scenery by Vladimir Dimitriev.

PREMIERE: May 9, 1923, Institute of Art History, Petrograd.

CAST: Unavailable.

16 LA MORT DU CYGNE

MUSIC: By Camille Saint-Saëns (*Le Cygne* [cello solo] from *Le Carnaval des Animaux: Fantaisie Zoologique* for small orchestra, 1886).

CHOREOGRAPHY: By Michel Fokine (1905?); staged by George Balanchine.

PREMIERE: June 1, 1923, Young Ballet, Alexandrovsky Hall, Duma, Petrograd.

CAST: Nina Stukolkina.

NOTE: First performed on the opening program of the Young Ballet, which also included the premiere of *Adagio* [17] and performances of *Romance* [1, earlier titled *La Nuit*], *Waltz and Adagio* [7], *Matelotte* [11]; and may have included the premieres of *Spanish Dance* [18], *Marche Funèbre* [19], *Waltz* [20], and *Extase* [21]. Works by Marius Petipa and N. Lisovskaya were also performed. The concert seems not to have been reviewed in the Soviet press or theater journals, but was announced for this date by a poster which lists the following participants: Alexandra Danilova, E. V. Eliseyeva, Lydia Ivanova, Vera Kostrovitskaya, N. Lisovskaya, Nina Mlodzinskaya, Olga Mungalova, N. A.

Nikitina, Nina Stukolkina, L. M. Tiuntina, Georgi Balanchivadze, L. Balashov, Pëtr Gusev, Nicholas Efimov, D. K. Kirsanov, Leonid Lavrovsky, and Mikhail Mikhailov.

See 263

17 ADAGIO

Music: By Camille Saint-Saëns (adagio excerpt from the ballet *Javotte*, produced 1896).

Premiere: June 1, 1923, Young Ballet, Alexandrovsky Hall, Duma, Petrograd.

Cast: Alexandra Danilova, George Balanchine?

Note: Also performed by Danilova and Balanchine at the final concert of the Young Ballet, June 15, 1924, Pavlovsk.

18 SPANISH DANCE

Music: Probably by Alexander Glazounov (from *Raymonda*, Op. 57, produced 1898).

Premiere: June 1, 1923, Young Ballet, Alexandrovsky Hall, Duma, Petrograd.

Cast: Nina Stukolkina, Mikhail Mikhailov.

Note: Although *Spanish Dance* does not appear on the poster announcing the first Evening of the Young Ballet, Slonimsky quotes Vera Kostrovitskaya's recollection that it was presented at the concert. *Adagio*, with Balanchine choreography to the music of Glazounov, does appear on the announcement poster; no other mention has been found: possibly it was retitled *Spanish Dance* for the performance.

See 233, 309, 339, 384

19 MARCHE FUNÈBRE

Music: By Frédéric Chopin (second movement [1837] of Sonata No. 1 in B-flat minor, Op. 35, 1839).

PRODUCTION: Scenery by Boris Erbshtein. Costumes by Vladimir Dimitriev.

PREMIERE: June 1, 1923, Young Ballet, Alexandrovsky Hall, Duma, Petrograd.

CAST: FIRST MOVEMENT, TRAGIC: Olga Mungalova or Tamara Geva, 3 men, 6 women; SECOND MOVEMENT, LYRIC: Alexandra Danilova, ensemble; THIRD MOVEMENT, TRAGIC: Entire cast.

NOTE: Although *Marche Funèbre* is not listed on the announcements for the initial program of the Young Ballet, Balanchine planned it for the first performance and believes that it had its premiere June 1, 1923. It was mentioned (although not reviewed) on June 24, 1923, in *Krasnaya gazeta*. There is some indication that it was first performed as a school work. Soon after joining the Ballets Russes in 1924, Balanchine taught *Marche Funèbre* to members of the company for presentation to Serge Diaghilev, Boris Kochno and S. L. Grigoriev in the studio of Serafima Astafieva.

20 WALTZ

MUSIC: By Maurice Ravel (one of the waltzes from *Valses Nobles et Sentimentales*, 1911, orchestrated 1912).

PREMIERE: 1923?

CAST: Nina Stukolkina or Nina Mlodzinskaya, male partner.

NOTE: Balanchine recalls that this dance was originally performed on the first Evening of the Young Ballet, June 1, 1923, at the Duma, Petrograd, although the poster announcing the program does not list it.

See 277

21 EXTASE

MUSIC: By George Balanchine.

PREMIERE: 1923?

CAST: Unavailable (pas de deux for ballerina and partner).

NOTE: Balanchine does not remember for whom he created this pas de deux, which he thinks may possibly have been included in the first Evening of the Young Ballet, June 1, 1923, at the Duma, Petrograd, although it does not appear on the poster announcing the concert. Alexandra Danilova thinks it might have been made for Lydia Ivanova and Rostislav Slavianinov.

22 PAS DE DEUX

MUSIC: By Fritz Kreisler (*Liebesleid* from *Alt Wiener Tanzweisen*, 1911).

PREMIERE: July 31, 1923, evening with dancers from the academic theaters, Petrograd.

CAST: Lydia Ivanova, Nicholas Efimov.

NOTE: Newspapers do not specify the location of this concert or whether a special event was involved. All the dancers were participants in the Young Ballet, and were also members of the State Theater (formerly Maryinsky) company. Balanchine is known to have choreographed two works for the concert: this duet to music of Kreisler and a polka by Rachmaninoff for Ivanova [23]. He thinks he probably also choreographed a duet to Tschaikovsky's *Romance without Words* (Op. 40, no. 6) for Ivanova and Efimov, and may have created a dance for Efimov to Dulov's *Variation Classique*, presented the same evening.

See 2

23 POLKA

MUSIC: By Sergei Rachmaninoff.

PREMIERE: July 31, 1923, evening with dancers from the academic theaters, Petrograd.

CAST: Lydia Ivanova.

NOTE: See 22.

24 LE COQ D'OR

Opera in Three Acts by Nicolai Rimsky-Korsakov
ACT II VISION; ACT III MARCH

PRODUCTION: Directed by S. A. Samosud. Choreography and movement direction by George Balanchine (uncredited).

PREMIERE: September 15, 1923, Maly Opera Theater, Petrograd. Danced by the resident ballet troupe.

CAST: VISION: Uspenskaya. MARCH: Orlova, Uspenskaya, Kobeleva, Dikushina, Baranovich, Komarov, Rykhliakov, Chesnakov, Kobelev, Shuisky.

NOTE: Balanchine also devised movement sequences in Act II for the Queen of Shemakha, the choral group, and Dodon and the pupils.

See 172

25 ENIGMA

MUSIC: By Anton Arensky (*The Exit of Cleopatra* from *Egyptian Nights*, Op. 50, produced 1900).

PREMIERE: 1923?

CAST: Lydia Ivanova, George Balanchine.

NOTE: Danced in bare feet. Although no documentation has been found, Balanchine believes that he and Ivanova originally performed the work. He and Tamara Geva danced it at a benefit at the State Theater of Opera and Ballet (formerly Maryinsky); there are also records of their performing it in the floorshow at the Donon Restaurant in Petrograd on September 29, 1923. The work was danced by Geva and Balanchine during the Principal Dancers of the Russian State Ballet tour of Germany in the summer of 1924, at the Empire Theatre in London that October, and in audition for Diaghilev later that autumn in Paris. It was performed by Diaghilev's Ballets Russes at least three times in 1925 on programs of divertissements in the Nouvelle Salle de Musique (Salle Ganne) in the Casino at Monte Carlo. The work was still performed in the Soviet Union during the 1930s. *Enigma* is Balanchine's title for the work.

26 CAESAR AND CLEOPATRA

Play by George Bernard Shaw

MUSIC: By Yuri Shaporin.

CHOREOGRAPHY: Pantomime and dances choreographed by George Balanchine.

PRODUCTION: Produced and directed by V. R. Rappaport. Scenery and costumes by Vladimir A. Schouko.

PREMIERE: September 30, 1923, Petrograd Drama Theater [group], Maly Opera Theater, Petrograd.

CAST: *Cleopatra*, Eugenia Wolf-Israel; others.

NOTE: Balanchine choreographed the pantomime and dances in Act I, and movements for Cleopatra.

27 EUGENE THE UNFORTUNATE (THE BROKEN BROW)
Play by Ernst Toller, translated by Adrian Piotrovsky

PRODUCTION: Directed by Sergei Radlov. Pantomime directed by Levitsky. Scenery by Vladimir Dimitriev.

PREMIERE: December 15, 1923, Maly Opera Theater, Petrograd. Conductor: Max Kuper.

CAST: *Eugene Brokenbrow*, Vivien; *Margaret Brokenbrow, His Wife*, Yureneva; *Mrs. Brokenbrow, His Mother*, Gribunina; *Jock Rooster*, Andreivsky; and others. *Dancers*: Berestorskaya, Orlova, Charova, Dikushina, Rykhliakov, Shiryayev, Morosov, Petrushenko.

NOTE: Balanchine contributed Act II dances in silhouette.

28 CHORUS READING

PREMIERE: Late 1923?, Young Ballet, Duma, Petrograd.

CAST: 10-12 members of the Young Ballet.

NOTE: Choreography by Balanchine to the chanting of Alexander Blok's *The Twelve* and other poems by a chorus of fifty voices, without music, with the performers dressed in national costumes. This was a single number in an evening of works, the rest of which had music. No certain information regarding the premiere date or location has been obtained; the suggested date is provided by Bernard Taper in his biography of Balanchine. Possibly this work and others as yet undocumented were first performed on the second program of the Young Ballet. Pëtr Gusev recalls that this work, with *Marche Funèbre* [19], was given on a program at the Cineselli Circus, Petrograd, by the Young Ballet.

29 [CABARET ENTERTAINMENT]

In December, 1923, The Carousel, an 'intellectual cabaret,' opened in Petrograd. For this occasion and subsequently, Balanchine devised movement for poems set to music. The Soviet periodical *Teatr* reported Balanchine's collaboration with the directors Evreinov, Petrov, Tversky, and Miklashevsky, the artists Akimov and Nicolas Benois, and also with Olga Mungalova, Armfeld and Volkov.

30 ÉTUDE

MUSIC: By Alexander Scriabin (probably *Caresse Dansée*, Op. 57, 1908, and one of the preludes, both for piano).

PREMIERE: 1923/24, Young Ballet.

CAST: Tamara Geva, George Balanchine.

NOTE: Pëtr Gusev recalls that Balanchine had intended a far more ambitious work, but was only able to complete the pas de deux. This was probably performed by Balanchine and Geva as an audition piece for Diaghilev in Paris in the autumn of 1924, and appears on matinee programs of divertissements performed by Diaghilev's Ballets Russes in the Nouvelle Salle de Musique (Salle Ganne) in the Casino at Monte Carlo. In 1925, Balanchine choreographed a new work to this music for Ruth Page and Chester Hale.

See 50

31 ORIENTAL DANCE

MUSIC: By Modest Moussorgsky (from the unfinished opera *Khovan-shchina*, 1872-80, completed by Nicolai Rimsky-Korsakov, 1886).

PREMIERE: 1923/24, Young Ballet.

CAST: Tamara Geva, George Balanchine.

See 97

32 ELEGY

MUSIC: By Sergei Rachmaninoff (*Élégie* for piano, 1892).

PREMIERE: 1923/24, Young Ballet?

CAST: Unavailable (a woman and two men).

NOTE: No information about the premiere has been located. The ballet was danced at the final concert of the Young Ballet, Pavlovsk, June 15, 1924, by Tamara Geva, Nicholas Efimov and Balanchine. It was also performed on the German tour of the Principal Dancers of the Russian State Ballet in the summer of 1924, and may have been one of the audition pieces for Diaghilev in Paris in the autumn of 1924.

1924

33 PAS DE DEUX

MUSIC: By Alexander Glazounov (slow movement from Violin Concerto in A Minor, Op. 82, 1904).

PREMIERE: May 7, 1924, State Theater of Opera and Ballet (formerly Maryinsky), Petrograd.

CAST: Elizaveta Gerdt, Mikhail Dudko.

NOTE: This pas de deux followed a performance of *La Bayadère* at a benefit for Elizaveta Gerdt. Balanchine and Gerdt then danced a pas de deux (excluding the male variation) to the music of Nicolas Tcherepnine's *Le Pavillon d'Armide*, which may or may not have had choreography by Balanchine: Gerdt's variation was by Fokine, who had choreographed a complete ballet to this music in 1907; Balanchine's contribution, if he made one, would have been the opening adagio and the closing coda.

34 INVITATION TO THE DANCE

MUSIC: By Carl Maria von Weber (*Aufforderung zum Tanz* for piano, Op. 65, 1819).

PREMIERE: Spring, 1924.

CAST: Alexandra Danilova, George Balanchine, Mikhail Mikhailov.

NOTE: Premiere information and original casting are given by Mikhailov in *My Life in Ballet*. Balanchine thinks this was probably first performed at Pavlovsk, where there was an open-air platform for performances. The ballet was danced by the Principal Dancers of the Russian State Ballet during the tour of Germany in the summer of 1924. The music had been used by Fokine for *Le Spectre de la Rose* (1911), which Balanchine staged and performed in Copenhagen in 1930.

See 105

35 LE BŒUF SUR LE TOIT and PULCINELLA

During the period 1923-24, at least two works were rehearsed by Balanchine but not performed. The four-hand piano score to Stravinsky's *Pulcinella* had been smuggled into Russia; Balanchine began preparing the ballet in January 1924, but the project proved to be beyond the resources of the Young Ballet and had to be abandoned. He also rehearsed the Milhaud-Cocteau *Le Bœuf sur le Toit*.

See 379

1925

36 PIZZICATO POLKA

MUSIC: By Léo Delibes (from *Sylvia, ou la Nymphe de Diane*, produced 1876).

CHOREOGRAPHY: By George Balanchine after Serafima Astafieva.

PREMIERE: February 1925 (before February 21), the Royal Palace, Monte Carlo.

CAST: Alicia Markova.

NOTE: First performed at a party given by the Princesse Héréditaire. Earliest program found (February 21, 1925, matinee) lists the work, then entitled *Variation*, as part of the 'Suite de Danses' under the general title *Le Festin*, in the series of concert performances by Diaghilev's Ballets Russes given in the Nouvelle Salle de Musique (Salle Ganne) of the Monte Carlo Casino.

See 273, 350, 387

37 VALSE CAPRICE

MUSIC: By Anton Rubinstein (Op. 118).

CHOREOGRAPHY: By George Balanchine after Serafima Astafieva.

PREMIERE: February 1925 (before February 21), the Royal Palace, Monte Carlo.

CAST: Alicia Markova.

NOTE: First performed at a party given by the Princesse Héréditaire. Earliest program found (March 4, 1925, matinee) lists the work as part of the 'Suite de Danses' under the general title *L'Assemblée*, in the series of concert performances by Diaghilev's Ballets Russes given in the Nouvelle Salle de Musique (Salle Ganne) of the Monte Carlo Casino.

See 14

38 CARMEN

Opera in Four Acts by Georges Bizet
ACT II SEGUIDILLA

PREMIERE: January 25, 1925, Opéra de Monte-Carlo. Danced by Diaghilev's Ballets Russes.

CAST: 4 couples.

NOTE: Diaghilev's dancers were employed between ballet seasons as the resident company of the Opéra de Monte-Carlo, and his first assignments to Balanchine were opera divertissements. Balanchine has said that all choreography for operas in Monte Carlo during his tenure with Diaghilev was newly created by him; programs occasionally include no credits for choreography, and it may be that some dances by Nijinska, resident choreographer with Diaghilev at Monte Carlo in 1923 and 1924, remained during Balanchine's early years. When choreography credits appear in the opera programs between 1925 and 1929, they are variously given as 'Maître de ballet: Georges Balanchine,' 'Chorégraphie de Georges Balanchine,' or 'Ballet reglé par Georges Balanchine'; the significance of these differences is unknown.

See 127, 155, 248

39 THAÏS
Opera in Three Acts and Six Scenes by Jules Massenet
ACT I DIVERTISSEMENT

PREMIERE: January 27, 1925, Opéra de Monte-Carlo. Danced by Diaghilev's Ballets Russes. Conductor: Léon Jehin.

CAST: 13 women.

40 MANON
Opera in Four Acts by Jules Massenet
ACT III BALLET

PREMIERE: February 5, 1925, Opéra de Monte-Carlo. Danced by Diaghilev's Ballets Russes.

CAST: Alexandra Danilova, Thadée Slavinsky, corps de ballet.

See 122, 159

41 LE HULLA
Oriental Lyric Tale in Four Acts by Marcel Samuel-Rousseau
ACT III DIVERTISSEMENT

PREMIERE: February 12, 1925, Opéra de Monte-Carlo. Danced by Diaghilev's Ballets Russes. Conductor: Marcel Samuel-Rousseau.

CAST: Vera Nemtchinova, 4 women.

42 LE DÉMON

Fantastic Opera in Three Acts by Anton Rubinstein
ACT II BALLET

PREMIERE: February 14, 1925, Opéra de Monte-Carlo. Danced by Diaghilev's Ballets Russes. Conductor: Victor de Sabata.

CAST: Lubov Tchernicheva, Léon Woizikowsky, 8 men.

NOTE: The dance from *Le Démon*, a lezghinka, was performed as part of the 'Suite de Danses' under the general title *L'Assemblée* (March 7, 1925, matinee), in the series of concert performances by Diaghilev's Ballets Russes given in the Nouvelle Salle de Musique (Salle Ganne) of the Monte Carlo Casino.

43 HOPAC

MUSIC: By Modest Moussorgsky (from *The Fair at Sorochinsk*, 1874-80 [unfinished]).

PREMIERE: February 21, 1925 (matinee), Diaghilev's Ballets Russes, Nouvelle Salle de Musique (Salle Ganne), Monte Carlo Casino.

CAST: Lubov Tchernicheva, Nicolas Kremnev, 4 couples.

See 208

44 FAY-YEN-FAH

Opera in Three Acts by Joseph Redding
ACT II, SCENE I BALLET DIVERTISSEMENT; BALLET VOLANT

PREMIERE: February 26, 1925, Opéra de Monte-Carlo. Danced by Diaghilev's Ballets Russes. Conductor: Victor de Sabata.

CAST: BALLET DIVERTISSEMENT: *Lilies*, 6 women; *Veils*, 8 women; *Chinese Woman*, Vera Nemtchinova; *Chinese Man*, Nicolas Kremnev; *Poppies*, Nemtchinova, 6 women; *White Peacocks*, 2 women; *Gold Peacocks*, 4 women. BALLET VOLANT: 5 women.

NOTE: World premiere.

See 125

45 FAUST

Opera in Five Acts by Charles Gounod
ACT II KERMESSE

PREMIERE: March 5, 1925, Opéra de Monte-Carlo. Danced by Diaghilev's Ballets Russes. Conductor: Marc-César Scotto.

CAST: Corps de ballet.

See 117, 151, 227, 397, 413

46 HÉRODIADE

Opera in Four Acts and Six Scenes by Jules Massenet
ACT III BALLET

PREMIERE: March 7, 1925, Opéra de Monte-Carlo. Danced by Diaghilev's Ballets Russes. Conductor: Marc-César Scotto.

CAST: Lubov Tchernicheva, George Balanchine, Thadée Slavinsky, 14 women, 8 men.

See 119

47 UN DÉBUT

Opera in Two Acts by Philippe Bellenot
ACT II BALLET (DANCES IN RESTAURANT)

PREMIERE: March 21, 1925, Opéra de Monte-Carlo. Danced by Diaghilev's Ballets Russes. Conductor: Léon Jehin.

CAST: Corps de ballet.

NOTE: This brief opera was performed as curtain-raiser for the premiere of Maurice Ravel's *L'Enfant et les Sortilèges*.

48 L'ENFANT ET LES SORTILÈGES
Lyric Fantasy in Two Parts

MUSIC: By Maurice Ravel (1920-25). Libretto by Colette.

PRODUCTION: Directed by Raoul Gunsbourg. Scenery by Alphonse Visconti. Costumes by Georgette Vialet.

PREMIERE: March 21, 1925, Opéra de Monte-Carlo. Danced by Diaghilev's Ballets Russes. Conductor: Victor de Sabata.

CAST: Singers and dancers appeared together on stage. Individual dancers were listed for the first time in the program for February 15, 1926: ACT I: *Shepherds and Shepherdesses*, Alexandra Danilova, Constantin Tcherkas, 2 couples; *Ashes*, Alicia Markova; *3 Sheep*; *Goat*; *Dog*. ACT II: *Butterflies*, Danilova, Tcherkas, 2 women; *4 Squirrels*; *4 Dragonflies*; *5 Frogs*. Sung parts included *The Child*, *2 Cats*, *Easy Chair*, *Princess*, *Mother*, *Nightingale*, *Fire*, *Chinese Cup*, *Dragonfly*, *Bat*, *Squirrel*, *Shepherd and Shepherdess*, *Teacher Arithmetic*, *Clock*, *Armchair*, *Teapot*, *Tree*, *Frog*, *3 Beasts*, *Owl*.

NOTE: A naughty child, confined to his room, smashes the teapot, mistreats his pet squirrel, tears the wallpaper, assaults the fireplace, the clock, his school books. The objects come to life, assert themselves, rebuke him. Transported into a magic garden, the child is confronted by animals and trees that in the past have suffered from his cruelties; they attack him. During the fray a small squirrel is injured; moved to compassion, the child dresses its wound. The animals are astonished; when in despair the child cries out for his mother, they assist him, and lead him to her.

World premiere. Diaghilev's first major assignment to Balanchine, and the first of four Balanchine productions of this work, each a different staging with new décor; the 1981 version, conceived especially for television, used elements from the 1975 production.

OTHER VERSIONS: 1946, Ballet Society (*The Spellbound Child* [*L'Enfant et les Sortilèges*]). 1975, New York City Ballet (*L'Enfant et les Sortilèges*, Ravel Festival). 1981, for the PBS television series Dance in America (*The Spellbound Child / L'Enfant et les Sortilèges*).

See 235, 390, 416

49 LA DAMNATION DE FAUST

'La Taverne' and 'Les Sylphes' from the Opera by Hector Berlioz

BALLET VOLANT (LES SYLPHES)

PREMIERE: March 24, 1925, Opéra de Monte-Carlo. Danced by Diaghilev's Ballets Russes. Conductor: Léon Jehin.

CAST: Corps de ballet.

See 69

50 ÉTUDE

MUSIC: By Alexander Scriabin (probably *Caresse Dansée*, Op. 57, 1908, and one of the preludes, both for piano).

PREMIERE: March 1925, Monte Carlo.

CAST: Ruth Page, Chester Hale.

NOTE: *Étude* and *Polka Mélancolique* [51], the first works commissioned from Balanchine by an American, were choreographed at the request of the dancer Ruth Page during her brief time as a member of the Diaghilev company. They were given unofficial concert performances and were soon lost.

See 30

51 POLKA MÉLANCOLIQUE

MUSIC: By Anton Rubinstein.

PREMIERE: March 1925, Monte Carlo.

CAST: Ruth Page.

NOTE: See 50.

52 LE CHANT DU ROSSIGNOL
(also called THE SONG OF THE NIGHTINGALE)

Ballet in One Act, after Hans Christian Andersen's Fairy Tale

MUSIC: By Igor Stravinsky (symphonic poem for orchestra in three parts, 1917; adapted from his 1913 opera *Le Rossignol*).

CHOREOGRAPHY: Originally choreographed by Léonide Massine (1920); rechoreographed by George Balanchine.

PRODUCTION: Curtain, scenery and costumes by Henri Matisse (from the 1920 production).

PREMIERE: June 17, 1925, Diaghilev's Ballets Russes, Théâtre Gaieté Lyrique, Paris. Conductor: Marc-César Scotto.

CAST: *Nightingale*, Alicia Markova; *Death*, Lydia Sokolova; *Emperor*, Serge Grigoriev; *Mechanical Nightingale*, George Balanchine; *Japanese Maestro*, Nicolas Kremnev; *16 Ladies of the Court*; *6 Warriors*; *6 Mandarins*; *4 Chamberlains*.

NOTE: Stravinsky prefixed a ballet scenario to the score based on quotations from Andersen, with the following headings: 1. The Fête in the Emperor of China's Palace; 2. The Two Nightingales; 3. Illness and Recovery of the Emperor of China.

Balanchine's first choreography for performance in the regular seasons of Diaghilev's Ballets Russes, and his first choreography in the West to music by Stravinsky; in Leningrad he had choreographed *Ragtime* [3], and rehearsed *Pulcinella* [35]. On one occasion when Markova was ill, Balanchine danced the role of the Nightingale.

53 BARABAU
Ballet with Chorus

MUSIC: Music and book by Vittorio Rieti (expanded to an orchestral score with chorus from an existing *a cappella* cantata, *Barabau*, on commission from Serge Diaghilev, 1925).

PRODUCTION: Scenery and costumes by Maurice Utrillo. Scenery executed by Prince A. Schervashidze; costumes executed by Alias and Morris Angel.

PREMIERE: December 11, 1925, Diaghilev's Ballets Russes, Coliseum, London. Conductor: Roger Desormière.

CAST: *Barabau*, Léon Woizikowsky; *Sergeant*, Serge Lifar; *Servants of Barabau*, Alice Nikitina, Alexandra Danilova, Tamara Geva; *Peasants*, 3 men, 3 women; *6 Soldiers*. Chorus on stage.

Note: Balanchine's first original ballet for Diaghilev. Rieti based the plot on an Italian nursery rhyme: When a village party in Barabau's garden is disrupted by soldiers, Barabau feigns death; the villagers carry him mournfully to church, but as soon as the soldiers depart he revives, and they return him to his home in triumph.

Revisions: Soon after London opening, role of one female peasant enlarged, with additional solo to new music.

Stagings: 1931, Royal Danish.

1926

54 BORIS GODUNOV
Opera in Four Acts and Nine Scenes by Modest Moussorgsky
ACT III POLONAISE

Premiere: February 9, 1926, Opéra de Monte-Carlo. Danced by Diaghilev's Ballets Russes. Conductor: Victor de Sabata.

Cast: 9 women, 10 men.

See 298, 388

55 JUDITH
Opera in Three Acts and Four Scenes by Arthur Honegger
ACT III, SCENE 2 BALLET

Premiere: February 13, 1926, Opéra de Monte-Carlo. Danced by Diaghilev's Ballets Russes. Conductor: Arthur Honegger.

Cast: 12 women, 12 men.

Note: World premiere.

56 L'HIRONDELLE (LA RONDINE)
Opera in Three Acts by Giacomo Puccini
ACT II VALSE

PREMIERE: February 20, 1926, Opéra de Monte-Carlo. Danced by Diaghilev's Ballets Russes. Conductor: Victor de Sabata.

CAST: Lydia Sokolova, Léon Woizikowsky, corps de ballet.

See 161

57 LAKMÉ
Opera in Three Acts by Léo Delibes
ACT II BALLET

PREMIERE: March 2, 1926, Opéra de Monte-Carlo. Danced by Diaghilev's Ballets Russes. Conductor: Léon Jehin.

CAST: Lubov Tchernicheva, 12 women.

See 115, 153

58 LES CONTES D'HOFFMANN
Opera in Three Acts and Five Scenes by Jacques Offenbach
SCENE 2 BALLET

PREMIERE: March 7, 1926, Opéra de Monte-Carlo. Danced by Diaghilev's Ballets Russes. Conductor: Léon Jehin.

CAST: VALSE: 4 women; PAS DE DEUX: Alexandra Danilova, Stanislas Idzikowsky; VARIATION: Idzikowsky; VARIATION: Danilova; POLKA: Tamara Geva, Thadée Slavinsky; GRANDE VALSE: 6 couples.

See 112, 260

59 JEANNE D'ARC
Mystery in Seven Parts by Charles Gounod
ACT III BALLET

PREMIERE: March 28, 1926, Opéra de Monte-Carlo. Danced by Diaghilev's Ballets Russes. Conductor: Léon Jehin.

CAST: DANCE OF THE SOLDIERS AND BOHEMIAN WOMEN: 4 women, 4 men; DANCE OF THE KNIGHTS AND LADIES OF THE COURT: 8 couples.

NOTE: Presented with *La Fête du Printemps* from Ambroise Thomas' *Hamlet*.

60 HAMLET

'La Fête du Printemps' from the Opera by Ambroise Thomas

BALLET DIVERTISSEMENT

PREMIERE: March 28, 1926, Opéra de Monte-Carlo. Danced by Diaghilev's Ballets Russes. Conductor: Léon Jehin.

CAST: ANDANTINO: Lubov Tchernicheva, Léon Woizikowsky, 14 women; VARIATION: Woizikowsky; ALLEGRETTO: 9 women; VALSE-MAZURKA: 3 women; VARIATION: Nadejda Nicolaeva, 4 women; ADAGIO: Tchernicheva, Woizikowsky; VARIATION: Alexandra Danilova; VALSE: Tchernicheva; CODA: Tchernicheva, Woizikowsky, 5 women.

61 ROMEO AND JULIET

A Rehearsal, without Scenery, in Two Parts

ENTR'ACTE

MUSIC: By Constant Lambert (*Adam and Eve* ballet score, 1924-25, retitled by Diaghilev).

CHOREOGRAPHY: By Bronislava Nijinska; choreography of the entr'acte by George Balanchine.

PRODUCTION: 'Night' and 'Day' curtains by Max Ernst; front curtain and stage pieces by Joan Miró. Curtains and stage pieces executed by Prince A. Schervashidze; costumes executed by Georgette Vialet.

PREMIERE: May 4, 1926, Diaghilev's Ballets Russes, Opéra de Monte-Carlo. Conductor: Marc-César Scotto.

CAST: PART I: Tamara Karsavina, Serge Lifar; *Maestro*, Thadée Slavinsky; 14 women, 12 men. PART II: *Juliet*, Karsavina; *Romeo*, Lifar; *Nurse*, Lydia Sokolova; *Pierre, Servant to Capulet*, Léon Woizikowsky; *The Maestro, Rehearsing as Tybalt*, Slavinsky; *Paris*, Constantin Tcherkas; 14 women, 12 men.

NOTE: Balanchine's entr'acte was staged without music between the two parts. A drop-curtain was lowered to within a foot or two of the ground so that only the dancers' legs and feet were visible.

62 LA PASTORALE

MUSIC: By Georges Auric (1926, commissioned by Serge Diaghilev). Book by Boris Kochno.

PRODUCTION: Curtain, scenery and costumes by Pedro Pruna. Curtain and scenery executed by Prince A. Schervashidze; costumes executed by La Maison Jules Muelle. Bicycle by Olympique.

PREMIERE: May 29, 1926, Diaghilev's Ballets Russes, Théâtre Sarah-Bernhardt, Paris. Conductor: Roger Desormière.

CAST: *The Star*, Felia Doubrovska; *A Young Lady*, Tamara Geva; *4 Young Ladies*; *Telegraph Boy*, Serge Lifar; *Régisseur*, Thadée Slavinsky; *2 Actors*; *2 Operators*.

NOTE: While a telegraph delivery boy takes an impromptu swim, a young girl as a prank steals his messages from his bicycle. The boy takes a nap on the stream bank; a movie company appears and sets up a scene; the boy awakens to find himself in a duet with the movie star. Villagers seeking their telegrams disrupt the scene and the boy runs away; returning at nightfall for his bicycle he finds the young girl, and they ride off together.

63 JACK IN THE BOX

MUSIC: By Erik Satie (unpublished piano score for pantomime, 1899; orchestrated after Satie's death in 1925 by Darius Milhaud).

PRODUCTION: Scenery and costumes by André Derain. Scenery executed by Prince A. Schervashidze; costumes executed by La Maison Jules Muelle.

PREMIERE: June 8, 1926, Diaghilev's Ballets Russes, Théâtre Sarah-Bernhardt, Paris. Conductor: Roger Desormière.

CAST: *The Puppet*, Stanislas Idzikowsky; *The Black Dancer*, Alexandra Danilova; *2 Dancers* (women); *2 Cloud Bearers* (men).

NOTE: The principal dancer is a comic puppet with whom the Black Dancer and two others perform as if they are attending a ball. In the background large cardboard clouds are moved by mimes.

64 THE TRIUMPH OF NEPTUNE
(also called LE TRIOMPHE DE NEPTUNE)

English Pantomime in Twelve Tableaux

MUSIC: By Lord Berners (1926, commissioned by Serge Diaghilev). Book by Sacheverell Sitwell.

PRODUCTION: Scenery and costumes after historical prints by George and Robert Cruikshank, Tofts, Honigold, and Webb, collected by B. Pollock and H. J. Webb. Costumes designed by Pedro Pruna; scenery and costumes adapted and executed by Prince A. Schervashidze.

PREMIERE: December 3, 1926, Diaghilev's Ballets Russes, Lyceum Theatre, London. Conductor: Henri Defosse.

CAST: *The Fairy Queen*, Alexandra Danilova; *Tom Tug, a Sailor*, Serge Lifar; *W. Brown, a Journalist*, Michael Fedorov; *Goddess [Britannia]*, Lydia Sokolova; *Emerald Fairy*; *Ruby Fairy*; *Fairies*, 16 women; *Sylphs*, Lubov Tchernicheva, Vera Petrova; *Street Dancer*, Tatiana Chamié; *The Sailor's Wife*; *The Sailor's Mother*; *Snowball, a Blackman*, George Balanchine; *Harlequins*, 6 men; *Pages*, 9 men; *Dandy*, Constantin Tcherkas; *2 Journalists*; *2 Policemen*; *Cab Driver*; *2 Telescope Keepers*; *Waiter*; *Beggar*; *2 Street Hawkers*; *3 Workmen*; *2 News Vendors*; *3 Newspaper Boys*; *Officer*; *Chimney Sweep*; *King of the Ogres*, Michel Pavloff; *10 Ogres*; *2 Clowns*; *3 Neptune Attendants*; *Voice*, Enrico Garcia.

Act I: CURTAIN [dance]. SCENE 1: London Bridge. SCENE 2: Cloudland. SCENE 3: Farewell. SCENE 4: Shipwreck. SCENE 5: Fleet Street. SCENE 6: The Frozen Wood.

Act II: CURTAIN [dance]. SCENE 7: The Giant Hand. SCENE 8: The Evil Grotto. SCENE 9: The Ogres' Castle. SCENE 10: Sunday Morning in London. SCENE 11: The Triumph of Neptune. SCENE 12: Apotheosis.

NOTE: Based on English pantomimes of the 1850s, the ballet follows the voyage to fairyland of a sailor and a journalist, and events back in London, where they are observed through a magic telescope. In the Apotheosis the sailor, deserted by his London wife, weds Neptune's daughter. Balanchine sometimes danced the roles of the tipsy Snowball, the Beggar and the leading Harlequin.

REVISIONS: 1927: *Cupid* (Stanislas Idzikowsky) added, with new variation. Within six months of the premiere (Paris, May 1927), Scenes 5, 8 and 9 had been deleted, as had several minor characters.

1927

65 AURORA'S WEDDING: ARIADNE AND HER BROTHERS

In 1926 or 1927 Balanchine replaced the pas de trois for a man and two women in *Aurora's Wedding* (divertissements from Act III of Petipa's *The Sleeping Beauty* [Tschaikovsky]) known as 'Florestan and His Sisters,' with a pas de trois for a woman and two men called 'Ariadne and Her Brothers.' The earliest program found is for the January 10, 1927, performance of Diaghilev's Ballets Russes at La Scala, Milan.

Throughout his tenure as ballet master to Diaghilev, Balanchine made frequent adjustments to repertory pieces, from minor alterations to entire new variations; most of these changes are not noted on printed programs. During the frequent periods between the seasons of the Ballets Russes, Balanchine is also known to have created choreography for productions in provincial opera houses in France; these are no longer possible to document.

See 225, 259, 281, 404, 418

66 SAMSON ET DALILA

Opera in Three Acts and Four Scenes by Camille Saint-Saëns
ACT III DIVERTISSEMENT

PREMIERE: January 27, 1927, Opéra de Monte-Carlo. Danced by Diaghilev's Ballets Russes. Conductor: Léon Jehin.

CAST: Lubov Tchernicheva, 16 women.

See 116, 171, 228

67 LA TRAVIATA

Opera in Four Acts by Giuseppe Verdi
ACT III BALLET

PREMIERE: February 8, 1927, Opéra de Monte-Carlo. Danced by Diaghilev's Ballets Russes. Conductor: Victor de Sabata.

CAST: Vera Petrova, Nicholas Efimov, 6 couples.

See 123, 150, 252

68 TURANDOT

Opera in Three Acts and Four Scenes by Giacomo Puccini
ACT II DIVERTISSEMENT, LES PORCELAINES DE CHINE

PREMIERE: February 22, 1927, Opéra de Monte-Carlo. Danced by Diaghilev's Ballets Russes. Conductor: Victor de Sabata.

CAST: Lubov Tchernicheva, Alexandra Danilova, Stanislas Idzikowsky, Léon Woizikowsky, George Balanchine, corps de ballet.

See 120

69 LA DAMNATION DE FAUST

Opera in Five Acts and Ten Scenes by Hector Berlioz
SCENE 2 BALLET (PEASANT DANCE); SCENE 4 BALLET VOLANT

PREMIERE: February 26, 1927, Opéra de Monte-Carlo. Danced by Diaghilev's Ballets Russes. Conductor: Léon Jehin.

CAST: PEASANT DANCE: 6 couples. BALLET VOLANT: 5 women; *Sylphs*, 8 women; *Those with Lanterns*, 10 women.

See 49

70 IVAN LE TERRIBLE

Opera in Three Acts by Raoul Gunsbourg
ACT III BALLET DIVERTISSEMENT

PREMIERE: March 3, 1927, Opéra de Monte-Carlo. Danced by Diaghilev's Ballets Russes. Conductor: Léon Jehin.

CAST: Lydia Sokolova, Léon Woizikowsky, 12 women, 11 men.

71 OBÉRON

Comic and Fantastic Opera in Three Acts and Eleven Scenes
by Carl Maria von Weber

ACT II BALLET

PREMIERE: March 26, 1927, Opéra de Monte-Carlo. Danced by Diaghilev's Ballets Russes. Conductor: Léon Jehin.

CAST: 21 women, 16 men.

72 LA CHATTE (also called THE CAT)

Ballet in One Act

MUSIC: By Henri Sauguet (1927, commissioned by Serge Diaghilev). Book by Sobeka [Boris Kochno] (after one of Aesop's Fables).

PRODUCTION: Architecture and sculpture constructed by Naum Gabo and Antoine Pevsner.

PREMIERE: April 30, 1927, Diaghilev's Ballets Russes, Opéra de Monte-Carlo. Conductor: Marc-César Scotto.

CAST: *The Cat*, Olga Spessivtseva; *The Young Man*, Serge Lifar; *His Companions*, 6 men.

NOTE: Deserting his male companions, a young man in love with a cat persuades Aphrodite to change the cat into a beautiful girl. Tempted by the goddess, the girl gives chase to a mouse, and is turned into a cat again; the boy dies broken-hearted. The cast of seven men and one woman danced around and through transparent Constructivist forms against a black background. Lifar's 1933 version, which retained his solos but little more, was produced without the collaboration of the choreographer.

STAGINGS: 1933, Serge Lifar and His Russian Ballets (American tour).

73 GROTESQUE ESPAGNOL

MUSIC: By Isaac Albéniz (*Córdoba*).

PRODUCTION: Presented by F. Ray Comstock and Morris Guest.

PREMIERE: October 10, 1927, Balieff's Chauve-Souris (The Bat Theatre of Moscow), Cosmopolitan Theater, New York.

CAST: Tamara Geva.

NOTE: *Grotesque Espagnol* and *Sarcasm* [74] were two of nineteen numbers in the 1927 version of Chauve-Souris, annual productions by Nikita Balieff of evenings of Russian cabaret which toured Europe and America. Balanchine choreographed the two pieces before the company departed from Paris for a New York season, where they became the first Balanchine works to be performed in America, and the first Balanchine choreography seen by Lincoln Kirstein.

74 SARCASM

MUSIC: By Sergei Prokofiev (Op. 17, 1912).

PRODUCTION: Presented by F. Ray Comstock and Morris Guest.

PREMIERE: October 10, 1927, Balieff's Chauve-Souris (The Bat Theatre of Moscow), Cosmopolitan Theater, New York.

CAST: Tamara Geva.

NOTE: See 73.

75 SWAN LAKE

At some time in the mid-1920s (1927?), Balanchine made minor alterations in Diaghilev's one-act *Swan Lake* (Tschaikovsky, choreographed by Ivanov and Petipa), deleting part of the Swan Queen's mime and rearranging ensemble movements for a decreased corps de ballet. Olga Spessivtseva was probably the first ballerina to dance the Swan Queen in this revised version.

See 191, 262, 285, 331, 367

1928

76 MIREILLE
Opera in Three Acts by Charles Gounod
ACT II FARANDOLE

PREMIERE: January 28, 1928, Opéra de Monte-Carlo. Danced by Diaghilev's Ballets Russes. Conductor: Marc-César Scotto.

CAST: Henriette Maikerska, Nicolas Kremnev, 8 couples.

77 LES MAÎTRES CHANTEURS
(DIE MEISTERSINGER VON NÜRNBERG)
Opera in Three Acts by Richard Wagner
ACT III DANSE

PREMIERE: February 5, 1928, Opéra de Monte-Carlo. Danced by Diaghilev's Ballets Russes. Conductor: Michel Steiman.

CAST: Dora Vadimova, Henriette Maikerska, Nicholas Efimov, Constantin Tcherkas.

See 163

78 VENISE
Opera in Three Acts and Four Scenes by Raoul Gunsbourg
ACT II, LE CARNAVAL

PREMIERE: February 23, 1928, Opéra de Monte-Carlo. Danced by Diaghilev's Ballets Russes. Conductor: Michel Steiman.

CAST: Alexandra Danilova, Léon Woizikowsky, 12 couples.

79 SIOR TODÉRO BRONTOLON

Comic Opera in One Act and Two Scenes by Gian Francesco Malipiero

BALLET

PREMIERE: March 8, 1928, Opéra de Monte-Carlo. Danced by Diaghilev's Ballets Russes. Conductor: Michel Steiman.

CAST: 3 couples.

80 UN BAL MASQUÉ (UN BALLO IN MASCHERA)

Opera in Three Acts by Giuseppe Verdi

ACT III DIVERTISSEMENT

PREMIERE: March 10, 1928, Opéra de Monte-Carlo. Danced by Diaghilev's Ballets Russes. Conductor: Marc-César Scotto.

CAST: 10 couples.

81 DON JUAN (DON GIOVANNI)

Opera in Three Acts and Seven Scenes by Wolfgang Amadeus Mozart

ACT II BALLET

PREMIERE: March 17, 1928, Opéra de Monte-Carlo. Danced by Diaghilev's Ballets Russes. Conductor: Michel Steiman.

CAST: 4 couples.

See 181, 253

82 LA FILLE D'ABDOUBARAHAH

Comic Opera in One Act by Sanvel

BALLET

PREMIERE: March 20, 1928, Opéra de Monte-Carlo. Danced by Diaghilev's Ballets Russes. Conductor: Florian Weiss.

CAST: Felia Doubrovska, Nicholas Efimov, Nicolas Kremnev, Michael Fedorov, Jean Yazvinsky, corps de ballet.

83 ALEKO and POLKA GROTESQUE

Probably in the spring of 1928, when both the Pavlova and Diaghilev companies were in Paris, Balanchine choreographed *Aleko* (a gypsy dance to music by Sergei Rachmaninoff) and *Polka Grotesque* (music unknown) for Nina Kirsanova and Thadée Slavinsky, at the request of Anna Pavlova, for her company's tour to South America in the fall of that year. A Balanchine work for Pavlova herself, possibly to Scarlatti, was discussed but not choreographed.

84 APOLLON MUSAGÈTE

(also called APOLLO MUSAGETES; APOLLO, LEADER OF THE MUSES; APOLLO; APOLO MUSAGETA)
Ballet in Two Scenes

MUSIC: Music and book by Igor Stravinsky (*Apollo Musagetes*, 1927-28, commissioned by Mrs. Elizabeth Sprague Coolidge, 1927).

PRODUCTION: Scenery and costumes by André Bauchant. (New costumes by Chanel, 1929.) Scenery executed by Prince A. Schervashidze; costumes executed under the direction of Mme A. Youkine.

PREMIERE: June 12, 1928, Diaghilev's Ballets Russes, Théâtre Sarah-Bernhardt, Paris. Conductor: Igor Stravinsky. Violinist: Marcel Darrieux.

CAST: *Apollo*, Serge Lifar; *Terpsichore*, Alice Nikitina; *Calliope*, Lubov Tchernicheva; *Polyhymnia*, Felia Doubrovska; *2 Goddesses*; *Leto, Mother of Apollo*, Sophie Orlova.

SCENE I: THE BIRTH OF APOLLO. SCENE 2: Apollo; PAS D'ACTION (Apollo and Muses): Calliope; Polyhymnia; Terpsichore; Apollo; PAS DE DEUX (Apollo and Terpsichore); CODA; APOTHEOSIS (Apollo and Muses).

NOTE: SCENE I: Leto's labor, and the birth and youth of Apollo; two goddesses present him with a lute and teach him music. SCENE 2: Apollo plays the lute and dances. The three Muses enter; he presents each with an emblem of her art: Calliope, receiving the stylus and tablet, personifies poetry and rhythm; Polyhymnia, finger to lips, represents mime; Terpsichore combines both poetry and gesture in dance and is honored by Apollo. He dances a solo variation and a pas de deux with Terpsichore. APOTHEOSIS: Apollo and the Muses join in a final dance and ascend toward Parnassus.

Stravinsky conceived and composed *Apollo Musagetes* as a ballet; the music was commissioned for a festival of contemporary music in Washington, D. C., with choreography by Adolph Bolm. Balanchine's production was his first collaboration with the composer; he later described the choreography as the turning point in his creative life.

REVISIONS: 1928, Ballets Russes: Variation for Alexandra Danilova (alternating as Terpsichore in the original production) differed from Nikitina's. 1978, Second International Dance Festival: SCENE I omitted. 1979, New York City Ballet: For a revival with Mikhail Baryshnikov as Apollo, SCENE I and Apollo's first variation omitted; ending of APOTHEOSIS rechoreographed to conclude with earlier tableau of Muses posing beside Apollo in arabesque, visually suggesting the sun and its rays, instead of ascending Mount Parnassus. 1980, New York City Ballet: Apollo's first variation restored.

NEW PRODUCTIONS BY BALANCHINE COMPANIES: 1937, American Ballet: Scenery and costumes by Stewart Chaney. 1941, American Ballet Caravan: Scenery and costumes by Tomás Santa Rosa. 1951, New York City Ballet: Costumes by Karinska. 1957, New York City Ballet: Danced in practice clothes with minimal scenery; scenery omitted entirely since 1979.

STAGINGS: 1931, Royal Danish; 1937, American Ballet; 1941, American Ballet Caravan; 1942, Colón; 1943, Ballet Theatre; 1946, Sociedad Pro-Arte Musical; 1947, Paris; 1948, Cuba; late 1940s?, La Plata; 1950, Ballet Nacional; 1951, New York City Ballet; 1955, San Francisco; 1958, Civic Ballet Society; 1960, Uruguay; 1962, Hamburg; 1965, Boston, São Paulo; 1966, Dutch National, Norway, Royal; 1967, Stuttgart, Vienna; 1969, Berlin, Geneva; 1970, Florence, Royal Ballet Touring; 1971, Düsseldorf, La Scala; 1973, Wisconsin, Rome; 1974, Nureyev and Friends, Munich, Royal Flemish; 1975, Palermo; 1976, Chicago Lyric Opera (excerpts), Turin; 1977, Gothenburg, Hungary; 1978, Second International Dance Festival, Catania; 1979, Bologna; 1981, San Juan.

TELEVISION: 1960 (CBC, Montreal); 1962 (BBC, London); 1963 (excerpts, Bell Telephone Hour, NBC); 1967 (rehearsal and performance, BBC, London); 1969 (L'Heure du Concert, CBC, Montreal); 1972 (rehearsal, PBS); ca. 1974 (German television; rebroadcast 1976, BBC, London); 1979 (pas de deux, The Magic of Dance, BBC, London).

See 176, 198, 284

85 THE GODS GO A-BEGGING
(also called LES DIEUX MENDIANTS)
Pastorale

MUSIC: By George Frederick Handel, arranged by Sir Thomas Beecham on commission from Serge Diaghilev (selections from the following compositions written between 1707 and 1739: *Rodrigo*; *Il Pastor Fido*; *Teseo*; *Admeto*; *Alcina* [four numbers]; two of the Opus 6 concerti grossi, including the Hornpipe movement from No. 7). Book by Sobeka [Boris Kochno].

PRODUCTION: Scenery by Léon Bakst (backcloth from first part of *Daphnis et Chloé* [Fokine], 1912). Costumes (with two exceptions) by Juan Gris (from *Les Tentations de la Bergère* [Nijinska], 1924).

PREMIERE: July 16, 1928, Diaghilev's Ballets Russes, His Majesty's Theatre, London. Conductor: Sir Thomas Beecham.

CAST: *The Serving Maid* and *The Shepherd* [divinities in disguise], Alexandra Danilova, Léon Woizikowsky; *Two Ladies*, Lubov Tcherni-cheva, Felia Doubrovska; *A Nobleman*, Constantin Tcherkas; *6 Ladies*; *6 Noblemen*; *4 Servants*.

NOTE: In the spirit of a *fête champêtre* by Watteau or Lancret. A shepherd wanders in among noble guests at an elaborate picnic; two aristocratic ladies invite him to dance with them, but he chooses to dance with a serving-girl. When indignant noblemen begin to chastise him, the shepherd and the maid cast off their humble dress and reveal themselves to be divinities in disguise.

STAGINGS: 1930, Ballet Club (Shepherd's hornpipe); 1931, Ballet Club (pas de deux, retitled *Shepherd's Wooing*).

TELEVISION: 1935 (excerpts, BBC, London).

1929

86 ROMÉO ET JULIETTE
Opera in Five Acts by Charles Gounod
ACT I DIVERTISSEMENT

PREMIERE: January 24, 1929, Opéra de Monte-Carlo. Danced by Diaghilev's Ballets Russes. Conductor: Gabriel Grovlez.

CAST: 8 couples.

See 124, 180

87 LA GIOCONDA
Opera in Four Acts by Amilcare Ponchielli
ACT I TARANTELLA; ACT III DANCE OF THE HOURS

PREMIERE: January 26, 1929, Opéra de Monte-Carlo. Danced by Diaghilev's Ballets Russes. Conductor: Michel Steiman.

CAST: TARANTELLA: Vera Petrova, Nicholas Efimov, 4 women. DANCE OF THE HOURS: *Morning (Dawn)*, Felia Doubrovska, Mezeslav Borovsky, 4 women; *Day*, Alexandra Danilova, Léon Woizikowsky, 4 women; *Evening*, Petrova, Efimov, 4 women; *Night*, Lubov Tchernicheva, Constantin Tcherkas, 4 women.

See 174

88 RIGOLETTO
Opera in Four Acts by Giuseppe Verdi
ACT I DIVERTISSEMENT

PREMIERE: February 28, 1929, Opéra de Monte-Carlo. Danced by Diaghilev's Ballets Russes. Conductor: Michel Steiman.

CAST: 6 couples.

See 121, 156

89

89 LA FEMME NUE

Opera in Four Acts by Henri Février

ACT II DIVERTISSEMENT

PREMIERE: March 23, 1929, Opéra de Monte-Carlo. Danced by Diaghilev's Ballets Russes. Conductor: Victor de Sabata.

CAST: Alexandra Danilova, Eugenia Lipkowska, Henriette Maikerska, corps de ballet.

NOTE: World premiere.

90 MARTHA

Opera in Four Acts by Friedrich von Flotow

SCENE 4 BALLET

PREMIERE: March 27, 1929, Opéra de Monte-Carlo. Danced by Diaghilev's Ballets Russes. Conductor: Marc-César Scotto.

CAST: Vera Petrova, Eugenia Lipkowska, Léon Woizikowsky, 8 couples.

91 WAKE UP AND DREAM!

Charles B. Cochran's 1929 Revue

MUSIC AND BOOK: Music and lyrics by Cole Porter. Book by John Hastings Turner.

CHOREOGRAPHY: Dances and ensembles by Tilly Losch, Max Rivers and George Balanchine (uncredited).

PRODUCTION: Produced under the personal direction of Charles B. Cochran. Staged by Frank Collins.

PREMIERE: March 29, 1929, London Pavilion. (Out-of-town preview: March 5, Palace Theatre, Manchester [titled *Charles B. Cochran's 1929 Revue*].)

CAST: Tilly Losch, Jessie Matthews, Sonnie Hale, Elsie Carlisle, Toni Birkmayer, and others.

NOTE: Balanchine's initial choreography for British and American musical revues.

WHAT IS THIS THING CALLED LOVE? (Part II, Scene 16): *Choreography*: By George Balanchine, credited to Tilly Losch. *Production*: Setting and The

Idol designed by Oliver Messel. *Cast: Singer*, Elsie Carlisle; *The Girl*, Tilly Losch; *The Man*, Toni Birkmayer; *The Other Woman*, Alanova; *The Idol*, William Cavanagh.

OTHER PRODUCTIONS: New York premiere December 30, 1929, Selwyn Theatre, produced by Arch Selwyn.

92 LA CROISADE DES DAMES (DIE VERSCHWORENEN)
Comic Opera in One Act by Franz Schubert
BALLET

PREMIERE: April 1, 1929, Opéra de Monte-Carlo. Danced by Diaghilev's Ballets Russes. Conductor: Marc-César Scotto.

CAST: Felia Doubrovska, Vera Petrova, Eugenia Lipkowska, corps de ballet.

93 LE BAL (also called THE BALL)
Ballet in Two Tableaux

MUSIC: By Vittorio Rieti (1928, commissioned by Serge Diaghilev). Book by Boris Kochno (suggested by a story by Count Vladimir Sologub).

PRODUCTION: Scenery and costumes by Giorgio de Chirico. Costumes executed under the direction of Mme A. Youkine.

PREMIERE: May 7, 1929, Diaghilev's Ballets Russes, Opéra de Monte-Carlo. Conductor: Marc-César Scotto.

CAST: *The Lady*, Alexandra Danilova; *The Young Man*, Anton Dolin; *The Astrologer*, André Bobrow; SPANISH ENTRANCE: Felia Doubrovska, Léon Woizikowsky, George Balanchine; ITALIAN ENTRANCE: Eugenia Lipkowska, Serge Lifar; *The Sylphides*, 4 women; *The Guests*, 12 women, 13 men; *The Statues*, 2 men.
    I. Prologue. II. The Ball.

NOTE: In the midst of a ball a Young Man seeks out a Lady accompanied by an Astrologer and begs her to remove her mask; she complies, and to his horror reveals the face of an old woman; he flees, she pursues him, and he hides. After the ball the Young Man is alone in the ballroom. The Lady returns with the Astrologer, unmasks, but then pulls off her face, which is only a second mask—and is revealed as a young and beautiful woman. The Astrologer, too, unmasks and appears a handsome youth; he embraces the Lady and they depart, as the Young Man falls swooning.

REVISIONS: Two Archeologists added for London season, July 1929.

94 LE FILS PRODIGUE (also called PRODIGAL SON)
Ballet in Three Scenes

MUSIC: By Sergei Prokofiev (Op. 46, 1928-29, commissioned by Serge Diaghilev, 1927). Book by Boris Kochno (after the biblical parable).

PRODUCTION: Scenery and costumes by Georges Rouault. Scenery executed by Prince A. Schervashidze; costumes executed by Vera Soudeikina.

PREMIERE: May 21, 1929, Diaghilev's Ballets Russes, Théâtre Sarah-Bernhardt, Paris. Conductor: Sergei Prokofiev.

CAST: *The Prodigal Son,* Serge Lifar; *The Father,* Michael Fedorov; *The Siren,* Felia Doubrovska; *The Servants,* Eleanora Marra, Nathalie Branitzka; *Confidants of the Prodigal Son,* Léon Woizikowsky, Anton Dolin; *Friends of the Prodigal Son,* 12 men.

    I. 1. The Prodigal Son leaves the paternal home, accompanied by his two Confidants.

    II. 2. The Prodigal Son meets his friends and takes part in their festival. 3. Entry and dance of the Siren, which takes place beside the Prodigal Son. 4. The Confidants of the Prodigal Son entertain the guests. 5. The Prodigal Son dances with the Siren. 6. The Siren and the Friends of the Prodigal Son force him to drink. 7. The Confidants, the Friends and the Siren strip the sleeping Prodigal Son and take flight. 8. The awakening and lamentations of the Prodigal Son. 9. Promenade of the Siren, the Confidants, and the Friends of the Prodigal Son, laden with their spoils.

    III. 10. Return of the repentant Prodigal Son to the paternal home.

REVISIONS: After the death of Diaghilev and the disbanding of his Ballets Russes, the Balanchine choreography for *Le Fils Prodigue* was not seen until it was revived for the New York City Ballet in 1950 as *Prodigal Son.* At that time and subsequently the cast of characters was listed somewhat differently: Servants became Sisters; Confidants became

Servants; Friends became Drinking Companions. The number of Drinking Companions was smaller (12 in the original, 9 in the New York City Ballet revival). In 1977, the dances of the two Servants (men) were omitted from the New York City Ballet production; they were restored in the 1980 American Ballet Theatre staging. Long-time observers have noticed other changes, but Balanchine has said that the choreography remains essentially the same.

STAGINGS: 1950, New York City Ballet; 1966, Boston, Dutch National, Tokyo Ballet Geikijo; 1967, National; 1968, Royal Danish; 1973, Paris, Royal, Royal Ballet Touring; 1974, Houston, Geneva; 1975, Chicago; 1978, Pittsburgh; 1980, American Ballet Theatre.

TELEVISION: 1973 (Wide World of Entertainment, ABC); 1978 (Dance in America, PBS).

See 267

95 PAS DE DEUX (later called MOODS)

MUSIC: By Raie da Costa, orchestrated by De Caillaux.

PRODUCTION: Production supervised by Anton Dolin. Costumes by Phyllis Dolton, executed by Sims.

PREMIERE: September 2, 1929, Anton Dolin with Anna Ludmila and Company, Coliseum, London. Conductor: Alfred Dove.

CAST: Anton Dolin, Anna Ludmila.

NOTE: Anton Dolin formed a small company after the death of Diaghilev on August 19, 1929. For an engagement at the London Coliseum the troupe performed five numbers (of which the Balanchine pas de deux was the fifth) on a variety program with eleven other acts.

96 LES CRÉATURES DE PROMÉTHÉE
Ballet in Two Acts

MUSIC: By Ludwig van Beethoven (*Die Geschöpfe des Prometheus,* produced 1801, commissioned by Salvatore Viganò).

CHOREOGRAPHY: By George Balanchine and Serge Lifar.

PRODUCTION: Scenery and costumes by Quelvée. Scenery executed by Mouveau.

PREMIERE: December 30, 1929, Paris Opéra Ballet, Théâtre National de l'Opéra, Paris. Conductor: J.-E. Szyfer.

CAST: Olga Spessivtseva, Serge Lifar; Mlles Lorcia, Lamballe, Cérès, M. Peretti; 5 demi-soloists, 13 women, 9 men.

NOTE: Jacques Rouché, director of the Paris Opéra, engaged Balanchine to choreograph the ballet. Balanchine conceived the basic outline and created some of the dances, then became ill; Lifar completed the ballet and received credit on the printed program.

97 DARK RED ROSES

Film

PRODUCTION: Produced by Era Films; British International Film Distributors. Directed by Sinclair Hill. From a story by Stacy Aumonier.

RELEASED: 1929.

CAST: Stewart Rome, Frances Doble, Hugh Eden, Kate Cutler, Jack Clayton, Jill Clayton, Una O'Connor, Sydney Morgan, and others.

NOTE: The first feature-length talking motion picture made in England. During the filming, Balanchine, Dolin and Lopokova learned of Diaghilev's death in Venice.

TARTAR BALLET, 'JEALOUSY': *Music*: By Modest Moussorgsky (selections from *Khovanshchina*, 1872-80 [unfinished]). *Cast*: *Tartar*, George Balanchine; *His Wife*, Lydia Lopokova; *Minstrel*, Anton Dolin.

See 31

1930

98 AUBADE

MUSIC: By Francis Poulenc (*Aubade* for piano and 18 instruments, 1929, commissioned by Vicomte and Vicomtesse de Noailles).

PRODUCTION: Scenery and costumes by Angèles Ortiz, executed by Mme A. Youkine (uncredited).

PREMIERE: January 21, 1930, Ballets Russes de Vera Nemtchinova, Théâtre des Champs-Élysées, Paris. Conductor: Alexandre Labinsky. Pianist: Francis Poulenc.

CAST: *Diana*, Vera Nemtchinova; *Actaeon*, Alexis Dolinoff; *Diana's Companions*, 6 women.

NOTE: A Greek myth: At dawn, the hunter Actaeon surprises the goddess Diana bathing; she transforms him into a deer, wounds him, and turning her companions into dogs, sets them upon him. With a pang of regret, the goddess resumes her course through the forest; day has come.

STAGINGS: 1936, Les Ballets de Monte-Carlo (René Blum).

99 CHARLES B. COCHRAN'S 1930 REVUE

MUSIC AND BOOK: Music by Vivian Ellis and Beverley Nichols. Ballet music by Lord Berners and Henri Sauguet. Book by Beverley Nichols. Ballet libretti by Boris Kochno.

CHOREOGRAPHY: Dances and ensembles by George Balanchine, Serge Lifar and Ralph Reader.

PRODUCTION: Entire production under the personal direction of Charles B. Cochran. Staged by Frank Collins.

PREMIERE: March 27, 1930, London Pavilion. (Out-of-town preview: March 4, Palace Theatre, Manchester.)

CAST: Maisie Gay, Ada-May, Serge Lifar, Alice Nikitina, Fowler and Tamara, Roy Royston, Eric Marshall, and others.

IN A VENETIAN THEATRE (Part I, Scene 8): *Music*: By Vivian Ellis. *Production*: Costumes executed by Reville, Ltd. *Cast*: Mr. Cochran's Young Ladies.

LUNA PARK, OR THE FREAKS (Part I, Scene 10): *Music*: By Lord Berners. Book by Boris Kochno. *Production*: Scenery and costumes by Christopher Wood. Scenery executed by E. Delany; costumes executed by C. Alias, Ltd. *Cast*: *The Showman*, Nicholas Efimov; *The Three-headed Man*, Constantin Tcherkas; *The Three-legged Man*, Richard Domonsky; *The One-legged Woman*, Alice Nikitina; *The Six-armed Man*, Serge Lifar.

PICCADILLY, 1830 (Part I, Scene 13): *Music*: By Ivor Novello. *Production*: Scenery and costumes by Oliver Messel. Scenery executed by Alick Johnstone; costumes executed by C. Alias, Ltd. *Cast*: *The Dancers*, Fowler and Tamara; *The Singer*, Eric Marshall; *Some Promenaders*, Mr. Cochran's Young Ladies and Gentlemen; *A Highlander*, Lifar; *An Elderly Invalid*, Efimov; *His Wife*, Nikitina; *His Servants*, Tcherkas, Domonsky.

HEAVEN (Part I, Scene 14): *Music*: By Beverley Nichols and Ivor Novello. *Production*: Scenery and costumes by Oliver Messel. Scenery executed by Alick Johnstone; costumes executed by Eleanor Abbey. *Cast*: *Nell Gwynn*; *Lord Byron*; *Lady Hamilton*; *The Duke of Wellington*; *Mr. Gladstone*; *The Empress Josephine*; *Lola Montez*; *Lord Nelson*; *The Flower Woman*; *The Dancers*, Fowler and Tamara; *The Thieves*, Roy Royston, Ada-May; *A Policeman*; *The Lover and His Lady*, Lifar, Nikitina; *A Boy Scout*; *The Soldiers*, Mr. Cochran's Young Gentlemen; *Angels*, Mr. Cochran's Young Ladies; *2 Singers*.

THE WIND IN THE WILLOWS (Part II, Scene 20): *Music*: By Desmond Carter and Vivian Ellis. *Production*: Costumes by Ada Peacock; executed by H. & L. Nathan, Ltd. *Cast*: Royston, Mr. Cochran's Young Ladies.

REVISIONS: Programs of September 1930 include two additional pieces choreographed by Balanchine, which may have been added at an earlier date.

PAS DE DEUX (Part II, Scene 26): *Music*: By Peter Ilyitch Tschaikovsky. *Production*: Costumes by Oliver Messel. *Cast*: Nikitina, Efimov.

TENNIS (Part II, Scene 28): *Music*: By Vivian Ellis. *Production*: Scenery by Rex Whistler. Scenery executed by Alick Johnstone; costumes executed by Reville, Ltd. *Cast*: *Referee*, Efimov; *Tennis Players*, Mr. Cochran's Young Ladies.

100 [DUET and TRIO]

MUSIC: By Franz Liszt (*Liebestraum*, ca. 1850).

PREMIERE: September 16, 1930, members of the Royal Danish Ballet, Nimb's Restaurant, Tivoli Gardens, Copenhagen. Conductor: Victor Schiøler.

CAST: [DUET]: Elna Jørgen-Jensen, George Balanchine. [TRIO]: Elna Lassen, Ulla Poulsen, Balanchine.

NOTE: Untitled pieces performed once as part of Princess Margarethe's Høstfest (Harvest Festival).

See 107

101 DEN TREKANTEDE HAT (LE TRICORNE)

MUSIC: By Manuel de Falla (*El Sombrero de Tres Picos*, produced 1919).

CHOREOGRAPHY: Originally choreographed by Léonide Massine (1919); rechoreographed by George Balanchine.

PRODUCTION: Scenery and costumes by Kjeld Abell.

PREMIERE: October 12, 1930, Royal Danish Ballet, Royal Theater, Copenhagen. Conductor: Victor Schiøler.

CAST. *The Miller*, Leif Ørnberg; *The Miller's Wife*, Ulla Poulsen; *The Corregidor*, Karl Merrild; *The Corregidor's Wife*, Tony Madsen; *The Red Lady*, Ragnhild Rasmussen; *Policemen*; *Townspeople*.

NOTE: Performed, with *Schéhérazade* and *La Boutique Fantasque*, in the first of two Royal Danish Ballet series called *Ballet Evening by George Balanchine* presented during his six months as guest ballet master.

102 SCHÉHÉRAZADE

MUSIC: By Nicolai Rimsky-Korsakov (Op. 35, 1888).

CHOREOGRAPHY: Originally choreographed by Michel Fokine (1910); rechoreographed by George Balanchine.

PRODUCTION: Scenery and costumes by Kay Nielsen.

PREMIERE: October 12, 1930, Royal Danish Ballet, Royal Theater, Copenhagen. Conductor: Victor Schiøler.

CAST: *The Sultan*, Svend Methling (actor); *Sultan's Brother*, Richard Jensen; *Sultan's Wife*, Ulla Poulsen; *Sultan's Dancing Girls*, 3 women; *A Negro*, Leif Ørnberg; *A Eunuch*, Storm Petersen (actor); *Slave Girls*; *Wives*; *Negroes*; *Captives*.

NOTE: Balanchine changed the location from the original interior scene to a Persian garden, and included actors in the cast.

103 LEGETØJSBUTIKEN (LA BOUTIQUE FANTASQUE)

MUSIC: By Gioacchino Rossini (selections from *Les Péchés de Vieillesse*, orchestrated by Ottorino Respighi, 1918, on commission from Serge Diaghilev).

CHOREOGRAPHY: Originally choreographed by Léonide Massine (1919); rechoreographed by George Balanchine.

PRODUCTION: Scenery and costumes by Kjeld Abell.

PREMIERE: October 12, 1930, Royal Danish Ballet, Royal Theater, Copenhagen. Conductor: Victor Schiøler.

CAST: *Storekeeper*, Storm Petersen (actor); *Englishman*, Aage Winther-Jørgensen; *Wife*, Ragnhild Rasmussen; *Russian Merchant*, Richard Jensen; *His Wife*, Edel Pedersen; *Bananaman*; *Thief*; *Fop*; *Dolls*; *Dogs*; *Cossacks*; TARANTELLA: Elna Jørgen-Jensen, Leif Ørnberg; MAZURKA: Magda Allan Dahl, Gerda Karstens, Karl Merrild, Hans Brenaa; COSSACK DANCE: 5 men; DOGS DANCE: Maren Eschelsen, Niels Bjørn-Larsen; CAN-CAN: Kirsten Nellemose, Børge Ralov; INTERMEZZO: Else Højgaard, Gertrud Jensen, 12 women; GALOP: Entire cast.

104 FYRST IGOR (PRINCE IGOR)

Polovtsian Dances from the Opera 'Prince Igor'

MUSIC: By Alexander Borodin (1875).

CHOREOGRAPHY: By Michel Fokine (1909); staged by George Balanchine.

PRODUCTION: Scenery and costumes by K. Korovin.

PREMIERE: December 3, 1930, Royal Danish Ballet, Royal Theater, Copenhagen. Conductor: Victor Schiøler.

CAST: *Prince Igor*, Richard Jensen; *Khan Kontchak*, Albrecht Delfs; *Polovtsian Warrior Chief*, Karl Merrild; *16 Polovtsian Warriors*; *13 Polovtsian Women*; *17 Captured Persian Women*; *The Khan's Warriors*; *Polovtsian Women*; *Boys*.

NOTE: Balanchine appeared twice in the role of the Warrior Chief as guest artist in later performances.

See 383

105 ROSENDROMMEN (LE SPECTRE DE LA ROSE)

MUSIC: By Carl Maria von Weber (*Aufforderung zum Tanz* for piano, Op. 65, 1819).

CHOREOGRAPHY: By Michel Fokine (1911); staged by George Balanchine.

PREMIERE: December 14, 1930, Koncert Palæet, Copenhagen.

CAST: Ulla Poulsen, George Balanchine.

NOTE: Given once, at the annual Christmas charity performance sponsored by the newspaper *Politiken*.

See 34

1931

106 JOSEF-LEGENDE (LA LÉGENDE DE JOSEPH)
Choreographic Narrative in Eight Scenes

MUSIC: By Richard Strauss (Op. 63, 1913-14, commissioned by Serge Diaghilev).

CHOREOGRAPHY: Originally choreographed by Michel Fokine (1914); rechoreographed by George Balanchine.

PRODUCTION: Scenery and costumes by Kjeld Abell. Scenery executed by Axel Bruun.

PREMIERE: January 18, 1931, Royal Danish Ballet, Royal Theater, Copenhagen. Conductor: Victor Schiøler.

CAST: *Josef*, Børge Ralov; *Father*, Karl Merrild; *Mother*, Edel Pedersen; *Josef's Brothers*, 10 men; *2 Young Women*; *3 Merchants*; *4 Slave Girls*; *Leader of Pharaoh's Bodyguard*, Richard Jensen; *His Wife*, Ulla Poulsen; *Bodyguards*; *Slaves*; *Guests*; *Onlookers*.
    SCENE 1: Joseph's Home. SCENE 2: The Well. SCENE 3: The Father. SCENE 4: The Masked Ball. SCENE 5: Interlude. SCENE 6: Temptation. SCENE 7: Interlude. SCENE 8: Pharaoh.

NOTE: Balanchine abandoned the original libretto by Hugo von Hofmannsthal (used by Fokine) and based his work on the story of

Joseph as recounted in the Old Testament. Presented with Balanchine's restaging of *Apollon Musagète* [84, with Leif Ørnberg] and *Barabau* [53, with Harald Lander] in the second of two Royal Danish Ballet series called *Ballet Evening by George Balanchine.*

107 DANCES FOR SIR OSWALD STOLL'S
VARIETY SHOWS

A NOVEL INTERPRETATION OF LIEBESTRAUM: *Music*: By Franz Liszt (*Liebestraum*, ca. 1850). *Production*: Costumes by Hedley Briggs. Scenery by Frederick Stafford. *Premiere*: February 16, 1931, Sir Oswald Stoll's Variety Shows, Coliseum, London. *Cast*: 16 women. *Note*: LIEBESTRAUM appears on programs for the weeks beginning February 16, 23, and March 2, along with 'other dances produced by George Balanchine (Director of Serge Diaghileff's Russian Ballet).' The Coliseum was distinguished by having 'the finest revolving stage in the world.' In his setting of LIEBESTRAUM, Balanchine used the stage as a giant phonograph record, with a small dog in the center as 'His Master's Voice,' and the women as phonograph needles. *See 100*

WALTZ FANTASY IN BLUE: *Music*: By Mikhail Glinka (*Valse Fantaisie* in B minor, 1839; orchestrated 1856). *Premiere*: March 9, 1931, Sir Oswald Stoll's Variety Shows, Coliseum. *Cast*: Doris Sonne, corps de ballet. *Note*: Balanchine choreographed works to this music in 1953 (*Valse Fantaisie*) and 1967 (as a section of *Glinkiana*, soon after performed alone as *Valse Fantaisie*), both for the New York City Ballet. *See 293, 359, 366*

A SKIT ON MARLENE DIETRICH IN THE FILM 'THE BLUE ANGEL': *Music*: By Sammy Lerner and Frederick Hollander ('Falling in Love Again' from *The Blue Angel*, 1930). *Premiere*: March 9, 1931, Sir Oswald Stoll's Variety Shows, Coliseum. *Cast*: 6-8 women.

STATUES: *Music*: By Felix Mendelssohn (one of the *Songs without Words*). *Production*: Produced by Sir Oswald Stoll. *Premiere*: April?, 1931, *Varieties en Fête*, Alhambra, London. *Cast*: Hedley Briggs, Dorothy Jackson, Anna Roth.

PAPILLONS: *Music*: Perhaps by Frédéric Chopin (possibly the 'Butterfly' Étude in G-flat major, Op. 25, no. 9, 1832-34). *Production*: Produced by

Sir Oswald Stoll. *Premiere*: April?, 1931, *Varieties en Fête*, Alhambra. *Cast*: Sonne, Natasha Gregorova, Maria Gaya, corps de ballet. *Note*: Sonne remembers a pas de six to this étude, which may be *Papillons*, or (as the program does not specify music) a separate work.

DIE FLEDERMAUS: *Music*: By Johann Strauss the Younger (overture to *Die Fledermaus*, produced 1874). *Production*: Produced by Sir Oswald Stoll. *Premiere*: May 18, 1931, *Varieties en Fête*, Alhambra. *Cast*: Bat, Sonne; *Pas de Deux*: Jackson, Briggs; corps de ballet. *See 169, 199, 206, 294*

NOTE: In addition to these works documented from programs of Sir Oswald Stoll's variety shows at the London Coliseum (February 16-March 21) and Alhambra (April 6-May 30), reviews and conversations with dancers identify the following: *Tango* (Sonne and Briggs); Rimsky-Korsakov's *Flight of the Bumble Bee* (Gregorova, Sonne, Gaya); can-can from Offenbach's *Orphée aux Enfers* for a corps de girls in front of the curtain; a short jazz number for four women to the recorded music of Jack Hilton and His Dance Orchestra, performed in front of the curtain; an ensemble number to Tschaikovsky's *1812 Overture*, and a pas de deux for Briggs and Betty Scorer to Lord Berners' *Scottish Rhapsody*. Publicity material suggests that costumes were designed by Hedley Briggs and scenery by Frederick Stafford, but Natasha Gregorova remembers that Barbara Karinska was also involved with costuming. Dennis Stoll (son of Sir Oswald) conducted some of the performances. Balanchine's group of sixteen women (Hedley Briggs was the single male performer) was variously billed as the Balanchine Ballet, Balanchine's Girls, Balanchine's Sixteen Novelty Dancers, George Balanchine's Sixteen Delightful Dancers, and 16 Delightful Balanchine Girls 16. *See 109*

108 CHARLES B. COCHRAN'S 1931 REVUE

MUSIC: By Noel Coward and others.

CHOREOGRAPHY: Dances and ensembles by Buddy Bradley, Billy Pierce and George Balanchine.

PRODUCTION: The whole produced under the direction of Charles B. Cochran. Staged by Frank Collins.

PREMIERE: March 19, 1931, London Pavilion. (Out-of-town preview: February 18, Palace Theatre, Manchester.)

CAST: Bobby Clark, Ada-May, Melville Cooper, Paul McCullough, Queenie Leonard, Edward Cooper, Effie Atherton, and others.

STEALING THROUGH (Part I, Scene 6): *Music and Sketch*: By Douglas Byng and Melville Gideon. *Production*: Scenery and costumes by Oliver Messel. Scenery executed by E. Delany; costumes executed by Reville, Ltd., Eleanor Abbey, L. & H. Nathan, Ltd. *Cast*: Ada-May, Mr. Cochran's Young Ladies; *A Satyr*, Bobby Clark.

SCARAMOUCHE: AN IMPRESSION OF THE COMMEDIA DELL'ARTE (Part I, Scene 11 [Finale]): *Music*: By Elsie April, from an air of Pergolesi. Lyrics by Douglas Byng. *Production*: Scenery and costumes by Oliver Messel. Scenery executed by Alick Johnstone; costumes executed by Eleanor Abbey and C. Alias, Ltd. *Cast*: *Scaramouche*, Bernardi; *Sylvia*, Kathryn Hamill; *Capitano*, Henry Mollison; *Pierrettes*, Mr. Cochran's Young Ladies, The John Tiller Girls; *Zanni*, 8 men; *Clown*, Charles Farey; *Sprite*, Eve; *2 Pages*; *Mezzetin*, Edward Cooper; *Coralline*, Jane Welsh; *Pantalone*, Melville Cooper; *Jacqueline*, Effie Atherton; *Arlochino*, John Mills; *Isabel*, Molly Molloy; *Pulcinella*, Al Marshall; *Trivellino*, Queenie Leonard; *Columbine*, Ada-May; *Two Sailors*, Clark, Paul McCullough.

109 ORPHÉE AUX ENFERS
Comic Opera in Three Acts and Nine Scenes

MUSIC: By Jacques Offenbach (produced 1874). Libretto by Hector Crémieux and Ludovic Halévy.

PRODUCTION: Produced by Les Frères Isola. Directed by Max Dearly.

PREMIERE: December 24, 1931, Théâtre Mogador, Paris. Danced by Les Ballets Russes de Georges Balanchine. Conductor: M. Diot.

CAST: *Jupiter*, Max Dearly; *Aristaeus-Pluto*, Lucien Muratore; *Eurydice*, Marise Beaujon; *Diana*, Jeanne Saint-Bonnet; *Public Opinion*, Rose Carday; *Orpheus*, Adrien Lamy; *Mercury*, Maurice Porterat; *Mars*, José Dupuis (fils); *Cupid*, Monette Diney; *Venus*, Raymonde Allain; *Juno*, Alice Soulie; *Morpheus*, Lucien Brouet; *John Styx*, Félix Oudart; *Premiere Danseuse* (and *Aurora*), Felia Doubrovska; *Premier Danseur*, Anatole Vilzak; *The Twelve Small Virtuosi* (child violinists); and others. Corps de ballet: 24 women, 4 men.

DIVERTISSEMENT PASTORALE (Act I): Corps de ballet.

DIVERTISSEMENT DES SONGES ET DES HEURES (Act II): Felia Doubrovska, corps de ballet.

GRAND BALLET DES NYMPHES (Act II): Doubrovska, Anatole Vilzak, Irina Baronova, Tatiana Semanova, Irène Lucezarska.

DIVERTISSEMENT DES MOUCHES (Act III): Corps de ballet.

CHŒUR INFERNAL (Act III, chorus and dance): Vilzak.

BACCHANALE (Act III): Doubrovska, Vilzak.

See 107

1932

110 LES AMOURS DU POÈTE

Comedy with Music in Five Acts by René Blum and G. Delaquys

ACT III SONG, LE PAUVRE PIERRE

MUSIC: By Robert Schumann ('Chopin' section of *Carnaval*, Op. 9, no. 3, 1834-35).

PRODUCTION: Scenery by Alphonse Visconti and Georges Geerts. Costumes by Georgette Vialet.

PREMIÈRE: January 5, 1932, Théâtre de Monte-Carlo [group], Opéra de Monte-Carlo. Danced by members of Ballets [Russes] de Monte-Carlo. Conductor: Marc-César Scotto.

CAST: 4 women, 2 men.

NOTE: Balanchine's first work as ballet master of the company that was to become Les Ballets Russes de Monte-Carlo. The play is about the poet Heinrich Heine; the chief characters in the song choreographed by Balanchine are lady admirers of the poet.

See 3

111 TANNHÄUSER
Opera in Three Acts and Four Scenes by Richard Wagner
ACT I VENUSBERG BALLET

PREMIERE: January 21, 1932, Opéra de Monte-Carlo. Danced by Ballets [Russes] de Monte-Carlo. Conductor: Gabriel Grovlez.

CAST: Valentina Lanina [Blinova], Léon Woizikowsky, 14 women, 7 men.

See 154

112 LES CONTES D'HOFFMANN
Opera in Three Acts with Prologue and Epilogue by Jacques Offenbach
SCENE 2 BALLET

PREMIERE: January 24, 1932, Opéra de Monte-Carlo. Danced by Ballets [Russes] de Monte-Carlo. Conductor: Gabriel Grovlez.

CAST: VALSE: 4 women; PAS DE DEUX: Valentina Blinova, Valentin Froman; POLKA: Eleanora Marra, Léon Woizikowsky; GRANDE VALSE: 6 couples.

See 58, 260

113 LE PROPHÈTE
Opera in Five Acts by Giacomo Meyerbeer
ACTS I, III, IV, V BALLETS

PREMIERE: January 26, 1932, Opéra de Monte-Carlo. Danced by Ballets [Russes] de Monte-Carlo. Conductor: Gabriel Grovlez.

CAST: ACT I VILLAGE BALLET: 4 couples. ACT III SKATING BALLET: 2 women, 4 men; *Two Skaters*, Eleanora Marra, Léon Woizikowsky; *Snow*, Valentina Blinova, Valentin Froman, 12 women. ACT IV, YOUNG GIRLS THROWING FLOWERS: 6 women. ACT V BACCHANALE: Marra, 10 women.

114 UNE NUIT À VENISE (EINE NACHT IN VENEDIG)
Comic Opera in Three Acts and Five Scenes by Johann Strauss the Younger
ACTS I, II, III BALLETS
PREMIERE: February 2, 1932, Opéra de Monte-Carlo. Danced by Ballets [Russes] de Monte-Carlo. Conductor: Gabriel Grovlez.
CAST: ACT I BALLET: 12 women. ACT II VALSE: 6 couples. ACT III MAZURKA: 3 couples. GRAND PAS CLASSIQUE: Valentina Blinova, Léon Woizikowsky, 3 women.

115 LAKMÉ
Opera in Three Acts by Léo Delibes
ACT II BALLET
PREMIERE: February 9, 1932, Opéra de Monte-Carlo. Danced by Ballets [Russes] de Monte-Carlo. Conductor: Marc-César Scotto.
CAST: Eleanora Marra, 12 women.

See 57, 153

116 SAMSON ET DALILA
Opera in Three Acts and Five Scenes by Camille Saint-Saëns
ACT I BALLET; ACT III BACCHANALE
PREMIERE: February 11, 1932, Opéra de Monte-Carlo. Danced by Ballets [Russes] de Monte-Carlo. Conductor: Gabriel Grovlez.
CAST: BALLET: 12 women. BACCHANALE: Eleanora Marra, 16 women.

See 66, 171, 228

117 FAUST
Opera in Five Acts by Charles Gounod
ACT II KERMESSE: VALSE
PREMIERE: February 13, 1932, Opéra de Monte-Carlo. Danced by Ballets [Russes] de Monte-Carlo. Conductor: Gabriel Grovlez.
CAST: 6 couples.

See 45, 151, 227, 397, 413

118 PATRIE

Opera-Ballet in One Act by Émile Paladilhe

BALLET

PREMIERE: February 20, 1932, Opéra de Monte-Carlo. Danced by Ballets [Russes] de Monte-Carlo. Conductor: Marc-César Scotto.

CAST: NEAPOLITAN DANCE: Tatiana Lipkovska, Roland Guérard; INDIAN DANCE: 1 woman, 3 men; AFRICAN DANCE: 5 women; FLEMISH DANCE: 2 couples; SPANISH DANCE: Eleanora Marra, Léon Woizikowsky; CLASSICAL BALLET: Valentina Blinova, Tamara Toumanova, Valentin Froman, 6 women; 'LA MONÉGASQUE' (music by Raoul Gunsbourg): corps de ballet.

NOTE: Performed once, with Act III of *Hérodiade*, for the benefit of the Caisse de Bienfaisance de la Colonie Française à Monaco.

119 HÉRODIADE

Act III of the Opera by Jules Massenet

DIVERTISSEMENT

PREMIERE: February 20, 1932, Opéra de Monte-Carlo. Danced by Ballets [Russes] de Monte-Carlo. Conductor: Gabriel Grovlez.

CAST: 6 women.

See 46

120 TURANDOT

Opera in Three Acts and Four Scenes by Giacomo Puccini

ACT II DIVERTISSEMENT, LES PORCELAINES DE CHINE

PREMIERE: February 21, 1932, Opéra de Monte-Carlo. Danced by Ballets [Russes] de Monte-Carlo. Conductor: Gabriel Grovlez.

CAST: Valentina Blinova, Tamara Toumanova, Léon Woizikowsky, Marian Ladré, Roland Guérard, 16 women.

See 68

121 RIGOLETTO
Opera in Four Acts by Giuseppe Verdi
ACT I DIVERTISSEMENT
PREMIERE: February 23, 1932, Opéra de Monte-Carlo. Danced by
Ballets [Russes] de Monte-Carlo. Conductor: Michel Steiman.
CAST: 4 couples.

See 88, 156

122 MANON
Opera in Four Acts by Jules Massenet
ACT III BALLET
PREMIERE: February 28, 1932, Opéra de Monte-Carlo. Danced by
Ballets [Russes] de Monte-Carlo. Conductor: Gabriel Grovlez.
CAST: Valentina Blinova, Léon Woizikowsky, 6 couples.

See 40, 159

123 LA TRAVIATA
Opera in Four Acts by Giuseppe Verdi
ACT III BALLET
PREMIERE: March 3, 1932, Opéra de Monte-Carlo. Danced by Ballets
[Russes] de Monte-Carlo. Conductor: Michel Steiman.
CAST: Tatiana Lipkovska, Metek [Mezeslav] Borovsky, 6 couples.

See 67, 150, 252

124 ROMÉO ET JULIETTE
Opera in Five Acts, Six Scenes and Prologue by Charles Gounod
ACT I DIVERTISSEMENT
PREMIERE: March 6, 1932, Opéra de Monte-Carlo. Danced by Ballets
[Russes] de Monte-Carlo. Conductor: Gabriel Grovlez.
CAST: 8 couples.

See 86, 180

125 FAY-YEN-FAH

Opera in Three Acts and Four Scenes by Joseph Redding
SCENE 3 BALLET DIVERTISSEMENT; BALLET VOLANT

PREMIERE: March 8, 1932, Opéra de Monte-Carlo. Danced by Ballets [Russes] de Monte-Carlo. Conductor: Michel Steiman.

CAST: BALLET DIVERTISSEMENT: *Lilies*, 6 women; *Veils*, 6 women; *Chinese Woman*, Tamara Toumanova; *Chinese Man*, Marian Ladré; *Poppies*, Toumanova, 6 women; *White Peacocks*, 2 women; *Gold Peacocks*, 4 women. BALLET VOLANT: 5 women.

See 44

126 AÏDA

Opera in Four Acts by Giuseppe Verdi
ACTS I AND II BALLETS

PREMIERE: March 19, 1932, Opéra de Monte-Carlo. Danced by Ballets [Russes] de Monte-Carlo. Conductor: Alfredo Padovani.

CAST: ACT I BALLET: 8 women. ACT II BALLET: 12 women, 6 men.

See 152, 226, 255

127 CARMEN

Opera in Four Acts by Georges Bizet
ACT II SEGUIDILLA

PREMIERE: March 24, 1932, Opéra de Monte-Carlo. Danced by Ballets [Russes] de Monte-Carlo. Conductor: Michel Steiman.

CAST: 4 couples.

See 38, 155, 248

128 LA PÉRICHOLE

Comic Opera in Three Acts and Four Scenes by Jacques Offenbach
ACT III BALLET

PREMIERE: March 31, 1932, Opéra de Monte-Carlo. Danced by Ballets [Russes] de Monte-Carlo. Conductor: Michel Steiman.

CAST: 12 couples, Juan Martínez trio of Spanish Dancers.

129 COTILLON

MUSIC: By Emmanuel Chabrier (*Dix Pièces Pittoresques*, 1880 [piano pieces, some orchestrated by Chabrier, others by Vittorio Rieti] and the third of the *Trois Valses Romantiques* for piano, 1883 [orchestrated by Felix Mottl]). Book by Boris Kochno.

PRODUCTION: Scenery and costumes by Christian Bérard. Scenery executed by Prince A. Schervashidze; women's costumes executed by Karinska, men's costumes executed by Lidvall.

PREMIERE: April 12, 1932, Ballets Russes de Monte-Carlo, Opéra de Monte-Carlo. Conductor: Pierre Kolpikoff. (Preview: January 17, 1932, Ballets [Russes] de Monte-Carlo, Opéra de Monte-Carlo, with George Balanchine in the role later danced by David Lichine. Conductor: Marc-César Scotto.)

CAST: THE TOILETTE: THE BALLROOM, WHERE THE FINAL PREPARATIONS ARE INTERRUPTED BY THE ARRIVAL OF GUESTS: Tamara Toumanova, Natalie Strakhova, David Lichine; THE INTRODUCTIONS: Valentina Blinova, 12 women, 6 men; THE MASTER OF CEREMONIES RUNS IN LATE: Léon Woizikowsky; THE PLEASURE GARDEN: THE MASTER AND MISTRESS OF CEREMONIES DEMONSTRATE THE FIGURES OF THE FIRST DANCE, WHICH ARE REPEATED BY ALL THE GUESTS: Blinova, Woizikowsky, corps de ballet; NEW ENTRÉE AND DANCE OF HATS: *Harlequins, Jockeys and Spaniards*, Toumanova, Strakhova, 4 women; Lichine, 2 men; THE HANDS OF FATE: THE CAVALIER COMES UP TO THE CURTAIN TO CHOOSE ONE OF THE HANDS THAT ARE REVEALED ABOVE IT, BUT IS STOPPED BY THE SUDDEN APPARITION OF A HAND GLOVED IN BLACK: Lubov Rostova, Valentin Froman; THE MAGIC LANTERN: A YOUNG GIRL TELLS THE FORTUNES OF THE GUESTS; APPEARANCE OF THE BAT AND THE CUP OF CHAMPAGNE: Toumanova, Blinova, Rostova, Froman, Lichine, corps de ballet; GRAND ROND AND END OF COTILLION: Entire cast.

NOTE: Amid the program of festivities at a cotillion, Fate appears in the guise of a vampire wearing black gloves. A Young Girl telling fortunes is rebuffed by the Mistress of Ceremonies and runs off, but reappears to lead the Grand Rond, in which she pirouettes around the ballroom by herself, until the guests join her spinning and the curtain falls.

The preview performance marked the debut of the Ballets de Monte-Carlo, which within six weeks became the Ballets Russes de

Monte-Carlo. *Cotillon* and Balanchine's other major work for the company, *La Concurrence*, were performed by the several Ballets Russes companies in Europe, North America, Australia (and in the case of *Cotillon*, South America) until 1939 (*La Concurrence*) and 1943 (*Cotillon*), providing the base for Balanchine's early reputation in the United States.

In 1967, Balanchine choreographed Chabrier's *Trois Valses Romantiques* for the New York City Ballet.

STAGINGS (THE HANDS OF FATE pas de deux): 1954, Danilova Concert Company; 1968, Tulsa.

See 357

130 LA CONCURRENCE

MUSIC: By Georges Auric (1932, commissioned by René Blum). Book by André Derain.

PRODUCTION: Curtain, scenery and costumes by André Derain. Curtain executed by André Derain; scenery executed by Prince A. Schervashidze; costumes executed by Karinska, Paris.

PREMIERE: April 12, 1932, Ballets Russes de Monte-Carlo, Opéra de Monte-Carlo. Conductor: Marc-César Scotto.

CAST: *First Tailor*, Metek [Mezeslav] Borovsky; *Second Tailor*, Yurek Shabelevsky; *First Tailor's Wife*, Tatiana Lipkovska; *Second Tailor's Wife*, Gala Chabelska; *First Couple*, Louise Lyman, Roman Jasinsky; *Second Couple*, Lara Obidenna, Marian Ladré; *Their Daughter*, Irène Stepanova; *Two Friends*, Valentina Blinova, Eleanora Marra; *The Vagabond*, Léon Woizikowsky; *The Girl*, Tamara Toumanova; *The Girls*, 10 women; *Neighbors*, 6 women, 5 men.

NOTE: The theme is fashion and human vanity. Two rival tailors, both selling fashionable apparel in an imaginary town, vie for the attention of eager shoppers. The tailors begin to quarrel, and the customers are drawn into the commotion. Citizens of the town intervene and disperse the crowd; the two tailors, finding themselves alone with their profits, are pleased and become reconciled.

STAGINGS (VAGABOND DANCE, retitled *Hobo Dance*): 1945, Ballet Russe Highlights.

131 LE BOURGEOIS GENTILHOMME

Music: By Richard Strauss (concert suite, ca. 1917). Book by Sobeka [Boris Kochno] after Molière.

Production: Curtain, scenery and costumes by Alexandre Benois. Curtain executed by Georges Geerts; scenery executed by Prince A. Schervashidze; costumes executed by Karinska, Paris.

Premiere: May 3, 1932, Ballets Russes de Monte-Carlo, Opéra de Monte-Carlo. Conductor: Paul Paray.

Cast: *Cléonte*, David Lichine; *Covielle, His Valet*, Jasht Dolotine; *Two Gypsy Tailors*; *Monsieur Jourdain, le Bourgeois Gentilhomme*, Marian Ladré; *His Retinue*, 4 women, 2 men; *Cléonte's Friends Disguised as Slaves*, 4 men; *Lucille*, Tamara Toumanova; *Nicole, Her Servant*, Eleanora Marra; BALLET GIVEN BY M. JOURDAIN IN HONOR OF THE SON OF THE GRAND TURK: Valentina Blinova, 6 women; TURKISH DIVERTISSEMENT: I. Olga Morosova, Yurek Shabelevsky, Léonide Katchourovsky; II. Natalie Strakhova, Metek [Mezeslav] Borovsky; III. *Acrobats*, Roman Jasinsky, 3 women.

    1. Cléonte disguises himself as the son of the Grand Turk. 2. Cléonte enters the house of Monsieur Jourdain. 3. Dance of Cléonte and his friends disguised as slaves. 4. Ballet given by Monsieur Jourdain in honor of the son of the Grand Turk. 5. Entrance of Lucille, accompanied by her servant Nicole. 6. Turkish ceremony to ennoble Monsieur Jourdain. 7. Turkish Divertissement. 8. Lucille, not recognizing Cléonte, attempts to flee. 9. Betrothal of Lucille to Cléonte, who removes his disguise.

Other versions (each subsequent version was a complete resetting of staging and décor): 1944, Ballet Russe de Monte Carlo. 1979, New York City Opera.

See 221, 410, 414

132 SUITES DE DANSE

Music: By Mikhail Glinka.

Premiere: May 5, 1932, Ballets Russes de Monte-Carlo, Opéra de Monte-Carlo. Conductor: Marc-César Scotto.

CAST: JOTA ARAGONESA: Eleanora Marra, Léon Woizikowsky, 6 couples; TARANTELLA: Nina Verchinina, Lena Kirsova, David Lichine, Metek [Mezeslav] Borovsky, Yurek Shabelevsky; VALSE: Valentina Blinova, Tamara Toumanova, Tatiana Riabouchinska, 6 women; KOMARINSKAIA: Irène Kervily, Woizikowsky, 8 couples.

NOTE: In 1967, Balanchine choreographed the JOTA ARAGONESA as part of Glinkiana for the New York City Ballet.

See 359

133 NUMÉRO LES CANOTIERS

MUSIC: 'The Waves of the Danube' (a waltz tune popular in Russia).

PRODUCTION: Costumes by Christian Bérard (after Renoir).

PREMIERE: Spring?, 1932, costume ball at the Villa Blanche, home of Édouard and Denise Bourdet at Tamaris, near Toulon.

CAST: Mme Georges Auric, George Balanchine, Boris Kochno.

NOTE: Performed once, at the Bal de la Préfecture.

1933

134 MOZARTIANA

MUSIC: By Peter Ilyitch Tschaikovsky (Suite No. 4, Mozartiana, Op. 61, 1887; based on Mozart's Gigue in G major [K. 574], Minuet in D major [K. 355], the motet 'Ave, Verum Corpus' [K. 618], and variations on 'Les Hommes Pieusement' from Gluck's comic opera La Rencontre Imprévue [K. 455]).

PRODUCTION: Curtain, scenery and costumes by Christian Bérard.

PREMIERE: June 7, 1933, Les Ballets 1933, Théâtre des Champs-Élysées, Paris. Conductor: Maurice Abravanel.

CAST: GIGUE: Ludovic Matlinsky; MENUETTO: 6 women; PREGHIERA: Lucienne Kylberg; TEMA CON VARIAZIONI: Tamara Toumanova, Roman Jasinsky, corps de ballet; FINALE: Toumanova, Kylberg, Jasinsky, 7 women, 1 man.

NOTE: A suite of dances in stylized eighteenth-century costumes, set in an Italian town. A young man dances a solo and is joined by village girls. A sad girl enters carried by two veiled figures; she dances a gentle 'Prayer.' A series of dances follows featuring town characters, then a grand adagio, and a country-dance finale. The forecurtain showed a silhouette of the child Mozart seated at a harpsichord.

Mozartiana was one of six new ballets created by Balanchine during the six-months' existence of Les Ballets 1933, the company he formed with Boris Kochno. It was performed in Paris and London with Les Sept Péchés Capitaux, Les Songes, Fastes, L'Errante, Les Valses de Beethoven, and other musical works without choreography. In 1981, Balanchine choreographed a new ballet to Mozartiana for the New York City Ballet Tschaikovsky Festival, changing the order of the movements to place the PREGHIERA first.

REVISIONS: 1935, American Ballet: Sections originally danced by Toumanova and Jasinsky differently apportioned, with single pas de deux for leading couple; pas de six in THEME AND VARIATIONS danced by six women (three in men's costumes). 1945, Ballet Russe de Monte Carlo: Original form more closely followed, with two pas de deux for leading couple; corps de ballet entirely women; one male soloist instead of two. 1956, Danilova Concert Company: Presented without MENUETTO by cast of four dancers.

STAGINGS: 1935, American Ballet; 1945, Ballet Russe de Monte Carlo; 1956, Danilova Concert Company.

See 149, 417

135 LES SONGES

MUSIC: By Darius Milhaud (1933, commissioned by Boris Kochno). Book by André Derain.

PRODUCTION: Scenery and costumes by André Derain.

PREMIERE: June 7, 1933, Les Ballets 1933, Théâtre des Champs-Élysées, Paris. Conductor: Maurice Abravanel.

CAST: The Ballerina, Tamara Toumanova; 1. POLKA: Kyra Blank, Karl Scheibe; 2. MONSTRE (ACROBAT): Roman Jasinsky; 3. THE KNAVES: Ludovic Matlinsky, Serge Ismaïloff; 4. THE CORYPHÉES: 5 women;

5. HIGH-LIFE AND THE DEMI-MONDE: Jasinsky, Lucienne Kylberg;
6. FINALE: Entire cast.

NOTE: Exhausted after a triumphant performance, the ballerina falls asleep and is assailed by nightmares and visions. The fragrance of flowers brings an intimation of loveliness; she awakens reassured to find herself in her own room.

STAGINGS (titled *Dreams*): 1935, American Ballet.

See 145

136 LES SEPT PÉCHÉS CAPITAUX (also called ANNA ANNA, OR THE SEVEN CAPITAL SINS)

MUSIC: By Kurt Weill (*Die sieben Todsünden*, produced 1933, commissioned by Boris Kochno and Edward James). Text by Bertolt Brecht from a suggestion by Boris Kochno and Edward James.

PRODUCTION: Produced and directed by George Balanchine. Scenery and costumes by Caspar Rudolph Neher.

PREMIÈRE: June 7, 1933, Les Ballets 1933, Théâtre des Champs-Élysées, Paris. Conductor: Maurice Abravanel.

CAST: *The Two Annas*, Lotte Lenya (singer), Tilly Losch; *The Family*, Heinrich Gretler, Otto Pasetti, Albert Peters, Erich Ruchs (singers); corps de ballet. Singers and dancers appeared together on stage.
I. Introduction. II. Sloth. III. Pride. IV. Anger. V. Gluttony. VI. Lust. VII. Avarice. VIII. Envy.

NOTE: An ironic morality play, the story of Anna, who leaves Louisiana to travel across the United States, intending to make her fortune and build a family home. Anna-Anna's double nature is portrayed by a dancer and a singer; in cabaret-style song and dance with pantomime, the two performers dramatize the opposing tendencies of Anna's nature: idealism and cynicism, generosity and meanness. As she goes from city to city (with her family onstage intoning Lutheran pieties) she betrays her art for success, love for money, justice for power.

OTHER VERSIONS: 1958, New York City Ballet (*The Seven Deadly Sins*).

See 322

137 FASTES

Music: By Henri Sauguet (1933, commissioned by Boris Kochno).
Book by André Derain.

Production: Scenery and costumes by André Derain.

Premiere: June 10, 1933, Les Ballets 1933, Théâtre des Champs-Élysées,
Paris. Conductor: Maurice Abravanel.

Cast: *The Genii*, Serge Ismaïloff, Ludovic Matlinsky; *The Matrons*,
6 women; *Two Persian Saltateurs*, Lucienne Kylberg, Tamara Sidorenko;
Two Buffoons, Ismaïloff, Matlinsky; *The Courtesan*, Tamara Tchinarova;
The Young Girl, Tamara Toumanova; *The Lupercalian Priest*, Roman
Jasinsky.

Note: The scene is a Latin feast in Etruscan Italy; two genii attend
pagan rites performed by matrons, buffoons, acrobats. The Young Girl
encounters a priest of Lupercal; wearing a three-faced mask, he dances
for her a parable of youth, maturity and old age. A final scene of orgy
ends in ridicule with the entrance of the donkey of Silenus.

138 L'ERRANTE (also called ERRANTE; ALMA ERRANTE;
THE WANDERER)
Choreographic Fantasy

Music: By Franz Schubert (*The Wanderer*, fantasy for piano, Op. 15,
1822, transcribed by Franz Liszt, orchestrated by Charles Koechlin).
Book by Pavel Tchelitchew.

Production: Costumes, lighting and dramatic effects by Pavel
Tchelitchew. Tilly Losch's dress by Molyneux.

Premiere: June 10, 1933, Les Ballets 1933, Théâtre des Champs-Élysées,
Paris. Conductor: Maurice Abravanel.

Cast: Tilly Losch; Roman Jasinsky; 8 women, 3 men; child.

Note: As in Schmidt von Lübeck's poem, set by Schubert, a wanderer
seeks lost love amid phantom dreams; she encounters figures of hope,
despair and memory in an atmosphere of dark shadow and diffused
light. Scenic effects achieved by lighting and silks dramatized the
actions of the dancers. In later productions, characters were identified
as Woman in Green, Youths, Shadows, Angels, Revolutionaries, and
others.

REVISIONS: 1935, American Ballet: A second male role made more prominent.

STAGINGS: 1935, American Ballet (*Errante*); 1941, American Ballet Caravan (*Alma Errante*); 1943, Ballet Theatre (*The Wanderer*).

See 143, 197

139 LES VALSES DE BEETHOVEN
(also called THE WALTZES OF BEETHOVEN)

MUSIC: By Ludwig van Beethoven (several waltzes, orchestrated by Nicolas Nabokov, and one of the *Scottish Songs* for cello and male voice).

PRODUCTION: Scenery and costumes by Emilio Terry.

PREMIERE: June 19, 1933, Les Ballets 1933, Théâtre des Champs-Élysées, Paris. Conductor: Maurice Abravanel.

CAST: *Daphne*, Tilly Losch; *The Elements, Companions of Daphne: Earth*, Diana Gould; *Water*, T. Ouchkova; *Air*, Prudence Hyman; *Fire*, Tamara Sidorenko; *Eros*, Lucienne Kylberg; *Apollo*, Roman Jasinsky; *The Train of Apollo*, 4 women; *The Shade of Apollo*, Fernando Gusso.

NOTE: A Greek myth: Eros, with an arrow shot from his bow, inflames the god Apollo with love for the maiden Daphne. Seeking to escape Apollo's embraces, Daphne prays to the gods and is transformed into a laurel tree. Apollo grieves his loss at the foot of the laurel and is mocked in song by his own shadow: The laurel is thereafter consecrated to poetry.

140 DANS L'ÉLYSÉE

MUSIC: By Jacques Offenbach.

PRODUCTION: Presented by Edward James.

PREMIERE: July 3, 1933, Ballets Serge Lifar, Savoy Theatre, London. Conductor: Alexander Labinsky.

CAST: Felia Doubrovska.

NOTE: Neither Balanchine nor Doubrovska remembers this piece, but a program for the Lifar engagement at the Savoy lists *Dans l'Élysée*, danced by Doubrovska, with choreography uncredited. A review of Lifar's London appearances (*Dancing Times*, August 1933, pp. 439-40) mentions a 'solo *sur les pointes* to music of Offenbach choreographed by Balanchine' for Doubrovska.

1935

141 SERENADE

MUSIC: By Peter Ilyitch Tschaikovsky (Serenade in C for string orchestra, Op. 48, 1880, first three movements; arranged and reorchestrated by George Antheil).

PRODUCTION: Scenery by Gaston Longchamp. Costumes by Jean Lurçat.

PREMIERE: March 1, 1935, American Ballet, Adelphi Theater, New York. Conductor: Sandor Harmati. (First performed by students of the School of American Ballet, June 10, 1934, at Woodland, the estate of Felix Warburg, near White Plains, New York, in rehearsal costumes; then by the Producing Company of the School of American Ballet, December 8, 1934, Avery Memorial Theater, Hartford, Connecticut, with costumes by William B. Okie, Jr.).

CAST: SONATINA: Leda Anchutina, Holly Howard, Elise Reiman, Elena de Rivas, 13 women; WALTZ: Anchutina, Howard, Sylvia Giselle [Gisella Caccialanza], Helen Leitch, Annabelle Lyon, 10 women; ELEGY: Howard, Kathryn Mullowny, Heidi Vosseler, Charles Laskey, 8 women, 4 men.

NOTE: Created for students during the first year of the School of American Ballet, *Serenade* is the first work Balanchine choreographed for American dancers; it has come to be considered the signature piece of the New York City Ballet and is one of Balanchine's most widely performed works. A ballet of patterns that newly explores academic ballet technique; the choreography, as the music, has overtones of love, loss, yearning. During the inaugural season of the American Ballet, the company formed by Balanchine, Lincoln Kirstein and Edward M. M. Warburg, *Serenade* was performed in repertory with *Alma Mater*,

Errante, Reminiscence, Dreams, and *Transcendence.* A ballet to the same music, Fokine's *Eros,* was in the repertory of the Maryinsky Theater during Balanchine's youth.

REVISIONS: 1936, American Ballet Ensemble at the Metropolitan Opera: male dancer added to WALTZ. 1940, Ballet Russe de Monte Carlo: solo parts (originally divided among several dancers) reworked for single ballerina, two male dancers and supporting female dancer (with full corps de ballet); fourth movement of the Serenade (*Tema Russo* [with some passages omitted]), called RUSSIAN DANCE, inserted before concluding ELEGY, danced by four demi-soloists and ballerina; Tschaikovsky's original scoring adopted, rather than Antheil's; these revisions incorporated in all subsequent stagings. 1970-71, New York City Ballet: Slight additions at beginning and extensive new material added at end of RUSSIAN DANCE, with all previous omissions in score of *Tema Russo* restored.

Although the steps have remained basically the same, solo measures have been allocated in various ways, most frequently to three ballerinas and two male dancers (New York City Ballet variations have included, among others, five ballerinas [1950, London]; four ballerinas [1953, 1955, 1958], three ballerinas [1959]).

NEW PRODUCTIONS BY BALANCHINE COMPANIES: From 1936, American Ballet: Performed without décor. 1941, American Ballet Caravan: Costumes by Candido Portinari. New York City Ballet: 1948, costumes uncredited, lighting by Jean Rosenthal; 1952, costumes by Karinska; 1964, lighting by Ronald Bates.

STAGINGS: 1940, Ballet Russe de Monte Carlo; 1941, American Ballet Caravan; 1947, Paris; 1948, New York City Ballet; 1952, San Francisco; 1957, Royal Danish; 1960, Hamburg, La Scala, Netherlands; 1961, Atlanta, Ballet Borealis; 1962, National Ballet of Canada; 1964, Ballet of Los Angeles, National, Utah, Royal; 1965, Munich; 1966, Boston, Düsseldorf, Tokyo Ballet Geikijo, Vienna; 1968, Ballet la Jeunesse; 1969, Pennsylvania; 1970, Australia, Berlin, Geneva, Norway, Royal Swedish; 1973, Cincinnati; 1974, Frankfurt; 1975, Israel, Les Grands Ballets Canadiens, New Zealand; 1976, Iran, Rome; 1977, Washington, Hungary; 1978, Pacific Northwest, Zagreb, Zürich; 1979, Dance Theatre of Harlem; 1981, Cleveland, Eglevsky; 1982, Kansas City, Milwaukee, Matsuyama.

TELEVISION: 1956 (excerpts, ABC); 1957 (L'Heure du Concert, CBC, Montreal).

See 193, 254

142 ALMA MATER

MUSIC: By Kay Swift, orchestrated by Morton Gould (1935, commissioned by Lincoln Kirstein and Edward M. M. Warburg). Book by Edward M. M. Warburg.

PRODUCTION: Scenery by Eugene Dunkel. Costumes by John Held, Jr. Scenery constructed and painted by New York Studios; costumes executed by Helene Pons Studio.

PREMIERE: March 1, 1935, American Ballet, Adelphi Theater, New York. Conductor: Sandor Harmati. (First performed by the Producing Company of the School of American Ballet, December 6, 1934, Avery Memorial Theater, Hartford, Connecticut.)

CAST: 1. INTRODUCTION: *The Heroine*, Sylvia Giselle [Gisella Caccialanza]; *The Villain*, William Dollar; *6 Girls*; 2. ENTRANCE OF THE HERO—SNAKE DANCE: *The Hero*, Charles Laskey; *The Photographer*, Eugene Loring; *6 Girls, 4 Boys*; 3. WALTZ: Giselle, Laskey, Dollar; 4. THE KNOCK-OUT-DREAM-WEDDING AND NIGHTMARE: *The Bride*, Heidi Vosseler; *The Groom*, Laskey; *14 Girls, 5 Boys*; 5. MORNING PAPERS, AND THE DUEL: *The Janitor*, Dollar; entire cast; 6. SALVATION RHUMBA: *Nell*, Kathryn Mullowny; 7. FINALE: Entire cast.

NOTE: Balanchine's first ballet with an American theme and American music: a fantasy satire on college life—the heroine a flapper, the hero a football halfback, the villain in a coonskin coat.

143 ERRANTE
Choreographic Fantasy

MUSIC: By Franz Schubert (*The Wanderer*, fantasy for piano, Op. 15, 1822, transcribed by Franz Liszt, orchestrated by Charles Koechlin). Book by Pavel Tchelitchew.

PRODUCTION: Costumes, lighting and dramatic effects by Pavel Tchelitchew (from the 1933 production).

PREMIERE: March 1, 1935, American Ballet, Adelphi Theater, New York. Conductor: Sandor Harmati.

CAST: Tamara Geva (guest artist); William Dollar, Charles Laskey; *3 Youths*; *Shadows, Angels, Revolutionaries, and Others*, 13 women, child.

NOTE: Originally presented by Les Ballets 1933, Paris.

See 138*, 197

144 REMINISCENCE

MUSIC: By Benjamin Godard, orchestrated by Henry Brant.

PRODUCTION: Scenery and costumes by Sergei Soudeikine. Scenery constructed by New York Studios; costumes executed by Helene Pons Studio.

PREMIERE: March 1, 1935, American Ballet, Adelphi Theater, New York. Conductor: Sandor Harmati.

CAST: *Brighella*, Eugene Loring; ENTRÉE: 12 women; PAS D'ACTION: Kathryn Mullowny, Charles Laskey, 4 men, 12 women; VALSE CHROMATIQUE: Leda Anchutina; BARCAROLE: Elena de Rivas; CANZONETTA: Gisella Caccialanza; FRAGMENT POÉTIQUE: Annabelle Lyon; TARANTELLA: Ruthanna Boris, Joseph Levinoff; SATURN: Paul Haakon (guest artist); PAS DE TROIS: William Dollar, Holly Howard, Elise Reiman; FINALE: Entire cast.

NOTE: A classical divertissement set in a ballroom: A welcome to the audience is followed by the entrée of the corps, principals in variations, coda, grand finale.

REVISIONS: Role of Brighella deleted soon after premiere. 1936, American Ballet Ensemble at the Metropolitan Opera: PAS D'ACTION and SATURN dance omitted; MAZURKA added for Anatole Vilzak and Rabana Hasburgh; VALSE and GRAND ADAGIO added.

145 DREAMS

MUSIC: By George Antheil (1935, commissioned by Lincoln Kirstein). Book by André Derain.

PRODUCTION: Scenery and costumes by André Derain (from *Les Songes* [135]).

PREMIERE: March 5, 1935, American Ballet, Adelphi Theater, New York. Conductor: Sandor Harmati. (First performed in America by students of the School of American Ballet, June 10, 1934, at Woodland, the estate of Felix Warburg, near White Plains, New York.)

CAST: *The Ballerina*, Leda Anchutina; THE POLKA: Gisella Caccialanza, Paul Haakon (guest artist); *The Acrobat*, William Dollar; THE MARCH: *The Knave*, Edward Caton; *2 Buffoons, 6 Pages* (women); THE CAN-CAN: Holly Howard, 8 women; *The Lady and the Prince*, Kathryn Mullowny, Charles Laskey; THE FINALE: Entire cast; EPILOGUE: *The Fairy Queen*, Mary Sale.

NOTE: Originally presented as *Les Songes* by Les Ballets 1933, Paris, with commissioned music by Darius Milhaud. Since this music could not be obtained for performance in America, a new score was commissioned; most of the choreography was from the 1933 production.

See 135

146 TRANSCENDENCE

MUSIC: By Franz Liszt ('Mephisto' Waltz; Ballade; 10th, 13th, 19th Hungarian Rhapsodies), arranged and orchestrated by George Antheil. Book by Lincoln Kirstein.

PRODUCTION: Scenery by Franklin Watkins (through union restrictions credited to Gaston Longchamp). Costumes by Franklin Watkins. Scenery constructed and painted by William H. Mensching Studios; costumes executed by Eaves Costume Company.

PREMIERE: March 5, 1935, American Ballet, Adelphi Theater, New York. Conductor: Sandor Harmati. (First performed by the Producing Company of the School of American Ballet, December 6, 1934, Avery Memorial Theater, Hartford, Connecticut.)

CAST: I. MEPHISTO WALTZ: *The Young Girl*, Elise Reiman; *The Young Man*, Charles Laskey; *The Man in Black*, William Dollar; 10 women, 4 men; II. BALLADE: THE MESMERISM: Reiman, Dollar; *Witches*, 15 women; THE END OF THE MAN IN BLACK: Dollar, 4 men; III. THE RESURRECTION: *The Possessed*: 16 women, 6 men.

NOTE: Inspired by the virtuosity of Liszt and Paganini, the ballet centers on the hypnotic powers of a virtuoso dancer; disguised as a monk, he mesmerizes a young girl. The girl's lover and friends manage to overcome him, but resurrected by his seemingly unlimited energy, the diabolical dancer leaps up and leads them all in a frenzied, Mephistophelean finale.

147 [SOLO]

MUSIC: By Frédéric Chopin (unknown).

PREMIERE: May 3, 1935, Park Theater, New York.

CAST: William Dollar.

NOTE: Performed once; the single classical work in a modern dance concert, *Men in Dance*.

148 JEANNE D'ARC

MUSIC: By Claude Debussy?

PREMIERE: July 4, 1935, His Majesty's Theatre, London. Pianist: Stephen Kovacs.

CAST: Alanova.

NOTE: Balanchine recalls choreographing a work called *Joan of Arc* for Alanova, but does not think the music was by Debussy. The program for Alanova's solo recital of July 4, 1935, lists Debussy as the composer of a work called *Joan of Arc* but gives no choreographer.

149 MOZARTIANA

MUSIC: By Peter Ilyitch Tschaikovsky (Suite No. 4, *Mozartiana*, Op. 61, 1887; based on Mozart's Gigue in G major [K. 574], Minuet in D major [K. 355], the motet 'Ave, Verum Corpus' [K. 618], and variations on 'Les Hommes Pieusement' from Gluck's comic opera *La Rencontre Imprévue* [K. 455]).

PRODUCTION: Scenery and costumes by Christian Bérard (from the 1933 production). Costumes executed by Karinska.

PREMIERE: September 28, 1935, Westchester County Center, White Plains, New York. Conductor: Sandor Harmati. (First performed in America by students of the School of American Ballet, June 9, 1934, at

Woodland, the estate of Felix Warburg, near White Plains, New York; then by the Producing Company of the School of American Ballet, December 6, 1934, Avery Memorial Theater, Hartford, Connecticut.)

CAST: 1. GIGUE: Hortense Kahrklin, Joseph Levinoff, Jack Potteiger; 2. MENUET: 8 women; 3. PREGHIERA: Annabelle Lyon; 4. THEME AND VARIATIONS: PAS DE SIX: 6 women; PROMENADE: 5 women, 2 men; SCHERZANDO: Annia Breyman, Elise Reiman; PAS DE QUATRE: 4 women; CLOCHETTES: Gisella Caccialanza, Elena de Rivas, Potteiger; PAS DE DEUX: Holly Howard, Charles Laskey; 5. FINALE: Entire cast.

NOTE: Originally presented by Les Ballets 1933, Paris.

See 134*, 417

150 LA TRAVIATA

Opera in Four Acts by Giuseppe Verdi
ACT III BALLET DIVERTISSEMENT (GYPSY DANCE)

PREMIERE: December 16, 1935, Metropolitan Opera, New York. Danced by American Ballet Ensemble. Conductor: Ettore Panizza.

CAST: Anatole Vilzak, Gisella Caccialanza, Ruthanna Boris, Constantine Iolas, Joseph Levinoff, corps de ballet.

NOTE: Balanchine's first choreography for the Metropolitan Opera during the three-year residence of the American Ballet as American Ballet Ensemble.

See 67, 123, 252

151 FAUST

Opera in Four Acts and Five Scenes by Charles Gounod
ACT I, SCENE 2 INCIDENTAL DANCE (KERMESSE)

PREMIERE: December 19, 1935, Metropolitan Opera, New York. Danced by American Ballet Ensemble. Conductor: Louis Hasselmans.

CAST: Corps de ballet.

See 45, 117, 227, 397, 413

152 AÏDA

Opera in Four Acts by Giuseppe Verdi
ACTS I AND II BALLETS

PREMIERE: December 20, 1935, Metropolitan Opera, New York. Danced by American Ballet Ensemble. Conductor: Ettore Panizza.

CAST: ACT I, SCENE 2 TEMPLE DANCE: Corps de ballet. ACT II, SCENE I NEGRO DANCE: Corps de ballet. ACT II, SCENE 2 VICTORY DANCE: Daphne Vane, William Dollar, corps de ballet.

NOTE: At least three versions of *Aïda* were danced by the American Ballet Ensemble at the Metropolitan Opera. Choreography was variously credited to Balanchine, William Dollar, and Marius Petipa.

See 126, 226, 255

153 LAKMÉ

Opera in Three Acts by Léo Delibes
ACT II BALLET

PREMIERE: December 23, 1935, Metropolitan Opera, New York. Danced by American Ballet Ensemble. Conductor: Louis Hasselmans.

CAST: TERANA: Kathryn Mullowny, Betty Eisner, Nora Koreff [Kaye], Yvonne Patterson, Mary Sale; REKTAH: Elise Reiman, Lew Christensen, Douglas Coudy; PERSANE: Holly Howard, Charles Laskey; ENSEMBLE DANCE; FINALE: Entire cast.

See 57, 115

154 TANNHÄUSER

Opera in Three Acts and Four Scenes by Richard Wagner
ACT I BALLET

PREMIERE: December 26, 1935, Metropolitan Opera, New York. Danced by American Ballet Ensemble. Conductor: Artur Bodanzky.

CAST: BACCHANALE: Anatole Vilzak, Rabana Hasburgh, corps de ballet; VISION: Annia Breyman, Kathryn Mullowny, Helen Stuart, Heidi Vosseler, Charles Laskey.

REVISIONS: In the printed program for January 25, 1937, VISION is replaced by THREE GRACES, danced by Mullowny, Daphne Vane and Elise Reiman.

See 111

155 CARMEN

Opera in Four Acts by Georges Bizet

ACT IV BALLET

PREMIERE: December 27, 1935, Metropolitan Opera, New York. Danced by American Ballet Ensemble. Conductor: Louis Hasselmans.

CAST: GITANE: Ruthanna Boris, corps de ballet; FARUCCA: Anatole Vilzak, Betty Eisner, corps de ballet; FARANDOLE: Vilzak, Boris, Madeline Leweck, corps de ballet.

NOTE: Rosa Ponselle, who sang Carmen, was partnered by Lew Christensen; the choreography was not by Balanchine.

REVISIONS: A review dated December 31, 1936, states that Balanchine changed the FARUCCA. The program for January 2, 1937, lists a MENUETTO danced by Annabelle Lyon between the FARUCCA and the FARANDOLE.

See 38, 127, 248

156 RIGOLETTO

Opera in Four Acts by Giuseppe Verdi

ACT I INCIDENTAL DANCE

PREMIERE: December 28, 1935, Metropolitan Opera, New York. Danced by American Ballet Ensemble. Conductor: Ettore Panizza.

CAST: Corps de ballet.

See 88, 121

157 [PAS DE DEUX]

In the middle or late 1930s, for a party at the Persian Room of the Plaza Hotel, New York City, Balanchine choreographed a pas de deux for Marie-Jeanne and William Dollar to a Mozart adagio, with costumes by Pavel Tchelitchew.

1936

158 MIGNON

Opera in Three Acts and Four Scenes by Ambroise Thomas
GYPSY DANCE

PREMIERE: January 4, 1936, Metropolitan Opera, New York. Danced by American Ballet Ensemble. Conductor: Louis Hasselmans.

CAST: William Dollar, corps de ballet.

NOTE: Although programs give no act for the GYPSY DANCE, it probably occurred in Act I.

159 MANON

Opera in Five Acts by Jules Massenet

PREMIERE: January 10, 1936, Metropolitan Opera, New York. Conductor: Louis Hasselmans.

NOTE: Although choreographer and ballet cast are omitted from the printed program, reference in a review to 'a blithe ballet divertissement' indicates choreography by Balanchine for the American Ballet Ensemble. It may have occurred in Act III, Scene 1, COURS LA REINE.

See 40, 122

160 LA JUIVE

Opera in Four Acts and Five Scenes by Jacques Halévy
ACT I VALSE; ACT III BALLET PANTOMIME

PREMIERE: January 11?, 1936, Metropolitan Opera, New York. Danced by American Ballet Ensemble. Conductor: Wilfred Pelletier.

CAST: VALSE: Gisella Caccialanza, William Dollar, corps de ballet.
BALLET PANTOMIME: *Death*, Anatole Vilzak; *The Good Lady*, Annabelle Lyon; *The Imp*, Ruthanna Boris; *The Knights*, Dollar, Charles Laskey; *The Heralds*, Lew Christensen, Douglas Coudy; *The Acrobats*, Kathryn

Mullowny, Daphne Vane, Audrey Guerard; *Masked Ladies, Juggler, Musicians*, corps de ballet.

NOTE: The first performance of the 1936 revival of *La Juive* occurred on January 11; the printed program does not credit dancing. Balanchine's choreography may have been inadvertently omitted from the program, or may have been added to the production later, as listed in the program of January 20, 1936. The casting given here is from the program of a Grand Concert of the Metropolitan Opera on January 12, at which the ballets from *La Juive* were performed.

161 LA RONDINE

Opera in Three Acts by Giacomo Puccini
ACT II WALTZ

PREMIERE: January 17, 1936, Metropolitan Opera, New York. Danced by American Ballet Ensemble. Conductor: Ettore Panizza.

CAST: Kyra Blank, Daphne Vane, Douglas Coudy, corps de ballet.

See 56

162 ZIEGFELD FOLLIES: 1936 EDITION

A National Institution, Glorifying the American Girl
Revue in Two Acts and Twenty-four Scenes

MUSIC AND BOOK: Music by Vernon Duke. Lyrics by Ira Gershwin. Sketches by David Freedman. Orchestrations by Hans Spialek; additional orchestrations by Conrad Sallinger, Russell Bennett and Don Walker.

CHOREOGRAPHY: Ballets by George Balanchine. Modern dances by Robert Alton.

PRODUCTION: Produced by Lee Shubert. Sketches directed by Edward Clarke Lilley. Entire production staged by John Murray Anderson. Scenery and costumes by Vincente Minnelli. Scenery executed by James Surridge; costumes executed by Brooks Costume Company and others.

PREMIERE: January 30, 1936, Winter Garden, New York. Conductor: John McManus. (Out-of-town preview: December 30, 1935, Opera House, Boston.)

CAST: Fannie Brice, Bob Hope, Josephine Baker, Eve Arden, Harriet Hoctor, and others. Corps de ballet (7 women), Dancers (17 women), Boys (8 men). Dancers, in addition to those appearing in the Balanchine ballets, included the Nicholas Brothers.

WEST INDIES (Act I, Scene 5): Gertrude Niesen and The Varsity Eight (singers); Josephine Baker and ensemble (dancers).

WORDS WITHOUT MUSIC: A SURREALIST BALLET (Act I, Scene 7): *The Singer*, Niesen; *The Dancer*, Harriet Hoctor; *The Figures in Green*, Milton Barnett, George Church, Tom Draper; *The Figures in Black*, Gene Ashley, Eddie Browne, Prescott Brown, Howard Morgan; *The Figure with the Light*, Willem van Loon; corps de ballet.

NIGHT FLIGHT (Act I, Scene 10): Hoctor.

MOMENT OF MOMENTS (Act II, Scene 1, The Foyer of an Opera House in the 'Sixties'): Niesen and Rodney McLennan with The Varsity Eight (singers); *The Ballerina*, Hoctor; *Grand Duke*, Herman Belmonte; ensemble (dancers).

SENTIMENTAL WEATHER (Act II, Scene 2): *Production*: Costumes designed by Raoul Pène du Bois. *Cast*: Sung and danced by Cherry and June Preisser and Duke McHale.

5 A. M. (Act II, Scene 6): Sung and danced by Josephine Baker; *The Shadows*, 4 men.

163 DIE MEISTERSINGER VON NÜRNBERG

Opera in Three Acts and Four Scenes by Richard Wagner
ACT III, SCENE 2 INCIDENTAL DANCE (DANCE OF THE APPRENTICES)

PREMIERE: February 3, 1936, Metropolitan Opera, New York. Danced by American Ballet Ensemble. Conductor: Artur Bodanzky.

CAST: Corps de ballet.

See 77

164 SERENATA: 'MAGIC'

MUSIC: By Wolfgang Amadeus Mozart.

PRODUCTION: Scenery and costumes by Pavel Tchelitchew.

PREMIERE: February 14, 1936, Avery Memorial Theater, Hartford, Connecticut. Conductor: Alexander Smallens.

CAST: *The Lady*, Felia Doubrovska; *The Boy*, Lew Christensen; *5 Girls*.

NOTE: Performed once at the Hartford Festival. The music was an unidentified Mozart composition for eight instruments; the subtitle 'Magic' referred to illusionistic devices used in the décor.

165 CONCERTO (later called CLASSIC BALLET)

MUSIC: By Frédéric Chopin (Piano Concerto No. 2 in F minor, Op. 21, 1829).

CHOREOGRAPHY: By William Dollar and George Balanchine.

PREMIERE: March 8, 1936, American Ballet Ensemble, Metropolitan Opera, New York. Conductor: Wilfred Pelletier. Pianist: Nicholas Kopeikine.

CAST: MAESTOSO: Gisella Caccialanza, Rabana Hasburgh, Kathryn Mullowny, Yvonne Patterson, Daphne Vane, Annia Breyman; LARGHETTO: Holly Howard, Charles Laskey; William Dollar; ALLEGRO VIVACE: Leda Anchutina, Elise Reiman, Helen Leitch, Lew Christensen, corps de ballet.

NOTE: Balanchine choreographed the LARGHETTO.

166 ON YOUR TOES

Musical Comedy in Two Acts and Thirteen Scenes

MUSIC AND BOOK: Music by Richard Rodgers. Lyrics by Lorenz Hart. Book by Richard Rodgers, Lorenz Hart and George Abbott. Orchestrations by Hans Spialek.

CHOREOGRAPHY: By George Balanchine. Assistants to Mr. Balanchine: William Dollar and Herbert Harper.

PRODUCTION: Entire production under the supervision of Dwight Deere Wiman. Produced by Dwight Deere Wiman. Staged by

Worthington Miner. Scenery by Jo Mielziner. Costumes by Irene
Sharaff. Scenery built by Turner Scenic Construction Company
and painted by Triangle Scenic Studio; costumes executed by Helene
Pons Studio, Brooks Costume Company, Eaves Costume Company,
and others.

PREMIERE: April 11, 1936, Imperial Theatre, New York. Conductor:
Gene Salzer. Pianists: Edgar Fairchild and Adam Carroll. (Out-of-town
preview: March 21, Shubert Theatre, Boston.)

CAST: *Phil Dolan III*, Ray Bolger; *Frankie Frayne*, Doris Carson; *Vera
Barnova*, Tamara Geva; *Peggy Porterfield*, Luella Gear; *Sergei Alexandrovitch*,
Monty Woolley; and others. Dancers: Demetrios Vilan, George Church,
12 Ladies of the Ballet, 8 Gentlemen of the Ballet.

LA PRINCESSE ZENOBIA BALLET (Act I, Scene 8): *Princesse Zenobia*, Tamara
Geva; *Beggar*, Demetrios Vilan; *Old Prince*, William Baker; *Young
Prince*, George Church.

ON YOUR TOES (Act II, Scene 2): Doris Carson, Ray Bolger, David Morris,
ensemble.

SLAUGHTER ON TENTH AVENUE BALLET (Act II, Scene 4): *Hoofer*, Bolger;
Strip Tease Girl, Geva; *Big Boss*, Church.

NOTE: LA PRINCESSE ZENOBIA BALLET parodies the Oriental-style ballet.
In SLAUGHTER ON TENTH AVENUE, a narrative ballet within the play, a
nightclub stripteaser and a dancer fall in love; a rival arranges for the
young man to be killed by a gangster, but the girl saves him.

At Balanchine's insistence, *On Your Toes* was the first Broadway
musical to credit staged dances as choreography (a practice already
customary in Europe), and is considered the first musical in which the
dances were integrated into the plot, performed by dancers who were
also dramatic characters. In choreographing for Broadway musicals,
Balanchine often used ballet, tap and ballroom steps, in combination
and separately.

OTHER PRODUCTIONS: February 5, 1937, Palace Theatre, London, and
April 19, 1937, London Coliseum ('dances' by Andy Anderson; 'ballets'
by William Baker, 'based on the choreography by George Balanchine').
Broadway revival October 11, 1954, Forty-sixth Street Theatre, New
York (out-of-town preview September 25, Shubert Theatre, New Haven).

TELEVISION: 1956 (excerpts from SLAUGHTER ON TENTH AVENUE, Omnibus, ABC).

See 186, 361

167 THE BARTERED BRIDE

Opera in Three Acts by Bedřich Smetana
ACTS I, II AND III BALLETS

PREMIERE: May 15, 1936, Metropolitan Opera, New York. Danced by American Ballet Ensemble. Conductor: Wilfred Pelletier. (DANCE OF THE COMEDIANS first performed as a concert work on a Metropolitan Opera Gala Program, February 9, 1936.)

CAST: ACT I POLKA: Ruthanna Boris, William Dollar, corps de ballet. ACT II WALTZ: Helen Leitch, corps de ballet. ACT III DANCE OF THE COMEDIANS (Gala Program, February 9): Anatole Vilzak, Dollar, Rabana Hasburgh, Gisella Caccialanza, Leitch, Kyra Blank, Leda Anchutina, corps de ballet.

NOTE: DANCE OF THE COMEDIANS was given separately as part of a Metropolitan Opera Gala Program (principally of operatic arias) which also included a performance of *Serenade* [141].

REVISIONS: 1937, Metropolitan Opera: WALTZ replaced by FURIANTE.

168 LUCIA DI LAMMERMOOR

Opera in Three Acts and Four Scenes by Gaetano Donizetti
ACT III, SCENE I INCIDENTAL DANCE

PREMIERE: May 20, 1936, Metropolitan Opera, New York. Danced by American Ballet Ensemble. Conductor: Gennaro Papi.

CAST: Corps de ballet.

NOTE: Presented with the premiere performance of *The Bat*.

169 THE BAT (also called EL MURCIÉLAGO)

Character Ballet, from 'Die Fledermaus'

MUSIC: By Johann Strauss the Younger (from *Die Fledermaus*, produced 1874, with unidentified additions). Book by Lincoln Kirstein.

PRODUCTION: Costumes and lighting by Keith Martin.

PREMIERE: May 20, 1936, American Ballet Ensemble, Metropolitan Opera, New York. Conductor: Wilfred Pelletier.

CAST: *The Bat*, Holly Howard, Lew Christensen; *The Poet*, Charles Laskey; *The Masked (Identical) Ladies*, Leda Anchutina, Annabelle Lyon; *The Gypsies* (later called *Hungarian Dancers*), Helen Leitch, William Dollar; *The Can-Can Dancer*, Rabana Hasburgh; *The Ladies of Fashion*, 4 women; *2 Coachmen, Can-Can Dancers, Officers, Ladies and Gentlemen*, corps de ballet.

NOTE: Balanchine conceived The Bat as a couple, girl and boy, each wearing a huge spangled wing. The ballet is an evocation of Vienna, set in a park; a young poet seeking inspiration is confounded by two beautiful but identical ladies; a band of gypsies invades the scene. At the end the park is empty, except for the shadow of The Bat.

STAGINGS: 1941, American Ballet Caravan.

See 107, 199, 206, 294

170 ORPHEUS AND EURYDICE
Opera in Two Acts and Four Scenes

MUSIC: By Christoph Willibald Gluck (*Orfeo ed Euridice*, produced 1762, with ballet music from the Paris production of 1774). Libretto by Raniero da Calzabigi.

PRODUCTION: Stage production conceived by George Balanchine and Pavel Tchelitchew. Scenery and costumes by Pavel Tchelitchew. Scenery painted by Joseph Novak.

PREMIERE: May 22, 1936, Metropolitan Opera, New York. Danced by American Ballet Ensemble. Conductor: Richard Hageman.

CAST: SINGERS: *Orpheus*, Anna Kaskas; *Eurydice*, Jeanne Pengelly; *Amor*, Maxine Stellman; and others. DANCERS: *Orpheus*, Lew Christensen; *Eurydice*, Daphne Vane; *Amor*, William Dollar; *Shepherds and Nymphs, Furies and Ghosts from Hades, Heroes from Elysium, Followers of Orpheus*, corps de ballet.

Act I: SCENE 1. At the tomb of Eurydice. SCENE 2. Entrance to Hades.
Act II: SCENE 1. The Elysian Fields. SCENE 2. The Gardens of the Temple of Love.

NOTE: An original production staged by Balanchine at the Metropolitan; the singers were invisible in the orchestra pit while the dancers performed the action on stage; intense atmospheric scenic effects ended with a vast night-sky of stars. The innovative and controversial production was presented only twice.

Balanchine reconceived and directed *Orpheus and Eurydice* for the Hamburgische Staatsoper in 1963; this choreography, with some revision, was performed in a new production of the Théâtre National de l'Opéra, Paris, in 1973, and forms the basis for the ballet *Chaconne* [400], first presented by the New York City Ballet in 1976. Balanchine created different choreography for the Chicago Lyric Opera production of the opera in 1975.

OTHER VERSIONS: 1963, Hamburgische Staatsoper.

See 345, 399, 400

171 SAMSON ET DALILA
Opera in Three Acts and Four Scenes by Camille Saint-Saëns
ACT I INCIDENTAL DANCES; ACT III, SCENE 2 BACCHANALE

PREMIERE: December 26, 1936, Metropolitan Opera, New York. Danced by American Ballet Ensemble. Conductor: Maurice Abravanel.

CAST: INCIDENTAL DANCES: corps de ballet. BACCHANALE: Daphne Vane, corps de ballet.

See 66, 116, 228

1937

172 LE COQ D'OR
Opera in Three Acts

MUSIC: By Nicolai Rimsky-Korsakov (produced 1909). Libretto by Vladimir Bielski after a fairy tale by Alexander Pushkin.

PRODUCTION: Staged and choreographed by George Balanchine (uncredited). Stage direction by Herbert Graf. Scenery by Willy Pogany (uncredited). Miss Pons' costume by Mme Valentina (uncredited).

PREMIERE: February 4, 1937, Metropolitan Opera, New York. Danced by American Ballet Ensemble. Conductor: Gennaro Papi.

CAST: *The Queen of Shemakha*, Lily Pons; *King Dodon*, Ezio Pinza; *Prince Guidon*, Giordano Paltrinieri; *General Polk*, Norman Cordon; *Prince Aphron*, Wilfred Engelman; *Amelfa*, Doris Doe; *The Astrologer*, Nicholas Massue; *The Voice of the Golden Cockerel*, Thelma Votipka; and others.

NOTE: Although printed programs do not list dances or credit choreography, Balanchine choreographed and staged the production, which included a comic Russian dance for King Dodon, oriental movement for the Queen of Shemakha, and ensemble dances. Pons also consulted Michel Fokine about choreography for her role.

See 24

173 CAPONSACCHI

Opera in Three Acts with Prologue and Epilogue by Richard Hageman
ACT I BALLET

PREMIERE: February 4, 1937, Metropolitan Opera, New York. Danced by American Ballet Ensemble. Conductor: Richard Hageman.

CAST: TARANTELLA: Kyra Blank, Rabana Hasburgh, Joseph Levinoff, corps de ballet; ADAGIO: Elise Reiman, Charles Laskey, Heidi Vosseler, corps de ballet; VALSE: Leda Anchutina, William Dollar, Kathryn Mullowny, Daphne Vane, Lew Christensen, Douglas Coudy, corps de ballet.

174 LA GIOCONDA

Opera in Four Acts and Five Scenes by Amilcare Ponchielli
ACT I FURLANA; ACT III DANCE OF THE HOURS

PREMIERE: February 18, 1937, Metropolitan Opera, New York. Danced by American Ballet Ensemble. Conductor: Ettore Panizza. (DANCE OF THE HOURS first performed at a Metropolitan Opera Gala Concert, February 2, 1936.)

CAST: FURLANA: Corps de ballet. DANCE OF THE HOURS (Gala Concert, February 2): *Dawn*: Annia Breyman; *Morning*: Leda Anchutina; *Dusk*: Elise Reiman; *Night*: Rabana Hasburgh; *Day*: Anatole Vilzak, Gisella Caccialanza, Holly Howard, Kathryn Mullowny, corps de ballet.

NOTE: For the February 18th premiere, Mona Montes replaced Annia Breyman as *Dawn* in DANCE OF THE HOURS.

See 87

175 BABES IN ARMS

Musical Comedy in Two Acts and Fourteen Scenes

MUSIC AND BOOK: Music by Richard Rodgers. Lyrics by Lorenz Hart. Book by Richard Rodgers and Lorenz Hart. Orchestrations by Hans Spialek.

CHOREOGRAPHY: By George Balanchine. Assistant to Mr. Balanchine: Johnny Pierce.

PRODUCTION: Production under the supervision of Dwight Deere Wiman. Produced by Dwight Deere Wiman. Staged by Robert Sinclair. Scenery by Raymond Sovey. Costumes by Helene Pons. Scenery built by Turner Scenic Construction Company and painted by Robert Bergman Studio and Triangle Studio; costumes executed by Helene Pons Studio.

PREMIERE: April 14, 1937, Shubert Theatre, New York. Conductor: Gene Salzer. Pianists: Edgar Fairchild and Adam Carroll. (Out-of-town preview: March 25, Shubert Theatre, Boston.)

CAST: *Val LaMar*, Ray Heatherton; *Marshall Blackstone*, Alfred Drake; *Billie Smith*, Mitzi Green; *Lee Calhoun*, Dana Hardwick; *Peter*, Duke McHale; *Baby Rose*, Wynn Murray; *Ivor and Irving de Quincy*, Harold and Fayard Nicholas; and others.

LEE CALHOUN'S FOLLIES (Act I): *The Singer*, Wynn Murray; *The Child*, Douglas Perry; *The High Priest*, Alfred Drake; *The Priestess*, Elenore Tennis; *The Nubians*, The Nicholas Brothers; *The Acrobat*, Bobby Lane; *The Specialty Dancers*, Mitzi Green and Duke McHale; ensemble. This dance sequence included an Egyptian ballet.

ALL DARK PEOPLE (Act I): The Nicholas Brothers.

BALLET: PETER'S JOURNEY (Act II, Dream Ballet to the song 'Imagine'): *The Prince*, McHale; *His Attendants*, Kenneth Wilkins, Leroy James; *Rockefeller*, Rolly Pickert; *The Mermaid*, Tennis; *Greta Garbo*, Gedda Petry; *Marlene Dietrich*, Ursula Seiler; *Clark Gable*, Ted Gary; ensemble.

DUET (untitled): Grace and Ray McDonald.

NOTE: PETER'S JOURNEY is considered to be the first dream ballet on Broadway, introducing a form that was to become popular in American musicals. Peter dreams an imaginary journey around the world, to Hollywood, to Europe, to the African wilds, and back to reality.

176 APOLLON MUSAGÈTE

MUSIC: Music and book by Igor Stravinsky (*Apollo Musagetes*, 1927-28, commissioned by Mrs. Elizabeth Sprague Coolidge).

PRODUCTION: Scenery and costumes by Stewart Chaney. Scenery executed by Studio Alliance; costumes executed by Helene Pons Studio. Wigs executed by Barris.

PREMIERE: April 27, 1937, American Ballet, Metropolitan Opera, New York. Conductor: Igor Stravinsky.

CAST: *Apollo, Leader of the Muses*, Lew Christensen; *Terpsichore*, Elise Reiman; *Calliope*, Daphne Vane; *Polyhymnia*, Holly Howard; *2 Nymphs*; *Leto, Mother of Apollo*, Jane Burkhalter.

NOTE: Originally presented by Diaghilev's Ballets Russes, Paris, 1928. Performed with the new works *The Card Party* and *Le Baiser de la Fée* as a Stravinsky Festival (April 27 and 28, 1937) by the American Ballet while in residence at the Metropolitan Opera House as the American Ballet Ensemble.

See 84*, 198, 284

177 THE CARD PARTY
(also called THE CARD GAME, POKER GAME)
A Ballet in Three Deals

MUSIC: By Igor Stravinsky (*Jeu de Cartes – A Card Game – Das Kartenspiel*, 1936, commissioned by Lincoln Kirstein and Edward M. M. Warburg). Book by Igor Stravinsky and M. Malaieff.

PRODUCTION: Scenery and costumes by Irene Sharaff. Scenery executed by Triangle Scenic Studio and painted by Joseph Novak; costumes executed by Eaves Costume Company and the American Ballet Studio: Eudoxia Mironova, Marie Striga. Wigs by Lucien.

PREMIERE: April 27, 1937, American Ballet, Metropolitan Opera, New York. Conductor: Igor Stravinsky.

CAST: *Joker*, William Dollar; *Queens: Hearts*, Annabelle Lyon; *Spades*, Leda Anchutina; *Diamonds*, Ariel Lang [Helen Leitch]; *Clubs*, Hortense Kahrklin; *4 Aces* (women); *4 Kings*; *4 Jacks*; *10, 9, 8, 7, 6, 5 of Hearts*; *10, 9, 8, 7 of Spades*.

NOTE: Conceived by Stravinsky: The principal characters are the chief cards in a game of poker; each of the three deals is complicated by the endless tricks of the perfidious Joker, who believes himself invincible because of his ability to become any desired card.

REVISIONS: In later productions by the Ballet Russe de Monte Carlo and the New York City Ballet, the Aces were danced by men.

STAGINGS: 1940, Ballet Russe de Monte Carlo (*Poker Game*); 1951, New York City Ballet (*The Card Game*).

See 275

178 LE BAISER DE LA FÉE (also called THE FAIRY'S KISS)
Ballet-Allegory in Four Scenes

MUSIC: Music and book by Igor Stravinsky (1928, commissioned by Ida Rubinstein, dedicated to Peter Ilyitch Tschaikovsky). Based on a tale by Hans Christian Andersen (*The Ice Maiden*).

PRODUCTION: Scenery and costumes by Alice Halicka. Scenery painted by Joseph Novak; costumes executed by Theatrical Costume Company and American Ballet Studio: Eudoxia Mironova, Marie Striga.

PREMIERE: April 27, 1937, American Ballet, Metropolitan Opera, New York. Conductor: Igor Stravinsky.

CAST: *The Fairy*, Kathryn Mullowny; *The Bride*, Gisella Caccialanza; *Her Friend*, Leda Anchutina; *The Bridegroom*, William Dollar; *His Mother*, Annabelle Lyon. FIRST TABLEAU, PROLOGUE: *Mother*; *2 Winds*; *Snowflakes*, Anchutina, 21 women; *Fairy*; *Her Shadow*, Rabana Hasburgh; *8 Mountaineers*. SECOND TABLEAU, THE VILLAGE FESTIVAL:

Peasant Boys and Girls; *Bridegroom*; *Bride*; *Bridesmaids*, Anchutina, 7 women; *A Gypsy (Disguised Fairy)*. THIRD TABLEAU, INSIDE THE MILL: DANCE OF THE PEASANT GIRLS: Anchutina, 16 women; PAS DE DEUX; BRIDE'S VARIATION; CODA (*Bride, Bridegroom, Friend*, corps de ballet); SCENE: *Fairy, Bridegroom*. FOURTH TABLEAU, EPILOGUE (BERCEUSE DE DEMEURES ETERNELLES): *Fairy, Bridegroom*.

NOTE: Stravinsky used the story of *The Ice Maiden*, with its theme of the muse's fatal kiss, to compose an homage to Tschaikovsky. The Fairy implants her magic kiss on a child at birth. When the child has grown to young manhood and good fortune, the Fairy reappears at his wedding fête; repeating the kiss, she leads the young man (the artist in allegory) to abandon his bride and dwell with her forever.

The score was first choreographed by Bronislava Nijinska in 1928 for Ballets Ida Rubinstein. Balanchine created a new ballet in 1937. In 1972, he choreographed *Divertimento from 'Le Baiser de la Fée'* for the New York City Ballet Stravinsky Festival, using *Divertimento*, a concert suite Stravinsky based on the ballet, with additions from the full ballet score.

REVISIONS: 1940, Ballet Russe de Monte Carlo: Final scene changed several times. 1947, Paris Opéra: Final scene changed. 1950, New York City Ballet: Dance sequences in entr'actes between the tableaux lengthened; new pas de deux for Bride and Bridegroom; new EPILOGUE (changed several times to better create illusion of Fairy and Bridegroom swimming through space).

STAGINGS: 1940, Ballet Russe de Monte Carlo; 1947, Paris; 1950, New York City Ballet; 1953, La Scala.

See 271, 376

179 MÂROUF

Opera in Four Acts by Henri Rabaud
ACT II ORIENTAL DANCES

PREMIERE: May 21, 1937, Metropolitan Opera, New York. Danced by American Ballet Ensemble. Conductor: Wilfred Pelletier.

CAST: Ruthanna Boris, Rabana Hasburgh, Eugene Loring, corps de ballet.

See 204

180 ROMÉO ET JULIETTE
Opera in Five Acts and Seven Scenes by Charles Gounod
ACT I INCIDENTAL DANCE

PREMIERE: December 16, 1937, Metropolitan Opera, New York. Danced by American Ballet Ensemble. Conductor: Maurice Abravanel.

CAST: Corps de ballet.

See 86, 124

1938

181 DON GIOVANNI
Opera in Two Acts and Ten Scenes by Wolfgang Amadeus Mozart
ACT II INCIDENTAL DANCE

PREMIERE: January 1, 1938, Metropolitan Opera, New York. Danced by American Ballet Ensemble. Conductor: Ettore Panizza.

CAST: Corps de ballet.

See 81, 253

182 I MARRIED AN ANGEL
Musical Comedy in Two Acts and Eleven Scenes

MUSIC AND BOOK: Music by Richard Rodgers. Lyrics by Lorenz Hart. Book by Richard Rodgers and Lorenz Hart, adapted from the play by John Vaszary. Orchestrations by Hans Spialek.

PRODUCTION: Produced by Dwight Deere Wiman. Staged by Joshua Logan. Scenery by Jo Mielziner. Costumes by John Hambleton. Scenery executed by Turner Scenic Construction Company; costumes executed by Mildred Manning, George Pons and Eaves Costume Company.

PREMIERE: May 11, 1938, Shubert Theatre, New York. Conductor: Gene Salzer. (Out-of-town preview: April 14, Shubert Theatre, New Haven.)

CAST: *Peter Mueller*, Charles Walters; *Count Willy Palaffi*, Dennis King; *Countess Peggy Palaffi*, Vivienne Segal; *Anna Murphy*, Audrey Christie; *Angel*, Vera Zorina; *Harry Mischka Szigetti*, Walter Slezak; and others. *Premier Danseur*, Charles Laskey; 19 Ladies of the Ballet, 10 Gentlemen of the Ballet.

HONEYMOON BALLET (Act I, Scene 4): Vera Zorina, Dennis King, Charles Laskey, corps de ballet.

HOW TO WIN FRIENDS AND INFLUENCE PEOPLE (Act I, Scene 6): Audrey Christie, Charles Walters, corps de ballet.

ROXY'S MUSIC HALL (Act II, Scene 4): Christie, Vivienne Segal, Zorina, Laskey, other cast members, corps de ballet.

SOLO ('Charlie McCarthy'): Walters.

183 THE BOYS FROM SYRACUSE
Musical Comedy in Two Acts and Nine Scenes

MUSIC AND BOOK: Music by Richard Rodgers. Lyrics by Lorenz Hart. Book by George Abbott, based on Shakespeare's *The Comedy of Errors*. Orchestrations by Hans Spialek.

CHOREOGRAPHY: By George Balanchine. Assistants to Mr. Balanchine: David Jones and Duke McHale.

PRODUCTION: Produced and directed by George Abbott. Scenery and lighting by Jo Mielziner. Costumes by Irene Sharaff. Scenery built by T. B. McDonald Construction Company and painted by Studio Alliance; costumes executed by Helene Pons.

PREMIERE: November 23, 1938, Alvin Theatre, New York. Conductor: Harry Levant. (Out-of-town preview: November 3, Shubert Theatre, New Haven.)

CAST: *Antipholus of Ephesus*, Ronald Graham; *Dromio of Ephesus*, Teddy Hart; *Antipholus of Syracuse*, Eddie Albert; *Dromio of Syracuse*, Jimmy Savo; *Luce*, Wynn Murray; *Adriana*, Muriel Angelus; *Luciana*, Marcy Wescott; *Dancing Policeman*, George Church; *Courtezan*, Betty Bruce; *Secretary to Courtezan*, Heidi Vosseler; and others. Dancers: 17 women, 11 men.

DEAR OLD SYRACUSE (Act I, Scene 1): Eddie Albert, Alice Craig, Vivien Moore, Lita Lede, dancers.

SHORTEST DAY OF THE YEAR (Act I, Scene 3): Betty Bruce, Heidi Vosseler, George Church.

LADIES OF THE EVENING (Act II, Scene 1): Vosseler, Church.

THE BALLET (Act II, Scene 2): Jimmy Savo, Albert, Buddy Douglas, Vosseler, Robert Howard, Wynn Murray, dancers.

SING FOR YOUR SUPPER (Act II, Scene 3): Bruce, ensemble.

OH, DIOGENES (Act II, Scene 4): Church, Bruce, ensemble.

184 GREAT LADY
Musical Comedy in Two Acts and Fourteen Scenes

MUSIC AND BOOK: Music by Frederick Loewe. Lyrics by Earle Crooker. Book by Earle Crooker and Lowell Brentano. Orchestrations by Hans Spialek.

CHOREOGRAPHY: By George Balanchine (for contractual reasons credited in the printed program to William Dollar).

PRODUCTION: Produced by Dwight Deere Wiman and J. H. Del Bondio by arrangement with Frank Crumit. Staged by Bretaigne Windust. Scenery by Albert R. Johnson. Costumes by Lucinda Ballard and Scott Wilson. Scenery built by Turner Scenic Construction Company and painted by Studio Alliance, Inc.; costumes executed by Brooks Costume Company.

PREMIERE: December 1, 1938, Majestic Theatre, New York. Conductor: John Fredhoven. (Out-of-town preview: October 21, Forrest Theatre, Philadelphia.)

CAST: *Eliza Bowen (later Elsa de la Croix)*, Norma Terriss; *Stephen Jumel*, Tullio Carminati; *Madame Colette*, Irene Bordoni; and others. *Premier Danseur*, André Eglevsky; *Premieres Danseuses*, Leda Anchutina, Annabelle Lyon; 19 Ladies of the Ballet, 11 Gentlemen of the Ballet.

MADAME COLETTE'S DRESSMAKING SHOP (Act I, Scene 5): *Floorwalker*, André Eglevsky; *Shop Forewoman*, Annabelle Lyon; *Shop Assistant*, Leda Anchutina; *Betty Bowen*, Norma Terriss; corps de ballet.

SISTERS UNDER THE SKIN (Act II, Scene 3): Helen Ford, Gentlemen of the Ballet.

ELSA'S REVERIE: THERE HAD TO BE THE WALTZ (Act II, Scene 3):
1. *The Waltz*: Napoleon, Ray Schultz; corps de ballet. 2. *Pas de Sept*: Holly

Howard; Albia Kavan, Yvonne Patterson, Nora Kaye, Olga Suárez, Hortense Kahrklin, Doris Jane Solly. *3. Pas de Trois and Variations*: Anchutina, Lyon, Eglevsky.

185 THE GOLDWYN FOLLIES
Film

PRODUCTION: United Artists. Produced by Samuel Goldwyn. Associate Producer: George Haight. Directed by George Marshall. Screenplay by Ben Hecht.

MUSIC: By George Gershwin. Lyrics by Ira Gershwin. Ballet music and additional songs by Vernon Duke (WATER NYMPH BALLET orchestrated by Ray Golden and Sid Kuller).

CHOREOGRAPHY: By George Balanchine. Tap Consultant: Sammy Lee.

RELEASED: 1938.

CAST: Adolphe Menjou, Ritz Brothers, Vera Zorina, Kenny Baker, Andrea Leeds, Helen Jepson, Phil Baker, Ella Logan, Bobby Clark, Jerome Cowan, Edgar Bergen and 'Charlie McCarthy,' and others.

ROMEO AND JULIET BALLET: Vera Zorina, William Dollar, corps de ballet.

WATER NYMPH BALLET: Zorina, Dollar, corps de ballet.

NOTE: Balanchine directed the filming of the choreography for his first Hollywood work. The corps de ballet was composed of members of the American Ballet. In the ROMEO AND JULIET BALLET, the Montagues (ballet dancers) and the Capulets (tap dancers) engage in a mock duel. In the WATER NYMPH BALLET, Zorina rises out of a pool; this dance was later the model for the dance of the hippos and ostriches (to the DANCE OF THE HOURS from *La Gioconda*) in Walt Disney's film *Fantasia* (RKO Radio, 1940). Balanchine also created a ballet to Gershwin's *An American in Paris*, which Goldwyn rejected.

1939

186 ON YOUR TOES
Film

PRODUCTION: Warner Brothers. Produced by Hal B. Wallis and Robert Lord. Directed by Ray Enright. Screenplay by Jerry Wald and Richard Macaulay from the Broadway show by George Abbott, Richard Rodgers and Lorenz Hart. Art direction by Robert Haas. Costumes by Orry-Kelly.

MUSIC: By Richard Rodgers. Lyrics by Lorenz Hart. Musical direction by Leo F. Forbstein.

RELEASED: 1939.

CAST: *Vera,* Vera Zorina; *Phil Dolan, Jr.,* Eddie Albert; *Sergei Alexandrovitch,* Alan Hale; *Konstantine Morrosine,* Erik Rhodes; *Phil Dolan, Sr.,* James Gleason; *Mrs. Dolan,* Queenie Smith; *Peggy Porterfield,* Gloria Dickson; *Ivan Boultonoff,* Leonid Kinsky; and others.

LA PRINCESSE ZENOBIA BALLET: Vera Zorina and others.

SLAUGHTER ON TENTH AVENUE BALLET: Zorina, Eddie Albert; Lew Christensen, André Eglevsky and others.

NOTE: Balanchine directed the filming of his dance sequences. He describes the choreography as essentially the same as that for the stage play of 1936.

See 166*, 361

1940

187 KEEP OFF THE GRASS
Revue in Two Acts

MUSIC AND BOOK: Music by James McHugh. *Raffles* ballet music by

Vernon Duke. Lyrics by Al Dubin. Sketches by Mort Lewis, Parke Levy and Alan Lipscott, S. Jay Kaufman, and Panama and Frank. Orchestrations by Hans Spialek and Don Walker. Vocal arrangements by Anthony R. Morelli.

PRODUCTION: Produced by the Shuberts. Book directed by Edward Duryea Dowling. Staged by Fred de Cordova. Scenery and costumes by Nat Karson. Scenery built by Nolan Brothers and painted by Van Ackerman Scenic Studios; costumes executed by Veronica. Lighting by Edward Duryea Dowling.

PREMIERE: May 23, 1940, Broadhurst Theatre, New York. Conductor: John McManus. (Out-of-town preview: April 30, Shubert Theatre, Boston.)

CAST: Jimmy Durante, Ray Bolger, Jane Froman, Ilka Chase, and others. Dancers: Betty Bruce, Sunnie O'Dea, José Limón, Daphne Vane, Marjorie Moore, 15 Dancing Young Ladies, 8 Dancing Young Men.

THIS IS SPRING (Act I): José Limón, Daphne Vane, Marjorie Moore, The Dancing Young Ladies [as ponies].

CRAZY AS A LOON (Act I): Ray Bolger, Sunnie O'Dea.

I'LL APPLAUD YOU WITH MY FEET (Act I): Betty Bruce, dancers.

THE FOUNTAIN (Act I): Bolger and others.

A LATIN TUNE, A MANHATTAN MOON, AND YOU (Act I): Bolger, Bruce, Limón, Vane, Moore, ensemble.

CLEAR OUT OF THIS WORLD (Act I): Limón, Vane, Moore, ensemble.

LOOK OUT FOR MY HEART (Act II): Bruce, Limón, The Dancing Young Ladies [as a chorus of fencers].

OLD JITTERBUG (Act II): Bolger, O'Dea, Moore, ensemble.

I'M IN THE MOOD (Act II): Bruce, Vane, Limón, Henry Dick.

RAFFLES (Act II): *Music*: By Vernon Duke. *Cast*: Bolger, Bruce, Vane, Moore, ensemble.

THIS IS WINTER (Act II): Bolger, Limón, Vane, Moore, entire company.

188 LOUISIANA PURCHASE

Musical Comedy in Two Acts and Fifteen Scenes

MUSIC AND BOOK: Music and lyrics by Irving Berlin. Book by Morrie Ryskind, based on a story by B. G. De Sylva. Orchestral arrangements by Russell Bennett. Vocal arrangements by Hugh Martin.

CHOREOGRAPHY: Ballets by George Balanchine. Modern dances by Carl Randall.

PRODUCTION: Produced by B. G. De Sylva. Book staged by Edgar MacGregor. Scenery and costumes by Tom Lee. Scenery built by Vail Scenic Construction Company and painted by Triangle Scenic Studios; costumes executed by Helene Pons and Eaves Costume Company.

PREMIERE: May 28, 1940, Imperial Theatre, New York. Conductor: Robert Emmett Dolan. (Out-of-town preview: May 2, Shubert Theatre, New Haven.)

CAST: *Marina Van Linden*, Vera Zorina; *Jim Taylor*, William Gaxton; *Madame Bordelaise*, Irene Bordoni; *Senator Oliver P. Loganberry*, Victor Moore; and others. *Premier Danseur*, Charles Laskey; 19 Dancing Girls, 15 Dancing Boys.

TONIGHT AT THE MARDI GRAS (Act I): *Queen of the Mardi Gras / Queen of the Creoles*, Vera Zorina; *Premier Danseur*, Charles Laskey.

OLD MAN'S DARLING—YOUNG MAN'S SLAVE? (Act II): *Marina*, Zorina; *Spirit of Jim Taylor*, Laskey; *Spirit of Senator Loganberry*, Harold Haskins.

NOTE: The film version of *Louisiana Purchase* (1941), with which Balanchine was not personally involved, included his Mardi Gras ballet but did not credit the choreographer.

189 PAS DE DEUX—BLUES

MUSIC: By Vladimir Dukelsky [Vernon Duke].

PREMIERE: August 6, 1940, Winter Garden, New York. Pianists: Vladimir Dukelsky and George Balanchine.

CAST: Vera Zorina, Anton Dolin.

NOTE: Performed once at an *All Star Dance Gala* for British War Relief.

190 CABIN IN THE SKY

Musical Comedy in Two Acts and Nine Scenes

MUSIC AND BOOK: Music by Vernon Duke. Lyrics by John Latouche. Book by Lynn Root. Orchestrations by Domenico Savino, Charles Cooke, Fudd Livingston, Nathan van Cleve. Vocal arrangements by Hugh Martin.

CHOREOGRAPHY: By George Balanchine in collaboration with Katherine Dunham.

PRODUCTION: Produced by Albert Lewis in association with Vinton Freedley. Entire production staged by George Balanchine. Dialogue directed by Albert Lewis. Scenery and costumes by Boris Aronson. Scenery executed by Studio Alliance; costumes executed by Karinska.

PREMIERE: October 25, 1940, Martin Beck Theatre, New York. Conductor: Max Meth.

CAST: *Petunia Jackson*, Ethel Waters; *'Little Joe' Jackson*, Dooley Wilson; *Georgia Brown*, Katherine Dunham; *Lucifer, Jr.*, Rex Ingram; *The Lawd's General*, Todd Duncan; and others. Katherine Dunham Dancers: 17 men and women.

DO WHAT YOU WANNA DO (Act I): *Lucifer, Jr.*, Rex Ingram; *Imps*, Archie Savage, Jieno Moxzer, Rajah Chardieno, Alexander McDonald.

EGYPTIAN BALLET (VISION) (Act II): Katherine Dunham and the Dunham Dancers.

LAZY STEPS (Act II): The Dunham Dancers.

BOOGY WOOGY (Act II): The Dunham Dancers.

SAVANNAH (Act II): *Petunia*, Ethel Waters; Savage.

NOTE: For this musical with a black cast, featuring the Katherine Dunham dancers, Balanchine combined classical ballet technique with their own highly developed dance forms and choreographed special dances for the leading players.

191 I WAS AN ADVENTURESS

Film

PRODUCTION: Twentieth-Century Fox. Produced by Darryl F. Zanuck. Associate Producer: Nunnally Johnson. Directed by Gregory Ratoff. Screenplay by Karl Tunberg, Don Ettlinger and John O'Hara.

MUSIC: Ballet music by Peter Ilyitch Tschaikovsky (primarily from *Swan Lake*, Act II, Op. 20, 1875-76).

RELEASED: 1940.

CAST: *Countess Tanya Vronsky*, Vera Zorina; *Paul Vernay*, Richard Greene; *André Desormeaux*, Erich von Stroheim; *Polo*, Peter Lorre; and others.

BALLET: *Swan Queen*, Vera Zorina; *Prince*, Lew Christensen; *Evil One*, Charles Laskey; 18 swans.

NOTE: An extremely abbreviated, rechoreographed version of *Swan Lake*, Act II, using elaborate camera techniques developed with the choreographer's collaboration. Some of the ideas for the corps de ballet were later used in the finale of Balanchine's New York City Ballet version of *Swan Lake* [285]. There are also rehearsal sequences with Zorina. Under the stage name Fortunio Bonanova, Balanchine plays the Orchestra Leader and is seen conducting.

See 75, 262, 285, 331, 367

1941

192 BALUSTRADE

MUSIC: By Igor Stravinsky (Concerto in D for violin and orchestra, 1931, commissioned by Blair Fairchild).

PRODUCTION: Scenery and costumes by Pavel Tchelitchew. Scenery executed by Eugene Dunkel; costumes executed by Karinska.

PREMIERE: January 22, 1941, Original Ballet Russe, Fifty-first Street Theatre, New York. Conductor: Igor Stravinsky. Violinist: Samuel Dushkin.

CAST: FIRST MOVEMENT, TOCCATA: Tatiana Leskova, Roman Jasinsky, 8 women; SECOND MOVEMENT, ARIA: Marina Svetlova, Paul Petroff, Sonia Orlova, Irina Zarova, 8 women; THIRD MOVEMENT, ARIA: Tamara Toumanova, Jasinsky, Petroff; FOURTH MOVEMENT, CAPRICCIO: Toumanova, Leskova, Svetlova, Jasinsky, Petroff, 12 women.

NOTE: A fantasy of contrasting moods expressed in a series of dialogues of movement, without story. The costumes and setting were surreal: two skeletal trees glowed as blood-red nerve ganglia. The title derives from a low balustrade onstage framing the action. In 1972, for the New York City Ballet Stravinsky Festival, Balanchine choreographed *Violin Concerto* (since 1973 called *Stravinsky Violin Concerto*), an entirely new work to this music performed in practice clothes without scenery.

See 374

193 SERENATA (SERENADE)

MUSIC: By Peter Ilyitch Tschaikovsky (Serenade in C for string orchestra, Op. 48, 1880, with third and fourth movements reversed).

PRODUCTION: Costumes by Candido Portinari.

PREMIERE: June 25, 1941, American Ballet Caravan, Teatro Municipal, Rio de Janeiro. Conductor: Emanuel Balaban.

CAST: Marie-Jeanne, William Dollar, Lorna London, corps de ballet.
SONATINA; WALTZ; TEMA RUSSO; ELEGY.

NOTE: Originally presented by the American Ballet, New York, 1935. At the invitation of Nelson A. Rockefeller, Co-ordinator of Inter-American Affairs, Balanchine and Lincoln Kirstein formed American Ballet Caravan, bringing together members of the former American Ballet and of Ballet Caravan for a five-months' tour of South America. *Serenade* was presented in repertory with other ballets, including Balanchine's *Ballet Imperial*, *Concerto Barocco*, *Divertimento*, *Errante*, *Apollo*, *The Bat*, and *Fantasia Brasileira*.

See 141*, 254

194 BALLET IMPERIAL (from 1973 called TSCHAIKOVSKY PIANO CONCERTO NO. 2)

MUSIC: By Peter Ilyitch Tschaikovsky (Piano Concerto No. 2 in G major, Op. 44, 1879, abridged, rewritten and rearranged by Alexander Siloti).

PRODUCTION: Scenery and costumes by Mstislav Doboujinsky.

PREMIERE: June 25, 1941, American Ballet Caravan, Teatro Municipal, Rio de Janeiro. Conductor: Emanuel Balaban. Pianist: Simon Sadoff. (Open dress rehearsal: May 29, Little Theatre of Hunter College, New York. Conductor: Fritz Mahler.)

CAST: Marie-Jeanne, William Dollar; Gisella Caccialanza; Fred Danieli, Nicholas Magallanes; 2 female demi-soloists; 16 women, 6 men.

ALLEGRO BRILLANTE–ANDANTE; ANDANTE NON TROPPO; ALLEGRO CON FUOCO.

NOTE: A tribute to St. Petersburg, Petipa and Tschaikovsky, set in the grandeur of a palace, the scenic view suggesting the splendors of the Imperial capital of Russia.

REVISIONS: 1950, Sadler's Wells [later Royal Ballet]: Pantomime deleted and new pas de deux added in second movement; somewhat different groupings in third movement; new scenery and costumes by Eugene Berman.

NEW PRODUCTIONS BY BALANCHINE COMPANIES: New York City Ballet: 1964, 1941 version with augmented corps de ballet and minor revisions, with new scenery by Rouben Ter-Arutunian (based on the 1941 production) and new costumes by Karinska; 1973, 1950 version (titled *Piano Concerto No. 2*, then *Tschaikovsky Piano Concerto No. 2*), staged without scenery, with new costumes by Karinska (classical tutus replaced by chiffon skirts), and lighting by Ronald Bates.

STAGINGS: 1942, New Opera Company; 1944, Ballet Russe de Monte Carlo; 1950, Sadler's Wells; 1952, La Scala; 1964, New York City Ballet; 1967, Australia; 1968, Berlin; 1973, Geneva; 1975, Naples; 1976, Norway; 1980, Mexico.

See 349, 382

195 CONCERTO BAROCCO

MUSIC: By Johann Sebastian Bach (Double Violin Concerto in D minor, B.W.V. 1043).

PRODUCTION: Scenery and costumes by Eugene Berman.

PREMIERE: June 27, 1941, American Ballet Caravan, Teatro Municipal, Rio de Janeiro. Conductor: Emanuel Balaban. Violinists: Edmundo

Blois, Salvador Piersant. (Open dress rehearsal: May 29, Little Theatre of Hunter College, New York. Conductor: Fritz Mahler.)

CAST: Marie-Jeanne, William Dollar; Mary Jane Shea; 8 women.

VIVACE; LARGO MA NON TANTO; ALLEGRO.

NOTE: The work was begun as a School of American Ballet exercise in stagecraft. When it entered the repertory of the Ballet Russe de Monte Carlo in 1945 the dancers were dressed in practice clothes, probably the first appearance of what has come to be regarded as the ballet uniform pioneered by Balanchine. Presented with *Orpheus* [246] and *Symphony in C* [244] at the first performance of the New York City Ballet, October 11, 1948.

NEW PRODUCTIONS BY BALANCHINE COMPANIES: New York City Ballet: 1948, using Berman's original costumes, molded of synthetic rubber; 1951, performed without scenery, in practice clothes (black for the women until ca. 1963; white thereafter).

STAGINGS: 1943, American Concert Ballet; 1945, Ballet Russe de Monte Carlo; 1948, New York City Ballet, de Cuevas; 1953, San Francisco; 1955, Royal Danish; 1956, Netherlands; 1960, Hamburg; 1961, Washington, La Scala, National Ballet of Canada; 1963, Paris; 1964, Boston, Pennsylvania; 1965, San Diego, Utah; 1967, National; 1968, Ballet la Jeunesse; 1969, Dayton, Cologne, Munich; 1970, Dallas, Geneva; 1971, Dance Theatre of Harlem, Houston; 1972, Cincinnati; 1973, Garden State, Los Angeles; 1974, Ballet Victoria, New Zealand; 1975, Chicago, Eglevsky; 1976, Chicago Lyric Opera, Les Grands Ballets Canadiens; 1977, Pacific Northwest, Frankfurt, Royal Ballet Touring; 1978, Minnesota, North Carolina, Zürich; 1979, Cleveland; 1980, Atlanta, Ohio, Belgrade, Bologna, Israel; 1981, Norway, Taller Coreográfico; 1982, Ballet Oklahoma, San Juan, Tulsa.

TELEVISION: 1964 (excerpts, Bell Telephone Hour, NBC); 1969 (L'Heure du Concert, CBC, Montreal); 1976 (second movement, Dance in America, PBS).

See 250

196 DIVERTIMENTO

MUSIC: By Gioacchino Rossini (*Matinées Musicales*; *Soirées Musicales*, 1830-35; overture to *La Cenerentola*, produced 1817; selected and orchestrated by Benjamin Britten at the request of Lincoln Kirstein).

PRODUCTION: Scenery and costumes by André Derain (from *Les Songes* [135]).

PREMIERE: June 27, 1941, American Ballet Caravan, Teatro Municipal, Rio de Janeiro. Conductor: Emanuel Balaban.

CAST: MARCH: *King*, Todd Bolender; *6 Attendants*; CANZONETTA: *Flower Lady*, Marjorie Moore; TYROLEAN DANCE: Marie-Jeanne; POLKA: *Couple in Black and White*, Gisella Caccialanza, John Kriza; BOLERO: *Lady in White*, Olga Suárez; TARANTELLA: *Ladies in Red*, 9 women; NOCTURNE: Marie-Jeanne, Fred Danieli; FINALE: Entire cast.

NOTE: A series of costume dances at a party. Near the end a guest costumed as a rat is chased by other guests; unmasked, he is discovered to be an acrobat. On at least one occasion, Balanchine appeared as the rat. Made for the South American tour and not performed elsewhere.

197 ALMA ERRANTE (ERRANTE)
Ballet Fantástico

MUSIC: By Franz Schubert (*The Wanderer*, fantasy for piano, Op. 15, 1882, transcribed by Franz Liszt, orchestrated by Charles Koechlin). Book by Pavel Tchelitchew.

PRODUCTION: Costumes, lighting and dramatic effects by Pavel Tchelitchew (from the 1933 production).

PREMIERE: June 27, 1941, American Ballet Caravan, Teatro Municipal, Rio de Janeiro. Conductor: Emanuel Balaban.

CAST: Marjorie Moore, William Dollar; *Shadows, Angels, Revolutionaries*, and others.

NOTE: Originally presented by Les Ballets 1933, Paris.

See 138*, 143

198 APOLO MUSAGETA (APOLLON MUSAGÈTE)
Ballet in Two Scenes

MUSIC: Music and book by Igor Stravinsky (*Apollo Musagetes*, 1927-28, commissioned by Mrs. Elizabeth Sprague Coolidge).

PRODUCTION: Scenery and costumes by Tomás Santa Rosa.

PREMIERE: June 30, 1941, American Ballet Caravan, Teatro Municipal, Rio de Janeiro. Conductor: Emanuel Balaban.

CAST: *Apollo*, Lew Christensen; *Terpsichore*, Marie-Jeanne; *Calliope*, Olga Suárez; *Polyhymnia*, Marjorie Moore; *2 Goddesses.*

NOTE: Originally presented by Diaghilev's Ballets Russes, Paris, 1928.

See 84*, 176, 284

199 EL MURCIÉLAGO (THE BAT)

MUSIC: By Johann Strauss the Younger (from *Die Fledermaus*, produced 1874, with unidentified additions). Book by Lincoln Kirstein.

PRODUCTION: Costumes and lighting by Keith Martin.

PREMIERE: June 30, 1941, American Ballet Caravan, Teatro Municipal, Rio de Janeiro. Conductor: Emanuel Balaban.

CAST: *The Bat*, Helen Kramer, Todd Bolender; *The Poet*, Lew Christensen; *The Masked (Identical) Ladies*, Gisella Caccialanza, Olga Suárez; *Hungarian Dancers* (formerly called *Gypsies*), Marie-Jeanne, William Dollar; *The Can-Can Dancer*, Beatrice Tompkins; *The Ladies of Fashion*, 4 women; *2 Coachmen*; *Can-Can Dancers, Officers, Ladies and Gentlemen*, corps de ballet.

NOTE: Originally presented by the American Ballet, New York, 1936.

See 107, 169*, 206, 294

200 FANTASIA BRASILEIRA

MUSIC: By Francisco Mignone (*Brazilian Fantasy No. 4*, 1941, commissioned by Lincoln Kirstein).

PRODUCTION: Scenery and costumes by Erico Bianco.

PREMIERE: August 27, 1941, American Ballet Caravan, Teatro Municipal, Santiago de Chile. Conductor: Emanuel Balaban. Pianist: Simon Sadoff.

CAST: Olga Suárez, Fred Danieli, Nicholas Magallanes, corps de ballet.

NOTE: The choreography employed Brazilian folk-dance motifs. Performed only in South America.

1942

201 THE LADY COMES ACROSS
Musical Comedy in Two Acts and Twelve Scenes

MUSIC AND BOOK: Music and lyrics by Vernon Duke and John Latouche. Book by Fred Thompson and Dawn Powell. Orchestrations supervised by Domenico Savino. Musical arrangements by Domenico Savino, Charles L. Cooke and staff.

CHOREOGRAPHY: By George Balanchine. Choreographic Assistant: William Holbrook.

PRODUCTION: Production under the supervision of Morrie Ryskind. Produced by George Hale in association with Charles R. Rogers and Nelson Seabra. Book directed by Romney Brent. Scenery and costumes by Stewart Chaney. Scenery built by Vail Construction Company and painted by Robert W. Bergman Studios, Inc.; costumes executed by Mme Karinska, Mme Berthe and Brooks Costume Company.

PREMIERE: January 9, 1942, Forty-fourth Street Theatre, New York. Conductor: Jacques Rabiroff. Pianist/Organist: Adam Carroll. (Out-of-town preview: December 17, 1941, Shubert Theatre, Boston.)

CAST: *Jill Charters*, Evelyn Wyckoff (Jessie Matthews, Boston); *Otis Kibber*, Joe E. Lewis; *Ernie Bustard*, Mischa Auer; *Mrs. Riverdale*, Ruth Weston; *Babs Appleway*, Wynn Murray; *Campbell*, Gower Champion; *Kay*, Jeanne Tyler; and others. *Ballerina Comique*, Eugenia Delarova; *Ballerina*, Lubov Rostova; *The Phantom Lover*, Marc Platt; Dancing Ensemble of 17 women and 8 men.

HIT THE RAMP (Act I, Scene 3): Wynn Murray, Mischa Auer, ensemble.

TANGO (Act I, Scene 4): Auer, Eugenia Delarova, ensemble.

CONEY ISLAND BALLET (Act II, Scene 1): Delarova, Lubov Rostova, Marc Platt, ensemble.

LADY (Act II, Scene 1): Gower Champion, Jeanne Tyler.

THIS IS WHERE I CAME IN (Act II, Scene 2): Champion, Tyler.

DAYBREAK (Act II, Scene 5): Evelyn Wyckoff (Jessie Matthews, Boston); *The Phantom Lover*, Platt.

202 THE BALLET OF THE ELEPHANTS

MUSIC: By Igor Stravinsky (*Circus Polka*, 1942, written at the request of George Balanchine, with the dedication 'For a young elephant').

PRODUCTION: Staged by John Murray Anderson. Costumes by Norman Bel Geddes. Elephants trained by Walter McClain.

PREMIERE: April 9, 1942, Ringling Brothers and Barnum & Bailey Circus, Madison Square Garden, New York. Conductor: Merle Evans.

CAST: The elephant Modoc as 'premiere ballerina,' and 'fifty elephants and fifty beautiful girls in an original choreographic *tour de force.*' In early performances, including an Armed Forces benefit, Vera Zorina rode at the head of the troupe in a specially choreographed addition to the circus routine.

NOTE: In 1945, for a program entitled *Adventure in Ballet*, Balanchine choreographed another work to this music with an all-human cast.

See 230

203 PAS DE TROIS FOR PIANO AND TWO DANCERS

MUSIC: By Theodore Chanler (1942, commissioned by Lincoln Kirstein).

PRODUCTION: Produced by Lincoln Kirstein. Costumes by Pavel Tchelitchew.

PREMIERE: May 10, 1942, Alvin Theatre, New York. Pianist: Theodore Chanler.

CAST: Mary Ellen Moylan, Nicholas Magallanes.

NOTE: Performed once on a program entitled *Music at Work*, in aid of Russian War Relief.

204 MARUF (MÂROUF)

Opera in Four Acts by Henri Rabaud

ACT II HAREM BALLET

PREMIERE: August 7, 1942, Opera of the Teatro Colón, Buenos Aires, Argentina. Conductor: A. Wolff.

CAST: Leticia de la Vega, Yurek Shabelevsky, corps de ballet.

NOTE: Presented with the premiere performance of *Concierto de Mozart* during Balanchine's two months as guest director of the ballet of the Teatro Colón. The season included a production of *Apollon Musagète* designed by Pavel Tchelitchew.

See 179

205 CONCIERTO DE MOZART (also called CONCIERTO)

MUSIC: By Wolfgang Amadeus Mozart (Violin Concerto in A major, K. 219, 1775).

PRODUCTION: Scenery and costumes by Pavel Tchelitchew.

PREMIERE: August 7, 1942, Ballet of the Teatro Colón, Buenos Aires, Argentina. Conductor: Juan José Castro. Violinist: Carlos Pessina.

CAST: ALLEGRO APERTO: Maria Ruanova, Michel [Mezeslav] Borovsky; Nelida Cendra, Estela Deporte, Jorge Tomin; 11 women, 11 men; ADAGIO: Ruanova, Yurek Shabelevsky; Tomin; 15 women, 7 men; MINUETO: Ruanova, Borovsky, Shabelevsky; Cendra, Deporte, Tomin; 19 women, 7 men.

NOTE: At least one section of this work has been seen in the United States, the pas de deux from the ADAGIO, performed in 1964 in Washington, D. C., and Montevideo, Minnesota.

STAGINGS: 1955?, La Plata; 1960, Berliner Ballett; 1964, Uruguay; 1965, São Paulo; 1980, Belo Horizonte.

206 ROSALINDA (DIE FLEDERMAUS)

Operetta in Three Acts and a Prologue

MUSIC AND BOOK: Music by Johann Strauss the Younger (produced 1874), in a version by Max Reinhardt (1920s). Music from other Strauss scores interpolated by Erich Wolfgang Korngold, including *Tales from the Vienna Woods, Knight Pazman* and *Wine, Women and Song*. Lyrics by Paul Kerby.

CHOREOGRAPHY: By George Balanchine. Ballet Master: William Dollar.

PRODUCTION: Produced by Lodewick Vroom. Staged by Felix Brentano and George Balanchine (uncredited). Scenery by Oliver Smith. Costumes by Ladislas Czettel. Scenery built by Vail Construction Company and painted by E. B. Dunkel Studios; costumes executed by Brooks Costume Company. Lighting by Jean Rosenthal.

PREMIERE: October 28, 1942, New Opera Company, Forty-fourth Street Theatre, New York. Conductor: Erich Wolfgang Korngold.

CAST: *Rosalinda von Eisenstein*, Dorothy Sarnoff; *Gabriel von Eisenstein*, Ralph Herbert; *Adele*, Virginia MacWatters; *Prince Orlofsky*, Oscar Karlweis; and others. *Premier Danseur*, José Limón; *Premiere Danseuse*, Mary Ellen Moylan; 10 women dancers, 7 men dancers.

WAITERS DANCE (Act I): Todd Bolender, Douglas Coudy.

BALLETS IN BALLROOM SCENE, INCLUDING GRAND WALTZ FINALE (Act II): Mary Ellen Moylan, José Limón, ensemble.

DANCE OF DRUNKEN GENTLEMEN IN PRISON (Act III): Male ensemble with flying ballerinas.

NOTE: Created during Balanchine's year-long association with the New Opera Company, for which he choreographed opera divertissements and mounted a production of *Ballet Imperial*.

See 107, 169, 199, 294

207 THE OPERA CLOAK
Operatic Fantasy in One Act by Walter Damrosch
RAGTIME BALLET [?]

PREMIERE: November 3, 1942, New Opera Company, Broadway Theatre, New York. Conductor: Walter Damrosch.

NOTE: World premiere and only performance. The RAGTIME BALLET was announced in press releases, but programs credit neither choreographer nor dancers. Balanchine recalls some association with this production. Presented with *The Fair at Sorochinsk*.

208 THE FAIR AT SOROCHINSK
Opera in Three Acts by Modest Moussorgsky
ACT III HOPAK BALLET

PREMIERE: November 3, 1942, New Opera Company, Broadway Theatre, New York. Conductor: Emil Cooper.

CAST: Gisella Caccialanza, William Dollar, 10 women, 4 men.

See 43

209 LA VIE PARISIENNE
Comic Opera in Three Acts and Four Scenes by Jacques Offenbach
ACT II, SCENE 2 BALLET

CHOREOGRAPHY: Dances staged by William Dollar under the supervision of George Balanchine.

PREMIERE: November 10, 1942, New Opera Company, Broadway Theatre, New York. Conductor: Paul Breisach.

CAST: Gisella Caccialanza, 10 women, 4 men.

210 THE QUEEN OF SPADES (PIQUE DAME)
Opera in Three Acts and Seven Scenes by Peter Ilyitch Tschaikovsky
ACT II, SCENE I BALLET

CHOREOGRAPHY: Dances staged by William Dollar under the supervision of George Balanchine.

PREMIERE: November 24, 1942, New Opera Company, Broadway Theatre, New York. Conductor: Emil Cooper.

CAST: Gisella Caccialanza, William Dollar, 10 women, 4 men.

211 MACBETH
Opera in Four Acts and Nine Scenes by Giuseppe Verdi
ACT I, SCENE I, AND ACT III, SCENE I DANCES OF THE WITCHES

CHOREOGRAPHY: Dances staged by William Dollar under the supervision of George Balanchine.

PREMIERE: December 2, 1942, New Opera Company, Broadway Theatre, New York. Conductor: Fritz Stiedry.

CAST: 10 women, 4 men.

212 [SOLO]

Gisella Caccialanza remembers performing a dance with Balanchine choreography to music by Prokofiev at the U. S. O. headquarters in New York City in 1942.

213 STAR SPANGLED RHYTHM
Film

PRODUCTION: Paramount Pictures. Produced by Joseph Sistrom. Directed by George Marshall. Screenplay by Melvin Frank, Norman Panama and Harry Tugend. Art direction by Hans Dreier and Ernst Fegte. Scenery by Stephen Seymour. Costumes by Edith Head.

MUSIC: Music and lyrics by Harold Arlen and Johnny Mercer. Musical Director: Robert Emmett Dolan, assisted by Arthur Franklin.

CHOREOGRAPHY: By George Balanchine, Danny Dare and Katherine Dunham.

RELEASED: 1942.

CAST: *Pop Webster*, Victor Moore; *Polly Judson*, Betty Hutton; *Jimmy Webster*, Eddie Bracken; and others. Stars playing themselves in the benefit performance scene include Bing Crosby, Bob Hope, Fred MacMurray, Franchot Tone, Ray Milland, Dorothy Lamour, Paulette Goddard, Vera Zorina, Mary Martin, Veronica Lake, Alan Ladd, Katherine Dunham, Cecil B. De Mille, and others.

THAT OLD BLACK MAGIC (sung by Johnny Johnston): Vera Zorina.

1943

214 HELEN OF TROY

Michel Fokine's last ballet, *Helen of Troy* (choreographed to excerpts from Offenbach's *La Belle Hélène*), was substantially revised by David Lichine, whose version was first performed by Ballet Theatre at the Masonic Auditorium, Detroit, November 29, 1942. Before the New York performances in April 1943, Balanchine assisted Lichine in devising a new ending for the ballet.

215 THE CRUCIFIXION OF CHRIST

Music: By Johann Sebastian Bach (*St. Matthew Passion*, 1729).

Production: Performance conceived by Leopold Stokowski, Robert Edmond Jones and George Balanchine. Groupings devised by George Balanchine.

Premiere: April 9, 1943, Metropolitan Opera, New York. Conductor: Leopold Stokowski.

Cast: Students of the School of American Ballet on stage, singers in the orchestra pit. *Maria Magdalena*, Lillian Gish; students from the School of American Ballet miming the roles of Peter, Pilate, the High Priest, Judas, Soldiers, the Crowd.

Note: Described in announcements as a modern form of miracle play, the work was performed once as a benefit for the American Friends Service Committee.

216 THE MERRY WIDOW

Operetta in Three Acts

Music and book: Music by Franz Lehár (produced 1905). New musical version by Robert Stolz. Lyrics by Adrian Ross. Special lyrics by Robert Gilbert. New book by Sidney Sheldon and Ben Roberts.

PRODUCTION: Produced by Yolanda Mero-Irion. Directed by Felix Brentano. Scenery by Howard Bay. Costumes by Walter Florell. Scenery built by William Kellam Company and painted by Centre Studios; costumes executed by Eaves and Brooks Costume Companies.

PREMIERE: August 4, 1943, New Opera Company, Majestic Theatre, New York. Conductor: Robert Stolz.

CAST: *Sonia Sadoya*, Marta Eggerth; *Prince Danilo*, Jan Kiepura; *Popoff*, Melville Cooper; *Jolidon*, Robert Field; *Natalie*, Ruth Matteson; *Clo-Clo*, Lisette Verea; and others. *Premieres Danseuses*, Lubov Roudenko, Milada Mladova; *Premiers Danseurs*, Chris Volkoff, James Starbuck; 6 women dancers, 5 men dancers.

POLKA (Act I): Lubov Roudenko, James Starbuck.

MARSOVIAN DANCE (Act II): Milada Mladova, Chris Volkoff, corps de ballet.

THE WOMEN (Act II): Melville Cooper, 6 men, 2 women dancers, 6 women singers.

I LOVE YOU SO (Act II): Mladova, Volkoff, corps de ballet.

THE GIRLS AT MAXIM'S [CAN-CAN] (Act III): Roudenko, ballet girls.

NOTE: The production featured the choreography, and added music for dance numbers not in the original score.

OTHER PRODUCTIONS: October 7, 1944 (New Opera Company) and April 9, 1957 (New York City Center Light Opera Company). Although Balanchine was not personally involved in these stagings, his name appears on the printed programs and his choreography was used, with modifications.

217 WHAT'S UP

Musical Comedy in Two Acts and Nine Scenes

MUSIC AND BOOK: Music by Frederick Loewe. Lyrics by Alan Jay Lerner. Book by Alan Jay Lerner and Arthur Pierson. Orchestrations by Van Cleave. Vocal arrangements by Bobby Tucker.

PRODUCTION: Produced by Mark Warnow. Book directed by Robert H. Gordon. Staged and choreographed by George Balanchine. Scenery by Boris Aronson. Costumes by Grace Houston. Scenery executed by

Studio Alliance, Inc.; costumes executed by Eaves Costume Company. Lighting by Al Alloy.

PREMIERE: November 11, 1943, National Theatre, New York. Conductor: Will Irwin. (Out-of-town preview: October 22, Playhouse, Wilmington, Delaware.)

CAST: *Rawa of Tanglinia*, Jimmy Savo; *Sgt. Moroney*, Johnny Morgan; *Virginia Miller*, Gloria Warren; and others. Featured dancers included Phyllis Hill, Don Weissmuller, Sondra Barrett, Kenneth Buffett, Honey Murray, Robert Bay, Jack Baker.

JOSHUA (Act I, Scene 3): Ensemble of men and women.

BALLET (Act I, Scene 4): Jimmy Savo, Phyllis Hill.

HOW FLY TIMES (Act I, Scene 4): Don Weissmuller.

YOU WASH AND I'LL DRY (Act II, Scene 1): Sondra Barrett, Kenneth Buffett, Honey Murray.

THE ILL-TEMPERED CLAVICHORD (Act II, Scene 3): Ensemble of men and women. Dance specialty: Robert Bay.

REPRISE: YOU'VE GOT A HOLD ON ME (Act II, Scene 3): Hill, Jack Baker.

NOTE: Among the dance numbers were two dream ballets: In JOSHUA, U. S. Army soldiers in pajamas dance with schoolgirls in nighties, combining ballet and tap styles; in BALLET, a pas de deux, the mime-comedian Jimmy Savo, small, pursues a large ballerina, his dream-girl.

1944

218 DREAM WITH MUSIC
Musical Comedy in Two Acts and Fourteen Scenes

MUSIC AND BOOK: Music by Clay Warnick (based on themes from Saint-Saëns' Violin Concerto in B minor, Rimsky-Korsakov's *Schéhérazade*, Schubert's Symphony No. 9, Beethoven's Symphony No. 7, Weber's *Oberon*, Grieg's Piano Concerto in A minor, Beethoven's Symphony No. 1, Borodin's *Prince Igor*, Moussorgsky's *A Night on Bald Mountain*, Wagner's 'Ride of the Valkyries' from *Die Walküre*, Chopin's

Twenty-four Preludes, Gluck's ballet music, Schumann's Piano Concerto, Dvořák's 'New World' Symphony, Haydn's Symphony No. 1, and Tschaikovsky's *The Nutcracker.*) Lyrics by Edward Eager. Book by Sidney Sheldon, Dorothy Kilgallen and Ben Roberts. Orchestrations by Russell Bennett, Hans Spialek, Ted Royal, and Clay Warnick. Vocal arrangements by Clay Warnick.

CHOREOGRAPHY: Ballet choreography by George Balanchine. Tap routines by Henry Le Tang.

PRODUCTION: Produced and directed by Richard Kollmar. Scenery by Stewart Chaney. Costumes by Miles White. Scenery built by Martin Turner and painted by Kaj Velden; costumes executed by Brooks Costume Company, Karinska and others.

PREMIERE: May 18, 1944, Majestic Theatre, New York. Conductor: Max Meth. (Out-of-town preview: April 17, Shubert Theatre, Boston.)

CAST: *Dinah,* Vera Zorina; *Michael,* Ronald Graham; *Marian,* Joy Hodges (June Knight, Boston). IN THE DREAM: *Scheherazade,* Zorina; *Jasmin,* Hodges; *Sultan,* Robert Brink; *Aladdin,* Graham; *Sinbad,* Leonard Elliott; and others. Dancers: Peter Birch and corps de ballet of 9 women and 4 men, 6 tap dancers.

SCHEHERAZADE'S DANCE (Act I): Vera Zorina, singing ensemble.

BE GLAD YOU'RE ALIVE (Act I): Alex Rotov, Peter Birch, ensemble.

I'LL TAKE THE SOLO (Act I): Corps de ballet, tap dancers.

BALLET IN THE CLOUDS (Act I): Zorina, Birch, Sunny Rice, corps de ballet.

THE LION AND THE LAMB (Act II): Ensemble.

219 SONG OF NORWAY
Operetta in Two Acts and Seven Scenes

MUSIC AND BOOK: Music by Edvard Grieg, adapted by Robert Wright and George Forrest. Lyrics by Robert Wright and George Forrest. Book by Milton Lazarus from a play by Homer Curran (based on the life of Grieg). Orchestral and vocal arrangements by Arthur Kay.

CHOREOGRAPHY: Choreography and vocal ensembles staged by George Balanchine.

PRODUCTION: Produced by Edwin Lester. Book directed by Charles K. Freeman. Scenery by Lemuel Ayers. Costumes by Robert Davison. Scenery supervised by Carl Kent. Scenery built by Curran Productions and painted by Harry Dworkin and Fritz Kraencke; costumes executed by Walter J. Israel.

PREMIERE: June 12, 1944, Los Angeles and San Francisco Civic Light Operas, Philharmonic Auditorium, Los Angeles, California. Conductor: Arthur Kay. Pianist: Rachel Chapman. (First New York performance, August 21, Imperial Theatre. Pianist: Louis Teicher.)

CAST: *Edvard Grieg*, Walter Cassel (Lawrence Brooks, New York); *Rikard Nordraak*, Robert Shafer; *Nina Hagerup*, Helena Bliss; *Count Peppi Le Loup*, Sig Arno; *Louisa Giovanni*, Irra Petina; *Maestro Pisoni*, Charles Judels (Robert Bernard, New York); *Freddy/Tito*, Frederic Franklin; *Adelina*, Alexandra Danilova; and others. Dancing ensemble from Ballet Russe de Monte Carlo: 11 women, 11 men.

IN THE HOLIDAY SPIRIT (Act I, Scene 2): Ruthanna Boris, Anna Istomina, Leon Danielian, Alexander Goudovitch, and others.

FREDDY AND HIS FIDDLE (Act I, Scene 2): *Music*: Adapted from *Norwegian Dances*, Op. 38, 1881. *Cast*: *Einar*, Kent Edwards; *Sigrid*, Janet Hamer; *Freddy*, Frederic Franklin; singers.

MARCH OF THE TROLLGERS (THE CAKE LOTTERY) (Act I, Scene 2): *Music*: Adapted from *Mountaineers Song*, *Halling* in G minor, and *March of the Dwarfs*. *Cast*: Singing and dancing ensemble.

CHOCOLATE PAS DE TROIS (Act II, Scene 2): *Music*: Adapted from *Fra Monte Pincio*, Op. 39, 1870, and *Rigaudon* from *Holberg Suite*, Op. 4, 1884. *Cast*: *Tito*, Franklin; *His Employees*, corps de ballet.

WALTZ ETERNAL (Act II, Scene 3): *Music*: Adapted from *Waltz Caprice*, Op. 37, 1883. *Cast*: Corps de ballet.

PEER GYNT BALLET (Act II, Scene 3): *Music*: Adapted from *Peer Gynt Suites* I and II, Opp. 46 and 55, 1876. *Cast*: Alexandra Danilova, Nathalie Krassovska, Danielian, corps de ballet. SOLVEIG'S SONG: Krassovska, Danielian; HALL OF THE DOVRE KING: Male ensemble; ANITRA'S DANCE: Danilova.

THE SONG OF NORWAY (Act II, Scene 5): *Music*: Adapted from A minor

Concerto, 1868. *Cast*: Danilova, Franklin, Nicholas Magallanes, corps de ballet.

NOTE: The production featured the Ballet Russe de Monte Carlo ensemble and its principal dancers, Danilova and Franklin.

OTHER PRODUCTIONS: May 26, 1952, Philharmonic Auditorium, Los Angeles. Although the choreography is credited to Balanchine and Aida Broadbent, Balanchine was not involved.

220 DANSES CONCERTANTES
(also called DANCE CONCERTO)

MUSIC: By Igor Stravinsky (*Danses Concertantes* for chamber orchestra, 1941-42, commissioned by Werner Janssen).

PRODUCTION: Scenery and costumes by Eugene Berman. Scenery executed by E. B. Dunkel Studios; costumes executed by Karinska, Inc.

PREMIERE: September 10, 1944, Ballet Russe de Monte Carlo, City Center of Music and Drama, New York. Conductor: Emanuel Balaban.

CAST: Alexandra Danilova, Frederic Franklin; I. VARIATION: Gertrude Svobodina, Nikita Talin, Nora White; II. VARIATION: Ruthanna Boris, Alexander Goudovitch, Dorothy Etheridge; III. VARIATION: Lillian Lanese, Herbert Bliss, Pauline Goddard; IV. VARIATION: Maria Tallchief, Nicholas Magallanes, Mary Ellen Moylan; PAS DE DEUX: Danilova, Franklin; FINALE: Entire cast.

NOTE: Stravinsky wrote the music for concert performance; Balanchine choreographed the score as his first new work for the Ballet Russe de Monte Carlo at the beginning of his two-year association with that company as choreographer.

REVISIONS: 1972, New York City Ballet (Stravinsky Festival): Choreography entirely reworked, but resembling the first production in style and effect, using Berman's original costumes and scenery.

See 375

221 LE BOURGEOIS GENTILHOMME

MUSIC: By Richard Strauss (concert suite, ca. 1917). Libretto after Molière.

PRODUCTION: Scenery and costumes by Eugene Berman. Scenery executed by E. B. Dunkel Studios; costumes executed by Karinska, Inc.

PREMIERE: September 23, 1944, Ballet Russe de Monte Carlo, City Center of Music and Drama, New York. Conductor: Emanuel Balaban.

CAST: *Cléonte*, Nicholas Magallanes; *Coviel, His Valet*, Peter Deign; *M. Jourdain*, Michel Katcharoff; *Lucile, His Daughter*, Nathalie Krassovska; *Nicola, Her Maid*, Vida Brown; *4 Ladies in Waiting*; *4 Blackamoors*; DIVERTISSEMENTS: *Fencers*, 2 men; PAS DE SEPT: Mary Ellen Moylan, 6 women; HARLEQUINADE: Ruthanna Boris, Leon Danielian, Nikita Talin; DANSE INDIENNE: Maria Tallchief, Yurek Lazowski; PAS DE DEUX D'AMOUR: Krassovska, Magallanes.

REVISIONS: 1945, Ballet Russe de Monte Carlo: Reviews imply some reworking.

OTHER VERSIONS: 1932, Ballets Russes de Monte-Carlo. 1979, New York City Opera.

See 131*, 410, 414

222 WALTZ ACADEMY

MUSIC: By Vittorio Rieti (orchestrated by the composer from his two-piano suite *Second Avenue Waltzes*, 1944, on commission from Ballet Theatre).

PRODUCTION: Scenery by Oliver Smith. Costumes by Alvin Colt. Scenery executed by Eugene B. Dunkel Studios; costumes executed by Karinska.

PREMIERE: October 5, 1944, Ballet Theatre, Opera House, Boston. Conductor: Antal Dorati.

CAST: PAS DE SIX: Margaret Banks, Mildred Ferguson, Barbara Fallis, Rozsika Sabo, June Morris, Fern Whitney; PAS DE QUATRE: Janet Reed, Albia Kavan, Harold Lang, Fernando Alonso; PAS DE TROIS: Miriam Golden, Diana Adams, John Kriza; PAS DE TROIS: Nora Kaye, John

Taras, Rex Cooper; PAS DE DEUX: Nana Gollner, Paul Petroff; FINALE: Entire cast.

NOTE: A suite of waltz variations, opening with morning ballet practice in a rehearsal room; the set suggested a loft under a cupola. Balanchine's first original work for Ballet Theatre.

REVISIONS: 1948, Ballet Theatre: Revised, retitled *Six Waltzes*.

223 SENTIMENTAL COLLOQUY

MUSIC: By Paul Bowles.

CHOREOGRAPHY: By George Balanchine, credited to André Eglevsky.

PRODUCTION: Scenery and costumes by Salvador Dali. Costumes executed by Karinska.

PREMIERE: October 30, 1944, Ballet International, International Theatre, New York. Conductor: Alexander Smallens.

CAST: Marie-Jeanne, André Eglevsky; 2 men.

NOTE: Titled after a poem by Verlaine and choreographed for two figures veiled in white who dance in surreal surroundings with a bicyclist and a figure costumed as a turtle. Dali's backdrop, filled with images of bearded bicyclists and a grand piano spouting water, was designed to suggest extreme loneliness experienced in the midst of a crowd.

1945

224 THE TEMPEST
Play by William Shakespeare

MUSIC: By David Diamond.

PRODUCTION: Produced by Cheryl Crawford, based on a production idea by Eva Le Gallienne. Directed by Margaret Webster. Scenery and costumes by Motley. Scenery built by Nolan Brothers and painted by Centre Studios; men's costumes executed by Eaves Costume

Company; other costumes executed by Edith Lutyens. Lighting by Moe Hack.

PREMIERE: January 25, 1945, Alvin Theatre, New York. Conductor: David Diamond. (Out-of-town preview: December 26, 1944, Shubert Theatre, Philadelphia.)

CAST: *Alonso*, Philip Huston; *Gonzalo*, Paul Leyssac; *Antonio*, Berry Kroeger; *Sebastian*, Eugene Stuckmann; *Prospero*, Arnold Moss; *Miranda*, Frances Heflin; *Ariel*, Vera Zorina; *Caliban*, Canada Lee; *Ferdinand*, Vito Christi; *Trinculo*, George Voskovec; *Stephano*, Jan Werich; and others.

NOTE: Although his name does not appear on the printed program, Balanchine arranged movement sequences for Vera Zorina.

See 308

225 PAS DE DEUX (also called GRAND ADAGIO)

MUSIC: By Peter Ilyitch Tschaikovsky (entr'acte from *The Sleeping Beauty*, 1890, orchestrated by Ivan Boutnikoff).

PREMIERE: March 14, 1945, Ballet Russe de Monte Carlo, City Center of Music and Drama, New York. Conductor: Emanuel Balaban.

CAST: Alexandra Danilova, Frederic Franklin.

NOTE: In 1955, Balanchine interpolated this music in its original form as a violin cadenza into Act I of his production of *The Nutcracker* for the New York City Ballet.

See 65, 259, 281, 302, 404, 418

226 AÏDA

Opera in Four Acts and Seven Scenes by Giuseppe Verdi
BALLET

CHOREOGRAPHY: By George Balanchine and William Dollar.

PREMIERE: ca. June 8, 1945, Ópera Nacional, Palacio de Bellas Artes, Mexico City. Danced by advanced students from the School of American Ballet and guest soloists. Conductor: Carl Alwin.

NOTE: Accompanying Balanchine and Dollar to Mexico were Marie-Jeanne, Nicholas Magallanes, and twelve girls from the School of American Ballet. Printed programs do not list dances or dancers. Balanchine choreographed *Aïda*, *Faust* and *Samson et Dalila*. He may also have choreographed *Carmen* and *Rigoletto*, but no documentation has been located. *Concerto Barocco* [195], *Apollo* [84], and Dollar's *Constantia* and staging of *Les Sylphides* were also performed.

See 126, 152, 255

227 FAUSTO (FAUST)

Opera in Four Acts by Charles Gounod

WALPURGISNACHT BALLET

PREMIERE: June 26, 1945, Ópera Nacional, Palacio de Bellas Artes, Mexico City. Danced by advanced students from the School of American Ballet and guest soloists. Conductor: Jean Morel.

NOTE: Patricia Wilde remembers performing a solo.

See 45, 117, 151, 397, 413

228 SANSÓN Y DALILA (SAMSON ET DALILA)

Opera in Three Acts by Camille Saint-Saëns

BALLETS

PREMIERE: July 3, 1945, Ópera Nacional, Palacio de Bellas Artes, Mexico City. Danced by advanced students from the School of American Ballet and guest soloists. Conductor: Jean Morel.

NOTE: Traditional choreography for *Samson et Dalila* includes the DANCE OF THE PRIESTESSES in Act I and BACCHANALE in Act III.

See 66, 116, 171

229 MR. STRAUSS GOES TO BOSTON

Musical Comedy in Two Acts and Nine Scenes

MUSIC AND BOOK: Music by Robert Stolz. Lyrics by Robert Sour. Book by Leonard L. Levinson, based on an original story by Alfred Gruenwald and Geza Herczeg. Orchestrations by George Lessner. Musical arrangements of Johann Strauss the Younger's melodies by Robert Stolz and George Lessner.

PRODUCTION: Produced, staged and directed by Felix Brentano. Scenery by Stewart Chaney. Costumes by Walter Florell. Scenery built by Vail Scenic Construction Company and painted by Robert Bergman Studios; costumes executed by Eaves Costume Company.

PREMIERE: September 6, 1945, Century Theatre, New York. Conductor: Robert Stolz. (Out-of-town preview August 13, Shubert Theatre, Boston.)

CAST: *Johann Strauss*, George Rigaud; *Brook Whitney*, Virginia MacWatters; *Dapper Dan Pepper*, Ralph Dumke; *Hetty Strauss*, Ruth Matteson; and others. *Solo Dancers*, Harold Lang, Babs Heath, Margit Dekova; corps de ballet of 9 women, 5 men.

RADETZKY MARCH-FANTASIE (Act I, music by Strauss): The Dancing Girls.

MIDNIGHT WALTZ (Act I, music by Strauss): Babs Heath, Harold Lang, corps de ballet.

THE GOSSIP POLKA (Act I, music by Strauss): Heath, Lang, corps de ballet; singers.

REPRISE: YOU NEVER KNOW WHAT COMES NEXT (Act II): Lang.

REPRISE: INTO THE NIGHT (Act II): Lang, Margit Dekova, corps de ballet.

THE GRAND AND GLORIOUS FOURTH (Act II): Lang, Helen Gallagher, corps de ballet.

WALTZ FINALE (Act II, music by Strauss): Entire company.

230 CIRCUS POLKA

MUSIC: By Igor Stravinsky (1942, written at the request of George Balanchine, with the dedication 'For a young elephant').

PREMIERE: November 5, 1945, Carnegie Hall, New York. National Orchestral Society, Leon Barzin, musical director. Danced by students of the School of American Ballet.

CAST: *A Little Elephant*, Judy Kursch; corps de ballet.

NOTE: Performed once, on a program arranged by Lincoln Kirstein entitled *Adventure in Ballet*, which also included *Élégie* [245] and *Symphonie Concertante* [241], danced by students of the School of American Ballet, with Todd Bolender as guest artist.

See 202

1946

231 RESURGENCE

Music: By Wolfgang Amadeus Mozart (from the Quintet in G minor, K. 516 [movements 1, 3, 4?]).

Premiere: January 22, 1946, Waldorf-Astoria Hotel, New York. Danced by students of the School of American Ballet.

Cast: *The Dancer*, Tanaquil Le Clercq; *4 Friends* (girls); *Children*; *The Teacher*, Elise Reiman; *The Angel*, Dorothy Bird; *Threat of Polio*, George Balanchine.

Note: Performed once at a March of Dimes benefit fashion show and luncheon, in which Vera Zorina and Gertrude Lawrence also participated.

232 THE NIGHT SHADOW
(also called NIGHT SHADOW, NIGHT SHADOWS, LA SOMNAMBULE, LA SONNAMBULA)

Music: Music and book by Vittorio Rieti, based on themes from operas by Vincenzo Bellini (1830-35, including *La Sonnambula*, *I Puritani*, *Norma*, and *I Capuletti ed i Montecchi*).

Production: Scenery and costumes by Dorothea Tanning. Scenery executed by E. B. Dunkel Studios; costumes executed by Karinska.

Premiere: February 27, 1946, Ballet Russe de Monte Carlo, City Center of Music and Drama, New York. Conductor: Emanuel Balaban.

Cast: *The Sleepwalker*, Alexandra Danilova; *The Poet*, Nicholas Magallanes; *The Coquette*, Maria Tallchief; *The Host* (Husband of the Sleepwalker), Michel Katcharoff; *Guests at the Ball*, 8 couples; ENTERTAINERS AT THE BALL: SHEPHERDS' DANCE: 2 couples; BLACKAMOORS' DANCE: Ruthanna Boris, Leon Danielian; HARLEQUIN DANCE: Marie-Jeanne; HOOP DANCE: 4 women.

NOTE: At a masked ball with entertainments, the Poet pays suit to the Coquette, who is escorted by the Host. After the guests go in to supper an apparition in white enters, a beautiful Sleepwalker. Entranced, the Poet tries to wake her, but she eludes him. The jealous Coquette informs the Host who, enraged, stabs the Poet. The Sleepwalker reappears and bears the Poet's body away.

REVISIONS: The Entertainers' dances (also called DIVERTISSEMENTS) have been changed often by the many companies that have staged the ballet. Examples in three principal companies include: Grand Ballet du Marquis de Cuevas: MOORISH DANCE sometimes substituted for BLACKAMOORS' DANCE; until about 1950, HARLEQUIN DANCE omitted; 1950, SHEPHERDS' DANCE (PASTORALE) changed from two couples to one, HOOP DANCE replaced by ACROBATS' DANCE for three (various combinations of men and women). New York City Ballet: 1960, name changed from *Night Shadow* to *La Sonnambula*, HARLEQUIN DANCE restored (for a man instead of a woman; frequently altered for various performers), ACROBATS' DANCE retained from de Cuevas production (HOOP DANCE omitted); 1967, SHEPHERDS' DANCE (PASTORALE) changed from two couples to a pas de trois for a virtuoso man and two women; 1979, BLACKAMOORS' DANCE eliminated. American Ballet Theatre, 1981: HOOP DANCE rechoreographed by John Taras as GYPSY DANCE, BLACKAMOORS' DANCE retitled DANSE EXOTIQUE.

STAGINGS: 1948, de Cuevas; 1955, Netherlands, Royal Danish; 1957, Ballets de Pâques; 1960, New York City Ballet; 1961, Ballet Rambert; 1964, Geneva; 1965, National; 1967, London Festival; 1972, Bordeaux (excerpt); 1973, San Juan; 1974, San Francisco; 1976, Paris (Sleepwalker pas de deux); 1977, Louisville, Turin; 1978, Ballet Théâtre Français; 1979, Dallas; 1980, Boston; 1981, American Ballet Theatre.

TELEVISION: 1948 (British television); 1958 (BBC, London); 1960s (Sleepwalker pas de deux, BBC); 1963 (Sleepwalker pas de deux, NBC); 1966 (excerpt, Camera Three, CBS).

See 328

233 RAYMONDA

Ballet in Three Acts

MUSIC: By Alexander Glazounov (Op. 57, produced 1898).

CHOREOGRAPHY: By George Balanchine and Alexandra Danilova after Marius Petipa.

PRODUCTION: Scenery and costumes by Alexandre Benois. Scenery executed by E. B. Dunkel Studios; costumes executed by Karinska.

PREMIERE: March 12, 1946, Ballet Russe de Monte Carlo, City Center of Music and Drama, New York. Conductor: Ivan Boutnikoff. Violinist: Earle Hummel. Harpist: Marjorie Call.

CAST: *Raymonda*, Alexandra Danilova; *Jean de Brienne*, Nicholas Magallanes; *Emir Abd-er-Raham, the Saracen Knight*, Nikita Talin. ACT I: *Raymonda*; *Brienne*; *Friends of Raymonda*, 3 women; *Raymonda's Page*; *Two Noblemen, Friends of Brienne*; *The White Lady, Protectress of the Castle*, Joy Williams; *The Seneschal of the Castle*, G. Alexandroff; *Peasant Girls*, Marie-Jeanne, Gertrude Tyven [Gertrude Svobodina], 8 women; *4 Knights*. ACT II: *Raymonda*; *Brienne*; *Emir*; *Emir's Favorite Slave*, Leon Danielian; *Slaves*, Pauline Goddard, 4 women, 2 men; *4 Jongleurs*; *Jongleuses*, Marie-Jeanne, 4 women. ACT III: DIVERTISSEMENTS: CZARDAS: Goddard, Stanley Zompakos, 6 couples; PAS DE TROIS: Tyven, Patricia Wilde, Danielian; PAS CLASSIQUE HONGROIS: Danilova, Magallanes; Marie-Jeanne, Ruthanna Boris, Maria Tallchief, Yvonne Chouteau, Herbert Bliss, Talin, Robert Lindgren, Ivan Ivanov (VARIATIONS: I. Tallchief; II. Chouteau; III. 4 men; IV. Marie-Jeanne; V. Boris; VI. Magallanes; VII. Danilova); FINALE: Entire cast.

NOTE: This version derives from the Petipa original at the Maryinsky as remembered by Balanchine and Danilova, abbreviated and rechoreographed by Balanchine, retaining the Petipa style. The male pas de quatre and the ballerina's variation in Act III (VARIATIONS III and VII of the PAS CLASSIQUE HONGROIS) are particularly close to the Petipa choreography. The original was a full evening's ballet, choreographed for more than two hundred performers; the Balanchine-Danilova version lasts three-quarters of an evening, omitting much of the Petipa mime, and used the entire Ballet Russe de Monte Carlo company of about forty dancers. The central pas de deux from the Act III PAS CLASSIQUE HONGROIS, usually called *Pas de Deux from*

Raymonda (and as often credited to Petipa as to Balanchine, who staged the Petipa choreography for Diaghilev in 1925), is frequently performed by a ballerina and cavalier as a concert piece.

In 1955, Balanchine choreographed *Pas de Dix* [309] for the New York City Ballet, using much of the PAS CLASSIQUE HONGROIS music, but adding a fast finale (coda). The choreography, for the most part new, retained VARIATION III exactly; VARIATION VII was retained in essence, although made more brilliant. In 1973, Balanchine incorporated this heightened VARIATION VII into *Cortège Hongrois* [384], a new work for the New York City Ballet using much of the *Pas de Dix* music.

In 1961, Balanchine choreographed a completely different work to other selections from the *Raymonda* score for the New York City Ballet: *Valses et Variations* [339, retitled *Raymonda Variations* in 1963].

REVISIONS: Ballet Russe de Monte Carlo: Numerous small revisions including omission of some Act III VARIATIONS on tour; by September, 1946, intermission between Acts I and II eliminated; 1947, White Lady and possibly other mime roles deleted; 1948, Act III given as *Divertissements from Raymonda*, although complete ballet remained in repertory.

STAGINGS (material from Act III divertissements performed under varying *Raymonda* titles [distinct from *Valses et Variations* (339, later retitled *Raymonda Variations*)]; most stagings include material from *Pas de Dix* [309]; choreography often not credited to Balanchine): 1959, Washington; 1961, American Ballet Theatre (titled *Grand Pas—Glazounov*); 1962, San Juan; 1964, National; 1967, Oklahoma City; 1969, Minnesota; 1970, North Carolina; 1972, Delta Festival; 1974, Chicago; 1975, Fairfax; 1976, Cincinnati; 1977, Louisville; 1978, Maryland; 1979, Princeton; 1980, Atlanta; 1982, Tulsa.

See 18, 309, 339, 384

234 GISELLE: ACT II GRAVE SCENE

MUSIC: By Adolphe Adam (produced 1841).

CHOREOGRAPHY: By Dimitri Romanoff, with contributions by George Balanchine and Antony Tudor.

PRODUCTION: Scenery and costumes by Eugene Berman.

PREMIERE: October 15, 1946, Ballet Theatre, Broadway Theatre, New York. Conductor: Max Goberman.

CAST: *Giselle*, Alicia Alonso; *Albrecht*, Igor Youskevitch; *Hilarion*, Stanley Herbertt; *Myrtha*, Nora Kaye; and others.

NOTE: Balanchine arranged the traditional Maryinsky staging of Giselle's grave scene in Act II: Albrecht prevents Giselle from disappearing into her grave and lays her on a bed of flowers; but Giselle sinks away, and only the flowers remain.

235 THE SPELLBOUND CHILD
(L'ENFANT ET LES SORTILÈGES)
Lyric Fantasy in Two Parts

MUSIC: By Maurice Ravel (1920-25). Libretto by Colette (translated by Lincoln Kirstein and Jane Barzin).

PRODUCTION: Scenery and costumes by Aline Bernstein. Costumes executed by Karinska. Lighting by Jean Rosenthal.

PREMIERE: November 20, 1946, Ballet Society, Central High School of Needle Trades, New York. Conductor: Leon Barzin.

CAST: Each role was performed by a singer off stage and a dancer on stage. *Child* (sung and danced), Joseph Connolly; *His Mother*; *Armchair*; *Bergère*; *Clock*; *Tea Pot*; *Chinese Cup*; *Fire*, Elise Reiman; *2 Shepherdesses*; *2 Shepherds*; *Princess*, Tanaquil Le Clercq; *Teacher Arithmetic*; *10 Numbers*; *Black Cat*, William Dollar; *White Cat*, Georgia Hiden; *Big Frog*; *4 Little Frogs*; *Tree* (sung only); *7 Dragonflies*; *Nightingale*; *Bat*; *Squirrel*; *Little Squirrel*; *Owl*.

NOTE: Presented with *The Four Temperaments* on the initial program of Ballet Society, the membership-supported non-profit organization formed by Balanchine and Lincoln Kirstein.

OTHER VERSIONS: 1925, Opéra de Monte-Carlo (*L'Enfant et les Sortilèges*, danced by Diaghilev's Ballets Russes). 1975, New York City Ballet (*L'Enfant et les Sortilèges*, Ravel Festival). 1981, for the PBS television series Dance in America (*The Spellbound Child/L'Enfant et les Sortilèges*).

See 48*, 390, 416

236 THE FOUR TEMPERAMENTS

MUSIC: By Paul Hindemith (*Theme with Four Variations [According to the Four Temperaments]* for string orchestra and piano, 1940, commissioned by George Balanchine).

PRODUCTION: Scenery and costumes by Kurt Seligmann. Lighting by Jean Rosenthal.

PREMIERE: November 20, 1946, Ballet Society, Central High School of Needle Trades, New York. Conductor: Leon Barzin. Pianist: Nicholas Kopeikine.

CAST: A. THEME: 1. Beatrice Tompkins, José Martinez; 2. Elise Reiman, Lew Christensen; 3. Gisella Caccialanza, Francisco Moncion; B. FIRST VARIATION: MELANCHOLIC: William Dollar; Georgia Hiden, Rita Karlin, 4 women; C. SECOND VARIATION: SANGUINIC: Mary Ellen Moylan, Fred Danieli, 4 women; D. THIRD VARIATION: PHLEGMATIC: Todd Bolender, 4 women; E. FOURTH VARIATION: CHOLERIC: Tanaquil Le Clercq, 3 THEME couples, Moylan, Danieli; Dollar, Bolender, entire cast.

NOTE: The three main themes are stated in the opening section by three successive couples. The variations are named after the four temperaments of medieval cosmology. The score, commissioned by Balanchine and completed in 1940, was partially choreographed during the 1941 American Ballet Caravan tour of South America for an entirely different ballet titled *The Cave of Sleep*; Pavel Tchelitchew created complete costumes and décor, but the work was never produced.

REVISIONS: The original MELANCHOLIC VARIATION was more acrobatic than it later became. Balanchine has made numerous changes in the finale, the most radical in 1977 for the Dance in America telecast; most television changes were retained in the stage version.

NEW PRODUCTIONS BY BALANCHINE COMPANIES: New York City Ballet: 1951, danced in practice clothes without scenery; 1964, lighting by David Hays.

STAGINGS: 1960, Netherlands, Royal Swedish; 1962, Hamburg, La Scala; 1963, Paris, Royal Danish; 1964, National, Vienna; 1966, Düsseldorf; 1967, Rome; 1968, Boston, Norway; 1969, Pennsylvania, National Ballet of Canada; 1970, Berlin, Geneva; 1973, Royal; 1974, San Francisco, Frankfurt, Les Grands Ballets Canadiens; 1975, Ballet West; 1976, Chicago Lyric Opera, Ballet Théâtre Contemporain, Royal Ballet

Touring, Strasbourg; 1977, Gothenburg, Zagreb, Zürich; 1978, Pacific Northwest, East Berlin; 1979, Dance Theatre of Harlem; 1980, New York Dance Theatre (FIRST THEME), Munich; 1982, Los Angeles.

TELEVISION: 1962 (Dutch television); 1963 (excerpt, NBC); 1964 (L'Heure du Concert, CBC, Montreal); 1977 (Dance in America, PBS).

1947

237 RENARD

Ballet-Burlesque for Singers and Dancers

MUSIC: Music and libretto by Igor Stravinsky (*Le Renard*, 1915-16, commissioned by Princesse Edmond de Polignac). Derived from a tale by Alexander Afanasiev. English version by Harvey Officer.

PRODUCTION: Scenery and costumes by Esteban Francés. Scenery painted by Centre Studios under the supervision of Gilbert Hancox, and built by Martin Turner; costumes executed by Karinska. Lighting by Jean Rosenthal.

PREMIERE: January 13, 1947, Ballet Society, Hunter College Playhouse, New York. Conductor: Leon Barzin. Singers: William Hess, William Upshaw (tenors); William Gephart, Leon Lishner (baritones).

CAST: *The Fox*, Todd Bolender; *The Rooster*, Lew Christensen; *The Cat*, Fred Danieli; *The Ram*, John Taras.

NOTE: *Le Renard* was first choreographed by Bronislava Nijinska for Diaghilev's Ballets Russes in 1922, and rechoreographed for that company by Serge Lifar in 1929. Balanchine's version was first presented on the second Ballet Society program, which also included the premiere of *Divertimento*.

REVISIONS: 1955, San Francisco Ballet: Rechoreographed by Lew Christensen, based on Balanchine's version.

238 DIVERTIMENTO

MUSIC: By Alexei Haieff (*Divertimento* for small orchestra, 1944).

PRODUCTION: Lighting by Jean Rosenthal.

PREMIERE: January 13, 1947, Ballet Society, Hunter College Playhouse, New York. Conductor: Leon Barzin.

CAST: Mary Ellen Moylan, Francisco Moncion; Gisella Caccialanza, Tanaquil Le Clercq, Elise Reiman, Beatrice Tompkins, Todd Bolender, Lew Christensen, Fred Danieli, John Taras.

PRELUDE; ARIA; SCHERZO; LULLABY; FINALE.

NOTE: Choreographed for a leading couple and four supporting couples, each dancer a principal with solos, and featuring a blues pas de deux. The ballet combines popular American dance idioms and modern concert dance with classic ballet.

239 THE CHOCOLATE SOLDIER
Operetta in Three Acts

MUSIC AND BOOK: Music by Oscar Straus. Book by Rudolph Bernauer and Leopold Jacobson. American version by Stanislaus Stange. Revised book by Guy Bolton. Revised and additional lyrics by Bernard Hanighen. Orchestrations by Jay Blackton.

CHOREOGRAPHY: By George Balanchine. Assistant to Mr. Balanchine: Edward Brinkman.

PRODUCTION: Produced by J. H. Del Bondio and Hans Bartsch for the Delvan Company. Directed by Felix Brentano. Scenery and lighting by Jo Mielziner. Costumes by Lucinda Ballard. Scenery built by Martin Turner Studios and painted by Studio Alliance; costumes executed by Eaves Costume Company.

PREMIERE: March 12, 1947, New Century Theatre, New York. Conductor: Jay Blackton. (Out-of-town preview: February 6, Forrest Theatre, Philadelphia.)

CAST: *Nadina*, Frances McCann; *Mascha*, Gloria Hamilton; *Bumerli*, Keith Andes; *Popoff*, Billy Gilbert; and others. *Premiere Danseuse*, Mary Ellen Moylan; *Premier Danseur*, Francisco Moncion; 7 Ladies of the Ballet, 7 Gentlemen of the Ballet.

SLAVIC DANCE (Act II): Mary Ellen Moylan, Francisco Moncion, corps de ballet.

WALTZ BALLET (Act III): Moylan, Moncion, corps de ballet.

AFTER TODAY GALA POLKA (Act III): Moylan, Moncion, corps de ballet.

240 LE PALAIS DE CRISTAL (later called SYMPHONY IN C)

MUSIC: By Georges Bizet (Symphony No. 1 in C major, 1855).

PRODUCTION: Scenery and costumes by Leonor Fini.

PREMIERE: July 28, 1947, Paris Opéra Ballet, Théâtre National de l'Opéra, Paris. Conductor: Roger Desormière.

CAST: FIRST MOVEMENT (ALLEGRO VIVO): Lycette Darsonval, Alexandre Kalioujny; SECOND MOVEMENT (ADAGIO): Tamara Toumanova, Roger Ritz; THIRD MOVEMENT (ALLEGRO VIVACE): Micheline Bardin, Michel Renault; FOURTH MOVEMENT (ALLEGRO VIVACE): Madeleine Lafon, Max Bozzoni (in each movement: 2 demi-solo couples, 6 women); FINALE: Entire cast.

NOTE: During six months as guest ballet master for the Paris Opéra, Balanchine choreographed Bizet's Symphony in C, and staged *Apollo, Serenade* and *Le Baiser de la Fée. Le Palais de Cristal* was staged for Ballet Society as *Symphony in C* [244] the following year, and was presented with *Concerto Barocco* [195] and *Orpheus* [246] at the first performance of the New York City Ballet, October 11, 1948. When the Paris Opéra Ballet performed this work at the Bolshoi Theater, Moscow, in June 1958, it became the first ballet made by Balanchine in the West to be seen in the Soviet Union since his departure in 1924.

REVISIONS: 1948, Ballet Society (titled *Symphony in C*): Original corps of 48 reduced, with doubling of corps members from movement to movement due to limited size of company. New York City Ballet: By 1968, larger company eliminated duplication of cast, allowing full finale; 8 corps members in FIRST MOVEMENT instead of 6; by 1971, 8 corps members in FOURTH MOVEMENT for total cast of 52; 1971?, musical repeat in FOURTH MOVEMENT, danced by FIRST MOVEMENT cast in exact repetition of FOURTH MOVEMENT cast steps (cut entirely at various times), completely rechoreographed for FIRST MOVEMENT cast. Male solos in FIRST and THIRD MOVEMENTS rechoreographed several times for various performers.

STAGINGS (in America, and usually in other countries, titled *Symphony in C*): 1948, Ballet Society, New York City Ballet; 1952, Royal Danish; 1955, La Scala; 1960, Royal Swedish; 1961, San Francisco; 1962, Dutch National; 1965, Garden State (FIRST, SECOND and THIRD MOVEMENTS), Hamburg; 1967, Ballet of Los Angeles, Boston, Pennsylvania, Norway; 1968, Atlanta, Ballet West, Memphis (SECOND MOVEMENT); 1969, Berlin; 1970, Geneva, Kirov (THIRD MOVEMENT); 1972, Rome, Vienna; 1973, Tokyo; 1975, Munich; 1976, East Berlin, Stuttgart; 1977, Hungary; 1978, Zürich.

TELEVISION: 1963 (SECOND and FOURTH MOVEMENTS, CBS); ca. 1963 (Dutch television).

See 244

241 SYMPHONIE CONCERTANTE
Classic Ballet in One Act

MUSIC: By Wolfgang Amadeus Mozart (Symphonie Concertante in E-flat for violin, viola and orchestra, K. 364, 1779).

PRODUCTION: Scenery and costumes by James Stewart Morcom. Costumes executed by Edith Lutyens. Lighting by Jean Rosenthal.

PREMIERE: November 12, 1947, Ballet Society, City Center of Music and Drama, New York. Conductor: Leon Barzin. Violinist: Hugo Fiorato. Violist: Karl Braunstein.

CAST: ALLEGRO MAESTOSO: Tanaquil Le Clercq, Maria Tallchief, 22 women; ANDANTE: Le Clercq, Tallchief, Todd Bolender, 6 women; PRESTO: Le Clercq, Tallchief, Bolender, 22 women.

NOTE: Created for students a year before its professional premiere to show the relationship between a classical symphony and classical dance. Originally presented (with *Élégie* [245] and *Circus Polka* [230]) on the program of the National Orchestral Society entitled *Adventure in Ballet*, November 5, 1945, danced by students of the School of American Ballet, with Todd Bolender as guest artist. The scenery for the Ballet Society production was a literal transcription of a design by the Baroque artist Giuseppe Galli Bibiena.

242 THEME AND VARIATIONS

MUSIC: By Peter Ilyitch Tschaikovsky (final movement of Suite No. 3 for orchestra in G major, 1884).

PRODUCTION: Scenery and costumes by Woodman Thompson. Scenery executed by Eugene B. Dunkel Studios; costumes executed by Karinska.

PREMIERE: November 26, 1947, Ballet Theatre, City Center of Music and Drama, New York. Conductor: Max Goberman.

CAST: Alicia Alonso, Igor Youskevitch; Anna Cheselka, Melissa Hayden, Paula Lloyd, Cynthia Riseley, Fernando Alonso, Eric Braun, Fernand Nault, Zachary Solov; 8 women, 8 men.

NOTE: An intensive development of the classic ballet lexicon. In 1970, incorporated (with minor revisions) as the fourth movement of the full *Suite No. 3* [369, later called *Tschaikovsky Suite No. 3*].

REVISIONS: Choreography for male principal changed several times for various performers.

STAGINGS: 1960, New York City Ballet; 1967, Mexico; 1969, Les Grands Ballets Canadiens; 1970, Cuba (pas de deux); 1971, Geneva; 1981, Dutch National.

TELEVISION: 1978 (American Ballet Theatre: Live from Lincoln Center, PBS).

See 330, 369

1948

243 THE TRIUMPH OF BACCHUS AND ARIADNE
Ballet-Cantata

MUSIC: By Vittorio Rieti (1947, commissioned by Ballet Society). Words from a Florentine carnival song by Lorenzo de' Medici.

PRODUCTION: Scenery and costumes by Corrado Cagli.

PREMIERE: February 9, 1948, Ballet Society, City Center of Music and

Drama, New York. Conductor: Leon Barzin. Singers: Ellen Faull, soprano; Leon Lishner, bass; chorus of 40.

CAST: INTRODUCTION (PRELUDE AND CHORUS): *Major Domo*, Lew Christensen; *Spectators*, 6 couples; BACCHUS AND ARIADNE (CHORUS): *Bacchus*, Nicholas Magallanes; *Ariadne*, Tanaquil Le Clercq; SATYRS AND NYMPHS (TARANTELLA WITH CHORUS): *Satyr*, Herbert Bliss; *Nymph*, Marie-Jeanne; *6 Satyrs, 6 Nymphs*; SILENUS (ARIA FOR SOLO BASS): *Silenus*, Charles Laskey; MIDAS (CHORUS): *Midas*, Francisco Moncion; *2 Discoboles*; *Little Girl*, Claudia Hall; *Young Girl*, Pat McBride; INVITATION TO THE DANCE (ARIA FOR SOLO SOPRANO); BACCHANALE (CHORUS): Ensemble.

NOTE: The work consists of songs and pageantry, and dance episodes celebrating Youth and Age and sacred and profane love, in an Italianate setting. At the premiere, the singers were visible in the windows of the scenic façade; in later performances they sang from the orchestra pit.

244 SYMPHONY IN C
Classic Ballet

MUSIC: By Georges Bizet (Symphony No. 1 in C major, 1855).

PRODUCTION: Lighting by Jean Rosenthal.

PREMIERE: March 22, 1948, Ballet Society, City Center of Music and Drama, New York. Conductor: Leon Barzin.

CAST: FIRST MOVEMENT (ALLEGRO VIVO): Maria Tallchief, Nicholas Magallanes; SECOND MOVEMENT (ADAGIO): Tanaquil Le Clercq, Francisco Moncion; THIRD MOVEMENT (ALLEGRO VIVACE): Beatrice Tompkins, Herbert Bliss; FOURTH MOVEMENT (ALLEGRO VIVACE): Elise Reiman, John Taras (in each movement, 2 demi-solo couples, 6 women; FINALE: Entire cast.

NOTE: Originally presented by the Paris Opéra Ballet, 1947, titled *Le Palais de Cristal*. Presented with *Concerto Barocco* [195] and *Orpheus* [246] at the first performance of the New York City Ballet, October 11, 1948.

NEW PRODUCTIONS BY BALANCHINE COMPANIES: 1950, New York City Ballet: Costumes by Karinska.

See 240*

245 ÉLÉGIE

MUSIC: By Igor Stravinsky (*Élégie-Elegy* for solo viola, 1944).

PREMIERE: April 28, 1948, Ballet Society, City Center of Music and Drama, New York. Violist: Emanuel Vardi.

CAST: Tanaquil Le Clercq, Pat McBride.

NOTE: As described by the choreographer, the music is reflected through the interlaced bodies of two dancers rooted to a central spot on the stage; referred to by the composer as a kind of preview of the *Orpheus* pas de deux. Originally presented (with *Symphonie Concertante* [241] and *Circus Polka* [230]) on the program of the National Orchestral Society entitled *Adventure in Ballet*, November 5, 1945, danced by students of the School of American Ballet, with Todd Bolender as guest artist. The Ballet Society premiere was part of an evening which included the premiere of *Orpheus*.

In 1966, and in 1982 for the New York City Ballet Stravinsky Centennial Celebration, Balanchine choreographed new works to this music, also called *Élégie*.

See 355, 423

246 ORPHEUS

Ballet in Three Scenes

MUSIC: By Igor Stravinsky (1947, commissioned by Ballet Society).

PRODUCTION: Scenery and costumes by Isamu Noguchi. Lighting by Jean Rosenthal.

PREMIERE: April 28, 1948, Ballet Society, City Center of Music and Drama, New York. Conductor: Igor Stravinsky.

CAST: *Orpheus*, Nicholas Magallanes; *Dark Angel*, Francisco Moncion; *Eurydice*, Maria Tallchief; *Leader of the Furies*, Beatrice Tompkins; *Leader of the Bacchantes*, Tanaquil Le Clercq; *Apollo*, Herbert Bliss; *Pluto*; *Satyr*; *Nature Spirits*; *Friends to Orpheus*; *Furies*, 9 women; *Lost Souls*, 7 men; *Bacchantes*, 8 women.

Synopsis of the action (from Stravinsky's score): SCENE 1: 1. Orpheus weeps for Eurydice. He stands motionless, with his back to the audience. Some friends pass, bringing presents and offering him sympathy.

2. AIR DE DANSE. 3. DANCE OF THE ANGEL OF DEATH. The Angel leads Orpheus to Hades. 4. *Interlude*. The Angel and Orpheus reappear in the gloom of Tartarus.

SCENE 2: 5. PAS DE FURIES (their agitation and their threats). 6a. AIR DE DANSE (Orpheus). 7. *Interlude*. The tormented souls in Tartarus stretch out their fettered arms toward Orpheus and implore him to continue his song of consolation. 6b. AIR DE DANSE (concluded). Orpheus continues his air. 8. PAS D'ACTION. Hades, moved by the song of Orpheus, grows calm. The Furies surround him, bind his eyes, and return Eurydice to him. (Veiled curtain.) 9. PAS DE DEUX (Orpheus and Eurydice before the curtain). Orpheus tears the bandage from his eyes. Eurydice falls dead. 10. *Interlude* (veiled curtain, behind which the décor of the first scene is placed). 11. PAS D'ACTION. The Bacchantes attack Orpheus, seize him, and tear him to pieces.

SCENE 3: 12. ORPHEUS' APOTHEOSIS. Apollo appears. He wrests the lyre from Orpheus and raises his song heavenwards.

NOTE: In composing *Orpheus*, Stravinsky worked in close collaboration with Balanchine. The ballet led Morton Baum, chairman of the Executive Committee of the City Center of Music and Drama, to invite Ballet Society to become its permanent ballet company: the New York City Ballet. *Orpheus* was presented with *Concerto Barocco* [195] and *Symphony in C* [244] at the first performance of the New York City Ballet, October 11, 1948.

REVISIONS: 1980, New York City Ballet: DANCE OF THE FURIES slightly revised by Peter Martins.

NEW PRODUCTIONS BY BALANCHINE COMPANIES: 1972, New York City Ballet (Stravinsky Festival): Designs rescaled by Noguchi for the New York State Theater.

STAGINGS: 1962, Hamburg; 1964, La Scala; 1974, Paris.

TELEVISION: 1956 (pas de deux, CBS); 1960 (CBC, Montreal).

247 PAS DE TROIS CLASSIQUE

MUSIC: By Léon Minkus (from *Paquita*, 1881).

PRODUCTION: Costumes by Jean Robier.

PREMIERE: August 9, 1948, Grand Ballet du Marquis de Cuevas, Royal Opera House, Covent Garden, London.

CAST: Rosella Hightower, Marjorie Tallchief, André Eglevsky.

NOTE: Balanchine considers his *Pas de Trois Classique* essentially a restaging of Petipa's pas de trois from *Paquita*. He changed some steps for the 1951 New York City Ballet version; the ballet possibly contains additional original Balanchine choreography, as is usual in his remounting of the classics.

REVISIONS: 1951, New York City Ballet: Variation created for Marjorie Tallchief revised.

STAGINGS (variant names include *Minkus Pas de Trois* and *Paquita Pas de Trois*; most stagings incorporate 1951 revisions; choreography credited to André Eglevsky in some later stagings): 1951, New York City Ballet; 1954, Rio de Janeiro; 1955, Ballet Russe de Monte Carlo; 1958, Vienna; 1961, Eglevsky; 1963, San Juan; 1965, Grand Ballet Classique de France, Hamburg, Uruguay; 1967, Joffrey; by 1967, Ballets Janine Charrat; 1968, Harkness, London Festival; 1970, Minnesota, Bordeaux; 1971, American Ballet Theatre, Newburgh, Paris; 1972, New Jersey; 1974, Augusta, Israel; 1975, Dover; 1976, Chicago Lyric Opera; 1979, Bernhard; 1982, Delta Festival.

TELEVISION: 1963 (Bell Telephone Hour, NBC).

See 276

248 CARMEN

Opera in Four Acts by Georges Bizet
ACT II TAVERN SCENE BALLET

PREMIERE: October 10, 1948, New York City Opera, City Center of Music and Drama, New York. Danced by New York City Ballet. Conductor: Jean Morel.

CAST: Maria Tallchief, Francisco Moncion, 2 women.

NOTE: Balanchine's first work for the New York City Ballet, which for two seasons served as resident ballet company for the New York City Opera.

See 38, 127, 155

249 WHERE'S CHARLEY?

Musical Comedy in Two Acts and Nine Scenes

MUSIC AND BOOK: Music and lyrics by Frank Loesser. Book by George Abbott, based on the play *Charley's Aunt*, by Brandon Thomas. Orchestrations by Ted Royal, Hans Spialek and Phil Lang. Vocal arrangements and direction by Gerry Dolin.

CHOREOGRAPHY: By George Balanchine, assisted by Fred Danieli.

PRODUCTION: Produced by Cy Feuer and Ernest H. Martin in association with Gwen Rickard. Directed by George Abbott. Scenery and costumes by David Ffolkes. Scenery executed by Studio Alliance; costumes executed by Brooks Costume Company.

PREMIERE: October 11, 1948, St. James Theatre, New York. Conductor: Max Goberman. (Out-of-town preview: September 13, Forrest Theatre, Philadelphia.)

CAST: *Charley Wykeham*, Ray Bolger; *Amy Spettigue*, Allyn McLerie; *Jack Chesney*, Byron Palmer; *Kitty Verdun*, Doretta Morrow; and others. Dancers: 9 women, 9 men.

THE NEW ASHMOLEAN MARCHING SOCIETY AND STUDENTS' CONSERVATORY BAND (Act I, Scene 2): Byron Palmer, Allyn McLerie, Doretta Morrow, Bobby Harrell, ensemble.

MAKE A MIRACLE (Act I, Scene 3): Ray Bolger, McLerie.

PERNAMBUCO (Act I, Scene 4): Bolger, McLerie, ensemble.

ONCE IN LOVE WITH AMY (Act II, Scene 2): Bolger.

AT THE RED ROSE COTILLION (Act II, Scene 4): Bolger, McLerie, ensemble.

OTHER PRODUCTIONS: January 21, 1951, Broadway Theatre, New York. Basically unchanged; ONCE IN LOVE WITH AMY performed with audience participation and expanded dance sequence.

250 CONCERTO BAROCCO

MUSIC: By Johann Sebastian Bach (Double Violin Concerto in D minor, B.W.V. 1043).

PRODUCTION: Scenery and costumes by Eugene Berman, executed by Centre Studios and Karinska under the supervision of George Balanchine. Lighting by Jean Rosenthal.

PREMIERE: October 11, 1948, New York City Ballet, City Center of Music and Drama, New York. Conductor: Leon Barzin.

CAST: Marie-Jeanne, Francisco Moncion; Ruth Gilbert; 8 women.

NOTE: Originally presented by American Ballet Caravan, Rio de Janeiro, 1941. *Concerto Barocco* was the first ballet danced by the New York City Ballet in its inaugural performance, October 11, 1948, which also included *Orpheus* [246] and *Symphony in C* [244].

See 195*

251 THE MARRIAGE OF FIGARO (LE NOZZE DI FIGARO)
Opera in Four Acts by Wolfgang Amadeus Mozart
ACT III FANDANGO

PREMIERE: October 14, 1948, New York City Opera, City Center of Music and Drama, New York. Danced by New York City Ballet. Conductor: Joseph Rosenstock.

CAST: Corps de ballet.

252 LA TRAVIATA
Opera in Four Acts by Giuseppe Verdi
ACT III BALLET

PREMIERE: October 17, 1948, New York City Opera, City Center of Music and Drama, New York. Danced by New York City Ballet. Conductor: Jean Morel.

CAST: Marie-Jeanne, Herbert Bliss, 4 women.

See 67, 123, 150

253 DON GIOVANNI
Opera in Two Acts and Six Scenes by Wolfgang Amadeus Mozart
ACT II DANCE

PREMIERE: October 21, 1948, New York City Opera, City Center of

Music and Drama, New York. Danced by New York City Ballet.
Conductor: Laszlo Halasz.

CAST: Corps de ballet.

See 81, 181

254 SERENADE

MUSIC: By Peter Ilyitch Tschaikovsky (Serenade in C for string orchestra, Op. 48, 1880, with third and fourth movements reversed).

PRODUCTION: Lighting by Jean Rosenthal.

PREMIERE: October 26, 1948, New York City Ballet, City Center of Music and Drama, New York. Conductor: Leon Barzin.

CAST: Marie-Jeanne, Pat McBride, Herbert Bliss, Nicholas Magallanes; 4 female demi-soloists; 12 women, 4 men.

SONATINA; WALTZ; TEMA RUSSO; ELEGY.

NOTE: Originally presented by the American Ballet, New York, 1935.

See 141*, 193

255 AÏDA

Opera in Three Acts by Giuseppe Verdi
ACT II, SCENE 2 TRIUMPHAL BALLET

PREMIERE: October 28, 1948, New York City Opera, City Center of Music and Drama, New York. Danced by New York City Ballet. Conductor: Laszlo Halasz.

CAST: Maria Tallchief, Nicholas Magallanes, 6 women, 4 men.

NOTE: In addition to the Scene 2 ballet, reviews mention the Ritual of the Priestesses and dance entertainment for Amneris.

See 126, 152, 226

256 EUGEN ONEGIN

Opera in Three Acts and Six Scenes by Peter Ilyitch Tschaikovsky

INCIDENTAL SOCIAL DANCES

PREMIERE: November 7, 1948, New York City Opera, City Center of Music and Drama, New York. Danced by New York City Ballet. Conductor: Laszlo Halasz.

CAST: 4 couples.

See 341

257 THE MADWOMAN OF CHAILLOT
(LA FOLLE DE CHAILLOT)

Play by Jean Giraudoux, adapted by Maurice Valency

MUSIC: By Albert Hague (mazurka, Act I) and Alexander Haas ('La Belle Polonaise,' Act II), arranged by Alexander Haas.

PRODUCTION: Produced and directed by Alfred de Liagre, Jr. Movement direction by George Balanchine (uncredited). Scenery and costumes by Christian Bérard (from the Paris production, 1945). American reproductions of original French costumes executed by Karinska. Lighting by Samuel Leve.

PREMIERE: December 27, 1948, Belasco Theatre, New York. Conductor: Alexander Haas.

CAST: *Countess Aurelia, the Madwoman of Chaillot,* Martita Hunt; *The Ragpicker,* John Carradine; *Mme Constance, the Madwoman of Passy,* Estelle Winwood; *The Prospector,* Vladimir Sokoloff; *The President,* Clarence Derwent; *Mlle Gabrielle, the Madwoman of St. Sulpice,* Nydia Westman; *Mme Josephine, the Madwoman of La Concorde,* Doris Rich; *The Deaf Mute,* Martin Kosleck; and others.

1949

258 TROUBLED ISLAND

Opera in Three Acts by William Grant Still

ACT II, SCENE 2 COURT BALLET

PREMIERE: March 31, 1949, New York City Opera, City Center of Music and Drama, New York. Danced by the company of Jean-Léon Destiné. Conductor: Laszlo Halasz.

NOTE: World premiere. The printed program does not list dancers.

259 PRINCESS AURORA

MUSIC: By Peter Ilyitch Tschaikovsky (excerpts from *The Sleeping Beauty*, produced 1890, most from Act III).

CHOREOGRAPHY: Originally choreographed by Marius Petipa; staged and adapted by George Balanchine. Choreography of the THREE IVANS by Bronislava Nijinska.

PRODUCTION: Scenery by Michel Baronoff and costumes by Barbara Karinska after designs by Léon Bakst (1921).

PREMIERE: April 2, 1949, Ballet Theatre, Opera House, Chicago. Conductor: Max Goberman.

CAST: *Princess Aurora*, Nana Gollner; *Prince Charming*, John Kriza; *The Queen*, Charlyne Baker; *The King*, Peter Rudley; *Master of Ceremonies*, Edward Caton; *Six Fairies*, Lillian Lanese, Janet Reed, Dorothy Scott, Ruth Ann Koesun, Diana Adams, Mary Burr (the first five danced VARIATIONS I-V); *6 Attendants*; PAS DE TROIS: Norma Vance, Jocelyn Vollmar, Wallace Seibert; BLUEBIRD AND THE PRINCESS: Maria Tallchief, Igor Youskevitch; THREE IVANS: Eric Braun, Fernand Nault, Nicolas Orloff; *4 Pages*; *Ensemble*, 4 women, 4 men.

NOTE: The printed program indicates that this selection of excerpts from *The Sleeping Beauty* included the FAIRY VARIATIONS from the PROLOGUE and divertissements from Act III. Balanchine staged Petipa's choreography of the BLUEBIRD pas de deux, but altered much of the rest. A duet (presumably for two fairies, which would have given each of the six Fairies a variation) is mentioned in a review by Lillian Moore (*Dancing Times*, June 1949, p. 497); printed programs list only five solo variations.

REVISIONS: 1950, Ballet Theatre: One, later two, FAIRY VARIATIONS omitted.

See 65, 225, 281, 404, 418

260 THE TALES OF HOFFMANN (LES CONTES D'HOFFMANN)

Opera in Three Acts with Prologue and Epilogue by Jacques Offenbach
BALLET

PREMIERE: April 6, 1949, New York City Opera, City Center of Music and Drama, New York. Danced by New York City Ballet. Conductor: Jean Morel.

NOTE: The printed program does not list dances or dancers.

See 58, 112

261 CINDERELLA

Made for Television

MUSIC: By Peter Ilyitch Tschaikovsky (excerpts from Symphonies No. 1 [1866, revised 1874] and 2 [1872, revised 1879]; adagio from Symphony No. 3 [1875]).

PRODUCTION: Produced by Paul Belanger.

FIRST TELECAST: April 25, 1949, Through the Crystal Ball, CBS.

CAST: *Cinderella*, Tanaquil Le Clercq; *Fairy*, Jimmy Savo; *Ugly Sisters*, Ruth Sobotka, Pat McBride; *Prince*, Herbert Bliss; corps de ballet.

262 DON QUIXOTE and SWAN LAKE (BLACK SWAN) PAS DE DEUX

During the 1949 Ballet Theatre spring tour and New York season, Balanchine staged and to some degree altered the pas de deux from

Don Quixote (Minkus, choreographed by Petipa), danced by Maria Tallchief and John Kriza, and the Black Swan pas de deux from *Swan Lake* Act III (Tschaikovsky, choreographed by Petipa), danced by Tallchief and Igor Youskevitch.

See 75, 191, 285, 331, 367

263 LA MORT DU CYGNE

MUSIC: By Camille Saint-Saëns (*Le Cygne* [cello solo] from *Le Carnaval des Animaux: Fantaisie Zoologique* for small orchestra, 1886).

CHOREOGRAPHY: Choreographed by Michel Fokine (1905?); staged by George Balanchine.

PREMIERE: June 20, 1949, Grand Ballet du Marquis de Cuevas, Stadsschouwburg, Amsterdam.

CAST: Tamara Toumanova.

NOTE: Performed at the Holland Festival, 1949.

See 16

264 FIREBIRD

MUSIC: By Igor Stravinsky (1909-10, dedicated to Andrei Rimsky-Korsakov [third ballet suite, for reduced orchestra, 1945]). Derived from ancient Russian legends and fairy tales.

PRODUCTION: Scenery and costumes by Marc Chagall (from the Ballet Theatre production, 1945). Scenery executed by Eugene B. Dunkel Studios; costumes executed by Edith Lutyens. Lighting by Jean Rosenthal.

PREMIERE: November 27, 1949, New York City Ballet, City Center of Music and Drama, New York. Conductor: Leon Barzin.

CAST: *Firebird*, Maria Tallchief; *Prince Ivan*, Francisco Moncion; *Prince's Bride*, Pat McBride; *Kastchei*, Edward Bigelow; *Chief Monster*, Beatrice Tompkins; *8 Maidens*, *19 Monsters*.

NOTE: Balanchine's 1949 production of *Firebird* was made with the assistance of Stravinsky. Balanchine had seen Lopukhov's production in Petrograd in 1921, and during his years with Diaghilev's Ballets

Russes performed Kastchei in Fokine's ballet, which was the original from 1910; Lincoln Kirstein saw him dance this role in 1926.

REVISIONS: New York City Ballet: 1970, largely rechoreographed; choreography for Monsters by Jerome Robbins; 1972 (Stravinsky Festival), choreography for Firebird made more stately, with few dance steps; new costume with long train and large wings (modified in 1974); 1980, revised choreography for Firebird incorporating some passages from 1949 version; gold costume and lighter train.

NEW PRODUCTIONS BY BALANCHINE COMPANIES: New York City Ballet: 1970, new scenery from Chagall designs executed under the supervision of Volodia Odinokov, costumes by Karinska, lighting by Ronald Bates; 1972, 1980, new costumes for Firebird by Karinska (uncredited on programs).

STAGINGS (based on 1949 version): 1965, Ballet of Los Angeles; 1981, Chicago City; 1982, Kansas City.

TELEVISION: 1952? (pas de deux, BBC, London); 1954 (pas de deux, NBC); 1956 (BERCEUSE, CBS).

265 BOURRÉE FANTASQUE

MUSIC: By Emmanuel Chabrier (*Marche Joyeuse*, 1888; *Bourrée Fantasque*, 1891; 'Prélude' from the opera *Gwendoline*, 1885; 'Fête Polonaise' from the opera *Le Roi Malgré Lui*, 1887).

PRODUCTION: Costumes by Karinska.

PREMIERE: December 1, 1949, New York City Ballet, City Center of Music and Drama, New York. Conductor: Leon Barzin.

CAST: BOURRÉE FANTASQUE: Tanaquil Le Clercq, Jerome Robbins; 8 women, 4 men; PRÉLUDE: Maria Tallchief, Nicholas Magallanes; 2 female demi-soloists; 8 women; FÊTE POLONAISE: Janet Reed, Herbert Bliss; 2 demi-solo couples; 6 women, 4 men; followed by full cast.

STAGINGS: 1960, London Festival; 1961, La Scala; 1963, Paris, Royal Danish; 1981, American Ballet Theatre.

See 403

266 [PAS DE DEUX]
Made for Television

In the late 1940s or early 1950s, Balanchine choreographed a pas de deux for Tanaquil Le Clercq and Nicholas Magallanes, telecast by CBC Television, Montreal. The ballet had elements of the *Coppélia* story.

See 291, 387

1950

267 PRODIGAL SON
Ballet in Three Scenes

MUSIC: By Sergei Prokofiev (Op. 46, 1928-29, commissioned by Serge Diaghilev, 1927). Book by Boris Kochno (after the biblical parable).

PRODUCTION: Lighting by Jean Rosenthal.

PREMIERE: February 23, 1950, New York City Ballet, City Center of Music and Drama, New York. Conductor: Leon Barzin.

CAST: *Prodigal Son*, Jerome Robbins; *Siren*, Maria Tallchief; *Father*, Michael Arshansky; *Servants to the Prodigal Son*, Frank Hobi, Herbert Bliss; *Two Sisters*, Jillana, Francesca Mosarra; *Drinking Companions*, 9 men.

NOTE: Originally presented by Diaghilev's Ballets Russes, Paris, 1929, titled *Le Fils Prodigue*. The New York City Ballet production was danced in improvised costumes from February 1950 until July, when scenery and costumes were added for the Company's first London season, recreated by Esteban Francés from Rouault sketches in the Wadsworth Atheneum, Hartford, Connecticut. For the 1978 Dance in America television production, the costume for the Prodigal Son was redesigned following that of the original Diaghilev production and was used for a limited period in staged performances. From time to time Balanchine appeared in the role of the Father.

See 94*

268 PAS DE DEUX ROMANTIQUE

MUSIC: By Carl Maria von Weber (Concertino for clarinet and orchestra, 1811).

PRODUCTION: Costumes by Robert Stevenson, executed by Angie Costumes, Inc.

PREMIERE: March 3, 1950, New York City Ballet, City Center of Music and Drama, New York. Conductor: Leon Barzin.

CAST: Janet Reed, Herbert Bliss.

269 JONES BEACH

MUSIC: By Jurriaan Andriessen (*Berkshire Symphonies* [Symphony No. 1], 1949, commissioned by the Royal Government of the Netherlands, dedicated to Serge Koussevitsky).

CHOREOGRAPHY: By George Balanchine and Jerome Robbins.

PRODUCTION: Bathing suits by Jantzen.

PREMIERE: March 9, 1950, New York City Ballet, City Center of Music and Drama, New York. Conductor: Leon Barzin.

CAST: SUNDAY [ALLEGRO]: Melissa Hayden, Yvonne Mounsey, Beatrice Tompkins, Herbert Bliss, Frank Hobi, 22 women, 9 men; RESCUE FROM DROWNING [ANDANTE]: Tanaquil Le Clercq, Nicholas Magallanes, 2 couples; WAR WITH MOSQUITOES [SCHERZO]: William Dollar, Hobi, Roy Tobias, 7 women; HOT DOGS [ALLEGRO]: Maria Tallchief, Jerome Robbins, entire cast.

NOTE: In SUNDAY, a small aggressive female gives chase to a big handsome male; RESCUE includes artificial respiration and a love duet; seven mosquitoes dance on pointe in WAR WITH MOSQUITOES; in the HOT DOGS finale, ballabile technique is employed in scenes of male rivalry over a hot dog and a girl. Balanchine's first collaboration with Robbins; both worked on all sections.

270 TRUMPET CONCERTO

MUSIC: By Franz Joseph Haydn (Trumpet Concerto in E-flat major, 1796).

PRODUCTION: Scenery and costumes by Vivienne Kernot. Scenery painted by Alick Johnstone; costumes executed under the direction of Eileen Anderson.

PREMIERE: September 14, 1950, Sadler's Wells Theatre Ballet, Opera House, Manchester. (First London performance, Sadler's Wells, September 19. Trumpet: Harry Wild.)

CAST: Svetlana Beriosova, David Blair; Elaine Fifield, Maryon Lane; David Poole, Pirmin Trecu; 8 women.

NOTE: *Trumpet Concerto* was choreographed at the request of Ninette de Valois, founder and director of the Sadler's Wells Ballet.

271 THE FAIRY'S KISS (LE BAISER DE LA FÉE)
Ballet-Allegory in Four Scenes

MUSIC: Music and book by Igor Stravinsky (1928, commissioned by Ida Rubinstein, dedicated to Peter Ilyitch Tschaikovsky). Based on a tale by Hans Christian Andersen (*The Ice Maiden*).

PRODUCTION: Scenery and costumes by Alice Halicka (from the 1937 production). Lighting by Jean Rosenthal.

PREMIERE: November 28, 1950, New York City Ballet, City Center of Music and Drama, New York. Conductor: Leon Barzin.

CAST: *The Fairy*, Maria Tallchief; *The Bride*, Tanaquil Le Clercq; *Her Friend*, Patricia Wilde; *The Bridegroom*, Nicholas Magallanes; *His Mother*, Beatrice Tompkins; *Shadow*, Helen Kramer; *Winds, Snowflakes, Mountaineers, Bridesmaids, Peasants.*

NOTE: Originally presented by the American Ballet (Stravinsky Festival), New York, 1937.

See 178*, 376

272 MAZURKA FROM 'A LIFE FOR THE TSAR'

MUSIC: By Mikhail Glinka (*A Life for the Tsar*, produced 1836).

PRODUCTION: Costumes by Karinska. Lighting by Jean Rosenthal.

PREMIERE: November 30, 1950, New York City Ballet, City Center of Music and Drama, New York. Conductor: Leon Barzin.

CAST: Janet Reed, Yurek Lazowski (guest artist); Vida Brown, George Balanchine; Barbara Walczak, Harold Lang; Dorothy Dushock, Frank Hobi.

NOTE: A brief character dance in which Balanchine performed on opening night.

273 SYLVIA: PAS DE DEUX

MUSIC: By Léo Delibes (from *Sylvia, ou la Nymphe de Diane*, produced 1876 [Act I VALSE LENTE and Act III pas de deux]).

PRODUCTION: Costumes by Karinska.

PREMIERE: December 1, 1950, New York City Ballet, City Center of Music and Drama, New York. Conductor: Leon Barzin.

CAST: Maria Tallchief, Nicholas Magallanes.

NOTE: In the tradition of a grand pas de deux, with entrée, adagio, two solos, and coda. In 1965, incorporated (with minor changes) into *Pas de Deux and Divertissement* [350], choreographed for the New York City Ballet. The male variation is reproduced in the Balanchine-Danilova *Coppélia* [387], Act III (PEACE pas de deux).

STAGINGS (choreography credited to André Eglevsky in some later stagings): 1963, National; 1964, American Ballet Theatre; 1965, Eglevsky; 1968, Harkness; 1979, Royal Winnipeg; 1980, Pennsylvania; 1981, Matsuyama.

TELEVISION: 1950 (CBS); 1955 (Ed Sullivan Show, CBS); 1959-60 (excerpts, PBS); 1960 (ABC); 1963 (CBC, Montreal); 1965 (Bell Telephone Hour, NBC).

See 36, 350, 387

1951

274 MUSIC AND DANCE:
NUMBERS IV, VI, VII, VIII, IX, XI, XII

MUSIC: As given below.

CHOREOGRAPHY: By George Balanchine (eight of thirteen dances), Todd Bolender, Frank Hobi, and Francisco Moncion.

PRODUCTION: Presented by the National Orchestral Society, Leon Barzin, Musical Director. Artistic Director: George Balanchine. Lighting Director: Jean Rosenthal.

PREMIERE: February 10, 1951, Carnegie Hall, New York. Danced by members of the New York City Ballet and students of the School of American Ballet. Conductor: Leon Barzin.

CAST: IV. SARABANDE from *Louis XIV Suite* (François Couperin, orchestrated by Wood-Hill): 4 women; VI. MINUET from Symphony No. 39, K. 543 (Wolfgang Amadeus Mozart): Doris Breckenridge, Robert Barnett; VII. GAVOTTE from *Ladies of the Ballet* (Alfred Edward Moffat): 2 couples; VIII. BOURRÉE from *Concerto for String Orchestra* (Jean-Baptiste Lully): 2 couples; IX. RIGAUDON from the Lully *Concerto*: 4 couples; XI. WALTZ from *Naïla* (*La Source*, Léo Delibes): Maria Tallchief, 11 women; XII. TANGO from *Le Carnaval d'Aix* (Darius Milhaud): Tanaquil Le Clercq.

NOTE: Each musical selection was played by the orchestra alone and then repeated with dances. *Mazurka from 'A Life for the Tsar'* [272] was performed as Number XIII, closing the program.

See 350, 364, 387

275 THE CARD GAME (THE CARD PARTY)
A Ballet in Three Deals

MUSIC: By Igor Stravinsky (*Jeu de Cartes–A Card Game–Das Kartenspiel*, 1936, commissioned by Lincoln Kirstein and Edward M. M. Warburg). Book by Igor Stravinsky and M. Malaieff.

PRODUCTION: Scenery and costumes by Irene Sharaff.

PREMIERE: February 15, 1951, New York City Ballet, City Center of Music and Drama, New York. Conductor: Leon Barzin.

CAST: *Joker*, Todd Bolender; *Queens*: *Hearts*, Janet Reed; *Spades*, Jillana; *Diamonds*, Patricia Wilde; *Clubs*, Doris Breckenridge; *4 Aces* (men); *4 Kings*; *4 Jacks*; *10, 9, 8, 7, 6, 5 of Hearts*; *10, 9, 8, 7 of Spades*.

NOTE: Originally presented by the American Ballet (Stravinsky Festival), New York, 1937.

REVISIONS: On at least one occasion, Joker danced by a woman (Janet Reed).

See 177*

276 PAS DE TROIS

MUSIC: By Léon Minkus (from *Paquita*, 1881).

PRODUCTION: Costumes by Karinska. Lighting by Jean Rosenthal.

PREMIERE: February 18, 1951, New York City Ballet, City Center of Music and Drama, New York. Conductor: Leon Barzin.

CAST: Nora Kaye, Maria Tallchief, André Eglevsky.

NOTE: Originally presented (in somewhat different form) by the Grand Ballet du Marquis de Cuevas, London, 1948, as *Pas de Trois Classique*.

See 247*

277 LA VALSE

MUSIC: By Maurice Ravel (*Valses Nobles et Sentimentales*, 1911, orchestrated 1912; *La Valse*, 1920, commissioned by Serge Diaghilev).

PRODUCTION: Costumes by Karinska. Lighting by Jean Rosenthal.

PREMIERE: February 20, 1951, New York City Ballet, City Center of Music and Drama, New York. Conductor: Leon Barzin.

CAST: VALSES NOBLES ET SENTIMENTALES: FIRST WALTZ, Overture (not danced); SECOND WALTZ: Vida Brown, Edwina Fontaine, Jillana; THIRD WALTZ: Patricia Wilde, Frank Hobi; FOURTH WALTZ: Yvonne Mounsey, Michael Maule; FIFTH WALTZ: Diana Adams, Herbert Bliss; SIXTH WALTZ: Adams; SEVENTH WALTZ: Bliss, Brown, Fontaine, Jillana; EIGHTH WALTZ: Tanaquil Le Clercq, Nicholas Magallanes; LA VALSE: Le Clercq, Magallanes, Francisco Moncion, 16 women, 9 men.

NOTE: The eight *Valses Nobles et Sentimentales* establish a mood of disturbed gaiety and impending catastrophe. In *La Valse* the stage becomes a ballroom of waltzing couples. The figure of Death, in black, enters; a girl in white dances with him. Waltzing ever faster, unable to resist, she dies.

REVISIONS: 1974, New York City Ballet: Figure of Death makes momentary appearance in EIGHTH WALTZ, foreshadowing events of LA VALSE.

STAGINGS: 1965, Stuttgart; 1966, Royal Swedish; 1967, Dutch National, Hamburg; 1969, Geneva; 1975, Paris; 1977, Berlin, Frankfurt; 1978, East Berlin, Vienna, Zürich; 1981, Pacific Northwest.

TELEVISION: 1951 (excerpts, CBS, on first commercial color telecast).

See 20

278 ROMEO AND JULIET
Play by William Shakespeare

MUSIC: By David Diamond.

PRODUCTION: Produced by Dwight Deere Wiman. Directed by Peter Glenville. Scenery and costumes by Oliver Messel. Scenery executed by Studio Alliance; costumes executed by Karinska.

PREMIERE: March 10, 1951, Broadhurst Theatre, New York. Conductor: Robert Stanley. (Out-of-town preview: January 22, Cass Theatre, Detroit.)

CAST: *Romeo,* Douglas Watson; *Juliet,* Olivia de Havilland; *Mercutio,* Jack Hawkins; *Tybalt,* William Smithers; *Capulet,* Malcolm Keen; *Lady Capulet,* Isobel Elsom; *Nurse to Juliet,* Evelyn Varden; *Friar Laurence,* James Hayter; and others.

NOTE: Balanchine choreographed a pavane for the Capulet ball, Act I, Scene 5.

See 325

279 CAPRICCIO BRILLANT

MUSIC: By Felix Mendelssohn (*Capriccio Brillant* for piano and orchestra, Op. 22, 1825-26).

PRODUCTION: Costumes by Karinska. Lighting by Jean Rosenthal.

PREMIERE: June 7, 1951, New York City Ballet, City Center of Music and Drama, New York. Conductor: Leon Barzin. On-stage pianist: Nicholas Kopeikine.

CAST: Maria Tallchief, André Eglevsky; Barbara Bocher, Constance Garfield, Jillana, Irene Larsson.

280 COURTIN' TIME
Musical Comedy in Two Acts and Nine Scenes

MUSIC AND BOOK: Music and lyrics by Jack Lawrence and Don Walker. Book by William Roos, based on the play *The Farmer's Wife*, by Eden Phillpotts. Musical and vocal arrangements by Don Walker.

PRODUCTION: Produced by James Russo and Michael Ellis in association with Alexander H. Cohen. Directed by Alfred Drake. Scenery and lighting by Ralph Alswang. Costumes by Saul Bolasni. Scenery built by Nolan Brothers and painted by Triangle Studios; costumes executed by Eaves Costume Company.

PREMIERE: June 13, 1951, National Theatre, New York. Conductor: Bill Jonson. (Out-of-town preview: April 9, Shubert Theatre, Boston.)

CAST: *Samuel Rilling*, Joe E. Brown (Lloyd Nolan, Boston); *Araminta*, Billie Worth; *Theresa Tapper*, Carmen Mathews; and others. Dancers: Gloria Patrice, Peter Conlow, 6 women, 6 men.

TODAY AT YOUR HOUSE, TOMORROW AT MINE (Act I): Gloria Patrice, Peter Conlow, ensemble.

REPRISE: THE WISHBONE SONG (Act I): Patrice, Conlow.

CHOOSE YOUR PARTNER (Act I): Patrice, Conlow, ensemble.

BALLET: JOHNNY AND THE PUCKWUDGIES (Act II): *Johnny-Ride-the-Sky*, Conlow; Patrice, ensemble.

NOTE: CHOOSE YOUR PARTNER, a square dance around a gazebo, used the American dance form on which Balanchine later based a ballet [315].

281 THE SLEEPING BEAUTY:
VARIATION from AURORA'S WEDDING

In the summer of 1951, at Jacob's Pillow, Diana Adams performed a variation from *Aurora's Wedding* (divertissements from Act III of *The Sleeping Beauty* [Tschaikovsky]), with choreography credited to Balanchine.

See 65, 225, 259, 404, 418

282 À LA FRANÇAIX

MUSIC: By Jean Françaix (*Serenade for Small Orchestra*, 1934).

PRODUCTION: Scenery by Raoul Dufy. Lighting by Jean Rosenthal.

PREMIERE: September 11, 1951, New York City Ballet, City Center of Music and Drama, New York. Conductor: Leon Barzin.

CAST: Janet Reed, Maria Tallchief, André Eglevsky; Frank Hobi, Roy Tobias.

NOTE: As the pun of the title implies, a humorous and anecdotal ballet: A tennis-playing athlete flirts with a pretty girl until a ballerina dressed as a winged sylph appears and fascinates him; in the end the sylph, stripping down to a bathing suit, reveals herself to be an athlete, too.

STAGINGS: 1953, San Francisco; 1964, Eglevsky; 1965, San Diego; 1981, American Festival; 1982, Kansas City.

TELEVISION: 1953 (Kate Smith Hour, NBC).

283 TYL ULENSPIEGEL

MUSIC: By Richard Strauss (*Till Eulenspiegels lustige Streiche*, Op. 28, 1895).

PRODUCTION: Scenery and costumes by Esteban Francés. Scenery executed by Triangle Studios and Nolan Brothers. Lighting by Jean Rosenthal.

PREMIERE: November 14, 1951, New York City Ballet, City Center of Music and Drama, New York. Conductor: Leon Barzin.

CAST: *Tyl Ulenspiegel*, Jerome Robbins; *Nell, His Wife*, Ruth Sobotka; *Philip II, King of Spain*, Brooks Jackson; *Duke and Duchess*, Frank Hobi,

Beatrice Tompkins; *Woman*, Tomi Wortham; *Tyl as a Child*, Alberta Grant; *Philip II as a Child*, Susan Kovnat; *Spanish Nobility*, 2 women, 2 men; *Soldiers*, 6 men; *Peasants*, 8 women; *Inquisitors*, 4 men; *Crowd*, 8 women.

NOTE: Fantastic pantomime-ballet depicting the medieval prankster as liberator of Flanders from Spanish invaders; set in elaborate décor, with many changes of costume.

284 APOLLO, LEADER OF THE MUSES
Ballet in Two Scenes

MUSIC: Music and book by Igor Stravinsky (*Apollo Musagetes*, 1927-28, commissioned by Mrs. Elizabeth Sprague Coolidge).

PRODUCTION: Costumes by Karinska. Lighting by Jean Rosenthal.

PREMIERE: November 15, 1951, New York City Ballet, City Center of Music and Drama, New York. Conductor: Leon Barzin.

CAST: *Apollo*, André Eglevsky; *Terpsichore*, Maria Tallchief; *Calliope*, Diana Adams; *Polyhymnia*, Tanaquil Le Clercq; *Leto*, Barbara Milberg; *Handmaidens*, Irene Larsson, Jillana.

NOTE: Originally presented by Diaghilev's Ballets Russes, Paris, 1928, titled *Apollon Musagète*. From 1957, titled *Apollo*.

See 84*, 176, 198

285 SWAN LAKE

MUSIC: By Peter Ilyitch Tschaikovsky (excerpts from *Swan Lake*, Op. 20, 1875-76).

CHOREOGRAPHY: By George Balanchine after Lev Ivanov.

PRODUCTION: Scenery and costumes by Cecil Beaton. Scenery executed by Triangle Studios and Nolan Brothers; costumes executed by Karinska. Lighting by Jean Rosenthal.

PREMIERE: November 20, 1951, New York City Ballet, City Center of Music and Drama, New York. Conductor: Leon Barzin.

CAST: *Odette, Queen of the Swans*, Maria Tallchief; *Prince Siegfried*, André Eglevsky; *Benno, the Prince's Friend*, Frank Hobi; PAS DE TROIS: Patricia

Wilde, 2 women; PAS DE NEUF: Yvonne Mounsey, 8 women; *Von Rothbart, a Sorcerer*, Edward Bigelow; *Swans*, 24 women; *Hunters*, 8 men.

NOTE: Balanchine's version of *Swan Lake* is essentially Act II of the original four-act production, reproducing Ivanov's WHITE SWAN ADAGIO (the pas de deux), the Swan Queen's solo and coda entrance, and the DANCE OF THE FOUR CYGNETS (the pas de quatre); the entrance of the Swans derives from traditional versions. Balanchine removed all mime, greatly enlarged the role of the corps de ballet, and choreographed a new finale to music from Act IV.

REVISIONS: New York City Ballet, changes from first years in repertory: 1956, traditional ending of pas de deux replaced by coda for corps de ballet (to Tschaikovsky's original score rather than the traditional Drigo interpolation); 1959, PAS DE TROIS omitted and new Prince's solo added to that music (Grand Waltz from Act II) replacing original Prince's solo to fourth variation of pas de six (Act III), and traditional entrance of Swan Queen in coda rechoreographed; 1964, traditional Swan Queen solo replaced by new choreography (to *Un Poco di Chopin*, Op. 72, no. 15, 1893, orchestrated by Drigo) and subsequently changed several times, Prince's solo rechoreographed (to music from Act I pas de trois) and subsequently changed several times and often omitted, pas de quatre (DANCE OF THE FOUR CYGNETS) replaced by WALTZ BLUETTE for 12 Swans (to orchestrated version of a composition for piano in E-flat), role of Benno omitted; 1980, traditional Swan Queen solo and entrance in coda restored.

NEW PRODUCTIONS BY BALANCHINE COMPANIES: 1964, New York City Ballet: New scenery, costumes and lighting by Rouben Ter-Arutunian for the New York State Theater.

STAGINGS: 1954, San Francisco; 1961, La Scala; 1965, Ballet of Los Angeles; 1979, Los Angeles; 1981, Eglevsky; 1982, Kansas City.

TELEVISION: 1954 (excerpt, Kate Smith Show, NBC); 1956 (pas de deux, CBS); 1959-60 (pas de deux, PBS).

See 75, 191, 262, 331, 367

.

1952

286 CARACOLE

MUSIC: By Wolfgang Amadeus Mozart (Divertimento No. 15 in B-flat major, K. 287, second minuet [fifth movement] and andante from sixth movement omitted).

PRODUCTION: Costumes by Christian Bérard (from *Mozartiana* [134]). Lighting by Jean Rosenthal.

PREMIERE: February 19, 1952, New York City Ballet, City Center of Music and Drama, New York. Conductor: Leon Barzin.

CAST: Diana Adams, Melissa Hayden, Tanaquil Le Clercq, Maria Tallchief, Patricia Wilde, André Eglevsky, Nicholas Magallanes, Jerome Robbins, 8 women.

ALLEGRO; THEME AND VARIATIONS; MINUET; ANDANTE; FINALE.

NOTE: The French title denotes a form of turning or circling, and is used as a term in horsemanship, to which the costumes made reference. The ballet, an intricate work set to music for which Balanchine has expressed special admiration, could not be remembered in 1956 when a revival was planned. Balanchine then choreographed a new ballet to the same score, titled *Divertimento No. 15*, without programmatic context.

See 314

287 BAYOU

MUSIC: By Virgil Thomson (*Acadian Songs and Dances*, 1947).

PRODUCTION: Scenery and costumes by Dorothea Tanning. Costumes executed by Karinska. Lighting by Jean Rosenthal.

PREMIERE: February 21, 1952, New York City Ballet, City Center of Music and Drama, New York. Conductor: Leon Barzin.

CAST: *Boy of the Bayou*, Francisco Moncion; *Girl of the Bayou*, Doris Breckenridge; *Leaves and Flowers*, Melissa Hayden, Hugh Laing, 2 couples; *Starched White People*, Diana Adams, Herbert Bliss, 2 couples.

NOTE: At the opening and close, the Boy poles a small boat through the mysterious bayou; the dancers are Acadians from country and town whom the Boy encounters. The music was composed for Robert Flaherty's documentary film *Louisiana Story*.

288 SCOTCH SYMPHONY

MUSIC: By Felix Mendelssohn (Symphony No. 3 in A minor, Op. 56, 'Scotch,' 1842 [first movement omitted]).

PRODUCTION: Scenery by Horace Armistead; painted by Scenic Studios. Women's costumes by Karinska. Men's costumes by David Ffolkes. Lighting by Jean Rosenthal.

PREMIERE: November 11, 1952, New York City Ballet, City Center of Music and Drama, New York. Conductor: Leon Barzin.

CAST: Maria Tallchief, André Eglevsky; Patricia Wilde; 8 couples.

NOTE: An homage to Scotland in the form of a classic ballet, with allusions to the elusive sylph of Romantic ballet.

STAGINGS: 1962, New England Civic; 1963, Paris; 1964, Munich; 1965, Pennsylvania, La Scala; 1966, San Francisco; 1967, Joffrey, Hamburg; 1970, Eglevsky (pas de deux); 1971, Geneva; 1973, San Juan; 1976, Pacific Northwest; 1978, Washington; 1979, Milwaukee; 1980, Los Angeles; 1982, Atlanta.

TELEVISION: 1959 (excerpts, Bell Telephone Hour, NBC).

289 METAMORPHOSES

MUSIC: By Paul Hindemith (*Symphonic Metamorphoses on Themes of Carl Maria von Weber*, 1943).

PRODUCTION: Costumes by Karinska. Décor by Jean Rosenthal.

PREMIERE: November 25, 1952, New York City Ballet, City Center of Music and Drama, New York. Conductor: Leon Barzin.

CAST: Tanaquil Le Clercq, Todd Bolender, Nicholas Magallanes, 16 women, 8 men.

ALLEGRO; TURANDOT SCHERZO; ANDANTINO; MARCH.

NOTE: A fantasy on insectile life: The dancers are costumed as bug-inspired, winged beings with antennae, in a décor formed of series of light-reflective coat hangers and Chinese panels. The adagio features a beetle and a sort of butterfly; the sky-swept finale, wings in motion. A principal theme of Hindemith's music is based on a Chinese melody used by Weber.

290 HARLEQUINADE PAS DE DEUX

MUSIC: By Riccardo Drigo (from *Les Millions d'Arlequin*, Act I, produced 1900).

PRODUCTION: Costumes by Karinska. Lighting by Jean Rosenthal.

PREMIERE: December 16, 1952, New York City Ballet, City Center of Music and Drama, New York. Conductor: Leon Barzin.

CAST: Maria Tallchief, André Eglevsky.

NOTE: In 1965, Balanchine choreographed the complete *Harlequinade* for the New York City Ballet, creating new choreography for this pas de deux.

STAGINGS: 1961, Eglevsky (female variation, retitled *Columbine*).

See 351

291 ONE, YULETIDE SQUARE
Made for Television

MUSIC: By Léo Delibes (from *Coppélia, ou la Fille aux Yeux d'Émail*, produced 1870).

PRODUCTION: Produced by L. Leonidoff. Costumes by Karinska.

FIRST TELECAST: December 25, 1952, NBC.

CAST: *Swanilda/Coppélia*, Tanaquil Le Clercq; *Frantz*, Jacques d'Amboise; *Dr. Coppélius*, Robert Helpmann; corps de ballet.

NOTE: An abridged treatment of the *Coppélia* story.

See 266, 387

292 CONCERTINO

Music: By Jean Françaix (Concertino for piano and orchestra, 1932).

Production: Costumes by Karinska. Lighting by Jean Rosenthal.

Premiere: December 30, 1952, New York City Ballet, City Center of Music and Drama, New York. Conductor: Leon Barzin. Pianist: Nicholas Kopeikine.

Cast: Diana Adams, Tanaquil Le Clercq, André Eglevsky.

Note: The two ballerinas, costumed as can-can dancers in black tutus, keep the male dancer, in formal dress, close company throughout; they permit him one brief solo variation.

1953

293 VALSE FANTAISIE

Music: By Mikhail Glinka (*Valse Fantaisie* in B minor, 1839; orchestrated 1856).

Production: Costumes by Karinska. Lighting by Jean Rosenthal.

Premiere: January 6, 1953, New York City Ballet, City Center of Music and Drama, New York. Conductor: Leon Barzin.

Cast: Diana Adams, Melissa Hayden, Tanaquil Le Clercq, Nicholas Magallanes.

Note: The three ballerinas, wearing headdresses reminiscent of Glinka's Russia, move together in a *perpetuum mobile*, attended by the male dancer.

Stagings (sometimes as *Waltz Fantasy*): 1964, Eglevsky; 1970, San Juan; 1974, Philippines; 1982, New York Dance Theatre.

See 107*, 359, 366

294 THE COUNTESS BECOMES THE MAID
Made for Television

MUSIC: By Johann Strauss the Younger (excerpts from *Die Fledermaus*, produced 1874).

FIRST TELECAST: February 3, 1953, Kate Smith Hour, NBC.

CAST: *Countess*, Melissa Hayden; *Maid*, Janet Reed; André Eglevsky.

See 107, 169, 199, 206

295 THE RAKE'S PROGRESS
Opera in Three Acts and Nine Scenes

MUSIC: By Igor Stravinsky (produced 1951). Libretto by W. H. Auden and Chester Kallman, a fable and epilogue after William Hogarth's paintings.

PRODUCTION: Stage direction by George Balanchine. Scenery and costumes by Horace Armistead. Scenery constructed by Metropolitan Opera Studio and painted by Studio Alliance; costumes executed by Helene Pons Studio.

PREMIERE: February 14, 1953, Metropolitan Opera, New York. Conductor: Fritz Reiner.

CAST: *Trulove*, Norman Scott; *Anne*, Hilde Gueden; *Tom Rakewell*, Eugene Conley; *Nick Shadow*, Mack Harrell; *Mother Goose*, Martha Lipton; *Baba the Turk*, Blanche Thebom; *Sellem, Auctioneer*, Paul Franke; *Keeper of the Madhouse*, Lawrence Davidson; and others.

NOTE: American premiere. Although the staging was noted for its choreographic qualities, particularly in the brothel scene at Mother Goose's house and the last act in the Madhouse, there were no actual dance sequences.

296 [COTILLION PROMENADE]

On February 20, 1953, Tanaquil Le Clercq and Jacques d'Amboise led some five hundred couples in a promenade arranged by Balanchine for the Negro Debutante Ball, at the 369th Armory, Harlem, New York City, an event sponsored by the *New Amsterdam News*.

297 LA FAVORITA

Opera in Four Acts and Five Scenes by Gaetano Donizetti

BALLET

PREMIERE: April 16, 1953, Teatro alla Scala, Milan. Conductor: Antonino Votto.

CAST: Olga Amati, Giulio Perugini, Vera Colombo, Gilda Maiocchi, Mario Pistoni.

NOTE: The ballet probably occurred in the Act II scene in the gardens of the Palace of the Alcazar.

298 BORIS GODUNOV

Opera in Prologue, Four Acts and Seven Scenes by Modest Moussorgsky

POLONAISE

PREMIERE: April 20, 1953, Teatro alla Scala, Milan. Conductor: Antonino Votto.

NOTE: Although the printed program credits no dance or dancers, the ballet was probably a POLONAISE performed in the scene set in the Polish castle.

See 54, 388

299 ADRIANA LECOUVREUR

Opera in Four Acts by Francesco Cilea

BALLET

PREMIERE: May 7, 1953, Teatro alla Scala, Milan. Conductor: Carlo Maria Giulini.

CAST: *Paris,* Walter Marconi; *Mercury,* Mario Pistoni; *Juno,* Tilde Baroni; *Pallas,* Gilda Maiocchi; *Venus,* Carla Calzati; *Wisdom,* Nuccy Muti; *Purity,* Maria Bazzolo; corps de ballet.

NOTE: The ballet occurred in Act III, in the scene set in the palace of the Prince of Bouillon.

300 AMAHL AND THE NIGHT VISITORS
Opera in One Act by Gian Carlo Menotti
SHEPHERDS' DANCE

PREMIERE: May 9, 1953, Teatro della Pergola, Florence. Conductor: Leopold Stokowski.

CAST: Raimonda Orselli, Alberto Moro.

NOTE: Performed at the XVI° Maggio Musicale.

1954

301 OPUS 34

MUSIC: By Arnold Schoenberg (*Accompaniment-Music for a Motion Picture*, Op. 34, 1930).

PRODUCTION: Costumes by Esteban Francés. Scenery and lighting by Jean Rosenthal.

PREMIERE: January 19, 1954, New York City Ballet, City Center of Music and Drama, New York. Conductor: Leon Barzin.

CAST: THE FIRST TIME: Diana Adams, Patricia Wilde, Nicholas Magallanes, Francisco Moncion, 9 women; THE SECOND TIME: Tanaquil Le Clercq, Herbert Bliss, 6 women, 10 men.

NOTE: The sections of the twelve-tone score are titled 'Threat,' 'Danger,' 'Fear,' 'Catastrophe.' The music is performed twice without pause.
THE FIRST TIME is performed in an extreme vocabulary of dance motion.
THE SECOND TIME is an endurance of horror, a grisly symbolic surgery in pantomime, with dancers costumed in bandages and as cadavers.

302 THE NUTCRACKER
Classic Ballet in Two Acts, Four Scenes, and Prologue

MUSIC: By Peter Ilyitch Tschaikovsky (*The Nutcracker*, produced 1892; violin cadenza from *The Sleeping Beauty* added 1955). Based on the Alexandre Dumas *père* version of E. T. A. Hoffmann's tale, *The Nutcracker and the Mouse King* (1816).

CHOREOGRAPHY: By George Balanchine. CANDY CANE variation (TREPAK) and Little Prince's mime choreographed by Lev Ivanov. BATTLE BETWEEN THE NUTCRACKER AND THE MOUSE KING choreographed by Jerome Robbins.

PRODUCTION: Scenery by Horace Armistead, executed by Century Scenic Studios. Costumes by Karinska. Masks by Vlady. Lighting and production by Jean Rosenthal.

PREMIERE: February 2, 1954, New York City Ballet with students from the School of American Ballet, City Center of Music and Drama, New York. Conductor: Leon Barzin.

CAST: ACT I, SCENE I, CHRISTMAS PARTY AT THE HOME OF DR. STAHLBAUM, NUREMBERG, CA. 1816: *Dr. and Frau Stahlbaum*, Frank Hobi, Irene Larsson; *Their Children, Clara and Fritz*, Alberta Grant, Susan Kaufman; *Maid*; *Guests: 4 Parents, 11 Children, 2 Grandparents*; *Herr Drosselmeyer*, Michael Arshansky; *His Nephew (The Nutcracker)*, Paul Nickel; *Toys: Harlequin and Columbine*, Gloria Vauges, Kaye Sargent; *Toy Soldier*, Roy Tobias; SCENE 2, THE BATTLE BETWEEN THE NUTCRACKER AND THE MOUSE KING: *Mouse King*, Edward Bigelow; *Nutcracker*; *Clara*; *8 Mice*; *19 Child Soldiers*; SCENE 3, THE WHITE FOREST AND THE SNOWFLAKE WALTZ: *Nutcracker*; *Clara*; *Snowflakes*, 16 women. Boys choir (40 voices) from St. Thomas Episcopal Church. ACT II, CONFITUERENBURG (THE KINGDOM OF THE SUGAR PLUM FAIRY): *Sugar Plum Fairy*, Maria Tallchief; *Her Cavalier*, Nicholas Magallanes; *Little Princess*, Grant; *Little Prince*, Nickel; *Angels*, 8 girls; DIVERTISSEMENTS: HOT CHOCOLATE (SPANISH DANCE): Yvonne Mounsey, Herbert Bliss, 4 couples; COFFEE (ARABIAN DANCE): Francisco Moncion, 4 children; TEA (CHINESE DANCE): George Li, 2 women; CANDY CANES (BUFFOONS): Robert Barnett, 6 girls; MARZIPAN SHEPHERDESSES (MIRLITONS): Janet Reed, 4 women; BONBONNIÈRE (MOTHER GINGER AND HER POLICHINELLES): Bigelow, 8 children; WALTZ OF THE CANDY FLOWERS: *Dewdrop*, Tanaquil Le Clercq; *Flowers*, 2 demi-soloists; 12 women.

NOTE: Balanchine danced the roles of The Nutcracker/Little Prince, Mouse King, and others in productions by the Maryinsky Theater in Petrograd (later State Theater of Opera and Ballet), and was especially noted for his solo in the BUFFOONS' DANCE (TREPAK [CANDY CANE] variation). He chose the ballet to be the first full-length work presented by the New York City Ballet; the overwhelming success of his production, with elaborate scenic effects, helped assure the permanence of the Company. The use of children from the School of American Ballet, recalling Balanchine's early experience at the Maryinsky, set a precedent for future New York City Ballet works. *The Sleeping Beauty* cadenza, interpolated into Act I by Balanchine in 1955, has the same theme as the 'tree growing' music from *The Nutcracker* which occurs later in Act I.

REVISIONS: New York City Ballet: 1955, violin cadenza from *The Sleeping Beauty* added to extended pantomime in Act I; 1958, GRAND PAS DE DEUX (Sugar Plum Fairy and Cavalier, end of Act II), replaced by PAS DE CINQ with Cavalier omitted and Sugar Plum Fairy supported in adagio by men from CHOCOLATE, COFFEE, TEA, CANDY CANES; variation for Sugar Plum Fairy moved to beginning of Act II from traditional placement at climax of GRAND PAS DE DEUX; 1959, adagio and coda of GRAND PAS DE DEUX restored with Cavalier, replacing PAS DE CINQ, but without variation for Cavalier; Sugar Plum Fairy variation retained at beginning of Act II; 1964, COFFEE (ARABIAN DANCE), formerly featuring hookah-smoking nobleman fanned by four parrots, rechoreographed as solo for a woman; 1968, introduction of mechanical device allowing Sugar Plum Fairy to glide across stage on one pointe; 1972, eight child mice added; 1979, opening section of SNOWFLAKE WALTZ revised; COFFEE (ARABIAN DANCE) substantially rechoreographed.

NEW PRODUCTIONS BY BALANCHINE COMPANIES: 1964, New York City Ballet: New scenery and lighting by Rouben Ter-Arutunian for the New York State Theater, executed by Feller Scenery Studios, tree by Decorative Plant Corporation; some new costumes by Karinska.

STAGINGS: 1959, Atlanta (ACT I, SCENE 3 and ACT II), Joffrey (pas de deux); 1965, Cologne; 1966, Atlanta (full length); 1968, Pennsylvania (ACT II); 1973, Geneva (ACT II); 1976, Pacific Northwest (pas de deux); 1977, Prince George's (pas de deux); 1978, Chicago Lyric Opera (excerpts).

TELEVISION: 1954 (pas de deux, NBC); 1955 (Sugar Plum Fairy variation, NBC); 1956 (excerpts, rehearsal, CBS); 1956 (pas de deux, Ed Sullivan Show, CBS); 1957 (full length, Seven Lively Arts, CBS); 1957? (pas de deux, L'Heure du Concert, CBC, Montreal); 1958 (full length, with Balanchine as Drosselmeyer, Playhouse 90, CBS); 1959 (pas de deux, ABC); 1959-60 (pas de deux, PBS); 1961 (pas de deux, Bell Telephone Hour, NBC); 1963 (pas de deux, NBC); 1971 (excerpts, NBC).

See 225

303 WESTERN SYMPHONY

MUSIC: By Hershy Kay (1954, commissioned by the New York City Ballet; themes: 'Red River Valley,' 'Old Taylor,' 'Rye Whiskey,' 'Lolly-Too-Dum,' 'Good Night, Ladies,' 'Oh, Dem Golden Slippers,' 'The Girl I Left Behind Me').

PRODUCTION: Lighting by Jean Rosenthal.

PREMIERE: September 7, 1954, New York City Ballet, City Center of Music and Drama, New York. Conductor: Leon Barzin.

CAST: FIRST MOVEMENT, ALLEGRO: Diana Adams, Herbert Bliss, 8 women, 4 men; SECOND MOVEMENT, ADAGIO: Janet Reed, Nicholas Magallanes, 4 women; THIRD MOVEMENT, SCHERZO: Patricia Wilde, André Eglevsky, 4 women; FOURTH MOVEMENT, RONDO: Tanaquil Le Clercq, Jacques d'Amboise, 4 couples.

NOTE: A ballet deriving its flavor and character from the American West while moving rigorously within the framework of classic dance technique and the symphony form. Initially presented without scenery, in practice clothes.

REVISIONS: ca. 1960, New York City Ballet: SCHERZO permanently eliminated.

NEW PRODUCTIONS BY BALANCHINE COMPANIES: New York City Ballet: 1955, scenery by John Boyt (executed by Eugene B. Dunkel Studios), costumes by Karinska; 1968, scenery and costumes renewed in the same style, executed by Nolan Scenery Studios and Karinska.

STAGINGS: 1976, Geneva; 1978, Zürich; 1982, Pacific Northwest, San Francisco.

TELEVISION: 1958 (RONDO, Australian television).

304 IVESIANA

MUSIC: By Charles Ives, as given below (for chamber orchestra except as noted).

PRODUCTION: Lighting by Jean Rosenthal.

PREMIERE: September 14, 1954, New York City Ballet, City Center of Music and Drama, New York. Conductor: Leon Barzin.

CAST: CENTRAL PARK IN THE DARK (1906): Janet Reed, Francisco Moncion,

20 women; HALLOWE'EN (1907?, string quartet and piano): Patricia Wilde, Jacques d'Amboise, 4 women; THE UNANSWERED QUESTION (1906): Allegra Kent, Todd Bolender, 4 men; OVER THE PAVEMENTS (1906-13): Diana Adams, Herbert Bliss, 4 men; IN THE INN (1904-6?): Tanaquil Le Clercq, Bolender; IN THE NIGHT (1906): Entire cast.

NOTE: A series of dances to brief compositions, each presenting a dramatic situation in the manner of a tone poem. This homage to the composer was choreographed soon after his death; the music had rarely been performed prior to its use for the ballet.

REVISIONS: New York City Ballet: 1955, HALLOWE'EN replaced by ARGUMENTS (second movement of String Quartet No. 2, 1907); later that year ARGUMENTS replaced by BARN DANCE (from *Washington's Birthday*, 1909); 1961, OVER THE PAVEMENTS and BARN DANCE eliminated, IN THE INN rechoreographed, presented in the order CENTRAL PARK IN THE DARK, THE UNANSWERED QUESTION, IN THE INN, IN THE NIGHT; 1978, Peter Martins' *Calcium Light Night* (also to Ives) included in several performances presented in the order CENTRAL PARK IN THE DARK, IN THE INN, THE UNANSWERED QUESTION, CALCIUM LIGHT NIGHT, IN THE NIGHT.

STAGINGS: 1968, Dutch National; 1971, Berlin; 1975, Los Angeles.

TELEVISION: 1964 (L'Heure du Concert, CBC, Montreal).

305 HOUSE OF FLOWERS
Musical Comedy in Two Acts and Thirteen Scenes

MUSIC AND BOOK: Music by Harold Arlen. Lyrics by Truman Capote and Harold Arlen. Book by Truman Capote. Orchestrations by Ted Royal.

CHOREOGRAPHY: By George Balanchine. Banda dance choreographed by Geoffrey Holder.

PRODUCTION: Produced by Saint Subber. Directed by Peter Brook. Scenery and costumes by Oliver Messel. Scenery built by Messmore & Damon and painted by E. B. Dunkel Studios; costumes executed by Brooks Costume Company. Lighting by Jean Rosenthal.

PREMIERE: November 25, 1954, Erlanger Theatre, Philadelphia. Conductor: Jerry Arlen.

CAST: *Madame Fleur*, Pearl Bailey; *Ottilie alias Violet*, Diahann Carroll;

Madame Tango, Juanita Hall; *Tulip*, Josephine Premice; *Royal*, Rawn Spearman; and others.

WAITING (Act I): *Pansy*, Enid Mosier; *Tulip*, Josephine Premice; *Gladiola*, Ada Moore; *Do*, Winston George Henriques; *Don't*, Solomon Earl Green.

BAMBOO CAGE (Act I): *The Champion*, Geoffrey Holder; Henriques, Green; *Watermelon*, Phillip Hepburn; Mosier, Premice, Moore; *Madame Tango*, Juanita Hall; *Chief of Police*, Don Redman; ensemble.

TWO LADIES IN DE SHADE OF DE BANANA TREE (Act I): Premice, Moore, male ensemble.

CARNIVAL (Act I): Mosier, Premice, Moore, ensemble.

VOUDOU (Act II): *The Drummers*, Joseph Comadore, Michael Alexander, Alphonso Marshall; *Duchess of the Sea*, Miriam Burton; *Octopus*, Albert Popwell; *Shark*, Walter Nicks, Arthur Mitchell, Marshall; *Turtle*, Comadore, ensemble; *Baron of the Cemetery* (Banda dance), choreographed and danced by Geoffrey Holder.

MADAME TANGO'S TANGO (Act II): Hall, Tango Belles.

THE TURTLE SONG (Act II): *Royal*, Rawn Spearman; Henriques, Green, Hepburn, Holder, ensemble.

NOTE: Balanchine withdrew from the show before the New York opening. Herbert Ross rearranged some of the choreography, some was deleted, and the sequence of the numbers was changed.

1955

306 ROMA

MUSIC: By Georges Bizet (three of the four movements from *Roma Suite*, 1861-68: Andante omitted).

PRODUCTION: Scenery and costumes by Eugene Berman. Lighting by Jean Rosenthal.

PREMIERE: February 23, 1955, New York City Ballet, City Center of Music and Drama, New York. Conductor: Leon Barzin.

CAST: Tanaquil Le Clercq, André Eglevsky; Barbara Milberg, Barbara Walczak, Roy Tobias, John Mandia; 12 women, 8 men.

SCHERZO; ADAGIO (pas de deux); CARNAVAL (TARANTELLA).

NOTE: A celebration of Italy, the set combining vistas of a lofty ruin and a slum square.

307 PAS DE TROIS

MUSIC: By Mikhail Glinka (ballet music from *Ruslan and Ludmilla* [Act II vision scene], produced 1842).

PRODUCTION: Costumes by Karinska. Lighting by Jean Rosenthal.

PREMIERE: March 1, 1955, New York City Ballet, City Center of Music and Drama, New York. Conductor: Leon Barzin.

CAST: Melissa Hayden, Patricia Wilde, André Eglevsky.

STAGINGS (choreography credited to André Eglevsky in some later stagings): 1965, Pennsylvania; 1969, Eglevsky; 1971, Downtown; 1972, Dance Repertory Company, North Carolina; 1974, Georgia Dance Theatre; 1975, Syracuse; 1977, Royal Winnipeg; 1979, American Ballet Theatre; 1980, Ballet West.

See 365

308 THE TEMPEST

Play by William Shakespeare

MUSIC: By Ernst Bacon.

PRODUCTION: Produced by Chandler Cowles. Directed by Denis Carey. Scenery by Horace Armistead. Costumes by Robert Fletcher. Scenery executed by Chester Rakeman Studios; costumes executed by Brooks Costume Company. Lighting by Jean Rosenthal.

PREMIERE: August 1, 1955, American Shakespeare Festival, Stratford, Connecticut. Danced by members of the Festival company. Conductor and pianist: Andrew Heath. (Preview: July 26.)

CAST: *Prospero*, Raymond Massey; *Antonio*, Fritz Weaver; *Ferdinand*, Christopher Plummer; *Caliban*, Jack Palance; *Miranda*, Joan Chandler; *Ariel*, Roddy McDowall; and others. BALLET MASQUE (speaking roles):

Iris, Dorothy Whitney; *Ceres,* Leora Dana; *Juno,* Virginia Baker.

NOTE: Balanchine choreographed the ballet masque for nymphs and reapers in Act IV, Scene 1.

See 224

309 PAS DE DIX

MUSIC: By Alexander Glazounov (*Raymonda,* excerpts from Act III, Op. 57, produced 1898).

CHOREOGRAPHY: By George Balanchine, after Marius Petipa.

PRODUCTION: Costumes by Esteban Francés. Lighting by Jean Rosenthal.

PREMIERE: November 9, 1955, New York City Ballet, City Center of Music and Drama, New York. Conductor: Leon Barzin.

CAST: Maria Tallchief, André Eglevsky; Barbara Fallis, Constance Garfield, Jane Mason, Barbara Walczak, Shaun O'Brien, Roy Tobias, Roland Vazquez, Jonathan Watts.

NOTE: Using much of the same music as the PAS CLASSIQUE HONGROIS from Act III of *Raymonda* [233], the work is composed of solos, two pas de deux, a duet for two women, and a quartet for four men, concluding with bravura measures for the ballerina. In 1960, for the San Francisco Ballet *Variations de Ballet,* parts of *Pas de Dix* were combined with choreography by Lew Christensen to Glazounov's suite *Scènes de Ballet,* Op. 52 (revised 1981).

REVISIONS: Often performed without male pas de quatre and sometimes without first two of three variations for female soloists.

STAGINGS (occasionally titled *Raymonda, Raymonda Pas de Dix* or *Raymonda Variations* [distinct from *Valses et Variations* (339, later retitled *Raymonda Variations*)]; see also note and stagings list for *Raymonda* [233]; choreography credited to Petipa in later stagings): 1960, Joffrey, San Francisco (as part of Christensen's *Variations de Ballet*); 1961, New England Civic; 1962, Eglevsky, Hamburg, Royal Winnipeg; 1963, Pennsylvania; 1964, Dutch National; 1965, Ballet of Los Angeles, Cologne; 1968, Huntington Dance Ensemble; 1969, Houston; 1970, Dance Repertory Company; 1972, Pittsburgh; 1973, Ballet West; 1974, Los Angeles, New Zealand; 1975, Milwaukee, Stars of American Ballet; 1976, Arizona, Dallas, National Academy, Pacific

Northwest; 1977, Chicago Lyric Opera; 1978, Garden State, Philippines; 1980, Makarova and Company; 1981, Kansas City; 1982, Mesa Civic, North Carolina.

TELEVISION: 1957 (L'Heure du Concert, CBC, Montreal).

See 18, 233*, 339, 384

310 JEUX D'ENFANTS

MUSIC: By Georges Bizet (*Jeux d'Enfants*, 12 pieces for piano duet, Opp. 22-26, nos. 2, 3, 6, 11, and 12, 1871, orchestrated by the composer as *Petite Suite d'Orchestre*, 1873; remaining sections orchestrated by an unidentified English composer).

CHOREOGRAPHY: By George Balanchine, Francisco Moncion and Barbara Milberg.

PRODUCTION: Scenery and costumes by Esteban Francés. Scenery executed by Messmore & Damon; costumes executed by Helene Pons Studio. Lighting by Jean Rosenthal.

PREMIERE: November 22, 1955, New York City Ballet, City Center of Music and Drama, New York. Conductor: Leon Barzin.

CAST: I. OVERTURE; 2. BADMINTON: Barbara Fallis, Richard Thomas, Jonathan Watts; 3. HOBBY HORSES: 2 couples; 4. PAPER DOLLS: 4 women; *Scissors*, 1 man; 5. THE LION AND THE MOUSE: Ann Crowell, Eugene Tanner; 6. THE MUSIC BOX: Una Kai, Walter Georgov, Roland Vazquez; 7. THE AMERICAN BOX: 5 women; 8. THE TOPS: Barbara Walczak, Robert Barnett; 9. THE SOLDIER: Roy Tobias; 10. THE DOLL: Melissa Hayden; 11. PAS DE DEUX: Hayden, Tobias; 12. GALOP: Entire cast.

NOTE: A set of dances for toys and playthings which come to life, with costumes and décor based on eighteenth- and nineteenth-century wooden toys, and American playthings from the early part of the twentieth century. In 1975, Balanchine choreographed the Marche, Berceuse, Duo, and Galop (nos. 6, 3, 11, 12) from *Jeux d'Enfants* as a pas de deux, *The Steadfast Tin Soldier*, for the New York City Ballet, retaining the woman's variation from the 1955 work.

REVISIONS: 1959, New York City Ballet: Restaged with choreography credited to Francisco Moncion (2-8) and George Balanchine (9-12).

See 398

1956

311 THE MAGIC FLUTE (DIE ZAUBERFLÖTE)
Made for Television

MUSIC: By Wolfgang Amadeus Mozart (*Die Zauberflöte*, K. 620, produced 1791). Libretto by Emanuel Schikaneder and Karl Ludwig Giesecke. English translation and adaptation by W. H. Auden and Chester Kallman. Conductor and Artistic Director: Peter Herman Adler.

PRODUCTION: Produced by Samuel Chotzinoff. Associate Producer: Charles Polacheck. Special Production Assistant: Lincoln Kirstein. Directed by Kirk Browning. Stage Direction by George Balanchine.

FIRST TELECAST: January 15, 1956, NBC Opera Theatre.

CAST: *Queen of the Night*, Laurel Hurley; *Pamina*, Leontyne Price; *Sarastro*, Yi-kwei Sze; *Papageno*, John Reardon; *Tamino*, William Lewis; *Papagena*, Adelaide Bishop; *Monostatos*, Andrew McKinley; *Three Ladies* (singers), Frances Paige, Joan Maynagh, Helen Vanni; *Three Ladies* (dancers), Françoise Martinet, Barbara Milberg, Eda Lioy.

NOTE: Balanchine created dance sequences for the Queen of the Night's Three Ladies, and in the staging emphasized fluidity of action and clarity of vocal placement.

312 ALLEGRO BRILLANTE

MUSIC: By Peter Ilyitch Tschaikovsky (Piano Concerto No. 3 in E-flat major, Op. 75, 1892 [unfinished]).

PRODUCTION: Costumes by Karinska (uncredited). Lighting by Jean Rosenthal; David Hays (1964-70); Ronald Bates (from 1971).

PREMIERE: March 1, 1956, New York City Ballet, City Center of Music and Drama, New York. Conductor: Leon Barzin. Pianist: Nicholas Kopeikine.

CAST: Maria Tallchief, Nicholas Magallanes, 4 couples.

NOTE: A concentrated essay in the extended classical vocabulary.

STAGINGS: 1961, Joffrey; 1962, La Scala; 1964, Les Grands Ballets Canadiens; 1965, Pennsylvania, Stuttgart; 1966, Boston, Cologne, Royal Swedish; 1967, Ballet of Los Angeles, Garden State; 1970, Eglevsky; 1971, Hamburg, Noverre; 1973, Royal Ballet Touring; 1974, Los Angeles, Geneva; 1975, Dance Theatre of Harlem, Norway; 1976, Chicago Lyric Opera, Pacific Northwest; 1977, Hartford, North Carolina, Caracas, Frankfurt; 1978, Atlanta; 1979, Ballet West, San Francisco; 1980, Louisville, Milwaukee, Minnesota; 1981, Ballet Metropolitan, Matsuyama, Reggio Emilia, West Australian, Zürich; 1982, Tulsa, Royal Flemish.

TELEVISION: 1964 (excerpts, Bell Telephone Hour, NBC); 1979 (Dance in America, PBS).

313 A MUSICAL JOKE

MUSIC: By Wolfgang Amadeus Mozart (*Ein musikalischer Spaß*, sextet for strings and horns in F major, K. 522, 1787).

PRODUCTION: Costumes by Karinska. Lighting by Jean Rosenthal.

PREMIERE: May 31, 1956, Mozart Festival, American Shakespeare Festival Theatre, Stratford, Connecticut. Danced by members of the New York City Ballet. Musical Director: Erich Leinsdorf. Conductor: Hugo Fiorato.

CAST: Diana Adams, Tanaquil Le Clercq, Patricia Wilde, Herbert Bliss, Nicholas Magallanes, Francisco Moncion.

NOTE: Performed twice, with the ballet *Divertimento No. 15* [314] and the Mozart Serenade for 13 Wind Instruments (K. 361). The program, titled *A Serenade of Music and Dance*, was presented during the five-day bicentennial Mozart Festival of the American Shakespeare Festival.

314 DIVERTIMENTO NO. 15

MUSIC: By Wolfgang Amadeus Mozart (Divertimento No. 15 in B-flat major, K. 287; second minuet [fifth movement] and andante from sixth movement omitted; new cadenza for violin and viola by John Colman added late 1960s).

PRODUCTION: Scenery by James Stewart Morcom (from *Symphonie Concertante* [241]). Costumes by Karinska. Lighting by Jean Rosenthal.

PREMIERE: May 31, 1956, Mozart Festival, American Shakespeare Theatre, Stratford, Connecticut. Danced by members of the New York City Ballet. Musical Director: Erich Leinsdorf. Conductor: Hugo Fiorato. (First New York City Ballet performance December 19, City Center of Music and Drama, New York. Conductor: Leon Barzin.)

CAST: ALLEGRO: Diana Adams, Melissa Hayden, Allegra Kent, Tanaquil Le Clercq, Patricia Wilde, Herbert Bliss, Nicholas Magallanes, Roy Tobias, 8 women; THEME AND VARIATIONS: Bliss, Tobias; FIRST VARIATION: Kent; SECOND VARIATION: Hayden; THIRD VARIATION: Adams; FOURTH VARIATION: Le Clercq; FIFTH VARIATION: Magallanes; SIXTH VARIATION: Wilde; MINUET: 8 women; ANDANTE: 8 principals; FINALE: Entire cast.

NOTE: Balanchine planned to present Caracole [286] for the American Shakespeare Theatre bicentennial Mozart Festival. When he found that neither he nor the dancers could recall the choreography, he created a new work using some of the former steps. It was initially performed under the title Caracole, and titled Divertimento No. 15 from the first New York performance.

REVISIONS: Late 1960s, New York City Ballet: Choreography to new cadenza by John Colman added at end of ANDANTE section; VARIATIONS and ANDANTE reworked with minor changes for different casts.

NEW PRODUCTIONS BY BALANCHINE COMPANIES: New York City Ballet: 1966, new scenery and lighting by David Hays (scenery executed by Nolan Brothers), new costumes by Karinska; from mid-1970s, performed without scenery.

STAGINGS: 1969, Vienna; 1970, Munich; 1971, Cologne, Dutch National, Geneva, Hamburg; 1975, Frankfurt; 1977, Pacific Northwest; 1978, Chicago Lyric Opera, Pennsylvania, Paris, Royal Danish; 1979, San Francisco, Les Grands Ballets Canadiens.

TELEVISION: 1961 (L'Heure du Concert, CBC, Montreal); 1977 (excerpt, Dance in America, PBS).

See 286

1957

315 SQUARE DANCE

MUSIC: By Antonio Vivaldi (Concerto Grosso in B minor, Op. 3, no. 10; Concerto Grosso in E major, Op. 3, no. 12 [first movement]) and Arcangelo Corelli (*Sarabanda, Badinerie e Giga* [second and third movements]).

PRODUCTION: Lighting by Nananne Porcher.

PREMIERE: November 21, 1957, New York City Ballet, City Center of Music and Drama, New York. Leader of on-stage string ensemble: Louis Graeler.

CAST: Patricia Wilde, Nicholas Magallanes, 6 couples. Square dance caller: Elisha C. Keeler.

NOTE: Balanchine adapted patterns from the American folk dance to classic ballet, setting them to seventeenth- and eighteenth-century music, with fiddlers on stage and rhymed directions invented by the square dance caller.

REVISIONS: 1976, New York City Ballet: Staged with musicians (augmented chamber ensemble) in orchestra pit, no longer with caller; new male solo choreographed to first movement of Corelli's *Sarabanda, Badinerie e Giga*, not used in 1957; lighting by Ronald Bates.

STAGINGS (incorporating new male solo after 1976): 1962, Joffrey; 1972, Geneva; 1973, Ballet West; 1980, Eglevsky; 1981, Atlanta, North Carolina, Pacific Northwest, Pennsylvania.

TELEVISION: 1963 (Bell Telephone Hour, NBC).

316 AGON

MUSIC: By Igor Stravinsky (1953-56, commissioned by the New York City Ballet with funds from the Rockefeller Foundation and dedicated to Lincoln Kirstein and George Balanchine).

PRODUCTION: Lighting by Nananne Porcher.

PREMIERE: December 1, 1957, New York City Ballet, City Center of Music and Drama, New York. Conductor: Leon Barzin. (Preview: March of Dimes Benefit, November 27.)

CAST: PART I: PAS DE QUATRE: 4 men; DOUBLE PAS DE QUATRE: 8 women; TRIPLE PAS DE QUATRE: 8 women, 4 men; PART II: FIRST PAS DE TROIS: SARABANDE: Todd Bolender; GAILLIARD: Barbara Milberg, Barbara Walczak; CODA: Milberg, Walczak, Bolender; SECOND PAS DE TROIS: BRANSLE SIMPLE: Roy Tobias, Jonathan Watts; BRANSLE GAY: Melissa Hayden; BRANSLE DOUBLE (DE POITOU): Hayden, Tobias, Watts; PAS DE DEUX: Diana Adams, Arthur Mitchell; PART III: DANSE DES QUATRE DUOS: 4 duos; DANSE DES QUATRE TRIOS: 4 trios; CODA: 4 men.

NOTE: *Agon* is the Greek word for contest; the movements of the ballet are named after French court dances. Although when commissioned the work was intended to complete a triad of ballets (with *Apollo* and *Orpheus*) on Greek themes, Stravinsky and Balanchine have noted that the historical references are pretexts. The composer and the choreographer together designed the structure of the ballet during the creation of the music. The outline for the score specifies in detail, with exact timings, the basic movements for twelve dancers.

REVISIONS: 1970s, New York City Ballet: Final arm sequence in GAILLIARD changed; final pose of ballet (in CODA) changed—four men face toward back of stage (repeating opening pose) rather than each other, following Stravinsky's original schematic manuscript indications in the outline for the score.

STAGINGS: 1967, San Francisco; 1970, Geneva, Hamburg, Stuttgart; 1971, Dance Theatre of Harlem; 1973, Royal; 1974, Dutch National, Paris; 1975, Israel (pas de deux); 1977, Berlin; 1978, Zürich; 1979, Hungary; 1980, New York Dance Theatre (pas de deux); 1982, Reggio Emilia.

TELEVISION: 1960 (CBC, Montreal); 1966 (excerpts, PBS); 1969 (excerpt, NBC).

1958

317 GOUNOD SYMPHONY

MUSIC: By Charles Gounod (Symphony No. 1 in D major, 1855).

PRODUCTION: Scenery by Horace Armistead (from *Lilac Garden* [Tudor], 1951). Costumes by Karinska. Scenery executed by Nolan Brothers. Lighting by Nananne Porcher.

PREMIERE: January 8, 1958, New York City Ballet, City Center of Music and Drama, New York. Conductor: Leon Barzin.

CAST: FIRST MOVEMENT, ALLEGRO MOLTO: Maria Tallchief, Jacques d'Amboise, 20 women, 10 men; SECOND MOVEMENT, ALLEGRETTO: Tallchief, d'Amboise, 8 women; THIRD MOVEMENT, MINUETTO: 6 couples; FOURTH MOVEMENT, ADAGIO AND ALLEGRO VIVACE: Entire cast.

NOTE: French in spirit, the ballet was choreographed soon after Gounod's First Symphony came to public attention following a century of neglect.

STAGINGS: 1959, Paris (retitled *Symphonie*).

318 STARS AND STRIPES
Ballet in Five Campaigns

MUSIC: By John Philip Sousa (as given below), adapted and orchestrated by Hershy Kay.

PRODUCTION: Scenery by David Hays. Costumes by Karinska. Lighting by Nananne Porcher (1958); David Hays (1964).

PREMIERE: January 17, 1958, New York City Ballet, City Center of Music and Drama, New York. Conductor: Leon Barzin.

CAST: FIRST CAMPAIGN, *1st Regiment* ('Corcoran Cadets'): Allegra Kent, 12 women; SECOND CAMPAIGN, *2nd Regiment* ('Thunder and Gladiator'): Robert Barnett, 12 men; THIRD CAMPAIGN, *3rd Regiment* ('Rifle Regiment'): Diana Adams, 12 women; FOURTH CAMPAIGN ('Liberty Bell' and 'El Capitan'): Melissa Hayden, Jacques d'Amboise; FIFTH CAMPAIGN, *All Regiments* ('Stars and Stripes').

Note: A kind of balletic parade based on the themes of Sousa's patriotic marching band music. The campaigns or movements feature each regiment in turn; following a grand pas de deux all combine in the finale as a giant American flag appears. Dedicated to the memory of Fiorello H. La Guardia, Mayor of New York City and founder of the City Center of Music and Drama.

Revisions: New York City Ballet: Order of Second and Third Campaigns reversed shortly after premiere.

Stagings (pas de deux unless otherwise noted): 1967, Garden State; 1969, Boston (complete); 1974, New York Dance Theatre; 1975, Dover; 1976, U. S. Terpsichore, Geneva; 1977, Princeton, Australia; ca. 1978, Eglevsky; 1979, Chicago Lyric Opera, Prince George's; 1981, New Jersey, San Francisco (complete).

Television: 1959 (excerpts, Bell Telephone Hour, NBC); 1963 (pas de deux, NBC); 1964 (excerpts, CBS); n.d. (pas de deux, German television).

319 A MIDSUMMER NIGHT'S DREAM
Play by William Shakespeare
Music: By Marc Blitzstein.

Production: Directed by Jack Landau. Scenery by David Hays. Costumes by Thea Neu. Lighting by Tharon Musser.

Premiere: June 20, 1958, American Shakespeare Festival, Stratford, Connecticut. Danced by members of the Festival company. Singer: Russell Oberlin.

Cast: *Titania*, June Havoc; *Oberon*, Richard Waring; *Puck*, Richard Easton; *Bottom*, Hiram Sherman; *Theseus*, Jack Bittner; and others.

Note: Balanchine choreographed dance passages for the fairies.

Stagings: American Shakespeare Festival, 1959, 1960 (Boston).

320 THE WINTER'S TALE
Play by William Shakespeare
Music: By Marc Blitzstein.

Production: Directed by John Houseman and Jack Landau. Scenery by David Hays. Costumes by Dorothy Jeakins. Lighting by Jean Rosenthal.

PREMIERE: July 20, 1958, American Shakespeare Festival, Stratford, Connecticut. Danced by members of the Festival company. Singer: Russell Oberlin.

CAST: *Polixenes*, Richard Waring; *Leontes*, John Colicos; *Hermione*, Nancy Wickwire; *Autolycus*, Earle Hyman; *Florizel*, Richard Easton; *Perdita*, Inga Swenson; and others.

NOTE: Balanchine choreographed dances in the pastoral scene, Act IV, Scene 3.

321 WALTZ-SCHERZO

MUSIC: By Peter Ilyitch Tschaikovsky (Waltz-Scherzo for violin and orchestra, Op. 34, 1877).

PRODUCTION: Costumes by Karinska. Lighting by Nananne Porcher.

PREMIERE: September 9, 1958, New York City Ballet, City Center of Music and Drama, New York. Conductor: Robert Irving. Violinist: Louis Graeler.

CAST: Patricia Wilde, André Eglevsky.

REVISIONS: 1964, New York City Ballet: Minor changes, including addition of some lifts.

322 THE SEVEN DEADLY SINS
Sloth, Pride, Anger, Gluttony, Lust, Avarice, Envy

MUSIC: By Kurt Weill (*Die sieben Todsünden*, produced 1933, commissioned by Boris Kochno and Edward James). Text by Bertolt Brecht, from a suggestion by Boris Kochno and Edward James, translated by W. H. Auden and Chester Kallman (translation commissioned by Lincoln Kirstein).

PRODUCTION: Scenery, costumes and lighting by Rouben Ter-Arutunian. Scenery executed by T. B. McDonald Construction Company.

PREMIERE: December 4, 1958, New York City Ballet, City Center of Music and Drama, New York. Conductor: Robert Irving.

CAST: *Anna I* (singer), Lotte Lenya; *Anna II* (dancer), Allegra Kent; *Characters* (dancers), 16 women, 15 men. *Family* (singers): *Mother*,

Stanley Carlson; *Father*, Gene Hollman; *Brother I*, Frank Poretta; *Brother II*, Grant Williams. Singers and dancers appeared together on stage.

NOTE: First presented by Les Ballets 1933, Paris. This revival for the New York City Ballet was sponsored by Ballet Society to celebrate the twenty-fifth year of association between Lincoln Kirstein and George Balanchine; Lotte Lenya played the role created for her in 1933. The staging, noted for its masque-like characteristics, consisted primarily of stylized movement rather than balletic dancing.

STAGINGS: 1964, San Francisco (based on Balanchine's 1958 version with new choreography by Lew Christensen).

OTHER VERSIONS: 1933, Les Ballets 1933 (*Les Sept Péchés Capitaux*).

*See 136**

1959

323 NATIVE DANCERS

MUSIC: By Vittorio Rieti (Symphony No. 5, 1945).

PRODUCTION: Scenery and lighting by David Hays. Women's costumes by Peter Larkin. Jockey silks by H. Kauffman & Sons Saddlery Company.

PREMIERE: January 14, 1959, New York City Ballet, City Center of Music and Drama, New York. Conductor: Robert Irving.

CAST: Patricia Wilde, Jacques d'Amboise; 6 women, 6 men.
ALLEGRO GIOCOSO; ANDANTE TRANQUILLO; PRESTO.

NOTE: Named after the famous race horse. The ladies are horses, with ponytails and jingling harnesses, put through their paces by men as jockeys.

324 EPISODES

Music: By Anton Webern (complete orchestral works, as given below).

Choreography: By Martha Graham (Part I) and George Balanchine (Part II).

Production: Scenery and lighting by David Hays. Costumes for Part I by Karinska. Scenery executed by Chester Rakeman Studios, S. C. Hansen and Decorator Plant Company; later by Nolan Brothers.

Premiere: May 14, 1959, New York City Ballet, City Center of Music and Drama, New York. Conductor: Robert Irving.

Cast: Part I. (*Passacaglia*, Op. 1, 1906, and *Six Pieces*, Op. 6, 1910): *Mary, Queen of Scots*, Martha Graham; *Bothwell*, Bertram Ross; *Elizabeth, Queen of England*, Sallie Wilson (of the New York City Ballet); *The Four Marys*, 4 women; *Darnley, Riccio, Chastelard*, 3 men; *Executioner*; 2 *Heralds*.

Part II. SYMPHONY (Op. 21, 1928): Violette Verdy, Jonathan Watts, 3 couples; FIVE PIECES (Op. 10, 1911-13): Diana Adams, Jacques d'Amboise; CONCERTO (Op. 24, 1934): Allegra Kent, Nicholas Magallanes, 4 women; VARIATIONS (Op. 30, 1940): Paul Taylor (of the Martha Graham Dance Company); RICERCATA (in 6 voices from Bach's *Musical Offering*, 1935): Melissa Hayden, Francisco Moncion, 14 women.

Note: A Ballet Society production. Conceived by Balanchine as an homage to the atonal composer Webern, *Episodes* is set to his complete orchestral works. Martha Graham by invitation choreographed Part I (a narrative, in period costume) for her company; Balanchine choreographed Part II (plotless, danced in practice clothes) for the New York City Ballet. The VARIATIONS FOR ORCHESTRA consists of a theme and six variations for a single male dancer, choreographed for Paul Taylor, then a member of the Graham Company. The final part, the RICERCATA, is a tribute by Webern to the music of Johann Sebastian Bach. The full ballet was performed by both companies for two seasons. In 1960, the New York City Ballet presented its part alone as *Episodes II*; from 1961 this was performed as *Episodes*, without the solo created for Paul Taylor.

Stagings (Part II): 1969, Berlin; 1971, Geneva; 1973, Dutch National; 1978, Chicago Lyric Opera (FIVE PIECES).

TELEVISION: 1963 (CONCERTO, NBC); 1970 (FIVE PIECES, CBC, Montreal); 1978 (BBC, London).

325 ROMEO AND JULIET
Play by William Shakespeare

MUSIC: By David Amram.

PRODUCTION: Directed by Jack Landau. Scenery by David Hays. Costumes by Dorothy Jeakins. Lighting by Tharon Musser.

PREMIERE: June 12, 1959, American Shakespeare Festival, Stratford, Connecticut. Danced by members of the Festival company.

CAST: *Romeo*, Richard Easton; *Juliet*, Inga Swenson; *Mercutio*, William Smithers; *Tybalt*, Jack Bittner; *Capulet*, Morris Carnovsky; *Lady Capulet*, Nancy Wickwire; *Nurse*, Aline MacMahon; *Friar Laurence*, Hiram Sherman; and others.

NOTE: Balanchine choreographed dances for the Capulet ball, Act I, Scene 5.

See 278

326 THE MERRY WIVES OF WINDSOR
Play by William Shakespeare

MUSIC: By Irwin Bazelon.

PRODUCTION: Directed by John Houseman and Jack Landau. Scenery by Will Steven Armstrong. Costumes by Motley. Lighting by Tharon Musser.

PREMIERE: July 2, 1959, American Shakespeare Festival, Stratford, Connecticut. Danced by members of the Festival company.

CAST: *Falstaff*, Larry Gates; *Mistress Page*, Nancy Marchand; *Mistress Ford*, Nancy Wickwire; *Mistress Quickly*, Sada Thompson; *Fenton*, Lowell Harris; *Anne Page*, Barbara Barrie; and others.

NOTE: Balanchine choreographed the fairies' dances in Windsor Park, Act V, Scene 5.

327 THE WARRIOR

MUSIC: By Sergei Rachmaninoff (Prelude in G minor, Op. 33, no. 5, 1911).

CHOREOGRAPHY: Originally choreographed by Léonide Massine (1945); rechoreographed by George Balanchine.

CAST: André Eglevsky.

NOTE: André Eglevsky recalled dancing this solo once in Miami during the 1950s.

1960

328 NIGHT SHADOW (from 1960 called LA SONNAMBULA)

MUSIC: Music and book by Vittorio Rieti, based on themes from operas by Vincenzo Bellini (1830-35, including *La Sonnambula*, *I Puritani*, *Norma*, and *I Capuletti ed i Montecchi*).

CHOREOGRAPHY: By George Balanchine. Staged by John Taras.

PRODUCTION: Scenery and lighting by Esteban Francés. Costumes by André Levasseur (from the Grand Ballet du Marquis de Cuevas production, 1948). Scenery and costumes executed by Nolan Brothers. Jewelry by Emmons.

PREMIERE: January 6, 1960, New York City Ballet, City Center of Music and Drama, New York. Conductor: Robert Irving.

CAST: *The Coquette*, Jillana; *The Baron*, John Taras; *The Poet*, Erik Bruhn; *The Sleepwalker*, Allegra Kent; *The Guests*, 8 couples; DIVERTISSEMENTS: PASTORALE: 2 couples; THE BLACKAMOORS: Suki Schorer, William Weslow; HARLEQUIN: Edward Villella; ACROBATS: 3 women.

NOTE: Originally presented as *The Night Shadow* by the Ballet Russe de Monte Carlo, New York, 1946.

*See 232**

329 PANAMERICA: NUMBERS II, IV, VIII

MUSIC: By Latin American composers (as given below), edited by Carlos Chávez.

CHOREOGRAPHY: By George Balanchine (three of eight dances), Gloria Contreras, Francisco Moncion, John Taras, and Jacques d'Amboise.

PRODUCTION: Scenery and lighting by David Hays. Costumes for Numbers II and VIII by Esteban Francés, executed by Brooks Costume Company; costumes for Number IV by Karinska.

PREMIERE: January 20, 1960, New York City Ballet, City Center of Music and Drama, New York. Conductor: Robert Irving. Guest Conductor for SINFONÍA NO. 5: Carlos Chávez.

CAST: II. PRELUDIOS PARA PERCUSIÓN (COLOMBIA), composed by Luis Escobar: Patricia Wilde, Erik Bruhn; IV. SINFONÍA NO. 5, FOR STRING ORCHESTRA (MEXICO), composed by Carlos Chávez: Diana Adams, Nicholas Magallanes, 6 couples; VIII. DANZAS SINFÓNICAS (CUBA), composed by Julián Orbón: Maria Tallchief, Conrad Ludlow, Arthur Mitchell, Edward Villella, 20 women, 10 men.

NOTE: A Ballet Society production. This salute to Pan America took the form of an evening-long collection of eight short ballets. During the following season (spring 1960), Number II, retitled *Colombia*, and Number VIII, retitled *Cuba*, were performed as independent works.

330 THEME AND VARIATIONS

MUSIC: By Peter Ilyitch Tschaikovsky (final movement of Suite No. 3 for orchestra in G major, 1884).

PRODUCTION: Costumes by Karinska (from *Symphony in C* [244]). Lighting by David Hays.

PREMIERE: February 5, 1960, New York City Ballet, City Center of Music and Drama, New York. Conductor: Robert Irving.

CAST: Violette Verdy, Edward Villella; Susan Borree, Judith Green, Francia Russell, Carol Sumner, Conrad Ludlow, Richard Rapp, Roy Tobias, William Weslow; 8 women, 8 men.

NOTE: Originally presented by Ballet Theatre, New York, 1947.

See 242*, 369

331 PAS DE DEUX
(also called TSCHAIKOVSKY PAS DE DEUX)

MUSIC: By Peter Ilyitch Tschaikovsky (*Swan Lake*, Op. 20, 1875-76; pas de deux originally intended for Act III, subsequently lost from 1877 until 1953).

PRODUCTION: Costumes by Karinska. Lighting by Jack Owen Brown; subsequently by David Hays.

PREMIERE: March 29, 1960, New York City Ballet, City Center of Music and Drama, New York. Conductor: Robert Irving.

CAST: Violette Verdy, Conrad Ludlow.

NOTE: A display piece for two leading dancers, choreographed to lost music intended for the third act of *Swan Lake*, rediscovered in 1953 in the Bolshoi archives. A fifty-second excerpt from this pas de deux appears in the film *The Turning Point* (Twentieth-Century Fox, 1977).

REVISIONS: Male variation and coda differ from performer to performer.

STAGINGS: 1962, Les Grands Ballets Canadiens; 1963, Royal Danish; 1964, Royal; 1969, Boston; 1970, American Ballet Theatre, Houston; 1971, Ballet West; 1972, San Francisco, London Festival; 1973, Los Angeles, Geneva; 1976, Joffrey, Caracas; ca. 1976, Eglevsky; 1977, Dance Theatre of Harlem, U. S. Terpsichore, Washington; 1978, Arizona, North Carolina; 1980, Connecticut, New Jersey, New York Dance Theatre, Alberta, Belgrade, La Scala, Matsuyama, Paris; 1981, Baltimore; 1982, Ballet Metropolitan, Kansas City.

TELEVISION: 1962 (Voice of Firestone, ABC); 1962 (BBC, London); 1964 (Bell Telephone Hour, NBC); 1965 (CBS); 1965 (CBC, Montreal); 1966 (PBS); 1968 (excerpts, Bell Telephone Hour, NBC); 1969 (WTTW, Chicago); 1970 (CBC, Montreal); 1979 (Dance in America, PBS).

See 75, 191, 262, 285, 367

332 THE FIGURE IN THE CARPET
Ballet in Five Scenes

MUSIC: By George Frederick Handel (from the *Royal Fireworks Music*, 1749, and *Water Music*, ca. 1717). Book by George Lewis; underlying

ideas in the organization of the sequence of scenes suggested by
Dr. Arthur Upham Pope.

PRODUCTION: Scenery, costumes and lighting by Esteban Francés.
Scenery executed by Nolan Brothers; costumes executed by Karinska.

PREMIERE: April 13, 1960, New York City Ballet, City Center of Music
and Drama, New York. Conductor: Robert Irving.

CAST: SCENE I, THE SANDS OF THE DESERT: Violette Verdy, 18 women;
SCENE II, THE WEAVING OF THE CARPET (PAS D'ACTION): Verdy, 12 women;
Nomad Tribesmen, Conrad Ludlow, 6 men; SCENE III, THE BUILDING OF THE
PALACE: ENTRANCE OF THE IRANIAN COURT: *Prince and Princess of Persia*,
Jacques d'Amboise, Melissa Hayden; *Their Courtiers*, 8 couples; THE
RECEPTION OF THE FOREIGN AMBASSADORS: *France: The Prince and Princesses
of Lorraine*, Edward Villella, Susan Borree, Suki Schorer; *Spain: The
Duke and Duchess of Granada*, Francisco Moncion, Judith Green;
America: The Princess of the West Indies, Francia Russell, 6 women; *China:
The Duke and Duchess of L'an L'ing*, Nicholas Magallanes, Patricia
McBride, 4 women; *Africa: The Oni of Ife and His Consort*, Arthur
Mitchell, Mary Hinkson (guest artist); *Scotland: The Four Lairds of the
Isles and Their Lady*, Diana Adams, 4 men; GRAND PAS DE DEUX: Hayden,
d'Amboise; SCENE IV, FINALE: THE GARDENS OF PARADISE; SCENE V,
APOTHEOSIS: THE FOUNTAINS OF HEAVEN.

NOTE: Devised in the style of an eighteenth-century court ballet, based
on Dr. Pope's relation of Handel's musical counterpoint to Persian
carpet weaving of the period. The title is from a tale by Henry James.
SCENE I evokes a desert atmosphere; in the APOTHEOSIS a large
fountain plays on stage; the décor and costumes for SCENES III, IV and V
were derived from Persian designs. Presented in honor of the
Fourth International Congress of Iranian Art and Archeology. In 1976,
Balanchine used the Scottish theme from the *Water Music* for the
Royal Canadian Air Force variation in *Union Jack* [401].

333 VARIATIONS FROM DON SEBASTIAN
(from 1961 called DONIZETTI VARIATIONS)

MUSIC: By Gaetano Donizetti (from *Dom Sébastien*, produced 1843).
PRODUCTION: Scenery and lighting by David Hays. Women's costumes
by Karinska; men's by Esteban Francés (from *Panamerica* [329]).

PREMIERE: November 16, 1960, New York City Ballet, City Center of Music and Drama, New York. Conductor: Robert Irving.

CAST: Melissa Hayden, Jonathan Watts, 6 women, 3 men.

NOTE: The premiere was part of a special *Salute to Italy*, which also included the premiere of *Monumentum pro Gesualdo*, and performances of *La Sonnambula* [232] and Lew Christensen's *Con Amore*.

REVISIONS: 1971, New York City Ballet: Some new choreography for principals.

NEW PRODUCTIONS BY BALANCHINE COMPANIES: 1971, New York City Ballet: Costumes by Karinska; lighting by Ronald Bates.

STAGINGS (usually titled *Donizetti Variations*): 1964, Boston, Pennsylvania; 1966, Joffrey; 1967, Hamburg; 1968, Royal Danish; 1972, Geneva; 1976, Dutch National; 1977, Maryland; 1978, Eglevsky; 1979, Chicago Lyric Opera; 1981, Connecticut, Louisville, New Jersey, Reggio Emilia.

TELEVISION: 1961 (excerpts, Omnibus, NBC).

334 MONUMENTUM PRO GESUALDO

MUSIC: By Igor Stravinsky (three madrigals by Gesualdo, recomposed for instruments, 1960).

PRODUCTION: Scenery and lighting by David Hays (1960); lighting by Ronald Bates (1974).

PREMIERE: November 16, 1960, New York City Ballet, City Center of Music and Drama, New York. Conductor: Robert Irving.

CAST: Diana Adams, Conrad Ludlow, 6 couples.

NOTE: Stravinsky made orchestral versions of Gesualdo's madrigals to honor the four-hundredth anniversary of the composer's birth. The ballet is in three parts, each lasting just over two minutes. Occasionally since 1965, and consistently since 1966, performed with *Movements for Piano and Orchestra* [344].

335 LIEBESLIEDER WALZER
Ballet in Two Parts

MUSIC: By Johannes Brahms (*Liebeslieder*, Op. 52, 1869, and *Neue Liebeslieder*, Op. 65, 1874, waltzes for piano duet and vocal quartet, all set to poems by Friedrich Daumer, except the last, by Goethe).

PRODUCTION: Scenery and lighting by David Hays. Costumes by Karinska.

PREMIERE: November 22, 1960, New York City Ballet, City Center of Music and Drama, New York. Pianists: Louise Sherman, Robert Irving. Singers: Angeline Rasmussen, Mitzi Wilson, Frank Poretta, Herbert Beattie.

CAST: Diana Adams, Bill Carter; Melissa Hayden, Jonathan Watts; Jillana, Conrad Ludlow; Violette Verdy, Nicholas Magallanes.

NOTE: Dancers and musicians in period costumes are on stage together. During the first set of eighteen waltzes the four couples, wearing formal evening dress and dancing slippers, dance in interweaving combinations in an intimate ballroom. After a brief lowering of the curtain they dance fourteen waltzes under a starry sky, the women wearing ballet dresses and toe shoes. They leave the stage; returning in the original costumes, they pause to listen to the final waltz. Within the strict three-quarter beat of music and dance, personal and romantic associations between the couples are implied.

STAGINGS: 1977, Vienna; 1979, Royal; 1981, Zürich.

TELEVISION: 1961 (L'Heure du Concert, CBC, Montreal).

336 RAGTIME (I)

MUSIC: By Igor Stravinsky (*Ragtime for Eleven Instruments*, 1918).

PRODUCTION: Scenery by Robert Drew (from *Blackface* [L. Christensen], 1947). Costumes by Karinska. Lighting by David Hays.

PREMIERE: December 7, 1960, New York City Ballet, City Center of Music and Drama, New York. Conductor: Robert Irving.

CAST: Diana Adams, Bill Carter.

NOTE: The choreography is jazz-inspired, in a cabaret style. One of a quartet of works by Balanchine, Todd Bolender, Francisco Moncion, and John Taras, collectively titled *Jazz Concert*. Balanchine first used this music for a dance in 1922; in 1966, he choreographed another work to this score, titled *Ragtime (II)*.

See 3, 356

1961

337 MODERN JAZZ: VARIANTS

MUSIC: By Gunther Schuller (*Variants* for orchestra and the Modern Jazz Quartet, 1960, commissioned by the New York City Ballet).

PRODUCTION: Lighting by David Hays.

PREMIERE: January 4, 1961, New York City Ballet, City Center of Music and Drama, New York. Conductor: Gunther Schuller. Modern Jazz Quartet: John Lewis (piano), Percy Heath (bass), Milt Jackson (vibraharp), Connie Kay (drums).

CAST: INTRODUCTION (orchestra): Diana Adams, Melissa Hayden, John Jones (guest artist), Arthur Mitchell, 6 women, 6 men; VARIANT 1 (piano): Adams, Jones; VARIANT 2 (bass): Adams, 6 men; VARIANT 3 (vibraharp): Hayden, Mitchell; VARIANT 4 (drums): Hayden; VARIANT 5 (quartet): Adams, Hayden, Jones, Mitchell; FINALE: Entire cast.

NOTE: The Modern Jazz Quartet played on stage, accompanied by a twelve-tone score performed by the orchestra. The choreography combines ballet with jazz action.

338 ELECTRONICS

MUSIC: Electronic tape by Remi Gassmann in collaboration with Oskar Sala (commissioned by Philip Johnson).

PRODUCTION: Scenery and lighting by David Hays. Scenery executed by Nolan Brothers. Fabrics by Dazian's.

PREMIERE: March 22, 1961, New York City Ballet, City Center of Music and Drama, New York.

CAST: Diana Adams, Violette Verdy, Jacques d'Amboise, Edward Villella, 8 women.

NOTE: The score is composed of sound material itself electronically created, not derived or adapted from conventional sound sources. The stage action takes place in an atmosphere of science fiction, the setting cellophane, the costumes white, silver, gold, black.

339 VALSES ET VARIATIONS
(from 1963 called RAYMONDA VARIATIONS)

MUSIC: By Alexander Glazounov (from *Raymonda*, Op. 57, produced 1898).

PRODUCTION: Scenery by Horace Armistead (from *Lilac Garden* [Tudor], 1951). Costumes by Karinska. Lighting by David Hays.

PREMIERE: December 7, 1961, New York City Ballet, City Center of Music and Drama, New York. Conductor: Robert Irving.

CAST: VALSE: Patricia Wilde, 12 women; PAS DE DEUX: Wilde, Jacques d'Amboise; VARIATION I: Victoria Simon; VARIATION II: Suki Schorer; VARIATION III: d'Amboise; VARIATION IV: Wilde; VARIATION V: Gloria Govrin; VARIATION VI: Carol Sumner; VARIATION VII: Patricia Neary; VARIATION VIII: d'Amboise; VARIATION IX: Wilde; CODA AND FINALE: Wilde, d'Amboise, ensemble.

NOTE: To selections from the score of *Raymonda*, Balanchine developed in his twentieth-century terms the heritage of the three-act Petipa original of 1898.

STAGINGS (distinct from the numerous stagings of excerpts from Act III of *Raymonda* [233] and *Pas de Dix* [309], also often performed under the title *Raymonda Variations*): 1966, Eglevsky; 1967, Atlanta; 1969, Geneva; 1971, Houston (titled *Waltz and Variations*), Pennsylvania; 1973, Los Angeles; 1976, Chicago Lyric Opera; 1982, Alabama.

See 18, 233*, 309, 384

1962

340 A MIDSUMMER NIGHT'S DREAM
Ballet in Two Acts and Six Scenes

MUSIC: By Felix Mendelssohn (Overture and incidental music to *Ein Sommernachtstraum*, Opp. 21 and 61, 1826, 1842; Overture to *Athalie*, Op. 74, 1845; Concert overture *Die schöne Melusine*, Op. 32, 1833; *Die erste Walpurgisnacht*, Op. 60; Symphony No. 9 for strings [first three of four movements], 1823; Overture to *Die Heimkehr aus der Fremde*, Op. 89, 1829).

PRODUCTION: Scenery and lighting by David Hays, assisted by Peter Harvey. Costumes by Karinska.

PREMIERE: January 17, 1962, New York City Ballet with children from the School of American Ballet, City Center of Music and Drama, New York. Conductor: Robert Irving. Singers: Veronica Tyler (soprano), Marija Kova (mezzo-soprano), 4 women.

CAST: ACT I: *Butterflies*, Suki Schorer, 4 women, 8 children; *Puck*, Arthur Mitchell; *Helena, in love with Demetrius*, Jillana; *Oberon, King of the Fairies*, Edward Villella; *Oberon's Pages*; *Titania, Queen of the Fairies*, Melissa Hayden; *Titania's Cavalier*, Conrad Ludlow; *Titania's Page*; *Bottom, a Weaver*, Roland Vazquez; *Bottom's Companions*, 4 men; *Theseus, Duke of Athens*, Francisco Moncion; *Courtiers to Theseus*; *Hermia, in love with Lysander*, Patricia McBride; *Lysander, beloved of Hermia*, Nicholas Magallanes; *Demetrius, Suitor to Hermia*, Bill Carter; *Titania's Retinue*, 12 women; *Oberon's Kingdom: Butterflies and Fairies*, 13 children; *Hippolyta, Queen of the Amazons*, Gloria Govrin; *Hippolyta's Hounds*, 6 women; ACT II: *Courtiers*, 18 women, 8 men; DIVERTISSEMENT: Violette Verdy, Ludlow, 6 couples.

NOTE: Balanchine's first wholly original full-length ballet. Act I relates the story of Shakespeare's play. Act II is a wedding divertissement, concluding with a brief return to the enchanted forest, and Shakespeare's ending. A film of the entire work, produced by Oberon Productions, Ltd., was released in 1967.

REVISIONS: New York City Ballet: Act II, third movement of Symphony

No. 9 deleted almost immediately; 1964, Act II, new choreography for courtiers, divertissement shortened (to first two movements of Symphony No. 9, omitting second movement fugue); 1978, Act I, new choreography for Hippolyta's Hounds.

NEW PRODUCTIONS BY BALANCHINE COMPANIES: New York City Ballet: 1964, scenery and costumes redesigned by David Hays and Karinska for the New York State Theater, with color scheme in Act II changed from white and gold to red; 1980, scenery adapted by David Hays to facilitate use in repertory, lighting by Ronald Bates.

STAGINGS: 1979, Zürich.

TELEVISION: n.d. (pas de deux from DIVERTISSEMENT, German television).

341 EUGEN ONEGIN
Opera in Three Acts and Six Scenes

MUSIC: By Peter Ilyitch Tschaikovsky (*Eugen Onegin*, produced 1879). Libretto based on a poem by Alexander Pushkin. German text by A. Bernhard and M. Kalbeck.

PRODUCTION: Directed and choreographed by George Balanchine. Scenery and costumes designed by H. M. Crayon.

PREMIERE: February 27, 1962, Hamburgische Staatsoper, Hamburg. Danced by Ballett der Hamburgischen Staatsoper. Conductor: Horst Stein.

CAST: *Larina*, Maria v. Ilosvay; *Tatiana*, Melitta Muszely; *Olga*, Cvetka Ahlin; *Filipevna*, Ursula Boese; *Eugen Onegin*, Vladimir Ruzdak; *Lensky*, Heinz Hoppe; *Count Gremin*, Arnold van Mill; and others.

NOTE: Printed programs list no dances or dancers; the choreography included the ball scenes in Acts II and III.

STAGINGS: 1971, Opéra du Grand Théâtre de Genève.

See 256

342 NOAH AND THE FLOOD
Made for Television

MUSIC: Dance-drama by Igor Stravinsky (*The Flood*, 1962). Text chosen and arranged by Robert Craft from *Genesis*, the *Te Deum* and *Sanctus* hymns, the fifteenth-century York and Chester miracle plays, and for Satan's final *Arietta* from several sources including Shakespeare and Dylan Thomas. Prologue written by Jack Richardson.

PRODUCTION: Produced by Sextant, Inc. Directed by Kirk Browning. Production Designer: Rouben Ter-Arutunian.

FIRST TELECAST: June 14, 1962, CBS. Danced by New York City Ballet. Columbia Symphony Orchestra and Chorus. Conductors: Igor Stravinsky and Robert Craft. Chorus Director: Gregg Smith.

CAST: VOICES: *Narrator*, Laurence Harvey; *Noah*, Sebastian Cabot; *Mrs. Noah*, Elsa Lanchester; *Caller*, Paul Tripp; *The Voice of God*, John Reardon and Robert Oliver; *Satan*, Robert Robinson. DANCERS: *Adam* and *Lucifer*, Jacques d'Amboise; *Eve*, Jillana; *Satan*, Edward Villella; *Noah*, Ramon Segarra; *Mrs. Noah*, Joysanne Sidimus; 8 women, 8 men.

NOTE: Conceived and written for television. Balanchine worked closely with the composer during the composition and production. The work is divided into six parts. Four sections are sung: *Prelude* (including the Creation, the Expulsion from the Garden, and God's Command to Noah), *The Catalogue of the Animals*, *The Comedy* (Noah and his wife and sons), and *The Covenant of the Rainbow*; two sections are choreographed: *The Building of the Ark* and *The Flood*. Balanchine did not choreograph a subsequent stage performance until the 1982 New York City Ballet production for the Stravinsky Centennial Celebration.

See 422

1963

343 BUGAKU

MUSIC: By Toshiro Mayuzumi (1962, commissioned by the New York City Ballet).

PRODUCTION: Scenery and lighting by David Hays. Costumes by Karinska. Scenery executed by Nolan Brothers.

PREMIERE: March 20, 1963, New York City Ballet, City Center of Music and Drama, New York. Conductor: Robert Irving.

CAST: Allegra Kent, Edward Villella, 4 couples.

NOTE: Following the appearance of the Imperial Gagaku company of musicians and dancers from Japan on programs of the New York City Ballet in 1959, Mayuzumi was invited to compose a piece in the spirit of Japanese court music (Bugaku), but with Western instrumentation. The ballet, in three movements, suggests ceremonial rites of courtship and marriage.

STAGINGS: 1975, Dance Theatre of Harlem; 1980, Zürich.

TELEVISION: 1977 (pas de deux, Dance in America, PBS); 1978 (CBC, Montreal).

344 MOVEMENTS FOR PIANO AND ORCHESTRA

MUSIC: By Igor Stravinsky (1958-59, dedicated to Margrit Weber).

PRODUCTION: Lighting by Peter Harvey.

PREMIERE: April 9, 1963, New York City Ballet, City Center of Music and Drama, New York. Conductor: Robert Irving. Pianist: Gordon Boelzner.

CAST: Suzanne Farrell, Jacques d'Amboise, 6 women.

NOTE: The music uses serial combinations and is divided into five concise parts. Stravinsky described the ballet as a double concerto for male and female solo dancers, both identified with the piano solo, accompanied by a corps de ballet. Occasionally since 1965, and consistently since 1966, performed with *Monumentum pro Gesualdo* [334].

TELEVISION: 1963 (CBS); 1971 (CBC, Montreal).

345 ORPHEUS UND EURYDIKE (ORFEO ED EURIDICE)
Opera in Three Acts and Five Scenes

MUSIC: By Christoph Willibald Gluck (*Orfeo ed Euridice*, produced 1762, with ballet music from the Paris production of 1774). Libretto by Raniero da Calzabigi, translated by Hans Swarowsky.

PRODUCTION: Directed and choreographed by George Balanchine. Scenery and costumes designed by Rouben Ter-Arutunian.

PREMIERE: November 16, 1963, Hamburgische Staatsoper, Hamburg. Danced by Ballett der Hamburgischen Staatsoper. Conductor: Janos Kulka.

CAST: SINGERS: *Orpheus*, Ursula Boese; *Eurydike*, Doris Jung; *Amor*, Ria Urban; and others. DANCERS: SCENE 1: *Shepherds and Shepherdesses*, 7 women, 4 men. SCENE 2: *Furies*, 12 women, 12 men. SCENE 3: *Night*, Angèle Albrecht; *8 Spirits* (women), *4 Shadows* (women). SCENE 5: CHACONNE: Christa Kempf, Heinz Clauss; Albrecht; Erika Czarnecki, Falco Kapuste; Wilfried Schumann; 9 women, 6 men; PAS DE TROIS: Uta Graf, Heidi Korf, Helmut Baumann; CUPID AND CHERUBS (PAS DE CINQ): Henni Vanhaiden, 4 women; PAS DE DEUX: Dulce Anaya, Rainer Kochermann; Marilyn Burr, Peter van Dyk.

NOTE: The CHACONNE of this production, directed and choreographed by Balanchine at the invitation of Rolf Liebermann, formed the basis for the ballet *Chaconne* [400], first performed by the New York City Ballet in 1976.

REVISIONS: 1973, Théâtre National de l'Opéra, Paris: Choreography from Hamburg, 1963, performed in a new production of the opera (not directed by Balanchine); changes included some new choreography in principal (second) pas de deux, pas de cinq, and ensemble passages.

STAGINGS (ballet sequences only): 1965, Hamburg; 1974, Geneva.

OTHER VERSIONS: 1936, Metropolitan Opera (danced by American Ballet, as American Ballet Ensemble).

See 170*, 399, 400

346 MEDITATION

MUSIC: By Peter Ilyitch Tschaikovsky (*Meditation*, Op. 42, no. 1, from *Souvenir d'un Lieu Cher*, three pieces for piano and violin, 1878, orchestrated by Alexander Glazounov).

PRODUCTION: Costumes by Karinska.

PREMIERE: December 10, 1963, New York City Ballet, City Center of Music and Drama, New York. Conductor: Robert Irving. Violinist: Marilyn Wright.

CAST: Suzanne Farrell, Jacques d'Amboise.

NOTE: On the darkened stage a solitary, troubled young man enters and kneels. He is approached by a young woman who seeks to comfort him. They dance together and embrace; in the end she departs, and he is again alone.

STAGINGS: 1973, Ballet du XXe Siècle.

TELEVISION: 1966 (PBS).

1964

347 TARANTELLA

MUSIC: By Louis Moreau Gottschalk (*Grande Tarantelle*, ca. 1866, reconstructed and orchestrated by Hershy Kay).

PRODUCTION: Costumes by Karinska.

PREMIERE: January 7, 1964, New York City Ballet, City Center of Music and Drama, New York. Conductor: Robert Irving. Pianist: Jean-Pierre Marty.

CAST: Patricia McBride, Edward Villella.

STAGINGS: 1973, Los Angeles, Geneva; 1974, Boston; 1975, Dayton; 1977, Arizona, Garden State, Joffrey; 1978, North Carolina, Zürich; 1979, Eglevsky; 1980, Royal.

TELEVISION: 1966 (PBS); 1968 (excerpts, Bell Telephone Hour, NBC); 1971 (CBC, Montreal); 1979 (WETA, Washington, D.C.).

348 CLARINADE

MUSIC: By Morton Gould (*Derivations for Clarinet and Jazz Band*, 1954-55, composed for Benny Goodman).

PRODUCTION: Costumes (practice clothes) assembled by Karinska in consultation with George Balanchine (uncredited).

PREMIERE: April 29, 1964, New York City Ballet, New York State Theater. Conductor: Robert Irving. Clarinetist: Benny Goodman.

CAST: WARM-UP: Gloria Govrin, Arthur Mitchell, 5 couples; CONTRA-PUNTAL BLUES: Suzanne Farrell, Anthony Blum, 2 couples; RAG: Govrin, 4 women; RIDE-OUT: Entire cast.

NOTE: The first work choreographed by Balanchine for the New York City Ballet after the move from City Center of Music and Drama to establish residency at the New York State Theater, Lincoln Center.

349 BALLET IMPERIAL (from 1973 called TSCHAIKOVSKY PIANO CONCERTO NO. 2)

MUSIC: By Peter Ilyitch Tschaikovsky (Piano Concerto No. 2 in G major, Op. 44, 1879, abridged, rewritten and rearranged by Alexander Siloti).

CHOREOGRAPHY: By George Balanchine. Staged by Frederic Franklin.

PRODUCTION: Scenery by Rouben Ter-Arutunian (based on the 1941 production). Costumes by Karinska.

PREMIERE: October 15, 1964, New York City Ballet, New York State Theater. Conductor: Robert Irving. Pianist: Gordon Boelzner.

CAST: Suzanne Farrell, Jacques d'Amboise; Patricia Neary; Frank Ohman, Earle Sieveling; 2 female demi-soloists; 16 women, 6 men.
   ALLEGRO BRILLANTE–ANDANTE; ANDANTE NON TROPPO; ALLEGRO
   CON FUOCO.

NOTE: Originally presented by American Ballet Caravan, Rio de Janeiro, 1941. This production used the original choreography with minor revisions and an augmented corps de ballet.

See 194*, 382

1965

350 PAS DE DEUX AND DIVERTISSEMENT

MUSIC: By Léo Delibes (excerpts from La Source [Naïla], 1866, and Sylvia, ou la Nymphe de Diane, 1876).

PRODUCTION: Costumes by Karinska. Lighting by David Hays.

PREMIERE: January 14, 1965, New York City Ballet, New York State Theater. Conductor: Robert Irving.

CAST: VALSE LENTE AND PAS DE DEUX: Melissa Hayden, André Prokovsky; ALLEGRO VIVACE: Suki Schorer, 8 women; VARIATION: Prokovsky; PIZZICATI: Hayden; VALSE DES FLEURS: Entire cast.

NOTE: VALSE LENTE AND PAS DE DEUX was originally choreographed for the New York City Ballet in 1950, titled *Sylvia: Pas de Deux* [273]. In 1969, the ALLEGRO VIVACE and VALSE DES FLEURS were incorporated in *La Source* [364], choreographed for the New York City Ballet.

See 36, 273*, 274, 364, 387

351 HARLEQUINADE

Ballet in Two Acts

MUSIC: By Riccardo Drigo (from *Les Millions d'Arlequin*, produced 1900).

PRODUCTION: Scenery (partially from the New York City Opera production of *La Cenerentola*, 1953), costumes and lighting by Rouben Ter-Arutunian. Scenery executed by Feller Scenery Studios.

PREMIERE: February 4, 1965, New York City Ballet with children from the School of American Ballet, New York State Theater. Conductor: Robert Irving.

CAST: *Harlequin*, Edward Villella; *Colombine*, Patricia McBride; *Pierrot, Servant to Cassandre*, Deni Lamont; *Pierrette, Wife of Pierrot*, Suki Schorer; *Cassandre, Father of Colombine*, Michael Arshansky; *Léandre, Wealthy Suitor to Colombine*, Shaun O'Brien; *La Bonne Fée*, Gloria Govrin; *Les Scaramouches, Friends to Harlequin*, 4 couples; *Les Sbires, Hired by Cassandre to Capture Harlequin*, 3 men; *La Patrouille*, 5 men; *Le Laquais; Alouettes*, Carol Sumner, 8 women; *Les Petits Harlequins*, 8 children.

    Act I: House of Cassandre
    Act II: An Enchanted Park

NOTE: As a student in Petrograd, Balanchine danced in Petipa's *Les Millions d'Harlequin*. Balanchine's production follows the tradition of the commedia dell'arte, in the spirit of Petipa. In Act I, Harlequin outwits his adversaries, and with the help of the Good Fairy wins Colombine's hand. Act II is a divertissement of celebration. The décor was taken from Pollock's toy theaters of London.

REVISIONS: New York City Ballet: 1966, CARNIVAL NUMBER added to Act I, BALLABILE DES INVITÉS (8 couples) added to Act II; 1973, lengthened version using complete score, with addition of 12 couples, 24 children.

TELEVISION: 1966 (pas de deux, Bell Telephone Hour, NBC); 1968 (pas de deux, Bell Telephone Hour, NBC); 1979 (pas de deux, PBS).

See 290

352 DON QUIXOTE
Ballet in Three Acts

MUSIC: By Nicolas Nabokov (commissioned by the New York City Ballet).

PRODUCTION: Scenery, costumes and lighting by Esteban Francés, assisted by Peter Harvey. Scenery executed by Feller Scenery Studios; costumes executed by Karinska. Giant by Kermit Love and Peter Saklin. Masks and armor by Lawrence Vlady.

PREMIERE: May 28, 1965, New York City Ballet with children from the School of American Ballet, New York State Theater. Conductor: Robert Irving. (Preview: Annual New York City Ballet Gala Benefit, May 27, with George Balanchine as Don Quixote.)

CAST: *Don Quixote*, Richard Rapp; *Dulcinea*, Suzanne Farrell; *Sancho Panza*, Deni Lamont. PROLOGUE (DON QUIXOTE'S STUDY): *Don Quixote*; *Dulcinea*; *Sancho Panza*; *Fantasies*, 6 children. ACT I, SCENE I (LA MANCHA): *Don Quixote*; *Sancho Panza*; *A Peasant*; *A Boy*; *6 Slaves*; *2 Guards*; SCENE 2 (A VILLAGE SQUARE): *3 Market Vendors*; *2 Waitresses*; *Cafe Proprietor*; *Townspeople*, 16 women, 8 men; *Dead Poet*; *His Friend*; *2 Pallbearers*; *Marcela*, Farrell; *2 Policemen*; *Organ Grinder*; *Puppeteer*; *Puppets* (children): *5 Saracens, Christian Girl, Christian Boy*; *4 Palace Guards*; *2 Ladies in Waiting*; *2 Gentlemen in Waiting*; *Duke*, Nicholas Magallanes; *Duchess*, Jillana. ACT II (THE PALACE): *Don Quixote*; *Sancho Panza*; *Vision of Dulcinea*; *Duke*; *Duchess*; *2 Ladies in Waiting*; *Major Domo*; *Ladies and Gentlemen of the Court*, 8 couples; *Merlin*, Francisco Moncion; DIVERTISSEMENTS: DANZA DE LA CACCIA: Patricia Neary, Conrad Ludlow, Kent Stowell; PAS DE DEUX MAURESQUE: Suki Schorer, John Prinz; COURANTE SICILIENNE: Sara Leland, Kay Mazzo, Carol Sumner, Frank Ohman, Robert Rodham, Earle Sieveling; RIGAUDON FLAMENCO: Gloria Govrin,

Arthur Mitchell; RITORNEL: Patricia McBride, child. ACT III, SCENE I (A GARDEN OF THE PALACE): *Don Quixote*; *Sancho Panza*; PAS D'ACTION: *Knight of the Silver Moon*, Ludlow; *Maidens*, Marnee Morris, Mimi Paul, 16 women; *Cavaliers*, Anthony Blum, Ohman; VARIATION I: Paul; VARIATION II: Morris; VARIATION III: Blum; VARIATION IV: Farrell; *Merlin*; *Night Spirit*, Govrin; SCENE 2 (LA MANCHA): *Don Quixote*; *Sancho Panza*; *Pigs*; *4 Bearers*; SCENE 3 (DON QUIXOTE'S STUDY): *Don Quixote*; *Sancho Panza*; *Housekeeper*; *Priest*; entire cast.

Prologue and Act I: In which Don Quixote reads—Dreams and fantasies—Vision of Dulcinea—The attainment of knighthood and beginning of the quest—Incident of the boy and the peasant—Adventure of the slaves—Sancho's adventure in the market place—Marcela and the murdered poet—Performance at the puppet theater—Arrival of the Duke and Duchess.

Act II: In which Don Quixote and Sancho Panza come to Court—Entertainment at Court—A Masque and other diversions—Merlin makes magic—Vision of Dulcinea.

Act III: Of knights, ladies and sorcery—Further adventures and a stampede—How Don Quixote comes home—Apotheosis and death.

NOTE: The Balanchine-Nabokov full-length production is an original work without reference to nineteenth-century Russian versions. The ballet depicts episodes in the hero's search for perfection, and for his ideal woman, Dulcinea, who appears as housemaid, shepherdess, the Virgin Mary, and in other guises. Balanchine performed the role of Don Quixote on several occasions.

REVISIONS: There were many revisions, including the composition of additional music and scenery alterations. Major changes:
ACT I, SCENE 2 (A VILLAGE SQUARE): 1967, Role of Zoraida (Dulcinea) added, with gypsy solo, JUGGLER'S DANCE added, Dead Poet omitted; 1968, Zoraida omitted; 1969, RIGAUDON FLAMENCO from Act II inserted (restored to Act II in 1972), Juggler omitted; 1972, PAS CLASSIQUE ESPAGNOL added (pas de deux with ensemble of 12 women), Belly Dancer added; 1973, four variations added to PAS CLASSIQUE ESPAGNOL, including one for leading man and one for leading woman; 1978, JOTA added as prelude to PAS CLASSIQUE ESPAGNOL.
ACT II (THE PALACE): 1965, order of divertissements changed, DANZA DE LA CACCIA changed from pas de trois to pas de deux; 1969, RIGAUDON

FLAMENCO inserted in Act I, Scene 2 (restored to Act II in 1972).

ACT III, SCENE I (A GARDEN OF THE PALACE): VARIATION III (male) changed several times; eliminated in 1975.

1966

353 VARIATIONS

MUSIC: By Igor Stravinsky (*Variations in Memory of Aldous Huxley*, 1965).

PRODUCTION: Lighting by Ronald Bates.

PREMIERE: March 31, 1966, New York City Ballet, New York State Theater. Conductor: Robert Irving.

CAST: I. 12 women; II. 6 men; III. Suzanne Farrell.

NOTE: The music is played three times, each time with different choreography and cast. In 1982, for the New York City Ballet Stravinsky Centennial Celebration, Balanchine rechoreographed the solo; it was presented alone, titled *Variations for Orchestra*.

See 425

354 BRAHMS–SCHOENBERG QUARTET

MUSIC: By Johannes Brahms (Piano Quartet No. 1 in G minor, Op. 25, 1861, orchestrated by Arnold Schoenberg, 1937).

PRODUCTION: Scenery by Peter Harvey, executed by Feller Scenery Studios. Costumes by Karinska. Lighting by Ronald Bates.

PREMIERE: April 21, 1966, New York City Ballet, New York State Theater. Conductor: Robert Irving. (Preview: Annual New York City Ballet Gala Benefit, April 19.)

CAST: ALLEGRO: Melissa Hayden, André Prokovsky; Gloria Govrin; 8 women, 4 men; INTERMEZZO: Patricia McBride, Conrad Ludlow, 3 women; ANDANTE: Allegra Kent, Edward Villella, 3 female demi-soloists, 12 women; RONDO ALLA ZINGARESE: Suzanne Farrell, Jacques d'Amboise, 8 couples.

NOTE: Brahms' First Piano Quartet was given the power of the full orchestra by Schoenberg; it was choreographed by Balanchine for dancers in ballroom gowns, court uniforms and gypsy regalia.

355 ÉLÉGIE

MUSIC: By Igor Stravinsky (*Élégie-Elegy* for solo viola, 1944).

PREMIERE: July 15, 1966, Philharmonic Hall, New York. Violist: Jesse Levine. (First New York City Ballet performance July 28, Saratoga Performing Arts Center. Violist: Jesse Levine.)

CAST: Suzanne Farrell.

NOTE: The premiere formed part of *A Festival of Stravinsky: His Heritage and His Legacy*, directed by Lukas Foss, which also included the premiere of Balanchine's *Ragtime (II)*.

See 245*, 423

356 RAGTIME (II)

MUSIC: By Igor Stravinsky (*Ragtime for Eleven Instruments*, 1918).

PREMIERE: July 15, 1966, Philharmonic Hall, New York. Conductor: Richard Dufallo. (First New York City Ballet performance January 17, 1967, New York State Theater.)

CAST: Suzanne Farrell, Arthur Mitchell.

See 3, 336*

1967

357 TROIS VALSES ROMANTIQUES

MUSIC: By Emmanuel Chabrier (*Trois Valses Romantiques* for piano, 1883, orchestrated by Felix Mottl).

PRODUCTION: Costumes by Karinska (from *Bourrée Fantasque* [265], with additions). Lighting by Ronald Bates.

PREMIERE: April 6, 1967, New York City Ballet, New York State Theater. Conductor: Hugo Fiorato.

CAST: Melissa Hayden, Arthur Mitchell; Gloria Govrin, Frank Ohman; Marnee Morris, Kent Stowell; 6 couples.

REVISIONS: 1968, New York City Ballet: Music performed by two pianists on stage, without orchestra.

See 129

358 JEWELS

MUSIC: EMERALDS: By Gabriel Fauré (from *Pelléas et Melisande*, 1898, and *Shylock*, 1889). RUBIES: By Igor Stravinsky (*Capriccio* for piano and orchestra, 1929). DIAMONDS: By Peter Ilyitch Tschaikovsky (from Symphony No. 3 in D major, Op. 29, 1875 [first movement omitted]).

PRODUCTION: Scenery by Peter Harvey, executed by Feller Scenery Studios. Costumes by Karinska. Lighting by Ronald Bates.

PREMIERE: April 13, 1967, New York City Ballet, New York State Theater. Conductor: Robert Irving. Pianist: Gordon Boelzner.

CAST: EMERALDS: Violette Verdy, Conrad Ludlow; Mimi Paul, Francisco Moncion; Sara Leland, Suki Schorer, John Prinz; 10 women.
RUBIES: Patricia McBride, Edward Villella; Patricia Neary; 8 women, 4 men.
DIAMONDS: Suzanne Farrell, Jacques d'Amboise; 4 demi-solo couples; 12 women, 12 men.

NOTE: Each section is a separate work, the costumes green for EMERALDS, red for RUBIES, white for DIAMONDS. The ballet lasts a full evening.

REVISIONS: 1976, New York City Ballet: EMERALDS extended by new pas de deux (to additional music from *Shylock*) and new pas de sept (to additional music from *Pelléas et Melisande*); second ballerina variation altered.

STAGINGS: RUBIES (usually retitled *Capriccio*): 1974, Paris; 1977, Dutch National; 1980, Les Grands Ballets Canadiens, Zürich; 1981, Chicago City; 1982, Los Angeles.

TELEVISION: 1968 (RUBIES pas de deux, Bell Telephone Hour, NBC); 1977 (excerpts, Dance in America, PBS); 1979 (RUBIES pas de deux, PBS).

359 GLINKIANA (later called GLINKAIANA)

MUSIC: By Mikhail Glinka.

PRODUCTION: Scenery, costumes and lighting by Esteban Francés.

PREMIERE: November 23, 1967, New York City Ballet, New York State Theater. Conductor: Robert Irving.

CAST: POLKA: Violette Verdy, Paul Mejia, 3 couples; VALSE FANTAISIE: Mimi Paul, John Clifford, 4 women; JOTA ARAGONESE: Melissa Hayden, 6 women, 8 men; DIVERTIMENTO BRILLANTE: Patricia McBride, Edward Villella.

NOTE: The curtain was lowered after each section and the décor changed. *Glinkiana* was seldom performed with the full four movements. From June 1, 1969, *Valse Fantaisie* was presented as a separate work; the other movements were eliminated.

STAGINGS: See 366.

TELEVISION: 1968 (DIVERTIMENTO BRILLANTE, Bell Telephone Hour, NBC); 1969 (DIVERTIMENTO BRILLANTE, L'Heure du Concert, CBC, Montreal).

See 107*, 132, 293, 366

1968

360 METASTASEIS & PITHOPRAKTA

MUSIC: By Iannis Xenakis (*Metastaseis*, 1953-54; *Pithoprakta*, 1955-56).

PRODUCTION: Lighting by Ronald Bates.

PREMIERE: January 18, 1968, New York City Ballet, New York State Theater. Conductor: Robert Irving.

CAST: METASTASEIS: 22 women, 6 men; PITHOPRAKTA: Suzanne Farrell, Arthur Mitchell, 7 women, 5 men.

NOTE: The music of both brief pieces by the modern Greek composer-architect is based on a calculus of sound, the orchestra of sixty-one instruments playing sixty-one different parts. In the ballet METASTASEIS (Greek, meaning 'a state of standstill') the dancers, in white, form a mass in the shape of a giant wheel that moves and changes, ending as it began. In PITHOPRAKTA (meaning 'action by probabilities'), the two leading dancers, dressed in white and gold, perform a pas de deux during which they simulate partnering but seldom touch; the corps is in black.

361 SLAUGHTER ON TENTH AVENUE

MUSIC: By Richard Rodgers (from *On Your Toes*, 1936, with new orchestration by Hershy Kay).

PRODUCTION: Scenery and lighting by Jo Mielziner, executed by Feller Scenery Studios. Costumes by Irene Sharaff.

PREMIÈRE: May 2, 1968, New York City Ballet, New York State Theater. Conductor: Robert Irving. (Preview: Annual New York City Ballet Gala Benefit, April 30.)

CAST: *Hoofer*, Arthur Mitchell; *Strip Tease Girl*, Suzanne Farrell; *Big Boss*, Michael Steele; *2 Bartenders*; *Thug*; *3 Policemen*; *Morosine, Premier Danseur Noble*, Earle Sieveling; *Gangster*; 7 Ladies of the Ballet; 4 Gentlemen of the Ballet.

NOTE: Originally choreographed in 1936 for the Broadway musical *On Your Toes*, the ballet was mounted for the New York City Ballet as a separate work, following the original ideas but with different steps.

STAGINGS: 1974, New York Dance Theatre (pas de trois).

TELEVISION: 1969 (excerpt, NBC).

See 166*, 186

362 REQUIEM CANTICLES

In Memoriam: Martin Luther King, Jr. (1929-68)

MUSIC: By Igor Stravinsky (*Requiem Canticles* for contralto, bass, chorus, and orchestra, 1966).

PRODUCTION: Costumes and candelabra by Rouben Ter-Arutunian. Lighting by Ronald Bates.

PREMIERE: May 2, 1968, New York City Ballet, New York State Theater. Conductor: Robert Irving. Singers: Margaret Wilson (contralto); John Ostendorf (bass).

CAST: Suzanne Farrell, Arthur Mitchell, corps de ballet.

NOTE: Choreographed as a religious ceremony and performed once. The corps de ballet, in long white robes and bearing three-branched candelabra, moved on the darkened stage; a lone woman seemed to search among them, and at the end a figure in purple representing Martin Luther King, Jr. was raised aloft.

363 DIANA AND ACTAEON PAS DE DEUX
Made for Television

MUSIC: By Cesare Pugni?

FIRST TELECAST: June 2, 1968, Ed Sullivan Show, CBS.

CAST: Patricia McBride, Edward Villella.

364 LA SOURCE
(briefly called PAS DE DEUX: LA SOURCE)

MUSIC: By Léo Delibes (excerpts from *La Source* [*Naïla*], 1866).

PRODUCTION: Costumes by Karinska. Lighting by Ronald Bates.

PREMIERE: November 23, 1968, New York City Ballet, New York State Theater. Conductor: Robert Irving.

CAST: Violette Verdy, John Prinz.

NOTE: Varying the conventional structure of a pas de deux, *La Source* begins with solos for the man and woman rather than a supported adagio.

REVISIONS: 1969, New York City Ballet: Expanded to include ALLEGRO VIVACE for female soloist and ensemble of 8 women and VALSE DES FLEURS from *Pas de Deux and Divertissement* [350].

STAGINGS: 1971, San Francisco, Geneva; 1982, Los Angeles.

See 274, 350, 387

1969

365 RUSLAN UND LUDMILLA
Opera in Three Acts

MUSIC: By Mikhail Glinka (produced 1842). Libretto based on the work by Alexander Pushkin. German version by Kurt Honolka.

PRODUCTION: Directed and choreographed by George Balanchine. Scenery and costumes by Nicolas Benois.

PREMIERE: March 30, 1969, Hamburgische Staatsoper, Hamburg. Danced by the Ballett der Hamburgischen Staatsoper. Conductor: Charles Mackerras.

CAST: SINGERS: *Svetosar*, Carl Schultz; *Ludmilla*, Jeanette Scovotti; *Ruslan*, Hubert Hofmann; *Ratmir*, Ursula Boese; *Farlaf*, Noël Mangin; *Gorislava*, Judith Beckmann; *Finn*, Helmut Melchert; *Naïna*, Maria v. Ilosvay; and others. DANCERS: ACT II VISION: 3 women; ACT III ORIENTAL DANCES: 5 women, 5 men.

See 307

366 VALSE FANTAISIE

MUSIC: By Mikhail Glinka (*Valse Fantaisie* in B minor, 1839; orchestrated 1856).

PRODUCTION: Scenery, costumes and lighting by Esteban Francés.

PREMIERE: June 1, 1969, New York City Ballet, New York State Theater. Conductor: Robert Irving.

CAST: Suki Schorer, John Prinz, 4 women.

NOTE: *Valse Fantaisie* was originally presented by the New York City Ballet in 1967 as the second section of *Glinkiana* [359].

STAGINGS (sometimes as *Waltz Fantasy*): 1968, Boston; 1973, Garden State, Los Angeles; 1975, Pacific Northwest; 1976, U. S. Terpsichore; 1977, Stars of American Ballet; 1978, Berkshire, Chicago Lyric Opera,

Dallas, North Carolina, Princeton; 1979, Connecticut; 1980, New Jersey; 1981, American Festival, Baltimore, Richmond; 1982, Kansas City, Festival, Toledo.

See 107*, 293, 359

367 LE LAC DES CYGNES
Ballet in Four Acts

MUSIC: By Peter Ilyitch Tschaikovsky (*Swan Lake*, 1875-76).

CHOREOGRAPHY: Staged by George Balanchine after Lev Ivanov, Marius Petipa, and Nicholas Beriozoff. Choreography for the WALTZ (Act I) and for the MAZURKA, CZARDAS and DANCE OF THE PRINCESSES (Act III) by George Balanchine.

PRODUCTION: Scenery and costumes by Alexandre Benois, executed in the workshops of La Scala, Milan, and by Marie Gromtseff.

PREMIERE: September 11, 1969, Ballet du Grand Théâtre, Geneva. Conductor: Jean Meylan.

CAST: *Odette, Queen of the Swans*, Patricia Neary; *The Evil Genius*, Carlos Kloster; *Prince Siegfried*, Karl Musil; *Jester*, Jean-Marie Sosso; corps de ballet.

See 75, 191, 262, 285, 331

1970

368 WHO CARES?

MUSIC: By George Gershwin (songs as given below), orchestrated by Hershy Kay.

PRODUCTION: Costumes by Karinska. Lighting by Ronald Bates.

PREMIERE: February 5, 1970, New York City Ballet, New York State Theater. Conductor: Robert Irving. Pianist on opening night (orchestration had been completed only for *Strike Up the Band* and *I Got Rhythm*): Gordon Boelzner. *Clap Yo' Hands* played by George Gershwin, recorded.

CAST: Karin von Aroldingen, Patricia McBride, Marnee Morris, Jacques d'Amboise, 15 women, 5 men.

STRIKE UP THE BAND (1927): Ensemble. SWEET AND LOW DOWN (1925): Ensemble. SOMEBODY LOVES ME (1924): Deborah Flomine, Susan Hendl, Linda Merrill, Susan Pilarre, Bettijane Sills. BIDIN' MY TIME (1930): Deni Lamont, Robert Maiorano, Frank Ohman, Richard Rapp, Earle Sieveling. 'S WONDERFUL (1927): Pilarre, Rapp. THAT CERTAIN FEELING (1925): Flomine, Lamont; Sills, Sieveling. DO DO DO (1926): Hendl, Ohman. LADY BE GOOD (1924): Merrill, Maiorano. REPEAT: Ensemble. THE MAN I LOVE (1924): McBride, d'Amboise. I'LL BUILD A STAIRWAY TO PARADISE (1922): von Aroldingen. EMBRACEABLE YOU (1930): Morris, d'Amboise. FASCINATIN' RHYTHM (1924): McBride. WHO CARES? (1931): von Aroldingen, d'Amboise. MY ONE AND ONLY (1927): Morris. LIZA (1929): d'Amboise. CLAP YO' HANDS (1926): von Aroldingen, McBride, Morris, d'Amboise. I GOT RHYTHM (1930): Entire cast.

NOTE: Balanchine and Gershwin had discussed a collaboration before the composer's death in 1937. Thirty-three years later, Balanchine selected and formed into this ballet seventeen of Gershwin's classic songs from Broadway musicals. First presented with costumes but without décor; from November, 1970, with scenery by Jo Mielziner.

REVISIONS: 1976, New York City Ballet: CLAP YO' HANDS eliminated.

STAGINGS: 1980, Zürich; 1982, Chicago City (excerpts).

TELEVISION: 1971 (CBC, Montreal); 1975 (THE MAN I LOVE, NBC).

369 SUITE NO. 3

(from 1971 called TSCHAIKOVSKY SUITE NO. 3)

MUSIC: By Peter Ilyitch Tschaikovsky (Suite No. 3 in G major, Op. 55, 1884).

PRODUCTION: Scenery and costumes by Nicolas Benois; costumes for TEMA CON VARIAZIONI later redesigned by Ben Benson. Lighting by Ronald Bates.

PREMIERE: December 3, 1970, New York City Ballet, New York State Theater. Conductor: Robert Irving.

CAST: ÉLÉGIE: Karin von Aroldingen, Anthony Blum, 6 women; VALSE MÉLANCOLIQUE: Kay Mazzo, Conrad Ludlow, 6 women; SCHERZO:

Marnee Morris, John Clifford, 8 women; TEMA CON VARIAZIONI: Gelsey Kirkland, Edward Villella, 4 demi-solo couples, 8 women, 8 men.

NOTE: Danced until the final movement in a darkened ballroom, the women's dresses long and flowing, their hair unbound; in the first movement they are barefoot. In the finale the stage brightens, the women appear in tutus and tiaras, and the men are dressed as cavaliers.

TELEVISION: 1979 (ÉLÉGIE, Dance in America, PBS).

See 242*, 330

1971

370 CONCERTO FOR JAZZ BAND AND ORCHESTRA

MUSIC: By Rolf Liebermann (Concerto for jazz band and orchestra, 1954).

CHOREOGRAPHY: By George Balanchine and Arthur Mitchell.

PRODUCTION: Lighting by Ronald Bates.

PREMIERE: May 6, 1971 (Annual New York City Ballet Gala Benefit), New York City Ballet and Dance Theatre of Harlem, New York State Theater. Conductor: Robert Irving. On stage: Tonight Show orchestra, conducted by 'Doc' Severinsen.

CAST: 21 New York City Ballet dancers, 23 Dance Theatre of Harlem dancers. I. INTRODUCTION AND JUMP: New York City Ballet women, men from both companies; II. SCHERZO I: New York City Ballet; III. BLUES: Dance Theatre of Harlem; IV. SCHERZO II: New York City Ballet women; V. BOOGIE WOOGIE: Dance Theatre of Harlem; VI. INTERLUDIUM: women from both companies, Dance Theatre of Harlem men; VII. MAMBO: Entire cast.

NOTE: Performed once, in practice clothes.

371 PAMTGG

MUSIC: By Roger Kellaway (based on themes by Stan Applebaum and Sid Woloshin, commissioned by the New York City Ballet).

PRODUCTION: Scenery and lighting by Jo Mielziner. Costumes by Irene Sharaff.

PREMIERE: June 17, 1971, New York City Ballet, New York State Theater. Conductor: Robert Irving.

CAST: Kay Mazzo, Victor Castelli, 24 women, 16 men; Karin von Aroldingen, Frank Ohman, 6 women, 6 men; Sara Leland, John Clifford, 16 women, 12 men.

NOTE: The title is an acronym of a radio and television jingle for an airline commercial; the ballet, a futuristic fantasy on airport procedures.

1972

372 SONATA

MUSIC: By Igor Stravinsky (Scherzo from Sonata in F-sharp minor, 1903-4).

PREMIERE: June 18, 1972, New York City Ballet, New York State Theater. Pianist: Madeleine Malraux. (Annual New York City Ballet Gala Benefit.)

CAST: Sara Leland, John Clifford.

NOTE: Unlisted in the program, *Sonata* was presented as a surprise, the first danced work of the Stravinsky Festival of the New York City Ballet (detailed in *Festivals Directed by Balanchine*, page 311), which included the premieres of ten Balanchine works [372-381].

373 SYMPHONY IN THREE MOVEMENTS

MUSIC: By Igor Stravinsky (1942-45, dedicated to the New York Philharmonic).

PRODUCTION: Lighting by Ronald Bates.

PREMIERE: June 18, 1972, New York City Ballet, New York State Theater. Conductor: Robert Craft. (Annual New York City Ballet Gala Benefit.)

CAST: I. Sara Leland, Marnee Morris, Lynda Yourth, Helgi Tomasson, Edward Villella, Robert Weiss; 5 demi-solo women; 5 demi-solo men; 16 women; II. Leland, Villella; III. Entire cast.

NOTE: An ensemble ballet of driving energy, the first and third movements contrasting with a meditative pas de deux in the second movement.

STAGINGS: 1981, Zürich.

374 VIOLIN CONCERTO
(from 1973 called STRAVINSKY VIOLIN CONCERTO)

MUSIC: By Igor Stravinsky (Concerto in D for violin and orchestra, 1931, commissioned by Blair Fairchild).

PRODUCTION: Lighting by Ronald Bates.

PREMIERE: June 18, 1972, New York City Ballet, New York State Theater. Conductor: Robert Irving. Violinist: Joseph Silverstein. (Annual New York City Ballet Gala Benefit.)

CAST: TOCCATA: Karin von Aroldingen, Kay Mazzo, Jean-Pierre Bonnefous, Peter Martins, 8 women, 8 men; ARIA I: von Aroldingen, Bonnefous; ARIA II: Mazzo, Martins; CAPRICCIO: Entire cast.

NOTE: The first movement is in eight parts, each overlapping into the next. Both the second and third movements are pas de deux showing contrasting relationships between the partners. The finale includes references to Russian motifs in the score. Balanchine had previously used this music for the ballet *Balustrade* with scenery and costumes; *Violin Concerto* was performed in practice clothes, without décor.

REVISIONS: 1977, New York City Ballet: entry of first male dancer altered and other changes made for Dance in America telecast; changes retained in stage version.

TELEVISION: 1977 (Dance in America, PBS).

See 192

375 DANSES CONCERTANTES

MUSIC: By Igor Stravinsky (*Danses Concertantes* for chamber orchestra, 1941-42, commissioned by Werner Janssen).

PRODUCTION: Scenery and costumes by Eugene Berman (from the Ballet Russe de Monte Carlo production, 1944), courtesy of the Ballet Foundation. Costumes executed by Barbara Matera.

PREMIERE: June 20, 1972, New York City Ballet, New York State Theater. Conductor: Robert Irving.

CAST: Lynda Yourth, John Clifford, 8 women, 4 men.
MARCHE; PAS D'ACTION; THÈME VARIÉ (4 variations); PAS DE DEUX; MARCHE.

NOTE: Originally presented by the Ballet Russe de Monte Carlo, New York, 1944, with similar choreography.

See 220*

376 DIVERTIMENTO FROM 'LE BAISER DE LA FÉE'

MUSIC: By Igor Stravinsky (excerpts from *Divertimento*, concert suite, 1934, and the full-length ballet, *Le Baiser de la Fée*, 1928).

PRODUCTION: Costumes by Eugene Berman (from *Roma* [306]). Lighting by Ronald Bates.

PREMIERE: June 21, 1972, New York City Ballet, New York State Theater. Conductor: Robert Irving.

CAST: Patricia McBride, Helgi Tomasson; Bettijane Sills, Carol Sumner, 10 women.

NOTE: Unlike Balanchine's earlier staging of the full score, the *Divertimento* tells no story, although certain sections suggest quest and foreboding.

REVISIONS: 1974, New York City Ballet: New pas de deux (with ensemble) added; two principal dancers bid farewell in elegiac conclusion to music from the score of *Le Baiser de la Fée* that incorporates Tschaikovsky's 'None But the Lonely Heart.'

See 178*, 271

377 SCHERZO À LA RUSSE

Music: By Igor Stravinsky (1925).

Production: Costumes by Karinska. Lighting by Ronald Bates.

Premiere: June 21, 1972, New York City Ballet, New York State Theater. Conductor: Hugo Fiorato.

Cast: Karin von Aroldingen, Kay Mazzo, 16 women.

Note: Reminiscent of Russian women's folk ensembles; performed in nursemaid costumes with aristocratic headdresses.

Revisions: 1982, New York City Ballet (Stravinsky Centennial Celebration): Substantially rechoreographed in the same style.

378 DUO CONCERTANT

Music: By Igor Stravinsky (*Duo Concertant* for violin and piano, 1939).

Production: Lighting by Ronald Bates.

Premiere: June 22, 1972, New York City Ballet, New York State Theater. Pianist: Gordon Boelzner. Violinist: Lamar Alsop. Both instrumentalists on stage.

Cast: Kay Mazzo, Peter Martins.
   I. CANTILENA; II. ECLOGUE I; III. ECLOGUE II; IV. GIGUE; V. DITHYRAMB.

Note: The performance of the musicians on stage is integral to the conception of the ballet. Standing at the piano with the musicians, the dancers listen to the first movement. During the next three movements they dance, mirroring the music and each other, and pause several times to rejoin the musicians and to listen. In the final movement, the stage is darkened; within circles of light the dancers enact a love story.

379 PULCINELLA

Music: By Igor Stravinsky (*Pulcinella: Ballet with Song in One Act after Pergolesi*, 1919-20).

Choreography: By George Balanchine and Jerome Robbins.

Production: Scenery and costumes by Eugene Berman. Scenery executed by Nolan Scenery Studios. Lighting by Ronald Bates. Masks and props by Kermit Love.

PREMIERE: June 23, 1972, New York City Ballet with children from the School of American Ballet, New York State Theater. Conductor: Robert Irving.

CAST: *Pulcinella*, Edward Villella; *Girl*, Violette Verdy; *Pulcinella's Father*, Michael Arshansky; *Devil*, Francisco Moncion, Shaun O'Brien; *Beggars*, George Balanchine, Jerome Robbins; *Concubines*, 2 men; *2 Policemen*; *Little Boy*; *6 Musicians*; *Townspeople*, 7 women, 5 men; *Pulcinellas*, Deni Lamont, Robert Weiss, 10 men, 12 children.

NOTE: Balanchine created a libretto of his own, working with Robbins. Beginning with Pulcinella's funeral procession, the ballet depicts his resurrection through a pact with the devil, his continued career of mockery, petty crime and debauchery, his defeat of the devil at a spaghetti feast, and a celebration of his victory by dancing. *Pulcinella* was first choreographed by Léonide Massine in 1920 for Diaghilev's Ballets Russes.

REVISIONS: New York City Ballet: Numerous early revisions.

See 35

380 CHORAL VARIATIONS
ON BACH'S 'VOM HIMMEL HOCH'

MUSIC: By Igor Stravinsky (Variations on two treatments of *Vom Himmel Hoch* by Johann Sebastian Bach [from his *Christmas Oratorio*, 1734, and his *Canonic Variations on Vom Himmel Hoch* for organ, 1748] for mixed chorus and orchestra, 1956, dedicated to Robert Craft).

PRODUCTION: Scenery by Rouben Ter-Arutunian. Lighting by Ronald Bates.

PREMIERE: June 25, 1972, New York City Ballet with children from the School of American Ballet, New York State Theater. Conductor: Robert Irving. Chorus: Gregg Smith Singers.

CAST: Karin von Aroldingen, Melissa Hayden, Sara Leland, Violette Verdy, Anthony Blum, Peter Martins, 15 women, 13 men, 12 children.

NOTE: The choral variations are accompanied by danced variations leading to a grand défilé. At the end, the dancers kneel.

381 SYMPHONY OF PSALMS

MUSIC: By Igor Stravinsky (for mixed voices and orchestra, 1930, commissioned by Serge Koussevitsky).

PRODUCTION: Staged by George Balanchine. Scenery by Rouben Ter-Arutunian.

PREMIERE: June 25, 1972, New York City Ballet, New York State Theater. Conductor: Robert Craft. Chorus: Gregg Smith Singers.

NOTE: This work, performed by the Gregg Smith Singers with the dancers assembled on stage behind the chorus, closed the Stravinsky Festival of the New York City Ballet.

1973

382 TSCHAIKOVSKY PIANO CONCERTO NO. 2
(briefly called PIANO CONCERTO NO. 2)

MUSIC: By Peter Ilyitch Tschaikovsky (Piano Concerto No. 2 in G major, Op. 44, 1879, abridged, rewritten and rearranged by Alexander Siloti).

PRODUCTION: Costumes by Karinska. Lighting by Ronald Bates.

PREMIERE: January 12, 1973, New York City Ballet, New York State Theater. Conductor: Robert Irving. Pianist: Gordon Boelzner.

CAST: Patricia McBride, Peter Martins; Colleen Neary; Tracy Bennett, Victor Castelli; 2 female demi-soloists; 16 women, 6 men.
ALLEGRO BRILLANTE–ANDANTE; ANDANTE NON TROPPO; ALLEGRO CON FUOCO.

NOTE: Originally presented by American Ballet Caravan, Rio de Janeiro, 1941, titled *Ballet Imperial*. While the choreography is essentially the same as the Sadler's Wells (Royal Ballet) presentation of 1950, the Imperial Russian décor and tutus of the 1964 New York City Ballet production were replaced in 1973 by simple chiffon dresses and a plain backdrop.

New productions by Balanchine companies: 1979, New York City Ballet: New costumes by Ben Benson.

See 194*, 349

383 FÜRST IGOR (PRINCE IGOR)

Opera in Four Acts and Prologue by Alexander Borodin
ACT II POLOVTSIAN DANCES

Choreography: Original choreography by Michel Fokine (1909); staged by George Balanchine.

Premiere: February 23, 1973, Deutsche Oper, Berlin. Danced by Ballett der Deutschen Oper. Conductor: Gerd Albrecht.

Cast: 4 women, 7 men.

See 104

384 CORTÈGE HONGROIS

Music: By Alexander Glazounov (from *Raymonda*, Op. 57, produced 1898).

Production: Scenery and costumes by Rouben Ter-Arutunian. Lighting by Ronald Bates.

Premiere: May 17, 1973, New York City Ballet, New York State Theater. Conductor: Robert Irving. (Preview: Annual New York City Ballet Gala Benefit, May 16.)

Cast: Melissa Hayden, Jacques d'Amboise [classical]; Karin von Aroldingen, Jean-Pierre Bonnefous [character]; 16 couples. CZARDAS: von Aroldingen, Bonnefous; PAS DE QUATRE: 4 women; VARIATION I: Colleen Neary; VARIATION II: 4 men; VARIATION III: Merrill Ashley; PAS DE DEUX: Hayden, d'Amboise.

Note: Created to honor Melissa Hayden on the occasion of her retirement. A suite of dances alternating classical and character styles, conceived in the tradition of the late works of Petipa. In the apotheosis the entire cast pays homage to the ballerina.

See 18, 233*, 309, 339

385 BEGIN THE BEGUINE

Music: By Cole Porter.

CHOREOGRAPHY: By George Balanchine (uncredited), one of five sections of the ballet *Salute to Cole*, choreographed by Edward Villella.

PRODUCTION: Produced by Hal de Windt. Costumes by Peter Wexler.

PREMIERE: May 31, 1973, Philharmonic Hall, New York. Conductor: André Kostelanetz.

CAST: Patricia McBride, Edward Villella.

NOTE: Performed as part of a New York Philharmonic Promenade concert.

1974

386 VARIATIONS POUR UNE PORTE ET UN SOUPIR

Music: Sonority by Pierre Henry (14 of 25 numbers from *Variations pour une Porte et un Soupir*, first performed 1963).

PRODUCTION: Scenery and costumes by Rouben Ter-Arutunian. Lighting by Ronald Bates.

PREMIERE: February 17, 1974, New York City Ballet, New York State Theater.

CAST: Karin von Aroldingen, John Clifford.

NOTE: The ballet is a set of fourteen variations in pas de deux form, for a female 'Door' and a male 'Sigh.' The dancers' movements are in precise accord with the separate sounds and vibrations that form the score. An integral part of the choreography is an enormous black cape attached to the 'Door,' which in the end envelops the 'Sigh.'

387 COPPÉLIA

Music: By Léo Delibes (*Coppélia, ou la Fille aux Yeux d'Émail*, produced 1870, with excerpts from *Sylvia, ou la Nymphe de Diane*, produced 1876, and *La Source* [*Naïla*], 1866). Book by Charles Nuitter, after E. T. A. Hoffmann's *Der Sandmann* (1815).

CHOREOGRAPHY: Choreography by Alexandra Danilova and George Balanchine after Marius Petipa (1884; revised 1894 by Lev Ivanov and Enrico Cecchetti), with additional choreography by George Balanchine.

PRODUCTION: Scenery and costumes by Rouben Ter-Arutunian. Costumes executed by Karinska and Barbara Matera, Ltd. Lighting by Ronald Bates.

PREMIERE: July 17, 1974, New York City Ballet, Saratoga Performing Arts Center, Saratoga Springs, New York. Conductor: Robert Irving. (First New York State Theater performance, with children from the School of American Ballet, November 20.)

CAST: *Swanilda/Coppélia*, Patricia McBride; *Frantz*, Helgi Tomasson; *Dr. Coppélius*, Shaun O'Brien. ACT I: *The Doll Coppélia*; *Villagers*, 8 couples; *Mayor*, Michael Arshansky; *Swanilda's Friends*, 8 women. ACT II: *Swanilda and Her Friends*; *The Automatons*: *Astrologer, Juggler, Acrobat, Chinaman*. ACT III: *Burgomaster*; *Villagers, Brides, Grooms*, and *Friends*, 8 women, 6 men; DEDICATION OF THE BELLS: WALTZ OF THE GOLDEN HOURS: Marnee Morris, 24 children; *Dawn*, Merrill Ashley; *Prayer*, Christine Redpath; *Spinner*, Susan Hendl; *Jesterettes*, 4 women; DISCORD AND WAR: Colleen Neary, Robert Weiss, 8 couples; PEACE (pas de deux): McBride, Tomasson; FINALE.

Act I. A Village Square in Galicia.

Act II. Dr. Coppélius' Secret Workshop.

Act III. A Village Wedding and Festival of Bells.

NOTE: Balanchine and Danilova collaborated to reproduce parts of Petipa's choreography for *Coppélia*, which they had learned while students at the Imperial Ballet School; Danilova had later become a leading interpreter of the role of Swanilda. Balanchine created entirely new choreography for Act III, and for the mazurka and czardas in Act I, and made slight revisions in other dances in Act I. Because the leading male role was originally danced by a woman, there is no provision for male variation or supported pas de deux in the score. Using music from *Sylvia*, Balanchine created a male variation for Act I and a complete pas de deux for Act III, in which the male variation is taken from his *Sylvia: Pas de Deux* [273]. The production was partially commissioned by the Saratoga Performing Arts Center.

REVISIONS: 1974, New York City Ballet: Act III costumes altered before first New York performance and new children's costumes designed by Karinska; coda added to Act III PEACE pas de deux.

STAGINGS: 1977, Geneva.

TELEVISION: 1978 (Live from Lincoln Center, PBS).

See 36, 266, 273, 274, 291, 350, 364

388 BORIS GODUNOV

Opera in Three Acts and Ten Scenes by Modest Moussorgsky
ACT II, SCENE 2 POLONAISE

PREMIERE: December 16, 1974, Metropolitan Opera, New York. Danced by Metropolitan Opera Ballet. Conductor: Thomas Schippers.

CAST: Corps de ballet.

See 54, 298

1975

389 SONATINE

MUSIC: By Maurice Ravel (1906).

PRODUCTION: Lighting by Ronald Bates.

PREMIERE: May 15, 1975, New York City Ballet, New York State Theater. Pianist: Madeleine Malraux. (Preview: Annual New York City Ballet Gala Benefit, May 14.)

CAST: Violette Verdy, Jean-Pierre Bonnefous.

NOTE: *Sonatine* was first presented as the opening work of the Ravel Festival of the New York City Ballet (detailed in *Festivals Directed by Balanchine*, page 312), which included the premieres of eight Balanchine works [389-396].

STAGINGS: 1975, Paris; 1976, Geneva.

390 L'ENFANT ET LES SORTILÈGES
Lyric Fantasy in Two Parts

MUSIC: By Maurice Ravel (1920-25). Libretto by Colette (translated by Catherine Wolff).

PRODUCTION: Scenery and costumes by Kermit Love. Supervising Designer: David Mitchell. Lighting by Ronald Bates.

PREMIERE: May 15, 1975, New York City Ballet, New York State Theater. Conductor: Manuel Rosenthal. (Preview: Annual New York City Ballet Gala Benefit, May 14.)

CAST: Each role performed by a singer off stage (six singers) and a dancer on stage. *Child* (sung and danced), Paul Offenkranz; *His Mother*; *Armchair*; *Bergère*; *Clock*; *Tea Pot*; *Chinese Cup*; *Fire*, Marnee Morris; *Cinder*; *3 Shepherdesses*; *3 Shepherds*; *Princess*, Christine Redpath; *Little Math Man*; *10 Numbers*; *Black Cat*, Jean-Pierre Frohlich; *Gray Cat*, Tracy Bennett; *Dragonflies and Moths*, Colleen Neary, 7 women; *Big Frog*; *5 Little Frogs*; *Tree* (sung only); *Squirrels and 2 Trees*, Stephanie Saland, 5 women, 2 men.

OTHER VERSIONS: 1925, Opéra de Monte-Carlo (*L'Enfant et les Sortilèges*, danced by Diaghilev's Ballets Russes). 1946, Ballet Society (*The Spellbound Child* [*L'Enfant et les Sortilèges*]). 1981, for the PBS television series Dance in America (*The Spellbound Child / L'Enfant et les Sortilèges*).

See 48*, 235, 416

391 SHÉHÉRAZADE

MUSIC: By Maurice Ravel (*Shéhérazade: Ouverture de Féerie*, 1898).

PRODUCTION: Lighting by Ronald Bates.

PREMIERE: May 22, 1975, New York City Ballet, New York State Theater. Conductor: Robert Irving.

CAST: Kay Mazzo, Edward Villella, 2 couples, 8 women.

392 LE TOMBEAU DE COUPERIN

MUSIC: By Maurice Ravel (four movements orchestrated by the composer from the six-part suite originally written for piano, 1919).

PRODUCTION: Lighting by Ronald Bates.

PREMIERE: May 29, 1975, New York City Ballet, New York State Theater. Conductor: Robert Irving.

CAST: LEFT QUADRILLE: Judith Fugate, Jean-Pierre Frohlich; Wilhelmina Frankfurt, Victor Castelli; Muriel Aasen, Francis Sackett; Susan Hendl, David Richardson; RIGHT QUADRILLE: Marjorie Spohn, Hermes Condé; Delia Peters, Richard Hoskinson; Susan Pilarre, Richard Dryden; Carol Sumner, Laurence Matthews.

PRÉLUDE; FORLANE; MENUET; RIGAUDON.

NOTE: The two quadrilles perform in geometric patterns, often with identical steps and gestures, simultaneous or canonic.

STAGINGS: 1975, Paris; 1976, Geneva; 1977, Dutch National; 1981, Zürich.

393 PAVANE

MUSIC: By Maurice Ravel (*Pavane pour une Infante Défunte* for piano, 1899; orchestral version, 1911).

PRODUCTION: Lighting by Ronald Bates.

PREMIERE: May 29, 1975, New York City Ballet, New York State Theater. Conductor: Robert Irving.

CAST: Patricia McBride.

NOTE: A lament, choreographed for a solo dancer and a piece of chiffon she holds.

394 TZIGANE

MUSIC: By Maurice Ravel (1924).

PRODUCTION: Costumes by Joe Eula and Stanley Simmons (from *Koddly Dances* [Clifford], 1971, uncredited). Lighting by Ronald Bates.

PREMIERE: May 29, 1975, New York City Ballet, New York State Theater. Conductor: Robert Irving. Violinist: Lamar Alsop.

CAST: Suzanne Farrell, Peter Martins, 4 couples.

NOTE: A choreographic fantasy on gypsy dance styles and personality.

STAGINGS: 1975, Paris.

TELEVISION: 1977 (Dance in America, PBS).

395 GASPARD DE LA NUIT

MUSIC: By Maurice Ravel (*Gaspard de la Nuit*, three poems for piano solo, 1908, inspired by poems of the same name by Aloysius Bertrand).

PRODUCTION: Scenery and costumes by Bernard Daydé; execution supervised by David Mitchell. Lighting by Bernard Daydé in association with Ronald Bates.

PREMIERE: May 29, 1975, New York City Ballet, New York State Theater. Pianist: Jerry Zimmerman.

CAST: ONDINE: Colleen Neary, Victor Castelli, 5 women; LE GIBET: Karin von Aroldingen, Nolan T'Sani, 8 women, 3 men; SCARBO: Sara Leland, Robert Weiss, 3 men.

NOTE: Bertrand's Gaspard represents the evils of the night. The ballet's atmosphere is black magic; mirrors figure importantly in each of the three sections, which bear the titles of the poems.

396 RAPSODIE ESPAGNOLE

MUSIC: By Maurice Ravel (1907).

PRODUCTION: Costumes by Michael Avedon. Lighting by Ronald Bates.

PREMIERE: May 29, 1975, New York City Ballet, New York State Theater. Conductor: Robert Irving.

CAST: Karin von Aroldingen, Peter Schaufuss, Nolan T'Sani, 12 couples.
PRÉLUDE DE LA NUIT; MALAGUEÑA; HABAÑERA (pas de deux); FERIA.

397 FAUST

Opera in Five Acts by Charles Gounod
ACT III, SCENE I WALPURGISNACHT BALLET

PREMIERE: June 3, 1975, Théâtre National de l'Opéra, Paris. Danced by Paris Opéra Ballet. Conductor: Michel Plasson.

CAST: Claudette Scouarnec, Sylvie Clavier, Jean-Paul Gravier; Joysane Conşoli, Janine Guiton, corps de ballet.

NOTE: In 1980, the WALPURGISNACHT BALLET entered the New York City Ballet repertory as an independent work.

STAGINGS: 1979, Chicago Lyric Opera; 1980, New York City Ballet (WALPURGISNACHT BALLET only).

See 45, 117, 151, 227, 413

398 THE STEADFAST TIN SOLDIER

MUSIC: By Georges Bizet (from *Jeux d'Enfants*, Opp. 22-26, 1871: no. 6, TROMPETTE ET TAMBOUR; no. 3, LA POUPÉE; no. 11, PETIT MARI, PETITE FEMME; no. 12, LE BAL).

PRODUCTION: Scenery and costumes by David Mitchell. Lighting by Ronald Bates.

PREMIERE: July 30, 1975, New York City Ballet, Saratoga Performing Arts Center, Saratoga Springs, New York. Conductor: Robert Irving. (First New York State Theater performance January 22, 1976.)

CAST: Patricia McBride, Peter Schaufuss.
MARCHE; BERCEUSE; DUO; GALOP.

NOTE: Balanchine transformed the Hans Christian Andersen story into a pas de deux recounting the courtship and love between the tin soldier and the paper-doll ballerina. The soldier gives the ballerina his tin heart, but a draft pulls her into the fire in the fireplace and she is consumed. All that remains is the heart, which the soldier, weeping, rescues. The production was commissioned by the Saratoga Performing Arts Center.

STAGINGS: 1981, Zürich.

TELEVISION: 1979 (Dance in America, PBS).

See 310*

399 ORFEO ED EURIDICE

Opera in Two Acts and Five Scenes by Christoph Willibald Gluck

DANCES OF SHEPHERDS AND SHEPHERDESSES; FURIES AND DEMONS;
BLESSED SPIRITS

PREMIERE: November 22, 1975, Chicago Lyric Opera. Danced by
Chicago Lyric Opera Ballet. Conductor: Jean Fournet.

CAST: Corps de ballet.

See 170*, 345, 400

1976

400 CHACONNE

MUSIC: By Christoph Willibald Gluck (ballet music from *Orfeo ed
Euridice*, produced 1762, with music from the Paris production of 1774).

CHOREOGRAPHY: By George Balanchine, staged by Brigitte Thom.

PRODUCTION: Lighting by Ronald Bates.

PREMIERE: January 22, 1976, New York City Ballet, New York State
Theater. Conductor: Robert Irving.

CAST: Suzanne Farrell, Peter Martins; PAS DE TROIS: Renee Estopinal,
Wilhelmina Frankfurt, Jay Jolley; PAS DE DEUX: Susan Hendl, Jean-
Pierre Frohlich; PAS DE CINQ: Elise Flagg; Bonita Borne, Elyse Borne,
Laura Flagg, Nichol Hlinka; PAS DE DEUX: Farrell, Martins; CHACONNE:
Farrell, Martins; Susan Pilarre, Marjorie Spohn, Tracy Bennett, Gerard
Ebitz, corps de ballet.

NOTE: The finale of Gluck's opera is in the form of a dance, rather
than song. This choreography, first performed in the 1963 Hamburg
State Opera production of *Orfeo ed Euridice* [345], was somewhat
altered for presentation as the ballet *Chaconne*, particularly the
sections for Farrell and Martins. Initially danced in practice clothes;
costumes by Karinska were added in the spring of 1976.

REVISIONS: New York City Ballet, spring 1976: Opening ensemble
added to 'The Dance of the Blessed Spirits.'

STAGINGS: 1978, Paris.

TELEVISION: 1978 (excerpts, Dance in America, PBS); 1979 (CBC, Montreal).

See 170*, 345, 399

401 UNION JACK

MUSIC: By Hershy Kay (adapted from traditional British sources as given below, 1976, commissioned by the New York City Ballet).

PRODUCTION: Scenery and costumes by Rouben Ter-Arutunian, including a drop curtain for Part II from the New York City Opera production of *La Cenerentola* (1953). Scottish costumes by Sheldon M. Kasman of Toronto. Lighting by Ronald Bates.

PREMIERE: May 13, 1976, New York City Ballet, New York State Theater. Conductor: Robert Irving. (Preview: Annual New York City Ballet Gala Benefit, May 12.)

CAST: I. SCOTTISH AND CANADIAN GUARDS REGIMENTS: ('Keel Row') LENNOX: Helgi Tomasson, 9 men; DRESS MACLEOD: Jacques d'Amboise, 9 men. ('Caledonian Hunt's Delight') GREEN MONTGOMERIE: Sara Leland, 9 women. ('Dance wi' My Daddy') MENZIES: Peter Martins, 9 men; DRESS MACDONALD: Kay Mazzo, 9 women. ('Regimental Drum Variations') MACDONALD OF SLEAT: Karin von Aroldingen, 9 women. (Scottish theme from the *Water Music* by George Frederick Handel) R.C.A.F. (ROYAL CANADIAN AIR FORCE): Suzanne Farrell, 9 women. ('Amazing Grace,' 'A Hundred Pipers') FINALE: Entire cast. II. COSTERMONGER PAS DE DEUX (music-hall songs, ca. 1890-1914: 'The Sunshine of Your Smile,' 'The Night the Floor Fell In,' 'Our Lodger's Such a Naice Young Man,' 'Following in Father's Footsteps,' 'A Tavern in the Town'): *Pearly King*, Jean-Pierre Bonnefous; *Pearly Queen*, Patricia McBride; 2 young girls, donkey. III. ROYAL NAVY (traditional hornpipe melodies, 'Rule Britannia'): von Aroldingen, Victor Castelli, Bart Cook; d'Amboise, 8 women, 8 men; Leland, Mazzo, Tomasson; Martins, 8 women, 8 men; WRENS (WOMEN'S ROYAL NAVAL SERVICE): Farrell, 8 women; FINALE: Entire cast.

NOTE: Created to honor the British heritage of the United States on the occasion of its Bicentennial. Part I is based on Scottish military tattoos and folk-dance forms performed in an open castle square.

Part II is a music-hall pas de deux for the costermonger Pearly King and Queen of London, with two little girls and a donkey, danced before a drop suggesting Pollock's toy theaters. Part III is a series of variations employing hornpipes, sea songs, work chants, jigs, and drill orders of the Royal Navy, in a quay-side setting. For the finale, hand flags signal 'God Save the Queen' in a marine semaphore code as the British Union Jack appears.

REVISIONS: 1976, New York City Ballet: March sections shortened immediately after premiere; second half of GREEN MONTGOMERIE section completely rechoreographed; ending of COSTERMONGER scene redone several times.

402 PAL JOEY
Musical Theater

Balanchine worked with Edward Villella (as Joey) on choreography for 'Bewitched, Bothered and Bewildered' in the 1976 Circle in the Square production of Richard Rodgers and Lorenz Hart's *Pal Joey*. Villella withdrew from the production before the premiere.

403 THE RELUCTANT KING (LE ROI MALGRÉ LUI)
Comic Opera in Three Acts by Emmanuel Chabrier
ACT II FÊTE POLONAISE; DANCE OF THE ROYAL POLISH GUARDS

PREMIERE: November 19, 1976, Juilliard American Opera Center, The Juilliard Theater, New York. Danced by students of the School of American Ballet. Conductor: Manuel Rosenthal.

CAST: Corps de ballet.

See 265

1977

404 THE SLEEPING BEAUTY: AURORA'S SOLO, VISION SCENE

MUSIC: By Peter Ilyitch Tschaikovsky (produced 1890).

CHOREOGRAPHY: After the choreography of Marius Petipa. Choreography for the GARLAND DANCE by Michael Vernon. Choreography for Aurora's solo in the VISION SCENE by George Balanchine.

PRODUCTION: Staged and directed by André Eglevsky. Scenery and costumes by Peter Farmer.

PREMIERE: April 14, 1977, The Eglevsky Ballet, Hofstra University, Hempstead, New York.

CAST: *Princess Aurora*, Patricia McBride; *Prince*, Peter Schaufuss; *Lilac Fairy*, Leslie Peck; corps de ballet.

See 65, 225, 259, 281, 418

405 ÉTUDE FOR PIANO

MUSIC: By Alexander Scriabin (Étude in C-sharp minor, Op. 8, no. 1).

PRODUCTION: Costumes by Christina Giannini.

PREMIERE: June 4, 1977, Spoleto Festival U.S.A., Charleston, South Carolina. Pianist: Boris Bloch. (First New York City Ballet performance June 12, New York State Theater. Pianist: Gordon Boelzner.)

CAST: Patricia McBride, Jean-Pierre Bonnefous.

406 VIENNA WALTZES (briefly called WIENER WALZER)

MUSIC: By Johann Strauss the Younger, Franz Lehár and Richard Strauss (as given below).

PRODUCTION: Scenery by Rouben Ter-Arutunian, executed by Nolan Scenery Studios. Costumes by Karinska. Lighting by Ronald Bates.

PREMIERE: June 23, 1977, New York City Ballet, New York State Theater. Conductor: Robert Irving. (Preview: Annual New York City Ballet Gala Benefit, June 15, with Jean-Pierre Bonnefous in the role later danced by Jorge Donn.)

CAST: TALES FROM THE VIENNA WOODS (J. Strauss, Op. 325, 1868): Karin von Aroldingen, Sean Lavery, 10 couples; VOICES OF SPRING (J. Strauss, Op. 410, 1885): Patricia McBride, Helgi Tomasson, 8 women; EXPLOSION POLKA (J. Strauss, Op. 43, ca. 1848): Sara Leland, Bart Cook, 3 couples; GOLD AND SILVER WALTZ (Lehár, 1905): Kay Mazzo, Peter Martins, 8 couples; FIRST SEQUENCE OF WALTZES FROM 'DER ROSEN-KAVALIER' (R. Strauss, arranged 1944): Suzanne Farrell, Jorge Donn (guest artist); von Aroldingen, Lavery; McBride, Tomasson; Leland, Cook; Mazzo, Martins; entire cast.

NOTE: Each waltz suggests a different mood. The first three take place in the Vienna Woods: a formal dance, wood spirits, a comic polka. The scenery evolves: The trees develop tendrils of décor to form the dancing-room of the 'Merry Widow' (GOLD AND SILVER WALTZ); in the finale, the roots of the trees become the chandeliers of a gala, mirrored ballroom for WALTZES FROM 'DER ROSENKAVALIER.'

REVISIONS: New York City Ballet: GOLD AND SILVER WALTZ changed many times; minor revisions in VOICES OF SPRING.

1978

407 BALLO DELLA REGINA

MUSIC: By Giuseppe Verdi (ballet music from *Don Carlos*, Act III, produced 1867, with some additions from the same score).

PRODUCTION: Costumes by Ben Benson. Lighting by Ronald Bates.

PREMIERE: January 12, 1978, New York City Ballet, New York State Theater. Conductor: Robert Irving. (Preview: Opening Night New York City Ballet Gala Benefit, November 15, 1977.)

CAST: Merrill Ashley, Robert Weiss; Debra Austin, Bonita Borne, Stephanie Saland, Sheryl Ware; 12 women.

NOTE: Using the ballet music from *Don Carlos*, with reference through lighting and costumes to the original tale of a fisherman's search for the perfect pearl, Balanchine created a work for a ballerina and her partner, with solos for four women.

TELEVISION: 1979 (Dance in America, PBS).

408 KAMMERMUSIK NO. 2

MUSIC: By Paul Hindemith (1924).

PRODUCTION: Costumes by Ben Benson. Lighting by Ronald Bates.

PREMIERE: January 26, 1978, New York City Ballet, New York State Theater. Conductor: Robert Irving.

CAST: Karin von Aroldingen, Colleen Neary, Sean Lavery, Adam Lüders; 8 men.

NOTE: In four movements (I.; II.; III. KLEINES POTPOURRI; IV. FINALE), performed without interruption.

409 TRICOLORE

MUSIC: By Georges Auric (1978, commissioned by the New York City Ballet).

CHOREOGRAPHY: Ballet conceived and supervised by George Balanchine. Choreography by Peter Martins, Jean-Pierre Bonnefous and Jerome Robbins.

PRODUCTION: Scenery and costumes by Rouben Ter-Arutunian. Lighting by Ronald Bates.

PREMIERE: May 18, 1978, New York City Ballet, New York State Theater. Conductor: Robert Irving. (Preview: Annual New York City Ballet Gala Benefit, May 17.)

CAST: PAS DE BASQUE (choreographed by Martins): Colleen Neary, Adam Lüders, 4 couples, 8 women, 8 men; PAS DEGAS (choreographed by Bonnefous): Merrill Ashley, Sean Lavery, 2 female demi-soloists, 10 women, 6 men; MARCHE DE LA GARDE RÉPUBLICAINE (choreographed by Robbins): *La Garde Républicaine*, 2 couples, 18 women, 18 men; *Majorettes*, Karin von Aroldingen, 8 women; APOTHEOSIS: *Mademoiselle Marianne*, Nina Fedorova; entire cast.

NOTE: A salute to France in music and dance: With *Stars and Stripes* [318] and *Union Jack* [401], the work completes a trio of ballets projected as an 'Entente Cordiale.' Balanchine chose Auric to compose the score for the occasion; they had first collaborated under Diaghilev in 1924 on *La Pastorale* [62], and again in 1932 on *La Concurrence* [130].

1979

410 LE BOURGEOIS GENTILHOMME

MUSIC: By Richard Strauss (concert suite, ca. 1917). Libretto after Molière.

CHOREOGRAPHY: By George Balanchine and Jerome Robbins. COOKS DANCE by Peter Martins (uncredited). Assistant to the Choreographers: Susan Hendl.

PRODUCTION: Scenery and costumes designed by Rouben Ter-Arutunian. Costumes executed by Karinska. Lighting by Gilbert Hemsley, Jr.

PREMIERE: April 8, 1979, New York City Opera, New York State Theater. Corps de ballet composed of students of the School of American Ballet. Conductor: Cal Stewart Kellogg.

CAST: *Lucile*, Patricia McBride; *M. Jourdain*, Jean-Pierre Bonnefous; *Cléonte*, Rudolf Nureyev; DIVERTISSEMENT: Darla Hoover, Michael Puleo, six women; *Maid*; *6 Lackeys*; *4 Cooks*; *2 Attendants to Cléonte*.

NOTE: Performed with Henry Purcell's opera *Dido and Aeneas*.

REVISIONS: 1980, New York City Ballet: Choreography credited to Balanchine alone; several dancing passages for Cléonte removed, replaced by mime passages for Cléonte and Lucile.

STAGINGS: 1979, Paris; 1980, Zürich.

OTHER VERSIONS: 1932, Ballets Russes de Monte-Carlo. 1944, Ballet Russe de Monte Carlo.

See 131*, 221, 414

411 DIDO AND AENEAS

Opera in a Prologue and Three Acts by Henry Purcell
PANTOMIME

CHOREOGRAPHY: By Peter Martins. Pantomime scenes directed by Frank Corsaro in collaboration with George Balanchine.

PREMIERE: April 8, 1979, New York City Opera, New York State Theater. Danced by students of the School of American Ballet. Conductor: Cal Stewart Kellogg.

CAST: *Attendants to Dido,* 8 girls; *Attendants to Aeneas,* 4 boys; *Witches, Sailors, Animals, Torch Bearers.*

1980

412 BALLADE

MUSIC: By Gabriel Fauré (*Ballade* for piano and orchestra, Op. 19, 1881).

PRODUCTION: Scenery and costumes by Rouben Ter-Arutunian (from *Tricolore,* PAS DEGAS [409]), lighting by Ronald Bates.

PREMIERE: May 8, 1980, New York City Ballet, New York State Theater. Conductor: Robert Irving. Pianist: Gordon Boelzner.

CAST: Merrill Ashley, Ib Andersen, 10 women.

NOTE: The music (celebrated in Proust) is in one movement with three underlying sections; the ballet is a series of pas de deux and solos for a ballerina and her cavalier, accompanied from time to time by the corps of women.

NEW PRODUCTIONS BY BALANCHINE COMPANIES: 1982, New York City Ballet: Performed without décor; costumes by Ben Benson (from *Introduction and Fugue* [J. Duell], 1981), lighting by Ronald Bates.

413 WALPURGISNACHT BALLET

From Gounod's 'Faust'

MUSIC: By Charles Gounod (from *Faust*, produced with ballet music 1869).

CHOREOGRAPHY: By George Balanchine. Staged by Brigitte Thom.

PRODUCTION: Lighting by Ronald Bates.

PREMIERE: May 15, 1980, New York City Ballet, New York State Theater. Conductor: Robert Irving. (Preview: School of American Ballet Gala Benefit, January 24.)

CAST: Suzanne Farrell, Adam Lüders; Heather Watts; Stephanie Saland, Judith Fugate; 20 women.

NOTE: Balanchine's presentation as an independent ballet of the work he originally staged as part of the Paris Opéra production of Gounod's *Faust* [397] in 1975.

See 45, 117, 151, 227, 397

414 LE BOURGEOIS GENTILHOMME

MUSIC: By Richard Strauss (concert suite, ca. 1917). Libretto after Molière.

CHOREOGRAPHY: By George Balanchine. Assistant to the Choreographer: Susan Hendl.

PRODUCTION: Scenery and costumes by Rouben Ter-Arutunian. Lighting by Ronald Bates.

PREMIERE: May 22, 1980, New York City Ballet, New York State Theater. Conductor: Robert Irving.

CAST: *M. Jourdain*, Frank Ohman; *Cléonte*, Peter Martins; *Lucille*, Suzanne Farrell; DIVERTISSEMENT: Heather Watts, Victor Castelli, 6 women; *Maid*; *6 Lackeys*; *4 Cooks*; *2 Assistants to Cléonte*.

NOTE: Originally presented by the New York City Opera, 1979.

OTHER VERSIONS: 1932, Ballets Russes de Monte-Carlo. 1944, Ballet Russe de Monte Carlo.

See 131*, 221, 410*

415 ROBERT SCHUMANN'S 'DAVIDSBÜNDLERTÄNZE'

Music: By Robert Schumann (Op. 6, 1837).

Production: Scenery and costumes by Rouben Ter-Arutunian. Lighting by Ronald Bates.

Premiere: June 19, 1980, New York City Ballet, New York State Theater. On-stage pianist: Gordon Boelzner. (Preview: Annual New York City Ballet Gala Benefit, June 12.)

Cast: Karin von Aroldingen, Adam Lüders; Suzanne Farrell, Jacques d'Amboise; Heather Watts, Peter Martins; Kay Mazzo, Ib Andersen.

Note: Four couples perform the eighteen *Dances of the League of David*, choreographed to Schumann's piano music written to Clara Wieck, who later became his wife. The original bylines expressing Schumann's multiple selves were expunged by him from later editions of the score. Although the dances suggest facets of Schumann and Clara's personalities, the ballet is in essence musical, not biographical.

Television: 1982 (CBS Cable).

1981

416 THE SPELLBOUND CHILD / L'ENFANT ET LES SORTILÈGES
Made for Television

Music: By Maurice Ravel (1920-25). Lyric fantasy in two parts based on a poem by Colette (translated by Catherine Wolff).

Production: Produced by Emile Ardolino and Judy Kinberg. Conceived for television and with choreography by George Balanchine, in collaboration with Kermit Love. Directed by Emile Ardolino. Design concept, puppets, models, and costumes by Kermit Love. Supervising Designer: David Mitchell. Lighting by Ralph Holmes.

First telecast: May 25, 1981, Dance in America, PBS. Danced by New York City Ballet, students from the School of American Ballet, and others. Conductor of New York City Ballet orchestra: Manuel Rosenthal. Singers off-camera.

CAST: *Boy*, Christopher Byars; *Mother*; *Armchair*; *Lady Chair* (2 women); *Clock*; *Teapot*; *Chinese Cup*; *Fire*, Karin von Aroldingen; *5 Shepherds*; *5 Shepherdesses*; *2 Cats*; *Wounded Tree*; *Dragonflies*, 4 women; *Bats*, 2 women, 1 man; *Moths*, 6 women; *2 Frogs*; *2 Owls*; *Toads*, 8 boys.

NOTE: Created for color television, this production used elements of the 1975 staging, and employed special effects, including animation for certain parts of the narrative.

OTHER VERSIONS: 1925, Opéra de Monte-Carlo (*L'Enfant et les Sortilèges*, danced by Diaghilev's Ballets Russes). 1946, Ballet Society (*The Spellbound Child* [*L'Enfant et les Sortilèges*]). 1975, New York City Ballet (*L'Enfant et les Sortilèges*, Ravel Festival).

See 48*, 235, 390

417 MOZARTIANA

MUSIC: By Peter Ilyitch Tschaikovsky (Suite No. 4, *Mozartiana*, Op. 61, 1887; based on Mozart's Gigue in G major [K. 574], Minuet in D major [K. 355], the motet 'Ave, Verum Corpus' [K. 618], and variations on 'Les Hommes Pieusement' from Gluck's comic opera *La Rencontre Imprévue* [K. 455]).

PRODUCTION: Costumes by Rouben Ter-Arutunian.

PREMIERE: June 4, 1981, New York City Ballet with students from the School of American Ballet, New York State Theater. Conductor: Robert Irving. (Annual New York City Ballet Gala Benefit.)

CAST: PREGHIERA: Suzanne Farrell, 4 young girls; GIGUE: Christopher d'Amboise; MENUET: 4 women; THÈME ET VARIATIONS: Farrell, Ib Andersen; FINALE: Entire cast.

NOTE: The ballet is completely different from the work Balanchine created to this music in 1933, and modified thereafter. The order of the first two movements is reversed to begin with the PREGHIERA (based on the motet 'Ave, Verum Corpus'), in which the ballerina dances a prayer, attended by four young girls. The 1981 *Mozartiana* was first presented on the opening night of the Tschaikovsky Festival of the New York City Ballet (detailed in *Festivals Directed by Balanchine*, page 313), which included the premieres of four Balanchine works [417-420]. Throughout the festival and until the end of the New York season on June 28, the scenery was an architectural structure with movable ranks of translucent plastic cylinders by Philip Johnson and John Burgee, in arrangements and with lighting designs by Ronald Bates.

See 134*, 149

418 TEMPO DI VALSE:
GARLAND DANCE from THE SLEEPING BEAUTY

MUSIC: By Peter Ilyitch Tschaikovsky (as given below).

CHOREOGRAPHY: By George Balanchine (two of five parts), Jacques d'Amboise and John Taras.

PRODUCTION: Costumes for GARLAND DANCE by Karinska (from DIAMONDS in *Jewels* [358] and *Chaconne* [400]) and Rouben Ter-Arutunian (from *Coppélia* [387]).

PREMIERE: June 9, 1981, New York City Ballet with students from the School of American Ballet, New York State Theater. Conductor: Robert Irving.

CAST: GARLAND DANCE from *The Sleeping Beauty*, Act I (produced 1890): 25 women, 16 men, 16 young girls.

NOTE: Sixteen couples dance, each couple holding aloft a garland of flowers in the form of an arch; a chain of little girls enters, weaving under the garlands, and is joined by nine older girls. In addition to the GARLAND DANCE, the short works presented under the general title *Tempo di Valse* during the Tschaikovsky Festival (and later in the season) were the WALTZ OF THE FLOWERS from *The Nutcracker* [302] by Balanchine, VALSE-SCHERZO by d'Amboise, and VARIATION VI FROM TRIO IN A MINOR and WALTZ FROM EUGEN ONEGIN, ACT II by Taras.

See 65, 225, 259, 281, 404

419 HUNGARIAN GYPSY AIRS

MUSIC: By Sophie Menter (*Hungarische Zigeuner Weisen*), orchestrated by Peter Ilyitch Tschaikovsky.

PRODUCTION: Costumes by Ben Benson.

PREMIERE: June 13, 1981, New York City Ballet, New York State Theater. Conductor: Robert Irving. Pianist: Richard Moredock.

CAST: Karin von Aroldingen, Adam Lüders; 4 women, 4 men.

420 SYMPHONY NO. 6—PATHÉTIQUE: FOURTH MOVEMENT, ADAGIO LAMENTOSO

MUSIC: By Peter Ilyitch Tschaikovsky (Symphony No. 6 in B minor, Op. 74, 1893 [first movement omitted]).

CHOREOGRAPHY: By George Balanchine (ADAGIO LAMENTOSO) and Jerome Robbins.

PRODUCTION: Costumes for ADAGIO LAMENTOSO by Rouben Ter-Arutunian.

PREMIERE: June 14, 1981, New York City Ballet, New York State Theater. Conductor: Robert Irving.

CAST: FOURTH MOVEMENT, ADAGIO LAMENTOSO: Karin von Aroldingen, Judith Fugate, Stephanie Saland; 16 women; 12 Angels; group of hooded figures; child.

NOTE: The first movement of the symphony was omitted; the second, ALLEGRO CON GRAZIA, was choreographed by Robbins; the third, ALLEGRO MOLTO VIVACE, was played by the orchestra with curtain lowered. The fourth and final movement was Balanchine's ADAGIO LAMENTOSO: Women mourners dance in grief; angels with tall white wings and hooded figures in purple are followed by a procession of monks who prostrate themselves to form a living cross; a child enters carrying a candle. To the final chords, the child extinguishes the candle. The ADAGIO LAMENTOSO closed the Tschaikovsky Festival of the New York City Ballet.

1982

421 TANGO

Music: By Igor Stravinsky (1940 [1953 instrumentation by Stravinsky]).

Premiere: June 10, 1982, New York City Ballet, New York State Theater. Conductor: Robert Irving. (Annual New York City Ballet Gala Benefit.)

Cast: Karin von Aroldingen, Christopher d'Amboise.

Note: The dancers perform in vaudeville-style costumes, the woman in abbreviated black lace, the man in Spanish dress. The premiere used Stravinsky's orchestration for jazz ensemble; subsequent performances were danced to the composer's score for solo piano, with the pianist on stage. *Tango* was first presented on the opening night of the Stravinsky Centennial Celebration of the New York City Ballet (detailed in *Festivals Directed by Balanchine*, page 316), which included the premieres of four Balanchine works [421-424]. The décor throughout the Centennial Celebration incorporated the architectural settings created by Johnson/Burgee for the Tschaikovsky Festival of 1981, arranged and lighted by Ronald Bates.

422 NOAH AND THE FLOOD

Music: Dance-drama by Igor Stravinsky (*The Flood*, 1962, written for television). Text chosen and arranged by Robert Craft from *Genesis*, the *Te Deum* and *Sanctus* hymns, and the fifteenth-century York and Chester miracle plays.

Choreography: Staged by George Balanchine and Jacques d'Amboise.

Production: Designed by Rouben Ter-Arutunian (costumes and masks from the 1962 television production [342]; hanging backdrop based on the 1962 designs; some new décor).

Premiere: June 11, 1982, New York City Ballet with students from the School of American Ballet, New York State Theater. Conductor:

Robert Craft. Off-stage singers: Members of the New York City Opera chorus; Chorus Master: Lloyd Walser.

CAST: VOICES: *Narrator* (spoken), John Houseman; *Voices of God* (basses), Robert Brubaker, Barry Carl; *Voice of Satan* (tenor), John Lankston. DANCERS: *Adam*, Adam Lüders; *Eve*, Nina Fedorova; *Lucifer*, Bruce Padgett; *Noah*, Francisco Moncion; *Noah's Wife*, Delia Peters; *The Family*, 2 women, 3 men; *Builders of the Ark*, 8 women, 8 men.

NOTE: Balanchine's staged presentation for the Stravinsky Centennial Celebration of the morality play originally conceived for television, reproducing almost exactly the choreographed sections of the original production. THE PROLOGUE and SATAN'S ARIETTA were omitted; the narration, divided among several actors on television, was spoken solely by John Houseman on stage. The décor was based on the designs for television, but the animals, which in the original production had been miniature toys belonging to Balanchine, were replaced by large cut-outs carried in procession by students of the School of American Ballet.

See 342*

423 ÉLÉGIE

MUSIC: By Igor Stravinsky (*Élégie-Elegy* for solo viola, 1944).

PREMIERE: June 13, 1982, New York City Ballet, New York State Theater. On-stage violist: Warren Laffredo.

CAST: Suzanne Farrell.

NOTE: Balanchine first choreographed Stravinsky's *Élégie* as a pas de deux in 1948, and then as a solo in 1966. At the opening and closing of this newly choreographed work the dancer kneels in a circle of light on the darkened stage.

See 245*, 355

424 PERSÉPHONE

MUSIC: By Igor Stravinsky (*Mélodrame* in three scenes for tenor, narrator, mixed chorus, children's choir, and orchestra, commissioned by Ida Rubinstein, 1933). Text by André Gide.

CHOREOGRAPHY: Staged by George Balanchine, John Taras and Vera Zorina.

PRODUCTION: Designed by Kermit Love.

PREMIERE: June 18, 1982, New York City Ballet, New York State Theater. Conductor: Robert Craft. Singers: Members of the New York City Opera chorus; Chorus Master: Lloyd Walser. The American Boychoir prepared by Brad Richmond and Robert Hobbs.

CAST: *Perséphone* (spoken), Vera Zorina; *Eumolpus the Eleusinian Priest* (tenor), Joseph Evans; *Spirit of Perséphone*, Karin von Aroldingen; *Pluto*, Mel Tomlinson; *Mercury*, Gen Horiuchi; *Nymphs*, 9 women; *Shades of the Underworld*, 9 women, 6 men.

NOTE: Presented by Balanchine on the one-hundredth anniversary of the composer's birth as the last ballet of the Stravinsky Centennial Celebration, forty-nine years after its first production, which Stravinsky had hoped Balanchine would choreograph. *Perséphone* was originally presented by Ballets Ida Rubinstein in 1934, choreographed by Kurt Jooss and narrated by Ida Rubinstein. In the Balanchine staging, the costumed chorus is grouped on both sides of the stage, framing the action. Perséphone, abducted by Pluto, dwells in the underworld during Autumn and Winter, but is restored to earth each year to bless mankind in Spring and Summer. Gide's text ends:

> No spring can ever live again
> Unless the seed beneath the ground
> Consents to die, and wakens then
> To make the future's field abound.

425 VARIATIONS FOR ORCHESTRA

MUSIC: By Igor Stravinsky (*Variations in Memory of Aldous Huxley*, 1965).

PRODUCTION: Lighting by Ronald Bates.

PREMIERE: July 2, 1982, New York City Ballet, New York State Theater. Conductor: Robert Irving.

CAST: Suzanne Farrell.

NOTE: The premiere of this ballet intended for the Stravinsky Centennial Celebration took place two weeks after its official close. Balanchine had first choreographed a solo for Suzanne Farrell to this music as the final section of his 1966 work for the New York City Ballet, in which the music was played three times. The 1982 work was entirely rechoreographed. This is the last ballet choreographed by Balanchine.

See 353

SOURCE NOTES

Entries in the *Catalogue* have been compiled from printed programs, and information from critical reviews in newspapers, periodicals, and the published works cited in the *Bibliography*. Additional information has been provided by the persons named in the notes that follow. Printed sources are included in the notes only when the information is available from a single source; author, title and page reference are given for books cited in the *Bibliography*, with publisher and date provided for other works.

Principal archives and public collections consulted include the Bibliothèque de l'Arsenal (Collection Rondel), Paris; Bibliothèque et Musée de l'Opéra, Paris; Bibliothèque Ste. Geneviève (Collection Doucet), Paris; Garrick Club, London; Harvard Theatre Collection; Lenin State Library, Moscow; Leningrad State Institute of Theater, Music and Cinematography; Moscow Institute of the History of the Arts; Moscow Theater (Bakrushin) Museum; Museum of the Vaganova Choreographic School, Leningrad; The New York Public Library Dance Collection and Slavonic Division; Opéra de Monte-Carlo Archives; library of the Royal Theater, Copenhagen; Theatre Museum at the Victoria and Albert Museum, London.

1 - 35 Full documentation of Balanchine's activities before he left the Soviet Union in 1924 is not possible. Although printed programs of official performances at the Maryinsky Theater and School in St. Petersburg (later State Theater of Opera and Ballet/Petrograd Theater [Ballet] School, now Kirov Theater and School) exist, none have been found for the performances given by the Young Ballet; a single poster announcing the opening concert is in the Museum of the Vaganova Choreographic School, Leningrad.

Research was carried out in the Soviet Union by Elizabeth Souritz (Moscow: Moscow Institute of the History of the Arts) and Vera Krasovskaya (Leningrad: State Institute of Theater, Music and Cinematography); and by Gunhild Schüller of the Institut für Theaterwissenschaft, University of Vienna, who visited Moscow and Leningrad in 1981. Major printed resources consulted were the newspapers *Krasnaya gazeta* and *Zhizn' iskusstva*, the periodicals *Teatr* and *Teatr i iskusstvo*, and the weekly of the Petrograd/Leningrad Academic Theaters: *Evhenedel'nik petrogradskikh gosudarstvenniykh akademicheskikh teatrov; Evhenedel'nik akademicheskikh teatrov v Leningrade*. Entries 1-35 are based on the research of Souritz, Krasovskaya and Schüller; on interviews conducted with Pëtr Gusev in Leningrad (Poel Karp, 1980), and with Balanchine, Alexandra Danilova and Tamara Geva in New York (Nancy Reynolds and Gunhild Schüller, 1979-81); and on material from publications cited in full in the *Bibliography: Balanchine's Complete Stories of the Great Ballets*, Tamara Geva's *Split Seconds*, Mikhail Mikhailov's *My Life in Ballet*, Natalia Roslavleva's *Era of the Russian*

Ballet, Yuri Slonimsky's *Balanchine: The Early Years,* Bernard Taper's *Balanchine: A Biography,* and A. E. Twysden's *Alexandra Danilova.*

Information about the Rhineland tour of the Principal Dancers of the Russian State Ballet (ending with an engagement at the Empire Theatre, London) comes primarily from announcements and reviews in the local press.

36, 37 Grigoriev, *The Diaghilev Ballet,* p. 209; amplified by Balanchine, Alicia Markova, Anton Dolin.

38 Balanchine.

48 Boris Kochno.

50, 51 John Martin, *Ruth Page: An Intimate Biography* (New York: Dekker, 1977), p. 61; corroborated by Balanchine, Ruth Page. Additional music information provided by Balanchine.

53 Revisions information in Hillary Ostlere, 'Rieti and Balanchine,' *Ballet Review* 10:1 (Spring 1982), p. 8.

61 Additional production information in Buckle, *Diaghilev,* p. 466.

64 Revisions information in Macdonald, *Diaghilev Observed,* p. 348. Additional information provided by Boris Kochno, David Vaughan.

65 Alicia Markova.

73, 74 Tamara Geva, Lincoln Kirstein. Although contained in a revue, these pieces were reviewed by the dance critic of the *New York Times,* December 11, 1927.

75 Balanchine, Alicia Markova.

83 Information provided by Keith Money; corroborated by Balanchine.

84 Additional information provided by Alexandra Danilova; additional revisions information provided by Nancy Goldner, Allegra Kent.

85 Additional production information in Macdonald, *Diaghilev Observed,* p. 364.

91 Uncredited choreography acknowledged by Balanchine.

94 Boris Kochno has corrected the general misunderstanding that the book for the ballet is based on a story by Pushkin. The printed program for the premiere performance names the conductor as *l'auteur,* Sergei Prokofiev; this is repeated by Prokofiev in his *Autobiography* (Moscow: Foreign Languages Publishing House, 1959, p. 74), and by Robert Craft in *Stravinsky in Pictures and Documents* (p. 287). Grigoriev (*The Diaghilev Ballet,* p. 278) gives Roger Desormière as conductor, which Balanchine believes to be correct.

95 Additional information provided by Alicia Markova and Anton Dolin, who danced *Moods* together for several years.

97 Boris Kochno.

98 Scenery and costumes credited to Angèles Ortiz in later programs.

100 Additional music information provided by Ulla Poulsen.

105 Ulla Poulsen.

107 Balanchine, Elizabeth Baron [Betty Scorer], Natasha Gregorova Cookson, Alicia Markova, Doris Sonne Toye, and brief reviews in *Era.*

110 Music information provided by Balanchine.

129 Music information provided by Balanchine and Vittorio Rieti; additional information provided by Kathrine Sorley Walker.

131 Note corroborated by Balanchine.

133 Balanchine, Georges Auric, Boris Kochno.

134 Revisions information provided by Balanchine and Patricia Wilde (who performed in the Ballet Russe de Monte Carlo version); additional information provided by Lincoln Kirstein.

135 Balanchine.

136 Boris Kochno.

139 Music information provided by Balanchine.

141 Additional music information provided by Balanchine. Revisions information provided by Balanchine, Ruthanna Boris, Rosemary Dunleavy, Annabelle Lyon, Marie-Jeanne.

142 Additional music information provided by Kay Swift, Morton Gould.

143 Tamara Geva, Marie-Jeanne.

144 Ruthanna Boris.

146 Lincoln Kirstein.

147 Mentioned in the *New York Times*, May 4 and 12, 1935. Additional information provided by William Dollar.

155 Information about scenery provided by Lincoln Kirstein.

157 Information provided by William Dollar, at the suggestion of Gisella Caccialanza.

160 Structure of ballet divertissement clarified by Ruthanna Boris.

164 Music information provided by Balanchine; date verified in Balanchine-Kirstein-A. Everett Austin correspondence, Wadsworth Atheneum, through the assistance of Jill Silverman; additional information provided by Lincoln Kirstein.

165 Structure of ballet clarified by William Dollar.

166 Balanchine.

167 Ruthanna Boris.

172 Balanchine.

178 Additional revisions information provided by Maria Tallchief.

182 Additional information about dance numbers provided by Balanchine.

185 Balanchine.

186 Balanchine.

190 Additional information provided by Katherine Dunham: The collaboration was so complete that it is impossible to be specific about individual contributions.

192 Kathrine Sorley Walker, Lincoln Kirstein.

194 Additional revisions and stagings information provided by Balanchine, Una Kai, Patricia McBride.

202 *New York Times*, June 18, 1982.

205 *Washington Post*, March 1, 6, 7, 1964. Margaret Graham.

206 Edward Bigelow.

212 Gisella Caccialanza.

214 Information provided by Balanchine; corroborated by André Eglevsky.

215 Tanaquil Le Clercq.

216 Balanchine.

218 Additional information about dance numbers provided by Balanchine.

219 Structure of dance numbers clarified by Alexandra Danilova, Maria Tallchief, Frederic Franklin.

220 Balanchine, Nikita Talin.

222 Additional music information provided by Vittorio Rieti.

223 Marie-Jeanne.

224 Balanchine.

225 Additional music information provided by Balanchine, Gordon Boelzner.

226 - 228 Balanchine, Marie-Jeanne, Patricia Wilde.

231 Balanchine, Tanaquil Le Clercq, March of Dimes.

232 Additional music information provided by Vittorio Rieti; additional revisions and stagings information provided by Rosemary Dunleavy, John Taras.

233 Additional information about the conception of the ballet provided by Balanchine, Alexandra Danilova; additional revisions information provided by Nikita Talin, Maria Tallchief; additional stagings information provided by Frederic Franklin, Lew Christensen; structure of *Pas de Dix* clarified by Maria Tallchief.

234 Balanchine.

237 Lew Christensen.

241 Lincoln Kirstein.

243 Betty Cage.

244 John Taras.

246 Nancy Goldner.

247 Balanchine, Maria Tallchief, Marjorie Tallchief, Victoria Simon, André Eglevsky, George Skibine.

249 Fred Danieli.

257 Uncredited movement direction acknowledged by Balanchine.

259 Balanchine, Maria Tallchief.

261 Balanchine, Tanaquil Le Clercq.

262 Balanchine, Maria Tallchief.

264 Additional information about choreography for the Firebird provided by Maria Tallchief.

266 Tanaquil Le Clercq.

267 Additional information about costumes provided by Barbara Horgan, Edward Bigelow.

273 Arlene Croce, David Vaughan.

274 Balanchine, Melissa Hayden.

275 David Vaughan.

285 Additional music information provided by Robert Irving; additional revisions information provided by Merrill Ashley, Arlene Croce, Rosemary Dunleavy, Robert Irving.

290 Balanchine.

291 Balanchine, Tanaquil Le Clercq, Jacques d'Amboise.

294 Information provided by Virginia Brooks, New York Public Library Dance Collection; corroborated by Melissa Hayden.

296 Tanaquil Le Clercq, Jacques d'Amboise.

297 - 299 Tanaquil Le Clercq.

302 Additional music information provided by Balanchine, Gordon Boelzner, Robert Irving; revisions information provided by Balanchine, Rosemary Dunleavy.

305 Tanaquil Le Clercq, Arthur Mitchell.

309 Additional revisions information provided by Arlene Croce.

311 Kirk Browning.

314 Additional music information provided by Balanchine, Robert Irving; additional revisions information provided by Arlene Croce, Rosemary Dunleavy, Suki Schorer.

316 Revisions information provided by Nancy Goldner.

323 Additional music information provided by Vittorio Rieti.

332 Additional music information provided by Gordon Boelzner.

340 Additional music information provided by Gordon Boelzner, Robert Irving.

345 Derivation of the ballet *Chaconne* and additional revisions information provided by Balanchine.

348 Information about costumes provided by Barbara Horgan.

350 Structure of ballet and its relationship to *Sylvia: Pas de Deux* [273] and *La Source* [364] clarified by Arlene Croce, Melissa Hayden, Suki Schorer, Jacques d'Amboise.

351 Additional revisions information provided by Arlene Croce.

358 Additional revisions information provided by Rosemary Dunleavy.

363 Patricia McBride.

367 Alfonso Catá, Karl Reuling.

369 Rosemary Dunleavy.

375 Balanchine.

376 Additional music information provided by Gordon Boelzner; additional revisions information provided by Nancy Goldner, Patricia McBride.

385 Patricia McBride.

387 Additional music information provided by Gordon Boelzner, Robert Irving; additional revisions information provided by Betty Cage, Arlene Croce, Nancy Goldner.

390 Barbara Horgan, Deborah Koolish.

400 Balanchine, Arlene Croce, Nancy Goldner.

402 Information corroborated by Edward Villella.

404 Information corroborated by Patricia McBride.

405 Additional music information provided by Gordon Boelzner, Joseph Wishey.

410 Rosemary Dunleavy.

414 Susan Hendl.

417 Balanchine.

420 Music information provided by Gordon Boelzner.

422 Deborah Koolish, Gordon Boelzner.

423 Gordon Boelzner.

425 Gordon Boelzner.

APPENDIXES

AMERICAN COMPANY ITINERARIES

Producing Company of the School of American Ballet

1934   December 6-8, Hartford, Connecticut: Avery Memorial Theater

American Ballet

1935   February 7-8, Bryn Mawr College: Goodhart Hall
March 1-17, NEW YORK SEASON: Adelphi Theatre
August 10-11, Philadelphia: Robin Hood Dell
August 12, 19, New York: Lewisohn Stadium
September 28, White Plains, New York: Westchester County Center
EASTERN UNITED STATES TOUR
    October 14-15, Greenwich, Connecticut: Greenwich High School
        Auditorium
    October 16, Bridgeport, Connecticut: Central High School
        Auditorium
    October 17, New Haven, Connecticut: Shubert Theatre
    October 18, Allentown, Pennsylvania: Lyric Theatre
    October 19, Princeton, New Jersey: McCarter Theatre
    October 21, Harrisburg, Pennsylvania: Majestic Theatre
    October 22, Scranton, Pennsylvania: Temple Theatre
RESIDENT COMPANY OF THE METROPOLITAN OPERA, NEW YORK, AS
    AMERICAN BALLET ENSEMBLE, December 1935 - April 1938
1936   February 14, Hartford, Connecticut: Avery Memorial Theater

American Ballet Caravan

1941   SOUTH AMERICAN TOUR
    June 25 - July 6, Rio de Janeiro, Brazil: Teatro Municipal
    July 8-11, São Paulo, Brazil: Teatro Municipal
    July 18-30, Buenos Aires, Argentina: Politeama
    August 1-4, Montevideo, Uruguay: Estudio Auditorio del S.O.D.R.E.
    August 6-7, Rosario, Argentina: Teatro Colón
    August 9-10, Córdoba, Argentina: Teatro Rivera Indarte
    August 12-15, Mendoza, Argentina: Teatro Independencia
    August 19-27, Santiago, Chile: Teatro Municipal

August 28, Viña del Mar, Chile
September 10-23, Lima, Peru: Teatro Municipal
September 30 - October 2, Cali, Colombia
October 4-5, Manizales, Colombia
October 7-9, Medellín, Colombia
October 14-21, Bogotá, Colombia: Teatro Colombia
October 31 - November 4, Caracas, Venezuela: Teatro Municipal

Ballet Society

1946　November 20, New York: Central High School of Needle Trades
1947　January 13-14, New York: Hunter College Playhouse
February 18-20, New York: Heckscher Theater (operas, *The Medium,*
The Telephone)
March 26, New York: Central High School of Needle Trades
May 18, New York: Ziegfeld Theater
November 12, New York: City Center
November 20, New York: Museum of Modern Art Auditorium
(film, Cocteau's *La Belle et la Bête*)
1948　January 22-23, New York: Hunter College Playhouse (opera,
Far Harbour)
February 9, New York: City Center
March 22, New York: City Center
April 28 - May 1, New York: City Center

New York City Ballet

1948　RESIDENT COMPANY OF THE NEW YORK CITY OPERA, October 1948 -
May 1949
October 11 - November 23, NEW YORK SEASON: City Center
1949　January 13-23, NEW YORK SEASON: City Center
November 23 - December 11, NEW YORK SEASON: City Center
1950　February 21 - March 19, NEW YORK SEASON: City Center
ENGLISH TOUR
July 10 - August 19, London: Royal Opera House, Covent Garden
August 28 - September 2, Manchester: Palace Theatre
September 4-9, Liverpool: Empire Theatre
September 11-16, Croydon: Davis Theatre
November 21 - December 10, NEW YORK SEASON: City Center

1951 February 13 - March 11, New York Season: City Center
      April 23 - May 6, Chicago: Opera House
      June 5-24, New York Season: City Center
      September 4-23, New York Season: City Center
      November 13 - December 16, New York Season: City Center
1952 February 12 - March 16, New York Season: City Center
      European Tour
         April 15 - May 8, Barcelona: Gran Teatro del Liceo
         May 10, Paris: Théâtre National de l'Opéra (Exposition Inter-
            nationale des Arts: L'Oeuvre du XXe Siècle; sous les auspices du
            Congrès pour la liberté de la culture)
         May 11-15, Paris: Théâtre des Champs-Élysées (Exposition Inter-
            nationale des Arts . . . .)
         May 18-30, Florence: Teatro Comunale (Maggio Musicale
            Fiorentino)
         June 1-4, Lausanne: Théâtre Municipal (Grandes Fêtes du Juin)
         June 6-7, Zürich: Stadttheater (Zürcher Juni-Festwochen)
         June 9-25, Paris: Théâtre des Champs-Élysées
         June 27 - July 3, The Hague: Gebouw voor Kunsten en
            Wetenschappen (Holland Festival)
         July 7 - August 23, London: Royal Opera House, Covent Garden
         August 25-30, Edinburgh: Empire Theatre (Edinburgh Festival)
         September 3, 6, Berlin: Schiller Theater (Berliner Festwochen)
         September 4-5, 7, Berlin: Städtische Oper (Berliner Festwochen)
      November 4 - January 25, 1953, New York Season: City Center
1953 February 12-13, Baltimore: Lyric Theatre
      February 14-16, Washington, D. C.: Constitution Hall
      May 5 - June 14, New York Season: City Center
      Western United States Tour
         July 2-3, Red Rocks, Colorado: Red Rocks Theater
         July 6 - August 1, Los Angeles: Greek Theatre
         August 3-14, San Francisco: War Memorial Opera House
      European Tour
         September 8-13, Milan: Teatro alla Scala
         September 18-20, Venice: Teatro La Fenice
         September 22-27, Milan: Teatro alla Scala
         September 28-29, Como: Teatro Sociale
         October 3-11, Naples: Teatro di San Carlo

October 13-16, Rome: Teatro dell'Opera
October 18-20, Florence: Teatro Comunale
October 22-25, Trieste: Teatro Comunale Giuseppe Verdi
October 27-28, Bologna: Teatro Duse
October 30 - November 1, Genoa: Teatro Carlo Felice
November 3-5, Munich: Bayerische Staatsoper, Prinzregenten-
theater
November 7-8, Stuttgart: Württembergische Staatstheater,
Stuttgart Staatsoper
November 11-17, Brussels: Théâtre Royale de la Monnaie
1954 January 12 - March 21, NEW YORK SEASON: City Center
UNITED STATES TOUR
May 26 - June 6, Chicago: Opera House
June 10-16, Seattle: Orpheum Theatre
June 19 - July 3, San Francisco: War Memorial Opera House
July 5 - August 15, Los Angeles: Greek Theatre
August 31 - September 26, NEW YORK SEASON: City Center
November 3 - December 19, NEW YORK SEASON: City Center
1955 February 15 - March 13, NEW YORK SEASON: City Center
EUROPEAN TOUR
April 9-17, Monte Carlo: Grand Théâtre du Casino de Monte-Carlo
(Salle Garnier)
April 20-24, Marseilles: Opéra Municipal
April 28-30, Lyons: Opéra de Lyon
May 6-9, Florence: Teatro Comunale (Maggio Musicale Fiorentino)
May 11-15, Rome: Teatro dell'Opera
May 18-20, Bordeaux: Grand-Théâtre (Mai Musical de Bordeaux)
May 2 - June 5, Lisbon: Teatro Nacional de San Carlos
June 8-14, Paris: Théâtre des Champs-Élysées (Salut à la France)
June 16-18, Lausanne: Théâtre de Beaulieu
June 20-22, Zürich: Stadttheater (Zürcher Juni-Festwochen)
June 24-27, Stuttgart: Württembergische Staatstheater,
Stuttgart Staatsoper
June 29 - July 3, Amsterdam: Stadsschouwburg (Holland Festival)
July 4-8, The Hague: Gebouw voor Kunsten en Wetenschappen
(Holland Festival)
UNITED STATES TOUR
July 20 - August 13, Los Angeles: Greek Theatre

August 15-28, San Francisco: War Memorial Opera House
August 30 - September 3, Seattle: Moore Theatre
September 7-18, Chicago: Opera House
November 8 - January 1, 1956, NEW YORK SEASON: City Center
1956 February 28 - March 25, NEW YORK SEASON: City Center
April 3-22, Chicago: Opera House
May 31 - June 1, Stratford, Connecticut: American Shakespeare
Festival Theatre (Mozart Festival)
EUROPEAN TOUR
August 26-30, Salzburg: Festspielhaus (Salzburger Festspiele)
September 1-9, Vienna: Staatsoper
September 12-15, Zürich: Stadttheater
September 18-23, Venice: Teatro La Fenice (Biennale)
September 26-28, Berlin: Titania-Palast (Berliner Festwochen)
September 29, Berlin: Städtische Oper (Berliner Festwochen)
September 30 - October 1, Berlin: Titania-Palast (Berliner
Festwochen)
October 4-7, Munich: Bayerische Staatsoper, Prinzregententheater
October 9-10, Frankfurt: Städtische Oper
October 12-14, Brussels: Théâtre de la Monnaie
October 15, Antwerp: Koninklijke Vlaamse Opera/Théâtre Royal
Flammande
October 17-21, Paris: Théâtre National de l'Opéra
October 23-24, Cologne: Aula der Universität
October 26-31, Copenhagen: Det Kongelige Teater
November 3-11, Stockholm: Operan
December 18 - March 3, 1957, NEW YORK SEASON: City Center
1957 April 23 - May 12, Chicago: Opera House
November 3, Philadelphia: Academy of Music
November 19 - January 19, 1958, NEW YORK SEASON: City Center
1958 January 20-24, Washington, D. C.: Loew's Capitol Theatre
FAR EASTERN TOUR
March 17-30, Tokyo: Shinjuku Koma Theatre
April 1-6, Tokyo: Sankei Hall
April 10-13, Osaka: Festival Hall (Osaka International Festival of
Music, Art and Drama)
April 17 - June 14, Sydney: Empire Theatre
June 16 - August 5, Melbourne: Her Majesty's Theatre

August 8-10, Manila: U. P. [University of the Philippines] Theater
September 2-28, NEW YORK SEASON: City Center
UNITED STATES TOUR
  October 11-12, Lafayette, Indiana: Purdue University, Edward C. Elliott Hall of Music
  October 13-15, East Lansing, Michigan: Michigan State University Auditorium
  October 16-17, Bloomington, Indiana: Indiana University Auditorium
  October 20-22, Washington, D. C.: Loew's Capitol Theatre
  October 23-25, Philadelphia: Academy of Music
November 25 - February 1, 1959, NEW YORK SEASON: City Center

1959 January 1, Albany, New York (Governor's Inaugural Ball)
May 12 - June 14, NEW YORK SEASON: City Center
UNITED STATES TOUR
  July 27 - August 8, Los Angeles: Greek Theatre
  August 11-16, Ravinia (Ravinia Festival)
August 25 - September 20, NEW YORK SEASON: City Center
October 19-21, Washington, D. C.: Loew's Capitol Theatre
October 22-24, Philadelphia: Academy of Music
December 8 - February 7, 1960, NEW YORK SEASON: City Center

1960 March 29 - April 24, NEW YORK SEASON: City Center
UNITED STATES TOUR
  July 16-20, Bear Mountain, New York (Empire State Music Festival)
  July 25 - August 6, Los Angeles: Greek Theatre
  August 9-14, Ravinia (Ravinia Festival)
November 8 - January 15, 1961, NEW YORK SEASON: City Center

1961 January 21-22, Baltimore: Lyric Theatre
January 24-26, Washington, D. C.: Loew's Capitol Theatre
March 14 - April 9, NEW YORK SEASON: City Center
UNITED STATES/CANADIAN TOUR
  July 13-19, Bear Mountain, New York: Anthony Wayne Recreation Area (Empire State Music Festival)
  July 24-29, Vancouver, British Columbia, Canada: Queen Elizabeth Theatre (Vancouver International Festival)
  July 31 - August 2, San Francisco: War Memorial Opera House
  August 4-12, Los Angeles: Greek Theatre
  August 15-20, Ravinia (Ravinia Festival)

August 29 - September 17, NEW YORK SEASON: City Center
UNITED STATES TOUR
  October 5-8, Cleveland, Ohio: Music Hall-Public Auditorium
  October 10-12, East Lansing, Michigan: Michigan State University
    Auditorium
  October 13-15, Detroit, Michigan: Masonic Auditorium
  October 17, Corning, New York
  October 19, Farmingdale, Long Island, New York: Farmingdale
    Senior High School
  October 20-21, Mineola, Long Island, New York: Mineola Theatre
  October 23-25, Raleigh, North Carolina: North Carolina State
    College, William Neal Reynolds Coliseum
December 5 - February 4, 1962, NEW YORK SEASON: City Center

1962 UPSTATE NEW YORK TOUR
  February 10, Rochester, New York: Eastman Theatre
  February 11, Buffalo, New York: Kleinhans Music Hall
  February 13, Albany, New York: Fabian's Palace Theatre
April 24 - May 13, NEW YORK SEASON: City Center
UNITED STATES TOUR
  July 2-14, Los Angeles: Greek Theatre
  July 16-21, San Francisco: War Memorial Opera House
  July 24 - August 4, Seattle: Seattle World's Fair Opera House
  August 7-12, Ravinia (Ravinia Festival)
EUROPEAN/RUSSIAN TOUR
  September 1-2, Hamburg: Staatsoper
  September 5-8, Berlin: Deutsche Oper
  September 11-15, Zürich: Stadttheater
  September 18-20, Stuttgart: Württembergische Staatstheater
  September 22-23, Cologne: Opernhaus
  September 25-26, Frankfurt: Grosses Haus
  September 29 - October 4, Vienna: Theater an der Wien
  October 9, Moscow: Bolshoi Theater
  October 10-17, Moscow: Palace of Congresses
  October 18, Moscow: Bolshoi Theater
  October 19-25, Moscow: Palace of Congresses
  October 26-28, Moscow: Bolshoi Theater
  October 31 - November 1, Leningrad: Kirov Theater
  November 2-8, Leningrad: Lensoviet Palace of Culture

November 11-18, Kiev: Opera House
November 21-25, Tbilisi: Opera House
November 28 - December 1, Baku
December 14-31, NEW YORK SEASON: City Center

1963 January 18, Washington, D. C.: National Guard Armory (Second Inaugural Anniversary Salute)
March 12 - April 21, NEW YORK SEASON: City Center
UNITED STATES TOUR
July 27-28, Brookville, Long Island, New York: C. W. Post College, Festival Tent (Long Island Festival of the Arts)
July 29 - August 4, Washington, D. C.: Carter Barron Amphitheatre
August 6-11, Ravinia (Ravinia Festival)
August 27 - September 29, NEW YORK SEASON: City Center
December 3 - January 26, 1964, NEW YORK SEASON: City Center

1964 April 24 - May 17, NEW YORK SEASON: New York State Theater
UNITED STATES TOUR
July 20 - August 1, Washington, D. C.: Carter Barron Amphitheatre
August 3-8, Ravinia (Ravinia Festival)
August 10-23, Los Angeles: Greek Theatre
September 22 - November 8, NEW YORK SEASON: New York State Theater
November 10-12, Raleigh, North Carolina: North Carolina State College, William Neal Reynolds Coliseum
December 11 - February 21, 1965, NEW YORK SEASON: New York State Theater

1965 SOUTHWESTERN UNITED STATES TOUR
February 24-28, Houston, Texas: Music Hall
March 2, San Antonio, Texas: Municipal Auditorium
March 3, Austin, Texas: University of Texas, Municipal Auditorium
March 5-7, Dallas, Texas: State Fair Music Hall
March 10-11, Bloomington, Indiana: Indiana University Auditorium
March 13-14, St. Louis, Missouri: Kiel Opera House
March 15, Urbana, Illinois: University of Illinois, University Assembly Hall
April 20 - June 13, NEW YORK SEASON: New York State Theater
EUROPEAN/MIDDLE-EASTERN TOUR
June 28 - July 3, Paris: Théâtre National de l'Opéra
July 8-12, Milan: Teatro alla Scala

July 15-18, Spoleto: Teatro Nuovo (Festival dei due Mondi)
July 21-24, Venice: Teatro La Fenice
July 28 - August 2, Dubrovnik: Terasa Tvradve Revelin
   (Dubrovačke Ljetne Igre)
August 5-8, Athens: Herodes Atticus Theater (Athens Festival)
August 11, Jerusalem: Binyenei Ha'ooma (Israel Festival)
August 12-17, Tel Aviv: Fredric R. Mann Auditorium (Israel Festival)
August 20-23, Salzburg: Festspielhaus (Salzburger Festspiele)
August 26-27, Amsterdam: Stadsschouwburg
August 30 - September 11, London: Royal Opera House, Covent
   Garden
September 23 - October 31, NEW YORK SEASON: New York
   State Theater
December 24 - January 16, 1966, NEW YORK SEASON: New York
   State Theater
1966 March 8-10, Philadelphia: Academy of Music
March 12-13, Newark, New Jersey: Symphony Hall
March 29 - May 22, NEW YORK SEASON: New York State Theater
July 8-31, SARATOGA SPRINGS SEASON: Saratoga Performing
   Arts Center
August 4-14, Washington, D. C.: Carter Barron Amphitheatre
August 16-21, Ravinia (Ravinia Festival)
UNITED STATES/CANADIAN TOUR
   September 22-25, Montreal: Place des Arts
   October 3-4, East Lansing, Michigan: Michigan State University
      Auditorium
   October 6, Columbus, Ohio: Veterans' Memorial Hall
   October 8-9, Cincinnati, Ohio: Music Hall
   October 14-15, St. Louis, Missouri: Kiel Opera House
   October 18-19, Lafayette, Indiana: Purdue University, Edward
      C. Elliott Hall of Music
   October 21-22, Detroit, Michigan: Masonic Auditorium
   October 24-29, Toronto: O'Keefe Centre for the Performing Arts
November 18 - February 5, 1967, NEW YORK SEASON: New York
   State Theater
1967 March 28 - May 7, NEW YORK SEASON: New York State Theater
May 9-11, Boston: Music Hall
May 13-14, Newark, New Jersey: Symphony Hall

July 2-5, Montreal: Salle Wilfrid-Pelletier, Place des Arts (Expo 67)

July 7-30, SARATOGA SPRINGS SEASON: Saratoga Performing Arts Center

August 3-12, Columbia, Maryland: Merriweather Post Pavilion of Music

August 14-19, Ravinia (Ravinia Festival)

August 28 - September 2, Edinburgh: Empire Theatre (Edinburgh Festival)

October 31 - November 5, Chicago: Auditorium Theatre

November 14 - February 18, 1968, NEW YORK SEASON: New York State Theater

1968 April 23 - June 16, NEW YORK SEASON: New York State Theater

July 4-28, SARATOGA SPRINGS SEASON: Saratoga Performing Arts Center

July 31 - August 4, Columbia, Maryland: Merriweather Post Pavilion of Music

August 12-17, Ravinia (Ravinia Festival)

August 30 - September 1, Cuyahoga Falls, Ohio: Blossom Music Center

November 19 - February 16, 1969, NEW YORK SEASON: New York State Theater

1969 April 22 - June 15, NEW YORK SEASON: New York State Theater

June 20-26, Monte Carlo: Grand Théâtre du Casino de Monte-Carlo (Salle Garnier) (Festival International de Ballets)

July 3-27, SARATOGA SPRINGS SEASON: Saratoga Performing Arts Center

July 30 - August 3, Columbia, Maryland: Merriweather Post Pavilion of Music

August 12-17, Ravinia (Ravinia Festival)

August 21-24, Cuyahoga Falls, Ohio: Blossom Music Center

November 18 - February 15, 1970, NEW YORK SEASON: New York State Theater

1970 May 19 - June 14, NEW YORK SEASON: New York State Theater

July 1-26, SARATOGA SPRINGS SEASON: Saratoga Performing Arts Center

August 4-8, Columbia, Maryland: Merriweather Post Pavilion of Music

August 11-18, Ravinia (Ravinia Festival)

August 20-23, Cuyahoga Falls, Ohio: Blossom Music Center

August 25 - September 6, NEW YORK SEASON: New York State Theater

November 2-7, Toronto: O'Keefe Centre for the Performing Arts

November 17 - February 14, 1971, NEW YORK SEASON: New York State Theater

1971   April 27 - June 27, NEW YORK SEASON: New York State Theater
July 6-31, SARATOGA SPRINGS SEASON: Saratoga Performing Arts Center
August 9-15, Ravinia (Ravinia Festival)
August 17-29, NEW YORK SEASON: New York State Theater
November 16 - February 20, 1972, NEW YORK SEASON: New York State Theater

1972   May 2 - July 2, NEW YORK SEASON: New York State Theater
July 5-29, SARATOGA SPRINGS SEASON: Saratoga Performing Arts Center
August 11-14, Munich: Bayerische Staatsoper Nationaltheater München (Münchner Opernfestspiele)
August 21-26, Ravinia (Ravinia Festival)
August 29 - September 3, Vienna, Virginia: Wolf Trap Farm for the Performing Arts
RUSSIAN/POLISH TOUR
   September 21-24, Kiev: Palace of Culture
   September 27 - October 1, Leningrad: Lensoviet Theater
   October 4-8, Tbilisi: New Philharmonic Concert Hall
   October 10-14, Moscow: Palace of Congresses
   October 17-18, Łodz, Poland: Teatr Wielki
   October 20-21, Warsaw: Teatr Wielki
November 14 - February 18, 1973, NEW YORK SEASON: New York State Theater

1973   May 1 - July 1, NEW YORK SEASON: New York State Theater
July 3-28, SARATOGA SPRINGS SEASON: Saratoga Performing Arts Center
August 13-25, Los Angeles: Greek Theatre
August 28 - September 2, Vienna, Virginia: Wolf Trap Farm for the Performing Arts
December 12 - February 17, 1974, NEW YORK SEASON: New York State Theater

1974   February 19 - March 3, Washington, D. C.: Kennedy Center
April 30 - June 30, NEW YORK SEASON: New York State Theater
July 3-27, SARATOGA SPRINGS SEASON: Saratoga Performing Arts Center
August 12-24, Los Angeles: Greek Theatre
September 5-8, Philadelphia: Academy of Music
November 12 - February 16, 1975, NEW YORK SEASON: New York State Theater

1975 March 25 - April 6, Washington, D. C.: Kennedy Center
April 29 - June 29, NEW YORK SEASON: New York State Theater
July 9 - August 2, SARATOGA SPRINGS SEASON: Saratoga Performing
Arts Center
September 3-7, Vienna, Virginia: Wolf Trap Farm for the
Performing Arts
November 11 - February 15, 1976, NEW YORK SEASON: New York State
Theater

1976 February 17-29, Washington, D. C.: Kennedy Center
April 27 - June 27, NEW YORK SEASON: New York State Theater
July 14-31, SARATOGA SPRINGS SEASON: Saratoga Performing
Arts Center
September 22 - October 10, Paris: Théâtre des Champs-Élysées
(International Festival de Danse de Paris)
November 16 - December 12, NEW YORK SEASON: New York State
Theater

1977 January 25 - February 20, NEW YORK SEASON: New York State Theater
February 22 - March 13, Washington, D. C.: Kennedy Center
March 16-19, Santo Domingo, Dominican Republic: Teatro Nacional
May 3 - July 3, NEW YORK SEASON: New York State Theater
July 5-30, SARATOGA SPRINGS SEASON: Saratoga Performing Arts Center
November 15 - February 19, 1978, NEW YORK SEASON: New York State
Theater

1978 February 21 - March 5, Washington, D. C.: Kennedy Center
March 23-25, West Palm Beach, Florida: West Palm Beach Auditorium
(Palm Beach Festival)
May 2 - July 2, NEW YORK SEASON: New York State Theater
July 5-22, SARATOGA SPRINGS SEASON: Saratoga Performing Arts Center
August 8-13, Copenhagen: Concert Hall, Tivoli Gardens
November 14 - February 18, 1979, NEW YORK SEASON: New York State
Theater

1979 February 20 - March 4, Washington, D. C.: Kennedy Center
UPSTATE NEW YORK TOUR
March 16-18, Rochester, New York: Eastman Theatre
March 22-25, Syracuse, New York: Civic Center
March 28-31, Buffalo, New York: Shea's Buffalo Theatre
April 18-29, Chicago: Auditorium Theatre
May 1 - July 1, NEW YORK SEASON: New York State Theater

July 3-21, SARATOGA SPRINGS SEASON: Saratoga Performing Arts Center
September 4-22, London: Royal Opera House, Covent Garden
October 2-21, Washington, D. C.: Kennedy Center
November 13 - February 17, 1980, NEW YORK SEASON: New York State Theater

1980 March 11-16, Chicago: Auditorium Theatre
March 21-26, West Palm Beach, Florida: West Palm Beach Auditorium (Palm Beach Festival)
April 29 - June 29, NEW YORK SEASON: New York State Theater
July 8-26, SARATOGA SPRINGS SEASON: Saratoga Performing Arts Center
EUROPEAN TOUR
August 19-30, Copenhagen: Concert Hall, Tivoli Gardens
September 2-6, Berlin: Deutsche Oper (Berliner Festwochen)
September 10-21, Paris: Théâtre des Champs-Élysées (International Festival de Danse de Paris)
October 8-19, Washington, D. C.: Kennedy Center
November 11 - February 15, 1981, NEW YORK SEASON: New York State Theater

1981 March 23-28, West Palm Beach, Florida: West Palm Beach Auditorium (Palm Beach Festival)
April 28 - June 28, NEW YORK SEASON: New York State Theater
July 7-25, SARATOGA SPRINGS SEASON: Saratoga Performing Arts Center
October 7-11, Fort Worth, Texas: Tarrant County Convention Center
October 27 - November 1, Boston: Metropolitan Center
November 17 - February 21, 1982, NEW YORK SEASON: New York State Theater

1982 UPSTATE NEW YORK TOUR
March 10-14, Rochester, New York: Eastman Theatre
March 17-21, Syracuse, New York: Crouse-Hinds Concert Theatre
May 4 - July 4, NEW YORK SEASON: New York State Theater

FESTIVALS DIRECTED BY BALANCHINE

Asterisks indicate world premieres. Choreography, costume and scenic design, and lighting credits follow title, with *Catalogue* number for Balanchine works.

STRAVINSKY FESTIVAL, April 27 and 28, 1937
American Ballet, Metropolitan Opera House, New York City

> *Apollon Musagète*, Balanchine/Chaney, 176
> *The Card Party*, Balanchine/Sharaff, 177
> *Le Baiser de la Fée*, Balanchine/Halicka, 178

STRAVINSKY FESTIVAL, June 18-25, 1972
New York City Ballet, New York State Theater

JUNE 18, GALA BENEFIT
> *Fanfare for a New Theater*, Orchestra
> *Greeting Prelude: Happy Birthday*, Orchestra
> *Fireworks*, Orchestra
> *Sonata*, Balanchine, 372
> *Scherzo Fantastique*, Robbins/Bates
> *Symphony in Three Movements*, Balanchine/Bates, 373
> *Violin Concerto*, Balanchine/Bates, 374
> *Firebird*, Balanchine-Robbins/Chagall/Bates, 264

JUNE 20
> *Symphony in E Flat*, Clifford/Simmons/Bates
> *The Cage*, Robbins/Rosenthal/Sobotka
> *Concerto for Piano and Winds*, Taras/Ter-Arutunian/Bates
> *Danses Concertantes*, Balanchine/Berman, 375

JUNE 21
> *Octuor*, Tanner/Bates
> *Serenade in A*, Bolender/Simmons/Bates
> *The Faun and the Shepherdess*, Mezzo-soprano and Orchestra
> *Divertimento from 'Le Baiser de la Fée,'* Balanchine/Berman/Bates, 376
> *Ebony Concerto*, Taras/Bates
> *Scherzo à la Russe*, Balanchine/Karinska/Bates, 377
> *Circus Polka*, Robbins/Bates

JUNE 22

> *Scènes de Ballet*, Taras/Karinska/Bates
> *Duo Concertant*, Balanchine/Bates, 378
> *The Song of the Nightingale*, Taras/Ter-Arutunian/Bates
> Capriccio for Piano and Orchestra, Balanchine/Harvey/Karinska/Bates
>   [RUBIES from *Jewels*, 358]

JUNE 23

> Concerto for Two Solo Pianos, Tanner/Simmons/Bates
> *Piano-Rag-Music*, Bolender/Simmons/Bates
> *Ode*, Lorca Massine/Bates
> *Dumbarton Oaks*, Robbins/Zipprodt/Bates
> *Pulcinella*, Balanchine–Robbins/Berman/Bates, 379

JUNE 24

> Apollo, Balanchine/Bates, 284
> Orpheus, Balanchine/Noguchi/Bates, 246
> Agon, Balanchine/Bates, 316

JUNE 25

> *Choral Variations on Bach's 'Vom Himmel Hoch,'* Balanchine/
>   Ter-Arutunian/Bates, 380
> Monumentum pro Gesualdo, Balanchine/Ter-Arutunian, 334
> Movements for Piano and Orchestra, Balanchine/Ter-Arutunian, 344
> *Requiem Canticles*, Robbins/Bates
> *Symphony of Psalms*, Orchestra and Chorus, with dancers assembled
>   on stage, 381

RAVEL FESTIVAL, May 14-31, 1975
New York City Ballet, New York State Theater

MAY 14, GALA BENEFIT

> Sonatine, Balanchine/Bates [preview]
> Concerto in G, Robbins/Ter-Arutunian/Bates [preview]
> L'Enfant et les Sortilèges, Balanchine/Love/Bates [preview]

MAY 15-17

> *Sonatine*, Balanchine/Bates, 389
> La Valse, Balanchine/Rosenthal/Karinska, 277
> *L'Enfant et les Sortilèges*, Balanchine/Love/Bates, 390
> *Concerto in G*, Robbins/Ter-Arutunian/Bates

MAY 22-24

*Introduction and Allegro for Harp, Robbins/Scaasi/Bates
*Shéhérazade, Balanchine/Bates, 391
*Alborada del Gracioso, d'Amboise/Braden/Bates
*Ma Mère l'Oye, Robbins/Simmons/Bates
*Daphnis and Chloe, Taras/Eula/Bates

MAY 29-31

*Le Tombeau de Couperin, Balanchine/Bates, 392
*Pavane, Balanchine/Bates, 393
*Un Barque sur l'Océan, Robbins/Welles/Bates
*Tzigane, Balanchine/Eula/Bates, 394
*Gaspard de la Nuit, Balanchine/Daydé–Bates, 395
*Sarabande and Danse [Debussy, orchestrated by Ravel], d'Amboise/
   Braden/Bates
*Chansons Madécasses, Robbins/Bates
*Rapsodie Espagnole, Balanchine/Avedon/Bates, 396

TSCHAIKOVSKY FESTIVAL, June 4-14, 1981
New York City Ballet, New York State Theater

Throughout the Festival the principal scenery was an architectural
structure with movable ranks of translucent plastic cylinders by Philip
Johnson and John Burgee, in arrangements and with lighting designs by
Ronald Bates.

JUNE 4, GALA BENEFIT

Lisa's aria from Pique Dame, Soprano and Orchestra
Lensky's aria from Eugen Onegin, Tenor and Orchestra
Duet from Undine, Soprano, Tenor and Orchestra
Overture-Fantasy from Romeo and Juliet, Orchestra
*Mozartiana, Balanchine/Ter-Arutunian, 417
*Capriccio Italien, Martins/Ter-Arutunian
*Pas de Deux [from Piano Concerto No. 1, 2nd movement], Robbins/
   Benson
Tempo di Polacca, Balanchine/Karinska [DIAMONDS Polonaise from
   Jewels, 358]

JUNE 5

Capriccio Italien
Pas de Deux [from Piano Concerto No. 1, 2nd movement]

Souvenir de Florence, Taras/Ter-Arutunian
Tschaikovsky Piano Concerto No. 2, Balanchine/Karinska, 382

JUNE 6, MATINEE
Capriccio Italien
Pas de Deux [from Piano Concerto No. 1, 2nd movement]
Souvenir de Florence
Tschaikovsky Piano Concerto No. 2

JUNE 6, EVENING
Serenade, Balanchine/Karinska, 254
Concert Fantasy, d'Amboise/Ter-Arutunian
Symphony No. 1, Martins/Benson

JUNE 7, MATINEE
Capriccio Italien
Pas de Deux [from *Swan Lake*, Act III], Balanchine/Karinska, 331
Scherzo Opus 42, d'Amboise/Ter-Arutunian
Concert Fantasy
Symphony No. 1

JUNE 7, EVENING
Swan Lake, Balanchine/Ter-Arutunian, 285
Concert Fantasy
Souvenir de Florence

JUNE 9
Concert Fantasy
Andante Elegiaco, Balanchine/Karinska [DIAMONDS pas de deux from
    Jewels, 358]
Capriccio Italien
Piano Concerto No. 3 [*Allegro Brillante*], Balanchine/Karinska, 312
Tempo di Valse
    *GARLAND DANCE FROM THE SLEEPING BEAUTY, Balanchine/Ter-
        Arutunian–Karinska, 418
    *VALSE-SCHERZO, d'Amboise/Ter-Arutunian
    WALTZ OF THE FLOWERS FROM THE NUTCRACKER, Balanchine/
        Ter-Arutunian, 302
    *VARIATION VI FROM TRIO IN A MINOR, Taras
    *WALTZ FROM EUGEN ONEGIN, ACT II, Taras/Ter-Arutunian
    The sequence of dances was altered in subsequent performances.

314

JUNE 10
> *Capriccio Italien*
> *Pas de Deux* [from Piano Concerto No. 1, 2nd movement]
> *Souvenir de Florence*
> *Tempo di Valse*

JUNE 11
> *Divertimento from 'Le Baiser de la Fée'* [Stravinsky, based on and
> dedicated to Tschaikovsky], Balanchine/Berman, 376
> *Inmitten des Balles*, Op. 38, no. 3; *Versöhnung*, Op. 25, no. 1; *Lied der
> Mignon: Nur wer die Sehnsucht kennt*, Op. 6, no. 6, Soprano and Piano
> *Piano Pieces*, Robbins/Benson
> *Tempo di Valse*

JUNE 12
> *Introduction and Fugue* [from Suite No. 1 in D major], Duell/Benson
> A selection of songs, as performed June 11
> *Scherzo Opus 42*
> *Piano Pieces*
> *Suite No. 3*, Balanchine/Benois, 369

JUNE 13, MATINEE
> *Divertimento from 'Le Baiser de la Fée'*
> *Hungarian Gypsy Airs* [Sophie Menter, orchestrated by
> Tschaikovsky], Balanchine/Benson, 419
> *Suite No. 2*, d'Amboise/Braden
> *Tempo di Valse*

JUNE 13, EVENING
> *Suite No. 2*
> *Piano Concerto No. 3* [*Allegro Brillante*]
> *Andante Elegiaco*
> *Symphony No. 1*

JUNE 14, MATINEE
> *Introduction and Fugue*
> A selection of songs, as performed June 11 and 12
> *Scherzo Opus 42*
> *Piano Pieces*
> *Suite No. 3*

JUNE 14, EVENING
> *Souvenir de Florence*

ÉLÉGIE from *Suite No. 3*
Andante Elegiaco
Symphony No. 6—Pathétique
ALLEGRO CON GRAZIA, Robbins/Benson
ALLEGRO MOLTO VIVACE, Orchestra
ADAGIO LAMENTOSO, Balanchine/Ter-Arutunian, 420

STRAVINSKY CENTENNIAL CELEBRATION, June 10-18, 1982
New York City Ballet, New York State Theater

The décor throughout the Festival incorporated the architectural setting created by Johnson/Burgee for the Tschaikovsky Festival of 1981, arranged and lighted by Ronald Bates.

JUNE 10, GALA BENEFIT
Fanfare for Two Trumpets
Circus Polka, Robbins
Fireworks, Orchestra
Tango, Balanchine, 421
Piano-Rag-Music, Martins/Benson
Duo Concertant, Balanchine, 378
Pastorale, d'Amboise/Benson
Capriccio for Piano and Orchestra, Balanchine/Karinska [RUBIES from *Jewels*, 358]
Concerto for Piano and Wind Instruments, Taras/Ter-Arutunian
Symphony in Three Movements, Balanchine, 373

JUNE 11
Noah and the Flood, Balanchine–d'Amboise/Ter-Arutunian, 422
Suite from Histoire du Soldat, Martins/Benson
Eight Easy Pieces, Martins/Benson
Stravinsky Violin Concerto, Balanchine, 374

JUNE 12, MATINEE
Noah and the Flood
Monumentum pro Gesualdo, Balanchine, 334
Movements for Piano and Orchestra, Balanchine, 344
Pastorale
Serenade en La, d'Amboise/Benson
Symphony in Three Movements

316

JUNE 12, EVENING
> *Divertimento from 'Le Baiser de la Fée,'* Balanchine/Berman, 376
> *Scherzo à la Russe,* Balanchine, 377
> *Norwegian Moods,* Christensen
> *Concerto for Piano and Wind Instruments*
> *Agon,* Balanchine, 316

JUNE 13, MATINEE
> *Circus Polka*
> *Fireworks,* Orchestra
> *Monumentum pro Gesualdo*
> *Movements for Piano and Orchestra*
> *Piano-Rag-Music*
> *Élégie,* Balanchine, 423
> *Tango*
> *Concerto for Two Solo Pianos,* Martins/Benson
> *Noah and the Flood*

JUNE 13, EVENING
> *Noah and the Flood*
> *Concerto for Piano and Wind Instruments*
> *The Cage,* Robbins/Sobotka
> *Agon*

JUNE 15
> *Divertimento from 'Le Baiser de la Fée'*
> *The Cage*
> *Monumentum pro Gesualdo*
> *Movements for Piano and Orchestra*
> *Pastorale*
> *Serenade en La*
> *Symphony in Three Movements*

JUNE 16
> *Orpheus,* Balanchine/Noguchi, 246
> *Four Chamber Works,* Robbins/Miller
> *Capriccio for Piano and Orchestra*

JUNE 17
> *Suite from Histoire du Soldat*

Four Chamber Works
Divertimento from 'Le Baiser de la Fée'

JUNE 18

Zvezdoliki [*Le Roi des Étoiles*], Orchestra and Chorus
Apollo, Balanchine, 284
*Perséphone, Balanchine–Taras–Zorina/Ter-Arutunian, 424
Symphony in Three Movements

ROLES PERFORMED BY BALANCHINE

Roles are listed chronologically by year of first performance, and alphabetically by title of work within each year. Final parentheses refer to sources other than printed programs, identified in the key which follows the *Roles* listing; published sources with reference to page number precede unpublished. Numbers in brackets refer to *Catalogue* entries.

1915-1917

1916 *La Jota Aragonesa* (Glinka/Fokine); Maryinsky; ROLE UNDETERMINED. First character role. (Balanchine, p. 749; Taper, p. 49)

1917 *Tarantella* (unknown); Alexandrinsky; DUET with Mara Dolinskaya. (*Petrogradskaya gazeta*, January 4, 1917, p. 4)

The Bear [*Medved'*] (Chekhov); St. Petersburg/Petrograd ballet school theater; OLD MAN. (Taper, p. 45; Kisselgoff, *New York Times*, November 10, 1975. Balanchine)

Don Quixote (Minkus/Petipa); Maryinsky; SPANISH BOY (Act I). (Slonimsky, p. 5)

The Fairy Doll (Bayer/Legat); 1) Maryinsky; MARCH OF THE TOY SOLDIERS. (Slonimsky, p. 6). 2) Place undetermined; PAS DE TROIS with O. Barysheva and Nicholas Efimov. Later performed with Lydia Ivanova and Efimov in the Chinese theater at Tsarskoye Selo. (Slonimsky, p. 31)

La Fille du Pharaon (Pugni/Petipa); Maryinsky; MONKEY. First named role in a printed program. (Taper, p. 47)

A Midsummer Night's Dream (Shakespeare/Mendelssohn); Mikhailovsky; BUG. (Balanchine, p. 749; Reynolds, p. 216)

The Nutcracker (Tschaikovsky/Ivanov); Maryinsky; TOY SOLDIER; KING OF MICE; CHILD PRINCE; GRAND DIVERTISSEMENT. (Balanchine, p. 748; Slonimsky, p. 6; Taper, p. 49)

Orfeo ed Euridice (Gluck/Fokine/Meyerhold); Maryinsky; FURY IN HADES. (Balanchine, p. 749; Slonimsky, p. 26. Krasovskaya)

Paquita (Deldevez–Minkus/Petipa); Maryinsky; MAZURKA (Act III). (Slonimsky, p. 5. Balanchine)

Le Pavillon d'Armide (Tcherepnine/Fokine); Maryinsky; JESTER. (Reynolds; Balanchine)

Polovtsian Dances from Prince Igor (Borodin/Fokine); Maryinsky; YOUNG
  BOY. (Slonimsky, p. 6)

Professor Storitsyn (Andreyev); Alexandrinsky; YOUNG STUDENT.
  (Balanchine, p. 749; Kisselgoff, *New York Times*, November 10, 1975)

Raymonda (Glazounov/Petipa); Maryinsky; DANCE OF THE ARAB BOYS
  (Act II). (Slonimsky, p. 5)

The Sleeping Beauty (Tschaikovsky/Petipa); Maryinsky; RETINUE OF
  CARABOSSE (Prologue), PEASANT [GARLAND] WALTZ (Act I), PAS D'ACTION
  (Act I), HOP O' MY THUMB AND THE SEVEN BROTHERS (Act III), A CUPID
  (Act III). Balanchine's first appearance on stage was in a performance
  of *The Sleeping Beauty*. (Balanchine, p. 746; Slonimsky, p. 6)

The Storm or *The Thunderstorm* [*Groza*] (Ostrovsky); St. Petersburg/
  Petrograd ballet school theater; ROLE UNDETERMINED. (Taper, p. 45)

Woe from Wit or *Wit Works Woe* or *The Trouble with Reason* [*Gore ot
  uma*] (Griboyedov); Alexandrinsky and/or St. Petersburg/Petrograd
  ballet school theater; CHATSKY. (Taper, p. 45; Slonimsky, p. 6;
  Kisselgoff, *New York Times*, November 10, 1975)

1918 - October 1924

1919 *Harlequinade* (Drigo/Petipa); Petrograd Theater (Ballet) School
      graduation performance; FRIEND. (Slonimsky, p. 26. Balanchine;
      Schüller)

      Paquita (Deldevez–Minkus/Petipa); Petrograd Theater (Ballet) School
      graduation performance; PAS DE TROIS with Alexandra Danilova and
      Lydia Ivanova. (Balanchine; Schüller)

1920 *The Magic Flute* (Drigo/Ivanov); Petrograd Theater (Ballet) School
      graduation performance; LUKE, with Lydia Ivanova as LISE.
      (Slonimsky, p. 31. Balanchine; Schüller)

1920? *La Nuit* (Rubinstein/Balanchine [1]); Petrograd Theater (Ballet) School;
      DUET with Olga Mungalova. Also performed *La Nuit* while a
      student with Lydia Ivanova, Tamara Geva and Alexandra
      Danilova; with the Young Ballet; in nightclubs in the Soviet Union;
      and on the 1924 tour of the Principal Dancers of the Russian State
      Ballet. (Taper, p. 58. Balanchine; Reynolds; Schüller)

1921   *Chopiniana* [*Les Sylphides*] (Chopin/Fokine); Tavrichesky Garden,
        Petrograd; POET, with Elizaveta Gerdt. Possibly performed in an
        earlier production. (Slonimsky, p. 26. Schüller)

        Le Corsaire (Adam–Drigo–Minkus–Pugni/Petipa); place undetermined;
        ENSEMBLE. (Balanchine)

        Javotte (Saint-Saëns/Mariquita–Gerdt–Chekrygin); Petrograd Theater
        (Ballet) School, for his graduation performance; JEAN, with Nina
        Vdovina as JAVOTTE. (Slonimsky, p. 30. Schüller)

        Lezghinka (music unknown); Petrograd Theater (Ballet) School, for his
        graduation performance; traditional Georgian dance (SOLO) staged
        by Alexander Shiryaev. (*Petrogradskaya pravda*, May 26, 1921, p. 4.
        Balanchine)

        [*Pas de Deux*] (Schubert/Preobrajenska); Petrograd Theater (Ballet)
        School graduation performance; DUET with Nina Stukolkina.
        (Balanchine; Schüller)

        Poème (Fibich/Balanchine [4]); Petrograd Theater (Ballet) School; DUET
        with Alexandra Danilova? (Slonimsky, p. 50; Taper, p. 59)

        Swan Lake (Tschaikovsky/Petipa–Ivanov); Pavlovsk, near Petrograd;
        PRINCE SIEGFRIED, with Elizaveta Gerdt as ODETTE and Soliannikov as
        ROTHBART. Balanchine replaced an injured dancer on a program
        in which he was to have been one of eight HUNTERS. (Balanchine;
        Schüller)

1921?   *Firebird* (Stravinsky/Lopukhov); place undetermined; MONSTER DANCE.
        (Balanchine)

1922   *The Nutcracker* (Tschaikovsky/Ivanov); State Theater of Opera and
        Ballet, Petrograd; SOLOIST, BUFFOONS' DANCE (TREPAK). Later
        interpolated into Balanchine's version of *The Nutcracker* [302].
        (Slonimsky, p. 32. Reynolds; Schüller)

        Solveig (Grieg–Asafiev/Petrov), State Theater of Opera and Ballet,
        Petrograd; NOCTURNE (Act I), NORWEGIAN DANCE (Act II); MIME SCENE
        (Act III). (Schüller; Souritz)

        Tarantella (unknown); Red Army charity performance; DUET with
        Olga Preobrajenska. (Taper, p. 59. Balanchine; Reynolds)

        Waltz (unknown/Balanchine [9]); resort at Sestroretsk, near Petrograd;
        DUET with Alexandra Danilova. (Balanchine; Schüller)

Waltz and Adagio (Balanchine/Balanchine[7]); place undetermined; DUET with Alexandra Danilova. (Slonimsky, p. 54. Schüller)

1922? *Harlequinade* (Drigo/Petipa); Moscow recital; PAS DE TROIS with Tamara Geva and Nicholas Efimov. (Geva, p. 287)

Matelotte or *Sailor's Hornpipe* (Traditional, arranged by Zuev/ Balanchine [11]); place undetermined; TRIO for a woman and two men. Performed with Alexandra Danilova and Nicholas Efimov on the 1924 tour of the Principal Dancers of the Russian State Ballet. (Beaumont, p. 220. Reynolds; Schüller)

1922-1923 *Orientalia* (Cui/Balanchine [12]); place undetermined; BLIND OLD BEGGAR, with Nina Mlodzinskaya as YOUNG ORIENTAL DANCER. (Slonimsky, p. 40; Mikhailov, April 1967, p. 6)

1923 *Adagio* (Saint-Saëns [from *Javotte*]/Balanchine [17]); Young Ballet, Alexandrovsky Hall, Duma, Petrograd; JEAN, with Alexandra Danilova as JAVOTTE. (Slonimsky, p. 64. Reynolds; Schüller; Souritz)

Coppélia (Delibes/Petipa–Lopukhov?); State Theater of Opera and Ballet, Petrograd; MAZURKA and CZARDAS (Act I). (Schüller)

Dance Symphony (Beethoven [Symphony No. 4]/Lopukhov); State Theater of Opera and Ballet, Petrograd; ENSEMBLE. (Kirstein, p. 218-19; Slonimsky, p. 42-44. Schüller)

Don Quixote (Minkus/Petipa); State Theater of Opera and Ballet, Petrograd; SEGUIDILLA. (Slonimsky, p. 26. Schüller)

Enigma (Arensky [from *Egyptian Nights*]/Balanchine [25]); place undetermined; DUET with Lydia Ivanova. Later performed with Tamara Geva in the Soviet Union, on the 1924 tour of the Principal Dancers of the Russian State Ballet, and in the 1924 audition for Diaghilev in Paris. (Balanchine; Reynolds; Schüller)

La Fille du Pharaon (Pugni/Petipa); State Theater of Opera and Ballet, Petrograd; KEEPER OF THE PYRAMIDS (later revealed as GENIE), SCÈNE MIMIQUE, GRAND PAS DE CROTALES. (Schüller; Souritz)

La Fille Mal Gardée (Hertel/Petipa–Ivanov); State Theater of Opera and Ballet, Petrograd; DANSE BOHÉMIENNE. (Schüller)

La Halte de Cavalerie (Armsheimer/Petipa); State Theater of Opera and Ballet, Petrograd; HUSSAR. (Schüller)

Internationale (unknown/Petrov); place and role undetermined. (Balanchine; Schüller)

Polovtsian Dances from Prince Igor (Borodin/Fokine); State Theater of
Opera and Ballet, Petrograd; POLOVTSIAN. (Slonimsky, p. 60)

The Sleeping Beauty (Tschaikovsky/Petipa–Lopukhov); State Theater of
Opera and Ballet, Petrograd; MINUET, BLIND MAN'S BUFF (Act II).
(Slonimsky, p. 30. Schüller; Souritz)

Swan Lake (Tschaikovsky/Petipa–Ivanov); State Theater of Opera
and Ballet, Petrograd; VALSE CHAMPÊTRE (Act I). (Slonimsky, p. 30.
Schüller; Souritz)

Tannhäuser (Wagner); State Theater of Opera and Ballet, Petrograd;
YOUTH IN LOVE in the Grotto of Venus. (Slonimsky, p. 30. Schüller)

1923-1924 *Étude* (Scriabin/Balanchine [30]); Young Ballet, place undetermined; DUET with Tamara Geva. Probably performed in the 1924
audition for Diaghilev in Paris; performed on programs of
Diaghilev's Ballets Russes in 1925.

Oriental Dance (Moussorgsky [from *Khovanshchina*]/Balanchine [31]);
Young Ballet, place undetermined; DUET with Tamara Geva.
(Reynolds)

Elegy (Rachmaninoff/Balanchine [32]); Young Ballet, Pavlovsk, near
Petrograd; TRIO with Tamara Geva and Nicholas Efimov.
Possibly performed earlier at another location; performed on the
1924 tour of the Principal Dancers of the Russian State Ballet;
possibly performed in the 1924 audition for Diaghilev in Paris.
(Slonimsky, p. 64. Schüller)

1924, JANUARY-OCTOBER *La Bayadère* (Minkus/Petipa), State Theater
of Opera and Ballet, Petrograd/Leningrad; FIRE DANCE (Scene 3).
(Slonimsky, p. 26. Schüller)

Le Corsaire (Adam–Drigo–Minkus–Pugni/Petipa); State Theater
of Opera and Ballet, Petrograd/Leningrad; DANCE OF THE CORSAIRS.
(Schüller)

Dutch Dance (Grieg or Lortzing/Balanchine or Petrov or Lopukhov [3]);
Principal Dancers of the Russian State Ballet, Empire Theatre,
London; DUET with Alexandra Danilova. Possibly performed earlier
in the Soviet Union. (Reynolds)

The End of the Fifth Act (variety show); Vol'naia Komediiă, Petrograd/
Leningrad; ROLES UNDETERMINED. (Souritz)

Four Seasons (Glazounov/Leontiev); State Theater of Opera and Ballet, Petrograd/Leningrad; BACCHANT (AUTUMN). (Balanchine; Schüller)

Hungarian Gypsy Dance (Brahms/Balanchine [13]); Principal Dancers of the Russian State Ballet, Schwechtasaal, Berlin; DUET with Tamara Geva. (Reynolds)

Invitation to the Dance (Weber/Balanchine [34]); Young Ballet, Pavlovsk?, near Petrograd; TRIO with Alexandra Danilova and Mikhail Mikhailov. Performed on the 1924 tour of the Principal Dancers of the Russian State Ballet. (Mikhailov; Reynolds)

Le Pavillon d'Armide (Tcherepnine/Fokine–Balanchine? [33, NOTE]); State Theater of Opera and Ballet, Petrograd/Leningrad; DUET with Elizaveta Gerdt. (Gusev; Reynolds; Schüller)

Spanish Dance (probably Glazounov [from *Raymonda*]/Balanchine [18]); Young Ballet, Pavlovsk, near Petrograd; DUET with Tamara Geva. (Schüller)

Year Undetermined

Carnaval (Schumann/Fokine); State Theater of Opera and Ballet, Petrograd/Leningrad; EUSEBIUS, THE POET. (Slonimsky, p. 26. Reynolds)

La Esmeralda (Pugni–Drigo/Petipa); State Theater of Opera and Ballet, Petrograd/Leningrad; BEGGAR. (Slonimsky, p. 30, 33; Taper, p. 68-69)

The Magic Flute (Drigo/Ivanov); State Theater of Opera and Ballet, Petrograd/Leningrad; MARQUIS. Possibly performed earlier. (Balanchine)

Le Pavillon d'Armide (Tcherepnine/Fokine); State Theater of Opera and Ballet, Petrograd/Leningrad; JESTER. Possibly the role first danced in 1915-1917.

November 1924 - August 1929, Diaghilev's Ballets Russes

Listings for the years of Balanchine's association with the Ballets Russes are limited to roles identified in programs in the collections of the Theatre Museum of the Victoria and Albert Museum and the library of the Garrick Club in London, the Collection Rondel of the Bibliothèque de l'Arsenal in Paris, the Archives of the Opéra de Monte-Carlo, and in the collection of Nathalie Branitzka, now in the possession of her son, André von Hoyer, of Pittsfield, Massachusetts.

1924 *Aurora's Wedding* (Tschaikovsky [from *The Sleeping Beauty*]/Petipa–
Sergeyev–Nijinska); Coliseum, London; POLONAISE.
Contes Russes (Liadov/Massine); Coliseum, London; FOLK DANCE.
Polovtsian Dances from Prince Igor (Borodin/Fokine); Coliseum, London;
POLOVTSIAN WARRIOR.
Soleil de Nuit (Rimsky-Korsakov/Massine); Coliseum, London;
BUFFOON.

1925 *Aurora's Wedding* (Tschaikovsky [from *The Sleeping Beauty*]/Petipa–
Sergeyev–Nijinska); 1) Opéra de Monte-Carlo; SCÈNE ET DANSE DES
DUCHESSES; probably also FARANDOLE and MAZURKA. 2) Nouvelle Salle
de Musique (Salle Ganne), Monte Carlo; PRINCE CHARMING with Vera
Nemtchinova as PRINCESS AURORA. Also danced this role with
Nemtchinova at the Coliseum, London, and in 1926 with Alexandra
Danilova at the Opéra de Monte-Carlo. 3) Coliseum, London; PAS
DE SEPT of the Maids of Honour and Their Cavaliers.
La Boutique Fantasque (Rossini–Respighi/Massine); Coliseum, London;
KING OF SPADES in the Mazurka.
Carnaval (Schumann/Fokine); 1) Nouvelle Salle de Musique (Salle
Ganne), Monte Carlo; PIERROT. 2) Coliseum, London; VALSE NOBLE.
Le Chant du Rossignol (Stravinsky/Balanchine [52]); Théâtre Gaieté
Lyrique, Paris; MECHANICAL NIGHTINGALE.
Cimarosiana (Cimarosa [from *Le Astuzie Femminili*]/Massine); Opéra
de Monte-Carlo; CONTREDANSE.
Contes Russes (Liadov/Massine); Opéra de Monte-Carlo; DANSES
POPULAIRES.
Les Fâcheux (Auric/Nijinska); Nouvelle Salle de Musique (Salle Ganne),
Monte Carlo; POLICEMAN.
Hérodiade (Massenet/Balanchine [46]); Opéra de Monte-Carlo; ACT III
BALLET.
Narcisse (Tcherepnine/Fokine); Nouvelle Salle de Musique (Salle
Ganne), Monte Carlo; GREEK.
Petrouchka (Stravinsky/Fokine); Coliseum, London; OLD FATHER OF THE
FAIR.
Schéhérazade (Rimsky-Korsakov/Fokine); Opéra de Monte-Carlo;
NEGRO.
Les Tentations de la Bergère (*The Faithful Shepherdess*) (Monteclair–
Casadesus/Nijinska); Opéra de Monte-Carlo; BARON.

Thamar (Balakirev/Fokine); Nouvelle Salle de Musique (Salle Ganne), Monte Carlo; LEZGHINKA.

Le Tricorne (*The Three-Cornered Hat*) (Falla/Massine); 1) Nouvelle Salle de Musique (Salle Ganne), Monte Carlo; ALGUAZIL (POLICEMAN). 2) Coliseum, London; GYPSY.

1926   *Cimarosiana* (Cimarosa [from *Le Astuzie Femminili*]/Massine); His Majesty's Theatre, London; PAS DE SIX, FINALE.

L'Oiseau de Feu (*Firebird*) (Stravinsky/Fokine); Lyceum Theatre, London; KASTCHEI.

Mazurka (Tschaikovsky/Petipa); Soirée Artistique, benefit for Grand Duc André, Monte Carlo?; ROLE UNDETERMINED.

Petrouchka (Stravinsky/Fokine); Opéra de Monte-Carlo; OLD SHOWMAN.

Pulcinella (Stravinsky/Massine); Théâtre Sarah Bernhardt, Paris; FOURBO.

Les Tentations de la Bergère (*The Faithful Shepherdess*) (Monteclair–Casadesus/Nijinska); Opéra de Monte-Carlo; HYMÉNÉE.

Thamar (Balakirev/Fokine); His Majesty's Theatre, London; SERVANT OF THAMAR.

Le Tricorne (*The Three-Cornered Hat*) (Falla/Massine); His Majesty's Theatre, London; GOVERNOR (CORREGIDOR).

The Triumph of Neptune (Berners/Balanchine [64]); Lyceum Theatre, London; SNOWBALL, LEADING HARLEQUIN, BEGGAR.

1926? *Le Chant du Rossignol* (Stravinsky/Balanchine [52]); Opéra de Monte-Carlo; NIGHTINGALE. Balanchine performed the role he had created for Alicia Markova, who was ill, at a command performance for the Princesse Héréditaire of Monaco. (Taper, p. 96-98, 339-40)

1927   *Barabau* (Rieti/Balanchine [53]); Opéra de Monte-Carlo; SERGEANT. (Balanchine)

Cimarosiana (Cimarosa [from *Le Astuzie Femminili*]/Massine); 1) La Scala; PAS DE SEPT. 2) Staatsoper, Vienna; PAS RUSTIQUE with Alexandra Danilova and Serge Lifar.

Turandot (Puccini/Balanchine [68]); Opéra de Monte-Carlo; LES PORCELAINES DE CHINE (Act II).

1928   *Carnaval* (Schumann/Fokine); His Majesty's Theatre, London;
        FLORESTAN.

        Cléopâtre (Arensky–Taneyev–Rimsky-Korsakov–Glinka–Glazounov/
        Fokine); Opéra de Monte-Carlo; CLEOPATRA'S FAVORITE SLAVE,
        with Alice Nikitina as the female FAVORITE SLAVE.

        Les Noces (Stravinsky/Nijinska); Théâtre Sarah Bernhardt, Paris;
        ENSEMBLE.

        Romeo and Juliet (Lambert/Nijinska–Balanchine [61]); Opéra de Monte-
        Carlo; THE MAESTRO, REHEARSING AS TYBALT.

        Soleil de Nuit (Rimsky-Korsakov/Massine); Opéra de Monte-Carlo;
        BOLBYL (THE INNOCENT).

1929   *Le Bal* (Rieti/Balanchine [93]); Opéra de Monte-Carlo; SPANISH ENTRANCE,
        with Felia Doubrovska and Léon Woizikowsky.

        Les Fâcheux (Auric/Massine); Théâtre Sarah Bernhardt, Paris;
        LA MONTAGNE (ERASTE'S VALET).

August 1929-1933

1929   *Dark Red Roses: Tartar Ballet, 'Jealousy'* (Moussorgsky [from
        Khovanshchina]/Balanchine [97]); TARTAR, with Lydia Lopokova as
        HIS WIFE and Anton Dolin as the MINSTREL. (Taper, p. 126)

1930   [*Duet* and *Trio*]. (Liszt/Balanchine [100]); Royal Danish Ballet, Tivoli
        Gardens, Copenhagen; DUET with Elna Jørgen-Jensen; TRIO with
        Elna Lassen and Ulla Poulsen.

        Polovtsian Dances from Prince Igor (*Fyrst Igor*) (Borodin/Fokine–
        Balanchine [104]); Royal Danish Ballet, Royal Theater, Copenhagen;
        WARRIOR CHIEF.

        Le Spectre de la Rose (*Rosendrømmen*) (Weber/Fokine–Balanchine [105]);
        Koncert Palæet, Copenhagen; SPIRIT OF THE ROSE, with Ulla Poulsen
        as the YOUNG GIRL.

        Les Sylphides (Chopin/Fokine); Royal Danish Ballet, Royal Theater,
        Copenhagen; POET.

1932   *Cotillon* (Chabrier/Balanchine [129]); Ballets Russes de Monte-Carlo,
        Opéra de Monte-Carlo; LA TOILETTE and CHAPEAU sections. In the

preview performance Balanchine danced the role later danced by David Lichine.

Numéro les Canotiers ('The Waves of the Danube' [a waltz tune popular in Russia]/Balanchine [133]); Villa Blanche, near Toulon; TRIO with Mme Georges Auric and Boris Kochno. (Kochno)

1933 *L'Errante* (Schubert/Balanchine [138]); Les Ballets 1933, Savoy Theatre, London; LEADING MALE DANCER. (Reynolds)

From 1934

1940 *I Was an Adventuress* [191]; ORCHESTRA LEADER, under the stage name Fortunio Bonanova.

1941 *Divertimento* (Rossini/Balanchine [196]); American Ballet Caravan South American tour; RAT. (Reynolds, p. 70)

1946 *Resurgence* (Mozart/Balanchine [231]); March of Dimes Benefit, Waldorf Astoria Hotel, New York; THREAT OF POLIO. (March of Dimes)

1950 *Mazurka from 'A Life for the Tsar'* (Glinka/Balanchine [272]); New York City Ballet, City Center of Music and Drama, New York; ENSEMBLE, partnering Vida Brown.
Prodigal Son (Prokofiev/Balanchine [267]); New York City Ballet, City Center of Music and Drama, New York; FATHER.

1952 *The Pied Piper* (Copland/Robbins); New York City Ballet, Théâtre des Champs-Élysées?, Paris; CLARINETIST (mimed). Performed incognito. (*Dance Magazine*, March 1960, p. 63. Balanchine)

1956 *The Concert* (Chopin/Robbins); New York City Ballet, City Center of Music and Drama, New York; HUSBAND (mime portions). (Reynolds, p. 172)

1958 *The Nutcracker* (Tschaikovsky/Balanchine [302]); telecast, Playhouse 90 (CBS); DROSSELMEYER. (*Dance Magazine*, March 1959, p. 15-17)

1960s The Nutcracker (Tschaikovsky/Balanchine [302]); New York City Ballet, New York State Theater; GRANDFATHER. Appeared occasionally in this role with Karinska as GRANDMOTHER.

1965 Don Quixote (Nabokov/Balanchine [352]); New York City Ballet, New York State Theater; DON QUIXOTE. Also danced in subsequent years.

1972 Pulcinella (Stravinsky/Balanchine–Robbins [379]); New York City Ballet, New York State Theater; BEGGAR.

Published Sources
Full citations are given in the Bibliography

George Balanchine. Complete Stories of the Great Ballets.
Cyril Beaumont. The Diaghilev Ballet in London.
Tamara Geva. Split Seconds.
S. L. Grigoriev. The Diaghilev Ballet, 1909-1929.
Lincoln Kirstein. Movement & Metaphor.
Mikhail Mikhailov. My Life in Ballet.
Nancy Reynolds. Repertory in Review.
Yuri Slonimsky. Balanchine: The Early Years.
Bernard Taper. Balanchine: A Biography.

Unpublished Sources

Balanchine. Interviews with Nancy Reynolds, 1980, 1981.
Gusev. Pëtr Gusev, interview with Poel Karp, February 1981.
Kochno. Boris Kochno, interview with Hoyt Rogers and Harvey Simmonds, February 8, 1979.
Krasovskaya. Vera Krasovskaya, letter to Nancy Reynolds, March 13, 1980.
March of Dimes. Letter to Susan Au, March 16, 1981.
Reynolds. Dossier compiled by Nancy Reynolds.
Schüller. Dossier compiled by Gunhild Schüller.
Souritz. Letters from Elizabeth Souritz to Nancy Reynolds and Susan Summer, 1980, 1981.

BIBLIOGRAPHY

This selective bibliography provides an initial list for further study of the work of George Balanchine. Given here are Balanchine's writings, arranged chronologically; principal writings in book form about Balanchine's works and the companies with which he has been associated (including a selection from general guides to ballet), arranged alphabetically by author; and titles of the most important periodicals and newspapers consulted in the preparation of this catalogue. Annotated indexes to pertinent articles in *Era* and *Dancing Times* (London), *Dance Magazine* (New York), and the *New York Times* form part of the archives of the project, and appear in an edited form in *Ballet Review* 11: 2, 3 [Spring, Summer 1983]. Among important sources for the study of Balanchine's work not here included are notes and articles in the house and souvenir programs of the companies with which he has been associated, a collection of which is included in the project archives.

I. Writings by Balanchine

BOOKS

Balanchine's Complete Stories of the Great Ballets. Edited by Francis Mason. Garden City, New York: Doubleday, 1954.

Balanchine's New Complete Stories of the Great Ballets. Edited by Francis Mason. Garden City, New York: Doubleday, 1968.

Histoire des mes ballets. Translated by Patrick Thévenon. Paris: Fayard, 1969.
   Based on the 1968 *New Complete Stories of the Great Ballets*, but including only ballets choreographed by Balanchine.

101 Stories of the Great Ballets (with Francis Mason). Garden City, New York: Doubleday, 1975.
   Intermediary work between the 1968 and 1977 editions of the *Complete Stories of the Great Ballets*; adds fifty-one ballets choreographed between 1968 and 1974.

Balanchine's Complete Stories of the Great Ballets (with Francis Mason). Revised and enlarged edition. Garden City, New York: Doubleday, 1977.

CONTRIBUTIONS TO BOOKS

'Marginal Notes on the Dance.' In *The Dance Has Many Faces*, edited by Walter Sorell. Cleveland/New York: World, 1951, pp. 31-40. Second edition, revised and expanded, New York: Columbia University Press, 1966, pp. 93-102.

Preface to *The Classic Ballet: Basic Technique and Terminology*, by Lincoln Kirstein and Muriel Stuart. New York: Knopf, 1952.

Preface to *Labanotation*, by Ann Hutchinson. New York: New Directions, 1954. Revised and expanded edition, New York: Theatre Arts, 1970.

'Ballet in America.' In *The Book of Knowledge 1955 Annual*, pp. 145-48. New York/Toronto: The Grolier Society, 1955.

'The Purpose of Ballet Society' and 'A Summing Up.' In *A Conference on Ballet—A National Movement*, pp. 9-12, 58-62. New York: Ballet Society, 1960.

ARTICLES

'The Non-Commissioned Officer's Widow, or How A. L. Volinsky Whipped Himself.' *Teatr* 13 (25 December 1923), 7.

'Dance Your Way to Health.' *Sunday Chronicle* (London), 7 July 1929. Excerpts reprinted in *Dancing Times* n.s. 227 (August 1929), 434-35.

'Les "Ballets 1933."' *Excelsior* (Paris), 4 June 1933.

'Ballet Goes Native.' *Dance* [East Stroudsburg, Pa.] 3:3 (December 1934), 13.

'Dance Will Assert Its Importance.' *Dance* [East Stroudsburg, Pa.] 6:1 (April 1939), 10.

'Ballet on Record.' *Listen* 1:4 (February 1941), 6-7.

'Balanchine Defines Dance as Visual Art.' As told to Robert Sabin. *Musical America* 64:5 (25 March 1944), 27.

'The American Dancer.' *Dance News* 4:4 (April 1944), 3, 6.

'Ballet in Films.' *Dance News* 5:4 (December 1944), 8.

'Notes on Choreography.' *Dance Index* 4:2, 3 (February-March 1945), 20-31.

'The Dance Element in Strawinsky's Music.' In 'Strawinsky in the Theatre: A Symposium,' edited by Minna Lederman. *Dance Index* 6:10, 11, 12 (October-December 1947), 250-56. Reprinted in *Stravinsky in the Theatre*, edited by Minna Lederman. New York: Pellegrini & Cudahy, 1949, pp. 75-84.

'Diaghileff and His Period.' *Dance News* 15:2 (August 1949), 6.

'Recording the Ballet.' *Dance Observer* 17:9 (November 1950), 132-33.

'Création d'un ballet' [7 October 1931]. *Revue chorégraphique de Paris* (May 1952), 9.

'La Peinture et la danse.' *Le Figaro* (Paris), 10-11 May 1952.

'The Met at Work: Directing a Rake.' House program, Metropolitan Opera, New York, 16 February 1953 et seq.

'George Balanchine Writes' [guest columnist, Dorothy Kilgallen's syndicated 'Voice of Broadway']. *Times-Herald* (Olean, New York), 24 June 1954.

'From There I See Patterns . . .' *Greek Theatre Magazine* (Los Angeles) 19-31 July 1954.

'Ivesiana.' *Center* 1:5 (August-September 1954), 5.

'George Platt Lynes.' Souvenir program, New York City Ballet, 1957. Reprinted in *George Platt Lynes: Photographs 1931-1955*, by Jack Woody. Los Angeles: Twelvetrees Press, 1981.

'A Word from George Balanchine.' *Playbill* (New York), 25 November 1957 et seq. Reprinted in *Dance Magazine* 32:1 (January 1958), 34-35.

'At Last: Congress Listens' (with others). *Dance Magazine* 36:2 (February 1962), 34-35.

'Balanchine Talks to Russia about His Artistic Credo.' *Dance News* 41:4 (December 1962), 5. Excerpted from *The Soviet Artist* (Moscow), October 1962.

'Now Everybody Wants to Get Into the Act.' *Life* 58 (11 June 1965), 94A-98, 100, 102.

'From Ballet into Movie: Balanchine Tells How.' *World Journal Tribune* (New York), 16 April 1967.

'La Mauvaise Musique inspire . . .' and 'La Musique de Stravinsky et la danse.' House program, Paris Opéra, 7 April 1978 et seq.

II. Books Relating to Balanchine

Amberg, George. *Ballet in America: The Emergence of an American Art.* New York: Duell, Sloan and Pearce, 1949.
Includes discussions of Balanchine's work in the chapters 'The Ballet Russe III—Americanization,' 'Lincoln Kirstein I—The Foundations,' 'Lincoln Kirstein II—The Performance,' 'The Musical Comedy.'

Anderson, Jack. *The Nutcracker Ballet.* London: Bison, 1979.
Includes a discussion of Balanchine's 1954 New York City Ballet production.

———. *The One and Only: The Ballet Russe de Monte Carlo.* Brooklyn, New York: Dance Horizons, 1981.
Includes information on Balanchine's association with and choreography for the company.

The Ballet Society 1946-1947. New York: Ballet Society, 1947.
Includes general information on Ballet Society; sections on the ballets *The Spellbound Child, The Four Temperaments, Renard,* and *Divertimento,* and on the School of American Ballet.

Barnes, Clive. *Ballet in Britain Since the War.* London: C. A. Watts, 1953.
Chapter titled 'The American Visiting Companies' includes an analysis of Balanchine's work, pp. 75-77.

Baryshnikov, Mikhail. *Baryshnikov at Work: Mikhail Baryshnikov Discusses His Roles.* Edited and introduced by Charles Engell France. With photographs by Martha Swope. New York: Knopf, 1976.
Includes a chapter on *Theme and Variations.*

Beaton, Cecil. *Ballet.* London/New York: Wingate, 1951.
Describes Balanchine's work in Europe in the early 1930s, including *Cotillon,* 'Luna Park' from the 1930 Cochran Revue, *L'Errante,* and dances for Sir Oswald Stoll's variety shows, pp. 41, 48-49, 53-55.

Beaumont, Cyril W. *Complete Book of Ballets.* London: Putnam, 1937/ New York: Grosset and Dunlap, 1938.
Includes descriptions of *The Triumph of Neptune, La Chatte, The Gods Go A-Begging, Le Fils Prodigue,* and *Cotillon,* as well as a brief biography of Balanchine and an excerpt from an interview published in *Dance Journal,* August-October 1931.

———. *Ballets of Today: Being a Second Supplement to the Complete Book of Ballets.* London: Putnam, 1954.
Includes descriptions of *Ballet Imperial, Orpheus* and *Night Shadow.*

———. *The Diaghilev Ballet in London: A Personal Record.* Third edition. London: Adam and Charles Black, 1951.
Includes descriptions of Balanchine's work for Diaghilev.

Buckle, Richard. *Buckle at the Ballet: Selected Criticism.* London: Dance Books / New York: Atheneum, 1980.
Includes reviews of New York City Ballet performances.

———. *Diaghilev.* London: Weidenfeld and Nicolson / New York: Atheneum, 1979.
Includes information on Balanchine's association with the Ballets Russes.

Chujoy, Anatole. *The New York City Ballet.* New York: Knopf, 1953.

Clarke, Mary. *The Sadler's Wells Ballet: A History and an Appreciation.* London: A. and C. Black / New York: Macmillan, 1955.
Includes a description and analysis of Balanchine's 1950 staging of *Ballet Imperial* for the company, pp. 248-50, 254.

Crisp, Clement, and Clarke, Mary. *Making a Ballet*. London: Studio Vista, 1974 / New York: Macmillan, 1975.
Includes Balanchine among the choreographers analyzed and quoted.

Croce, Arlene. *Afterimages*. New York: Knopf, 1977.

———. *Going to the Dance*. New York: Knopf, 1982.
Both include reviews of New York City Ballet performances.

Dance Index 4:2, 3 (February-March 1945): 'George Balanchine.'
Includes 'Notes on Choreography' by George Balanchine, 'Balanchine's Choreography (1930)' by Agnes de Mille, 'A Note on Balanchine's Present Style' by Edwin Denby, 'Ballets by George Balanchine,' 'Musicals with Choreography by George Balanchine,' and 'Motion Pictures with Choreography by George Balanchine'.

Deakin, Irving. *Ballet Profile*. New York: Dodge, 1936.
Chapter titled 'Georgei Melitonovitch Balanchivadze' gives a detailed biography.

Denby, Edwin. *Dancers, Buildings and People in the Streets*. New York: Horizon, 1965.
Includes reviews of New York City Ballet performances; also the articles 'Some Thoughts about Classicism and George Balanchine' and 'Balanchine Choreographing.'

———. *Looking at the Dance*. New York: Horizon, 1949.
Includes reviews of Balanchine's works for the Ballet Russe de Monte Carlo in the 1940s, the Original Ballet Russe (*Balustrade*), and the New Opera Company (*Ballet Imperial*).

Detaille, Georges, and Mulys, Gérard. *Les Ballets de Monte-Carlo 1911-1944*. Paris: Éditions Arc-en-Ciel, 1954.
Includes information about, synopses and photographs of Balanchine ballets performed in Monte Carlo by Diaghilev's Ballets Russes, the Ballets Russes de Monte-Carlo, and Ballets de Monte-Carlo (René Blum).

de Valois, Ninette. *Come Dance with Me: A Memoir, 1898-1956*. London: H. Hamilton / Cleveland/New York: World, 1957.
Describes Balanchine's first days with Diaghilev's Ballets Russes, including his teaching *Marche Funèbre* to the company, pp. 83-84.

———. *Invitation to the Ballet*. London: Bodley Head, 1937 / New York: Oxford University Press, 1938.
Includes brief comments on Balanchine's work for Diaghilev's Ballets Russes and Les Ballets 1933.

———. *Step by Step*. London: W. H. Allen, 1977.
Chapter titled 'Diaghilev' contains a brief description of Balanchine's performance as Grandfather of the Fair in *Petrushka*.

Divoire, Fernand. *Pour la danse*. Paris: Éditions de la Danse, 1935.
Describes works choreographed for Les Ballets 1933, including *Fastes*,
L'Errante, *Les Sept Péchés Capitaux*, pp. 122-24.

Dolin, Anton. *Divertissement*. London: S. Low, Marston, 1931.
Briefly mentions Balanchine and his ballets in a description of the final years
of the Diaghilev company, pp. 195, 200-201, 205-6; describes how Dolin,
Balanchine and Lydia Lopokova learned of Diaghilev's death during the
filming of *Dark Red Roses*, pp. 212-15.

————. *The Sleeping Ballerina: The Story of Olga Spessivtzeva*. London:
Frederick Muller, 1966.
Describes her creation of the title role in *La Chatte*, pp. 46-49.

Drew, David (ed.). *The Decca Book of Ballet*. London: Frederick Muller, 1958.
Includes descriptions of many Balanchine ballets.

Duke, Vernon. *Passport to Paris*. Boston: Little, Brown, 1955.
Includes information on Balanchine's years with Diaghilev and on his
musical comedy collaborations with Duke.

Franks, A. H. *Twentieth Century Ballet*. London: Burke / New York:
Pitman, 1954.
Includes a chapter on Balanchine.

Geva, Tamara. *Split Seconds: A Remembrance*. New York: Harper & Row,
1972.
Describes Balanchine's life and early works in Russia, the tour of the Principal
Dancers of the Russian State Ballet, work for Diaghilev's Ballets Russes,
arrival in America, first performance of the American Ballet (1935), and the
musical comedy *On Your Toes* (1936).

Goldner, Nancy. *The Stravinsky Festival of the New York City Ballet*. New
York: Eakins, 1973.

Goldner, Nancy, and Kirstein, Lincoln. *Coppélia: New York City Ballet*.
New York: Eakins, 1974.

Goode, Gerald (ed.). *The Book of Ballets: Classic and Modern*. New York:
Crown, 1939.
Includes descriptions of *Le Bourgeois Gentilhomme*, *La Chatte*, *La Concurrence*,
Cotillon, and *Les Dieux Mendiants*.

Grigoriev, Serge Leonidovich. *The Diaghilev Ballet 1909-1929*. Translated
and edited by Vera Bowen. London: Constable, 1953. Reprinted,
Harmondsworth, Middlesex: Penguin, 1960; Brooklyn, New York:
Dance Horizons, 1974.
Includes information on Balanchine's association with the Ballets Russes,
1924-29.

Grigorovich, Yuri (ed.). *Balet entsiklopediĩa* (*Ballet Encyclopedia*). Moscow: Sovetskaĩa entsiklopediĩa, 1981.
Includes articles on Balanchine and a number of his associates.

Gruen, John. *Erik Bruhn: Danseur Noble*. New York: Viking, 1979.
Includes a chapter describing Bruhn's season with the New York City Ballet, 1959-60, and discusses his appearances with the company in 1963.

———. *The Private World of Ballet*. New York, Viking, 1975.
Includes an interview with Balanchine (1972), and interviews with a number of his associates, and dancers of the New York City Ballet.

Guest, Ivor. *Le Ballet de l'Opéra de Paris: Trois siècles d'histoire et de tradition*. Translated by Paul Alexandre. Paris: Théâtre National de l'Opéra/Flammarion, 1976.
Includes Balanchine's works choreographed and staged for the company.

Haddakin, Edward [A. V. Coton]. *A Prejudice for Ballet*. London: Methuen, 1938.
Includes descriptions of *Cotillon* and *Aubade*, pp. 73-76, 121.

———. *Writings on Dance, 1938-68*. Selected and edited by Kathrine Sorley Walker and Lilian Haddakin. London: Dance Books, 1975.
Includes reviews of New York City Ballet performances.

Haggin, Bernard H. *Ballet Chronicle*. New York: Horizon, 1970.
Reviews from 1947 to 1970 include discussions of Balanchine's works for Ballet Theatre, Ballet Society, and the New York City Ballet.

———. *Discovering Balanchine*. New York: Horizon, 1981.
Includes biographical material and accounts of personal encounters with Balanchine in a short text accompanied by many photographs.

Hall, Fernau. *An Anatomy of Ballet*. London: A. Melrose, 1953 / New York (titled *World Dance*): A. A. Wyn, 1954.
Chapter titled 'Post-Expressionist Pseudo-Classicism' includes a section on Balanchine and a section on his companies from Les Ballets 1933 to the New York City Ballet. Briefly discusses Balanchine's work for the Ballet Russe de Monte Carlo (1944-46), pp. 416-17.

———. *Modern English Ballet: An Interpretation*. London: Andrew Melrose, 1950.
Discusses Balanchine's work for Diaghilev and his choreographic style, pp. 59, 61-62.

Haskell, Arnold L. *Balletomania: The Story of an Obsession*. London: Gollancz / New York: Simon and Schuster, 1934. Reprinted with

additional material as *Balletomania: Then and Now*, London: Weidenfeld and Nicolson / New York: Knopf, 1977.
Chapter titled 'Four Choreographers' includes a section on Balanchine.

Howard, Ruth Eleanor. *The Story of the American Ballet*. New York: Ihra, 1936.
Discusses Balanchine's activities in founding the School of American Ballet and leading up to the formation of the American Ballet, with a history of the company until its association with the Metropolitan Opera. Provides lists and brief biographies of dancers; lists of repertory and opera ballets.

Jowitt, Deborah. *Dance Beat: Selected Views and Reviews, 1967-1976*. New York: Dekker, 1977.
Includes reviews of New York City Ballet performances.

Kameneff, Vladimir. *Russian Ballet through Russian Eyes*. London: Russian Books and Library, 1936.
Includes brief comments on *La Chatte*, *Cotillon* and *La Concurrence*, pp. 21-22, 31; description of the first scene of *Apollon Musagète*, p. 33.

Kanin, Garson. *Hollywood*. New York: Viking, 1974.
Includes reminiscences of Balanchine's meetings with Samuel Goldwyn during the filming of *The Goldwyn Follies*, pp. 108-13.

Kirstein, Lincoln. *Blast at Ballet: A Corrective for the American Audience*. New York: Lincoln Kirstein, 1938. Reprinted in *Three Pamphlets Collected*, Brooklyn, New York: Dance Horizons, 1967.
Includes information on Balanchine's early years in America and the activities of the American Ballet, including its association with the Metropolitan Opera.

———. *Dance: A Short History of Classic Theatrical Dancing*. New York: Putnam, 1935. Reprinted, Brooklyn, New York: Dance Horizons, 1969.
Discusses Balanchine's early life in Russia, his years with Diaghilev's Ballets Russes, his work for the Royal Danish Ballet and the Ballets Russes de Monte-Carlo, Les Ballets 1933, and his early work in America, pp. 309-11, 314-24.

———. *Flesh Is Heir: An Historical Romance*. New York: Brewer, Warren & Putnam, 1932. Reprinted, Carbondale and Edwardsville, Illinois: Southern Illinois University Press, 1975.
The chapter 'Flesh Was Fair: 1929' includes a description of *Le Fils Prodigue*, pp. 197-99.

———. 'For John Martin: Entries from an Early Diary.' *Dance Perspectives* 54 (1973).

Describes Balanchine during the Paris and London seasons of Les Ballets 1933 and the discussions leading to his coming to America.

——. *Movement & Metaphor: Four Centuries of Ballet*. New York: Praeger, 1970.
Includes chapters on *Apollon Musagète, Orpheus* and *Agon*.

——. *The New York City Ballet*. With photographs by George Platt Lynes and Martha Swope. New York: Knopf, 1973.

——. *Thirty Years: Lincoln Kirstein's The New York City Ballet*. New York: Knopf, 1978.
Text of the 1973 publication (without photographs) expanded to cover the period through 1978.

——. *Union Jack: The New York City Ballet*. New York: Eakins, 1977.

Kochno, Boris. *Diaghilev and the Ballets Russes*. New York: Harper & Row, 1970. (*Diaghilev et les Ballets Russes*. Paris: Fayard, 1973.)
Includes discussions of Balanchine's works for the company.

Kochno, Boris, and Luz, Maria. *Le Ballet*. Paris: Hachette, 1954.
Discusses Balanchine's ballets for Diaghilev, pp. 265-81; for the Ballets Russes de Monte-Carlo, pp. 293-98; for Les Ballets 1933, pp. 300-301; and for the Paris Opéra in 1947, pp. 338-39.

Koegler, Horst. *Balanchine und das moderne Ballett*. Velber bei Hannover: Friedrich, 1964.

Krokover, Rosalyn. *The New Borzoi Book of Ballets*. New York: Knopf, 1956.
Includes descriptions of many Balanchine ballets.

Lawrence, Robert. *The Victor Book of Ballets and Ballet Music*. New York: Simon and Schuster, 1950.
Includes descriptions of many Balanchine ballets.

Lawson, Joan. *A History of Ballet and Its Makers*. London: Pitman, 1964.
Includes sections on 'George Balanchine and the Neo-classical Ballet' (covering his work for Diaghilev) and 'George Balanchine and the Neo-classical Ballet in America.'

Levinson, André. *La Danse d'aujourd'hui: Études—Notes—Portraits*. Paris: Éditions Duchartre et Van Buggenhoudt, 1929.
Discusses Balanchine's work for Diaghilev in the chapter 'Grandeur et décadence des "Ballets Russes"'; *Le Chant du Rossignol* and *Apollon Musagète* are also discussed in the chapter 'Stravinsky et la danse théâtrale.'

——. *Les Visages de la danse*. Paris: Éditions Bernard Grasset, 1933.
Includes chapters on 'Derniers ballets de Diaghilew'; '"Les Ballets Nemtchinova" (1928-1930)' (*Aubade*, pp. 62-63); 'Georges Balanchine à

Mogador: Offenbach et Les Ballets Russes d'*Orphée aux Enfers*'; 'Les Ballets Russes de Monte-Carlo (1ʳᵉ saison 1932)' (*Cotillon, La Concurrence, Le Bourgeois Gentilhomme*, pp. 70-76); 'Les Ballets 1933 de Georges Balanchine.'

Lifar, Serge. *Histoire du ballet russe depuis les origines jusqu'à nos jours.* Paris: Éditions Nagel, 1950. (*A History of Russian Ballet from Its Origins to the Present Day.* Translated by Arnold L. Haskell. London: Hutchinson, 1954.)
Discusses Balanchine's work for Diaghilev's Ballets Russes, pp. 265-69, 273-75; and in the 1930s, p. 282 (London edition).

————. *Serge Diaghilev: His Life, His Work, His Legend.* New York: Putnam, 1940. (*Serge de Diaghilew, sa vie, son oeuvre, sa légende.* Monaco: Éditions du Rocher, 1954.)
Includes a section on 'Balanchine as Choreographer'; also discusses roles danced by Lifar in Balanchine ballets.

Lopukhov, Fëdor. *Puti baletmeĭstera (Paths of a Ballet Master).* Berlin: Petropolis, 1925.

————. *Shes'desiat let v balete: Vospominaniia i zapiski baletmeĭstera* (*Sixty Years in Ballet: A Balletmaster's Notes and Memoirs*). Moscow: Iskusstvo, 1966.
Lopukhov's works provide background information on ballet in Russia in the early twentieth century.

Macdonald, Nesta. *Diaghilev Observed by Critics in England and the United States 1911-1929.* Brooklyn, New York: Dance Horizons / London: Dance Books, 1975.
Includes reviews of Balanchine's works for Diaghilev from 1926.

Martin, John. *World Book of Modern Ballet.* Cleveland/New York: World, 1952.
Includes chapters titled 'Balanchine Discovers America' (1933-41) and 'America Discovers Balanchine' (1946-52).

Maynard, Olga. *The American Ballet.* Philadelphia: MacRae Smith, 1959.
Includes sections on 'George Balanchine,' 'Balanchine's American Ballet and Kirstein's Ballet Caravan,' 'Ballet Society,' 'The New York City Ballet,' and 'The School of American Ballet.'

Mazo, Joseph H. *Dance Is a Contact Sport.* New York: Saturday Review Press/Dutton, 1974.
Account of a season (1973) spent with the New York City Ballet.

Merlin, Olivier. *Stravinsky.* Paris: Hachette, 1968.
Includes an interview with Balanchine on *Agon* and the approaching New York City Ballet tour of the Soviet Union (1962).

Michaut, Pierre. *Le Ballet contemporain 1929-1950*. Paris: Librairie Plon, 1950.

Discusses Balanchine's work for Diaghilev, pp. 2-3; the unfinished *Créatures de Prométhée*, pp. 37-41; his work for the Ballets Russes de Monte-Carlo, pp. 66-75; for Les Ballets 1933, pp. 103-8; for the Grand Ballet du Marquis de Cuevas, pp. 341-43; for the Paris Opéra in 1947, pp. 352-59.

Mikhailov, Mikhail. *Zhizn' v balete (My Life in Ballet)*. Leningrad: Iskusstvo, 1966.

Excerpts from Chapter 2 published as 'My Classmate: Georges Balanchivadze' in *Dance News* 50:3, 4, 5 (March, April, May 1967), 12, 6, 8-9.

Minnelli, Vincente, and Arce, Hector. *I Remember It Well*. Garden City, New York: Doubleday, 1974.

Includes a description of Balanchine's choreography for the 'Words without Music' ballet in the 1936 Ziegfeld Follies, p. 79.

Moore, Lillian. *Artists of the Dance*. New York: Thomas Y. Crowell, 1938. Reprinted, Brooklyn, New York: Dance Horizons, 1969.

Chapter titled 'George Balanchine' gives his biography to 1937.

———. *Echoes of American Ballet*. Edited and introduced by Ivor Guest. Brooklyn, New York: Dance Horizons, 1976.

Chapter titled 'The Metropolitan Opera Ballet, 1883-1951' includes a brief discussion of Balanchine's work for that company.

Nabokov, Nicolas. *Old Friends and New Music*. Boston: Little, Brown, 1951.

Chapter titled 'Ode' includes mentions of Balanchine during his years with Diaghilev's Ballets Russes and briefly describes a rehearsal of *Apollon Musagète*. Chapters titled 'Christmas with Stravinsky' and 'Stravinsky in Hollywood' describe a visit made by the author, Balanchine and Maria Tallchief at the time of the composition of *Orpheus* (1947).

Newman, Barbara. *Striking a Balance: Dancers Talk about Dancing*. Boston: Houghton Mifflin, 1982.

Includes interviews with Felia Doubrovska, Serge Lifar, Lew Christensen, Tanaquil Le Clercq, Desmond Kelly, Jean-Pierre Bonnefous, Peter Martins, Merrill Ashley, and others, with commentary on the performance of roles in the Balanchine repertory.

Nikitina, Alice. *Nikitina, by Herself*. Translated by Baroness Budberg. London: Allan Wingate, 1959.

Includes descriptions of her participation in Balanchine's ballets for Diaghilev's Ballets Russes (*Barabau, La Chatte, Apollon Musagète, Le Bal*), Cochran's 1930 Revue ('Luna Park,' Tschaikovsky pas de deux), and her own 1932 recital in Paris.

Palmer, Winthrop. *Theatrical Dancing in America: The Development of the Ballet from 1900.* Second edition, revised. South Brunswick, New Jersey: A. S. Barnes / London: Thomas Yoseloff, 1978.
Includes sections on 'The Abstract Ballets of George Balanchine after 1945' and 'The Repertoire of New York City Ballet'; chapter on 'Lincoln Kirstein's "American Ballet."'

Payne, Charles, et al. *American Ballet Theatre.* New York: Knopf, 1978.
Includes information on works choreographed by Balanchine for the company.

Propert, Walter Archibald. *The Russian Ballet 1921-1929.* London: Bodley Head, 1931 / New York: Greenberg, 1932.
Includes discussions of Balanchine's works for Diaghilev's Ballets Russes.

Rebling, Eberhard. *Ballett A-Z: Ein Führer durch die Welt des Balletts.* Third edition. Wilhelmshaven: Heinrichsofen's Verlag, 1977.
Includes descriptions of *Agon, The Card Party, The Four Temperaments, Orpheus, Prodigal Son,* and *The Seven Deadly Sins.*

Regner, Otto Friedrich, and Schneiders, Heinz-Ludwig. *Reclams Ballett-führer.* Fifth edition, completely revised. Stuttgart: Reclam, 1972.
Includes descriptions of many Balanchine ballets.

Reynolds, Nancy. *Repertory in Review: Forty Years of the New York City Ballet.* New York: Dial, 1977.

Reynolds, Nancy, and Reimer-Torn, Susan. *In Performance: A Companion to the Classics of the Dance.* New York: Harmony, 1980.
Includes a chapter on Balanchine and the ballets *Apollo, Serenade, Concerto Barocco, The Four Temperaments, Pas de Dix, Agon,* and *Star and Stripes.*

Riobó, Julio F., and Cucullu, Carlos. *El Arte del ballet en el Teatro Colón.* Buenos Aires: Corletta & Castro, 1945.
Includes discussions of *Apollon Musagète* and *Concierto de Mozart.*

Robert, Grace. *The Borzoi Book of Ballets.* New York: Knopf, 1946.
Includes descriptions of *Apollon Musagète, Le Baiser de la Fée, Ballet Imperial, Danses Concertantes, Waltz Academy*; also discusses *Prodigal Son.*

Roslavleva, Natalia. *Era of the Russian Ballet.* London: Gollancz / New York: Dutton, 1966.
Provides background information on ballet in the Soviet Union in the 1920s.

Schaïkevitch, André. *Olga Spessivtzeva, magicienne envoutée.* Paris: Librairie les Lettres, 1954.
Includes discussions of *La Chatte,* pp. 87-90; *Les Créatures de Prométhée,* pp. 98-99.

Sharaff, Irene. *Broadway and Hollywood: Costumes Designed by Irene Sharaff*. New York: Van Nostrand Reinhold, 1976.
Includes a description of the 1936 production of *On Your Toes*, pp. 30, 33.

Siegel, Marcia B. *At the Vanishing Point: A Critic Looks at Dance*. New York: Saturday Review Press, 1972.
The section 'Balanchine's America' includes reviews of New York City Ballet performances.

———. *The Shapes of Change: Images of American Dance*. Boston: Houghton Mifflin, 1979.
The chapter 'Neoclassicism I' includes discussions of *Serenade* and *Concerto Barocco*; the chapter 'Balanchine's America' discusses *The Four Temperaments*, *Ivesiana*, *Agon*, and *Episodes*.

———. *Watching the Dance Go By*. Boston: Houghton Mifflin, 1977.
Includes reviews of New York City Ballet performances.

Slonimsky, Yuri. 'Balanchine: The Early Years.' Translated by John Andrews. Edited by Francis Mason. *Ballet Review* 5:3 (1975-76).

Smakov, Gennady. *Baryshnikov: From Russia to the West*. New York: Farrar, Straus & Giroux, 1981.
Includes a chapter titled 'With Balanchine and Robbins.'

Sokolova, Lydia. *Dancing for Diaghilev: The Memoirs of Lydia Sokolova*. Edited by Richard Buckle. London: Murray, 1960 / New York: Macmillan, 1961.
Includes descriptions of ballets choreographed by Balanchine for the Ballets Russes.

Souritz, Elizabeth J. *Khoregraficheskoe iskusstvo dvadtsatykh godov: Tendentsii, razvitiia (Choreographic Art of the Twenties: Tendencies, Developments)*. Moscow: Iskusstvo, 1979.
Includes a discussion of Balanchine's work, pp. 64-71.

Stokes, Adrian. *Russian Ballets*. London: Faber & Faber, 1935.
Includes descriptions of *Cotillon* and *La Concurrence*, with an analysis of Balanchine's choreographic style, pp. 184-96.

Stravinsky, Igor. *Chroniques de ma vie*. Paris: De Noël et Steele, 1935. (*Chronicles of My Life*. London: Gollancz, 1936. *An Autobiography*. New York: Simon and Schuster, 1936; reprinted, New York: Norton, 1962.)
Includes a description of the composition of the score and Balanchine's choreography for *Apollon Musagète*, pp. 210-15, 224-27 (New York edition).

————. *Selected Correspondence*, Volume I. Edited and with commentaries by Robert Craft. New York: Knopf, 1982.
Includes 'Correspondence with Lincoln Kirstein, 1946-1966,' pp. 263-95.

Stravinsky, Igor, and Craft, Robert. *Dialogues and a Diary*. Garden City, New York: Doubleday, 1963.
Includes a section on *Apollo*, pp. 16-20, and working notes for Stravinsky's collaboration with Balanchine on *The Flood*, pp. 89-98.

————. *Themes and Episodes*. New York: Knopf, 1966.
Section titled 'Eye Music' discusses Balanchine's *Movements for Piano and Orchestra*; Balanchine's choreography is also discussed in sections on *'Jeu de Cartes,' 'Danses Concertantes,'* and *'Orpheus.'*

Stravinsky, Vera, and Craft, Robert. *Stravinsky in Pictures and Documents*. New York: Simon and Schuster, 1978.
Includes information on collaborations with Balanchine.

Stravinsky and the Dance: A Survey of Ballet Productions, 1910-1962, in Honor of the Eightieth Birthday of Igor Stravinsky. Catalogue by Selma Jeanne Cohen, with an introduction by Herbert Read. New York: Dance Collection of The New York Public Library, 1962.
Includes ballets choreographed by Balanchine.

Stravinsky and the Theatre: A Catalogue of Decor and Costume Designs for Stage Productions of His Works 1910-1962. New York: Dance Collection of The New York Public Library, 1963.
Includes designs for ballets choreographed by Balanchine.

Swope, Martha. *A Midsummer Night's Dream: The Story of the New York City Ballet's Production Told in Photographs by Martha Swope*. Edited by Nancy Lassalle, with an introduction by Lincoln Kirstein. New York: Dodd, Mead, 1977.

————. *The Nutcracker: The Story of the New York City Ballet's Production Told in Pictures by Martha Swope*. Edited by Nancy Lassalle, with an introduction by Lincoln Kirstein. New York: Dodd, Mead, 1975.

Taper, Bernard. *Balanchine: A Biography*. Revised and updated edition. New York: Macmillan / London: Collier Macmillan, 1974.

Terry, Walter. *Ballet Guide*. New York: Dodd, Mead, 1976.
Includes descriptions of many Balanchine ballets.

————. *I Was There: Selected Dance Reviews and Articles 1936-1976*. Compiled and edited by Andrew Mark Wentink. New York: Dekker, 1978.

Includes reviews of Balanchine's works for Ballet Society, the New York City Ballet, the Original Ballet Russe (*Balustrade*), Ballet Theatre, and in musical comedy.

Twysden, Aileen Elizabeth. *Alexandra Danilova*. London: Beaumont, 1945 / New York: Kamin, 1947.

Describes Balanchine and his ballets in the Soviet Union in the 1920s, on tour with the Principal Dancers of the Russian State Ballet, with Diaghilev's Ballets Russes, and with the Ballet Russe de Monte Carlo. Provides an analysis of his choreography and Danilova's influence on it, pp. 86-87. Chapter titled 'Favourite Ballets' includes descriptions of *Les Dieux Mendiants* (*The Gods Go A-Begging*) and *Le Baiser de la Fée*.

Tyler, Parker. *The Divine Comedy of Pavel Tchelitchew: A Biography*. New York: Fleet, 1967.

Includes discussions of Balanchine's *L'Errante* (1933 version), *Magic*, *Orpheus*, *Balustrade*, and *Concerto*, pp. 353-68, 383-84, 385-87, 437, 442.

Vaillat, Léandre. *La Danse à l'Opéra de Paris*. Paris: Amiot-Dumont, 1951.

Includes a discussion of Balanchine's work as guest ballet master at the Opéra in 1947 in chapters titled 'M. Balanchine à l'Opéra,' '*Sérénade*,' '*Apollon Musagète*,' '*Le Baiser de la Fée*,' and '*Le Palais de Cristal*.'

Walker, Kathrine Sorley. *De Basil's Ballets Russes*. London: Hutchinson, 1982.

Includes information on Balanchine's work for the de Basil companies.

Ware, Walter. *Ballet Is Magic: A Triple Monograph—Harriet Hoctor, Paul Haakon, Patricia Bowman*. New York: Ihra, 1936.

Includes a description of 'Night Flight' from the Ziegfeld Follies of 1936 in the monograph on Hoctor, pp. 1-3.

Wentink, Andrew Mark. *The Steadfast Tin Soldier: The Story of George Balanchine's New York City Ballet Production, Told in Photographs by Steven Caras*. Brooklyn, New York: Dance Horizons, 1981.

White, Eric Walter. *Stravinsky: The Composer and His Works*. Second edition. Berkeley and Los Angeles: University of California Press, 1979.

Includes discussions of Balanchine's choreography to Stravinsky scores.

Williamson, Audrey. *Ballet of Three Decades*. London: Rockcliff / New York: Macmillan, 1958.

Includes comments on Balanchine's works for the Grand Ballet du Marquis de Cuevas (*La Sonnambula*), New York City Ballet, and Sadler's Wells Ballet (*Ballet Imperial*), pp. 113, 116-20, 170-71.

———. *Ballet Renaissance*. London: Golden Gallery / New York: Transatlantic Arts, 1948.

Includes comments on Balanchine's works for Ballet Theatre (*Waltz Academy*, *Apollo*), p. 81.

III. Principal Periodicals and Newspapers Consulted

Dance Magazine (New York)
Dancing Times (London)
Era (London)
Ezhenedel'nik akademicheskikh teatrov (Petrograd/Leningrad)
Krasnaya gazeta (Leningrad)
New York Herald Tribune
New York Times
Teatr (Leningrad)
Teatr i iskusstvo (Petrograd)
Theatre Arts (New York)
Variety (New York)
Zhizn' iskusstva (Petrograd/Leningrad)

ADDENDA
Revisions and Additional Information

CATALOGUE

p. 57 10 VALSE TRISTE

STAGINGS: 1984, Leningrad, Palace of the Arts (conference in honor of Balanchine).

p. 72 48 L'ENFANT ET LES SORTILÈGES

NOTE: This should not be called the first of four Balanchine productions of the work, since the conception and direction were Gunsbourg's, not the choreographer's, in 1925.
(*Source: Dale Harris*)

p. 82 72 LA CHATTE

REVISIONS: 1927, Ballets Russes: Balanchine made the role of the Cat more difficult, including the addition of double air turns, following an injury to Olga Spessivtseva on May 26, 1927, the day before the Paris premiere. On opening night in Paris, the role was danced by Alice Nikitina, who thereafter alternated with Alicia Markova.
(*Source: Markova*)

p. 86 84 APOLLON MUSAGÈTE (later called APOLLO)

STAGINGS: 1984 (planned), Ballet Théâtre Français.

TELEVISION: 1980 (excerpts, rehearsal, performance, CBS); 1982 (Live from Lincoln Center, PBS).

p. 88 85 THE GODS GO A-BEGGING

TELEVISION: 1936 (*Shepherd's Wooing*, BBC, London).

347

p. 92   94 LE FILS PRODIGUE (PRODIGAL SON)

STAGINGS: 1984 (planned), Dallas, Pacific Northwest, San Francisco.

p. 93   95 PAS DE DEUX (later MOODS)

TELEVISION: 1933 (BBC, London).

p. 105   114 UNE NUIT DE VENISE

CAST: The three women in the GRAND PAS CLASSIQUE were Tamara Toumanova, Hélène Slavinsky, and Olga Morosova. Toumanova remembers this as her first 'big variation.'

p. 109   129 COTILLON

MUSIC: The orchestration by Felix Mottl was not used; a new one was made by Vittorio Rieti.
(*Source: Rieti*)

p. 117   141 SERENADE

PREMIERE: The diaries of Lincoln Kirstein, according to Richard Buckle, note that *Serenade*, though announced and rehearsed in costume, was not performed at Hartford during the December 1934 engagement. However, a review of the performances there by John S. Kyes (*Musical America*, December 25, 1934) states that it was substituted for another ballet on the final program, December 8 (evening). At a 'preview' performance of the American Ballet, February 7, 1935, at Bryn Mawr College, *Serenade* was performed with *Alma Mater* [142] and *Transcendence* [146]. According to printed programs, on the following night *Mozartiana* [134] replaced *Serenade*; the other two ballets were repeated.

REVISIONS: 1977?, New York City Ballet: three ballerinas dance 'Dark Angel' section (beginning of ELEGY) with hair loose.
(*Source: Robert Greskovic*)

STAGINGS: 1982, Basel, Portugal; 1983, Houston, Los Angeles, Minnesota, Pittsburgh, Cape Town, Chile, Tokyo Star Dancers; 1984, Madrid.

p. 127 **162 ZIEGFELD FOLLIES: 1936 EDITION**

NOTE: Hoctor took NIGHT FLIGHT (in which she played a dead pilot) into her personal repertory, dancing it—among other places—in a Chicago theater that presented stage shows with movies.

(*Source: Selma Jeanne Cohen*)

p. 130 **166 ON YOUR TOES**

OTHER PRODUCTIONS: Broadway revival March 6, 1983, Virginia Theatre, New York (out-of-town preview December 19, 1982, Opera House, Kennedy Center, Washington, D. C.), with the 1968 version of SLAUGHTER ON TENTH AVENUE and additional choreography by Peter Martins.

TELEVISION: 1937 (abridged 'adaptation' including PRINCESS ZENOBIA and SLAUGHTER ON TENTH AVENUE, BBC, London).

p. 141 **184 GREAT LADY**

NOTE: Broadway debut of Jerome Robbins.

p. 146 **191 I WAS AN ADVENTURESS**

NOTE: Balanchine as the Orchestra Leader is uncredited. Fortunio Bonanova was a character actor of the period (perhaps originally assigned to the role).

(*Source: Arlene Croce, David Vaughan*)

p. 148 **194 BALLET IMPERIAL (later TSCHAIKOVSKY PIANO CONCERTO NO. 2)**

STAGINGS: 1982, Los Angeles.

p. 149 **195 CONCERTO BAROCCO**

STAGINGS: 1982, Milwaukee, Royal Flemish; 1983, Pittsburgh, Ballet du Nord, Tokyo Star Dancers; 1984 (planned), Düsseldorf, Finland.

p. 154   202 THE BALLET OF THE ELEPHANTS

CAST: According to the Circus World Museum, Baraboo, Wis., the Ringling Brothers troupe had more than forty—but fewer than fifty—elephants in 1942.

p. 159   214 HELEN OF TROY

According to Jerome Robbins (who danced Hermes), Lichine did not 'substantially revise' Fokine's work, but totally rechoreographed the ballet. Balanchine then made some changes, after which Lichine worked on it again.

p. 168   227 FAUST

NOTE: Marie-Jeanne remembers performing a pas de deux with Nicholas Magallanes.

p. 170   232 THE NIGHT SHADOW
                 (later LA SONNAMBULA)

STAGINGS: 1983, Ballet du Nord.

p. 172   233 RAYMONDA

STAGINGS (material from Act III divertissements): 1982, Richmond; 1983, Dance Theatre of Harlem.

p. 175   236 THE FOUR TEMPERAMENTS

REVISIONS: 1947, Ballet Society: Original finale, which resembled an undulating football huddle from which an erect figure (Dollar) was raised aloft, completely rechoreographed. Resulting linear formations have remained basically the same over the years, despite Balanchine's frequent small alterations. The 1977 changes for Dance in America retain the essence of the linear structure.
STAGINGS: 1983, Ballet du Nord, Cape Town; 1984 (planned), Cleveland.

p. 175   239A CHANSON RUSSE

Music: By Peter Ilyitch Tschaikovsky (*Chanson Russe*, Op. 39, no. 11, from *Children's Album: 24 Easy Pieces* for piano, 1878).

Première: May 16, 1947, Ambassadeur, Paris.

Cast: Tamara Toumanova.

Note: Performed once, at a gala for the Mutuelle des Artistes de la Danse de l'Opéra, organized by Prince A. Michaguine. (*Source: Toumanova*)

p. 179   241 SYMPHONIE CONCERTANTE

Stagings: 1983, American Ballet Theatre.

p. 180   242 THEME AND VARIATIONS

Stagings: 1983, Cleveland, Ballet du Nord.

p. 182   246 ORPHEUS

Television: 1982 (Live from Lincoln Center, PBS).

p. 183   247 PAS DE TROIS CLASSIQUE (Minkus)

Stagings: 1982, Ballet Théâtre Français.

p. 192   265 BOURRÉE FANTASQUE

Stagings: 1984 (planned), Ballet Théâtre Français.

p. 196   273 SYLVIA: PAS DE DEUX

Stagings: 1983, National Ballet of Canada.

p. 198   277 LA VALSE

Stagings: 1982, Munich.

p. 201   282   À LA FRANÇAIX

STAGINGS: 1983, Richmond.

p. 202   285   SWAN LAKE

REVISIONS: Music for VALSE BLUETTE is an orchestrated version of *Valse Bagatelle*, Op. 72, no. 11 (in E-flat).
(*Source: Jack Reed*)

p. 204   286   CARACOLE

NOTE: Le Clercq, Adams, and Robbins agree that the steps for *Caracole* and *Divertimento No. 15* [314] are virtually identical and that it is incorrect to say that no one could remember *Caracole* in 1956.

p. 205   288   SCOTCH SYMPHONY

STAGINGS: 1982, Kansas City; 1983, North Carolina, Düsseldorf; 1984 (planned), Minnesota.

p. 207   293   VALSE FANTAISIE

STAGINGS: 1984 (planned), Arizona Metropolitan.

p. 210   302   THE NUTCRACKER

REVISIONS: 1983, New York City Ballet: Two adult couples and a teenage couple (guests) and another maid added to PARTY SCENE, ACT I, SCENE I, following a plan of Balanchine's.

TELEVISION: 1975 (children's rehearsals, NBC); 1980 (excerpts, children's rehearsals, performance, NBC).

p. 213   303   WESTERN SYMPHONY

STAGINGS: 1984 (planned), Ballet West, Pennsylvania.

p. 216   307 PAS DE TROIS (Glinka)

STAGINGS: 1973, Ballet Repertory; 1983, Fort Worth.

p. 219   311 THE MAGIC FLUTE

PRODUCTION: Production Designer: Rouben Ter-Arutunian.

NOTE: The entire concept of the production, as well as the
movement direction, was Balanchine's.
(*Source: Ter-Arutunian*)

p. 219   312 ALLEGRO BRILLANTE

STAGINGS: 1982, Royal Winnipeg; 1983, New Jersey, Ohio,
Pittsburgh, San Juan, Washington; 1984 (planned), Ballet
Oklahoma.

p. 220   314 DIVERTIMENTO NO. 15

NOTE: See new Note for *Caracole* [286].

p. 222   315 SQUARE DANCE

STAGINGS: 1982, Ballet Metropolitan, Tulsa; 1983, Dance Theatre
of Harlem, Los Angeles, Louisville; 1984 (planned), Ballet du Nord.

p. 222   316 AGON

STAGINGS: 1976, San Francisco (*not* 1967).

TELEVISION: 1983 (Dance in America, PBS).

p. 224   318 STARS AND STRIPES

STAGINGS (pas de deux unless otherwise noted): 1983, Ballet West
(complete), Jacksonville, Pacific Northwest (complete),
Pennsylvania (complete), Royal Flemish; 1984 (planned), Dance
Alive, Dance Theatre of Harlem (complete).

TELEVISION: 1980 (pas de deux, Gala of Stars, PBS).

p. 228   324 EPISODES

STAGINGS: 1982, Zürich.

p. 230   328 NIGHT SHADOW (later LA SONNAMBULA)

PRODUCTION: Costumes by André Levasseur from Les Ballets de Pâques production, 1957.
(*Source: John Taras*)

p. 232   331 PAS DE DEUX (TSCHAIKOVSKY PAS DE DEUX)

STAGINGS: 1982, Zürich; 1983, Atlanta, Pennsylvania, Ballet du Nord, Berlin; 1984, Ballet Théâtre Français, Madrid, Hamburg; 1984 (planned), Hartford.

TELEVISION: 1980 (excerpts, rehearsal, performance, CBS).

p. 233   333 VARIATIONS FROM DON SEBASTIAN (later DONIZETTI VARIATIONS)

STAGINGS: 1982, Cincinnati; 1983, Tulsa; 1984 (planned), Hartford, San Juan, Ballet du Nord.

p. 235   335 LIEBESLIEDER WALZER

STAGINGS: 1984 (planned), Cleveland.

p. 237   339 VALSES ET VARIATIONS (later RAYMONDA VARIATIONS)

STAGINGS: 1983, Cincinnati, Pittsburgh; 1984 (planned), Louisville.

p. 240   343 BUGAKU

STAGINGS: 1983, Chicago City.

p. 242   346 MEDITATION

TELEVISION: 1980 (excerpts, CBS).

p. 243   347 TARANTELLA

STAGINGS: 1984, Washington.

p. 245   351 HARLEQUINADE

NEW PRODUCTIONS BY BALANCHINE COMPANIES: 1984, New York
City Ballet: eight new children's Scaramouche costumes designed
by Rouben Ter-Arutunian.

STAGINGS: HARLEQUINADE PAS DE DEUX (pas de deux from Act I,
variations from Act II): 1982, American Ballet Theatre, Pacific
Northwest (with children).

p. 246   352 DON QUIXOTE

REVISIONS: ca. 1970, New York City Ballet: ACT III, SCENE I, New
solo (with scarf) added for Dulcinea.
(*Source: David Daniel*)

p. 250   358 JEWELS

NEW PRODUCTIONS BY BALANCHINE COMPANIES: 1983, New York
City Ballet: Three new backdrops by Robin Wagner. (This was the
first production change in a Balanchine ballet to be commissioned
after his death; during his lifetime, he personally oversaw all
details of costume, scenery, and music.)

STAGINGS: RUBIES: 1983, Pennsylvania.

p. 254   366 VALSE FANTAISIE

STAGINGS: 1982, Dance Alive; 1983, Pennsylvania, Bari; 1984
(planned), Berkeley, Southwest.

p. 255   368   WHO CARES?

NEW PRODUCTIONS BY BALANCHINE COMPANIES: 1983, New York City Ballet: New costumes by Ben Benson.

TELEVISION: 1982 (excerpt, Gala of Stars, PBS); 1983 (Live from Lincoln Center, PBS).

p. 259   374   VIOLIN CONCERTO

STAGINGS: 1984, Zürich; 1984 (planned), Paris.

p. 261   379   PULCINELLA

REVISIONS: Very soon after premiere, Berman décor substantially reduced.

p. 268   390   L'ENFANT ET LES SORTILÈGES

CHOREOGRAPHY: By George Balanchine. TEA POT and LITTLE MATH MAN with 10 NUMBERS choreographed by Jerome Robbins.

p. 269   394   TZIGANE

STAGINGS: 1983, Chicago City.

p. 270   397   FAUST, WALPURGISNACHT BALLET

REVISIONS: 1979: Ballerina variation rechoreographed for Chicago. (*Source: Maria Tallchief*)

p. 272   400   CHACONNE

STAGINGS: 1983, Pacific Northwest, San Francisco.

TELEVISION: 1983 (excerpt, Gala of Stars, PBS).

p. 273   401   UNION JACK

TELEVISION: 1980 (excerpt, rehearsal, CBS); 1983 (COSTERMONGER PAS DE DEUX, Gala of Stars, PBS).

p. 275   406 VIENNA WALTZES

TELEVISION: 1983 (Live from Lincoln Center, PBS).

p. 278   410 LE BOURGEOIS GENTILHOMME

REVISIONS: 1980: Although choreography was credited to
Balanchine alone, substantial portions of Robbins's work remained.

p. 281   415 ROBERT SCHUMANN'S
               'DAVIDSBÜNDLERTÄNZE'

TELEVISION: 1980 (excerpt, CBS).

p. 282   417 MOZARTIANA

STAGINGS: 1983, Chicago City.

TELEVISION: 1983 (Live from Lincoln Center, PBS).

p. 287   424 PERSÉPHONE

TELEVISION: 1983 (Dance in America, PBS).

p. 287   425 VARIATIONS FOR ORCHESTRA

TELEVISION: 1983 (Dance in America, PBS).

AMERICAN COMPANY ITINERARIES

New York City Ballet

p. 309   1982 July 6-25, SARATOGA SPRINGS SEASON: Saratoga Performing
               Arts Center
               October 4-17, Washington, D. C.: Kennedy Center
               November 16 - February 20, 1983, NEW YORK SEASON: New York
               State Theater

1983   April 26 - June 26, NEW YORK SEASON: New York State Theater
    July 5-23, SARATOGA SPRINGS SEASON: Saratoga Performing
        Arts Center
    EUROPEAN TOUR
        August 22 - September 3, London: Royal Opera House,
            Covent Garden
        September 6 - September 18, Copenhagen: Concert Hall,
            Tivoli Gardens
        September 20 - October 2, Paris: Théâtre Musical de Paris/
            Châtelet
        November 15 - February 19, 1984, NEW YORK SEASON: New York
            State Theater
1984   February 29 - March 11, Washington, D. C.: Kennedy Center
    April 24 - June 24, NEW YORK SEASON: New York State Theater

ROLES PERFORMED BY BALANCHINE

p. 320   1918 - OCTOBER 1924: 1918 *Le Rossignol* (Stravinsky); State Theater of
    Opera and Ballet, Petrograd/Leningrad; WALK-ON. (Balanchine;
    Reynolds)

p. 323   1924, JANUARY - OCTOBER   *Le Corsaire* (Adam-Drigo-Minkus-Pugni/
    Petipa); State Theater of Opera and Ballet, Petrograd/Leningrad;.
    DANCE OF THE CORSAIRS. First performed by Balanchine in 1923.

p. 323   1924, JANUARY - OCTOBER   Balanchine danced in *Petrouchka* (Stravinsky/
    Fokine); State Theater of Opera and Ballet, Petrograd/Leningrad;
    ARTISAN.

BIBLIOGRAPHY

I. Writings by Balanchine

ARTICLES

'A Letter from George Balanchine.' *Ballet Annual* 15 (1961), 55. A tribute to Frederick Ashton.

II. Books Relating to Balanchine

Barnes, Clive. *Nureyev.* New York: Helene Obolensky, 1982.
Includes discussions of the dancer's interpretations of various Balanchine roles and his creation of the role of Cléonte in *Le Bourgeois Gentilhomme.*

Bentley, Toni. *Winter Season: A Dancer's Journal.* New York: Random House, 1982.
An account of the 1980-81 winter season of the New York City Ballet.

Buckle, Richard. *In the Wake of Diaghilev.* New York: Holt, Rinehart and Winston, 1983.

Cohen, Selma Jeanne (ed.). *Dance as a Theatre Art: Source Readings in Dance History from 1581 to the Present.* New York: Harper and Row, 1974.
Includes reprint of the article: Balanchine, George, 'Work in Progress' [interview with Louis Botto] (1972), pp. 187-92.

Copeland, Roger, and Cohen, Marshall (eds.). *What is Dance? Readings in Theory and Criticism.* New York: Oxford University Press, 1983.
Includes reprints of the following articles: Levin, David Michael, 'Balanchine's Formalism' (1973), pp. 123-45; Denby, Edwin, 'Three Sides of *Agon*' (1957), pp. 446-53, and 'A Balanchine Masterpiece (*Concerto Barocco*)' (1945), pp. 454-55; Croce, Arlene, 'Momentous (*The Four Temperaments*)' (1975), pp. 459-64.

d'Amboise, Christopher. *Leap Year: A Year in the Life of a Dancer.* Garden City, New York: Doubleday, 1982.

Hastings, Baird. *Choreographer and Composer: Theatrical Dance and Music in Western Culture.* Boston: Twayne, 1983.
Includes 'The Collaborations of George Balanchine and Igor Stravinsky,' pp. 122-60.

Keynes, Milo (ed.). *Lydia Lopokova*. New York: St. Martin's Press, 1983.

Kirstein, Lincoln. *Ballet—Bias & Belief: 'Three Pamphlets Collected' and Other Dance Writings of Lincoln Kirstein*. With Introduction and Comments by Nancy Reynolds. Brooklyn, New York: Dance Horizons, 1983.
A selection of Kirstein's writings from 1930 to 1978, with Postscript (1982).

—. *Portrait of Mr. B: Photographs of George Balanchine*. With additional material by Peter Martins, Edwin Denby, and Jonathan Cott. A Ballet Society Book. New York: Viking, 1984.

McDonagh, Don. *George Balanchine*. Boston: Twayne, 1983.

Mikhailov, Mikhail. *Molodyie gody leningradskogo baleta (Young Years of the Leningrad Ballet)*. Leningrad: Iskusstvo, 1978.

Martins, Peter, and Cornfield, Robert. *Far from Denmark*. Boston: Little, Brown, 1982.

Steinberg, Cobbett (ed.). *The Dance Anthology*. New York: New American Library, 1980.
Includes reprints of the articles: Balanchine, George, 'Notes on Choreography' (1945), pp. 28-35, and 'The Dance Element in Stravinsky's Music' (1947), pp. 149-52.

Switzer, Ellen. *Dancers! Horizons of American Dance*. New York: Atheneum, 1982.
Includes a discussion of Balanchine's place in the history of American dance; also, sections on several New York City Ballet dancers.

Tracy, Robert, and DeLano, Sharon. *Balanchine's Ballerinas: Conversations with the Muses*. New York: Linden Press, 1983.

Although space and time have precluded a listing of the enormous number of articles written about Balanchine, his ballets, his companies, and his dancers, a bibliography of the more substantive items, compiled by Marion-Clare Kahn and edited by Susan Au, appears in *Ballet Review* 11:2;3 (Summer-Fall 1983), 9-11, 97-99.

COMPANIES STAGING BALANCHINE WORKS

July 1982 - February 1984

Numbers refer to Catalogue entries. The Key to companies with Balanchine works in repertory prior to July 1982 begins on p. 373.

United States

American Ballet Theatre, 241, 351
Arizona Metropolitan Ballet (Phoenix), 293
Atlanta, 331
Ballet Metropolitan, 315
Ballet Oklahoma, 312
Ballet West, 303, 318
Berkeley Ballet Theatre (California), 366
Chicago City, 343, 394, 417
Cincinnati (since 1983 known as Cincinnati/New Orleans City Ballet), 333, 339
Cleveland, 236, 242, 335
Dallas, 94
Dance Alive (Gainesville, Florida), 318, 366
Dance Theatre of Harlem, 233, 315, 318
Forth Worth Ballet (Texas), 307
Hartford, 331, 333
Houston, 141
Jacksonville (Florida Ballet at Jacksonville), 318
Kansas City, 288
Los Angeles, 141, 194, 315
Louisville, 315, 339
Milwaukee, 195
Minnesota, 141, 288
New Jersey, 312
New Orleans City Ballet (see Cincinnati)
North Carolina, 288
Ohio, 312
Pacific Northwest, 94, 318, 351, 400
Pennsylvania, 303, 318, 331, 358, 366
Pittsburgh, 141, 195, 312, 339

Richmond, 233, 282
San Francisco, 94, 400
San Juan, 312, 333
Southwest Ballet Company (Albuquerque, New Mexico), 366
Tulsa, 315, 333
Washington, 312, 347

Other Countries

Ballet du Nord (Roubaix, France), 195, 232, 236, 242, 315, 331, 333
Ballet Théâtre Français, 84, 247, 265, 331
Basel (Ballett des Basler Theaters, Switzerland), 141
Bari (Balletto del Sol, Italy), 366
Berlin, 331
Cape Town (CAPAB, Cape Performing Arts Board), 141, 236
Chile (Teatro Municipal, Santiago), 141
Düsseldorf, 195, 288
Finland (National Ballet Company, Suomen Kansallis Baletti, Helsinki), 195
Hamburg, 331
Madrid (Ballet Nacional de España), 141, 331
Munich, 277
National Ballet of Canada, 273
Paris, 374
Portugal (Companhia Nacional de Bailado, Lisbon), 141
Royal Flemish, 195, 318
Royal Winnipeg, 312
Tokyo Star Dancers (Star Dancers Ballet Company, Tokyo), 141, 195
Zürich, 324, 331, 374

Particular thanks in the preparation of the Addenda are due to Elizabeth Souritz (letter from Moscow to Nancy Reynolds, 8/2/83), Vera Krasovskaya (letter from Leningrad to Selma Jeanne Cohen, 1/20/84), to Jerome Robbins, Barbara Horgan, Rosemary Dunleavy, and William Lawson of the New York City Ballet, and to Susan Au and Katherine Matheson.

N. R.

INDEXES

Numbers refer to Catalogue entries

TITLES BY CATEGORY

BALLET

À la Françaix, Françaix, 282

Adagio, Saint-Saëns, 17

Adagio Lamentoso, see *Symphony No. 6—Pathétique*

Agon, Stravinsky, 316

Allegro Brillante, Tschaikovsky, 312

Alma Errante, see *L'Errante*

Alma Mater, Swift, 142

Anna Anna, or The Seven Capital Sins, see *Les Sept Péchés Capitaux*

Apollo; Apollo, Leader of the Muses; Apolo Musageta, see *Apollon Musagète*

Apollon Musagète, Stravinsky, 84, 176, 198, 284

Aubade, Poulenc, 98

Aurora's Wedding: Ariadne and Her Brothers, Tschaikovsky, 65

Le Baiser de la Fée, Stravinsky, 178, 271

Le Bal, Rieti, 93

Ballade, Fauré, 412

Ballet Imperial, Tschaikovsky, 194, 349, 382

Ballo della Regina, Verdi, 407

Balustrade, Stravinsky, 192

Barabau, Rieti, 53

The Bat, J. Strauss II, 169, 199

Bayou, Thomson, 287

Le Bœuf sur le Toit, Milhaud, 35

Le Bourgeois Gentilhomme, R. Strauss, 131, 221, 410, 414

Bourrée Fantasque, Chabrier, 265

La Boutique Fantasque, Rossini, 103

Brahms–Schoenberg Quartet, 354

Bugaku, Mayuzumi, 343

Capriccio Brillant, Mendelssohn, 279

Caracole, Mozart, 286

The Card Game, see *The Card Party*

The Card Party, Stravinsky, 177, 275

Chaconne, Gluck, 400

Le Chant du Rossignol, Stravinsky, 52

La Chatte, Sauguet, 72

Chorus Reading, Blok, 28

Clarinade, Gould, 348

Classic Ballet, see *Concerto*

Concertino, Françaix, 292

Concerto, Chopin, 165

Concerto Barocco, Bach, 195, 250

Concerto for Jazz Band and Orchestra, Liebermann, 370

Concierto de Mozart, 205

La Concurrence, Auric, 130

Coppélia, Delibes, 387

Cortège Hongrois, Glazounov, 384

Cotillon, Chabrier, 129

Les Créatures de Prométhée, Beethoven, 96

Dance Concerto, see *Danses Concertantes*

Danses Concertantes, Stravinsky, 220, 375

Les Dieux Mendiants, see *The Gods Go A-Begging*

Divertimento, Haieff, 238

Divertimento, Rossini, 196

Divertimento from 'Le Baiser de la Fée,' Stravinsky, 376

Divertimento No. 15, Mozart, 314

Don Quixote, Nabokov, 352

Don Quixote: Pas de Deux, Minkus, 262

Donizetti Variations, see *Variations from Don Sebastian*

Dreams, Antheil, 145

Duo Concertant, Stravinsky, 378

Electronics, Gassmann/Sala, 338

Élégie, Stravinsky, 245, 355, 423

Elegy, Rachmaninoff, 32
Enigma, Arensky, 25
Episodes, Webern, 324
L'Errante, Schubert, 138, 143, 197
Étude, Scriabin, 30
Étude for Piano, Scriabin, 405
Extase, Balanchine, 21
The Fairy's Kiss, see *Le Baiser de la Fée*
Fantasia Brasileira, Mignone, 200
Fastes, Sauguet, 137
The Figure in the Carpet, Handel, 332
Le Fils Prodigue, Prokofiev, 94, 267
Firebird, Stravinsky, 264
The Four Temperaments, Hindemith, 236
Fyrst Igor, see *Prince Igor*
Garland Dance from *The Sleeping Beauty*, see *Tempo di Valse*
Gaspard de la Nuit, Ravel, 395
Giselle: Act II Grave Scene, Adam, 234
Glinkiana, 359
The Gods Go A-Begging, Handel, 85
Gounod Symphony, 317
Grand Adagio, see *Pas de Deux*, Tschaikovsky, from *The Sleeping Beauty*
Harlequinade, Drigo, 351
Harlequinade Pas de Deux, Drigo, 290
Helen of Troy, Offenbach, 214
Hungarian Gypsy Airs, Menter/ Tschaikovsky, 419
Hungarian Gypsy Dance, Brahms, 13
Invitation to the Dance, Weber, 34
Ivesiana, Ives, 304
Jack in the Box, Satie, 63
Jeux d'Enfants, Bizet, 310
Jewels, Fauré/Stravinsky/Tschaikovsky, 358
Jones Beach, Andriessen, 269
Josef-Legende, see *La Légende de Joseph*
Kammermusik No. 2, Hindemith, 408

Le Lac des Cygnes, see *Swan Lake*
La Légende de Joseph, R. Strauss, 106
Legetøjsbutiken, see *La Boutique Fantasque*
Liebeslieder Walzer, Brahms, 335
Marche Funèbre, Chopin, 19
Matelotte, traditional, 11
Mazurka from 'A Life for the Tsar,' Glinka, 272
Meditation, Tschaikovsky, 346
Metamorphoses, Hindemith, 289
Metastaseis & Pithoprakta, Xenakis, 360
A Midsummer Night's Dream, Mendelssohn, 340
Modern Jazz: Variants, Schuller, 337
Monumentum pro Gesualdo, Stravinsky, 334
La Mort du Cygne, Saint-Saëns, 16, 263
Movements for Piano and Orchestra, Stravinsky, 344
Mozartiana, Tschaikovsky, 134, 149, 417
El Murciélago, see *The Bat*
Native Dancers, Rieti, 323
The Night Shadow, Rieti, 232, 328
La Nuit, Rubinstein, 1
The Nutcracker, Tschaikovsky, 302
Opus 34, Schoenberg, 301
Oriental Dance, Moussorgsky, 31
Orientalia, Cui, 12
Orpheus, Stravinsky, 246
Le Palais de Cristal, Bizet, 240, 244
PAMTGG, Kellaway/Applebaum/ Woloshin, 371
Panamerica, Escobar/Chávez/Orbón, 329
Pas de Deux, Glazounov, 33
Pas de Deux, Kreisler, 22
Pas de Deux, Tschaikovsky, from *The Sleeping Beauty*, 225

Pas de Deux, Tschaikovsky, from
   Swan Lake, 331; see also 262
Pas de Deux and Divertissement,
   Delibes, 350
Pas de Deux Romantique, Weber, 268
Pas de Dix, Glazounov, 309
Pas de Trois, Glinka, 307
Pas de Trois, Minkus, see *Pas de Trois
   Classique*
Pas de Trois Classique, Minkus, 247,
   276
La Pastorale, Auric, 62
Pavane, Ravel, 393
Piano Concerto No. 2, see *Ballet
   Imperial*
Poème, Fibich, 4
Poker Game, see *The Card Party*
Polka, Rachmaninoff, 23
Polovtsian Dances, see *Prince Igor*
Prince Igor, Borodin, 104
Princess Aurora, Tschaikovsky, 259
Prodigal Son, see *Le Fils Prodigue*
Pulcinella, Stravinsky, 35, 379
Ragtime, Stravinsky, 3, 336, 356
Rapsodie Espagnole, Ravel, 396
Raymonda, Glazounov, 233
Raymonda Variations, see *Valses et
   Variations*
Reminiscence, Godard, 144
Renard, Stravinsky, 237
*Robert Schumann's 'Davidsbündler-
   tänze,'* 415
Roma, Bizet, 306
Romance, see *La Nuit*
Romanza, Balanchine, 8
Romeo and Juliet, Lambert, 61
Rosendrømmen, see *Le Spectre de la Rose*
Sailor's Hornpipe, see *Matelotte*
Schéhérazade, Rimsky-Korsakov, 102
Scherzo à la Russe, Stravinsky, 377
Schön Rosmarin, Kreisler, 2

Scotch Symphony, Mendelssohn, 288
Sentimental Colloquy, Bowles, 223
Les Sept Péchés Capitaux, Weill/Brecht,
   136, 322
Serenade, Tschaikovsky, 141, 193, 254
The Seven Deadly Sins, see *Les Sept
   Péchés Capitaux*
Shéhérazade, Ravel, 391
Slaughter on Tenth Avenue, Rodgers, 361
*The Sleeping Beauty: Aurora's Solo,
   Vision Scene*, Tschaikovsky, 404
The Sleeping Beauty: Variation from
   Aurora's Wedding, Tschaikovsky,
   281
The Sleeping Beauty, see also *Aurora's
   Wedding; Pas de Deux; Princess
   Aurora; Tempo di Valse.*
La Somnambule, see *The Night Shadow*
Sonata, Stravinsky, 372
Sonatine, Ravel, 389
The Song of the Nightingale, see *Le Chant
   du Rossignol*
Les Songes, Milhaud, 135
La Sonnambula, see *The Night Shadow*
La Source, Delibes, 364
Spanish Dance, Glazounov, 18
Le Spectre de la Rose, Weber, 105
Square Dance, Vivaldi/Corelli, 315
Stars and Stripes, Sousa, 318
The Steadfast Tin Soldier, Bizet, 398
Stravinsky Violin Concerto, see *Violin
   Concerto*
Suite No. 3, Tschaikovsky, 369
Suites de Danse, Glinka, 132
Swan Lake, Tschaikovsky, 75, 285, 367
Swan Lake: Black Swan Pas de Deux,
   Tschaikovsky, 262
Swan Lake, see also *Pas de Deux*
Sylvia: Pas de Deux, Delibes, 273
Symphonie Concertante, Mozart, 241
Symphony in C, see *Palais de Cristal*

Symphony in Three Movements,
Stravinsky, 373

*Symphony No. 6—Pathétique: Fourth
Movement, Adagio Lamentoso,*
Tschaikovsky, 420

Tango, Stravinsky, 421

Tarantella, Gottschalk, 347

Tempo di Valse: Garland Dance from
The Sleeping Beauty, Tschaikovsky,
418

Theme and Variations, Tschaikovsky,
242, 330

Le Tombeau de Couperin, Ravel, 392

Transcendence, Liszt, 146

Den Trekantede Hat, see *Le Tricorne*

Tricolore, Auric, 409

Le Tricorne, Falla, 101

The Triumph of Bacchus and Ariadne,
Rieti, 243

The Triumph of Neptune, Berners, 64

Trois Valses Romantiques, Chabrier,
357

Trumpet Concerto, Haydn, 270

Tschaikovsky Pas de Deux, see *Pas de
Deux,* Tschaikovsky, from *Swan
Lake*

Tschaikovsky Piano Concerto No. 2, see
Ballet Imperial

Tschaikovsky Suite No. 3, see *Suite No. 3*

Tyl Ulenspiegel, R. Strauss, 283

Tzigane, Ravel, 394

Union Jack, Kay, 401

La Valse, Ravel, 277

Valse Caprice, Rubinstein, 14

Valse Fantaisie, Glinka, 293, 366

Valse Triste, Sibelius, 10

Les Valses de Beethoven, 139

Valses et Variations, Glazounov, 339

Variations, Stravinsky, 353, 425

Variations from Don Sebastian,
Donizetti, 333

Variations pour une Porte et un Soupir,
Henry, 386

Vienna Waltzes, J. Strauss II/Lehár/
R. Strauss, 406

Violin Concerto, Stravinsky, 374

Walpurgisnacht Ballet, Gounod, 413

Waltz, Drigo, 6

Waltz, Ravel, 20

Waltz, unknown, 9

Waltz Academy, Rieti, 222

Waltz and Adagio, Balanchine, 7

Waltz-Scherzo, Tschaikovsky, 321

The Waltzes of Beethoven, see *Les Valses
de Beethoven*

The Wanderer, see *L'Errante*

Western Symphony, Kay, 303

Who Cares?, Gershwin, 368

BALLET FOR OPERA

Adriana Lecouvreur, Cilea, 299

Aïda, Verdi, 126, 152, 226, 255

Amahl and the Night Visitors, Menotti,
300

Un Bal Masqué, see *Un Ballo in Maschera*

Un Ballo in Maschera, Verdi, 80

The Bartered Bride, Smetana, 167

Boris Godunov, Moussorgsky, 54, 298,
388

Caponsacchi, Hageman, 173

Carmen, Bizet, 38, 127, 155, 248

Les Contes d'Hoffmann, Offenbach, 58,
112, 260

Le Coq d'Or, Rimsky-Korsakov, 24

Le Croisade des Dames, see *Die
Verschworenen*

La Damnation de Faust, Berlioz, 49, 69

Un Début, Bellenot, 47

Le Démon, Rubinstein, 42

Dido and Aeneas, Purcell, 411

Don Giovanni, Mozart, 81, 181, 253

Don Juan, see *Don Giovanni*

Eine Nacht in Venedig, J. Strauss II, 114

Eugen Onegin, Tschaikovsky, 256

The Fair at Sorochinsk, Moussorgsky, 208

Faust, Gounod, 45, 117, 151, 227, 397

La Favorita, Donizetti, 297

Fay-Yen-Fah, Redding, 44, 125

La Femme Nue, Février, 89

La Fille d'Abdoubarahah, Sanvel, 82

Fürst Igor, see *Prince Igor*

La Gioconda, Ponchielli, 87, 174

Hamlet, Thomas, 60

Hérodiade, Massenet, 46, 119

L'Hirondelle, see *La Rondine*

Le Hulla, Samuel-Rousseau, 41

Ivan le Terrible, Gunsbourg, 70

Jeanne d'Arc, Gounod, 59

Judith, Honegger, 55

La Juive, Halévy, 160

Lakmé, Delibes, 57, 115, 153

Lucia di Lammermoor, Donizetti, 168

Macbeth, Verdi, 211

Les Maîtres Chanteurs, see *Die Meistersinger von Nürnberg*

Manon, Massenet, 40, 122, 159

Mârouf, Rabaud, 179, 204

The Marriage of Figaro, see *Le Nozze di Figaro*

Martha, Flotow, 90

Die Meistersinger von Nürnberg, Wagner, 77, 163

Mignon, Thomas, 158

Mireille, Gounod, 76

Le Nozze di Figaro, Mozart, 251

Obéron, Weber, 71

The Opera Cloak, Damrosch, 207

Orfeo ed Euridice, Gluck, 399

La Périchole, Offenbach, 128

Pique Dame, Tschaikovsky, 210

Prince Igor, Borodin, 383

Le Prophète, Meyerbeer, 113

The Queen of Spades, see *Pique Dame*

The Reluctant King, see *Le Roi Malgré Lui*

Rigoletto, Verdi, 88, 121, 156

Le Roi Malgré Lui, Chabrier, 403

Roméo et Juliette, Gounod, 86, 124, 180

La Rondine, Puccini, 56, 161

Samson et Dalila, Saint-Saëns, 66, 116, 171, 228

Sior Todéro Brontolon, Malipiero, 79

The Tales of Hoffmann, see *Les Contes d'Hoffmann*

Tannhäuser, Wagner, 111, 154

Thaïs, Massenet, 39

La Traviata, Verdi, 67, 123, 150, 252

Troubled Island, Still, 258

Turandot, Puccini, 68, 120

Une Nuit à Venise, see *Eine Nacht in Venedig*

Venise, Gunsbourg, 78

Die Verschworenen, Schubert, 92

La Vie Parisienne, Offenbach, 209

OPERA

Le Coq d'Or, Rimsky-Korsakov, 172

Eugen Onegin, Tschaikovsky, 341

Orfeo ed Euridice, Gluck, 170, 345

Orpheus and Eurydice, Orpheus und Eurydike, see *Orfeo ed Euridice*

The Rake's Progress, Stravinsky, 295

Ruslan und Ludmilla, Glinka, 365

OPERA-BALLET

L'Enfant et les Sortilèges (*The Spellbound Child*), Ravel, 48, 235, 390

Patrie, Paladilhe, 118

STAGED CHORAL WORKS

Choral Variations on Bach's 'Vom Himmel Hoch,' Stravinsky, 380

The Crucifixion of Christ, Bach, 215

Noah and the Flood, Stravinsky, 422; see also 342
Perséphone, Stravinsky, 424
Requiem Canticles, Stravinsky, 362
Symphony of Psalms, Stravinsky, 381

OPERETTA

The Chocolate Soldier, O. Straus, 239
Die Fledermaus, see *Rosalinda*
The Merry Widow, Lehár, 216
Rosalinda, J. Strauss II, 206
Song of Norway, Grieg/Wright/Forrest, 219

CONCERT WORKS

Aleko, Rachmaninoff, 83
Begin the Beguine, Porter, 385
[*Cabaret Entertainment*], 29
Circus Polka, Stravinsky, 230
[*Cotillion Promenade*], 296
Dans l'Élysée, Offenbach, 140
[*Duet*], Liszt, 100
Dutch Dance, Grieg, 3
Étude, Scriabin, 50
Die Fledermaus, J. Strauss II, 107
Flight of the Bumble Bee, Rimsky-Korsakov, 107
[*Foxtrots*], 5
Grotesque Espagnol, Albéniz, 73
Hopac, Moussorgsky, 43
Jeanne d'Arc, Debussy?, 148
Moods, see *Pas de Deux* [*Moods*]
Music and Dance, 274
A Musical Joke, Mozart, 313
A Novel Interpretation of Liebestraum, Liszt, 107
Numéro les Canotiers, popular waltz, 133
Papillons, Chopin?, 107
[*Pas de Deux*], Mozart, 157
Pas de Deux [*Moods*], da Costa, 95

Pas de Deux—Blues, Duke, 189
Pas de Trois for Piano and Two Dancers, Chanler, 203
Pizzicato Polka, Delibes, 36
Polka Grotesque, unknown, 83
Polka Mélancolique, Rubinstein, 51
Resurgence, Mozart, 231
Sarcasm, Prokofiev, 74
Serenata: 'Magic,' Mozart, 164
A Skit on Marlene Dietrich in the Film 'The Blue Angel,' Lerner/Hollander, 107
[*Solo*], Chopin, 147
[*Solo*], Prokofiev, 212
Statues, Mendelssohn, 107
Tango, unknown, 107
[To a waltz perhaps by Johann Strauss], 3
[To can-can from *Orphée aux Enfers* by Offenbach], 107
[To jazz recorded by Jack Hilton and His Dance Orchestra], 107
[To music by Scriabin], 3
[To music by Chopin or Schumann], 3
[To music by Medtner], 3
[To music from *Salome* by Richard Strauss], 3
[To *Scottish Rhapsody* by Lord Berners], 107
[To the *1812 Overture* by Tschaikovsky], 107
[*Trio*], Liszt, 100
Valse Caprice, Rubinstein, 37
Variation, see *Pizzicato Polka*
Waltz Fantasy in Blue, Glinka, 107
The Warrior, Rachmaninoff, 327

MUSICAL THEATER

Babes in Arms, Rodgers/Hart, 175
The Boys from Syracuse, Rodgers/Hart/Abbott, 183

Cabin in the Sky, Duke/Latouche/Root, 190

Charles B. Cochran's 1929 Revue, see *Wake Up and Dream!*

Charles B. Cochran's 1930 Revue, 99: *In a Venetian Theatre; Luna Park, or The Freaks; Piccadilly, 1830; Heaven; The Wind in the Willows; Pas de Deux; Tennis*

Charles B. Cochran's 1931 Revue, 108: *Stealing Through; Scaramouche*

Courtin' Time, Lawrence/Walker/ Roos, 280

Dream with Music, Warnick/Eager, et al., 218

Great Lady, Loewe/Crooker/Brentano, 184

House of Flowers, Arlen/Capote, 305

I Married an Angel, Rodgers/Hart, 182

Keep Off the Grass, McHugh/Duke/ Dubin, et al., 187

The Lady Comes Across, Duke/ Latouche/Thompson/Powell, 201

Louisiana Purchase, Berlin/Ryskind, 188

Mr. Strauss Goes to Boston, Stolz/Sour/ Levinson, 229

On Your Toes, Rodgers/Hart/Abbott, 166

Orphée aux Enfers, Offenbach, 109

Pal Joey, Rodgers/Hart, 402

Wake Up and Dream!, Porter/Turner, 91: *What Is This Thing Called Love?*

What's Up, Loewe/Lerner/Pierson, 217

Where's Charley?, Loesser/Abbott, 249

Ziegfeld Follies: 1936 Edition, Duke/ Gershwin/Freedman, 162: *West Indies; Words without Music: A Surrealist Ballet; Night Flight;* *Moment of Moments; Sentimental Weather;* 5 A. M.

THEATER

Les Amours du Poète, Blum/Delaquys, 110

The Broken Brow, see *Eugene the Unfortunate*

Caesar and Cleopatra, Shaw, 26

Columbine's Veil, see *Der Schleier der Pierrette*

Eugene the Unfortunate, Toller, 27

La Folle de Chaillot (*The Madwoman of Chaillot*), Giraudoux, 257

The Merry Wives of Windsor, Shakespeare, 326

A Midsummer Night's Dream, Shakespeare, 319

Romeo and Juliet, Shakespeare, 278, 325

Der Schleier der Pierrette, Schnitzler/ Dohnanyi, 15

The Tempest, Shakespeare, 224, 308

The Winter's Tale, Shakespeare, 320

CIRCUS

The Ballet of the Elephants, Stravinsky, 202

FILM

Dark Red Roses, 97

Goldwyn Follies, 185

I Was an Adventuress, 191

On Your Toes, 186

Star Spangled Rhythm, 213

TELEVISION

Cinderella, Tschaikovsky, 261

The Countess Becomes the Maid, J. Strauss II, 294

Diana and Actaeon Pas de Deux, Pugni?, 363

The Magic Flute, see *Die Zauberflöte*
Noah and the Flood, Stravinsky, 342; see also 422
One, Yuletide Square, Delibes, 291

[Pas de Deux], 266
The Spellbound Child / L'Enfant et les Sortilèges, Ravel, 416
Die Zauberflöte, Mozart, 311

KEY TO COMPANIES
STAGING BALANCHINE WORKS

United States

Alabama (State of Alabama Ballet)

American Ballet (1935-38; resident Metropolitan Opera company as American
   Ballet Ensemble; see also New York City Ballet)

American Ballet Caravan (see also New York City Ballet)

American Ballet Ensemble (1935-38; see also New York City Ballet)

American Ballet Theatre (see also Ballet Theatre)

American Concert Ballet

American Festival Ballet Company (Idaho)

American Shakespeare Festival (Connecticut)

Arizona Ballet Theatre (disbanded)

Atlanta Ballet (until 1968 known as Atlanta Civic Ballet)

Augusta Ballet (Georgia)

Ballet Borealis (Minnesota; now called Andahazy Ballet Company)

Ballet International (de Cuevas company, 1944-45; see also *Other Countries*:
   de Cuevas)

Ballet la Jeunesse (Los Angeles)

Ballet Metropolitan (Ohio)

Ballet of Los Angeles (1964-67; also called Western Ballet)

Ballet Oklahoma

Ballet Russe de Monte Carlo (1938-62; in North America from 1939)

Ballet Russe Highlights (Massine company, 1945-47)

Ballet Society (1946-48; see also New York City Ballet)

Ballet Theatre (in 1957 became American Ballet Theatre)

Ballet West (see also Utah Civic Ballet)

Baltimore Ballet (see also Maryland Ballet)

Berkshire Ballet (Massachusetts)

Bernhard Ballet (Connecticut)

Boston Ballet (see also New England Civic Ballet)

Chicago Ballet

Chicago City Ballet (see also Chicago Lyric Opera Ballet)

Chicago Lyric Opera

Chicago Lyric Opera Ballet (in 1980 separated from Chicago Lyric Opera to
   form Chicago City Ballet)

Cincinnati Ballet Company

City Center Light Opera (New York City, 1954-68)

Civic Ballet Society (Washington, D. C.; disbanded)
Cleveland Ballet
Connecticut Ballet
Dallas Ballet
Dance Repertory Company (New York City; disbanded)
Dance Theatre of Harlem
Danilova Concert Company ('Great Moments of Ballet,' 1954-57)
Dayton Ballet (Ohio)
Delta Festival Ballet (New Orleans)
Dover Ballet Theatre Company (Delaware, 1975-77)
Downtown Ballet Company (New York City)
Eglevsky Ballet (Long Island, New York)
Fairfax Ballet (Virginia)
Festival Ballet (Rhode Island)
Garden State Ballet (New Jersey)
Georgia Dance Theatre (Augusta)
Harkness Ballet (1964-70)
Hartford Ballet (Connecticut)
Houston Ballet
Huntington Dance Ensemble (Long Island, New York; later became P. A. F. [Performing Arts Foundation] Dance Ensemble; disbanded)
Joffrey (Robert Joffrey Theatre Ballet, 1958-60; American Ballet Center Company, 1960; Robert Joffrey Ballet, 1961-66; City Center Joffrey Ballet, 1966-76; Joffrey Ballet, from 1976)
Kansas City Ballet (Missouri)
Los Angeles Ballet
Los Angeles Civic Light Opera
Louisville Ballet (Kentucky)
Makarova and Company (1980)
Maryland Ballet (in 1981 became Baltimore Ballet)
Memphis Civic Ballet (Tennessee)
Mesa Civic Ballet (Arizona)
Metropolitan Opera (New York City)
Metropolitan Opera Ballet (New York City)
Milwaukee Ballet
Minnesota Dance Theatre
National Academy Ballet (later became National Ballet of Illinois; disbanded)
National Ballet (Washington, D. C., 1963-74)
New England Civic Ballet (in 1964 became Boston Ballet)
New Jersey Ballet (West Orange)
New Opera Company (New York City, 1941-44)

New York City Ballet (see also American Ballet, American Ballet Caravan,
   American Ballet Ensemble, Ballet Society, Producing Company of the
   School of American Ballet)
New York City Opera (City Center Opera, 1943-66; New York City Opera,
   from 1966)
New York Dance Theatre
Newburgh Ballet (New York)
North Carolina Dance Theatre
Nureyev and Friends
Ohio Ballet
Oklahoma City Ballet
Pacific Northwest Dance Theatre (Seattle, Washington; in 1980 became Pacific
   Northwest Ballet)
Pennsylvania Ballet
Pittsburgh Ballet Theatre
Prince George's Ballet (Maryland; disbanded)
Princeton Ballet (New Jersey)
Producing Company of the School of American Ballet (1934; see also New
   York City Ballet)
Richmond Ballet (Virginia)
Ringling Brothers and Barnum & Bailey Circus
San Diego Ballet
San Francisco Ballet
San Francisco Civic Light Opera
San Juan (Ballets de San Juan, Puerto Rico)
Second International Dance Festival (Second North American International
   Dance Festival of Stars, Chicago, 1978)
Stars of American Ballet (disbanded)
Syracuse Ballet Theatre (disbanded)
Toledo Ballet (Ohio)
Tulsa Ballet Theatre
U. S. Terpsichore (New York City)
Utah Civic Ballet (in 1967 became Ballet West)
Washington Ballet (Washington, D. C.)
Wisconsin Ballet

Other Countries

Alberta Ballet Company (Canada)
Anton Dolin with Anna Ludmila and Company (1929)
Australian Ballet

Balanchine Ballet (1931)

Balieff's Chauve-Souris (The Bat Theatre of Moscow, 1908-36)

Ballet Club (early title of Rambert company, London)

Ballet du XXe Siècle (Brussels)

Ballet Nacional (Alberto Alonso company, Cuba, 1950-51)

Ballet Rambert (London)

Ballet Théâtre Contemporain (Angers; in 1978 merged with Ballet Théâtre Français in Nancy)

Ballet Théâtre Français (Nancy; see also Ballet Théâtre Contemporain)

Ballet Victoria (Australia; disbanded)

Les Ballets de Monte-Carlo (René Blum, 1936-37)

Ballets de Pâques (Monte Carlo, 1957)

Ballets Janine Charrat (later called Ballets de France)

Les Ballets 1933

Les Ballets Russes de Georges Balanchine (1931)

Ballets Russes de Monte-Carlo (1932-52, associated with de Basil under various names; after 1940, called Original Ballet Russe)

Ballets Russes de Serge Diaghilev (1909-29)

Ballets Russes de Vera Nemtchinova (1930)

Ballets Serge Lifar (1933)

Belgrade (National Theater Company, Balet Narodno Pozorište)

Belo Horizonte (Clovis Salgado Foundation, Brazil [Ballet])

Berlin (Ballett der Deutschen Oper, West Berlin)

Berlin (Deutsche Oper, West Berlin)

Berliner Ballett (West Berlin)

Bologna (Teatro Comunale [Ballet])

Bordeaux (Ballet du Grand Théâtre Municipal)

Caracas (Ballet Internacional de Caracas, Venezuela, renamed Ballet Nuevo Mundo de Caracas)

Catania (Teatro Massimo Bellini, Sicily [Ballet])

Cologne (Ballett der Bühnen Stadt Köln)

Colón (Teatro Colón, Buenos Aires [Ballet])

Colón (Teatro Colón, Buenos Aires [Opera])

Cuba (Ballet Alicia Alonso, 1948-55; Ballet de Cuba, 1955-59; Ballet Nacional de Cuba, from 1959)

de Cuevas (Grand Ballet de Monte-Carlo, 1947-51; Grand Ballet du Marquis de Cuevas, 1951-62; see also United States: Ballet International)

Düsseldorf (Ballett der Deutschen Oper am Rhein)

Dutch National Ballet (Het Nationale Ballet, Amsterdam; see also Netherlands Ballet)

East Berlin (Ballett der Deutschen Staatsoper)

Florence (Teatro Comunale [Ballet])
Frankfurt (Ballett der Städtischen Bühnen)
Geneva (Grand Théâtre de Genève [Ballet])
Geneva (Grand Théâtre de Genève [Opera])
Gothenburg (Stora Teaterns Balett, Sweden)
Grand Ballet Classique de France
Les Grands Ballets Canadiens (Montreal)
Hamburg (Ballett der Hamburgischen Staatsoper)
Hamburg (Hamburgische Staatsoper)
Hungary (State Opera Ballet, Magyar Allami Operahaz)
Iran (Iranian National Ballet; disbanded)
Israel Ballet (also known as Israel Classical Ballet)
Kirov Ballet (Leningrad; see also State Theater of Opera and Ballet)
La Plata (Teatro Argentino [Ballet])
London Festival Ballet
Maly Opera Theater (Petrograd)
Matsuyama Ballet Company (Japan)
Mexico (Ballet Clásico de Mexico, renamed Compañía Nacional de Danza)
Mexico (Ópera Nacional, Palacio de Bellas Artes)
Monte Carlo (Opéra de Monte-Carlo)
Monte Carlo (Théâtre de Monte-Carlo)
Munich (Ballett der Bayerischen Staatsoper)
Naples (Teatro San Carlo [Ballet])
National Ballet of Canada (Toronto)
Netherlands Ballet (Het Nederlands Ballet; in 1961 merged with Amsterdam
    Ballet to form Dutch National Ballet)
New Zealand Ballet
Norway (Den Norske Opera [Ballet])
Noverre Ballet (Stuttgart, 1971-73)
Original Ballet Russe (see also Ballets Russes de Monte-Carlo)
Palermo (Teatro Massimo [Ballet])
Paris (Théâtre National de l'Opéra)
Paris (Théâtre National de l'Opéra [Ballet])
Pavlova Company (1913-31)
Petrograd Drama Theater
Philippines (Cultural Center of the Philippines Dance Company; now also
    called Ballet Philippines)
Principal Dancers of the Russian State Ballet (1924)
Reggio Emilia (A.T.E.R., Associazione Teatri Emilia-Romagna [Ballet])
Rio de Janeiro (Teatro Municipal [Ballet])
Rome Opera Ballet (Teatro dell'Opera di Roma [Ballet])

Royal Ballet (see also Sadler's Wells Ballet)
Royal Ballet Touring company (Sadler's Wells Theatre Ballet, 1947-56; Royal Ballet Touring Section, 1956-70; New Group, 1970-76; Sadler's Wells Royal Ballet, from 1976)
Royal Danish Ballet (Den Kongelige Danske Ballet)
Royal Flemish Ballet (Koninklijk Ballet van Vlaanderen)
Royal Swedish Ballet (Kungliga Teaterns Balett)
Royal Winnipeg Ballet (Canada)
Sadler's Wells Ballet (in 1956 became Royal Ballet)
São Paulo (Halina Biernacka Ballet, renamed São Paulo Chamber Ballet)
La Scala (Teatro alla Scala, Milan [Ballet])
La Scala (Teatro alla Scala, Milan [Opera])
Serge Lifar and His Russian Ballets (1933-35)
Sociedad Pro-Arte Musical (Cuba)
State Theater of Opera and Ballet (Petrograd/Leningrad, 1917-35; formerly Maryinsky; from 1935, Kirov)
Strasbourg (Ballet de l'Opéra du Rhin)
Stuttgart (Ballett der Württembergischen Staatsoper)
Taller Coreográfico (Mexico)
Tokyo Ballet (also known as Tschaikovsky Memorial Tokyo Ballet)
Tokyo Ballet Geikijo (disbanded)
Turin (Teatro Regio [Ballet])
Uruguay (S.O.D.R.E., Servicio Oficial de Difusión Radio Eléctrica [Ballet])
Vienna (Ballett der Wiener Staatsoper)
West Australian Ballet Company
Young Ballet (Petrograd, 1922-24)
Zagreb (Croatian National Theater, Balet Hrvatsko Narodno Kazalište)
Zürich Ballet (Ballett des Opernhauses Zürich)

GENERAL INDEX

Catalogue entry titles appear in small capitals
For entries with plus sign (+), consult Addenda for additional information.

À LA FRANÇAIX (Françaix)+, 282
A.T.E.R. [Ballet], see Reggio Emilia
 (A.T.E.R. [Ballet])
Aasen, Muriel, 392
Abbey, Eleanor, 99, 108
Abbott, George, 166, 183, 186, 249
ABC (American Broadcasting Com-
 pany), 94, 141, 166, 273, 302, 331
Abell, Kjeld, 101, 103, 106
Abravanel, Maurice, 134-139, 171, 180
Ada-May, 99, 108
ADAGIO (Saint-Saëns), 16-18
ADAGIO LAMENTOSO (Tschaikovsky), see
 SYMPHONY NO. 6—PATHÉTIQUE
Adam, Adolphe, 234
Adams, Diana, 222, 259, 277, 281, 284,
 286, 287, 292, 293, 301, 303, 304,
 314, 316, 318, 324, 329, 332, 334-338
Adler, Peter Herman, 311
ADRIANA LECOUVREUR (Cilea), 299
Adventure in Ballet, 202, 230, 241, 245
Aesop, 72
Afanasiev, Alexander, 237
AGON (Stravinsky)+, 316
Ahlin, Cvetka, 341
AÏDA (Verdi), 126, 152, 226, 255
Akimov, 29
Alabama (State of Alabama Ballet),
 339
Alanova, 91, 148
Albéniz, Isaac, 73
Albert, Eddie, 183, 186
Alberta Ballet Company (Canada), 331
Albrecht, Angèle, 345
Albrecht, Gerd, 383
Alexander, Michael, 305
Alexandroff, G., 233
ALEKO (Rachmaninoff), 83
Alias, 53

Alias, C., Ltd., see C. Alias, Ltd.
All Star Dance Gala, 189
Allain, Raymonde, 109
ALLEGRO BRILLANTE (Tschaikovsky)+, 312
Alloy, Al, 217
ALMA ERRANTE (Schubert), see
 L'ERRANTE
ALMA MATER (Swift), 141, 142
Alonso, Alicia, 234, 242
Alonso, Fernando, 222, 242
Alsop, Lamar, 378, 394
Alswang, Ralph, 280
Alton, Robert, 162
Alwin, Carl, 226
AMAHL AND THE NIGHT VISITORS
 (Menotti), 300
Amati, Olga, 297
Amboise, Christopher d', 417, 421
Amboise, Jacques d', 291, 296, 303, 304,
 317, 318, 323, 324, 329, 332, 338, 339,
 342, 344, 346, 349, 354, 358, 368, 384,
 401, 415, 418, 422
American Ballet, 84, 134, 135, 138, 141-
 146, 150, 176-178, 185, 193, 199, 236,
 254, 271, 275, 345; see also American
 Ballet Ensemble, New York City
 Ballet
American Ballet Caravan, 84, 138, 141,
 169, 193-200, 250, 349, 382; see also
 New York City Ballet
American Ballet Center Company,
 see Joffrey Ballet
American Ballet Ensemble, 141, 144,
 150-156, 158-161, 163, 165, 167-174,
 176, 179-181, 345; see also American
 Ballet, New York City Ballet
American Ballet Stravinsky Festival,
 176-178, 271, 275
American Ballet Studio, 177, 178

American Ballet Theatre, 94, 232, 233, 242, 247, 265, 273, 307, 331; *see also* Ballet Theatre

American Ballet Theatre: Live from Lincoln Center (PBS), 242

American Boychoir (Princeton, New Jersey), 424

American Broadcasting Company, *see* ABC

American Concert Ballet, 195

American Festival Ballet Company (Idaho), 282, 366

American Friends Service Committee Benefit, 215

American Shakespeare Festival (Connecticut), 308, 313, 314, 319, 320, 325, 326

American Shakespeare Festival Mozart Festival, 313, 314

LES AMOURS DU POÈTE (Blum/Delaquys), 110

Amram, David, 325

Amsterdam Ballet, *see* Dutch National Ballet

Anaya, Dulce, 345

Anchutina, Leda, 141, 144, 145, 165, 167, 169, 173, 174, 177, 178, 184

Andahazy Ballet Company (Minnesota), *see* Ballet Borealis

Andersen, Hans Christian, 52, 178, 271, 398

Andersen, Ib, 412, 415, 417

Anderson, Andy, 166

Anderson, Eileen, 270

Anderson, John Murray, 162, 202

Andes, Keith, 239

Andreivsky, 27

Andriessen, Jurriaan, 269

Angel, Morris, 53

Angelus, Muriel, 183

Angie Costumes, Inc., 268

ANNA ANNA, OR THE SEVEN CAPITAL SINS (Weill/Brecht), *see* LES SEPT PÉCHÉS CAPITAUX

Anna Ludmila and Company, *see* Anton Dolin with Anna Ludmila and Company

Antheil, George, 141, 145, 146

Anton Dolin with Anna Ludmila and Company, 95

APOLLO; APOLLO, LEADER OF THE MUSES; APOLLO MUSAGETES; APOLO MUSAGETA (Stravinsky), *see* APOLLON MUSAGÈTE

APOLLON MUSAGÈTE (Stravinsky)+, **84**, 106, 176, 193, 198, 204, 226, 240, 284, 316

Applebaum, Stan, 371

April, Elsie, 108

Arden, Eve, 162

Ardolino, Emile, 416

Arensky, Anton, 25

ARIADNE AND HER BROTHERS (Tschaikovsky), *see* AURORA'S WEDDING: ARIADNE AND HER BROTHERS

Arizona Ballet Theatre, 309, 331, 347

Arlen, Harold, 213, 305

Arlen, Jerry, 305

Armfeld, 29

Armistead, Horace, 288, 295, 302, 308, 317, 339

Armstrong, Will Steven, 326

Arno, Sig, 219

Aroldingen, Karin von, 368, 369, 371, 374, 377, 380, 384, 386, 395, 396, 401, 406, 408, 409, 415, 416, 419-421, 424

Aronson, Boris, 190, 217

Arshansky, Michael, 267, 302, 351, 379, 387

Ashley, Gene, 162

Ashley, Merrill, 384, 387, 407, 409, 412

L'Assemblée, 37, 42

Associazione Teatri Emilia-Romagna [Ballet], *see* Reggio Emilia (A.T.E.R. [Ballet])

Astafieva, Serafima, 14, 19, 36, 37

Atherton, Effie, 108

Atlanta Ballet, 141, 195, 233, 240, 288, 302, 312, 315, 339

Atlanta Civic Ballet, *see* Atlanta Ballet
AUBADE (Poulenc), 98
Auden, W. H., 295, 311, 322
Auer, Mischa, 201
Augusta Ballet (Georgia), 247
Aumonier, Stacy, 97
Auric, Georges, 62, 130, 409
Auric, Nora Vilter, 133
AURORA'S WEDDING: ARIADNE AND HER
  BROTHERS (Tschaikovsky), 65
Austin, Debra, 407
Australian Ballet, 141, 194, 318
Avedon, Michael, 396
Ayers, Lemuel, 219
BABES IN ARMS (Rodgers/Hart), 175
Bach, Johann Sebastian, 195, 215, 250,
  324, 380
Bacon, Ernst, 308
Bailey, Pearl, 305
LE BAISER DE LA FÉE (Stravinsky), 176,
  178, 240, 271
Baker, Charlyne, 259
Baker, Jack, 217
Baker, Josephine, 162
Baker, Kenny, 185
Baker, Phil, 185
Baker, Virginia, 308
Baker, William, 166
Bakst, Léon, 85, 259
LE BAL (Rieti), 93
UN BAL MASQUÉ (Verdi), *see* UN BALLO IN
  MASCHERA
Balaban, Emanuel, 193-200, 220, 221,
  225, 232
Balanchine Ballet, 107
Balanchine's Girls; Balanchine's
  Sixteen Novelty Dancers, *see* Balan-
  chine Ballet
Balashov, L., 16
Balet Hrvatsko Narodno Kazalište,
  see Zagreb (Croatian National
  Theater, Balet Hrvatsko Narodno
  Kazalište)
Balet Narodno Pozorište, *see* Belgrade

(National Theater Company, Balet
  Narodno Pozorište)
Balieff, Nikita, 73
Balieff's Chauve-Souris, 73, 74
THE BALL (Rieti), *see* LE BAL
BALLADE (Fauré), 412
Ballard, Lucinda, 184, 239
Ballet Alicia Alonso, *see* Cuba (Ballet
  Alicia Alonso; Ballet de Cuba; Ballet
  Nacional de Cuba)
Ballet Borealis (Minnesota), 141
Ballet Caravan, 193
Ballet Clásico de Mexico, *see* Mexico
  (Ballet Clásico de Mexico)
Ballet Club (London), 85; *see also*
  Ballet Rambert
Ballet de Cuba, *see* Cuba (Ballet Alicia
  Alonso; Ballet de Cuba; Ballet
  Nacional de Cuba)
Ballet de l'Opéra du Rhin, *see*
  Strasbourg (Ballet de l'Opéra du
  Rhin)
Ballet du Grand Théâtre Municipal,
  see Bordeaux (Ballet du Grand
  Théâtre Municipal)
Ballet du XXe Siècle (Brussels), 346
Ballet Evening by George Balanchine
  (Copenhagen), 101, 106
Ballet Foundation, 375
BALLET IMPERIAL (Tschaikovsky)[+], 193,
  194, 206, 349, 382
Ballet Internacional de Caracas, *see*
  Caracas (Ballet Internacional de
  Caracas)
Ballet International, 223; *see also*
  Cuevas
Ballet la Jeunesse (Los Angeles), 141,
  195
Ballet Metropolitan (Ohio), 312, 331
Ballet Nacional, 84
Ballet Nacional de Cuba, *see* Cuba
  (Ballet Alicia Alonso; Ballet de
  Cuba; Ballet Nacional de Cuba)
Ballet Nuevo Mundo de Caracas, *see*

Caracas (Ballet Internacional de
Caracas)
Ballet of Los Angeles, 141, 240, 264,
285, 309, 312
THE BALLET OF THE ELEPHANTS (Stra-
vinsky)+, 202
Ballet Oklahoma, 195
Ballet Philippines, *see* Philippines
(Cultural Center of the Philippines
Dance Company)
Ballet Rambert (London), 232; *see also*
Ballet Club
Ballet Russe de Monte Carlo, 131, 134,
141, 177, 178, 194, 195, 219-221, 225,
232, 233, 247, 328, 375, 410, 414
Ballet Russe Highlights, 130
Ballet Society, 48, 235-238, 240-246, 322,
324, 329, 390, 416; *see also* New York
City Ballet
Ballet Theatre, 84, 138, 214, 222, 234,
242, 259, 262, 264, 330; *see also*
American Ballet Theatre
Ballet Théâtre Contemporain
(Angers), 236; *see also* Ballet Théâtre
Français
Ballet Théâtre Français (Nancy),
232; *see also* Ballet Théâtre Con-
temporain
Ballet Van Vlaanderen, *see* Royal
Flemish Ballet
Ballet Victoria (Australia), 195
Ballet West, 236, 240, 307, 309, 312, 315,
331; *see also* Utah Civic Ballet
Ballets de France, *see* Ballets Janine
Charrat
Les Ballets de Monte-Carlo (René
Blum), 98
Ballets de Pâques (Monte Carlo), 232
Ballets de San Juan, *see* San Juan
(Ballets de San Juan)
Ballets Ida Rubinstein, 178, 424
Ballets Janine Charrat, 247
Les Ballets 1933, 134-139, 143, 145, 149,
197, 322

Les Ballets Russes de Georges
Balanchine, 109
Ballets Russes de Monte-Carlo, 110-
132, 221, 410, 414; *see also* Original
Ballet Russe
Ballets Russes de Serge Diaghilev, 19,
25, 30, 36-50, 52-72, 76-90, 92-94, 107,
176, 198, 235, 237, 264, 267, 284, 379,
390, 416
Ballets Russes de Vera Nemtchinova,
98
Ballets Serge Lifar, 140
Ballett der Bayerischen Staatsoper,
see Munich (Ballett der Bayerischen
Staatsoper)
Ballett der Bühnen Stadt Köln, *see*
Cologne (Ballett der Bühnen Stadt
Köln)
Ballett der Deutschen Oper, *see*
Berlin (Ballett der Deutschen Oper)
Ballett der Deutschen Oper am Rhein,
see Düsseldorf (Ballett der Deut-
schen Oper am Rhein)
Ballett der Deutschen Staatsoper, *see*
East Berlin (Ballett der Deutschen
Staatsoper)
Ballett der Hamburgischen Staats-
oper, *see* Hamburg (Ballett der
Hamburgischen Staatsoper)
Ballett der Städtischen Bühnen, *see*
Frankfurt (Ballett der Städtischen
Bühnen)
Ballett der Wiener Staatsoper, *see*
Vienna (Ballett der Wiener Staats-
oper)
Ballett der Württembergischen Staats-
oper, *see* Stuttgart (Ballett der
Württembergischen Staatsoper)
Ballett des Opernhauses Zürich, *see*
Zürich Ballet
BALLO DELLA REGINA (Verdi), 407
UN BALLO IN MASCHERA (Verdi), 80
Baltimore Ballet, 331, 366; *see also*
Maryland Ballet

BALUSTRADE (Stravinsky), 192, 374
Banks, Margaret, 222
BARABAU (Rieti), 53, 106
Baranovich, 24
Barbara Matera, Ltd., 375, 387
Bardin, Micheline, 240
Barnett, Milton, 162
Barnett, Robert, 274, 302, 310, 318
Barnum & Bailey Circus, see Ringling Brothers and Barnum & Bailey Circus
Baroni, Tilde, 299
Baronoff, Michel, 259
Baronova, Irina, 109
Barrett, Sondra, 217
Barrie, Barbara, 326
Barris, 176
THE BARTERED BRIDE (Smetana), 167
Bartsch, Hans, 239
Barysheva, O., 2
Baryshnikov, Mikhail, 84
Barzin, Jane, 235
Barzin, Leon, 230, 235-238, 241, 243, 244, 250, 254, 264, 265, 267-269, 271-277, 279, 282-290, 292, 293, 301-304, 306, 307, 309, 310, 312, 314, 316-318
Basil, Colonel Vasily de, see Ballets Russes de Monte-Carlo; Original Ballet Russe
THE BAT (J. Strauss II), 168, 169, 193, 199
The Bat Theatre of Moscow, see Balieff's Chauve-Souris
Bates, Ronald, 141, 194, 264, 312, 315, 333, 334, 340, 353, 354, 357, 358, 360, 362, 364, 368-370, 373, 374, 376-380, 382, 384, 386, 387, 389-396, 398, 400, 401, 406-409, 412-415, 417, 421, 425
Bauchant, André, 84
Baum, Morton, 246
Baumann, Helmut, 345
Bay, Howard, 216
Bay, Robert, 217
La Bayadère (Petipa), 33
Bayerische Staatsoper [Ballet], see

Munich (Ballett der Bayerischen Staatsoper)
BAYOU (Thomson), 287
Bazelon, Irwin, 326
Bazzolo, Maria, 299
BBC (British Broadcasting Corporation), 84, 85, 232, 264, 324, 331
Beaton, Cecil, 285
Beattie, Herbert, 335
Beaujon, Marise, 109
Beckmann, Judith, 365
Beecham, Sir Thomas, 85
Beeness, D. I., 14
Beethoven, Ludwig van, 96, 139, 218
BEGIN THE BEGUINE (Porter), 385
Belanger, Paul, 261
Bel Geddes, Norman, 202
Belgrade (National Theater Company, Balet Narodno Pozorište), 195, 331
Bell Telephone Hour (NBC), 84, 195, 247, 273, 288, 302, 312, 315, 318, 331, 347, 351, 358, 359
Bellenot, Philippe, 47
Bellini, Vincenzo, 232, 328
Belmonte, Herman, 162
Belo Horizonte (Clovis Salgado Foundation, Brazil [Ballet]), 205
Bennett, Russell, 162, 188, 218
Bennett, Tracy, 382, 390, 400
Benois, Alexandre, 131, 233, 367
Benois, Nicolas, 29, 365, 369
Benson, Ben, 369, 382, 407, 408, 412, 419
Bérard, Christian, 129, 133, 134, 149, 257, 286
Berestorskaya, 27
Bergen, Edgar, 185
Bergman, Robert W., Studio, see Robert W. Bergman Studio
Beriosova, Svetlana, 270
Beriozoff, Nicholas, 367
Berkshire Ballet (Massachusetts), 366
Berlin, Irving, 188
Berlin (Ballett der Deutschen Oper, West Berlin), 84, 141, 194, 236, 240,

277, 304, 316, 324, 383
Berlin (Deutsche Oper, West Berlin), 383
Berliner Ballett (West Berlin), 205
Berlioz, Hector, 49, 69
Berman, Eugene, 194, 195, 220, 221, 234, 250, 306, 375, 376, 379
Bernard, Robert, 219
Bernardi, 108
Bernauer, Rudolph, 239
Berners, Gerald Hugh Tyrwhitt-Wilson, Baron, 64, 99, 107
Bernhard, A., 341
Bernhard Ballet (Connecticut), 247
Bernstein, Aline, 235
Berthe, 201
Bertrand, Aloysius, 395
Bianco, Erico, 200
Bibiena, Giuseppe Galli, 241
Bielski, Vladimir, 172
Bigelow, Edward, 264, 285, 302
Birch, Peter, 218
Bird, Dorothy, 231
Birkmayer, Toni, 91
Bishop, Adelaide, 311
Bittner, Jack, 319, 325
Bizet, Georges, 38, 127, 155, 240, 244, 248, 306, 310, 398
BLACK SWAN PAS DE DEUX (Tschaikovsky), see SWAN LAKE (BLACK SWAN) PAS DE DEUX
Blackface (L. Christensen), 336
Blackton, Jay, 239
Blair, David, 270
Blank, Kyra, 135, 161, 167, 173
Blinova, Valentina, 111-114, 118, 120, 122, 129-132
Bliss, Helena, 219
Bliss, Herbert, 220, 233, 243, 244, 246, 252, 254, 261, 265, 267-269, 277, 287, 301-304, 313, 314
Blitzstein, Marc, 319, 320
Bloch, Boris, 405
Blois, Edmundo, 195

Blok, Alexander, 28
The Blue Angel (film), 107
Blum, Anthony, 348, 352, 369, 380
Blum, René, 98, 110, 130
Bobrow, André, 93
Bocher, Barbara, 279
Bodanzky, Artur, 154, 163
Boelzner, Gordon, 344, 349, 358, 368, 378, 382, 405, 412, 415
Boese, Ursula, 341, 345, 365
LE BŒUF SUR LE TOIT (Milhaud), 35
Bois, Raoul Pène du, see du Bois, Raoul Pène
Bolasni, Saul, 280
Bolender, Todd, 196, 199, 206, 230, 236-238, 241, 245, 274, 275, 289, 304, 316, 336
Bolger, Ray, 166, 187, 249
Bolm, Adolph, 84
Bologna (Teatro Comunale [Ballet]), 84, 195
Bolton, Guy, 239
Bonanova, Fortunio, 191
Bondio, J. H. Del, see Del Bondio, J. H.
Bonnefous, Jean-Pierre, 374, 384, 389, 401, 405, 406, 409, 410
Bonnet, Jeanne Saint, see Saint-Bonnet, Jeanne
Bordeaux (Ballet du Grand Théâtre Municipal), 232, 247
Bordoni, Irene, 184, 188
Borealis (Minnesota), see Ballet Borealis
Boris, Ruthanna, 144, 150, 155, 160, 167, 179, 219-221, 232, 233
BORIS GODUNOV (Moussorgsky), 54, 298, 388
Borne, Bonita, 400, 407
Borne, Elyse, 400
Borodin, Alexander, 104, 218, 383
Borovsky, Mezeslav (Metek; Michel), 87, 123, 130-132, 205

Borree, Susan, 330, 332
Boston Ballet, 84, 94, 141, 195, 232, 236, 240, 312, 318, 331, 333, 347, 366; see also New England Civic Ballet
Bourdet, Denise, 133
Bourdet, Édouard, 133
LE BOURGEOIS GENTILHOMME (R. Strauss)+, 131, 221, 410, 414
BOURRÉE FANTASQUE (Chabrier)+, 265, 357
LA BOUTIQUE FANTASQUE (Rossini), 101, 103
Boutnikoff, Ivan, 225, 233
Bowles, Paul, 223
THE BOYS FROM SYRACUSE (Rodgers/ Hart/Abbott), 183
Boyt, John, 303
Bozzoni, Max, 240
Bracken, Eddie, 213
Bradley, Buddy, 108
Brahms, Johannes, 13, 335, 354
BRAHMS–SCHOENBERG QUARTET, 354
Branitzka, Nathalie, 94
Brant, Henry, 144
Braun, Eric, 242, 259
Braunstein, Karl, 241
Brecht, Bertolt, 136, 322
Breckenridge, Doris, 274, 275, 287
Breisach, Paul, 209
Brenaa, Hans, 103
Brent, Romney, 201
Brentano, Felix, 206, 216, 229, 239
Brentano, Lowell, 184
Breyman, Annia, 149, 154, 165, 174
Brice, Fannie, 162
Briggs, Hedley, 107
Brink, Robert, 218
Brinkman, Edward, 239
British Broadcasting Corporation, see BBC
British International Film Distributors, 97
Britten, Benjamin, 196
Broadbent, Aida, 219

THE BROKEN BROW (Toller), see EUGENE THE UNFORTUNATE
Brook, Peter, 305
Brooks, Lawrence, 219
Brooks Costume Company, 162, 166, 184, 201, 206, 216, 218, 249, 305, 308, 329
Brouet, Lucien, 109
Brown, Jack Owen, 331
Brown, Joe E., 280
Brown, Prescott, 162
Brown, Vida, 221, 272, 277
Browne, Eddie, 162
Browning, Kirk, 311, 342
Brubaker, Robert, 422
Bruce, Betty, 183, 187
Bruhn, Erik, 328, 329
Bruun, Axel, 106
Bühne Stadt Köln [Ballet], see Cologne (Ballett der Bühnen Stadt Köln)
Buffett, Kenneth, 217
BUGAKU (Mayuzumi)+, 343
Burgee, John, 417, 421
Burkhalter, Jane, 176
Burr, Marilyn, 345
Burr, Mary, 259
Burton, Miriam, 305
Byars, Christopher, 416
Byng, Douglas, 108
C. Alias, Ltd., 99, 108
CABIN IN THE SKY (Duke/Latouche/ Root), 190
Cabot, Sebastian, 342
Caccialanza, Gisella, 141, 142, 144, 145, 149, 150, 160, 165, 167, 174, 178, 194, 196, 199, 208-210, 212, 236, 238
CAESAR AND CLEOPATRA (Shaw), 26
Cagli, Corrado, 243
Caillaux, De, 95
Caisse de Bienfaisance de la Colonie Française à Monaco, 118
Calcium Light Night (Martins), 304
Call, Marjorie, 233
Calzabigi, Raniero da, 170, 345

Calzati, Carla, 299
Camera Three (CBS), 232
Canadian Broadcasting Corporation,
	see CBC
CAPONSACCHI (Hageman), 173
Capote, Truman, 305
CAPRICCIO (Stravinsky), see JEWELS
CAPRICCIO BRILLANT (Mendelssohn),
	279
Caracas (Ballet Internacional de Ca-
	racas, Venezuela), 312, 331
CARACOLE (Mozart)+, 286, 314
THE CARD GAME (Stravinsky), see THE
	CARD PARTY
THE CARD PARTY (Stravinsky), 176, 177,
	275
Carday, Rose, 109
Carey, Denis, 308
Carl, Barry, 422
Carlisle, Elsie, 91
Carlson, Stanley, 322
CARMEN (Bizet), 38, 127, 155, 226, 248
Carminati, Tullio, 184
Carnovsky, Morris, 325
Carradine, John, 257
Carroll, Adam, 166, 175, 201
Carroll, Diahann, 305
Carson, Doris, 166
Carter, Bill, 335, 336, 340
Carter, Desmond, 99
Cassel, Walter, 219
Castelli, Victor, 371, 382, 392, 395, 401,
	414
Castro, Juan José, 205
THE CAT (Sauguet), see LA CHATTE
Catania (Teatro Massimo Bellini
	[Ballet], Sicily), 84
Caton, Edward, 145, 259
Cavanagh, William, 91
The Cave of Sleep (Balanchine), 236
CBC (Canadian Broadcasting Cor-
	poration), 84, 141, 195, 236, 246, 266,
	273, 302, 304, 309, 314, 316, 324, 331,
	335, 343, 344, 347, 359, 368, 400

CBS (Columbia Broadcasting System),
	232, 240, 246, 261, 264, 273, 277, 285,
	302, 318, 331, 342, 344, 363
CBS Cable (television), 415
Cecchetti, Enrico, 387
Cendra, Nelida, 205
La Cenerentola (Rossini), 351, 401
Centre Studios, 216, 224, 237, 250
Century Scenic Studios, 302
Cérès, 96
Chabelska, Gala, 130
Chabrier, Emmanuel, 129, 265, 357,
	403
CHACONNE (Gluck)+, 170, 345, 400, 418
Chagall, Marc, 264
Chamié, Tatiana, 64
Champion, Gower, 201
Chandler, Joan, 308
Chanel, Coco, 84
Chaney, Stewart, 84, 176, 201, 218, 229
Chanler, Theodore, 203
LE CHANT DU ROSSIGNOL (Stravinsky), 52
Chapman, Rachel, 219
Chardieno, Rajah, 190
CHARLES B. COCHRAN'S 1929 REVUE, see
	WAKE UP AND DREAM!
CHARLES B. COCHRAN'S 1930 REVUE, 99
CHARLES B. COCHRAN'S 1931 REVUE, 108
Charlotte, Princesse Héréditaire de
	Monaco, 36, 37
Charova, 27
Charrat, Janine, see Ballet de France
	de Janine Charrat
Chase, Ilka, 187
LA CHATTE (Sauguet)+, 72
Chávez, Carlos, 329
Cheselka, Anna, 242
Chesnakov, 24
Chester Rakeman Studios, 308, 324
Chicago Ballet, 94, 195, 233
Chicago City Ballet, 264, 358, 368; see
	also Chicago Lyric Opera Ballet
Chicago Lyric Opera, 170, 397, 399
Chicago Lyric Opera Ballet, 84, 195,

236, 247, 302, 309, 312, 314, 318, 324, 333, 339, 366, 397, 399; *see also* Chicago City Ballet

Chirico, Giorgio de, 93

THE CHOCOLATE SOLDIER (O. Straus), 239

Chopin, Frédéric, 3, 19, 107, 147, 165, 218

CHORAL VARIATIONS ON BACH'S 'VOM HIMMEL HOCH' (Stravinsky), 380

CHORUS READING (Blok), 28

Chotzinoff, Samuel, 311

Chouteau, Yvonne, 233

Christensen, Lew, 153, 155, 160, 164, 165, 169, 170, 173, 176, 186, 191, 198, 199, 236-238, 243, 309, 322, 333, 336

Christi, Vito, 224

Christie, Audrey, 182

Church, George, 162, 166, 183

Cilea, Francesco, 299

Cincinnati Ballet Company, 141, 195, 233

CINDERELLA (Tschaikovsky), 261

Circle in the Square (New York City), 402

CIRCUS POLKA (Stravinsky), **230**, 241, **245**

City Center Joffrey, *see* Joffrey Ballet

City Center Light Opera Company, *see* New York City Center Light Opera Company

City Center of Music and Drama (New York City), 246, 318

City Center Opera, *see* New York City Opera

Civic Ballet Society (Washington, D. C.), 84

CLARINADE (Gould), 348

Clark, Bobby, 108, 185

CLASSIC BALLET (Chopin), *see* CONCERTO

Clauss, Heinz, 345

Clavier, Sylvie, 397

Clayton, Jack, 97

Clayton, Jill, 97

Cleave, Nathan van, *see* Van Cleave, Nathan

Cleveland Ballet, 141, 195

Clifford, John, 359, 369, 371, 372, 375, 386, 394

Clovis Salgado Foundation [Ballet], *see* Belo Horizonte (Clovis Salgado Foundation [Ballet])

Cochran, Charles B., 91, 99, 108

Cocteau, Jean, 35

Cohen, Alexander H., 280

Colette, 48, 235, 390, 416

Colicos, John, 320

Collins, Frank, 91, 99, 108

Colman, John, 314

Cologne (Ballett der Bühnen Stadt Köln), 195, 302, 309, 312, 314

COLOMBIA (Escobar), *see* PANAMERICA [Number II]

Colombo, Vera, 297

Colón (Teatro Colón, Buenos Aires [Ballet]), 84, 204, 205

Colón (Teatro Colón, Buenos Aires [Opera]), 204

Colt, Alvin, 222

Columbia Broadcasting System, *see* CBS

Columbia Symphony Orchestra and Chorus, 342

Columbine (Drigo), *see* HARLEQUINADE PAS DE DEUX

COLUMBINE'S VEIL (Schnitzler/Dohnanyi), *see* DER SCHLEIER DER PIERRETTE

Comadore, Joseph, 305

Compañía Nacional de Danza, *see* Mexico (Ballet Clásico de Mexico, renamed Compañía Nacional de Danza)

Comstock, F. Ray, 73, 74

Con Amore (L. Christensen), 333

CONCERTINO (Françaix), 292

CONCERTO (Chopin), 165

CONCERTO BAROCCO (Bach)+, 193, **195**, 226, 240, 244, 246, 250

CONCERTO FOR JAZZ BAND AND
ORCHESTRA (Liebermann), 370
CONCIERTO (Mozart), see CONCIERTO DE
MOZART
CONCIERTO DE MOZART, 204, **205**
LA CONCURRENCE (Auric), 129, 130, 409
Condé, Hermes, 392
Conley, Eugene, 295
Conlow, Peter, 280
Connecticut Ballet, 331, 333, 366
Connolly, Joseph, 235
Consoli, Joysane, 397
Constantia (Dollar), 226
LES CONTES D'HOFFMANN (Offenbach),
58, 112, 260
Contreras, Gloria, 329
Cook, Bart, 401, 406
Cooke, Charles L., 190, 201
Coolidge, Elizabeth Sprague, 84, 176,
198, 284
Cooper, Edward, 108
Cooper, Emil, 208, 210
Cooper, Melville, 108, 216
Cooper, Rex, 222
COPPÉLIA (Delibes), 266, 273, 291, **387**,
418
LE COQ D'OR (Rimsky-Korsakov), 24,
172
Cordon, Norman, 172
Cordova, Fred de, 187
Corelli, Arcangelo, 315
Corsaro, Frank, 411
CORTÈGE HONGROIS (Glazounov), 233,
384
Costa, Raie da, see da Costa, Raie
COTILLON (Chabrier)+, 129
Coudy, Douglas, 153, 160, 161, 173,
206
THE COUNTESS BECOMES THE MAID
(J. Strauss II), 294
Couperin, François, 274
COURTIN' TIME (Lawrence/Walker/
Roos), 280
Cowan, Jerome, 185

Coward, Noel, 108
Cowles, Chandler, 308
Craft, Robert, 342, 373, 380, 381, 422,
424
Craig, Alice, 183
Crawford, Cheryl, 224
Crayon, H. M., 341
LES CRÉATURES DE PROMÉTHÉE (Bee-
thoven), 96
Crémieux, Hector, 109
Croatian National Theater, see
Zagreb (Croatian National
Theater, Balet Hrvatsko Narodno
Kazalište)
LA CROISADE DES DAMES (Schubert),
see DIE VERSCHWORENEN
Crooker, Earle, 184
Crosby, Bing, 213
Crowell, Ann, 310
THE CRUCIFIXION OF CHRIST (Bach), 215
Cruikshank, George, 64
Cruikshank, Robert, 64
Crumit, Frank, 184
CUBA (Orbón), see PANAMERICA
[Number VIII]
Cuba (Ballet Alicia Alonso; Ballet
de Cuba; Ballet Nacional de Cuba),
84, 242
Cuevas (Grand Ballet de Monte-Carlo;
Grand Ballet du Marquis de
Cuevas), 195, 232, 247, 263, 276, 328;
see also Ballet International
Cui, César, 12
Cultural Center of the Philippines
Dance Company, see Philippines
(Cultural Center of the Philippines
Dance Company)
Curran, Homer, 219
Curran Productions, 219
Cutler, Kate, 97
Czarnecki, Erika, 345
Czettel, Ladislas, 206
da Calzabigi, Raniero, see Calzabigi,
Raniero da

da Costa, Raie, 95
Dahl, Magda Allan, 103
Dali, Salvador, 223
Dallas Ballet, 195, 232, 309, 366
d'Amboise, see Amboise
LA DAMNATION DE FAUST (Berlioz), 49, 69
Damrosch, Walter, 207
Dana, Leora, 308
DANCE CONCERTO (Stravinsky), see DANSES CONCERTANTES
Dance in America (PBS), 48, 94, 195, 235, 236, 267, 312, 314, 331, 343, 358, 369, 374, 390, 394, 398, 400, 407, 416
Dance Repertory Company (New York City), 307, 309
Dance Theatre of Harlem, 141, 195, 236, 312, 316, 331, 343, 370
Danieli, Fred, 194, 196, 200, 236-238, 249
Danielian, Leon, 219, 221, 232, 233
Danilova, Alexandra, 3, 4, 6, 7, 9-11, 16, 17, 19, 21, 34, 40, 48, 53, 58, 60, 63, 64, 68, 78, 84, 85, 87, 89, 93, 219, 220, 225, 232, 233, 273, 387
Danilova Concert Company ('Great Moments of Ballet'), 129, 134
DANS L'ÉLYSÉE (Offenbach), 140
DANSES CONCERTANTES (Stravinsky), 220, 375
Daphnis et Chloé (Fokine), 85
Dare, Danny, 213
DARK RED ROSES (film), 97
Darrieux, Marcel, 84
Darsonval, Lycette, 240
Daumer, Friedrich, 335
Davidson, Lawrence, 295
Davison, Robert, 219
Daydé, Bernard, 395
Dayton Ballet (Ohio), 195, 347
Dazian's, 338
Dearly, Max, 109
de Basil, Colonel Vasily, see Ballets

Russes de Monte-Carlo; Original Ballet Russe
Debussy, Claude, 148
UN DÉBUT (Bellenot), 47
De Caillaux, see Caillaux, De
de Chirico, Giorgio, see Chirico, Giorgio de
Decorative Plant Corporation, 302, 324
Decorator Plant Company, see Decorative Plant Corporation
de Cuevas (Grand Ballet du Marquis de Cuevas), see Cuevas (Grand Ballet de Monte-Carlo; Grand Ballet du Marquis de Cuevas)
de Falla, Manuel, see Falla, Manuel de
Defosse, Henri, 64
de Havilland, Olivia, 278
Deign, Peter, 221
Dekova, Margit, 229
Delany, E., 99, 108
Delaquys, Georges, 110
Delarova, Eugenia, 201
de la Vega, Leticia, see Vega, Leticia de la
Del Bondio, J. H., 184, 239
Delfs, Albrecht, 104
de Liagre, Alfred, Jr., 257
Delibes, Léo, 36, 57, 115, 153, 273, 274, 291, 350, 364, 387
Delta Festival Ballet (New Orleans), 233, 247
Delvan Company, 239
De Mille, Cecil B., 213
LE DÉMON (Rubinstein), 42
de Polignac, Princesse Edmond, see Polignac, Princesse Edmond de
Deporte, Estela, 205
Derain, André, 63, 130, 135, 137, 145, 196
de Rivas, Elena, see Rivas, Elena de
Derwent, Clarence, 257
de Sabata, Victor, see Sabata, Victor de
Desormière, Roger, 53, 62, 63, 240

Destiné, Jean-Léon, 258
De Sylva, B. G., 188
Deutsche Oper, *see* Berlin (Deutsche Oper)
Deutsche Oper am Rhein [Ballet], *see* Düsseldorf (Ballett der Deutschen Oper am Rhein)
Deutsche Staatsoper [Ballet], *see* East Berlin (Ballett der Deutschen Staatsoper)
de Valois, Ninette, *see* Valois, Ninette de
de Windt, Hal, 385
Diaghilev, Serge, 19, 25, 30, 32, 36-50, 52-72, 75-90, 92-95, 97, 103, 106, 107, 176, 198, 233, 235, 237, 264, 267, 277, 284, 379, 390, 409, 416
Diamond, David, 224, 278
DIAMONDS (Tschaikovsky), *see* JEWELS
DIANA AND ACTAEON PAS DE DEUX (Pugni?), 363
Dick, Henry, 187
Dickson, Gloria, 186
DIDO AND AENEAS (Purcell), 410, **411**
LES DIEUX MENDIANTS (Handel), *see* THE GODS GO A-BEGGING
Dikushina, 24, 27
Dimitriev, Vladimir, 1
Dimitriev, Vladimir (designer), 15, 19, 27
Diney, Monette, 109
Diot, 109
Disney, Walt, 185
DIVERTIMENTO (Haieff), 237, **238**
DIVERTIMENTO (Rossini), 193, **196**
DIVERTIMENTO FROM 'LE BAISER DE LA FÉE' (Stravinsky), 178, **376**
DIVERTIMENTO NO. 15 (Mozart)+, 286, 313, **314**
Divertissements from Raymonda (Glazounov), *see* RAYMONDA
Doble, Frances, 97
Doboujinsky, Mstislav, 194
Doe, Doris, 172

Dohnanyi, Ernst von, 15
Dolan, Robert Emmett, 188, 213
Dolin, Anton, 93-95, 97, 189
Dolin, Gerry, 249
Dolinoff, Alexis, 98
Dollar, William, 142-147, 152, 157, 158, 160, 165-167, 169, 170, 173, 177, 178, 184, 185, 193-195, 197, 199, 206, 208-211, 226, 235, 236, 269
Dolotine, Jasht, 131
Dolton, Phyllis, 95
Domonsky, Richard, 99
DON GIOVANNI (Mozart), 81, 181, 253
DON JUAN (Mozart), *see* DON GIOVANNI
DON QUIXOTE (Nabokov)+, 352
DON QUIXOTE PAS DE DEUX (Minkus), 262
Donizetti, Gaetano, 168, 297, 333
DONIZETTI VARIATIONS, *see* VARIATIONS FROM DON SEBASTIAN
Donn, Jorge, 406
Dorati, Antal, 222
Doubrovska, Felia, 62, 82, 84, 85, 87, 92-94, 109, 140, 164
Douglas, Buddy, 183
Dove, Alfred, 95
Dover Ballet Theatre Company (Delaware), 247, 318
Dowling, Edward Duryea, 187
Downtown Ballet Company (New York City), 307
Drake, Alfred, 175, 280
Draper, Tom, 162
DREAM WITH MUSIC (Warnick/Eager, et al.), 218
DREAMS (Antheil), 135, 141
Dreier, Hans, 213
Drew, Robert, 336
Drigo, Riccardo, 6, 285, 290, 351
Dryden, Richard, 392
Dubin, Al, 187
du Bois, Raoul Pène, 162
Dudko, Mikhail, 4, 33
Duell, Joseph, 412

Düsseldorf (Ballett der Deutschen
  Oper am Rhein), 84, 141, 236
Dufallo, Richard, 356
Dufy, Raoul, 282
Duke, Vernon, 162, 185, 187, 189, 190,
  201
Dukelsky, Vladimir, *see* Duke, Vernon
Dulov, 22
Dumas, Alexandre, *père*, 302
Dumke, Ralph, 229
Duncan, Todd, 190
Dunham, Katherine, 190, 213
Dunham, Katherine, Dancers, *see*
  Katherine Dunham Dancers
Dunkel, Eugene B., 142, 192
Dunkel, Eugene B., Studios, *see*
  E. B. Dunkel Studios
DUO CONCERTANT (Stravinsky), 378
Dupuis, José, *fils*, 109
Durante, Jimmy, 187
Dushkin, Samuel, 192
Dushock, Dorothy, 272
DUTCH DANCE (Grieg), 3
Dutch National Ballet (Het Nationale
  Ballet, Amsterdam), 84, 94, 240, 242,
  277, 304, 309, 314, 316, 324, 333, 358,
  392; *see also* Netherlands Ballet
Dvořák, Anton, 218
Dworkin, Harry, 219
E. B. Dunkel Studios, 206, 220-222, 232,
  233, 242, 264, 303, 305
Eager, Edward, 218
East Berlin (Ballett der Deutschen
  Staatsoper), 236, 240, 277
Easton, Richard, 319, 320, 325
Eaves Costume Company, 146, 166,
  177, 182, 188, 216, 217, 224, 229, 239,
  280
Ebitz, Gerard, 400
Ed Sullivan Show (CBS), 273, 302, 363
Eden, Hugh, 97
Edwards, Kent, 219
Efimov, Nicholas, 5, 11, 13, 16, 22, 32,
  67, 77, 82, 87, 99

Eggerth, Marta, 216
Eglevsky, André, 184, 186, 223, 247,
  273, 276, 279, 282, 284-286, 288, 290,
  292, 294, 303, 306, 307, 309, 321, 327,
  404
Eglevsky Ballet (Long Island, New
  York), 141, 195, 247, 273, 282, 285,
  288, 290, 293, 307, 309, 312, 315, 318,
  331, 333, 339, 347, 404
1812 Overture (Tschaikovsky; SIR
  OSWALD STOLL'S VARIETY SHOWS), 107
EINE NACHT IN VENEDIG (J. Strauss II),
  114
Eisner, Betty, 153, 155
ELECTRONICS (Gassmann/Sala), 338
ÉLÉGIE (Stravinsky), 230, 241, 245, 355,
  423
ELEGY (Rachmaninoff), 32
Eliseyeva, E. V., 16
Elliott, Leonard, 218
Ellis, Michael, 280
Ellis, Vivian, 99
Elsom, Isobel, 278
EMERALDS (Fauré), *see* JEWELS
Emmons, 328
L'ENFANT ET LES SORTILÈGES (Ravel)+, 47,
  48, 235, 390, 416
Engelman, Wilfred, 172
ENIGMA (Arensky), 25
Enright, Ray, 186
'Entente Cordiale,' 409
EPISODES (Webern)+, 324
Era Films, 97
Erbshtein, Boris, 1, 10, 19
Ernst, Max, 61
Eros (Fokine), 141
L'ERRANTE (Schubert), 134, 138, 141,
  143, 193, 197
Eschelsen, Maren, 103
Escobar, Luis, 329
Estopinal, Renee, 400
Etheridge, Dorothy, 220
Ettlinger, Don, 191
ÉTUDE (Scriabin), 30, 50

ÉTUDE FOR PIANO (Scriabin), 405
EUGEN ONEGIN (Tschaikovsky), 256,
341, 418
Eugene B. Dunkel Studios, see E. B.
Dunkel Studios
EUGENE THE UNFORTUNATE (Toller), 27
Eula, Joe, 394
Evans, Joseph, 424
Evans, Merle, 202
Eve, 108
Evreinov, 29
EXTASE (Balanchine), 16, 21
THE FAIR AT SOROCHINSK (Moussorgsky),
207, 208
Fairchild, Blair, 192, 374
Fairchild, Edgar, 166, 175
Fairfax Ballet (Virginia), 233
THE FAIRY'S KISS (Stravinsky), see
LE BAISER DE LA FÉE
Falla, Manuel de, 101
Fallis, Barbara, 222, 309, 310
Fantasia (film), 185
FANTASIA BRASILEIRA (Mignone), 193,
200
Farey, Charles, 108
Farmer, Peter, 404
Farrell, Suzanne, 344, 346, 348, 349,
352-356, 358, 360-362, 394, 400, 401,
406, 413-415, 417, 423, 425
FASTES (Sauguet), 134, 137
Faull, Ellen, 243
Fauré, Gabriel, 358, 412
FAUST (Gounod)+, 45, 117, 151, 226, 227,
397, 413
FAUSTO (Gounod), see FAUST
LA FAVORITA (Donizetti), 297
FAY-YEN-FAH (Redding), 44, 125
Fedorov, Michael, 64, 82, 94
Fedorova, Nina, 409, 422
Fegte, Ernst, 213
Feller Scenery Studios, 302, 351, 352,
354, 358, 361
LA FEMME NUE (Février), 89
Ferguson, Mildred, 222

Le Festin, 36
Festival Ballet (London), see London
Festival Ballet
Festival Ballet (Rhode Island), 366
A Festival of Stravinsky: His Heritage
and His Legacy, 355
Feuer, Cy, 249
Février, Henri, 89
Ffolkes, David, 249, 288
Fibich, Zdeněk, 4
Field, Robert, 216
Fifield, Elaine, 270
THE FIGURE IN THE CARPET (Handel), 332
LA FILLE D'ABDOUBARAHAH (Sanvel), 82
LE FILS PRODIGUE (Prokofiev)+, 94, 267
Fini, Leonor, 240
Fiorato, Hugo, 241, 313, 314, 357, 377
Firebird (Fokine), 264
Firebird (Lopukhov), 264
FIREBIRD (Stravinsky), 264
5 A. M. (Duke; ZIEGFELD FOLLIES: 1936
EDITION), 162
Flagg, Elise, 400
Flagg, Laura, 400
Flaherty, Robert, 287
DIE FLEDERMAUS (J. Strauss II), see
ROSALINDA
Die Fledermaus (J. Strauss II; SIR
OSWALD STOLL'S VARIETY SHOWS), 107
Fletcher, Robert, 308
Flight of the Bumble Bee (Rimsky-
Korsakov; SIR OSWALD STOLL'S
VARIETY SHOWS), 107
Flomine, Deborah, 368
Florell, Walter, 216, 229
Florence (Teatro Comunale [Ballet]),
84
Flotow, Friedrich von, 90
Fokine, Michel, 3, 16, 33, 34, 85, 102,
104-106, 141, 172, 214, 263, 264, 383
LA FOLLE DE CHAILLOT (Giraudoux),
257
Fontaine, Edwina, 277
Forbstein, Leo F., 186

Ford, Helen, 184
Forrest, George, 219
Foss, Lukas, 355
THE FOUR TEMPERAMENTS (Hindemith)+, 235, **236**
Fournet, Jean, 399
Fowler and Tamara, 99
Françaix, Jean, 282, 292
Francés, Esteban, 237, 267, 283, 301, 309, 310, 328, 329, 332, 333, 352, 359, 366
Frangopoulo, Marietta, 4
Frank, Melvin, 187, 213
Franke, Paul, 295
Frankfurt, Wilhelmina, 392, 400
Frankfurt (Ballett der Städtischen Bühnen), 141, 195, 236, 277, 312, 314
Franklin, Arthur, 213
Franklin, Frederic, 219, 220, 225, 349
Fredhoven, John, 184
Freedley, Vinton, 190
Freedman, David, 162
Freeman, Charles K., 219
Les Frères Isola, 109
Frohlich, Jean-Pierre, 390, 392, 400
Froman, Jane, 187
Froman, Valentin, 112, 113, 118, 129
FÜRST IGOR (Borodin), see PRINCE IGOR
Fugate, Judith, 392, 413, 420
FYRST IGOR (Borodin), see PRINCE IGOR
Gabo, Naum, 72
Gagaku, see Imperial Gagaku
Gallagher, Helen, 229
Garcia, Enrico, 64
Garden State Ballet (New Jersey), 195, 240, 309, 312, 318, 347, 366
Garfield, Constance, 279, 309
GARLAND DANCE from THE SLEEPING BEAUTY (Tschaikovsky), see TEMPO DI VALSE
Gary, Ted, 175
GASPARD DE LA NUIT (Ravel), 395
Gassmann, Remi, 338

Gates, Larry, 326
Gaxton, William, 188
Gay, Maisie, 99
Gaya, Maria, 107
Gear, Luella, 166
Geerts, Georges, 110, 131
Geneva (Grand Théâtre de Genève [Ballet]), 84, 94, 141, 194, 195, 232, 236, 240, 242, 277, 288, 302, 303, 312, 314-316, 318, 324, 331, 333, 339, 345, 347, 364, 367, 387, 389, 392
Geneva (Grand Théâtre de Genève [Opera]), 341
George Balanchine's Sixteen Delightful Dancers, see Balanchine Ballet
Georgia Dance Theatre, 307
Georgov, Walter, 310
Gephart, William, 237
Gerdt, Elizaveta, 33
Gershwin, George, 185, 368
Gershwin, Ira, 162, 185
Gesualdo, Carlo, Principe de Venosa, 334
Geva, Tamara, 10, 12, 13, 19, 25, 30-32, 53, 58, 62, 73, 74, 143, 166
Giannini, Christina, 405
Gide, André, 424
Gideon, Melville, 108
Giesecke, Karl Ludwig, 311
Gilbert, Billy, 239
Gilbert, Robert, 216
Gilbert, Ruth, 250
LA GIOCONDA (Ponchielli), 87, 174, 185
Giraudoux, Jean, 257
Giselle, Sylvia, see Caccialanza, Gisella
GISELLE: ACT II GRAVE SCENE (Adam), 234
Gish, Lillian, 215
Giulini, Carlo Maria, 299
Glazounov, Alexander, 18, 33, 233, 309, 339, 346, 384
Gleason, James, 186
Glenville, Peter, 278
Glinka, Mikhail, 107, 132, 272, 293, 307, 359, 365, 366

GLINKAIANA *see* GLINKIANA
GLINKIANA, 107, 132, **359**, 366
Gluck, Christoph Willibald, 134, 149, 170, 218, 345, 399, 400, 417
Goberman, Max, 234, 242, 249, 259
Godard, Benjamin, 144
Goddard, Paulette, 213
Goddard, Pauline, 220, 233
THE GODS GO A-BEGGING (Handel)+, 85
Goethe, Johann Wolfgang von, 335
Golden, Miriam, 222
Golden, Ray, 185
Goldwyn, Samuel, 185
GOLDWYN FOLLIES (film), 185
Gollner, Nana, 222, 259
Goodman, Benny, 348
Gordon, Robert H., 217
Gothenburg (Stora Teaterns Balett, Sweden), 84, 236
Gottschalk, Louis Moreau, 347
Goudovitch, Alexander, 219, 220
Gould, Diana, 139
Gould, Morton, 142, 348
Gounod, Charles, 45, 59, 76, 86, 117, 124, 151, 180, 227, 317, 397, 413
GOUNOD SYMPHONY, 317
Govrin, Gloria, 339, 340, 348, 351, 352, 354, 357
Graeler, Louis, 315, 321
Graf, Herbert, 172
Graf, Uta, 345
Graham, Martha, 324
Graham, Martha, Company, *see* Martha Graham Company
Graham, Ronald, 183, 218
GRAND ADAGIO (Tschaikovsky), *see* PAS DE DEUX (Tschaikovsky, from *The Sleeping Beauty*)
Grand Ballet Classique de France, 247
Grand Ballet de Monte-Carlo, *see* Cuevas (Grand Ballet de Monte-Carlo; Grand Ballet du Marquis de Cuevas)
Grand Ballet du Marquis de Cuevas, *see* Cuevas (Grand Ballet de Monte-Carlo; Grand Ballet du Marquis de Cuevas)
Grand Pas–Glazounov, see RAYMONDA
Grand Théâtre de Genève, *see* Geneva (Grand Théâtre de Genève)
Grand Théâtre Municipal, Bordeaux, *see* Bordeaux (Ballet du Grand Théâtre Municipal)
Les Grands Ballets Canadiens (Montreal), 141, 195, 236, 242, 312, 314, 331, 358
Grant, Alberta, 283, 302
Gravier, Jean-Paul, 397
GREAT LADY (Loewe/Crooker/Brentano), 184
'Great Moments of Ballet,' *see* Danilova Concert Company
Green, Judith, 330, 332
Green, Mitzi, 175
Green, Solomon Earl, 305
Greene, Richard, 191
Gregg Smith Singers, 380, 381
Gregorova, Natasha, 107
Gretler, Heinrich, 136
Gribunina, 27
Grieg, Edvard, 3, 218, 219
Grigoriev, Serge Leonidovich, 19, 52
Gris, Juan, 85
Gromtseff, Marie, 367
GROTESQUE ESPAGNOL (Albéniz), 73
Grovlez, Gabriel, 86, 111-114, 116, 117, 119, 120, 122, 124
Gruenwald, Alfred, 229
Gueden, Hilde, 295
Guerard, Audrey, 160
Guérard, Roland, 118, 120
Guest, Morris, 73, 74
Guimar, Marie-Jeanne, *see* Marie-Jeanne
Guiton, Janine, 397
Gunsbourg, Raoul, 48, 70, 78, 118
Gusev, Pëtr, 1, 5, 7, 8, 16, 28, 30
Gusso, Fernando, 139

H. & L. Nathan, Ltd., 99, 108
H. Kauffman & Sons Saddlery Company, 323
Haakon, Paul, 144, 145
Haas, Alexander, 257
Haas, Robert, 186
Hack, Moe, 224
Hageman, Richard, 170, 173
Hague, Albert, 257
Haieff, Alexei, 238
Haight, George, 185
Halasz, Laszlo, 253, 255, 256, 258
Hale, Alan, 186
Hale, Chester, 30, 50
Hale, George, 201
Hale, Sonnie, 91
Halévy, Jacques, 160
Halévy, Ludovic, 109
Halicka, Alice, 178, 271
Halina Biernacka Ballet, see São Paulo (Halina Biernacka Ballet)
Hall, Claudia, 243
Hall, Juanita, 305
Hambleton, John, 182
Hamburg (Ballett der Hamburgischen Staatsoper), 84, 141, 195, 236, 240, 246, 247, 277, 288, 309, 312, 314, 316, 333, 341, 345, 365
Hamburg (Hamburgische Staatsoper), 170, 341, 345, 365, 400
Hamer, Janet, 219
Hamill, Kathryn, 108
Hamilton, Gloria, 239
HAMLET (Thomas), 59, 60
Hancox, Gilbert, 237
Handel, George Frederick, 85, 332, 401
Hanighen, Bernard, 239
Hansen, S. C., 324
Hardwick, Dana, 175
Harkness Ballet, 247, 273
HARLEQUINADE (Drigo)+, 290, **351**
HARLEQUINADE PAS DE DEUX (Drigo), 290
Harmati, Sandor, 141-146, 149

Harper, Herbert, 166
Harrell, Bobby, 249
Harrell, Mack, 295
Harris, Lowell, 326
Hart, Lorenz, 166, 175, 182, 183, 186, 402
Hart, Teddy, 183
Hartford Ballet (Connecticut), 312
Hartford Festival, 164
Harvey, Laurence, 342
Harvey, Peter, 340, 344, 352, 354, 358
Hasburgh, Rabana, 144, 154, 165, 167, 169, 173, 174, 178, 179
Haskins, Harold, 188
Hasselmans, Louis, 151, 153, 155, 158, 159
Havilland, Olivia de, see de Havilland, Olivia
Havoc, June, 319
Hawkins, Jack, 278
Hayden, Melissa, 242, 269, 286, 287, 293, 294, 307, 310, 314, 316, 318, 324, 332, 333, 335, 337, 340, 350, 354, 357, 359, 380, 384
Haydn, Franz Josef, 218, 270
Hays, David, 236, 312, 314, 318-320, 323-325, 329-331, 333-340, 343, 350
Hayter, James, 278
Head, Edith, 213
Heath, Andrew, 308
Heath, Babs, 229
Heath, Percy, 337
Heatherton, Ray, 175
Heaven (Nichols/Novello; CHARLES B. COCHRAN'S 1930 REVUE), 99
Hecht, Ben, 185
Heflin, Frances, 224
Heine, Heinrich, 110
Held, John, Jr., 142
HELEN OF TROY (Offenbach)+, 214
Helene Pons Studio, 142, 144, 166, 175, 176, 295, 310
Helpmann, Robert, 291
Hemsley, Gilbert, Jr., 410

Hendl, Susan, 368, 387, 392, 400, 410, 414
Henriques, Winston George, 305
Henry, Pierre, 386
Hepburn, Phillip, 305
Herbert, Ralph, 206
Herbertt, Stanley, 234
Herczeg, Geza, 229
HÉRODIADE (Massenet), 46, 118, 119
Hess, William, 237
L'Heure du Concert (CBC), 84, 141, 195, 236, 302, 304, 309, 314, 335, 359
Hiden, Georgia, 235, 236
Hightower, Rosella, 247
Hill, Phyllis, 217
Hill, Sinclair, 97
Hilton, Jack, 107
Hindemith, Paul, 236, 289, 408
Hinkson, Mary, 332
L'HIRONDELLE (Puccini), see LA RONDINE
Hlinka, Nichol, 400
Hobbs, Robert, 424
Hobi, Frank, 267, 269, 272, 274, 277, 282, 283, 285, 302
Hoctor, Harriet, 162
Hodges, Joy, 218
Højgaard, Else, 103
Hoffmann, E. T. A., 302, 387
Hofmann, Hubert, 365
Hofmannsthal, Hugo von, 106
Hogarth, William, 295
Holbrook, William, 201
Holder, Geoffrey, 305
Holland Festival, 263
Hollander, Frederick, 107
Hollman, Gene, 322
Holmes, Ralph, 416
Honegger, Arthur, 55
Honigold, 64
Honolka, Kurt, 365
Hoover, Darla, 410
HOPAC (Moussorgsky), 43
Hope, Bob, 162, 213
Hoppe, Heinz, 341

Horiuchi, Gen, 424
Hoskinson, Richard, 392
HOUSE OF FLOWERS (Arlen/Capote), 305
Houseman, John, 320, 326, 422
Houston, Grace, 217
Houston Ballet, 94, 195, 309, 331, 339
Howard, Holly, 141, 144, 145, 149, 153, 165, 169, 174, 176, 184
Howard, Robert, 183
LE HULLA (Samuel-Rousseau), 41
Hummel, Earle, 233
HUNGARIAN GYPSY AIRS (Menter/Tschaikovsky), 419
HUNGARIAN GYPSY DANCE (Brahms), 13
Hungary (State Opera Ballet, Magyar Allami Operahaz), 84, 141, 240, 316
Hunt, Martita, 257
Huntington Dance Ensemble (Long Island, New York), 309
Hurley, Laurel, 311
Huston, Philip, 224
Hutton, Betty, 213
Hyman, Earle, 320
Hyman, Prudence, 139
I MARRIED AN ANGEL (Rodgers/Hart), 182
I WAS AN ADVENTURESS (film)+, 191
Idzikowsky, Stanislas, 58, 63, 64, 68
Ilosvay, Maria v., 341, 365
Imperial Gagaku company, 343
In a Venetian Theatre (Ellis; CHARLES B. COCHRAN'S 1930 REVUE), 99
Ingram, Rex, 190
International Congress of Iranian Art and Archeology, 332
International Dance Festival, see North American International Dance Festival of Stars
Introduction and Fugue (J. Duell), 412
INVITATION TO THE DANCE (Weber), 34
Iolas, Constantine, 150
Iranian National Ballet, 141
Irion, Yolanda Mero, see Mero-Irion, Yolanda
Irving, Robert, 321-324, 328-336, 339,

340, 343, 344, 346-354, 358-362, 364, 366, 368-371, 374-376, 379, 380, 382, 384, 387, 391-394, 396, 398, 400, 401, 406-409, 412-414, 417-421, 425
Irwin, Will, 217
Ismaïloff, Serge, 135, 137
Israel, Eugenia Wolf, see Wolf-Israel, Eugenia
Israel, Walter J., 219
Israel Ballet, 141, 195, 247, 316
Istomina, Anna, 219
IVAN LE TERRIBLE (Gunsbourg), 70
Ivanov, Ivan, 233
Ivanov, Lev, 75, 285, 302, 367, 387
Ivanova, Lydia, 1, 10, 11, 16, 21-23, 25
Ives, Charles, 304
IVESIANA, 304
JACK IN THE BOX (Satie), 63
Jackson, Brooks, 283
Jackson, Dorothy, 107
Jackson, Milt, 337
Jacobson, Leopold, 239
James, Edward, 136, 140, 322
James, Henry, 332
James, Leroy, 175
Janssen, Werner, 220, 375
Jantzen, Inc., 269
Jasinsky, Roman, 130, 131, 134, 135, 137-139, 192
Jazz Concert (Balanchine/Bolender/ Moncion/Taras), 336
Jeakins, Dorothy, 320, 325
JEANNE D'ARC (Debussy?), 148
JEANNE D'ARC (Gounod), 59
Jehin, Léon, 39, 47, 49, 57-60, 66, 69-71
Jensen, Elna Jørgen, see Jørgen-Jensen, Elna
Jensen, Gertrud, 103
Jensen, Richard, 102-104, 106
Jepson, Helen, 185
JEUX D'ENFANTS (Bizet), 310
JEWELS (Fauré/Stravinsky/Tschaikovsky)+, **358**, 418

Jillana, 267, 275, 277, 279, 284, 328, 335, 340, 342, 352
JOAN OF ARC (Debussy?), see JEANNE D'ARC
Jørgen-Jensen, Elna, 100, 103
Jørgensen, Aage Winther, see Winther-Jørgensen, Aage
Joffrey Ballet, 247, 288, 302, 309, 312, 315, 331, 333, 347
John Tiller Girls, 108
Johnson, Albert R., 184
Johnson, Nunnally, 191
Johnson, Philip, 338, 417, 421
Johnston, Johnny, 213
Johnstone, Alick, 99, 108, 270
Jolley, Jay, 400
Jones, David, 183
Jones, John, 337
Jones, Robert Edmond, 215
JONES BEACH (Andriessen), 269
Jonson, Bill, 280
Jooss, Kurt, 424
JOSEF-LEGENDE (R. Strauss), see LA LÉGENDE DE JOSEPH
Judels, Charles, 219
JUDITH (Honegger), 55
Juilliard American Opera Center, 403
LA JUIVE (Halévy), 160
Jung, Doris, 345
Kahrklin, Hortense, 149, 177, 184
Kai, Una, 310
Kalbeck, M., 341
Kalioujny, Alexandre, 240
Kallman, Chester, 295, 311, 322
KAMMERMUSIK NO. 2 (Hindemith), 408
Kansas City Ballet (Missouri), 141, 264, 282, 285, 309, 331, 366
Kapuste, Falco, 345
Karinska, Barbara, 84, 107, 129-131, 141, 149, 190, 192, 194, 201, 218, 220-223, 232, 233, 235, 237, 242, 244, 250, 257, 259, 264, 265, 272, 273, 276-279, 284, 285, 287-293, 302, 303, 307, 312-314, 317, 318, 321, 324, 329-333, 335,

336, 339, 340, 343, 346-350, 352, 354, 357, 358, 364, 368, 377, 382, 387, 400, 406, 410, 418
Karlin, Rita, 236
Karlweis, Oscar, 206
Karp, Poel, 7
Karsavina, Tamara, 61
Karson, Nat, 187
Karstens, Gerda, 103
Kaskas, Anna, 170
Kasman, Sheldon M., 401
Katcharoff, Michel, 221, 232
Katchourovsky, Léonide, 131
Kate Smith Hour (NBC), 282, 285, 294
Katherine Dunham Dancers, 190
Kauffman, H., & Sons Saddlery Company, see H. Kauffman & Sons Saddlery Company
Kaufman, S. Jay, 187
Kaufman, Susan, 302
Kavan, Albia, 184, 222
Kay, Arthur, 219
Kay, Connie, 337
Kay, Hershy, 303, 318, 347, 361, 368, 401
Kaye, Nora, 153, 184, 222, 234, 276
Keeler, Elisha C., 315
Keen, Malcolm, 278
KEEP OFF THE GRASS (McHugh/Duke/Dubin, et al.), 187
Kellam, William, Company, see William Kellam Company
Kellaway, Roger, 371
Kellogg, Cal Stewart, 410, 411
Kempf, Christa, 345
Kent, Allegra, 304, 314, 318, 322, 328, 343, 354
Kent, Carl, 219
Kerby, Paul, 206
Kernot, Vivienne, 270
Kervily, Irène, 132
Kiepura, Jan, 216
Kilgallen, Dorothy, 218
Kinberg, Judy, 416
King, Dennis, 182

King, Martin Luther, Jr., 362
Kinsky, Leonid, 186
Kirkland, Gelsey, 369
Kirov Ballet (Leningrad), 240
Kirsanov, D., 2
Kirsanov, D. K., 16
Kirsanova, Nina, 83
Kirsova, Lena, 132
Kirstein, Lincoln, 73, 141, 142, 145, 146, 169, 177, 193, 196, 199, 200, 203, 230, 235, 264, 275, 311, 316, 322
Kloster, Carlos, 367
Knight, June, 218
Kobelev, 24
Kobeleva, 24
Kochermann, Rainer, 345
Kochno, Boris, 19, 62, 72, 85, 93, 94, 99, 129, 131, 133-137, 267, 322
Koechlin, Charles, 138, 143, 197
Koesun, Ruth Ann, 259
Kollmar, Richard, 218
Kolpikoff, Pierre, 129
Komarov, 24
Den Kongelige Danske Ballet, see Royal Danish Ballet
Koninklijk Ballet Van Vlaanderen, see Royal Flemish Ballet
Kopeikine, Nicholas, 165, 236, 279, 292, 312
Koreff, Nora, see Kaye, Nora
Korf, Heidi, 345
Korngold, Erich Wolfgang, 206
Korovin, K., 104
Korsakov, Andrei Rimsky, see Rimsky-Korsakov, Andrei
Korsakov, Nicolai Rimsky, see Rimsky-Korsakov, Nicolai
Kosleck, Morris, 257
Kostelanetz, André, 385
Kostrovitskaya, Vera, 4, 16, 18
Koussevitsky, Serge, 269, 381
Kova, Marija, 340
Kovacs, Stephen, 148
Kovnat, Susan, 283

Kraencke, Fritz, 219
Kramer, Helen, 199, 271
Krasovskaya, Vera, 4
Krassovska, Nathalie, 219, 221
Kreisler, Fritz, 2, 22
Kremnev, Nicolas, 43, 44, 52, 76, 82
Kriza, John, 196, 222, 259, 262
Kroeger, Berry, 224
Kulka, Janos, 345
Kuller, Sid, 185
Kungliga Teaterns Balett, see Royal
    Swedish Ballet
Kuper, Max, 27
Kursch, Judy, 230
Kylberg, Lucienne, 134, 135, 137, 139
L. & H. Nathan, Ltd., see H. & L.
    Nathan, Ltd.
La Plata (Teatro Argentino [Ballet]),
    84, 205
Labinsky, Alexandre, 98, 140
LE LAC DES CYGNES (Tschaikovsky),
    see SWAN LAKE
Ladd, Alan, 213
Ladré, Marian, 120, 125, 130, 131
THE LADY COMES ACROSS (Duke/
    Latouche/Thompson/Powell), 201
Laffredo, Warren, 423
Lafon, Madeleine, 240
La Guardia, Fiorello H., 318
Laing, Hugh, 287
Lake, Veronica, 213
LAKMÉ (Delibes), 57, 115, 153
Lamballe, 96
Lambert, Constant, 61
Lamont, Deni, 351, 352, 368, 379
Lamour, Dorothy, 213
Lamy, Adrien, 109
Lanchester, Elsa, 342
Lancret, Nicolas, 85
Landau, Jack, 319, 320, 325, 326
Lander, Harald, 106
Lane, Bobby, 175
Lane, Maryon, 270
Lanese, Lillian, 220, 259

Lang, Ariel, see Leitch, Helen
Lang, Harold, 222, 229, 272
Lang, Phil, 249
Lanina, Valentina, see Blinova,
    Valentina
Lankston, John, 422
Larkin, Peter, 323
Larsen, Niels Bjørn, 103
Larsson, Irene, 279, 284, 302
Laskey, Charles, 141-146, 149, 153, 154,
    160, 165, 169, 173, 182, 188, 191, 243
Lassen, Elna, 100
Latouche, John, 190, 201
Lavery, Sean, 406, 408, 409
Lavrovsky, Leonid, 16
Lawrence, Gertrude, 231
Lawrence, Jack, 280
Lazarus, Milton, 219
Lazowski, Yurek, 221, 272
Le Clercq, Tanaquil, 231, 235, 236,
    238, 241, 243-246, 261, 265, 266, 269,
    271, 274, 277, 284, 286, 289, 291-293,
    296, 301-304, 306, 313, 314
Lede, Lita, 183
Lee, Canada, 224
Lee, Sammy, 185
Lee, Tom, 188
Leeds, Andrea, 185
Le Gallienne, Eva, 224
LA LÉGENDE DE JOSEPH (R. Strauss), 106
LEGETØJSBUTIKEN (Rossini), see LA
    BOUTIQUE FANTASQUE
Lehár, Franz, 216, 406
Leinsdorf, Erich, 313, 314
Leitch, Helen, 141, 165, 167, 169, 177
Leland, Sara, 352, 358, 371-373, 380,
    395, 401, 406
Lenin, Vladimir Il'ich, 5
Lenya, Lotte, 136, 322
Leonard, Queenie, 108
Leonidoff, Léon, 291
Lerner, Alan Jay, 217
Lerner, Sammy, 107
Leshevich, Tamara K., 13

Leskova, Tatiana, 192
Lessner, George, 229
Lester, Edwin, 219
Le Tang, Henry, 218
Levant, Harry, 183
Levasseur, André, 328
Leve, Samuel, 257
Levine, Jesse, 355
Levinoff, Joseph, 144, 149, 150, 173
Levinson, Leonard L., 229
Levitsky, 27
Levy, Parke, 187
Leweck, Madeline, 155
Lewis, Albert, 190
Lewis, George, 332
Lewis, Joe E., 201
Lewis, John, 337
Lewis, Mort, 187
Lewis, William, 311
Leyssac, Paul, 224
Li, George, 302
Liagre, Alfred de, Jr., see de Liagre,
    Alfred, Jr.
Lichine, David, 129, 131, 132, 214
Lidvall, 129
Liebermann, Rolf, 345, 370
LIEBESLIEDER WALZER (Brahms)+, 335
Lifar, Serge, 53, 61, 62, 64, 72, 84, 93,
    94, 96, 99, 140, 237
Lilac Garden (Tudor), 317, 339
Lilley, Edward Clarke, 162
Limón, José, 187, 206
Lindgren, Robert, 233
Lioy, Eda, 311
Lipkovska, Tatiana, 118, 123, 130
Lipkowska, Eugenia, 89, 90, 92, 93
Lipscott, Alan, 187
Lipton, Martha, 295
Lishner, Leon, 237, 243
Lisovskaya, N., 16
Liszt, Franz, 100, 107, 138, 143, 146, 197
Live from Lincoln Center (PBS), 242,
    387
Livingston, Fudd, 190

Lloyd, Paula, 242
Loesser, Frank, 249
Loewe, Frederick, 184, 217
Logan, Ella, 185
Logan, Joshua, 182
London, Lorna, 193
London Festival Ballet, 232, 247, 265,
    331
Longchamp, Gaston, 141, 146
Loon, Willem van, see Van Loon,
    Willem
Lopokova, Lydia, 97
Lopukhov, Andrei, 3
Lopukhov, Fëdor, 264
Lorcia, 96
Lord, Robert, 186
Loring, Eugene, 142, 144, 179
Lorre, Peter, 191
Lortzing, Albert, 3
Los Angeles Ballet, 195, 236, 285, 288,
    304, 309, 312, 331, 339, 347, 358, 364,
    366
Los Angeles Civic Light Opera, 219
Losch, Tilly, 91, 136, 138, 139
LOUISIANA PURCHASE (Berlin/Ryskind),
    188
Louisiana Story (film), 287
Louisville Ballet (Kentucky), 232, 233,
    312, 333
Love, Kermit, 352, 379, 390, 416, 424
Lucezarska, Irène, 109
LUCIA DI LAMMERMOOR (Donizetti), 168
Lucien, 177
Ludlow, Conrad, 329-332, 334, 335, 340,
    352, 354, 358, 369
Ludmila, Anna, 95
Lübeck, Georg Philipp Schmidt von,
    see Schmidt, Georg Philipp
Lüders, Adam, 408, 409, 413, 415, 419,
    422
Lully, Jean-Baptiste, 274
Luna Park, or The Freaks (Berners;
    CHARLES B. COCHRAN'S 1930 REVUE),
    99

Lurçat, Jean, 141
Lutyens, Edith, 224, 241, 264
Lyman, Louise, 130
Lyon, Annabelle, 141, 144, 149, 155, 160, 169, 177, 178, 184
Macaulay, Richard, 186
MACBETH (Verdi), 211
McBride, Pat, 243, 245, 254, 261, 264
McBride, Patricia, 332, 340, 347, 351, 352, 354, 358, 359, 363, 368, 376, 382, 385, 387, 393, 398, 401, 404-406, 410
McCann, Frances, 239
McCarthy, Charlie, 185
McClain, Walter, 202
McCullough, Paul, 108
McDonald, Alexander, 190
McDonald, Grace, 175
McDonald, Ray, 175
McDonald, T. B., Construction Company, see T. B. McDonald Construction Company
McDowall, Roddy, 308
MacGregor, Edgar, 188
McHale, Duke, 162, 175, 183
McHugh, James, 187
Mackerras, Charles, 365
McKinley, Andrew, 311
McLennan, Rodney, 162
McLerie, Allyn, 249
MacMahon, Aline, 325
McManus, John, 162, 187
MacMurray, Fred, 213
MacWatters, Virginia, 206, 229
Madsen, Tony, 101
THE MADWOMAN OF CHAILLOT (Giraudoux), see LA FOLLE DE CHAILLOT
Magallanes, Nicholas, 194, 200, 203, 219-221, 226, 232, 233, 243, 244, 246, 254, 255, 265, 266, 269, 271, 273, 277, 286, 289, 293, 301-303, 312-315, 324, 329, 332, 335, 340, 352
Maggio Musicale Fiorentino, 300
MAGIC (Mozart), see SERENATA: MAGIC

THE MAGIC FLUTE (Mozart), see DIE ZAUBERFLÖTE
The Magic of Dance (BBC), 84
Mahler, Fritz, 194, 195
Maikerska, Henriette, 76, 77, 89
Maiocchi, Gilda, 297, 299
Maiorano, Robert, 368
La Maison Jules Muelle, 62, 63
LES MAÎTRES CHANTEURS (Wagner), see DIE MEISTERSINGER VON NÜRNBERG
Makarova and Company, 309
Maklezova, Xenia, 14
Malaieff, M., 177, 275
Malipiero, Gian Francesco, 79
Malraux, Madeleine, 372, 389
Maly Opera Theater (Petrograd), 24, 27
Mandia, John, 306
Mangin, Noël, 365
Manning, Mildred, 182
MANON (Massenet), 40, 122, 159
March of Dimes, 231, 316
Marchand, Nancy, 326
MARCHE FUNÈBRE (Chopin), 16, 19, 28
Marconi, Walter, 299
Margarethe, Princess of Denmark, 100
Marie-Jeanne, 157, 193-196, 198, 199, 226, 232, 233, 243, 250, 252, 254
Markova, Alicia, 14, 36, 37, 48, 52
MÂROUF (Rabaud), 179, 204
Marra, Eleanora, 94, 112, 113, 115, 116, 118, 130-132
THE MARRIAGE OF FIGARO (Mozart), see LE NOZZE DI FIGARO
Marshall, Al, 108
Marshall, Alphonso, 305
Marshall, Eric, 99
Marshall, George, 185, 213
MARTHA (Flotow), 90
Martha Graham Dance Company, 324
Martin, Ernest H., 249
Martin, Hugh, 188, 190
Martin, Keith, 169, 199

Martin, Mary, 213
Martin Turner Studios, 239
Martinet, Françoise, 311
Martinez, José, 236
Martínez, Juan, 128
Martins, Peter, 246, 304, 374, 378, 380, 382, 394, 400, 401, 406, 409-411, 414, 415
Marty, Jean-Pierre, 347
MARUF (Rabaud), see MÂROUF
Maryinsky Theater and School (St. Petersburg), 141, 233, 234, 302, 387; see also Petrograd Theater (Ballet) School, State Theater of Opera and Ballet
Maryland Ballet, 233, 333; see also Baltimore Ballet
Mason, Jane, 309
Massenet, Jules, 39, 40, 46, 119, 122, 159
Massey, Raymond, 308
Massine, Léonide, 52, 101, 103, 327, 379
Massue, Nicholas, 172
MATELOTTE (traditional), 11, 16
Matera, Barbara, see Barbara Matera, Ltd.
Mathews, Carmen, 280
Matisse, Henri, 52
Matlinsky, Ludovic, 134, 135, 137
Matsuyama Ballet Company (Japan), 141, 273, 312, 331
Matteson, Ruth, 216, 229
Matthews, Jessie, 91, 201
Matthews, Laurence, 392
Maule, Michael, 277
Maynagh, Joan, 311
Mayuzumi, Toshiro, 343
MAZURKA FROM 'A LIFE FOR THE TSAR' (Glinka), 272, 274
Mazzo, Kay, 352, 369, 371, 374, 377, 378, 391, 401, 406, 415
Medici, Lorenzo de', 243
MEDITATION (Tschaikovsky)+, 346
Medtner, Nicolai, 3

DIE MEISTERSINGER VON NÜRNBERG (Wagner), 77, 163
Mejia, Paul, 359
Melchert, Helmut, 365
Memphis Civic Ballet (Tennessee), 240
Men in Dance, 147
Mendelssohn, Felix, 107, 279, 288, 340
Menjou, Adolphe, 185
Menotti, Gian Carlo, 300
Mensching, William H., Studios, see William H. Mensching Studios
Menter, Sophie, 419
Mercer, Johnny, 213
Mero-Irion, Yolanda, 216
Merrild, Karl, 101, 103, 104, 106
Merrill, Linda, 368
THE MERRY WIDOW (Lehár), 216
THE MERRY WIVES OF WINDSOR (Shakespeare), 326
Mesa Civic Ballet (Arizona), 309
Messel, Oliver, 91, 99, 108, 278, 305
Messmore & Damon, 305, 310
METAMORPHOSES (Hindemith), 289
METASTASEIS & PITHOPRAKTA (Xenakis), 360
Meth, Max, 190, 218
Methling, Svend, 102
Metropolitan Opera (New York City), 150-156, 158-161, 163, 167, 168, 170-174, 179-181, 295, 345, 388
Metropolitan Opera Ballet (New York City), 388
Metropolitan Opera Studio (New York City), 295
Mexico (Ballet Clásico de Mexico, renamed Compañía Nacional de Danza), 194, 242
Mexico (Ópera Nacional, Palacio de Bellas Artes), 226-228
Meyerbeer, Giacomo, 113
Meylan, Jean, 367
A MIDSUMMER NIGHT'S DREAM (Mendelssohn), 340

A MIDSUMMER NIGHT'S DREAM (Shakespeare), 319

Mielziner, Jo, 166, 182, 183, 239, 361, 368, 371

MIGNON (Thomas), 158

Mignone, Francisco, 200

Mikhailov, Mikhail, 1, 12, 13, 16, 18, 34

Miklashevsky, 29

Milberg, Barbara, 284, 306, 310, 311, 316

Milhaud, Darius, 35, 63, 135, 145, 274

Milland, Ray, 213

Mille, Cecil B. De, *see* De Mille, Cecil B.

Les Millions d'Harlequin (Petipa), 351

Mills, John, 108

Milwaukee Ballet, 141, 288, 309, 312

Miner, Worthington, 166

Minkus, Léon, 247, 262, 276

MINKUS PAS DE TROIS, *see* PAS DE TROIS CLASSIQUE

Minnelli, Vincente, 162

Minnesota Dance Theatre, 195, 233, 247, 312

MIREILLE (Gounod), 76

Miró, Joan, 61

Mironova, Eudoxia, 177, 178

MR. STRAUSS GOES TO BOSTON (Stolz/ Sour/Levinson), 229

Mitchell, Arthur, 305, 316, 329, 332, 337, 340, 348, 352, 356, 357, 360-362, 370

Mitchell, David, 390, 395, 398, 416

Mladova, Milada, 216

Mlodzinskaya, Nina, 12, 16, 20

MODERN JAZZ: VARIANTS (Schuller), 337

Modern Jazz Quartet, 337

Modoc, 202

Moffat, Alfred Edward, 274

Molière, 131, 221, 410, 414

Mollison, Henry, 108

Molloy, Molly, 108

Molyneux, 138

Moment of Moments (Duke; ZIEGFELD FOLLIES: 1936 EDITION), 162

Moncion, Francisco, 236, 238, 239, 243, 244, 246, 248, 250, 264, 274, 277, 287, 301, 302, 304, 310, 313, 324, 329, 332, 336, 340, 352, 358, 379, 422

Monte Carlo (Opéra de Monte-Carlo), 38-42, 44-49, 54-60, 66-71, 76-82, 86-90, 92, 111-128, 235, 390, 416

Monte Carlo (Théâtre de Monte-Carlo), 110

Montes, Mona, 174

MONUMENTUM PRO GESUALDO (Stravinsky), 333, **334**, 344

MOODS (da Costa), *see* PAS DE DEUX (da Costa)

Moore, Ada, 305

Moore, Lillian, 259

Moore, Marjorie, 187, 196-198

Moore, Victor, 188, 213

Moore, Vivien, 183

Morcom, James Stewart, 241, 314

Moredock, Richard, 419

Morel, Jean, 227, 228, 248, 252, 260

Morelli, Anthony R., 187

Morgan, Howard, 162

Morgan, Johnny, 217

Morgan, Sydney, 97

Moro, Alberto, 300

Morosov, 27

Morosova, Olga, 131

Morris, David, 166

Morris, June, 222

Morris, Marnee, 352, 357, 368, 369, 373, 387, 390

Morrow, Doretta, 249

LA MORT DU CYGNE (Saint-Saëns), 16, 263

Mosarra, Francesca, 267

Mosier, Enid, 305

Moss, Arnold, 224

Motley, 224, 326

Mottl, Felix, 129, 357

Mounsey, Yvonne, 269, 277, 285, 302

Moussorgsky, Modest, 31, 43, 54, 97, 208, 218, 298, 388

Mouveau, 96

MOVEMENTS FOR PIANO AND ORCHESTRA (Stravinsky), 334, **344**

Moxzer, Jieno, 190

Moylan, Mary Ellen, 203, 206, 220, 221, 236, 238, 239

Mozart, Wolfgang Amadeus, 81, 134, 149, 157, 164, 181, 205, 231, 241, 251, 253, 274, 286, 311, 313, 314, 417

Mozart Festival, see American Shakespeare Festival Mozart Festival

MOZARTIANA (Tschaikovsky)+, 134, 149, 286, 417

Mravinsky, Evgeny, 8

Muelle, Jules, see La Maison Jules Muelle

Mullowny, Kathryn, 141, 142, 144, 145, 153, 154, 160, 165, 173, 174, 178

Mungalova, Olga, 1, 7, 8, 16, 19, 29

Munich (Ballett der Bayerischen Staatsoper), 84, 141, 195, 236, 240, 288, 314

Muratore, Lucien, 109

EL MURCIÉLAGO (J. Strauss II), see THE BAT

Murray, Honey, 217

Murray, Wynn, 175, 183, 201

MUSIC AND DANCE, 274

Music at Work, 203

A MUSICAL JOKE (Mozart), 313

Musil, Karl, 367

Musser, Tharon, 319, 325, 326

Muszely, Melitta, 341

Muti, Nuccy, 299

Nabokov, Nicolas, 139, 352

Naples (Teatro San Carlo [Ballet]), 194

Nathan, H. & L., Ltd., see H. & L. Nathan, Ltd.

National Academy Ballet (Illinois), 309

National Ballet (Washington, D. C.), 94, 141, 195, 232, 233, 236, 273

National Ballet of Canada (Toronto), 141, 195, 236

National Ballet of Illinois, see National Academy Ballet

National Broadcasting Company, see NBC

National Orchestral Society, 230, 241, 245, 274

National Theater Company, see Belgrade (National Theater Company, Balet Narodno Pozorište)

Het Nationale Ballet, Amsterdam, see Dutch National Ballet

NATIVE DANCERS (Rieti), 323

Nault, Fernand, 242, 259

NBC (National Broadcasting Company), 84, 195, 232, 236, 247, 264, 273, 282, 285, 288, 291, 294, 302, 311, 312, 315, 316, 318, 324, 331, 333, 347, 351, 358, 359, 361, 368

NBC Opera Theatre, 311

Neary, Colleen, 382, 384, 387, 390, 395, 408, 409

Neary, Patricia, 339, 349, 352, 358, 367

Het Nederlands Ballet, see Netherlands Ballet

Negro Debutante Ball, 296

Neher, Caspar Rudolph, 136

Nellemose, Kirsten, 103

Nemtchinova, Vera, 41, 44, 98

Netherlands, 269

Netherlands Ballet, 141, 195, 232, 236; see also Dutch National Ballet

Neu, Thea, 319

New Amsterdam News, 296

New Group, see Royal Ballet Touring company

New England Civic Ballet, 288, 309; see also Boston Ballet

New Jersey Ballet (West Orange), 247, 318, 331, 333, 366

New Opera Company (New York City), 194, 206-211, 216

New York City Ballet, 48, 84, 94, 107, 129, 132, 134, 136, 141, 170, 177, 178,

191, 194, 195, 220, 225, 232, 233, 235, 236, 240, 242, 244, 246-248, 250-256, 260, 264, 265, 267-269, 271-277, 279, 282-290, 292, 293, 301-304, 306, 307, 309, 310, 312-318, 321-324, 328-340, 342-344, 346-362, 364, 366, 368-382, 384, 386, 387, 389-398, 400, 401, 405-410, 412-425; *see also* American Ballet, American Ballet Caravan, American Ballet Ensemble, Ballet Society, Producing Company of the School of American Ballet

New York City Ballet Gala Benefit, 1965: 352; 1966: 354; 1968: 361; 1971: 370; 1972: 372-374; 1973: 384; 1975: 389, 390; 1976: 401; 1977: 406, 407; 1978: 409; 1980: 415; 1981: 417; 1982: 421.

New York City Ballet Ravel Festival, 48, 235, 389-396, 416

New York City Ballet Stravinsky Centennial Celebration, 245, 342, 353, 377, 421-425

New York City Ballet Stravinsky Festival, 178, 192, 220, 246, 264, 372-381

New York City Ballet Tschaikovsky Festival, 134, 417-420

New York City Center Light Opera Company, 216

New York City Center of Music and Drama, *see* City Center of Music and Drama

New York City Opera, 131, 221, 248, 251-253, 255, 256, 258, 260, 351, 401, 411, 414, 422, 424

New York Dance Theatre, 236, 293, 316, 318, 331, 361

New York Philharmonic, 373

New York Philharmonic Promenade Concert, 385

New York Studios, 142, 144

New Zealand Ballet, 141, 195, 309

Newburgh Ballet (New York), 247

Nicholas Brothers (Fayard and Harold), 162, 175

Nichols, Beverley, 99

Nickel, Paul, 302

Nicks, Walter, 305

Nicolaeva, Nadejda, 60

Nielsen, Kay, 102

Niesen, Gertrude, 162

Night Flight (Duke; ZIEGFELD FOLLIES: 1936 EDITION), 162

THE NIGHT SHADOW (Rieti)[+], **232, 328,** 333

NIGHT SHADOWS (Rieti), *see* THE NIGHT SHADOW

Nijinska, Bronislava, 38, 61, 85, 178, 237, 259

Nikitina, Alice, 53, 84, 99

Nikitina, N. A., 16

NOAH AND THE FLOOD (Stravinsky), 342, 422

Noailles, Anna-Elisabeth, Vicomtesse de, and Mathieu, Vicomte de, 98

Noguchi, Isamu, 246

Nolan, Lloyd, 280

Nolan Brothers, 187, 224, 280, 283, 285, 314, 317, 324, 328, 332, 338, 343

Nolan Scenery Studios, 303, 379, 406

Den Norske Opera [Ballet], *see* Norway (Den Norske Opera [Ballet])

North American International Dance Festival of Stars, Second (Chicago), 84

North Carolina Dance Theatre, 195, 233, 307, 309, 312, 315, 331, 347, 366

Norway (Den Norske Opera [Ballet]) 84, 141, 194, 195, 236, 240, 312

Novak, Joseph, 170, 177, 178

A Novel Interpretation of Liebestraum (Liszt; SIR OSWALD STOLL'S VARIETY SHOWS), 107

Novello, Ivor, 99

Noverre Ballet (Stuttgart), 312

LE NOZZE DI FIGARO (Mozart), 251

LA NUIT (Rubinstein), 1, 16

Nuitter, Charles, 387
NUMÉRO LES CANOTIERS (composer unknown), 133
Nureyev, Rudolf, 410
Nureyev and Friends, 84
THE NUTCRACKER (Tschaikovsky)+, 225, 302, 418
Oberlin, Russell, 319, 320
OBÉRON (Weber), 71
Oberon Productions, Ltd., 340
Obidenna, Lara, 130
O'Brien, Shaun, 309, 351, 379, 387
O'Connor, Una, 97
O'Dea, Sunnie, 187
Odinokov, Volodia, 264
Ørnberg, Leif, 101-103, 106
Offenbach, Jacques, 58, 107, 109, 112, 128, 140, 209, 214, 260
Offenkranz, Paul, 390
Officer, Harvey, 237
O'Hara, John, 191
Ohio Ballet, 195
Ohman, Frank, 349, 352, 357, 368, 371, 414
Okie, William B., Jr., 141
Oklahoma City Ballet, 233
Oliver, Robert, 342
Olympique, 62
Omnibus (ABC), 166
Omnibus (NBC), 333
ON YOUR TOES (Rodgers/Hart/Abbott), 166, 186, 361
ONE, YULETIDE SQUARE (Delibes), 291
THE OPERA CLOAK (Damrosch), 207
Opéra de Monte-Carlo, see Monte Carlo (Opéra de Monte-Carlo)
Opéra du Rhin [Ballet], see Strasbourg (Ballet de l'Opéra du Rhin)
Ópera Nacional, see Mexico (Ópera Nacional, Palacio de Bellas Artes)
OPUS 34 (Schoenberg), 301
Orbón, Julián, 329
ORFEO ED EURIDICE (Gluck), 170, 345, 399, 400

ORIENTAL DANCE (Moussorgsky), 31
ORIENTALIA (Cui), 12
Original Ballet Russe, 192; see also Ballets Russes de Monte-Carlo
Orloff, Nicolas, 259
Orlova, 24, 27
Orlova, Sonia, 192
Orlova, Sophie, 84
Orphée aux Enfers [Can-Can] (Offenbach; SIR OSWALD STOLL'S VARIETY SHOWS), 107
ORPHÉE AUX ENFERS (Offenbach), 109
ORPHEUS (Stravinsky)+, 195, 240, 244, 245, 246, 250, 316
ORPHEUS AND EURYDICE; ORPHEUS UND EURYDIKE (Gluck), see ORFEO ED EURIDICE
Orry-Kelly, 186
Orselli, Raimonda, 300
Ortiz, Angèles, 98
Ostendorf, John, 362
Ouchkova, T., 139
Oudart, Félix, 109
P. A. F. Dance Ensemble, see Huntington Dance Ensemble
Pacific Northwest Ballet (Seattle, Washington), see Pacific Northwest Dance Theatre
Pacific Northwest Dance Theatre (Seattle, Washington), 141, 195, 236, 277, 288, 302, 303, 309, 312, 314, 315, 366
Padgett, Bruce, 422
Padovani, Alfredo, 126
Paganini, Niccolo, 146
Page, Ruth, 30, 50, 51
Paige, Frances, 311
PAL JOEY (Rodgers/Hart), 402
Palacio de Bellas Artes, see Mexico (Ópera Nacional, Palacio de Bellas Artes)
Paladilhe, Émile, 118
LE PALAIS DE CRISTAL (Bizet), 195, 240, 244, 246, 250, 330

Palance, Jack, 308
Palermo (Teatro Massimo [Ballet]), 84
Palmer, Byron, 249
Paltrinieri, Giordano, 172
PAMTGG (Kellaway/Applebaum/ Woloshin), 371
Panama, Norman, 187, 213
PANAMERICA (Escobar, Chávez, Orbón), 329, 333
Panizza, Ettore, 150, 152, 156, 161, 174, 181
Papi, Gennaro, 168, 172
Papillons (Chopin?; SIR OSWALD STOLL'S VARIETY SHOWS), 107
PAQUITA (Petipa), 247
PAQUITA PAS DE TROIS, see PAS DE TROIS CLASSIQUE
Paramount Pictures, 213
Paray, Paul, 131
Paris (Théâtre National de l'Opéra), 170, 345, 397, 413
Paris (Théâtre National de l'Opéra [Ballet]), 84, 94, 96, 141, 178, 195, 232, 236, 240, 244, 246, 247, 265, 277, 288, 314, 316, 317, 331, 358, 389, 392, 394, 397, 400, 410
PAS DE DEUX (da Costa)+, 95
PAS DE DEUX (Glazounov), 33
PAS DE DEUX (Kreisler), 22
PAS DE DEUX (Minkus, from Don Quixote), see DON QUIXOTE PAS DE DEUX
Pas de Deux (Tschaikovsky; CHARLES B. COCHRAN'S 1930 REVUE), 99
PAS DE DEUX (Tschaikovsky, from The Sleeping Beauty), 225
PAS DE DEUX (Tschaikovsky, from Swan Lake)+, 331
PAS DE DEUX (Tschaikovsky, from Swan Lake: BLACK SWAN), see SWAN LAKE (BLACK SWAN) PAS DE DEUX
PAS DE DEUX—BLUES (Duke), 189
PAS DE DEUX: LA SOURCE (Delibes), see LA SOURCE

PAS DE DEUX AND DIVERTISSEMENT (Delibes), 273, 350, 364
Pas de Deux from Raymonda (Glazounov), see RAYMONDA
PAS DE DEUX ROMANTIQUE (Weber), 268
PAS DE DIX (Glazounov), 233, 309, 339
PAS DE TROIS (Glinka)+, 307
PAS DE TROIS (Minkus), see PAS DE TROIS CLASSIQUE
PAS DE TROIS CLASSIQUE (Minkus)+, 247, 276
PAS DE TROIS FOR PIANO AND TWO DANCERS (Chanler), 203
Pasetti, Otto, 136
LA PASTORALE (Auric), 62, 409
Patrice, Gloria, 280
PATRIE (Paladilhe), 118
Patterson, Yvonne, 153, 165, 184
Paul, Mimi, 352, 358, 359
Le Pauvre Pierre (Schumann; LES AMOURS DU POÈTE), 110
PAVANE (Ravel), 393
Le Pavillon d'Armide (Fokine), 33
Pavloff, Michel, 64
Pavlova, Anna, 83
Pavlova Company, 83
PBS (Public Broadcasting Service), 48, 84, 94, 195, 235, 236, 242, 273, 285, 302, 312, 314, 316, 331, 343, 346, 347, 351, 358, 369, 374, 387, 390, 394, 398, 400, 407, 416
Peacock, Ada, 99
Peck, Leslie, 404
Pedersen, Edel, 103, 106
Pelletier, Wilfred, 160, 165, 167, 169, 179
Pengelly, Jeanne, 170
Pennsylvania Ballet, 141, 195, 236, 240, 273, 288, 302, 307, 309, 312, 314, 315, 333, 339
Peretti, 96
Performing Arts Foundation Dance Ensemble, see Huntington Dance Ensemble

Pergolesi, Giovanni Battista, 108, 379
LA PÉRICHOLE (Offenbach), 128
Perry, Douglas, 175
PERSÉPHONE (Stravinsky)+, 424
Perugini, Giulio, 297
Pessina, Carlos, 205
Peters, Albert, 136
Peters, Delia, 392, 422
Petersen, Storm, 102, 103
Petina, Irra, 219
Petipa, Marius, 6, 16, 65, 75, 152, 194,
    233, 247, 259, 262, 309, 339, 351, 367,
    384, 387, 404
Petroff, Paul, 192, 222
Petrograd Drama Theater, 26
Petrograd Theater (Ballet) School, 1, 2,
    4, 6, 7
Petrov, 29
Petrov, Pavel, 3
Petrova, Vera, 64, 67, 87, 90, 92
Petrushenko, 27
Petry, Gedda, 175
Pevsner, Antoine, 72
Philippines (Cultural Center of the
    Philippines Dance Company), 293,
    309
Phillpotts, Eden, 280
PIANO CONCERTO NO. 2, see BALLET
    IMPERIAL
Piccadilly, 1830 (Novello; CHARLES B.
    COCHRAN'S 1930 REVUE), 99
Pickert, Rolly, 175
Pierce, Billy, 108
Pierce, Johnny, 175
Piersant, Salvador, 195
Pierson, Arthur, 217
Pilarre, Susan, 368, 392, 400
Pinza, Ezio, 172
Piotrovsky, Adrian, 27
PIQUE DAME (Tschaikovsky), 210
Pistoni, Mario, 297, 299
PITHOPRAKTA, see METASTASEIS &
    PITHOPRAKTA
Pittsburgh Ballet Theatre, 94, 309

PIZZICATO POLKA (Delibes), 36
Plasson, Michel, 397
Platt, Marc, 201
Playhouse 90 (CBS), 302
Plummer, Christopher, 308
POÈME (Fibich), 4
Pogany, Willy, 172
POKER GAME (Stravinsky), see THE CARD
    PARTY
Polacheck, Charles, 311
Polignac, Princesse Edmond de, 237
Politiken, 105
POLKA (Rachmaninoff), 23
POLKA GROTESQUE (composer
    unknown), 83
POLKA MÉLANCOLIQUE (Rubinstein), 50,
    51
Pollock, Benjamin, 64, 351, 401
Ponchielli, Amilcare, 87, 174
Pons, George, 182
Pons, Helene, 175, 183, 188
Pons, Helene, Studio, see Helene Pons
    Studio
Pons, Lily, 172
Ponselle, Rosa, 155
Poole, David, 270
Pope, Arthur Upham, 332
Popwell, Albert, 305
Porcher, Nananne, 315-318, 321
Poretta, Frank, 322, 335
Porter, Cole, 91, 385
Porterat, Maurice, 109
Portinari, Candido, 141, 193
Potteiger, Jack, 149
Poulenc, Francis, 98
Poulsen, Ulla, 100-102, 105, 106
Powell, Dawn, 201
Preisser, Cherry, 162
Preisser, June, 162
Premice, Josephine, 305
Price, Leontyne, 311
Prince George's Ballet (Maryland), 302,
    318
PRINCE IGOR (Borodin), 104, 383

PRINCESS AURORA (Tschaikovsky), 259; *see also The Sleeping Beauty*
Princeton Ballet (New Jersey), 233, 318, 366
Principal Dancers of the Russian State Ballet, 1-3, 6, 10-13, 25, 32, 34
Prinz, John, 352, 358, 364, 366
PRODIGAL SON (Prokofiev), *see* LE FILS PRODIGUE
Producing Company of the School of American Ballet, 141, 142, 146, 149; *see also* New York City Ballet
Prokofiev, Sergei, 74, 94, 212, 267
Prokovsky, André, 350, 354
LE PROPHÈTE (Meyerbeer), 113
Proust, Marcel, 412
Pruna, Pedro, 62, 64
Puccini, Giacomo, 56, 68, 120, 161
Pugni, Cesare, 363
PULCINELLA (Stravinsky)+, 35, **52**, **379**
Puleo, Michael, 410
Purcell, Henry, 410, 411
Pushkin, Alexander, 172, 341, 365
THE QUEEN OF SPADES (Tschaikovsky), *see* PIQUE DAME
Quelvée, 96
Rabaud, Henri, 179, 204
Rabiroff, Jacques, 201
Rachmaninoff, Sergei, 22, 23, 32, 83, 327
Radlov, Sergei, 27
RAGTIME (Stravinsky), 3, 52
RAGTIME (I) (Stravinsky), 336
RAGTIME (II) (Stravinsky), 336, 355, **356**
Rakeman, Chester, Studios, *see* Chester Rakeman Studios
THE RAKE'S PROGRESS (Stravinsky), 295
Ralov, Børge, 103, 106
Rambert, Marie, *see* Ballet Club; Ballet Rambert
Randall, Carl, 188
Rapp, Richard, 330, 352, 368
Rappaport, V. R., 26
RAPSODIE ESPAGNOLE (Ravel), 396

Rasmussen, Angeline, 335
Rasmussen, Ragnhild, 101, 103
Ratoff, Gregory, 191
Ravel, Maurice, 20, 47, 48, 235, 277, 389-396, 416
Ravel Festival, *see* New York City Ballet Ravel Festival
RAYMONDA (Glazounov)+, **233**, 309, 339, 384
Raymonda Act III, see RAYMONDA
Raymonda Divertissements, see RAYMONDA
Raymonda Pas de Dix, see PAS DE DIX
Raymonda Variations, see PAS DE DIX; RAYMONDA; VALSES ET VARIATIONS
Reader, Ralph, 99
Reardon, John, 311, 342
Redding, Joseph, 44, 125
Redman, Don, 305
Redpath, Christine, 387, 390
Reed, Janet, 222, 259, 265, 268, 272, 275, 282, 294, 302-304
Reggio Emilia (A.T.E.R. [Ballet]), 312, 316, 333
Reiman, Elise, 141, 144, 146, 149, 153, 154, 165, 173, 174, 176, 231, 235, 236, 238, 244
Reiner, Fritz, 295
Reinhardt, Max, 206
THE RELUCTANT KING (Chabrier), *see* LE ROI MALGRÉ LUI
REMINISCENCE (Godard), 141, **144**
RENARD (Stravinsky), 237
Renault, Michel, 240
Renoir, Auguste, 133
REQUIEM CANTICLES (Stravinsky), 362
Respighi, Ottorino, 103
RESURGENCE (Mozart), 231
Reville, Ltd., 99, 108
Rhodes, Erik, 186
Riabouchinska, Tatiana, 132
Rice, Sunny, 218
Rich, Doris, 257
Richardson, David, 392

Richardson, Jack, 342
Richmond, Brad, 424
Richmond Ballet (Virginia), 366
Rickard, Gwen, 249
Rieti, Vittorio, 53, 93, 129, 222, 232, 243, 323, 328
Rigaud, George, 229
RIGOLETTO (Verdi), 88, 121, 156, 226
Rimsky-Korsakov, Andrei, 264
Rimsky-Korsakov, Nicolai, 24, 31, 102, 107, 172, 218
Ringling Brothers and Barnum & Bailey Circus, 202
Rio de Janeiro (Teatro Municipal [Ballet]), 247
Riseley, Cynthia, 242
Ritz, Roger, 240
Ritz Brothers, 185
Rivas, Elena de, 141, 144, 149
Rivers, Max, 91
RKO Radio, 185
Robbins, Jerome, 264, 265, 267, 269, 283, 286, 302, 379, 409, 410, 420
Robert Joffrey Ballet; Robert Joffrey Theatre Ballet, see Joffrey Ballet
ROBERT SCHUMANN'S 'DAVIDS-BÜNDLERTÄNZE'+, 415
Robert W. Bergman Studios, Inc., 175, 201, 229
Roberts, Ben, 216, 218
Robier, Jean, 247
Robinson, Robert, 342
Rockefeller, Nelson A., 193
Rockefeller Foundation, 316
Rodgers, Richard, 166, 175, 182, 183, 186, 361, 402
Rodham, Robert, 352
Rogers, Charles R., 201
LE ROI MALGRÉ LUI (Chabrier), 403
ROMA (Bizet), 306, 376
ROMANCE (Rubinstein), see LA NUIT
Romanoff, Dimitri, 234
ROMANZA (Balanchine), 8
Rome, Stewart, 97

Rome Opera Ballet (Teatro dell'Opera di Roma [Ballet]), 84, 141, 236, 240
ROMEO AND JULIET (Lambert), 61
ROMEO AND JULIET (Shakespeare), 278, 325
Romeo and Juliet Ballet (Gershwin; GOLDWYN FOLLIES), 185
ROMÉO ET JULIETTE (Gounod), 86, 124, 180
LA RONDINE (Puccini), 56, 161
Roos, William, 280
Root, Lynn, 190
Rosa, Tomás Santa, see Santa Rosa, Tomás
ROSALINDA (J. Strauss II), 206
ROSENDRØMMEN (Weber), see LE SPECTRE DE LA ROSE
Rosenstock, Joseph, 251
Rosenthal, Jean, 141, 206, 235-238, 241, 244, 246, 250, 254, 264, 267, 271, 272, 274, 276, 277, 279, 282-290, 292, 293, 301-310, 312-314, 320
Rosenthal, Manuel, 390, 403, 416
Ross, Adrian, 216
Ross, Bertram, 324
Ross, Herbert, 305
Rossini, Gioacchino, 103, 196
Rostova, Lubov, 129, 201
Roth, Anna, 107
Rotov, Alex, 218
Rouault, Georges, 94, 267
Rouché, Jacques, 96
Roudenko, Lubov, 216
Rousseau, Marcel Samuel, see Samuel-Rousseau, Marcel
Royal, Ted, 218, 249, 305
Royal Ballet, 84, 94, 141, 194, 236, 316, 331, 335, 347, 382; see also Sadler's Wells Ballet, Royal Ballet Touring company
Royal Ballet Touring company, 84, 94, 195, 236, 270, 312; see also Royal Ballet, Sadler's Wells Ballet

Royal Danish Ballet (Den Kongelige Danske Ballet), 53, 84, 94, 100-104, 106, 141, 195, 232, 236, 240, 265, 314, 331, 333
Royal Flemish Ballet (Koninklijk Ballet Van Vlaanderen), 84, 312
Royal Swedish Ballet (Kungliga Teaterns Balett), 141, 236, 240, 277, 312
Royal Winnipeg Ballet (Canada), 273, 307, 309
Royston, Roy, 99
Ruanova, Maria, 205
RUBIES (Stravinsky), see JEWELS
Rubinstein, Anton, 1, 14, 37, 42, 51
Rubinstein, Ida, 178, 271, 424
Ruchs, Erich, 136
Rudley, Peter, 259
RUSLAN UND LUDMILLA (Glinka), 365
Russell, Francia, 330, 332
Russo, James, 280
Ruzdak, Vladimir, 341
Rykhliakov, 24, 27
Ryskind, Morrie, 188, 201
S.O.D.R.E. [Ballet], see Uruguay (S.O.D.R.E. [Ballet])
Sabata, Victor de, 42, 44, 48, 54, 56, 67, 68, 89
Sabo, Rozsika, 222
Sackett, Francis, 392
Sadler's Wells Ballet, 194, 382; see also Royal Ballet, Royal Ballet Touring company
Sadler's Wells Royal Ballet; Sadler's Wells Theatre Ballet, see Royal Ballet Touring company
Sadoff, Simon, 194, 200
Saëns, Camille Saint, see Saint-Saëns, Camille
SAILOR'S HORNPIPE (traditional), see MATELOTTE
Saint-Bonnet, Jeanne, 109
Saint-Saëns, Camille, 16, 17, 66, 116, 171, 218, 228, 263

St. Thomas Episcopal Church Boys Choir (New York City), 302
Saklin, Peter, 352
Sala, Oskar, 338
Saland, Stephanie, 390, 407, 413, 420
Sale, Mary, 145, 153
Salgado, Clovis, see Belo Horizonte (Clovis Salgado Foundation, Brazil [Ballet])
Sallinger, Conrad, 162
Salute to Cole (Villella), 385
Salute to Italy, 333
Salzer, Gene, 166, 175, 182
Samosud, S. A., 24
SAMSON ET DALILA (Saint-Saëns), 66, 116, 171, 226, 228
Samuel-Rousseau, Marcel, 41
San Diego Ballet, 195, 282
San Francisco Ballet, 84, 141, 195, 232, 236, 237, 240, 282, 285, 288, 303, 309, 312, 314, 316, 318, 322, 331, 364
San Francisco Civic Light Opera, 219
San Juan (Ballets de San Juan), 84, 195, 232, 233, 247, 288, 293
SANSÓN Y DALILA (Saint-Saëns), see SAMSON ET DALILA
Santa Rosa, Tomás, 84, 198
Sanvel, 82
São Paulo (Halina Biernacka Ballet, renamed São Paulo Chamber Ballet), 84, 205
Saratoga Performing Arts Center, 387, 398
SARCASM (Prokofiev), 73, 74
Sargent, Kaye, 302
Sarnoff, Dorothy, 206
Satie, Erik, 63
Sauguet, Henri, 72, 99, 137
Savage, Archie, 190
Savino, Domenico, 190, 201
Savo, Jimmy, 183, 217, 261
La Scala (Teatro alla Scala, Milan [Ballet]), 84, 141, 178, 194, 195, 236,

240, 246, 265, 285, 288, 297-299, 312,
331
La Scala (Teatro alla Scala, Milan
[Opera]), 297-299
Scaramouche: An Impression of the
Commedia dell'Arte (April; CHARLES
B. COCHRAN'S 1931 REVUE), 108
Scarlatti, 83
Scenic Studios, 288
Schaufuss, Peter, 396, 398, 404
SCHÉHÉRAZADE (Rimsky-Korsakov),
101, 102
Scheibe, Karl, 135
Schervashidze, A., Prince, 53, 61-64, 84,
94, 129-131
SCHERZO À LA RUSSE (Stravinsky),
377
Schikaneder, Emanuel, 311
Schiøler, Victor, 100-104, 106
Schippers, Thomas, 388
DER SCHLEIER DER PIERRETTE
(Schnitzler/Dohnanyi), 15
Schmidt, Georg Philipp, 138
Schnitzler, Arthur, 15
SCHÖN ROSMARIN (Kreisler), 2
Schoenberg, Arnold, 301, 354
School of American Ballet, 141, 142,
145, 146, 149, 195, 215, 226-228, 230,
231, 241, 245, 274, 302, 340, 351, 352,
379, 380, 387, 403, 410, 411, 416-418,
422
School of American Ballet Gala
Benefit, 1980, 413
School of American Ballet Producing
Company, see Producing Company
of the School of American Ballet
Schorer, Suki, 328, 332, 339, 340,
350-352, 358, 366
Schouko, Vladimir A., 26
Schubert, Franz, 92, 138, 143, 197, 218
Schuller, Gunther, 337
Schultz, Carl, 365
Schultz, Ray, 184
Schumann, Robert, 3, 110, 218, 415

Schumann, Wilfried, 345
Scorer, Betty, 107
SCOTCH SYMPHONY (Mendelssohn)+, 288
Scott, Dorothy, 259
Scott, Norman, 295
Scottish Rhapsody (Berners; SIR OSWALD
STOLL'S VARIETY SHOWS), 107
Scotto, Marc-César, 45, 46, 52, 61, 72,
76, 80, 90, 92, 93, 110, 115, 118, 129,
130, 132
Scouarnec, Claudette, 397
Scovotti, Jeanette, 365
Scriabin, Alexander, 3, 30, 50, 405
Seabra, Nelson, 201
Second International Dance Festival,
see North American International
Dance Festival of Stars
Segal, Vivienne, 182
Segarra, Ramon, 342
Seibert, Wallace, 259
Seiler, Ursula, 175
Seligmann, Kurt, 236
Selwyn, Arch, 91
Semanova, Tatiana, 109
SENTIMENTAL COLLOQUY (Bowles), 223
Sentimental Weather (Duke; ZIEGFELD
FOLLIES: 1936 EDITION), 162
LES SEPT PÉCHÉS CAPITAUX (Brecht/
Weill), 134, 136, 322
SERENADE (Tschaikovsky)+, 141, 167,
193, 240, 254
A Serenade of Music and Dance, 313
SERENATA (Tschaikovsky), see SERENADE
SERENATA: 'MAGIC' (Mozart), 164
Serge Lifar and His Russian Ballets,
72
Servicio Oficial de Difusión Radio
Eléctrica [Ballet], see Uruguay
(S.O.D.R.E. [Ballet])
THE SEVEN DEADLY SINS (Weill/
Brecht), see LES SEPT PÉCHÉS
CAPITAUX
Seven Lively Arts (CBS), 302
Severinsen, 'Doc,' 370

Sextant, Inc., 342
Seymour, Stephen, 213
Shabelevsky, Yurek, 130-132, 204, 205
Shafer, Robert, 219
Shakespeare, William, 183, 224, 278, 308, 319, 320, 325, 326, 340, 342
Shaporin, Yuri, 26
Sharaff, Irene, 166, 177, 183, 275, 361, 371
Shaw, George Bernard, 26
Shcherbakov, N. A., 15
Shea, Mary Jane, 195
SHÉHÉRAZADE (Ravel), 391
Sheldon, Sidney, 216, 218
Sherman, Hiram, 319, 325
Sherman, Louise, 335
Shiryayev, 27
Shubert, Lee, 162
Shubert Brothers, 187
Shuisky, 24
Sibelius, Jean, 10
Sidimus, Joysanne, 342
Sidorenko, Tamara, 137, 139
Sieveling, Earle, 349, 352, 361, 368
Sills, Bettijane, 368, 376
Siloti, Alexander, 194, 349, 382
Silverstein, Joseph, 374
Simmons, Stanley, 394
Simon, Victoria, 339
Sims, 95
Sinclair, Robert, 175
SIOR TODÉRO BRONTOLON (Malipiero), 79
SIR OSWALD STOLL'S VARIETY SHOWS, 107
Sistrom, Joseph, 213
Sitwell, Sacheverell, 64
SIX WALTZES (Rieti), see WALTZ ACADEMY
16 Delightful Balanchine Girls 16, see Balanchine Ballet
A Skit on Marlene Dietrich in the Film 'The Blue Angel' (Lerner/Hollander; SIR OSWALD STOLL'S VARIETY SHOWS), 107

SLAUGHTER ON TENTH AVENUE (Rodgers) 166, 361
Slavianinov, Rostislav, 12, 13, 21
Slavinsky, Thadée, 40, 46, 58, 61, 62, 83
The Sleeping Beauty: ARIADNE AND HER BROTHERS from AURORA'S WEDDING (Tschaikovsky), 65
THE SLEEPING BEAUTY: AURORA'S SOLO, VISION SCENE (Tschaikovsky), 404
The Sleeping Beauty: GARLAND DANCE (Tschaikovsky), 418
The Sleeping Beauty: PAS DE DEUX (Tschaikovsky), 225
The Sleeping Beauty: PRINCESS AURORA (Tschaikovsky), 259
The Sleeping Beauty: VARIATION from AURORA'S WEDDING (Tschaikovsky), 281
Slezak, Walter, 182
Slonimsky, Yuri, 1, 12, 18
Smallens, Alexander, 164, 223
Smetana, Bedřich, 167
Smith, Gregg, 342
Smith, Gregg, Singers, see Gregg Smith Singers
Smith, Oliver, 206, 222
Smith, Queenie, 186
Smithers, William, 278, 325
Smolyakov, I. A., 14
Sobeka, see Kochno, Boris
Sobotka, Ruth, 261, 283
Sociedad Pro-Arte Musical (Cuba), 84
Sokoloff, Vladimir, 257
Sokolova, Lydia, 52, 56, 61, 64, 70
Solly, Doris Jane, 184
Sologub, Vladimir, Count, 93
Solov, Zachary, 242
LA SOMNAMBULE (Rieti), see THE NIGHT SHADOW
SONATA (Stravinsky), 372
SONATINE (Ravel), 389
SONG OF NORWAY (Grieg/Wright/ Forrest), 219

THE SONG OF THE NIGHTINGALE (Stravinsky), see LE CHANT DU ROSSIGNOL

LES SONGES (Milhaud), 134, **135**, 145, 196

LA SONNAMBULA (Rieti), see THE NIGHT SHADOW

Sonne, Doris, 107

Sosso, Jean-Marie, 367

Soudeikina, Vera, 94

Soudeikine, Sergei, 144

Soulie, Alice, 109

Sour, Robert, 229

LA SOURCE (Delibes), 350, 364

Sousa, John Philip, 318

Sovey, Raymond, 175

SPANISH DANCE (Glazounov), 16, 18

Spearman, Rawn, 305

Le Spectre de la Rose (Fokine), 34

LE SPECTRE DE LA ROSE (Weber), 105

THE SPELLBOUND CHILD (Ravel), see L'ENFANT ET LES SORTILÈGES

Spessivtseva, Olga, 72, 75, 96

Spialek, Hans, 162, 166, 175, 182-184, 187, 218, 249

Spohn, Marjorie, 392, 400

Spoleto Festival U. S. A., Charleston, South Carolina, 405

SQUARE DANCE (Vivaldi/Corelli)+, 315

Stafford, Frederick, 107

Stange, Stanislaus, 239

Stanley, Robert, 278

STAR SPANGLED RHYTHM (film), 213

Starbuck, James, 216

STARS AND STRIPES (Sousa)+, **318**, 409

Stars of American Ballet, 309, 366

State of Alabama Ballet, see Alabama (State of Alabama Ballet)

State Theater of Opera and Ballet (Petrograd/Leningrad), 22, 25, 33; see also Maryinsky Theater, Petrograd Theater (Ballet) School

Statues (Mendelssohn; SIR OSWALD STOLL'S VARIETY SHOWS), 107

THE STEADFAST TIN SOLDIER (Bizet), 310, 398

Stealing Through (Byng/Gideon; CHARLES B. COCHRAN'S 1931 REVUE), 108

Steele, Michael, 361

Steiman, Michel, 77-79, 81, 87, 88, 121, 123, 125, 127, 128

Stein, Horst, 341

Stellman, Maxine, 170

Stepanova, Irène, 130

Stevenson, Robert, 268

Stiedry, Fritz, 211

Still, William Grant, 258

Stokowski, Leopold, 215, 300

Stoll, Dennis, 107

Stoll, Oswald, Sir, 107

Stolz, Robert, 216, 229

Stora Teaterns Balett, Sweden, see Gothenburg (Stora Teaterns Balett, Sweden)

Stowell, Kent, 352, 357

Strakhova, Natalie, 129, 131

Strasbourg (Ballet de l'Opéra du Rhin), 236

Straus, Oscar, 239

Strauss, Johann, the Younger, 3, 107, 114, 169, 199, 206, 229, 294, 406

Strauss, Richard, 3, 106, 131, 221, 283, 406, 410, 414

Stravinsky, Igor, 3, 35, 52, 84, 176-178, 192, 198, 202, 220, 230, 237, 245, 246, 264, 271, 275, 284, 295, 316, 334, 336, 342, 344, 353, 355, 356, 358, 362, 372-381, 421-425

Stravinsky, Vera, see Soudeikina, Vera

Stravinsky Centennial Celebration, see New York City Ballet Stravinsky Centennial Celebration

Stravinsky Festival (1937), see American Ballet Stravinsky Festival

Stravinsky Festival (1972), see New York City Ballet Stravinsky Festival

STRAVINSKY VIOLIN CONCERTO, *see*
VIOLIN CONCERTO
Striga, Marie, 177, 178
Stroheim, Erich von, 191
Stuart, Helen, 154
Stuckmann, Eugene, 224
Studio Alliance, 176, 183, 184, 190, 217,
239, 249, 278, 295
Stukolkina, Nina, 16, 18, 20
Stuttgart (Ballett der Württember-
gischen Staatsoper), 84, 240, 277,
312, 316
Suárez, Olga, 184, 196, 198-200
Subber, Saint, 305
SUITE NO. 3 (Tschaikovsky), 242, **369**
SUITES DE DANSE (Glinka), 132
Sumner, Carol, 330, 339, 351, 352, 376,
392
Surridge, James, 162
Svetlova, Marina, 192
Svobodina, Gertrude, 220, 233
SWAN LAKE (Tschaikovsky)[+], 75, 191,
262, **285**, 331, 367
Swan Lake: PAS DE DEUX (Tschaikovsky),
331
SWAN LAKE (BLACK SWAN) PAS DE DEUX
(Tschaikovsky), 262
Swarowsky, Hans, 345
Swenson, Inga, 320, 325
Swift, Kay, 142
Les Sylphides (Fokine), 226
Sylva, B. G. De, *see* De Sylva, B. G.
SYLVIA: PAS DE DEUX (Delibes)[+], **273**, 350,
387
SYMPHONIE (Gounod), *see* GOUNOD
SYMPHONY
SYMPHONIE CONCERTANTE (Mozart)[+],
230, **241**, 245, 314
SYMPHONY IN C (Bizet), *see* LE PALAIS
DE CRISTAL
SYMPHONY IN THREE MOVEMENTS
(Stravinsky), 373
SYMPHONY NO. 6—PATHÉTIQUE
(Tschaikovsky), 420

SYMPHONY OF PSALMS (Stravinsky), 381
Syracuse Ballet Theatre, 307
Sze, Yi-kwei, 311
Szyfer, J.-E., 96
T. B. McDonald Construction
Company, 183, 322
THE TALES OF HOFFMANN (Offenbach), *see*
LES CONTES D'HOFFMANN
Talin, Nikita, 220, 221, 233
Tallchief, Maria, 220, 221, 232, 233,
241, 244, 246, 248, 255, 259, 262, 264,
265, 267, 269, 271, 273, 274, 276, 279,
282, 284-286, 288, 290, 302, 309, 312,
317, 329
Tallchief, Marjorie, 247
Taller Coreográfico (Mexico), 195
Tamara, *see* Fowler and Tamara
Tango (composer unknown; SIR
OSWALD STOLL'S VARIETY SHOWS), 107
TANGO (Stravinsky), 421
Tanner, Eugene, 310
TANNHÄUSER (Wagner), 111, 154
Tanning, Dorothea, 232, 287
Taper, Bernard, 28
TARANTELLA (Gottschalk)[+], 347
Taras, John, 222, 232, 237, 238, 244,
328, 329, 336, 418, 424
Taylor, Paul, 324
Tchelitchew, Pavel, 138, 143, 157, 164,
170, 192, 197, 203-205, 236
Tcherepnine, Nicolas, 33
Tcherkas, Constantin, 48, 61, 64, 77, 85,
87, 99
Tchernicheva, Lubov, 42, 43, 46, 57,
60, 64, 66, 68, 84, 85, 87
Tchinarova, Tamara, 137
Teatro alla Scala, Milan, *see* La Scala
(Teatro alla Scala)
Teatro Argentino, *see* La Plata (Teatro
Argentino [Ballet])
Teatro Colón, *see* Colón (Teatro
Colón)
Teatro Comunale (Bologna), *see*
Bologna (Teatro Comunale [Ballet])

Teatro Comunale (Florence), *see* Florence (Teatro Comunale [Ballet])

Teatro dell'Opera di Roma, *see* Rome Opera Ballet

Teatro Massimo, *see* Palermo (Teatro Massimo [Ballet])

Teatro Massimo Bellini, *see* Catania (Teatro Massimo Bellini [Ballet])

Teatro Municipal, *see* Rio de Janeiro (Teatro Municipal [Ballet])

Teatro Regio, *see* Turin (Teatro Regio [Ballet])

Teatro San Carlo, *see* Naples (Teatro San Carlo [Ballet])

Teicher, Louis, 219

THE TEMPEST (Shakespeare), 224, 308

TEMPO DI VALSE (Tschaikovsky), 418

Tennis, Elenore, 175

Tennis (Ellis; CHARLES B. COCHRAN'S 1930 REVUE), 99

Les Tentations de la Bergère (Nijinska), 85

Ter-Arutunian, Rouben, 194, 285, 302, 322, 342, 345, 349, 351, 362, 380, 381, 384, 386, 387, 401, 406, 409, 410, 412, 414, 415, 417, 418, 420, 422

Terriss, Norma, 184

Terry, Emilio, 139

THAÏS (Massenet), 39

Théâtre de Monte-Carlo, *see* Monte Carlo (Théâtre de Monte-Carlo)

Théâtre National de l'Opéra, *see* Paris (Théâtre National de l'Opéra)

Theatrical Costume Company, 178

Thebom, Blanche, 295

THEME AND VARIATIONS (Tschaikovsky)+, **242**, 330

Thom, Brigitte, 400, 413

Thomas, Ambroise, 59, 60, 158

Thomas, Brandon, 249

Thomas, Dylan, 342

Thomas, Richard, 310

Thompson, Fred, 201

Thompson, Sada, 326

Thompson, Woodman, 242

Thomson, Virgil, 287

Through the Crystal Ball (CBS), 261

Tiller, John, Girls, *see* John Tiller Girls

Tiuntina, L. M., 16

Tobias, Roy, 269, 282, 302, 306, 309, 310, 314, 316, 330

Tofts, 64

Tokyo Ballet, 240

Tokyo Ballet Geikijo, 94, 141

Toledo Ballet (Ohio), 366

Toller, Ernst, 27

Tomasson, Helgi, 373, 376, 387, 401, 406

LE TOMBEAU DE COUPERIN (Ravel), 392

Tomin, Jorge, 205

Tomlinson, Mel, 424

Tompkins, Beatrice, 199, 236, 238, 244, 246, 264, 269, 271, 283

Tone, Franchot, 213

Tonight Show orchestra, 370

Toumanova, Tamara, 118, 120, 125, 129-132, 134, 135, 137, 192, 239A, 240, 263

TRANSCENDENCE (Liszt), 141, **146**

LA TRAVIATA (Verdi), 67, 123, 150, 252

Trecu, Pirmin, 270

DEN TREKANTEDE HAT (Falla), *see* LE TRICORNE

Triangle Scenic Studio, 166, 175, 177, 188, 280, 283, 285

TRICOLORE (Auric), **409**, 412

LE TRICORNE (Falla), 101

LE TRIOMPHE DE NEPTUNE (Berners), *see* THE TRIUMPH OF NEPTUNE

Tripp, Paul, 342

THE TRIUMPH OF BACCHUS AND ARIADNE (Rieti), 243

THE TRIUMPH OF NEPTUNE (Berners), 64

TROIS VALSES ROMANTIQUES (Chabrier), 129, **357**

TROUBLED ISLAND (Still), 258

TRUMPET CONCERTO (Haydn), 270

T'Sani, Nolan, 395, 396

Tschaikovsky, Peter Ilyitch, 22, 65, 75, 99, 107, 134, 141, 149, 178, 191, 193, 194, 210, 218, 225, 242, 254, 256, 259,

261, 262, 271, 281, 285, 302, 312, 321, 330, 331, 341, 346, 349, 358, 367, 369, 382, 404, 417-420

Tschaikovsky Festival, *see* New York City Ballet Tschaikovsky Festival

Tschaikovsky Memorial Tokyo Ballet, *see* Tokyo Ballet

TSCHAIKOVSKY PAS DE DEUX, *see* PAS DE DEUX (Tschaikovsky, from *Swan Lake*)

TSCHAIKOVSKY PIANO CONCERTO NO. 2, *see* BALLET IMPERIAL

TSCHAIKOVSKY SUITE NO. 3, *see* SUITE NO. 3

Tucker, Bobby, 217

Tudor, Antony, 234, 317, 339

Tugend, Harry, 213

Tulsa Ballet Theatre, 129, 195, 233, 312

Tunberg, Karl, 191

TURANDOT (Puccini), 68, 120

Turin (Teatro Regio [Ballet]), 84, 232

Turner, John Hastings, 91

Turner, Martin, 218, 237

Turner, Martin, Studios, *see* Martin Turner Studios

Turner Scenic Construction Company, 166, 175, 182, 184

The Turning Point (film), 331

Tversky, 29

Twentieth-Century Fox, 191, 331

TYL ULENSPIEGEL (R. Strauss), 283

Tyler, Jeanne, 201

Tyler, Veronica, 340

Tyven, Gertrude, *see* Svobodina, Gertrude

TZIGANE (Ravel)[+], 394

U. S. Terpsichore (New York City), 318, 331, 366

UNE NUIT À VENISE (J. Strauss II), *see* EINE NACHT IN VENEDIG

UNION JACK (Kay), 332, **401**, 409

United Artists, 185

Upshaw, William, 237

Urban, Ria, 345

Uruguay (S.O.D.R.E. [Ballet]), 84, 205, 247

Uspenskaya, 24

Utah Civic Ballet, 141, 195; *see also* Ballet West

Utrillo, Maurice, 53

Vadimova, Dora, 77

Vail Scenic Construction Company, 188, 201, 206, 229

Valency, Maurice, 257

Valentina, 172

Valois, Ninette de, 270

LA VALSE (Ravel)[+], 277

VALSE CAPRICE (Rubinstein), 14, 37

VALSE FANTAISIE (Glinka)[+], 107, 293, 359, 366

Valse-Scherzo (J. d'Amboise), 418

VALSE TRISTE (Sibelius)[+], 10

LES VALSES DE BEETHOVEN, 134, 139

VALSES ET VARIATIONS (Glazounov)[+], 233, 309, **339**

Van Ackerman Scenic Studios, 187

Vance, Norma, 259

Van Cleave, Nathan, 190, 217

Van Dyk, Peter, 345

Vane, Daphne, 152, 154, 160, 161, 165, 170, 171, 173, 176, 187

Vanhaiden, Henni, 345

Van Loon, Willem, 162

Van Mill, Arnold, 341

Vanni, Helen, 311

Varden, Evelyn, 278

Vardi, Emanuel, 245

VARIATION (Delibes), *see* PIZZICATO POLKA

VARIATIONS (Stravinsky), 353

Variations de Ballet (L. Christensen), 309

VARIATIONS FOR ORCHESTRA (Stravinsky)[+], 353, 425

VARIATIONS FROM DON SEBASTIAN (Donizetti)[+], 333

VARIATIONS POUR UNE PORTE ET UN SOUPIR (Henry), 386

Varieties en Fête, 107
The Varsity Eight, 162
Vaszary, John, 182
Vauges, Gloria, 302
Vazquez, Roland, 309, 310, 340
Vega, Leticia de la, 204
Velden, Kaj, 218
VENISE (Gunsbourg), 78
Verchinina, Nina, 132
Verdi, Giuseppe, 67, 80, 88, 121, 123, 126, 150, 152, 156, 211, 226, 252, 255, 407
Verdy, Violette, 324, 330-332, 335, 338, 340, 358, 359, 364, 379, 380, 389
Verea, Lisette, 216
Verlaine, Paul, 223
Vernon, Michael, 404
Veronica, 187
DIE VERSCHWORENEN (Schubert), 92
Vialet, Georgette, 48, 61, 110
LA VIE PARISIENNE (Offenbach), 209
Vienna (Ballett der Wiener Staatsoper), 84, 141, 236, 240, 247, 277, 314, 335
VIENNA WALTZES (J. Strauss II/Lehár/R. Strauss)+, 406
Viganò, Salvatore, 96
Vilan, Demetrios, 166
Villella, Edward, 328-330, 332, 338, 340, 342, 343, 347, 351, 354, 358, 359, 363, 369, 373, 379, 385, 391, 402
Vilzak, Anatole, 109, 144, 150, 154, 155, 160, 167, 174
VIOLIN CONCERTO (Stravinsky)+, 192, **374**
Visconti, Alphonse, 48, 110
Vivaldi, Antonio, 315
Vivien, 27
Vlady, Lawrence, 302, 352
Voice of Firestone (ABC), 331
Volkoff, Chris, 216
Volkov, 29
Vollmar, Jocelyn, 259
von Dohnanyi, Ernest, *see* Dohnanyi, Ernest von

von Flotow, Friedrich, *see* Flotow, Friedrich von
von Hofmannsthal, Hugo, *see* Hofmannsthal, Hugo von
von Stroheim, Erich, *see* Stroheim, Erich von
von Weber, Carl Maria, *see* Weber, Carl Maria von
Vorobieva, Anna, 6
Voskovec, George, 224
Vosseler, Heidi, 141, 142, 154, 173, 183
Votipka, Thelma, 172
Votto, Antonino, 297, 298
Vroom, Lodewick, 206
Wagner, Richard, 77, 111, 154, 163, 218
WAKE UP AND DREAM! (Porter/Turner), 91
Walczak, Barbara, 272, 306, 309, 310, 316
Wald, Jerry, 186
Walker, Don, 162, 187, 280
Wallis, Hal B., 186
WALPURGISNACHT BALLET (Gounod)+, 397, **413**
Walser, Lloyd, 422, 424
Walters, Charles, 182
WALTZ (composer unknown), 9
WALTZ (Drigo), 6
WALTZ (Ravel), 16, **20**
WALTZ ACADEMY (Rieti), 222
WALTZ AND ADAGIO (Balanchine), **7**, 16
WALTZ AND VARIATIONS (Glazounov), *see* VALSES ET VARIATIONS
WALTZ FANTASY (Glinka), *see* VALSE FANTAISIE
Waltz Fantasy in Blue (Glinka; SIR OSWALD STOLL'S VARIETY SHOWS), 107
Waltz from Eugen Onegin, Act II (Taras), 418
WALTZ-SCHERZO (Tschaikovsky), 321
THE WALTZES OF BEETHOVEN, *see* LES VALSES DE BEETHOVEN

THE WANDERER (Schubert), *see*
L'ERRANTE
Warburg, Edward M. M., 141, 142,
177, 275
Warburg, Felix, 141, 145, 149
Ware, Sheryl, 407
Waring, Richard, 319, 320
Warner Brothers, 186
Warnick, Clay, 218
Warnow, Mark, 217
Warren, Gloria, 217
THE WARRIOR (Rachmaninoff), 327
Washington Ballet (Washington,
D. C.), 141, 195, 233, 288, 331
Water Nymph Ballet (Gershwin;
GOLDWYN FOLLIES), 185
Waters, Ethel, 190
Watkins, Franklin, 146
Watson, Douglas, 278
Watteau, Antoine, 85
Watts, Heather, 413-415
Watts, Jonathan, 309, 310, 316, 324,
333, 335
Weaver, Fritz, 308
Webb, 64
Webb, H. J., 64
Weber, Carl Maria von, 34, 71, 105,
218, 268, 289
Weber, Margrit, 344
Webern, Anton, 324
Webster, Margaret, 224
Weill, Kurt, 136, 322
Weiss, Florian, 82
Weiss, Robert, 373, 379, 387, 395, 407
Weissmuller, Don, 217
Welsh, Jane, 108
Werich, Jan, 224
Wescott, Marcy, 183
Weslow, William, 328, 330
West Australian Ballet Company, 312
West Indies (Duke; ZIEGFELD FOLLIES:
1936 EDITION), 162
Western Ballet, *see* Ballet of Los
Angeles

WESTERN SYMPHONY (Kay)+, 303
Westman, Nydia, 257
Weston, Ruth, 201
WETA (television station,
Washington, D. C.), 347
Wexler, Peter, 385
What Is This Thing Called Love? (Porter;
WAKE UP AND DREAM!), 91
WHAT'S UP (Loewe/Lerner/Pierson), 217
WHERE'S CHARLEY? (Loesser/Abbott),
249
Whistler, Rex, 99
White, Miles, 218
White, Nora, 220
Whitney, Dorothy, 308
Whitney, Fern, 222
WHO CARES? (Gershwin)+, 368
Wickwire, Nancy, 320, 325, 326
Wide World of Entertainment (ABC),
94
Wieck, Clara, 415
Wiener Staatsoper [Ballet], *see* Vienna
(Ballett der Wiener Staatsoper)
WIENER WALZER (J. Strauss II/Lehár/
R. Strauss), *see* VIENNA WALTZES
Wild, Harry, 270
Wilde, Patricia, 227, 233, 271, 275, 277,
285, 286, 288, 301, 303, 304, 307, 313-
315, 321, 323, 329, 339
Wilkins, Kenneth, 175
William H. Mensching Studios, 146
William Kellam Company, 216
Williams, Grant, 322
Williams, Joy, 233
Wilson, Dooley, 190
Wilson, Margaret, 362
Wilson, Mitzi, 335
Wilson, Sallie, 324
Wilson, Scott, 184
Wiman, Dwight Deere, 166, 175, 182,
184, 278
The Wind in the Willows (Carter/Ellis;
CHARLES B. COCHRAN'S 1930 REVUE), 99
Windt, Hal de, *see* de Windt, Hal

Windust, Bretaigne, 184
THE WINTER'S TALE (Shakespeare), 320
Winther-Jørgensen, Aage, 103
Winwood, Estelle, 257
Wisconsin Ballet, 84
Woizikowsky, Léon, 42, 53, 56, 60, 61, 68, 70, 78, 85, 87, 90, 93, 94, 111-114, 118, 120, 122, 129, 130, 132
Wolf-Israel, Eugenia, 26
Wolff, A., 204
Wolff, Catherine, 390, 416
Woloshin, Sid, 371
Wood, Christopher, 99
Wood-Hill, 274
Woolley, Monty, 166
Words without Music: A Surrealist Ballet (Duke; ZIEGFELD FOLLIES: 1936 EDITION), 162
Worth, Billie, 280
Wortham, Tomi, 283
Wright, Marilyn, 346
Wright, Robert, 219
WTTW (television station, Chicago), 331
Württembergische Staatsoper [Ballet], see Stuttgart (Ballett der Württembergischen Staatsoper)

Wyckoff, Evelyn, 201
Xenakis, Iannis, 360
Yazvinsky, Jean, 82
Youkine, A., 84, 93, 98
Young Ballet (Petrograd), 1, 4, 5-7, 11, 16-22, 28, 30-32, 35
Yourth, Lynda, 373, 375
Youskevitch, Igor, 234, 242, 259, 262
Yureneva, 27
Zagreb (Croatian National Theater, Balet Hrvatsko Narodno Kazalište), 141, 236
Zanuck, Darryl F., 191
Zarova, Irina, 192
DIE ZAUBERFLÖTE (Mozart)+, 311
ZIEGFELD FOLLIES: 1936 EDITION (Duke/Gershwin/Freedman)+, 162
Zimmerman, Jerry, 395
Zompakos, Stanley, 233
Zorina, Vera, 182, 185, 186, 188, 189, 191, 202, 213, 218, 224, 231, 424
Zürich Ballet (Ballett des Opernhauses Zürich), 141, 195, 236, 240, 277, 303, 312, 316, 335, 340, 343, 347, 358, 368, 373, 392, 398, 410
Zuev, 11

ACKNOWLEDGMENTS

The preparation and publication of *Choreography by George Balanchine* has been made possible by grants from Gillian Attfield, Ballet Society, Mr. and Mrs. Sid R. Bass, the Doll Foundation, the Eakins Press Foundation, the Ford Foundation, the Lassalle Fund, Earle I. Mack, the National Endowment for the Arts, Mr. and Mrs. Henry Paschen, Frances Schreuder, and the Wallace Fund.

From its beginning the project has been considered a collaborative effort. Mr. Balanchine's personal participation has been vital. Special thanks are due Barbara Horgan and Edward Bigelow of the New York City Ballet. Mrs. Mark Schorer made available the results of research toward a biography of Balanchine, and has served as valued consultant. Important assistance has been given by the following (and often in the case of persons with institutional associations, their staffs): Barbara J. Allen (Consulate General of the United States of America, Leningrad), Jacques d'Amboise, Peter Anastos, Leda Anchutina, Sergio Mascareñas del Angel (Instituto Nacional de Bellas Artes, Mexico City), Bene Arnold, Karin von Aroldingen, Dame Sonia Arova, Erik Aschengreen, Suzanne Aubert (Grand Théâtre de Genève), Daniel Aubry (Archives, Opéra de Monte-Carlo), Georges Auric, Irina Baronova, Ann Barzel, Nicole Beauséjour (RM Productions, Munich), Marika Besobrasova, Gordon Boelzner, Todd Bolender, Ruthanna Boris, Vida Brown, Kirk Browning, Richard Buckle, Gage Bush, Miguel Cabrera, Alfonso Catá, Yvonne Chouteau, Lew Christensen, Marie-Françoise Christout (Bibliothèque de l'Arsenal, Paris), Mary Clarke, Heinz Clauss, John Clifford, Selma Jeanne Cohen, Roberta Cooper (American Shakespeare Festival, Stratford, Connecticut), Mari Cornell, Fred Danieli, David Daniels, Alexandra Danilova, Karen Davidov, Kensington Davison, Roxanna Deane (Martin Luther King Memorial Library, Washington, D.C.), Carole Deschamps, Fernand Detaille, Deutsche Oper am Rhein (Berlin), Charles Dickson, Anton Dolin, William Dollar, Felia Doubrovska, Paul Draper, Lucille Duncan (Center for Inter-American Relations, New York), Katherine Dunham, Rosemary Dunleavy,

Marina Eglevsky, Richard Englund, Antonio José Faró, Olga Ferri, Enzo Valenti Ferro (Teatro Colón, Buenos Aires), Charles France, Frederic Franklin, Julia Gade, Beth Genné, Tamara Geva, Nancy Goldner, Solange Golovine, Edward Gorey, Susan Gould, Margaret Graham, Natasha Gregorova, Robert Greskovic, Nicholas Grimaldi (National Association for Regional Ballet), Ivor Guest, Pëtr Gusev, Marianna Hallar (Library of the Royal Theater, Copenhagen), Carolyn Harden (Theatre Museum, London), Camille Hardy, Russell Hartley (San Francisco Archives for the Performing Arts), Henley Haslam, Baird Hastings, Melissa Hayden, Susan Hendl, Laurie Horn, Marian Horosko, Olga and André von Hoyer, Merle Hubbard, Heinrich Huesmann (Theatermuseum, Munich), David Huntley (Boosey & Hawkes, Inc.), Robert Irving, George Jackson, Jillana, Robert Joffrey, Clark Jones, Martine Kahane (Bibliothèque et Musée de l'Opéra, Paris), Una Kai, Poel Karp, Tibor Katona (Orchestre National de Monte-Carlo), Allegra Kent, William P. Kiehl (United States International Communications Agency), Lincoln Kirstein, Anna Kisselgoff, Boris Kochno, Horst Koegler, Gabriella Komleva, Bernard L. Koten, Svend Kragh-Jacobsen, Nadia Lacoste (Centre de Presse, Principauté de Monaco), Moscelyne Larkin, Niels Bjørn Larsen, Juan Ubaldo Lavanga, George Laws, Tanaquil Le Clercq, Sara Leland, Tatiana Leskova, Library of Congress Newspaper Annex, Rolf Liebermann, Michael Lland, Lady Lousada, Conrad Ludlow, Pamela Lumsden (Library of the Garrick Club, London), Annabelle Lyon, Shona Dunlop MacTavish, Patricia McBride, Don McDonagh, Martha Mahard (Harvard Theatre Collection), John E. Malmstad (Department of Slavic Languages, Columbia University), Raymond Mander and Joseph Mitchenson (Mander and Mitchenson Collection, London), Giora Manor, Marie-Jeanne, Dame Alicia Markova, Francis Mason, Carlos Heria Massardo (Teatro Municipal, Santiago, Chile), Larry Miller, Arthur Mitchell, Yvonne Mounsey, John Mueller (Dance Film Archives, University of Rochester), Betty June Myers, Colleen Neary, Patricia Neary, Vera Nemtchinova, Barbara Newman, Jack L. Noordhorn (Columbia University Libraries), Frank Ohman, Arbie Orenstein, Genevieve Oswald (The New York Public Library Dance Collection), Ruth Page, Susan Pilarre, Freda Pitt, Richard Ploch

(Library of the Dance Notation Bureau, New York), Nina Popova, Ulla Poulsen, Ali Pourfarrokh, Denise Prézeau (Canadian Broadcasting Corporation), Børge Ralov, Dame Marie Rambert, Jack Reed, Janet Reed, Susan Reimer-Torn, Karl Reuling, Rupert Rhymes (London Coliseum), Vittorio Rieti, Claire Robilant (Library, London School of Contemporary Dance), Raúl Roger, Francis Rosset (Société des Bains de Mer, Monte Carlo), Francia Russell, Richard Temple Savage (Music Library, Royal Opera House, London), Jorgen Schiott, Suki Schorer, Betty Scorer, Joysanne Sidimus, Jill Silverman, Victoria Simon, George Skibine, Boris Skidelsky (Royal Opera House Archives, London), David R. Smith (Walt Disney Archives, Burbank, California), Arkadi Sokolow (Leningrad State Institute of Theater, Music and Cinematography), Zachary Solov, Doris Sonne, Marco Sorgetti, Mary Stuart (Slavic and East European Department, University of Illinois at Urbana-Champaign), Mark E. Swartz (Harvard Theatre Collection), Kay Swift, Nikita Talin, Maria Tallchief, Marjorie Tallchief, John Taras, Alberto Testa, Brigitte Thom, Giampiero Tintori (Museo Teatrale, La Scala, Milan), Roy Tobias, Rojelio Tristam (Argentine Consulate, New York), Alexander Trubizin, Hilda Soto U (Archivo Municipal de Ballet, Santiago, Chile), Dame Ninette de Valois, David Vaughan, Violette Verdy, Celida Parera Villalon, Edward Villella, Lynn Visson, Kathrine Sorley Walker, Barbara Weisberger, Andrew Mark Wentink, Joachim Wenzel (Hamburgische Staatsoper), Elaine Whitelaw (March of Dimes, White Plains, New York), Patricia Wilde, Roland John Wiley (School of Music, University of Michigan), E. Virginia Williams, Joseph Wishey, Sarah Woodcock (Theatre Museum, London), Rochelle Zide-Booth, Vera Zorina, and the artistic directors, administrators and archivists who assisted in establishing the record of stagings. The final quatrain of Gide's *Perséphone* has been translated by Richard Wilbur.

The manuscript of this *Catalogue* was read with essential corrective attention by Edward Bigelow, Gordon Boelzner, Betty Cage, Lew Christensen, Arlene Croce, Rosemary Dunleavy, Nancy Goldner, Barbara Horgan, Robert Irving, Lincoln Kirstein, Anna Kisselgoff, Boris Kochno, Deborah Koolish, Tanaquil Le Clercq, John Martin, Francis Mason, Ruth Schorer, John Taras, David Vaughan, and Henry Wisneski.